THE SCORNED ALLY

THE SCORNED ALLY

A Revisionist Novel of the Spanish-Cuban-American War

by

LEONARD BIRD

LOST SOULS PRESS
Grand Haven, Michigan
hawkdreaming@yahoo.com

LOST SOULS PRESS
1910 Grant Avenue
Grand Haven, Michigan 49417
hawkdreaming@ yahoo.com

This is a work of revisionist fiction. The leading characters and
much of the supporting cast are fictitious. Words and deeds of the
leading historical characters are based on what they did, and what they
might have said, given their histories, personalities and basic values.

Library of Congress Cataloging in-Publication Data
ISBN 978-0-578-06108-5

Book and cover design design by Ann Wassmann
Printed in the United State of America
10 9 8 7 6 5 4 3 2 1

Dedication
To the painter Jane Leonard, my wife and best friend.

With Gratitude
To my editor, Margaret Willey, novelist and editor, whose encouragement
and suggestions made *The Scorned Ally* far more readable.
And Ann Wassmann, the designer, who added graphic beauty
to the cover and the content it embraces.

And to fellow writers who critiqued various drafts
John Brandi, Carolyn Petersen, Renee Gregorio, Mark Coburn
and Doreen Mehs, "Alaska Jim" Misko, and the early encouragement
of Barbara Cover, my first wife and the mother of my two children.

Table of Contents

Preface

B y January 1898, of Spain's great American empire, only Puerto Rico, Cuba and a handful of smaller islands remained. In the Pacific, the Philippines were her last great bastion. By July Spain had lost both the Caribbean and Pacific, and the Spanish Empire ceased to exist. Although the U.S. Army and Navy received most of the credit for the *coup de grace* in Cuba, the Cuban revolutionary movement and its military arm provided the *coup de main, Cuba Libre!*, required enormous sacrifices from the Cuban people, rebels and civilians alike. Who were these rebels and civilians? How did they deal with despair? What vision helped them retain hope? Between 1896 and 1898 almost 200,000 civilians, mostly women and children, died in the *reconcentrados*. Toward the end of 1897 the enfeebled survivors wandered through a wasteland where, for three years, each side in the war had been destroying anything of possible use to the other.

Spain was exhausted. She had already wasted her gold, prestige and four generations of her youth grasping at a disintegrating empire. She had little left to spend. For the Spanish boy-conscripts, Cuba was a virtual death sentence. Far more of the recruits died of diseases (typhoid, cholera, malaria and particularly yellow fever) than from Cuban (and later American) machetes and bullets. In Spain there were draft riots. Both townsmen and peasants rose up in arms over the seemingly endless losses of their youth to the quagmire Cuba had become.

But *Cuba Libre!* too was struggling to survive. Though Cuban strategists distrusted the restless colossus to the north, by 1898 they knew—and argued—that American intervention was essential. *Cuba Libre!* could fight Spain to a standstill; it could not evict her.

On February 15 the *USS Maine*, the world's most modern battleship, exploded in Havana harbor. Who or what destroyed the *Maine?* and how? remains a mystery. Regardless, two hundred and thirty-three

American sailors and marines died in the blast. An enraged America, led by William Randolph Hearst and Joseph Pulitzer, immediately declared war on Spain. A great cry of vengeance, "Remember the *Maine*!" united an America still suffering from the divisions of the Civil War. The ensuing campaign and rapid victory destroyed one empire and created another.

On April 24, after waiting more than two months for McKinley to make a move, Congress declared war. Six days later Commodore Dewey destroyed Spain's Pacific fleet in Manila Bay. On May 8 the House and Senate debated their joint resolution to annex Hawaii. Three days later the Administration decided to keep the spoils of war and declared that it would retain the Philippines. The next day Admiral Sampson destroyed San Juan's Moro Fortress and Puerto Rico fell.

On June 22, sixteen thousand American soldiers landed on the south-eastern coast of Cuba. In late June and the first four days of July, in a series of short but intense battles, America and Cuba defeated Spain. With Commodore Dewey's easy naval victory, America became a Pacific power. With Commodore Schley's blockade and subsequent destruction of Spain's antiquated fleet at Santiago de Cuba, America became an Atlantic power. In the process *Cuba Libre!* was squashed by her colossal saviour.

Though all but its most historically important characters are fictitious, *The Scorned Ally* purports to tell the story of individual Cubans and Americans. How did they perceive themselves and each other? What drove them on? How did the war change their lives and the future of Cuba?

Leonard Bird

Significant Characters

*In order of appearance (* denotes historical person)*

*Jose Marti (1853–1895) is the great national hero. Though he does not appear in this novel, Marti's vision and strength fueled the aspirations of every Cuban rebel. Revolutionary idealist, theorist and co-founder of the Cuban Revolutionary Party, Marti was the only person killed in the battle of *Dos Rios*, the first skirmish of the 1895–98 war. A journalist and poet, he founded the *Modernismo* movement in poetry and strongly influenced poets like Ruben Dario and Gabriella Mistral. One of Marti's poems became the deeply felt and still popular song, "Guantanamera," the unofficial national anthem.

* Tomas Estrada Palma (1832–1908), a rebel general in the Ten Years War (1868–78) who worked closely with Jose Marti. In 1895, after the death of Marti, Palma became head of the Cuban Revolutionary Party and served as its spokesman in New York. In 1902 he became the first President of Cuba. Coerced by the U.S., Palma signed the new Cuban Constitution. That document both ceded Guantanamo and established permanent American control over Cuban foreign policy.

Joshua Vandervoort, private banker, the quietly effective scion of an old and powerful family.

* J. Pierpont Morgan (1837–1919), financier, industrialist, art collector and amateur archaeologist.

* Marcus Hanna (1837–1904), manager of William McKinley's successful 1896 presidential bid, a new but already powerful Republican senator.

* **Joseph Pulitzer** (1847–1911), founder of the *St. Lois Post- Dispatch* and publisher of the *New York World*, the most successful newspaper in the country, a tabloid that exemplified what came to be known as" yellow journalism."

* **William Randolph Hearst** (1863–1951), yellow journalist, builder of what was to become America's first communications empire, publisher of the *New York Journal*, arch-competitor to Pulitzer.

Armond Q. Adams, South Carolina expatriate, sugar planter from Pino del Rio Province and spokesman for many of the more conservative, anti-rebel planters.

* **William R. Shafter** (1835–1906), Medal of Honor winning veteran of the Civil and Indian Wars, the obese and incompetent General of the American invading army.

* **Winfield Scott Schley** (1829–1911), Roosevelt's friend and a free wheeling Commodore of the U.S. Atlantic Squadron; responsible for destroying Admiral Cervera's Spanish Fleet in the one day battle of Santiago de Cuba.

* **Theodore Roosevelt** (1858–1915), Assistant Secretary of the Navy, credited with its rapid reorganization, and with making the decision to send Commodore Dewey to the Philippines; later Lieutenant Colonel and then Colonel of the Rough Riders. Within two years of the Battle of San Juan Hill, Roosevelt became Governor of New York, Vice president during McKinley's second term and, upon the assassination of McKinley, President of the United States.

***Henry Moore Teller** (1830–1913), Republican Colorado Senator who switched to the Democrats in 1896, an anti-expansionist, later author of the Teller Amendment, which both authorized money for the war and forbade the formal annexation of Cuba.

Christopher Jackson, expatriate Georgian, a sometime sugar planter and captain (later colonel) in *Cuba Libre!*

SIGNIFICANT CHARACTERS

* *Cuba Libre!* The popular name and rallying cry of the Cuban Revolutionary Party and its rag tag army.

* *Mambises*, the soldiers of *Cuba Libre!* a montage of every Cuban race and class, including many European and American expatriates who considered themselves to be Cuban.

Fidel Federico, sergeant and later lieutenant, an ex-slave, Christopher's foreman, aide and sole friend.

Consuelo Valdez Jackson, the mulatto daughter of a rebel killed in the Ten Years War, Christopher's wife and the mother of three daughters.

Theresa Valdez, Consuelo's younger sister, a captain in *Cuba Libre!* and head of rebel intelligence in Havana.

Amos Jordan, Theresa's patron, the American Vice Consul in Havana.

* **Fitzhugh Lee** (1835–1905), former Confederate General, son of Robert E. Lee, an American expansionist, the American Consul in Havana.

Guillermo Morales, ex-foreman on the Valdez estate and a newly minted colonel serving under General Maximo Gomez; Christopher Jackson's immediate superior.

* **Maximo Gomez** (1836–1905), Commanding General of *Cuba Libre!* The sole survivor of the triumvirate (Gomez, Jose Marti and Antonio Maceo) that reignited the Cuban War of Independence. Gomez detested the idea of American involvement but by 1898 realized that his *Mambises* could not alone dislodge the Spanish Army. A master of asymmetrical warfare, Gomez invented the massed infantry machete charges that terrorized the Spanish conscripts. In 1901 General Gomez turned down the presidency of Cuba and returned to his home in the Dominican Republic.

Isaac Rabinski, watchmaker, a refugee Russian Jew, builder of delicate bombs for *Cuba Libre!*

Judith Sandoval, Joseph's stepdaughter, later a *mambi* nurse and ersatz surgeon, and a companion to Christopher, Theresa and Fidel.

Ignatius Alvarez, "the Beast," a Spanish Major and inquisitor, head of Spanish Intelligence in Havana.

Ephraim Pratt, runaway Mormon, former enlisted man, ensign on the *USS Maine*.

George Bedford, Harvard classmate of Christopher's younger brother Alex, also an ensign aboard the *Maine*.

Alexander Dumas Jackson, Christopher's younger brother, a procurement clerk in the War Department who helps supply Theodore Roosevelt and Leonard Wood and their dream regiment; later an officer in the First volunteer U.S. Cavalry, the "Rough Riders."

* General Russell A. Alger (1835–1907), former Union general and Governor of Michigan, currently Secretary of War.

* Leonard Wood (1860–1927), holder of the Congressional Medal of Honor for action against Geronimo; personal physician to President McKinley, co-organizer and Colonel of the Rough Riders; later Governor General of Cuba.

Charlotte Boggs, a Washington debutant, Alex's fiancée.

Richard Boggs, Charlotte's father, a Washington entrepreneur and power broker; a former Union officer and close friend to Amos Jordan.

Michael Archuletta, Alex's friend; a half Irish, half Mexican sheepherder who joins the Rough Riders to avenge the murder of his Navajo wife.

* Miguel Antonio Otero (1859–1924), Governor of New Mexico Territory.

Marty Mason, itinerant cowboy and Rough Rider.

SIGNIFICANT CHARACTERS

Bill Pike, itinerant trapper and miner and Rough Rider.

Shorty Norton, an itinerant drifter and Rough Rider.

David Vandervoort, Alex's roommate at Harvard, an officer in the Rough Riders.

Fred Anderson, lieutenant in the Missouri National Guard, Quartermaster for the Rough Riders.

* **General Calixto Garcia** (1839–1898), Commander of *Cuba Libre!* in eastern Cuba; aided the U.S. Marines who took Guantanamo, then provided close to 30,000 *Mambises* to block Spanish reinforcements from reaching Santiago de Cuba; supplied several thousand more to help General Lawton capture El Caney.

* **Richard P. Hobson** (1870–1937) volunteered to lead a small crew and sink a U.S. Navy collier in an attempt to block Santiago Harbor. He and his crew were captured by the Spanish. Thirty-five years later, as a retired rear admiral, Hobson was awarded the Medal of Honor for his 1898 feat.

* **Admiral William T. Sampson** (1840–1902), Commander of the fleet that surrounded Cuba; sometimes credited with the defeat of Admiral Cervera's Atlantic Squadron. The victory should be credited to Commodore Winfield Scott Schley.

* **William Owen "Bucky" O'Neill** (1860–1898), Sheriff and later Mayor of Prescott, Arizona, a captain in the Rough Riders.

* **General Joseph "Fighting Joe" Wheeler** (1836–1906), Alabama Congressman, ex-Confederate cavalry general, later Commanding General of the cavalry division that included the Rough Riders.

* **General Henry Ware Lawton** (1843–1899), a colonel in the last of the Indian Wars, credited with capturing Geronimo; later the commanding general of the 2nd Infantry Division and a bitter rival to General Wheeler, whom he held in ill-disguised contempt.

Prologue

New York City, January 5, 1898

Dr. Tomas Estrada Palma, former school teacher, lawyer, Havana postmaster and revolutionary general, and present Chairman of the New York Cuban Junta, paced nervously back and forth over the thick Persian carpet that spread the full length of the reception room he had occupied for more than an hour. The room led through carved cherry doors to the inner-sanctum of Joshua Vandervoort, a reclusive but powerful member of the New York business community. Estrada Palma was so anxious to be summoned through the huge doors that his hands shook. He had already swallowed one laudanum pill to soothe his screaming stomach; only his iron will kept him from swallowing a second. Even though he was not precisely sure what he would say once summoned into the assemblage of powerful men, he knew that as soon as he started talking he would be in control of both his body and his words. His eternally upset stomach and jangled nerves would recede back into the nether mists of his consciousness. Only later, after his task was completed, would he allow his body to rebel. Then he would stretch out on his bed in the small, lower east side hotel provided by William Randolph Hearst, and swallow laudanum pills for the two or three days his body required to unwind from any major crisis.

Estrada Palma was fifty-eight years old and reed thin. Though he still flaunted the full head of white hair, drooping white mustache and high, thin facial features that often denoted the well born Cuban of Spanish lineage, Palma was not a Spaniard and had never considered himself one. His pride, his sense of aloofness, his seeming arrogance and his idealism were the combined results of his social class and his Spanish education. In his political sentiments, however, he was no more Spanish than Thomas Jefferson, his one American hero, was English.

Eight years into the future, Estrada Palma's ill-disguised contempt for the unwashed and untutored peasants and his distrust of the more liberal revolutionary generals would drive him from the presidency of Cuba and plunge his country into a political abyss from which it has yet to crawl. But at the moment he was the revolution's spokesman, the Cuban Ben Franklin whose responsibility it was to enlist support at foreign courts, be they the courts of diplomacy or, as on this blustery January afternoon in New York, the courts of finance. Dr. Palma knew he had an opening, an unusual opportunity to change the balance of power in Cuba. He was anxious to get to work.

On the other side of the carved cherry doors, ten men sat around a highly polished table. Despite the presence of two well-known members of the press, Joseph Pulitzer and William Randolph Hearst, the meeting was private. And despite the wealth of the room's furnishings and the obvious power represented by its occupants, there were no servants. Vandervoort, the host and organizer of the meeting, demanded privacy. From time to time during the past two hours, various important personages had risen from the table and moved to the simply carved cherry buffet to refill a decanter or replenish a gold-trimmed plate from the platters of smoked meats, cheeses and fruits that decorated the buffet. Even as they moved about the room, however, each man attended to what his fellows were saying. Joshua Vandervoort had long been a very private yet substantive supporter of the Spanish—not because he was attached sentimentally to the collapsing Spanish empire, but because he equated the Spanish presence in Cuba with political—therefore economic—stability. However, because of what he was coming to see as increasing ineptitude on the part of a long series of Spanish Captain-Generals, coupled with almost total imbecility in the Spanish court, Vandervoort was thinking of changing sides. If the huge Spanish army in Cuba could not protect private property—and it couldn't—why prolong its existence? Vandervoort had invited this particular group of men to his house because of the various powers they wielded and the variety of their views.

On Vandervoort's right sat J. Pierpont Morgan, king of the millionaire robber barons, who was currently refurbishing his public image by endowing museums, and assuaging his twisted soul by searching for the secrets of eternal life in the winding sheets of Egyptian pharaohs.

Morgan opposed the Cuban revolution and was appalled by the war fever currently being stirred up by Hearst, Roosevelt and their expansionist friends. Like Vandervoort, however, he was worried about the incompetence of the Spanish government and its concomitant effect on trade.

Next to Morgan sat Marcus Hanna, political boss of Ohio, the man most responsible for getting his close friend, William McKinley, elected President of the United States, and a brand new but already powerful member of the U.S. Senate. Although a leading advocate of war with Spain, Hanna was not at all interested in Cuban independence. For almost two decades he had championed the cause of Manifest Destiny and Cuban annexation. The American lust for Cuba had been a passion, sometimes waxing, sometimes waning, that began with Thomas Jefferson. It first became a rallying cry during the War of 1812, and rose to fever pitch during many subsequent American crises. Senator Marcus Hanna rode the current crest of that old American wave.

Next to Hanna sat Joseph Pulitzer and William Randolph Hearst, the Rosencranz and Guildenstern of yellow journalism. The two fiercely competitive publishers despised each other almost as much as they despised the conservative Wall Streeters in whose presence they sat. Nevertheless, they were tied to each other by the symbiotic juices of the anti-Spanish, pro-Cuban sentiment that flowed across the front pages of their respective newspapers. Of the two men, Pulitzer was somewhat less wealthy, considerably less rapacious and infinitely less flamboyant. He dressed conservatively, spoke quietly, and wore the mien of a Methodist minister freshly deserted by his congregation. He was also the more conservative of the two on the issue of overseas expansion, especially in the Pacific: Pulitzer opposed annexation of Hawaii; Hearst trumpeted annexation as a logical extension of Manifest Destiny. Hearst wanted to invade Cuba forthwith and, eventually, to annex it. Pulitzer was against both steps but felt that food, medicine and munitions should be sent to the long-suffering Cuban people. William Randolph Hearst personified conspicuous consumption. He believed himself to be the reincarnation of Francis I, and lived accordingly. Although his taste was abominable, his opulence was dazzling. Should war break out with Spain, Hearst was prepared, in good Renaissance fashion, to recruit and equip a regiment for the cause, and to lead his own small navy to Cuba. In the meantime he was satisfying his imperial urges by building a baroque castle on the oak-covered heights of California's central coast. In dress, voice and demeanor Hearst was a Renaissance despot who had fallen asleep one day after drinking too much canary and awakened on the wrong side of the Age of Revolution. His journalistic tenets and success derived from his insights to what made the lumpen proletariat act and, more important, react.

At the foot of the table sat the one man then present most likely to be directly affected by what the assembled power brokers decided upon and in subsequent months accomplished. Armond Quincy Atkins, spokesman for the large Cuban-American planter community, was a first generation Cuban whose parents had emigrated from South Carolina in 1867 to a land where the institution of slavery would be appreciated and perpetuated for another twenty years. Atkins was a vial of poisonous juices barely contained by a cork of economic self-preservation. His earliest memories were of Charleston falling to the Yankees; his most recent were of the flames rising—for the third time in as many years—from his 10,000 hectare sugar plantation in Pinar del Rio Province. Atkins hated the Yankees for abolishing "the only civilized way of life America had ever known," and the South for surrendering. He hated the Cuban insurrectionists, whom he held responsible for the freeing of the slaves in '88 and for turning them loose with machetes to burn and kill in '95. Despite his connections through class and marriage, he hated the Spanish for their inability to suppress a ragged army soldiered by "hungry niggers and naive poets." He hated this group of Yankee millionaires upon whom his future seemed to depend. And most of all, he hated Maximo Gomez, the insurgents' Commander-in-Chief, and Tomas Estrada Palma, who was pacing nervously up and down a Persian carpet scarcely forty feet away.

Around the corner to Atkins' right sat the three representatives of American military might, led by William R. Shafter, General of the Army, the 323 pound, semi-senile Chief of Staff, a man whose time-and-desk bound mind could not comprehend the advanced degree of logistical rust afflicting his army.

On the general's right sat Winfield Scott Schley, Commodore, U.S. Navy, a talented and ambitious advocate of war with Spain. Schley had remained absolutely quiet throughout the meeting, but his mind had been busy photographing every sign of strength and weakness, every gesture, however apparently insignificant, of the powerful assembly.

On Schley's right sat his friend, Theodore Roosevelt, Assistant Secretary of the Navy, hell-bent-for-leather, bit-chomping, desk-pounding champion of Manifest Destiny and war with Spain "right bloody now!" Though always easy to parody, Roosevelt was the most energetic and talented and certainly the most charismatic public man of his era. Far more insightful, strong-willed and competent than his immediate superior, Secretary Long, Roosevelt was almost single-handedly reorganizing the Navy, vastly improving its logistical and strategic readiness and, before resigning his position to organize the First Volunteer Cavalry Regiment, giving the orders that enabled Commodore Dewey to easily defeat the Spanish in the Philippines.

The final member of the group, flanked on one side by Roosevelt, whom he despised, and on the other by the empty chair reserved for Tomas Estrada Palma, was William Teller, U.S. Senator from Colorado, a man whose Calvinistic sense of integrity and western sense of political acumen would, three months later, stymie forever America's drive to annex Cuba. Teller was a life-long friend of Amos Jordan, the Vice Consul-General in Cuba, whose insights he trusted considerably. More important, Teller represented a state still caroming off the walls of a depression in its fledgling sugar beet industry. As far as his constituents were concerned, Cuban annexation meant Cuban competition and quite likely, the *coup de grace* to Colorado's sick infant. Although Teller opposed annexation, he was not immune to the war fever sweeping the country and waiting under the table to ambush the assemblage of powerful men. Even his good friend, Amos Jordan, could not convince him that war with Spain, even if short and sweet, would change the character and destiny of America. Thus far, however, the Senator from Colorado had not been tempted to enter the conversation. He knew that the real issue had yet to be broached.

Joshua Vandervoort was the titular head of a large Sephardic family whose restraint, dignity and quiet grace most of the other men gathered in the room would never fully comprehend, despite their own very tangible wealth and or power. The Vandervoorts and their allies exercised great influence, in both America and Europe, and quietly enjoyed all the perquisites of such power. Unlike most of the men around the table, the Vandervoorts were interested in neither publicity nor public position. They shunned the former and both despised and manipulated the latter.

Other than introducing the topic of discussion, Vandervoort had said little. He was a creative listener who usually preferred to sit back and do just that. But it was past time to move this talkative crew along. As was his habit, he spoke quietly.

"Gentlemen!" His eyes slowly swept the room. "Let us look for a moment at the long term implications of war with Spain. What are the results likely to be for our economic and foreign policy ten, twenty, forty years down the road?"

"Well, your Excellency. It occurs to me that...," Marcus Hanna began in the sycophant's tone he reserved for men whose power exceeded his own.

"Excuse me, Senator," Vandervoort interrupted, already annoyed by Hanna's tone and language. "I would prefer, I think we would all prefer, to hear from those members of our little group who have, at least thus far, kept relatively quiet. Don't you agree?"

"Yes, sir," Hanna nodded amiably, as if he had been about to make the same suggestion.

Vandervoort continued. "Commodore Schley. I have heard a number of positive remarks concerning you, especially from your friend, Mr. Roosevelt. How do you view the implications of war with Spain?"

Schley replied slowly, but in clipped military cadence. Despite his own ambitions and his full awareness of the company, he was not at all awe-struck. He spoke forthrightly, without sugar and without salt, as if addressing a slightly confused group of junior officers in his wardroom. "Cuba is only part of the issue. We will be going to war with Spain. And we will win the war—easily."

"But Commodore?" J. P. Morgan interrupted. "Isn't it true that Spain has 200,000 soldiers in Cuba? And doesn't Admiral Cervera have a fleet steaming more or less continuously around the island?"

Theodore Roosevelt was immediately on his feet. "Most of those men are under age conscripts; they don't even know who they're fighting for. They're just little fellows, sixteen, seventeen years old. One American could lick four or five of them." Roosevelt finished his short tirade, glared belligerently around the room and resumed his seat.

Schley continued, unflustered, as if the interruption had not taken place. "We will win the war. We will be able—should we desire—

to annex Cuba, Puerto Rico, Guam, Wake Island, the Philippines and, obviously, Hawaii."

"My God, man! Are you mad?" Teller exploded. "We're not in the empire business. Nor should we be!"

"May I point out, my esteemed colleagues..." Hanna had been oiling his tongue since his recent setback with Vandervoort. He was prepared to tell most of the assembled men what he was sure they wanted to hear. He smiled benevolently at Teller, whom he considered a dangerous enemy. "We have reached our limits on this continent. We own Alaska, half of what was once Mexico, and our just share of Canada. Within the past two decades our industry has made us a great economic power. We must recognize our responsibility to the other countries of the world, just as we must, of course, recognize our potential for world greatness. We're a comer, gentlemen. Spain is on the way out, and has no further business in our hemisphere. Remember the Monroe Doctrine!"

"The Monroe Doctrine has nothing to do with this, Senator. And Guam and the Philippines are hardly in our hemisphere." Although Schley agreed with most of Hanna's sentiments, he prized accuracy.

Schley glanced around to make sure the brief tempest had settled back to the bottom of the teapot. "We already have a fleet in the far Pacific; Dewey is standing down at Hong Kong, ready to sail for the Philippines on short notice. We also have troops in Peking. The old Empress Dowager is dying; China is about to collapse. Whether we want to or not, we will probably become more involved in Asia. If so, we will obviously need coaling stations. Whether we annex Guam and the Philippines or not, we must control them! And we must continue to control Hawaii. Otherwise . . ." He looked around sternly. "Our Pacific fleet is useless."

Teller leaned back in his chair and glared at the ceiling. "If I may twist Mr. Vandervoort's question, Commodore, what will those coaling stations cost? Ultimately?"

"I don't know, sir. We will become responsible for the Aborigines, for educating and civilizing them. That will, of course, become a continuing part of our responsibility."

"What other costs, sir?" Teller was insistent.

"If we keep those islands we will become a major world power. Within a decade or two we will be so recognized."

"That's a cost?" Roosevelt shot out.

"Major powers have major responsibilities," Vandervoort insisted. "Power involves major risks, some dangers."

"Such as?" Teller leaned forward around Roosevelt and looked from Mahon to Vandervoort and back again to Schley, who had not changed expression during the entire exchange.

Schley answered. "A major war with one or more European powers. Perhaps a war in the Pacific. The risks here are small, but they should be recognized. In any case, we must have Cuba. She could become, quite easily, a major threat to our under belly, especially if she falls into the wrong hands.

"I agree with your assessments. And with yours, Senator," he added, nodding at Hanna. "We are . . . 'comers' . . . as you so eloquently phrase it. I do not believe we have to worry about Spain; she's been collapsing for most of the century. As far as the rest of Europe is concerned— France, Britain, Germany—we have too much in common ever again to get involved in a major conflict with any of them."

"What about Russia, gentlemen?" General Shafter had roused himself from a little nap.

Vandervoort was puzzled. "I don't see how that relates to the problem at hand, General. Russia is nothing more than a huge, harmless, hibernating bear ruled by Romanoff fools."

The fat general shrugged his shoulders and settled back down to what would quickly become another nap.

"Gentlemen? May I have a word?" All eyes turned to the plain grey face of Joseph Pulitzer, who spoke quietly, as if to belie the ferocity of his paper's headlines. "Mr. Hearst and I are not . . . friends. But our success as publishers is based on a shared perception about America, about Americans. My question is: How will war with Spain—and victory—affect the way we Americans perceive ourselves?"

Roosevelt winked at Hearst, a close friend, and smiled condescendingly at Pulitzer. "Certainly no one will be offended by a smashing victory, Mr. Pulitzer."

"Allow me, Theodore," Hearst interrupted, turning to address a short sermon to his rival. "War with Spain, Mr. Pulitzer, especially a short, victorious war, will serve, finally, to unite our country. A German like yourself might not understand that, but . . ."

Pulitzer turned white and rose from his chair. Vandervoort slammed his open palm down on the highly polished table and glared back and forth at the two giants of American publishing. "Mr. Hearst," he finally managed to hiss, "Remember where you are!"

After a long moment of silence, during which several members of the group refilled their goblets and plates, Hearst continued his sermon, albeit in a somewhat less strident tone. "We are still suffering from the sectionalism of the Civil War. A foreign war will, I am convinced, bring us together. Interestingly enough, Southerners particularly seem anxious to show their patriotism in Cuba. Theodore was telling me just the other day that Georgia's "Fighting Joe" Wheeler is ready to resign his seat in Congress and lead a cavalry division."

Several men chuckled at the idea of the white-bearded, ex-Confederate hero leading a Yankee division. J. P. Morgan was not one of those, however. Morgan had, somewhat uncharacteristically, sat quietly through most of the discussion. But he had come to the meeting with one all-consuming concern: Economic stability in Cuba—regardless of the means. Morgan was not yet convinced that war with Spain was either desirable or necessary; moreover, he was confident that Vandervoort and Teller felt the same way. War fever seemed already to have become a contagion. That unpleasant reality should, however, provide no excuse for the nation's more responsible leaders to allow themselves to be infected—by the press or by the likes of Hearst and Roosevelt. Revolutionaries, even starving revolutionaries, were a distasteful and dangerous breed. They should be stamped out rather than encouraged. Pity that Spain was too weak to do the job.

"Remember, Mr. Hearst," Morgan lectured. "We are discussing the implications of a theoretical war—not committing ourselves to a real one. We should go to war with Spain only if there exists no other way to insure our investments, present and potential."

Roosevelt shifted in his seat, unable to sit still. "War with Spain now is in our best interests, Mr. Morgan. We've tried every other means, including four solid years of diplomatic pressure. Nothing has worked thus far. Nothing will work. Except war. The field of Mars, gentlemen." Roosevelt looked around the room, thrust his jaw out slightly, and added: "There's where we'll settle this bloody problem—and settle it well. Victory will cover all of us—cover America—with glory."

"Ah, yes. Glory. Wonderful abstraction," Vandervoort muttered, glancing at the tall clock standing in the far corner of the room. But I'd rather win bank notes than glory, he thought. "Tell me, Mr. Secretary. Do you know that Crimean poem by the English poet, Mr. Tennyson?"

"The Charge of the Light Brigade?" Roosevelt replied. "Yes, sir. Marvelous poem. Glorious charge."

"And marvelously stupid generals," Teller snickered.

"Ah, yes. Precisely, Senator," Vandervoort continued, as General Shafter shifted his corpulence in the protesting chair. "Gloriously romantic and absolutely senseless."

Vandervoort stood up and stretched. "Gentlemen, let us move forward. We listened to Mr. Atkins earlier, and I have invited Dr. Tomas Estrada Palma, leader of the Cuban Junta, to share his views with us. Now seems to be an appropriate time to ask him in."

"You've what?" Armand Quincy Atkins, representative of the more conservative Cuban-American planters, was on his feet, livid. "That god damned nigger-loving radical. We wouldn't even be here today if it wasn't for him and his kind."

"Mr. Atkins, need I remind you that you were invited here to provide information, and invited to stay as an observer. You will be civil to Dr. Palma, or you will leave immediately." Atkins managed to get the cork back into his vial, which was turning apoplectic purple. "The trouble with you planters," Vandervoort continued, "is that you cannot distinguish between the various revolutionary factions. There is a world of difference between this man and General Maximo Gomez, as you should well know. If the Cubans win this 'war of liberation,' as they so quaintly call it, and they probably will, whether or not we enter the fray, you and your friends will have to deal with them. Dr. Palma is an aristocrat, a scholar—and a conservative. He is head of the Cuban Junta because he understands—and is understood by—the American business community. Court him, Mr. Atkins. Or . . . go down with the Spanish!"

Atkin's gaze dropped beneath Vandervoort's icy stare. Several members of the group, embarrassed by the confrontation, rose to take a turn around the room. They talked little and only pleasantries: about the steady rain that was slowly turning to grey snow, about their clubs, about the labor agitators who were slowing, albeit imperceptibly, the mighty wheels of industrial progress.

A hush fell over the room as Vandervoort returned, preceded by the slight, white-headed and extremely dignified Cuban. Several of the men present had met Dr. Palma before. All had heard of him. Hearst was his unofficial sponsor. Not only did the publisher contribute money and arms to *Cuba Libre!*; as important, he gave Palma space on the editorial pages of his newspapers. Vandervoort showed Palma to the seat reserved for him and took his own. As soon as the others had sat back down, he began. "Gentlemen, you are all acquainted with Dr. Palma and his cause. He now has the floor. Dr. Palma?"

Estrada Palma rose slowly to his feet and placed his hands, palms down and fingers extended, on the table so they wouldn't shake. His stomach was screaming. He began in a somewhat tremulous voice that only slowly gained the strength and authority he so absolutely required.

"Mr. Vandervoort. Distinguished gentlemen. Thank you for giving me—and the long-suffering Cuban people—this opportunity. I would like to speak of three related subjects: Cuba's potential. Her present condition. America's best interests." Dr. Palma could still feel the pain in his stomach, but he now knew where he was going, what he was going to say, and that the pain would slowly recede into the background.. "Many of you think of Cuba as an island, which she is, but she is an island as large as Mr. Hanna's Ohio, more than 700 miles long, more than 44,000 square miles of rich soil, abundant rainfall, and undeveloped mineral resources—such as copper and nickel. As you know, various parts of the island are perfect for coffee, tobacco and sugar cane. I do not want to berate you with facts already at your disposal. Just as you have a frontier, so do we, though ours is in the east rather than the west. Just as you have barely begun to tap the wealth of your country, so have we. Our countries are natural partners, scarcely ninety miles apart. We have raw materials; you have industrial power."

Palma paused for a moment to catch his breath. He knew that, thus far, he had affirmed both their knowledge and their sense of self-interest. What was required was to work on the latter. "Cuba's potential is great, both as a source of exotic crops and raw materials for you, our closest neighbor, and as a growing market for your fine industrial products. However, whatever Cuba's potential, her present situation is deplorable. Nor is her situation likely to change as long as she is ruled by the Spaniards. Because Spain has long demonstrated a self-defeating unwillingness to invest the required capital, our mines have not been developed to even a fraction of their real capacity. Despite ideal weather conditions, our exportable cash crops have decreased each of the last four years. And in a country blessed with much wild produce, between one and two hundred thousand people have already died of starvation and disease."

Atkins could no longer restrain himself. "Dr. Palma. Your account of the island's potential is accurate. But isn't your description of the deterioration of the economy a little self-serving? You and Gomez and Garcia and the rest of your *insurrectos* have destroyed the economy. You started the war up again after a decade of peace. Your soldiers are burning the fields and spreading terror. *Cuba Libre!*, your 'cause', is the great threat to order—and prosperity—in Cuba."

"Have you quite finished, Mr. Atkins?" Vandervoort chided.

Dr. Palma raised his slight hand and waved it back and forth slightly, shaking his head. "Please, Mr. Vandervoort. Mr. Atkins' words contain much truth." Palma was now in charge, and knew it. "As some of you know, the revolution has been proceeding off and on for more than fifty years. The periods of so-called peace have been little more than armed truces. Every Latin country from Mexico south has won its independence—except Cuba and Puerto Rico. Most Latin countries are prospering in gardens of independence and self-realization, while Cuba languishes in a desert of repression and exploitation. These realities do not sustain argument.

"Mr. Atkins is correct when he accuses us of burning plantations. We burn the fields—and factories—of those who side with the tyrant. The Spaniards, in turn, burn the fields of those who side with liberty. Nobody wins; Cuba loses. By now the world must realize, Spain must realize, even, Mr. Atkins, you should realize, that the New World, the Americas, Cuba included—are lands for free men rather than slaves, lands to be governed by their own citizens rather than by European oppressors, lands where the produce of labor is plowed back into the soil as seed for the future rather than hauled across the ocean to fertilize decay."

Palma stepped back from the table and moved slowly around the perimeter of the room, forcing his audience to shift in their seats. "Our methods are desperate because our cause is desperate. However much you may despise revolutionaries and their actions, you must remember that your own country was made possible by equally outrageous actions performed by equally desperate—and dedicated—men and women. Because of their actions, you have prospered. We believe that our actions will allow our children to prosper.

"As Spanish repression has increased in ferocity, so have our own efforts. This cannot be helped. Even though Spain has promised—repeatedly promised—your government that the mass executions would cease, and that the *reconcentrados*, the concentration towns, would be closed down, that has yet to happen. Hundreds of thousands of my people still starve. Your newspapers have made you aware of the torture and executions taking place in El Morro, La Punta and Los Cabanas, as well as elsewhere on the island. But do you know that most of the scores upon scores of thousands of Cubans who have died in the *reconcentrados* are non-combatants? The very old, the very young and the women? Still? After all Spain's empty promises and posturings? The water, if any, is bad. Prisoners must grow their own food. In those camps hundreds die daily—from typhoid, cholera, yellow fever, starvation—and beatings.

"As long as these conditions continue, 'domestic tranquility' is not possible. Chaos, suffering—and war—will continue to prevail. Spain must rule more wisely or give us our freedom. Because we despair of the former, we fight for the latter.

"In summary, gentlemen, Cuba is an island whose economic potential is immense—more than capable of bringing prosperity to her people and riches to the investor. Cuba needs capital to develop her potential. American businessmen are the logical suppliers of that capital. But without peace new investments will remain impractical, present investments unrewarded. Spain has been trying, for more than half a century, to suppress *Cuba Libre!* as we proudly call our revolution. Spain has failed. Now, should the revolution succeed, and with your help it can, quickly, peace will come. Peace! Order! Stability! Foreign—preferably American—capital will flow into the country. Cuba—and her investors—will prosper.

"But about *Cuba Libre!* there is one fact that you must understand!" Dr. Palma stopped for a moment and looked each member of the powerful assemblage straight in the eye. "You must realize that the movement is a coalition, and that, as such, it includes several irresponsible factions of peasants and ex-slaves. The longer the revolution continues, the more these factions, many of whom are absolutely desperate, will determine the outcome. Stand warned. We know that the American people favor Cuba, that many of you have favored Spain, and that your government is paralyzed by indecision. Help us! Help us now! By helping us, you will be helping yourselves."

And, having framed his appeal, as intended, primarily along economic rather than humanitarian grounds, Dr. Palma resumed his seat. For a very long moment the room was silent. Even Atkins was impressed with the speech. More important, he sensed that Palma was right, and that everyone present in the room knew that he was right. Spain had failed. If America wanted to annex Cuba, or at least influence the direction of her government, responsible Americans, including American-Cubans, must do everything possible to co-opt the revolution. Atkins was no idiot. He rose to his feet. "Dr. Palma. I have been your enemy. I would like to become your friend. I cannot afford to support you publicly; my ties with the Spanish are too numerous. I will, however, support you with American dollars. I must admit that I'm very worried about your 'irresponsible factions.' You control the niggers and the riffraff, Dr. Palma. You do that and I'll pledge the support of the American-Cuban business community."

Concealing a self-satisfied smile, Palma rose from his seat, floated to the far end of the table, and shook hands with a man he would never trust but whose economic and political support were priceless. "Mr. Atkins, we have welcomed support wherever we could find it. In the past we have been despised by many responsible people like yourself, who have preferred the known status quo of Spanish tyranny to the feared chaos of revolution. Your support, now and after Spain is beaten, will provide a tempering—and absolutely necessary—force in Cuban politics."

Dr. Tomas Estrada Palma, who would soon become the first President of The Republic of Cuba, had spent many years in America. He was sincere, but naive. Because of his education, his social class, his aloof, stern disposition and his long years in exile, he possessed little insight to the emotions and aspirations of the Cuban people. Nowhere during the ensuing discussion was his naivete more apparent than in his answers to the first questions from his audience.

Senator Marcus Hanna was the first to jump on the Atkins bandwagon. "That was a splendid speech, Dr. Palma, just splendid. But let me ask one question. How do you and your people feel about being annexed or, ah, admitted, to the Union?"

"My God!" Senator Teller mumbled begrudgingly. "That sure harnesses the horse." With the exception of General Shafter, who was slumbering at rotund attention in his chair, everyone waited expectantly while the Cuban framed his words.

"Senator Hanna," Palma began, "the philosophy and aims of *Cuba Libre!* are based on the writings of Jose Marti, the great Cuban poet and martyr. The cornerstones of his teachings are independence, universal suffrage, and free land for the landless."

Several members of the group shifted uncomfortably. Phipps glared at Palma, Atkins began to regret his hasty offer, and Morgan, deeply offended, wandered off into Egyptian mythology.

"Well-spoken—as a diplomat, Doctor." Hanna sensed an answer beyond the answer, and was as adept at spotting evasions as he was in committing them. "We should like to know what you think." Several of the powerful assemblage grunted their assent.

Palma was caught; he had no choice but to continue. "As I mentioned, gentlemen, the revolution is composed of factions: ex-slaves, creole peasants, young intellectuals, the sons of Spanish grandees, even a few American and European planters. Interestingly enough, many of those fighting Spain fear independence and what it could bring. Such men, and I consider myself among them, believe that our destiny is yoked to yours, to America's. We value your political and economic institutions, and we value your view of progress."

Palma paused for a moment and cleared his throat before continuing. "The confidentiality of my private opinions must be respected, gentlemen. However, I favor union with the United States, as do many committed, anti-Spanish revolutionaries of conservative background."

"Hear! Hear!" Atkins boomed, pounding his fist down hard on the polished table.

Does the man understand what he is saying? Senator Teller wondered. Damn! Yes, he knows exactly what he's doing, and he knows the effect his remarks will have—like putting out a forest fire with a hot, dry wind. Teller had long empathized with the Cuban revolutionaries. He was even sufficiently infected with war fever to support American intervention— if absolutely necessary—but only as a disinterested party. To benefit from such a war would deny basic American principles. It would also offend his powerful constituents in the sugar beet districts of eastern Colorado. Annexation was out of the question. America was not and—damn it— never would become a colonial power. At least not if he could help it. The senator looked around the room. He was already mulling over legislation that would, if necessary, keep America from annexing the island.

Everyone smelled war. Even General Shafter had returned from the fog to smile at the possibilities. Commodore Schley glimpsed an admiralcy just around the corner and a seat in Congress just down the street. Roosevelt, who had remained uncharacteristically quiet most of the afternoon, was playing political leap frog. Everyone else in the room was experiencing more tangible visions: money, expansion, Progress. Atkins and Hanna beamed. Pulitzer and Hearst conjured circulation figures a year ahead, although Pulitzer remained dubious about outright war and even more dubious about annexation. Even Morgan and Vandervoort, by far the most conservative members of the group, were convinced. Palma had pulled Spain's plug. After 400 years, her disintegrating hold on the New World was about to cease. Vandervoort brought the group back to the one remaining question. "You understand, Dr. Palma? We cannot speak for our government, although a few of us possess some little influence." Palma nodded. "We are merely interested parties—interested in domestic order, interested in protecting our southern coast from a foreign threat, interested in expanding and strengthening the American economy."

"Joshua? May I?" J. Pierpont Morgan had decided to get the show moving. He had a late afternoon appointment with a Central American archaeologist who claimed to have discovered proof of man's immortality. "We can not promise that America will enter your little scrap, Dr. Palma, although at least one of our friends from the press here is certainly leaving few stones unturned. As you know, McKinley is opposed to intervention."

"McKinley is 'chicken-livered and lacks gall,'" Roosevelt exploded, drawing chuckles from Hearst and Teller.

Morgan glared balefully at Roosevelt for a moment, then turned back to Palma and continued. "Barring our entry into the war, what can we do for you? Now?"

Palma quickly pulled his shopping list from the rear pocket of his mind. "Four things, Mr. Morgan, three of which I know are within your power. About the fourth I am not so sure."

Vandervoort smiled to himself. Palma was nobody's fool; he knew perfectly well what these men were capable of, and he knew that several of them, particularly Roosevelt, Hearst and Hanna, would take the slightest doubt as a personal challenge. "What are your four requests, Dr. Palma?"

"First, the Junta needs credits to buy arms, ammunition and medical supplies. You can under write such credits. Second, you can supply safe transport, say from Charleston or Tampa. Third, you can convince the rest of your business community that, distasteful as it may seem in the short run, a successful end to the revolution, now, is preferable to another ten or twenty years of guerilla warfare that Spain can never win." Brilliant! Teller thought to himself. "Finally, gentlemen, I have reason to believe that your Consul General in Havana, General Fitzhugh Lee, has requested your new president to send a battleship to Havana, as a show of American resolve. "Gentlemen, the fanatically pro-Spanish militia groups have been rioting for more than a week. Foreign, including American, lives and property are in danger. An American show of naval strength would, I believe, prove salutary.

"The Spanish are, as you know, absolutely terrified that you might enter the war, but a 'friendly visit' by an American warship could calm things down in Havana, may even encourage the Spanish to honor their past agreements—such as finally closing the *reconcentrados* and releasing several thousand political prisoners from El Morro, La Punta and Las Cabanas."

Vandervoort looked slowly around the table. Only Teller's face registered doubt. "Done, Dr. Palma—at least as far as your first three requests are concerned." Then, turning to Schley and Roosevelt, he asked: "Commodore Schley? Mr. Secretary? What about a battleship for Dr. Palma?" Schley and Roosevelt mumbled to each other for a moment before the latter responded: "It is up to McKinley, of course, and he's afraid of a bloody incident. The Navy and State departments are pushing him, though. I can almost guarantee that that incompetent, ex-Confederate ass, Fitzhugh Lee, will get his ship."

"Good." Vandervoort rose to his feet. "Let us take a stretch, gentlemen. Then we need to discuss the deplorable state of the army, especially the Supply Corps, with General Shafter here. Dr. Palma. Thank you for your time."

Well, that's done, Palma thought, gently massaging his complaining stomach. I've given Maximo Gomez everything he requested. He rose, shook hands and left the room, contemplating a physical collapse of three or four days.

Part I

VIVA CUBA LIBRE!

Chapter One

NEW SPANISH EVACUATION OF CUBA WOULD
MEAN WAR IN SPAIN
Spanish Prime Minister is Seeking for a Way Out
* * * *
THE NEXT OUTBREAK OF ANTI AUTONOMY SPANISH
LOYALISTS LIKELY TO BE DIRECTED AGAINST AMERICANS
* * * *

Havana, January 4—Spain has no army left. The Cuban climate and Spanish corruption have robbed Spain's greatest colonial army of food and supplies. This pitiful remnant of a 300,000-man army is only slightly larger than the revolutionary army Gen. Gomez has at his disposal. Spain's skeletal army is the legacy of Gen. Weyler, who destroyed so much of the Cuban agriculture that he starved his own troops. He did not succeed in starving the rebel army. As the World has often reported, however, he did succeed in starving to death more than 100,000 Cuban civilians, mostly women and children. *The World*, January 14.

Central Cuba

O ver the previous six days Christopher Jackson and his aide had descended from the relative safety of the *Sierra Maestra* and ridden west across the far more dangerous rolling hills, shallow valleys and open plains of central Cuba. Dressed as the struggling sugar planter he once was and hoped again to become, Captain Jackson wore a worn, white cotton shirt open at the collar and tan, whipcord britches stuffed into old riding boots. His companion, Sergeant Fidel Federico, a broad-shouldered Negro who had spent the first half of his thirty-two years as a slave and the last ten as Christopher's foreman, wore the loose, unbleached cotton blouse and trousers of the *camposino*. Unlike most *camposinos*, however, and as befitted his status as Jackson's sometime foreman, Fidel too wore boots. Other than reaching their destinations in the Zapata Swamp, the riders had two concerns: avoiding the Spanish and finding food in the burned over and weed-infested wasteland that Cuba had become. As was the case with most of the Spanish soldiers and many of the rebels, Christopher's large but emaciated frame had been thinned by repeated bouts of malaria made worse by chronic malnutrition. Deep vertical creases scored his gaunt face and, despite his thirty-eight years, streaks of white patterned his wavy brown hair and ragged beard.

A week before setting out on his dangerous odyssey across the devastated countryside, Christopher had been sitting in his sagging hammock, lost in maunderings of self-doubt and regret and only vaguely aware of the rain beating down on the palm-thatched roof of his *palapa*. Although he was recovering physically from the malaria attack that had again flattened him, his mind seemed stuck in the darkness. For most of the eight months he had spent with the rebels in the *Sierra Maestra*, the mountain range that dominates east central Cuba, his doubts and fears had sat quietly in the back of his mind like a watchful but patient vulture. But in the last few weeks loneliness and disillusionment had crept into the foreground and blossomed into a cancer of despair that was eating into his heart. Christopher placed his face in his hands and wished that he had been strong enough to go out on patrol with his men. Only when hunting or fighting Spaniards was he able to avoid his darker mind.

For the past three days Christopher's company, under the temporary command of his lieutenant, had been waiting on the edge of the mountains to ambush a detachment of Spaniards. The Cubans were a day late returning and tension in the camp was running high. But suddenly Christopher felt the atmosphere of the camp change. "They are back! They are back!" he heard someone yell from the far side of the clearing. He exhaled sharply, donned his slicker and straw hat and stumbled out into the rain.

Christopher's battalion of *mambises* numbered almost three hundred men and boys and a few women, divided into three companies of cavalry, one of which he commanded. Their camp was hidden deep in a pine and palm forest on the western edge of the Sierra, and consisted of a large meadow dotted with fire rings and *palapas*, the palm-thatched shanties used for centuries by Cuba's rural poor. Here the rebels were safe from the Spanish, though the poorly led patrols of dragooned Spanish soldiers were not safe from them.

Christopher joined the scores of other fighters and camp followers who surged toward the opening in the clearing where the first horsemen had appeared. The women crowded to the front of the circle, anxious to check on their men. They became aware that the returning troops were quiet, a sign that they had experienced losses. Toward the end of the column, the litters of eight wounded jolted between eight pairs of horses. Bringing up the rear, three riders, each with a dead fighter draped over his saddle, followed the company into the clearing.

Now it begins, Christopher thought, as he watched half a dozen women pull their eyes from the men still sitting upright in their saddles and focus on the faces of the wounded. Almost immediately the lamentations began as one woman after another grabbed the hand of a husband or son and screamed into the low hanging clouds. Since the rebels possessed only the most primitive medical supplies, over half of the wounded usually died, often slowly and in great pain.

One of the women now stood alone, Mama Sandoval, an old mulatto dressed in black to mourn the loss of her husband, barely three months dead. The passing soldiers avoided her eyes. She turned to the last three riders and their dead baggage. The last horseman rode over to her, dismounted and laid at her feet the body of her sixteen-year-old son, covered in mud and blood except around the face where someone had wiped it clean. "I am deeply sorry, Mama Sandoval. I tried to hold Felipe back, but he wanted to be brave. He was a good soldier. He died well."

The blank-faced mother stared into the eyes of the soldier and shook her head, as if listening to a fool. "My dear son is dead. For nothing. My sweet husband is dead. For nothing. For nothing." She collapsed to the ground next to her son, tried to fold his already stiff body into her arms, rocked slowly back and forth and broke into a keening lamentation that rose in pitch and volume, as she cursed God and Man.

The soldier turned away from the sound and led his horse across the clearing to the *ramada*. For several minutes the hushed crowd listened to Mama Sandoval's laments and curses, which sank into their hearts, but slowly they turned away to the tasks at hand. Many of them had suffered such losses and felt the old woman's pain, but there was work to be done, and keeping busy helped.

After receiving the battle report from his lieutenant, who resented serving under a *Yanqui* and yearned to replace him, Christopher returned to his *palapa*, stretched out on his hammock and stared at the roof, where a small, lime green iguana was flicking its tongue to catch flies and mosquitoes. He would let the lieutenant report to the colonel and, in the process, curry favor.

When will this madness ever end? He wondered. Will it ever end? He shut his eyes and prayed for sleep. But ten minutes later Fidel Federico shook his captain's leg. After waiting a long minute for a response, he shook the leg again

"What do you want?" Christopher grumbled.

"I am sorry, Captain, but the colonel requires your presence."

"Now?"

"Yes, now."

Christopher shifted his feet to the earth and mumbled, "I'll be there in five minutes." He rose, rinsed his face with water from the small calabash bowl that sat near the corner of his hut, donned his worn and patched officer's tunic and headed for the command tent. A few minutes later he stood at attention before Colonel Mendoza's dented and splintered camp desk.

At first the dark-bearded colonel ignored him and continued to stare intently at the scattered pages of a letter. He nodded twice, as if agreeing with the writer, lifted his eyes and waved the younger man to a chair. For a long moment he stared at the tall American, whose grey eyes and sandy hair contrasted so sharply with the dark skins of his Negro, mulatto and Spanish command. He is different from us, in so many ways, Mendoza thought, and said, "Let us share a glass of rum, Captain Jackson. You look like you could use it." The colonel bent over to rummage in a pack.

"Thank you, sir. Rum can be a weakness. Still, there is nothing better," Christopher added, laughing nervously, well aware that Mendoza distrusted the dozen or so American and European planters who had, for whatever conflicted motives, condescended to join *Cuba Libre!*

The colonel sat back up and poured each of them half a glass of dark rum. "So, Captain, you think of potential weaknesses as something to laugh at? In times of war, it is often our weaknesses that get us killed." Mendoza lifted his glass and nodded somberly. "So, my expatriate Georgian colleague, let us drink rather to our strengths." He lifted the glass again and added half mockingly, "Captain Jackson, I drink to your courage and endurance. And to your loyalty to our cause."

Christopher raised his glass. *Viva Cuba Libre!* he said dutifully, raised his glass and drained the rum.

The colonel took a small sip, studied Jackson through almost totally closed black eyes and returned his glass to the table. "I believe you need a little more, no?"

"No, sir. Thank you." Not after what you just implied about weaknesses, he added to himself.

"Please, Captain Jackson." The colonel smiled forcefully, as if to test his subordinate. "There is an appropriate time for everything. This is one of those times. I insist."

Christopher held out his glass and watched the colonel fill it almost to the brim.

"I think maybe we should have another toast, our last before I send you away."

"Sir?"

Mendoza lifted his glass, took another small sip and held the glass out in front of him, as if to examine the purity of the amber liquor. "You enjoy our little war. Is that not the truth, Captain?"

Jackson found the question startling, almost insulting. "I take pride in doing my job well, in taking care of my men, in out-fighting Spanish lice. But no. No, sir. I have come to hate…"

"Why are you bothering with *Cuba Libre*? Most of you American and European planters, even the few of you sympathetic to our cause, are sitting out the war in Paris or Charleston or at least Havana. Why are you not with your family in a safer place?"

Jackson felt the colonel's penetrating gaze as a blow. That is becoming the question, Christopher thought, but gave the response that had sucked him into the revolution. "I am a Cuban, Colonel Mendoza. Like you and the rest of the *mambises*, I fight for our freedom. I believe it is worth the effort, worth the sacrifices we are all making," he added, though he was less than sure that he still believed the words.

Without in any way ceasing the unrelenting scrutiny of his subordinate's face, the colonel said, "I drink to your loyalty, Captain. And I drink to the sacrifices you have made for our cause, and to the sacrifices you will be called upon to make in the future." He took two small sips then drained his glass and watched as the *Yanqui* drained his.

I need more rest, Christopher thought, not a pointless conversation with this lawyer colonel. And probably not the rum. "Are you returning me to duty, sir?"

Mendoza shook his head hard, as if shaking off a mood. "I have a letter from General Calixto Garcia, who has received a cable from General Maximo Gomez, our most illustrious leader."

Christopher felt a surge of excitement. Maximo Gomez was responsible for the campaign in western Cuba. Perhaps…

"It seems that Estrada Palma, our man in New York, has arranged a meeting with some of your people who would like to go to war with Spain."

Christopher was finding it increasingly difficult to mask his impatience and fatigue. "They are not my people, Colonel. Other than a young brother in Washington, I have no connections left in the States— and haven't for years."

Mendoza glanced at the letter again and smiled slightly. "No. Of course not. You are a Cuban now, no?" He tapped the letter and continued. "Estrada Palma believes that if the meeting goes well we will at least be getting more, much more, in the way of arms and medicine. That is what our esteemed General Garcia, was pleased to confide to me in this letter." Mendoza carefully folded the letter and placed it in his bag.

"I see, sir."

"So, you ask, why are you here in my tent?"

"I was wondering about that, Colonel."

"Our illustrious Commander-in-chief, General Maximo Gomez, has a special need for you back in the Western Command. I presume that such a request does not displease you."

Christopher shook his head and tried to conceal the rush of excitement and pleasure. "It was General Gomez who sent me here in the first place. He does not want the world to know that I am one of you." At the phrase 'one of you,' the colonel raised his eyebrows, but Christopher chose to ignore the taunt and continued. "If I return to the Western Command, I will have greater opportunity to see my family."

At the mention of family a shadow passed briefly across the colonel's face. "General Gomez was right to send you to the *Sierra*." Mendoza glanced at the letter in his bag. "But now he thinks he might have an important mission for you. Whatever our commanding general has in mind must be important to pull you back half way across this miserable island." Mendoza rose from his field desk and Christopher leaped to his feet. "You will leave first thing tomorrow, disguised as the sugar planter you once were. Take your sergeant with you. General Gomez orders you to proceed directly to the home of your sergeant's parents in the Zapata Swamp. The General will reach you there. You are absolutely to avoid any fighting with our Spanish cousins."

"Colonel Mendoza, can you tell me..."

"That was the entire message," Mendoza lied. "You have your orders. Neither Maximo Gomez nor Calixto Garcia takes me into their confidence unless it is required. You are dismissed." But when Jackson saluted and turned to leave the tent, the colonel's face softened slightly. "Christopher?"

Jackson turned, startled. Mendoza had never called him by his Christian name. "Sir?"

"General Garcia and I appreciate your contributions during the eight months you have been with us. You are a brave man and an effective officer. I am afraid that I do not understand your motives as clearly as you seem to think you do, but I have come to respect you. Go with God."

After the *Yanqui* left, Mendoza pulled the letter out, read it through slowly and shook his head. Perhaps I should have told him, he thought, then shook his head again, put the letter back in his pack, and refilled his glass.

* * * * *

The first six days of their ride had been hard, and they still had almost a hundred kilometers to go. As they rode carefully through the burned over and almost totally abandoned countryside, they watched both for Spanish patrols and, with increasing desperation, for food to supplement their dwindling supply of mixed rice and beans. During the long, jarring ride, Christopher tried to focus on the surrounding bush, partly because he was always hungry, but mostly because he needed to keep his mind shut down. He had been in Cuba for almost thirteen years, the first ten establishing a small sugar plantation in the rolling hills of Matanzas Province, much of the last three fighting Spaniards. For the past eight months he had been separated from his family by hundreds of kilometers and by a series of indeterminate battles that had both occupied his mind and forced his previous life into a background that seemed, day by day and month by month, to be receding into an impossible distance.

But now, as they rode slowly west, toward home and the familiar, the would-be planter discovered that his long shut down feelings had become an enemy. One night, flat on his back with his head resting on his saddle, painful images rose and danced before him. He could not understand his inability to control his thoughts. He wanted only to think of his reunion with Consuelo, and of the great physical passion for each other they had known before the war. But more recent images refused to move aside. The memory of their last night together tormented him. It was the night before he sent her and the girls north to the city of Cardenas, and the night before he and Fidel and their field hands, on the orders of General Gomez, started their long journey toward the *Sierra Maestra*.

They were in their bedroom. Consuelo had withdrawn into outraged silence. They had argued little during their years together. But each time he had ridden off to join the *mambises*, she had withdrawn from him. And each time a little of her love for him had died.

Keeping her back to Christopher as much as possible, Consuelo moved slowly around the room, inhaling the treasures she would leave behind. She ran her palm along the highly polished surface of her mother's tall cherry armoire; stood for a moment in front of the large portrait of her father, a mulatto lawyer, poet and friend of Jose Marti who had been executed by the Spanish in the Ten Years War. She collapsed into the rattan rocker in which she had nursed their three daughters. For a long time she stared out the window into the blackness of the night.

They had been fighting for most of the past three days. Prior to each of his other departures they had made love and reaffirmed their vows, but this time she hadn't allowed him to touch her. This time not only was he abandoning her and their daughters; worse, he was sending her away, depriving them not only of his presence but also of their home.

Christopher knew he was causing her great pain. But someday, he was confident, someday when their beloved Cuba had won her freedom, Consuelo would appreciate his strength and wisdom and all would be well. For a moment he had thought of changing his mind: No idea could be worth what they were sacrificing. Almost immediately, however, he had brushed the insight aside as unworthy of his sense of honor and the oath he had sworn to *Cuba Libre!* He packed and re-packed his saddlebags and tried to ignore her silent rocking. For one searing moment he was almost overcome by his love for her and his hunger for her respect and approval. He wanted desperately to take her slight frame in his arms, to relent, to reassure her that he would never again leave her, *Cuba Libre!* be damned. He wanted to bury his face in the dark curls that covered her lovely head and stay safely in her arms forever. But he knew that he could not do so and continue to live with himself. He fastened the flaps of his saddlebags and walked to Consuelo's rocker. Standing behind her, he placed his long hands on her thin shoulders and stopped the rocking. She did not respond.

"Listen to me, Consuelo mine. There is no other choice. You must take the girls to your aunt's town house." He spoke slowly, softly, almost as if he were talking to a child. Although he could hear her teeth grinding, he continued. "Your aunt is pure Spanish, Consuelo, and a Loyalist. You and the girls will be safe there. Cardenas is a far safer place for you than the countryside." He pushed the rocker slowly forward and back, wanting the motion to comfort her. "For now our life here has ended. When we free Cuba, then we can start over." He had been using the same arguments for three days now, ever since General Maximo Gomez had ordered him east to the *Sierra Maestra.*

She shook her head and planted her feet to stop the rocking. The fear and anger broke from her heart in a non-stop barrage. "It may be too late by then, Christopher. Why can't you see that? For us I think maybe it is already too late. We are partners in life. We are a family. God means us to stay together." She turned her head sharply and glared at him. "We are one!" she screamed. "How can you possibly believe that your desertion can help our family?"

He walked around in front of the rocker, knelt down and took her small hands in his. "Consuelo. My beloved. Trust in me. It is for the best," he entreated, in what he hoped was a firmly reassuring voice.

"For the best?" She jerked her hands away and leaped from the rocker. "How can you do this thing? How can you tear us asunder like this?" She lifted her two clenched fists, grabbed the collars of her blouse and ripped it half to the waist. "Don't you see, you blind, stupid hero? This is what you are doing to my heart. Ripping it apart! This is what you are doing to our family."

"Consuelo. My dearest one, I have my orders." Even to him his words sounded insipid, impotent in the face of her feelings, but they were all the tools he had. "I must go. It has become too dangerous for you and the girls to remain in the countryside. So you, too, must go." He did not have the heart to tell her that as soon as she left, he and Fidel and their *mambises,* again at the express orders of General Gomez, would burn the plantation they had worked so hard to build.

She bent forward and hissed, "Do not send us away, Christopher. Do not leave us. My dreams tell me that I will never see you again."

Christopher finally lost patience and grabbed her by the shoulders. "That is the African in you speaking. Dreams are nonsense." He put his face within inches of hers and shook her twice. "You will take the girls to Cardenas!" Almost immediately he released her and shuddered. He had never before touched her with force.

She sank to the edge of the bed and lifted her hand to her mouth as if to hold back a scream.

"I am sorry, my dearest." He stroked her forehead, cheek and lips with his palm. "Our General has come up with this plan. It is a very logical . . ."

"Logical?" She leaped from the edge of the bed and stood next to the door, her body taut, poised to flee. "Every few months you abandon us to fight your glorious revolution. Now you send us away. Us! who depend upon your wisdom and trust in your strength. You tear us apart and then puff out your chest with pride in that old man's LOGIC?"

"Goddamn it! Consuelo," he swore in English. "Because of *Cuba Libre!* and that 'old man's' leadership, our daughters will live better lives."

"*Cuba Libre!* is nothing but a blood-sucking slogan, nothing but a fine talking whore! Why is this whore, this slogan, more important to you than our daughters?"

"Your sister is a whore, Consuelo, and you know you love her very much."

"We are not discussing my sister, Christopher. Besides, she is just another fool like you, deluded by this great fantasy of *Cuba Libre!*"

"We do what we do so that the next generation will know freedom. I do what I do for them, for our daughters. And for you, heart of my heart."

She shook her head hard. "Your 'glorious' revolution is consuming our lives, Christopher."

The fight had gone on for hours. Shortly before dawn, just hours before she would leave her beloved home and husband, Consuelo fell into a fretful, half-sobbing sleep. Christopher stood at the window, exhausted and depressed by the pain he was causing, by her contempt for his honor, and by his own fear that she might be right. But he was resolved. As a man and as a *mambi* officer, he must do what he must do. Some day she would understand, and respect his strength.

* * * * *

At their mid-day break, which they always took a safe distance off the trail, Fidel returned from a foraging trip into the jungle with some over-ripe plantains, which they mixed with the cold beans they had cooked the night before. The day was cool and damp, and they sat on a flat rock in a place where the sun broke through the canopy. Because they were always hungry, they were tempted to gobble the mush Fidel had prepared, but because they were disciplined and hoped to appease their complaining stomachs for an hour or two, they alternated small, slowly chewed mouthfuls of mush with large drafts of water. When they were about to resume their trek, Fidel put his hand on his captain's shoulder, cocked his large round head at a concerned angle and said, "Christopher, my captain? And my friend?"

"Yes?" Christopher registered the expression on his sergeant's face. "Are you all right?"

Fidel nodded. "It is you I worry about."

Christopher laughed. "Don't. The fever is gone. Even with this wretched diet and this butt blistering ride, each day I get stronger."

Fidel shook his head. "It is not your body that worries me."

Christopher's expression flattened and he turned away. "There is nothing wrong with my mind."

"We are homeward bound," Fidel said, his voice still full of concern. "I feel my heart lighten as I think of seeing Mama Oinja and Papi and my little brothers and sisters. They will have found a wild pig for us and we will eat well. Why are you not happy?"

The captain exhaled sharply and turned back to face Fidel. "I am pleased that I will be able to spend a little time with Consuelo and the girls. It is just that...my mind keeps falling back to the night before I sent them away, the night before we burned our home."

Fidel nodded. He had led the small group of *mambises* who had escorted Consuelo and the girls to the house of the proud Spanish lady in Cardenas. By burning his plantation Christopher had gained great respect from the rebels. Now, like them, he had little to lose. "We can re-build the house, Captain. Some day, when the war ends."

Christopher shook his head. "It is not just the house, Fidelito. It is the way Consuelo and I parted. Every time I leave to fight, we have tears and anger. But always, at least before, we have a little love. We hold each other, and give each other strength and comfort. But not this time."

Fidel shrugged. "That is the way with women. You sent her away from her nest. But after the war, my friend...

"That's what I told Consuelo." Christopher rose to his feet, ended the conversation and started back toward the trail. For the rest of the day he focused on the good years before the war. And that night, before he fell into exhausted sleep, he tried to recollect their first meeting.

He had just turned twenty-five and had completed the first cutting of the cane he had planted on his hundred hectares of land. His rich neighbor, Juan Moreno Escriber, had invited him to dinner. The maid had set the table on the front veranda of Don Moreno's spacious ranch house. Brightly striped Zapotec carpets imported from southern Mexico almost covered the red tile floor. Potted poinsettias lined the archways and a large silver crucifix dominated the white-washed wall behind the long mahogany dining table.

Christopher was pleased to be invited into the rich man's home and, in an attempt to be at least minimally presentable, had worn his not quite threadbare linen suit. He sat directly across from Consuelo Valdez, a permanent guest in her uncle's home. Despite his Georgia background and her obvious mulatto heritage, he was immediately intrigued. The slight young woman's oval face and golden skin glistened with health, and her deep brown eyes seemed to inhale her surroundings. In an attempt to seem taller than her five feet, Consuelo wore her loose black curls piled on top of her head, held in place by a bright abalone comb.

God, she's beautiful, he thought, as he watched her move a bite of duck to her mouth. A tiny fleck of gravy stuck to the edge of her full lower lip, and he saw himself licking it away. He felt an erection starting and crossed his legs self-consciously. He could not help staring at her, but she said nothing and concentrated on her plate.

Señor Moreno was pontificating, his voice droning on and on. Though Christopher answered when necessary, his mind and aroused body inhaled the demure young woman across the table. Her mother sat at Consuelo's right, a haggard, broken woman of fifty who still mourned her husband's decade-old death by Spanish firing squad. Next to Christopher sat Theresa, Consuelo's twelve-year old sister who, a few years hence, would flee the estate in shame.

Consuelo sipped from a glass of white rose. Christopher felt an emptiness in the pit of his stomach, a great hunger for the young woman who had not even bothered to raise her eyes and acknowledge his presence. Even though they had exchanged less than a dozen words before sitting down to table, he was absolutely sure that she was playing coy. Almost without thinking, certainly without thinking about the possible consequences, he extended his leg and brushed the inside of his boot along the skirt of her dress. She slowly replaced her glass, placed both hands on the table and turned pink.

A few minutes later Señora Valdez rose from the table and left the room in tears. Christopher looked around. What had he missed?

As if in answer to his unspoken question, Señor Moreno turned to him: "You must excuse my sister, Señor Jackson. Everyone warned her when she did it. If she is upset with our political opinions, she has only herself to blame. "We knew what would happen if she married beneath her class. But to marry a rebel and a man whose mother was an African slave?" He raised his shoulders and shrugged. Christopher glanced back at Consuelo, who glared at her uncle. A moment later she excused herself from the table and went off to comfort her mother.

Soon afterwards, they sat again in the same places, eating boiled beef and listening to another of Don Moreno's monologues. This time Consuelo wore a high-collared dress with a lace ruffle that was bothering her chin. Every few minutes she shifted her neck, as if trying to rescue it from the starch.

I wish she would look at me just once, Christopher thought, as he allowed the top of his mind to carry on a conversation with the pompous old man. God but she must think I'm a fool. As he had been doing all evening, he winked every time she looked up to answer a question or address someone. Only Theresa, the skinny little girl on his left, seemed to sense what was going on. Though she said nothing, sometimes the girl giggled, apparently enjoying the game her sister and the *Yanqui* were playing.

"Cuba is not capable of self-government. We must stay with Spain, or, if God wills it, become part of your United States." Moreno smiled importantly at Christopher, who smiled absently back. Just like my father, he thought, totally indifferent to the old man's sentiments. A pompous blowhard. Christopher concentrated on the shadows and veins of Consuelo's right hand, imagined touching it.

At that moment, just as he was removing his fork from his mouth, he felt her foot on his knee. Though he looked straight at her, she continued to stare at her plate. She was smiling, as if recollecting a funny story. He felt the toe of her shoe hesitate slightly before descending several inches down his leg and pulling away. Every muscle in his body tightened, and then he coughed. He had swallowed a semi-masticated piece of beef. The one sharp cough resurrected the beef and sent it full force into the middle of the table.

Señor Moreno stopped in mid-sentence and frowned. Christopher turned red, looked around the table and listened to the breeze move through the trees on the other side of the veranda. Then, almost as if to mock him, the young woman lifted her face, smiled and winked at him. Little Theresa laughed so hard she had to leave the table.

"I am extremely sorry," Christopher mumbled. "Please excuse me." He started to rise from the table, realized with horror that he had an erection, and sank slowly back to his seat.

* * * *

When Christopher awoke just before dawn, his leg still burned where Consuelo's foot had touched him. He lay still for a moment, lost in the warm glow of mixed memories and dreams. But as he became aware of where he was and what he was trying to do, the glow faded. Today, as they moved further into central Cuba and onto the almost flat plains of Camuguey, the Spanish patrols would probably increase, protective cover would be scarce, and they would have to move more slowly, in fits and starts.

Fidel was already up. He had saddled their mounts and spread their small cold breakfast on a torn banana leaf. "How are you today, my captain?"

Christopher felt his forehead, nodded and rose unsteadily to his feet. "I still think I am getting stronger" He glanced at their breakfast and laughed. "A good meal would help."

"Yes," Fidel grunted, as he forced himself to drink deeply from his canteen between each meager bite of breakfast.

They spent the next three days moving slowly along stream beds and through slender tendrils of forest. When forced to move in the open, they spent long periods with Christopher using his binoculars to sweep slowly back and forth across the countryside. They moved quickly only in the early mornings and late evenings, and spent hours each day in hiding.

The first day on the plain they managed to trap a small rabbit, but after that they found nothing but an occasional bunch of plantains or mangoes. The few haciendas they came across were nothing but burned and looted ruins, and the once numerous cattle had disappeared, slaughtered by the competing armies for food. After three days of eating little but half-rotten fruit, they finally crossed the *Rio Jatabanico* and entered the low foothills north of the *Sierra Sancti Spiritus.* That evening, well into a forest of evergreens and giant ferns, they dismounted to stretch their legs and cool their horses . The light had already faded. All but the most luminous shades of green had been absorbed to black.

* * * *

As they walked slowly along a cart track, Fidel suddenly flung his right arm out across Christopher's chest. After twenty seconds of standing absolutely still, he turned and whispered, "You hear?"

Christopher shook his and shrugged his shoulders. "What?"

Fidel shook his head, handed over the reins to his mount and disappeared into the gloom. Ten long minutes later he re-emerged just far enough to beckon Christopher on. Christopher tied their horses to a royal palm, padded forward for a moment and stopped. In the distance he could hear unguarded voices and giggles, and knew immediately what they had stumbled onto. Only young Spanish soldiers, suffering from shoddy discipline and low morale, would be so careless. The two rebels turned their backs on the sounds and put their heads together. "Can we get by them?" Christopher whispered.

"Not tonight, not through this." Fidel shook his head at the all-encroaching darkness.

"How many are there?"

Fidel shrugged. "I do not know."

"We could go back half a kilometer and sleep off the trail," Christopher suggested without enthusiasm. "They will probably move on in the morning."

"Yes, we could do that," Fidel agreed with a noticeable lack of enthusiasm. He was having a hard time sustaining his large frame. The fruit was running right through him, his butt was almost too sore to put on the saddle, and his stomach hurt, particularly at night when his mind was not tied to the possible dangers. He had no desire to re-trace his steps. "They have food. I smelled roast pig."

"Sergeant, our orders are to avoid all contact with Spanish patrols."

"Yes, that is the truth. But I have a great need for some roast pig."

Christopher gave a few brief seconds of silent thought to the problem, then smiled. "Lead on, Sergeant." Fidel's wide grin shone in the darkness.

Around a bend the two Cubans halted again. Less than thirty meters away and in the middle of the trail, they counted four soldiers hunkered around the glowing coals of a carelessly large fire. Caught up in telling stories and chewing mouthfuls of pork, the squatting soldiers focused on the fire and the charred carcass of a small wild pig. Again the two *mambises* turned their backs away from the fire to confer, though the noisy and absorbed circle could not possibly have heard them. "Jesus and Maria," Fidel whispered. "Have you ever smelled anything that good?"

Christopher shook his head. "Not for a lifetime or two. How many guards are posted?"

Fidel shrugged. "There must be at least one."

"We will wait."

"They might eat it all."

Christopher barely suppressed a guffaw. "You don't really see that as a problem."

Fidel nodded. "The truth is the truth."

"We will wait, and watch them enjoy their last supper."

Within twenty minutes, after some argument, a short, skinny boy rose to his feet, withdrew his rifle from the pyramid stack and walked a few paces toward the Cubans. Immediately, a shape they had not noticed detached itself from the trees and rushed to the fire. Just a few minutes later the new guard appeared back in the trail and moved a few steps closer to the comfort of the fire and his companions.

"That is probably the only guard," Fidel whispered.

"We will wait."

Within the hour the soldiers around the still glowing fire had unstrapped their bedrolls and rolled up in fetal positions around the secure glow. The lone guard now sat at the side of the trail, his back against a large rock.

"I think you're right, Fidelito. There's no sign of another sentry."

Christopher nodded in the direction of the lone sitting soldier, whose head now rested on up-raised knees. The two rebels pulled out their machetes and their pistols, the latter of which long conditioning had taught them to use only when necessary. "Go!" Christopher signaled, and followed two paces later.

When Fidel got within two meters of the lazy soldier, the boy felt a shiver of fear run along his spine. He looked up just in time to see Fidel's machete bite into the bridge of his nose and well into his skull. The boy fell soundlessly back against the rock. Fidel moved around the fire to the left, Christopher to the right. Each had killed an additional soldier before the surviving two even reacted; the ambush was over in less than a minute. The last soldier, an under-age corporal, pulled a large pistol and pointed it at Christopher, who was leaping toward him. The boy blinked into the greyest, coldest eyes he had ever seen and pulled back the hammer with his thumb.

"MA-CHE-TEEEE!" Christopher hissed, as he nearly severed the pistol arm just above the wrist and back-handed the machete most of the way through the corporal's neck. Christopher's scream, the terrifying *Mambi* battle cry, was the only accompaniment to a few short gurgles and sighs.

Once sure that the Spaniards were dead, and breathless after their draining charges of adrenalin, the two Cubans withdrew a few steps and collapsed in the trail. After a few minutes of raspy breathing, Fidel rose to his feet and fetched the remnants of the charred pig. He placed the carcass on the grass alongside the cart ruts and sliced off short strips, the first of which he handed to Christopher. "Here. Eat. It will help."

Christopher shook his head. "Not yet." He was still shaking, exhausted and slightly nauseous from the sight and smell of blood. "Sometimes I think I am getting too old to be a warrior."

Fidel shook his head and snorted, "I hope that I never get too old to kill these pubic lice." He walked into the jungle for a moment and returned with two plantain leaves, which he wrapped around the small pile of boned pig, then ran back down the trail to fetch their horses.

Christopher continued to sit in the trail, slowly willing his rasping lungs and shaking hands back under control. "It has to be the malaria," he mumbled. "I'm just not that damned old." When Fidel returned, Christopher grabbed his horse's reins, led the horse slowly forward, and allowed himself a seldom-voiced moment of despair. "What will it take to end this God-cursed war?"

Fidel looked over and smiled. "It has only lasted for fifty years, my friend. Off and on."

"Yes. Mostly on."

When they finally bedded down an hour later, Christopher fell into a restless sleep. Early in the morning he dreamed of his son's death nine years earlier. He heard the voice again, Consuelo's voice, calling as from a great distance. He whispered, "I love you, Consuelo. I will love you until I die. Do not despair, my love." He leaned over and kissed her clammy, sleeping face. "We are young. We will have other sons."

The doctor turned his fat, white-suited body and nodded at Christopher. "Take the baby away. She must not see it again."

The doctor's voice came from far away, like a foghorn off the Georgia coast in winter. Christopher stared at Consuelo, who was lying on the blood-soaked bed; and at the purple little body of his son, curled lifeless on the towel, the umbilical cord a twisted noose around his neck; and at the doctor, who was trying to get his attention. The doctor's mouth kept opening and shutting, like a huge carp with three gold teeth. He flapped his hands. "Take it away and bury it."

Christopher picked up the tiny body and walked out into the early morning light that was slowly burning away the mists. "Be strong, my love," he mumbled. "Have faith. We have a lifetime together to raise sons."

He awoke before first light, shivering and apprehensive. He had never had that dream before, or seldom even thought of their lost son, who had not lived long enough to receive a name, or baptism, and who in Consuelo's heart was a tiny ghost that floated in the darkness between heaven and hell.

In the next three days they crossed the *Rio Sagua la Grande*, then headed west-southwest along the *Rio Janabanillo*. They were finally back in western Cuba, and in home country, though still riding through a burned over wasteland devoid of people. Since the land was even more open, Fidel led them off the main trail and concentrated on light tracks that skirted the northern edge of the mangrove swamps. The tracks were the paths of hope and terror traced over the centuries, first by runaway Indian slaves, then by their African successors, and more recently by the *mambises*. Fidel knew the paths well.

At mid-day they flushed three vultures squatting at the side of the trail and almost rode into a small group of refugees. Because of the silence and stillness of the refugees, the bird song from the canopy sounded normal. They rode around a bend at a slow trot and almost stepped on the first woman. Five others lay along the path and did not even attempt to move away from the horses. The seventh woman, a tall, black skeleton, stood in the middle of the trail, facing the riders. Like the others she was dressed in filthy rags. Her blouse was a sleeveless man's shirt without buttons. Running sores covered her face and shriveled breasts. The woman held out her hand, palm up, to stop them. No one spoke or even moaned, though all but one, who looked as if she might be dead, focused their deep-set eyes on the riders.

The two men stared back for a moment and dismounted. Christopher pulled from his saddlebag a shallow, yellow calabash bowl, two half-rotten potatoes and the remnants of the package of pork. Wordlessly, he chopped the strands of pork and the potatoes into mush, added water and stirred. He squatted next to a pale, rasping woman who wore the shreds of a once fancy black dress, dipped his middle three fingers into the bowl and placed them gently into the open mouth. Fidel nodded approvingly, pulled out his own bowl and joined his captain. His first patient was a woman who had lost most of her salt and pepper hair and whose lineless face had frozen into an open-mouthed but long-exhausted scream of horror. Only her sunken black eyes moved. When Fidel tried to drop the gruel directly into her throat, she choked it right back up.

"It will do no good."

The two men snapped their heads around and stared at the skeleton standing in the path. She stared back. Of the group she was the only one whose eyes still glowed, like lanterns flickering deep in an airless mine.

"It will do no good." Her voice was horse, frog-like, jarring.

Christopher turned back to his dying patient. Within the crook of his arm, sharing his breath, lay a set mask that radiated more concentrated horror than even he had ever seen.

"It is too late," the tall skeleton croaked.

At that moment the woman in Christopher' arms choked once then exhaled a long deep sigh and relaxed against his chest. He turned back to the woman in the road and nodded. "Yes. It is too late for this one."

"It is too late for everybody," the speaker croaked. "It is too late for us even to want to live."

"I think maybe that she is right." Fidel jerked his head around the group. "Look at these women."

Christopher let out a sigh almost as deep as that of the woman who had just expired against his chest. He placed the body in the grass and, struck by the horror, stood and turned to the speaker. "Where are the children?"

"They died in the *reconcentrado*. You brave *mambises* who hate the Spanish more than you value the lives of your families did not come soon enough."

Yes, Christopher thought, trying to divorce himself from her despair. *Cuba Libre!* far too often required unbearable sacrifices.

Fidel extended his calabash to the speaker. When she shook her head he mumbled, "I feel with your sorrow, Lady."

Christopher was overcome with a sense of impotence. There was little left they could do for these women, other than stay with them a few days and bury them. "What can we do?" he forced himself to ask, suddenly anxious to move on.

"You *mambises*," the black skeleton croaked. You brave patriots who were men enough to start this war. Are you men enough to shoot us?"

Christopher glanced at Fidel, whose eyes brimmed with huge tears, stared at the ground for a long moment, raised his eyes to scan the passive faces of the refugees, and looked directly into the anger-filled eyes of the speaker. "No." He shook his head. "I am sorry. We are not men enough to do this thing you ask of us."

"Please, Lady," Fidel mumbled. "Forgive us."

The speaker shook her head and tried to spit. "Then go!"

The two men nodded, silently remounted and rode on. They had taken fewer than a score of steps, however, when Fidel blinked, pulled his horse to a halt and turned back toward the women. "Ride on, my captain. Please. I will catch up with you in one moment."

He thought he knew the woman. "Please, Lady, he said as he came to a halt directly in front of her. "What can you tell us about the Spanish?" She did not speak. She was not seeing him but staring through him, as if he were a ghost He was ashamed to ask again. This woman no longer cared about them, or about the revolution. He felt a rush of anger at both himself and the woman for his shame. Who is she? He was a soldier and needed to know things. "Please, Lady. Have you seen any Spanish patrols?"

"The Spanish are always with us, Fidel."

At the sound of his name spoken by her deep croak, Fidel shivered. "Where are you people from?"

"Cardenas, Fidel." The skeleton's mouth tightened to a ghastly smile, and he saw that she had lost most of her teeth.

"Jesus and Maria!" Cardenas was their market town. Carmine. "Carmine?" She had been married to his cousin, who had died in battle two years earlier.

"We ran away from a *reconcentrado*."

"Ah, Carmine, my cousin. You are a long day's ride from Cardenas. Why are you out here in the jungle?"

"Only one day?" The skeleton shook her head. "For maybe two weeks now we have been wandering. There is nobody left in the country-side. Nowhere can we find any food." For the first time tears appeared in her hollow eyes. "I think maybe all our saints have abandoned Cuba."

Fidel's mouth went dry. One does not say such a thing, even if it is true. "Where are the others?" Carmine shook her head slowly. "Carmen! Where are the others?"

"The others?"

He tried again. "What happened?"

"Soldiers drove us from the town, everybody who wasn't Spanish." She pointed a long, crooked finger at the dead woman in the fancy black rags. "Even some of them. Two months ago." She shook her head, aware that she no longer tracked time.

"The others? Please, Carmine. What about them?"

Again she shook her head. "That is the *Yanqui*? That man with you?"

"Yes. Do you know what happened to his family? They were in Cardenas, staying with Doña Valdez."

Carmine shook her head and sat down in the path. "I did not see them in the *reconcentrado*, in *El Cajon del Muerto*. I cannot say. Many hundreds of people died in that place." She leaned back on one arm and held out the other, again imploring him. "Please kill us, Fidelito."

Fidel shook his head. "My heart is not strong enough."

"Your brother would have done this thing we ask."

"I am sorry, Carmine. May your spirits find rest with Mother Mary and all the saints." He turned his horse and cantered away.

"The Spanish will always be everywhere," she said, long after Fidel had disappeared. "Only we will have left."

"What was that about?" Christopher asked. Fidel shrugged and raised his canteen to take a long drink. Although it was a fairly cool day he was sweating. "Fidel?"

"I wanted to find out what she knew. About the Spanish." Fidel took another drink and carefully re-screwed the lid to his canteen. "And to get her story."

Christopher raised his eyebrows and shook his head. "Well, what did you find out?"

Fidel stared up the trail and again shrugged his shoulders. "Not much, my friend. She didn't know anything about Spanish patrols, but she said they were everywhere."

"That's not much help. Anything else?"

"Not that we want to hear," Fidel said, and changed the subject. "I think that if we stay on these old slave trails we will not see any Spanish patrols.

Chapter Two

NEW SPANISH EVACUATION OF CUBA WOULD MEAN
WAR IN SPAIN
*Our Two Most Powerful Battleships and a Great Auxiliary Fleet
Held in Readiness*

* * * *

Washington, January 13—The United States battleship *Maine*, the cruiser *Marblehead* and a flotilla of torpedo ships have been held all day at Key West, with steam up, ready to sail at a moment's notice to Havana.

The two powerful battle-ships *Indiana* and *Iowa*—either of which could fight alone the entire Spanish navy—and the swift cruiser *New York* are at Hampton Roads, only three days sail from Havana.

A dispatch was received late last night from Gen. Lee describing the riotous behavior of the Spanish loyalists. Gen. Lee, the American Consul-General, emphasized the seriousness of the situation and reiterated the need to have the fleet in readiness and at least one battle-ship in the immediate vicinity. *The World*, January 14.

Habana Viejo

A t first the knocking seemed a long way off and to have nothing to do with her. When it came closer she rolled over and moaned. The door opened and a dark, heavy-set woman dressed in black and carrying a pitcher of warm water entered.

"Captain Valdez?" Theresa opened her eyes and stared at the white-washed wall. Someone was calling her back. "Captain Theresa!" Theresa turned toward the door and blinked.

"I am very sorry, my captain, but you asked me to wake you by 6:00. Your patron will be here in an hour." The woman moved heavily across the darkened room to a walnut bureau and tall mirror. She poured the contents of the pitcher into a zinc basin and asked, "Are you strong enough for this? It is not too late to send a messenger."

Theresa groaned and sat up. "I'll be fine, Josefina." Her eyes brimmed with tears. She was still in her dream, still back in the *reconcentrado* with Consuelo, who had just died. She was stroking Consuelo's matted hair and staring at little Elizabeth, who was also dying.

Josefina glanced at her diminutive commanding officer and tears appeared in her own eyes. "You do not have to do this, Captain. General Gomez ordered you to return to duty only after regaining your strength."

Theresa bowed her head as if in agreement, then wiped her large brown eyes with the tips of her delicate fingers and placed her bare feet on the flowered carpet. She knew where she was now, and what it was that she must do. "We are at war, Josefina. Our General still needs information."

"But you have given so much recently. Your sister…"

"That will be all, Josefina." Clad only in her worn ivory chemise,

Theresa Valdez pulled her her ninety pounds to attention and gestured for her subordinate to leave.

Josefina placed her hand on the latch, cocked her head like a scolded puppy and left. Theresa sat back down on the edge of the bed for a moment, mumbled, "I'm sorry, Josefina," then pulled the chemise over her head and walked to her dresser. She dropped a sponge into the basin of warm, perfumed water, squeezed it semi-dry and rinsed and re-rinsed her face and daintily proportioned body.

Her twice-daily sponge baths were the one ritual that could bring her a moment or two of peace; she felt cleaner, freer than at any other time of the day or night. The rose-scented water helped to wash away the lingering scent of the influential men who purchased her evenings. The massaging motion of the sponge freed her mind to float backward to the few good years and forward into fantasy.

But this evening she stared into the mirror, oblivious to her massaging hands and the warm sponge. In the nine days she had spent in *El Cajon del Muerto*, she had lost ten of her hundred pounds. Almost three weeks after the breakout, her large, slightly slanted almond eyes still appeared huge in their deep sockets and her cheekbones jutted sharply from her oval face.

Theresa watched her eyes brim and overflow with large tears. "I must stop this." She bowed her head and watched the tears drop into the basin where, like liquid pebbles, their ripples marred the surface of the still water. Beneath the ripples, her older sister's rigid face stared back at her.

"Mother of God!" Theresa pleaded as she pulled her mind back to the present. "Please give me the strength of self-control." Her jaw rigidly set, she dried her body and concentrated on dressing for the evening. "Control!" she muttered. "Control!"

Josefina knocked lightly and stuck her head through the door. "I am sorry, Theresa. Isabella needs some medicine."

Theresa nodded curtly and continued brushing her loose black curls. "I still have some time."

A tall, full-breasted woman with henna stained hair entered. She was dressed in a green silk wrapper and she was in tears. "Theresa, I can't do this any more. Not with the Beast."

"Come on in, Little One." Theresa forced a smile for her much taller and more buxom associate and walked to her liquor cabinet. She extracted a blue bottle from which she poured laudanum into a whiskey glass and handed it to Isabella. "How else may I help thee?"

Isabella sat on the edge of the bed, grabbed the glass in both hands and took four long sips. "Theresa, I have been a whore since I was fourteen. It is not just what this evil man requires of my body. It's who he is, and what I know he does to our companions."

"Please, Isabella. Lie back. Relax. Do not think."

Although Isabella allowed her superior to push her gently back on the bed, her words came faster, and her normally alto voice rose half an octave. "When he is hurting me, I think of my two cousins, Alfredo and Guitterez. That fat devil tortured them in El Morro and then dropped their bodies through the trap door and allowed them to wash up on the beach for the land crabs. When…"

"Hush, Little One. You will only become more upset."

"When he is biting and twisting me, I…I see the land crabs eating my cousins."

"Hush, Isabella. Do not think of these horrors."

"Theresa, my dreams tell me that this man is the Devil. I am so frightened I think my heart will stop." Isabella took a deep breath and drained the glass. "Please, Captain. Just a little more?"

Theresa thought for a moment about the august personage of "the Beast," Major Ignacio Alvarez. He was the Spanish *Commandante* of Intelligence for *La Habana* and chief inquisitor at El Moro castle, the three hundred year old pile of mossy rock that sat on a guano-covered point overlooking the entrance to the harbor. She reached out to caress Isabella's tear-streaked cheek with her palm and shook her head. "I am sorry, my friend. You do not have to be with Alvarez. I cannot order you to do that. But if you go through with this assignment, you must—must—be fully alert.

"Please, my captain. I need…"

"After the major leaves, Little One. Ask Josefina." Theresa studied Isabella's eyes, waiting for the drug to take effect. "You do not have to lie with that corpulent pig. We will make an excuse." She patted her on the knee.

Isabella grunted and propped herself onto her elbow. She shook her head and her voice dropped from hysteria to sarcasm. "Do not lie to me, Captain. For me one drug is enough."

Theresa grabbed the larger woman by the shoulders and shook her. "Hope is not a drug, Isabella. It is our life force!

Isabella laughed and shook her head. "Hope for what? Peace? I am a soldier. I will do my job. But…no, Captain Valdez. Our war began long before we were born, and we are still dying faster than the Spaniards."

Theresa nodded and kissed Isabella on the forehead. "Do not despair. Our strength is deeper than theirs."

"No!" Isabella shook her head. "I do not fuck Spaniards because I believe we will win; it is all I have ever done. I fuck these bastards because of what we learn from them, and because we earn money for *Cuba Libre!* and because *Cuba Libre!* is my life."

"That is our hope, dear. Do not abandon it."

Josefina knocked and entered, visibly upset. "Major Morales is here.

"Guillermo?" Theresa's face hardened and she reached for her wrapper.

"Yes, I am sorry. I told him that you have a patron who will be arriving soon, but you know how he is, no? He demands to see you, immediately." Josefina nodded to Isabella. "Perhaps it is time for you to return to your station?"

"It is okay, Josefina from the cantina," Isabella giggled. "Our gracious captain wants you to give me some more medicine when the Beast finishes with me." She turned to Theresa and smiled charmingly.

Theresa nodded at Josefina. "Only after Alvarez leaves!" She looked directly into Isabella's dilated eyes, as if to measure her strength, and asked, "Will you be all right?"

Isabella rose from the bed. "Tell our major Morales that I would be pleased to receive him again sometime." She licked her lips and raised her eyebrows. "He is very strong."

"Yes." Yes, Theresa continued to herself, a strong, stupid pig.

The three women turned at the sound of quick, heavy steps. A broad-shouldered, pigeon-chested man dressed in white linen and worn boots entered the room. Long black hair and a heavy beard all but concealed his swarthy skin. In one smirking glance his bright but tiny black eyes surveyed the three women.

"Hello, Isabella. It is always my pleasure." He walked over, ran his stubby index finger between her large, partially exposed breasts and chucked her under the chin, then turned his attention to Theresa. Josefina grabbed Isabella by the arm and, clucking protectively, led her from the room.

Theresa collapsed into her favorite chair, a high-backed rattan rocker, and struggled to control her feelings. Seeing Morales always triggered old rage and disgust. "What do you want of me, Major?"

"Our General is bringing Christopher Jackson back from the *Sierra Maestra*."

"Christopher? Mother of God! Why?"

"He wants to see you."

"Christopher . . .?"

Guillermo Morales laughed. "Yes, Theresa, my sweetheart. Maybe he is like me. Maybe he would like to fuck you, hey?" He laughed a long, leering chuckle, then set his face hard. "Your *Yanqui* brother-in-law does not even care that you exist right now. He has other problems on his mind. It is our most illustrious General who requires your presence."

Morales stalked to her chair, placed his large square hands on its arms and leaned into her face. She smelled the stale garlic and the mint he used to subdue its power. "I am to bring you to him. When can you leave?"

Theresa squeezed her knees tightly together and tried to push his hands from her chair. "My patron will be here shortly. I will be ready to leave an hour after curfew."

The major nodded. "Who are you fucking tonight, Captain?"

"As a fellow officer in *Cuba Libre!*", she hissed, "I demand some respect."

"Demand?" He cleared his throat as if about to spit in her face. "You do not respect me, Captain Valdez. Do you?" He swallowed noisily and smiled, then dropped his hand and played at prying her knees apart. "I am a major, a rank I earned. Yet you have no respect for me. You are a whore who fucks fat Spanish turds and foreigners, yet you 'demand' my respect? Who is your client, Captain?"

Theresa leaped from her chair, glided to the door and pulled it open. "The American vice-consul, Amos Jordan."

Morales laughed. "Ah, the man who is less than a man, the talker, the one who buys your time but seldom takes you."

"Please, Major. I need a few minutes to prepare myself. I will be ready to leave one hour after curfew."

"Be dressed for a long ride. We will meet the General in the Zapata." Guillermo Morales feinted a grab at her breast, laughed again and left.

Shaking visibly, Theresa returned to her rocker. She glanced at the blue bottle of opium, which she also used on bad nights, then shook her head. "No!" But almost immediately she sank into a morass of self-doubt: When will I get my strength back? When will I get my heart back? How long before the Beast figures out that we're not just a covey of greedy whores? How much longer can we keep this pig sty open?

She thought of the three other whores she managed for *Cuba Libre!* and of all the men whom she had used and been used by during her long years in *La Habana*. She succumbed to a brief but sharp wave of self-revulsion, then moved quickly to the cabinet and took a stiff pull from the blue bottle.

A few minutes later Theresa stood at her narrow window and stared sightlessly down at the small patio. She concentrated on the comforting rush of the laudanum as it moved from her head to her toes and back up along her gradually relaxing body. For a moment she allowed her mind to wander to the tall *Yanqui* who was married to her sister. Have they told him? she wondered. It occurred to her that Christopher Jackson was the only member of her family still alive. She felt a desperate need to be near him, to partake of his strength and courage and commitment to their cause. Maybe, someday…Maybe someday what? Maybe someday we can share our pain?

* * * * *

Trying to ignore the excitement percolating from Havana's central plaza two floors down, Amos Jordan squinted through half glasses at the letter he had written almost two weeks earlier. Jordan's desktop never contained more than one document at a time, and this one rested squarely in the middle of a large green blotter. The Vice Consul valued neatness almost as much as he valued simplicity. He also valued integrity, and for the past half hour he had been re-reading his one page request for retirement from the Consular Corps, effective June 30. The request lacked only a current date and his signature. At the moment he was trying to comprehend why he had yet to supply the signature.

Jordan was startled from his reverie by a loud knock, followed immediately by the blustery entrance of the Consul-General, Fitzhugh Lee, a walrus-mustached, cigar chewing ex-Confederate general.

"Jordan!" Lee yelled, as if his Vice Consul were hiding fifty yards away. "I don't know why the sam hell I'm botherin' ta ask, but what do ya think of this?" He strode to Jordan's desk and dropped a cablegram on top of the green blotter. "Think this'll get their idiotic attention?"

It's not their idiotic attention we need, Jordan thought as he dropped his eyes from his superior to the cablegram. "Is this another request for the Marines?"

"Even better, damn it. Just read!" While his subordinate leaned back in his chair and studied the cablegram, Fitzhugh Lee buttoned and unbuttoned the loosely fitting, white linen coat that almost disguised his girth, adjusted the knot of his red, polka-dotted cravat and chomped on his unlighted cigar. "Well?"

Jordan stood, placed his hands on his desk and bent his slender form in the Consul's direction. "You're asking for a fleet?"

"I'm merely trying to protect American lives and property."

On the street below, what had been little more than a distracting murmur slowly increased to an angry roar. General Lee rushed to one of the windows that overlooked the plaza. As if pulled along against his will, Amos Jordan limped to another window just as a mob poured into the long plaza that separated their hotel from Havana's Central Park. Jordan pulled up one of the venetian blinds and gazed down at the excited mob, which stretched all the way down the tree-lined *Prado*. Ah yes, Jordan thought. Here they come, back from a hard day of destruction. The pride of Spain. The bane of the revolution. Los *anti-autonomistos*. Not that they look all that angry, he told himself. The mob of several hundred Volunteers appeared, rather, as if they had stolen a week on Carnival. Once again they had stood up for the Queen Regent and her infant son. Tonight they would drink Bacardi, and tomorrow, if they were not too tired, they would seek additional targets for their patriotic outrage.

"My God! Jordan. The consulate isn't safe."

Jordan smiled to himself and continued to stare down at the mob. "Perhaps not, General, but I rather doubt that we're in imminent peril."

"Every American on this island is in imminent peril, Jordan."

"Perhaps. But no Americans have been hurt thus far, and for a reason. The Spanish are terrified of any incident that might bring America into this war."

A block behind the plaza, in the breezeless evening, a pillar of smoke rose straight up from *El Autonomista*, one of the three newspapers that had enraged the pro-Spanish Volunteers, who prided themselves on the purity of their European blood and their unimpeachable loyalty to the Queen.

This must have been the way our own Tories responded in the last century, Jordan thought. If you think the umbilical cord to the glorious motherland is threatened—especially if you think your property is threatened by the great, unwashed and illiterate hordes—you fight back: Burn their rabble-rousing, pro-independence newspapers, hang their leaders, proclaim your undying allegiance to the avaricious idiots who surround the kings and queens. March, sing, burn, kill. "And lose anyway," he muttered.

"What's that?"

"You know what I think, General Lee. Cuba is a powder keg. The Spanish are already washed up here, although they have yet to accept the fact. Our job should be to calm things down. Take this riot as instance."

"Goddamnit, Jordan! What's your problem? And when the hell are ya gonna sign that damn resignation and get your pigeon-livered Yankee bones outta here?"

Jordan returned to his chair, placed the cablegram at the front of his desk and smiled slightly at his superior. "I think I'll stay awhile longer and try to keep you out of trouble. As far as your cable is concerned, General, it should get Washington's attention. I assume you will be sending a copy to that new Assistant Secretary of the Navy?"

Lee puffed out his chest as if preparing to attack, then nodded. "To Roosevelt? You damn right. I want action, a concept that Roosevelt damn well understands." He snatched the cablegram from the desk and marched to the door.

"Sir?" Jordan called. Lee stopped and half turned. "You really would enjoy war, wouldn't you?"

"We're in the process of annexing Hawaii, Jordan. Cuba is a helluva lot closer to home and a helluva lot richer. A little intimidation now might save a war later." Lee slammed the door behind him.

Amos Jordan stared at his unsigned resignation for a moment, glanced at the clock, noticed that it was almost 5:45 and prepared to leave. He was a man who hated to be late, even to the bordello.

Although widely recognized as the best hotel in Havana, Amos Jordan had recently come to see the Ingleterre's lobby as little more than a loud and increasingly smelly cockpit where he was clearly *persona non grata*. In addition to several foreign consulates and his personal apartment, the Inglettere also housed a score of wealthy planters driven from their coffee, tobacco and sugar plantations by the revolution. Almost without exception the planters prayed that William McKinley, the newly elected American president, would come to their aid.

This evening, as he descended the main stairs and limped through the high, vaulted lobby of the *Inglaterre*, his home for the past four years, Jordan stood as erect as his old wound would allow and tightened his grip on the black, steel-pointed umbrella that doubled as a cane.

Most of the crowd was discussing the riots and their implications. Two of the men and their wives pointed at Jordan and whispered. Feigning indifference, he moved through the loud crowd as quickly as possible.

"Mr. Jordan! Sir!" From behind, a hand grabbed him by the shoulder.

Damn! Jordan thought, as he turned to face a square-shaped, red-faced planter who a third of a century earlier had fled South Carolina for Cuba. "Good evening, York. What might I do for you?"

"Go hang yourself, sir," York spat. "Barring that, get your pacifist, milk toast posterior out of Cuba."

Jordan pushed his face closer and smiled. "Thank you for the solicitous advice, York. I've been contemplating the latter for some time now. As to the former?"

"What's that supposed to mean?" Their part of the lobby crowd had quieted and was crowding closer. York looked around for validation. "You know, Mr. Vice Consul, do you not, that every day America refuses to act costs a thousand lives."

"Hear! Hear!" chorused a trio of stern-faced women.

Jordan looked around the widening circle of hostile faces and smiled.

"Your prayers may well be answered, ladies and gentlemen. But someone ought first to ask what the bill will be for our intervention.'" Looking straight at York he added, "What will be the cost for you Cubans? What will be the cost for America?"

Without waiting for an answer, the Vice Consul turned and limped quickly to the large double doors, across the *Prado* and into Central Park.

He wove through the remnants of the mob and turned into a quiet glade where he collapsed onto a rotting, moss-covered bench, shut his eyes and rubbed his old wound. Although Jordan had lived with the limp ever since Gettysburg, the weakness still angered him. In the past year the pain had worsened, probably he told himself, because of the dampness.

Startled by a shuffling sound, he opened his eyes and peered into an arbor almost completely covered by a canopy of untrimmed, magenta bougainvillea. He faced a scrawny woman and three orange-headed, pot-bellied children who had made the arbor their shelter. I must get out of this cesspool of madness, he told himself.

While the children sat or sprawled in the dirt, the woman approached him, and silently held out a hand. He rose stiffly, pulled a ten peseta note from his pocket, dropped it on the bench and limped from the park.

Goddamned Spaniards! he thought. How can more than 100,000 civilians die of famine and disease on an island that's a natural paradise? He shuddered, as if to shake off the stone of foreboding that, day by day, grew in the pit of his stomach.

As Jordan turned up the narrow, cobblestone street that led to the Casa de Ponce de Leon, Havana's most exclusive bordello, he pulled his attention away from politics and studied the two and three story colonial houses. Most of the narrow, baroque facades were almost identical; Other than the varied colors of exterior stucco and variously carved wooden entries, individuality resided behind the facades, in the lush interior gardens where well off Spanish and creole Cubans lived their private lives. And though the once beautiful houses, like almost everything else these days in Cuba, suffered from long neglect, Jordan appreciated the ornate beauty of the ironwork , the bright colors of the peeling stucco, and the tiled roofs that glowed in the amber light of the setting winter sun. Such a beautiful place, he thought. So beautiful, so forlorn, and so deadly.

He stopped at the entrance to the Casa de Ponce de Leon, straight-ened slightly, then crossed the stone path that led through an over-grown garden of poinsettia and orange bougainvilla to a the small reception room where Josefina acted as chaperon. After chatting with Josefina for a moment and handing her a small envelope, Jordan followed her up an inside circular stairway to the large corner room occupied by the softly alive hands and melodious voice of Theresa Valdez, who made at least a good pretense of being his one remaining friend in Havana.

She met him at the door. "Good evening, Amos. I am pleased that you could come to visit me; I have been very lonesome, and I have missed you." She placed his warm hands between her cool ones and led him into her room. "Would you care for a little wine? I am sorry that it is not French." She shrugged her shoulders. "But what is one to do?"

He shook his head and smiled warmly, enchanted as always by the quiet tremolo of her voice and the delicate beauty of her dark hair and eyes and honey-colored skin. "No thank you, Theresa. But...do you have a little Bacardi? I need, that is I could use, something a little stiffer."

"But certainly, my friend." She glided to the cabinet and poured a large measure of rum into a water tumbler. "I am very sorry that I have no ice."

Her client shrugged. "It is the times. I have what I need." He sank into Theresa's rattan rocker, stared at the flowered carpeting for a moment and quickly drained the large glass while Theresa walked to the tall, narrow window and adjusted the louvers. The spaces between the louvers cast horizontal bars of light, like negative shadows, on the oppo-site wall, an effect that Jordan had more than once admired. She crossed back to her patron and rested her hands on his shoulders.

"May I have another?" he asked. He raised his eyes and noticed the hollowness of her cheeks.

"But of course."

While he sipped at the second glass of rum, Theresa moved around behind his chair and massaged his neck and the base of his skull. As his muscles loosened, he leaned his head back, smiled up at her and purred, "Mmmmmmmm, good."

"Yes, good." She walked around to the front of the chair, knelt between his legs and undid his cravat. He lifted his hand and stroked her thick curls.

Theresa frowned. "You seem worried, Amos."

He nodded and caressed her long neck. "And you, my dear, seem considerably thinner than before you left. The conditions in the country-side are not getting any better, are they?"

Theresa shuddered at the image of two death-workers casually flip-ping Elizabeth's still limpid body onto the lime-sprinkled layers of rigid corpses. "No," she whispered, "they are not." Then she added in a firm-er voice, "Let us not speak of our misery, my friend. Let us enjoy this little oasis of tenderness and peace."

She stepped back and, holding his agreeably enchanted eyes with hers, unfastened the two dozen mother-of-pearl buttons of her white, high-necked, cotton dress and shrugged it to the floor. Standing before him in her ivory chemise, which reached halfway down her slender thighs, Theresa seemed to him more like a pouting girl than a twenty-four year old woman. She was small boned and small breasted. Though her hair was curly rather than kinky and her skin relatively light, her African heritage revealed itself in her dark, almond-shaped eyes and full lips.

My God, she's exquisite, Jordan told himself, as he gazed at the proud, thoughtful woman standing before him—a sepia-toned doll. Theresa gazed back at him for a moment, gently removed the tumbler from his relaxing hand and led him to the high brass bedstead. When they were seated on the edge of the bed, Jordan put his arms around her and gave her a long kiss, needy but even less passionate than usual.

Something very important must have happened today, she thought. I must not allow him to keep this thing inside.

Jordan was comfortable with his nakedness and old enough to have lost any self-consciousness about his skinny, bone-protruding body, or even about the large blotch of scar tissue that disfigured his left buttock. He helped her undo his various buttons and watched smilingly as she removed his clothes.

Still wearing her chemise, Theresa slid into bed and caressed his body with her slender fingers. Jordan kissed her lips, hair and neck, and allowed one hand to move up under her chemise. With the other he pulled the ivory straps from her shoulders and, like the hungry infant he sometimes was, nuzzled her small breasts.

Even as he entered her, Theresa knew that her diplomat sought warmth and security rather than passion. She put her arms around him, pulled him deeply in and rocked back and forth. The thin bars of fading light flowed across their locked bodies.

After a long time of silent holding, during which she watched the light disappear completely into the shadows, Theresa carefully released him, and they lay on their backs, holding hands and staring at the now darkened ceiling.

"Please, Amos. Talk about it. I know there's nothing I can do but listen. Still…" She was unprepared for the urgency of his response.

"America is moving toward intervention. And that could lead to war."

Theresa barely managed to suppress a pleased gasp.

Although faint alarms sounded far back in his head, Jordan's hunger to be known and understood over-powered completely the pragmatic, soul-extinguishing caution of the diplomat. For the next twenty minutes, his words and worries poured forth, seemingly without direction.

Theresa listened to the words. More important, she listened to the tones and pauses. Lost in his anger and frustration, Jordan squeezed her hand so hard she could barely conceal the pain, but the last thing she wanted was for the flow of words to stop. Then her pain seemed, suddenly, to disappear. What was he saying?

"If President McKinley gives in to that idiot Lee, and sends even one battleship…Good Christ! One false move on anyone's part and we're in this filthy war."

He talked on and on, about the effects of colonialism on the Spanish, British and Germans, and about its probable impact on America. But Theresa was no longer listening. Her mind kept returning to Jordan's linked phrases: "even one battleship," "one false move," "one false move on anyone's part and we're in." We're in. We're in.

Chapter Three

AMERICANS NOT ATTACKED YET, BUT NAVAL FLEET
MAY BE ORDERED TO CUBA AT ANY HOUR

* * * *

*Spanish Government Using Every Means to Restore Peace,
and the United States Still Friendly, but Crisis Grave.
The World, January 14.*

Matanzas Province

Just beneath the crest of a low hill, they dismounted and Christopher crawled the rest of the way to a panoramic view of land they both knew well. He moved his binoculars in slow sweeps, left to right, right to left, back and forth until he had completely scanned the green and black rolling hills. All the way to the next sharp ridge an hour away, he saw nothing but burned fields softened by the ragged patches of volunteer cane and the creepers and brush of expanding jungle. The charred ruins of a few haciendas and outbuildings dotted the panorama. A kilometer or two away to the north, a line of refugees accompanied by four circling buzzards moved slowly along a footpath. Nowhere did he see any sign of a Spanish patrol.

After carefully re-scanning, Christopher motioned Fidel forward with the horses. "Doesn't look much better than when we left," he said as he re-mounted. "But it does seem to be empty of Spaniards." He spurred his horse forward at a walk.

"Yes. Free of Spanish, and free of almost everything else."

They rode in silence for awhile, the minds of both men caught back on the trail with the reconcentrados. Fidel thought of Carmen and his cousin, and the joy they used to share after the sugar harvest when everyone had money and rum. How many more have to die? he wondered.

"So, Fidel. What did you learn about those poor people back there?"

Fidel tensed. "They are from one of the *reconcentrados*, which they named *El Cajon del Muerto*. I will tell you their story later." He increased their pace to a canter. "If the valley is clear of *pendejos* we can make good time, no?"

Shortly after noon the next day, still half a day's ride to Federico's *bohio* and their rendezvous with the General, they arrived at the ruins of the plantation Christopher had devoted twelve years of his life to building. After examining the fields and ruins for any signs of danger, he dismounted and walked slowly to a small grove of royal palms.

"Do you mind, Fidelito? I would like a few minutes to think of my life in this place."

"But of course, my friend. We can easily make the Zapata before dark."

They sat under the partially burned timbers of an arbor covered with magenta bougainvillea. For what to Fidel seemed a long time, Christopher sat silently on the ground, his arms wrapped around his knees. Fidel sat to his rear, twenty meters away. They both stared out over the charred cane fields they had known so intimately. Resurgent jungle battled the volunteer cane. As usual, burning had temporarily helped the soil. Some day they would be able to begin again, some day, when they had won...

"Christopher?" Fidel finally ventured.

"Yes?" Christopher asked after another long silence. He had been thinking of her last words, "You will kill us all."

"I need to talk about this thing that we did to our homes."

Christopher caught his breath, shook his head, stood to his feet and walked downhill away from Fidel, his mind totally locked to the last moments he had spent with his family.

The three girls and their bags sat piled on one of their cane carts, which was hitched to their last yoke of oxen and surrounded by Fidel and four of their *mambi* colleagues. The girls were frightened. The five year old twins held hands. Maria was whimpering. Elizabeth, whose face showed her own fear, kept kissing her twin and repeating, "Jesus loves us, Jesus loves us." Anna Theresa, who was eight, stared at her angry, depressed parents. Do not fight with him, Mother, she prayed silently, afraid that if Mother made Father angry he might never let them come home.

Consuelo and Christopher stood at the side of the cart, his arms around her waist, hers around his shoulders, their bodies rigid. Her up-turned face was an open but doubting entreaty, as if she had already surrendered to her darkest fear: He was willing to desert their family and separate them from their roots.

"Please, Christopher, I ask you in the name of God."

He removed her arms and held her wrists in his palms. "You must go, my love. Please, be strong for our daughters."

"I used to love the fool in you," she half-whispered, shaking her head back and forth. "Even when you were strong and sometimes even wise, even then I would see the fool in you, and I loved that in you because it made me laugh."

She rose on her toes, kissed his cheek with lips that felt as cold as ice and pulled away. As he handed her up into the cart, she turned half around and hissed through tightly compressed lips, "Now I see that your fool will kill us all."

"I love you, Consuelo," he declared in what he hoped to be an assuring voice. "More than I would ever have thought possible." He stood tall and erect. "Anna-Theresa, Maria, Elizabeth! I love you, girls. Be brave for your mother."

Fidel nodded to the driver, the cart jerked and they began their slow, squeaking journey north to Cardenas, the large fishing and marketing town a full day away by ox-cart. For a long time Christopher stood in the road waving his hand and trying to smile. Consuelo and his daughters stared back at him with stricken, identical faces, as if they had been abandoned by hope.

* * * * *

"My Captain!" He jerked around and stared at Fidel, who stood ten paces behind him, the reins of their horses in his hand. "I am sorry. It will be dark. We must ride."

Christopher nodded, wiped the sweat from his face, took one more long look around his beloved valley and remounted. Fidel noticed that, though the temperature was pleasant, his captain was sweating heavily. "Please Mother Mary," he prayed, "just a few more hours to my father's home."

Less than an hour later Christopher's horse wandered off the path and he made no attempt to guide it back. He wiped his streaming face, dismounted and staggered over to the base of a royal palm.

Fidel was immediately at his side. "The fever, no?"

Christopher answered between gasps. "The sweats. I keep thinking of the morning you took my family to Cardenas. It felt like my heart seized."

"Rest here. Put your head between your legs. Do not speak. Breathe slowly."

A great hunger knotted Christopher's stomach. He could not pull his mind from the horrific face of the woman who had died in his arms. In his mind the woman's face became Consuelo's, and he was too weak to shake the image. When he finally felt as if he were regaining control, he lifted his head, looked directly into Fidel's compassionate eyes and said, "I have a great need to see my family, Fidelito."

Fidel felt like taking his *companero* into his arms. He put his huge hands on Christopher's shoulders. "I understand. Let us pray to all the saints that we will find them well."

As soon as they were back on the trail, Christopher announced, "I cannot go directly to our rendezvous with the General. I must go to Cardenas."

"No, my Captain. We must not follow that path."

"I need to check on my family, Fidel. It will take us only one extra day. General Gomez will understand."

"No, my friend. There are at least three strong reasons. We must not go that way."

"My heart pulls me strongly to the north, Fidelito. What are your reasons?"

Fidel rode a few steps along the trail that headed southwest to the northern edge of the Zapata, the great swamp. He turned around in his saddle. "You can not ride much further unless your sweats stop, and if you get chills you will soon be on your back. Unless you get a lot stronger very soon, my friend, you do not have an extra day's ride in you."

Christopher tried to sit a little straighter in the saddle. "That's one reason."

"I meant it as two, but that is fine. Our orders are to proceed directly from the Sierra to the Zapata and to meet the General at my father's *bohio*. We can make it before dark. If you remain sick, Mama Oinja can heal you."

Christopher stared off to the north for a moment, took a long drink from his canteen and turned to follow Fidel along the southwesterly path. Fidel was right on both counts, and Christopher knew that his fever was intensifying. Barring a miracle, wherever they stopped, he would need to be cared for.

But then his mind circled back to Consuelo. If the fever gets much worse, the General will have to wait regardless of where I am laid up. Consuelo could nurse me. At the thought of her cool hands on his body Christopher's heart swelled with love and desire. Now that he was so close, he felt how deeply he had missed her. He pulled his horse up short. "I need to get to my family, Fidelito. I need that very much."

Fidel turned and rode back, placed a hand on the pommel of Christopher's saddle and looked into Christopher's unhappy face. "My friend, I have still another reason why we should not go to Cardenas."

"Yes?"

"Your family may be in the Zapata. We must pray that they are already at my father's *bohio*."

Christopher's response was barely audible "What do you mean?"

"Those refugees on the trail? They were from Cardenas. The Spanish kicked them out. They rounded up many, many people and took them to the *reconcentrados*."

"What are you saying?"

Fidel jerked the pommel and pulled his captain closer. "Listen to me, my friend. That woman in the trail with the broken voice? She was married to one of my cousins."

"Forget that woman! What are you talking about?"

"She told me that there was no food . . ."

"Those people are from Cardenas? But it was a safe place."

Ah, my friend, Fidel thought. I cannot cause you this pain. "Many people were put in *reconcentrados*. Some headed for the swamp. If she had a chance, Consuelo would have headed for the swamp and our *bohio*." Fidel saw the horror dawning in Christopher's sweating face, and knew that he could not complete the rest of Carmen's story.

"Fidelito?" Christopher asked in the tone used by children when they first see cracks in their world. "She and the girls could not have made it to the swamp, not without help."

"Let us pray to all our saints that there was help." After a long pause Fidel placed his arm on his friend's shoulder and urged their horses along the trail. "Our best chance of finding your family is to go where our General ordered us to go. If they are not there, we will get help.

Maybe we can find them. Come, my friend. Come." He spoke gently, in a deep, loving voice. "If they are alive, they will most likely be at our *bohío*."

Christopher had become too weak to argue. He nodded and spurred his horse. He was numb, even to the fever. During their time with General Garcia in the Sierra he had derived great strength from his faith that Consuelo and the girls were secure at Consuelo's aunt's town home.

His mood changed to a deep, voiceless rage at all things Spanish. Although the rage further drained his energy, it helped to displace his increasing fear and self-anger. He tried simultaneously to hold onto the rage, to focus on the trail and to will Consuelo's presence in the Zapata.

Two hours before sunset they reached the outskirts of the great swamp. For the first time since leaving the burned plantation, Fidel was confident that he would get Christopher safely to his parents' clearing. But just as he exhaled a deep, congratulatory breath, he jerked his horse to a halt and raised his hand. Dismounting, he continued to hold his raised hand, palm outward, toward Christopher.

"From over there," he whispered, and moved quickly to help Christopher dismount. He pointed down a long meadow where a four-man infantry patrol waded toward them through lush, waist-high grass.

Fidel tethered their horses back in the trees and the two *mambises*, rifles in hand, crept through the dense ferns and creepers to a small lime-stone outcropping that offered both concealment and an unobstructed view of the meadow. If it kept coming, the advancing patrol should pass within fifty meters.

"When the man furthest to the left is opposite those three palms on the far side of the valley, shoot," Christopher whispered. The adrenalin charging through his body was giving him fresh power

Fidel stared at Christopher's sweating face for a moment and shook his head. "Killing those *pendejos* is not a necessary thing. We can stay here safely until they ride by."

Christopher's hatred swelled beyond containment. "This will not take very long," he whispered hoarsely.

"No, my captain," Fidel whispered. "We must let them pass."

He gripped Fidel's forearm." Are you crazy, Sergeant?" he hissed.

"How do we end this filthy little war if we refuse to kill their little boy soldiers?"

Ah, my friend, Fidel thought, this fever taints your judgment. "Our mission is to meet General Gomez, not ambush *pendejos.*"

Christopher felt a great need to be understood, but an even greater need to explode his rage. "Fidel, follow my order! Do as I say!"

"Why don't we just wait until they're gone, Captain?" Fidel reached over and pushed down the barrel of Christopher's Mauser, which jutted from the outcropping like a wavering flag.

Christopher felt his blood surging. The rage, which now embraced Fidel, was causing great pain in his head. "This won't take very long, Sergeant. You start from the left. I'll hit the leader then start from the right."

Fidel saw that Christopher's continued arguments would soon reveal their position. He exhaled sharply, nodded and turned to the on-coming soldiers.

The patrol was organized as a loose skirmish line designed to span the width of the narrow valley, as if it were out flushing rabbits. But the soldiers' fear of being alone acted as a magnet that kept drawing them back toward their corporal, who walked in the middle of the line. Another group of untrained, undisciplined boys, Christopher thought. More cannon fodder for the dying empire.

Every few moments the corporal stopped, extended his arms and flapped them wildly, as if trying to fly. The nervous recruits again fanned out for a moment and then, almost immediately and imperceptibly, glided slowly back through the knee-high grass toward their corporal and each other.

* * * * *

Corporal Rafael Martinez, their leader, scourge and protector, was bare-ly seventeen. He had been in Cuba for fifteen months, and his exalted rank testified more to the random chance of his survival than to any real ability, native or acquired. Corporal Martinez knew that he was sup-posed to keep his men spread out, at least twenty or thirty meters apart, but he didn't know how to accomplish this. He knew he was supposed to kill or capture any rebels he encountered, but he didn't know where they were or what they looked like. Many were women and many were boys far younger than himself. Corporal Martinez knew only that anyone who lacked a travel pass or who looked suspicious or who tried to run should be captured or shot, and that it was far safer to shoot than to capture.

Earlier that day they had flushed an old mulatto and his young wife, apparently walking to their squash patch, machetes in hand. The patrol had come upon the couple so suddenly and so surprised them that the frightened camposinos had dropped their machetes and run. All four of the privates, almost as frightened by the unexpected encounter as the couple, had fired at their fleeing backs. Most managed to get off three or four rounds before the corporal shouted, "Cease fire! Cease fire! Blood of the Devil, cease fire!"

The shots had blown the couple to opposite sides of the trail, the old mulatto curled up as if taking a nap, the young woman sprawled on her back with her head in a ditch. Two of the younger soldiers jostled their friends and giggled when Pablo used his rifle as a sharp extension of his curiosity to lift the woman's long skirt. No one would touch her, but the corporal used his machete to rip away her worn cotton blouse and skirt. The boys stared quietly at the forbidden mysteries of her body and the three peso-sized black punctures that contrasted so strangely with her brown skin.

Corporal Martinez could not get his mind off the incident. Even now, moving through this lush valley, his thoughts keep falling away from the present. He looked up, saw that his troops were once again converging on him, and lifted his arms to wave them away just as Christopher Jackson's first bullet entered his chest.

The corporal was on his back in the deep grass. He felt nothing. One leg was crossed over the other as if, once again a small boy, he was lying in a field daydreaming when he was supposed to be tending his father's goats. Corporal Martinez was aware of sharp sounds, pops and cracks, but they receded quickly over the hills, to other lands, other lifetimes. All his evaporating consciousness focused on a blue heron that flapped slowly across his vision.

* * * *

Christopher's first and best shot burned his concentration. By the time he turned to his next target, the Spaniard had disappeared in the grass.

At fifty meters it was almost impossible to miss, and Fidel easily downed his two soldiers, but Christopher was still shooting at his invisible target. The muzzle of his Mauser shook like a reed in the wind, and sweat poured from his hands and face.

What craziness! Fidel thought. "Stop firing!" he commanded, just as Christopher squeezed off another round. "Captain! He is not where you are shooting."

Glassy-eyed, Christopher glanced at his sergeant, then at the grass, which moved in the light breeze like gentle waves on a green sea. He saw with a flash of hard light that he had become incompetent, and that his sickness and rage had placed them in unnecessary jeopardy. "Fidel, I am very, very sorry," he mumbled as he turned and moved slowly off the limestone outcrop.

"Yes, my friend. I too am sorry," Fidel said. Christopher was staggering into the meadow. "Where are you going?"

"I have to kill that other bastard before he gets away."

Fidel could not suppress a laugh. "You?" He moved off the rock in one graceful vault and helped Christopher toward their horses. "Did you wound that *pendejo?*"

Christopher thought for a second and shook his head.

"Not to worry. That scared little rabbit knows where our shots came from, just as he knows that his companions are probably dead. He is crawling away from us as fast as he can. Come. Not to worry. We are almost home."

He helped Christopher back into the saddle. "Can you ride? Maybe less than two hours? I can make a litter and drag you."

Christopher nodded. He did not believe he could ride two minutes, let alone another two hours, but he knew that he had temporarily purged his rage. His thoughts returned to his loved ones. They would be at Federico's. He was sure. They knew he was finally coming back. They would be waiting. "I will ride as long as I can sit." Fidel shrugged, took a rag of a shirt from his saddlebags, tore it into strips and tied Christopher's hands to the pommel.

Within an hour, however, Christopher lost both will and conscious-ness and slumped from his saddle. A half hour later they started again, this time with Christopher on a three branch travois that Fidel led home.

Just before sunset Fidel stopped the horses. They were only a few minutes from his father's *bohio*, where he knew that Christopher's fam-ily would almost certainly not be. Fidel's parents would have heard the shots, or at least the alarm the birds had broadcast for miles in all direc-tions. They would have faded into the safety of the swamp to wait and listen. If they are still in the Zapata, he worried. If they are still alive.

After listening for a few minutes to the normal calls of the evening birds, he took a deep breath and in a rich but off-key voice sang the first line of an old planting song: "If you want to reap the sugar, you got to burn the field."

The bird song ceased. Then from not far ahead, a rich contralto picked up the tune: "If you want to reap the sugar, then burn the for-eign weeds."

Fidel turned to smile at Christopher's unconscious body, then leaned back in the saddle, pointed his head at the jungle canopy and belted out, "Burn the foreign creepers and plant good native seeds."

A tall, large-boned woman sprang from the bush. "Fidelito!" she screamed. "My Fidelito."

"Mama Oinja!" Fidel jumped from his saddle and took the mid-dle-aged woman in his arms. Even though he was the youngest son of Bettita, Oinja's predecessor, this woman had raised him; she was his mother.

"Aiee! Mama Oinja. Much love, much health." He lifted the large black woman and swung her around three times before returning her to the ground. Then he turned to embrace somewhat more gently his old father, who was scarcely half his size.

"My Papi," he said. "I hope my acts bring you pride."

For answer the slight but sinewy man gave him a big grin from a wide mouth missing a front tooth. "My son, your return will always bring me great heart pleasure."

"Federico! Fidelito?" The two men moved to the rear of the second horse, where Oinja leaned over Christopher. "It is the fever, no?"

Fidel nodded. "He was just recovering from an attack when we left the *Sierra Maestra*. I am afraid our journey has been hard for him. We have had little food. Also, he is afraid for his family and angry with himself.

Oinja gave Christopher a cold, hard look. "He should have gotten angry with himself before he rode off to be a hero."

Having spoken words that sounded harsh even to her, Oinja's face softened a little and she placed her palm on the unconscious man's sweating head. "Federico!" she snapped. "Go! Start some water boiling."

"Yes, Mama," the old man said to his much younger wife." He smiled happily at Fidel and ran into the jungle.

Fidel and Oinja walked side by side, leading the horses and travois. "What does he know about his family?" she asked.

Fidel tightened his jaw. Her tone had revealed all he needed to know. He glanced back at the travois and its baggage and felt a deep pain in his heart. "His hope was that they were safe, that they would be here with you."

"They are all dead, Fidelito." Tears welled in her eyes and her stepson took her to his breast. "I think maybe such news will kill him."

Fidel patted her broad back. "No, Mama Oinja. The news will cut away a part of his heart that already knows much pain, but I do not think he will die, unless maybe from the fever. He is very weak."

Later that evening, joined by four thin children of various ages, the three former slaves sat around a smokeless charcoal fire, where Oinja was brewing a thin soup. During her patient's brief returns to semi-consciousness, she had fed him quinine tea.

"So you did not eat well?" she asked, though her strong stepson showed no signs of having suffered. She shook her head. "No one in Cuba except maybe the rich people in *La Habana*, eat well anymore. Even the Spanish soldiers are starving."

Fidel grunted. "The first few days we had a little food from the camp. After that mostly fruit, a small rabbit and some nicely roasted pork we took from some Spanish soldiers." He thought of the refugees from Cardenas and of his dead cousin's wife. They must all be dead by now. He did not want to discuss food. "Mama Oinja, I saw Carmen."

Oinja's face lit up. "Where?"

"On the road here. I talked with her. She…"

"Ahhh, my Fidelito, I am so pleased." She stood and clapped her hands. "Two good things today. Our son returns and Carmen is safe. Praise be to all our saints, Fidelito."

"Mama Oinja..."

"So many people from Cardenas have died. So many people from the whole island have died." Her mind returned for a moment to their *bohio*, where Christopher lay in sickness, and of his dead family. She felt a sharp pang of sorrow but quickly shooed it away. It is not good to think of sorrows when the saints bring you good news.

Fidel looked down at the fire, at a loss for words.

"Our thanks to Mama Maria and all her saints," Oinja said as she fingered the small canvas bag of magical herbs that hung between her heavy breasts. "I thought maybe Carmen had been lost in that *reconcentrado*."

"They are dead, Mama," Fidel mumbled. He looked around the fire at his young siblings, thin but obviously healthy.

"But, you said..." Oinja squatted down next to Fidel, grabbed him by the chin, spun his head around and glared into his sad eyes. "You said you talked to her on the road."

"Yes, Mama Oinja, but she had been in that death place, and she and those with her were dying, and their children were already dead." He tried to put all his love for her into his eyes and added in a soft voice, "I am sorry, Mama."

Oinja shook her head, stood up and walked into the darkness.

"Fidelito," Federico said after a hard silence.

Fidel looked across the fire to see his father emerge from the anonymity he usually wore in the presence of his outspoken wife. "Yes, Papi?"

"We must tell him, you know. As soon as possible. He is one of us now."

"The *Yanqui* has always been one with us, Papi. His commitment to our cause is strong."

"All you say is true, my son. I honor him—and you." Federico reached across the fire and placed his thin palm against his son's cheek. "He is a good soldier. Even our General Gomez sees this truth. But it is only when we lose blood family that we truly become *mambises*. Our fight is not for freedom only, my son. *mambises* fight for blood, their blood for our blood. For our blood that they have already taken."

Fidel nodded assent. He had always hated the Spanish and what they stood for, but he knew the change that took place in his heart when his older brother had been killed along with Carlos Gomez and Antonio Maceo in the Battle of Three Sorrows. The blood of every Spaniard in Cuba could never fill the ache of that loss. "Yes, Papi," Fidel said in a voice that carried great sadness. "He is now a *mambi*. His loss will not make our *Yanqui* a better man. He will become a much harder man, but perhaps a stronger leader."

Oinja returned to the fire shaking her head. "If you tell him now while he is sick, his mind will not heal well." She poured some herbs into the simmering soup and glared at her two men folk.

Federico looked hard at his wife. Usually, she was right. Usually, she led and he followed. But in matters of war she was out of place. Her hatred for the war and what it had done to those she loved was so great that she could not understand. "We will tell him as soon as he awakens," Federico commanded.

"No! Your captain is sick and weak. What you say will kill his heart."

"Oinja!" Federico spoke in a flat, hard voice he seldom used with his strong wife, but one she usually submitted to. "This is what we will do. It is what our General would do if he were here."

"Your precious general is not here, husband. And his *Yanqui* captain is my patient. I..."

"Listen! Oinja. He must know. The sooner he receives the blow, the sooner you will be able to make him well."

"Papi is right, Mama Oinja. Our General has a need for this man."

"Then let your general tell him—when he is stronger."

"Oinja!" Her name came weakly from the darkness, as if spoken from a great distance. The family turned to see Christopher standing behind them on unsteady feet. "Where is my family? Why are they not here?"

Oinja looked around at her stern-faced men-folk and broke into tears. Federico rose, walked to Christopher's side and gently but forcefully led him to the fire and sat him next to Fidel. The old man hunkered down in front of Christopher, placed both hands on the captain's shoulders and stated in the strongest voice he could muster: "I am sorry, my friend. We are all sorry. You are now one of us."

Christopher stared into Federico's dark eyes, which reflected the flickering light from the fire. "Where is my family?"

"Our hearts bleed for you, Captain Jackson."

"They are dead!" Oinja howled, unable to take the tension. "Like so many we have loved, Captain. They are dead. Aiii-eee!" she keened, once again feeling the loss of so many she had loved. "Aiiiii-eeeeee!"

Federico spoke softly. "They died in *El Cajon del Muerto*, almost three weeks ago."

"They are all dead?"

"Yes, my friend," Fidel said, placing an arm around his captain, both to comfort and to suppress his shaking. "Our hearts break with yours."

"You must be strong, Captain," Federico said. Our general needs you. *Cuba Libre!* needs you."

Christopher stared into his friend's eyes, shook his head back and forth and whispered, "Fuck *Cuba Libre!*"

Chapter Four

SPANISH EVACUATION OF CUBA WOULD MEAN
WAR IN SPAIN

* * * *

Havana, January 14—Spain has no army left. The Cuban climate and Spanish corruption have robbed Spain's greatest colonial army of food and supplies. This pitiful remnant of a 300,000-man army is only slightly larger than the revolutionary army Gen. Gomez has at his disposal. *The World*, January 14.

The Zapata Swamp

Although they had broken the two day ride into stages, with long mid-day rests, Theresa's bone-deep fatigue was wearing her down. By the time they crossed into Matanzas Province and reached the edge of the Zapata, she was close to physical collapse. They carried forged passes but still avoided the relatively more comfortable main trail that dissected the long island from *La Habana* to Santiago de Cuba. Like Christopher Jackson and Fidel Federico moving toward them from the East, they opted for a slower and more arduous but safer route. Guillermo Morales still wore his white linen suit, now blotched with sweat and grime, and a broad panama hat. Theresa wore a green, ankle length cotton skirt; yellow, scoop-necked blouse; and a green and white polka-dot bandanna pulled tightly around her curly hair. Like any peasant woman, she rode astride, her long skirt hiked over her knees.

By noon of their second day out from *La Habana*, they had reached the small Contreras farm, a safe house where Theresa hoped to spend the afternoon resting. She followed the major over the brow of a low hill, pulled up short for a moment, then spurred her black pony alongside Guillermo's large chestnut gelding. "Major Morales." She pointed at a cluster of palms and a small patch of blackened ground. "Isn't that Mama Contreras's clearing?"

Morales blinked a couple of times and stared vacantly toward the clearing. He had been thinking of the old days when as a young overseer on the Valdez plantation, he had been able to seduce Theresa, then a wild and rebellious sixteen year old.

"Major?" Three vultures rose from the clearing, did a couple of slow turns to investigate the two riders, then returned to land in the long jungle grasses.

"I can see," he mumbled. "The Spanish have been here. Stay at least twenty meters behind me." He delivered the words as flat declarations of fact. Without waiting for Theresa to respond, he dismounted and pulled his Mauser from its scabbard. Theresa did the same. Keeping their horses between them and the black patch of clearing, they proceeded slowly along the slope.

Even in the winter the heavy humidity did its job; the pungent odors of charred and rotting flesh blended with the softer smell of pine and palm ashes. By the time they completed a cautious circling of the clearing, the stench had become overpowering.

"Jesus and Maria!" Theresa wrapped her scarf around her lower face. A chill of cold apprehension began at her toes and crawled up her back to the base of her neck. "Let us hurry."

Morales nodded and pulled a grimy blue neckerchief over his nose. "Wait here!" he commanded and handed his reins to Theresa.

Horses had trampled the old woman's small garden. Like the rest of the clearing, her pine and palm frond *bohio* was a pile of cold ashes. What a waste these bastards make, Morales thought as he poked through the ruins with a long stick. The half-starved Spanish soldiers had decapitated Mama's pig and thrown the head and entrails into the burning cabin.

Theresa could not will herself to stay on the hillside. But as her pony moved slowly toward the cabin, it suddenly whinnied, snapped its neck back and jerked the reins from her tired hand. Just in front of them a large vulture flapped its wings and rose awkwardly from the long grass.

"Major!" she tried to yell. The call came out as little more than a breathless squeak. She tried again, "Major! Guillermo!" Her voice rose from a low, half-choked wail to a raw screech. "Guillermo!"

Wedged in between the burnt rows of a small squash patch lay the semi-dissected body of Juan and Leonardo Contreras's mother. She was lying on her stomach. Buff and pink land crabs swarmed in the black gash along her split kidneys.

A moment later, out of breath but standing at her side, Morales stared hard at the butchered remains of a very poor, very strong old woman. He shook his head and glanced at Theresa, who had averted her head. "Fucking bastards." After staring sadly at the body of an old woman he, too, had been fond of, he grabbed Theresa's elbow. "Let us be on our way. There is nothing for us here."

"No! We must bury her, Major. What would her sons say?"

Guillermo ground his teeth, glanced at the sky and glared at Theresa. "Go back up on the far side of the ridge, keep out of sight, and scan both valleys. It should take me about an hour."

Theresa shook her head and staggered to her feet. "I, too, am a soldier, Guillermo, and I loved this woman. We will bury her together." She dropped to her knees and rolled up the sleeves of her loose yellow blouse. Disregarding her long, painted nails, she plunged her hands into the damp humus and began to scrape away the loosened soil.

Morales watched. Her blouse had fallen away and he could see most of her small breasts. As usual her anger excited him and he surrendered for a moment to the heat rising between his legs. But then he clenched his fists and willed himself back into control. "Suit yourself, Captain, but I think you should save your strength." He turned to loosening the earth but continued to stare at Theresa on her knees scooping away the soil.

Much later that evening, still an hour or two from Federico's *bohio*, they stopped again to allow Theresa a few minutes of rest. During the ride both riders had been absorbed by the problem of their uncomfortable proximity to each other. Now they sat two meters apart, their backs against separate trees, facing away from each other. Guillermo Morales tried to pull his mind from his sometimes violent feelings for this woman whose complexities he could not fathom. On the few occasions when he was ordered to spend time with her, all the old feelings came back. Her presence triggered both desire and a deep anger that he could no longer possess her. He was frustrated by his knowledge that this *puta* he had seduced as a girl was too strong and quick for him. He respected her far more than he was willing to admit.

Other than the depression she felt about the fact and nature of Mama Contreras's butchering, Theresa's thoughts were calmer. Although Guillermo Morales was a man of great strength and at times uncontrollable appetites and violent temper, he was also a good soldier. She would always be uncomfortable with him, and felt little but contempt for him as a man. Still, she felt safe in his company. He knew her worth to *Cuba Libre!* As much as he obviously wanted to possess her, she trusted that he would do nothing to incur the wrath of Maximo Gomez.

In the last hour or so, however, she had thought little of the crass, unsubtle warrior who was taking her to the Zapata. Rather, she had been

thinking about Christopher Jackson, with whom she had been infatuated since he had first entered their house to court her older sister. She
knew that she would have to share with him the details of Consuelo's
death, and the deaths of the girls. She gazed at the few tendrils of pink
and orange cloud sweeping west from the Sierra and set her jaw. Even
though she was bone weary from her recuperation and from the two day
ride, she rose to her feet, suddenly anxious to complete the journey.

Morales helped her to her mount and held her arm. "Theresa."
When she jerked it away, he mumbled, "I am sorry. Please. There is
something I must say."

She narrowed her eyes, examined his face for a moment, saw that
she was in no immediate danger, but decided she needed more distance
from his urgency. "Very well, Major. Is it something you cannot say
while we are riding?"

Guillermo's face reddened and his hands tightened to fists, but he took
a deep breath and moved to his horse. "I can say it while we are riding."

For almost ten minutes, however, he said nothing, and Theresa felt
the tension again mount between them. She knew that she could draw
him out; getting men to open their hearts was her one great skill. But
she would do nothing to make it easier for him.

"Theresa," he finally began, allowing his horse to drop back alongside her pony."

"Major Morales, I am a captain in *Cuba Libre!* Please show me the
respect to call me by my rank."

"Goddamnit!" Morales exploded. "Why do you do this to me? We
have known each other almost our entire lives. We have been lovers. We
are on the same side."

"We were never lovers, Major Morales. I was sixteen years old when
you seduced me. That was…"

"You seemed willing enough at…"

"That was many, many lifetimes ago. And, as you have pointed out,
often, even insultingly, I have been with many, many men since then."

"I am sorry for that," Morales mumbled. "I do not know how to act
when I am with you."

Theresa smiled. It was true. Guillermo could not help himself; he
was a creature of his passions. "It would be much easier if you would

treat me as an officer, rather than as the faint ghost of a young girl whose legs you still want to spread."

Morales nodded. He did not want to fight with her. He just wanted her to understand. Although he still desired her, he understood the danger of his desire. In a rare flash of insight he understood what it was that he most needed from her. "Theresa?"

"Captain Valdez."

He remained calm. "I am sorry. I truly respect what you do for our revolution, and at what cost. Believe that, Captain. I may never say it again. But it is to Theresa Valdez that I must speak. Please." His tone was quiet, almost beseeching.

She took in the tone and the boy-like wistfulness of his expression. This was a side of Guillermo that she had not seen for years. She relented and nodded curtly.

"What I, too, need is respect, Theresa. A man needs that. I have killed men because they showed me disrespect."

"Or at least you thought they had."

He held up his hand to stop her. "In my heart it is the same. I know you hold me in contempt as a man."

She reached over and touched his arm. "The old anger comes out only, only when you treat me like a cheap *puta*." He started to interrupt. "No! Do not ruin this chance between us, Major Morales." She pulled her arm away but spurred her pony across the trail and turned in the saddle so they were face to face. "Yes, I have been a whore for too long. But I have never been cheap. And I became a whore only because you ran away, and because after I went to the *bruja* for an abortion and was *excomminicado*, I could not go home anymore. I do not want you—ever—to touch me again like a man touches a woman. I want you to treat me with respect as a fellow officer. Can you do that?"

He jutted out his jaw. "Blood of Christ! Theresa. Can't you hear me? A man needs respect!"

She shook her head and cried. "Guillermo! Can you do that?"

He blinked twice, slowly, as if he finally understood the source of her rage. Then he cocked his head, narrowed his eyes and tried to look into her soul. "Yes. I can do that, Captain Theresa Valdez."

"Thank you," she said, exhaling a long breath. "You are a strong man. You can do anything you put your mind to." She smiled and added to herself, As long as your appetites do not get in the way.

"Now. What about me?" he asked, drumming his fingers against his barrel chest.

Theresa smiled. She had won. "Major Guillermo Morales. I am glad to have you as a colleague in *Cuba Libre!* and I am glad to have you as my protector on this visit to our General." Guillermo sat a little straighter in his saddle and smiled in agreement. "You are sometimes rash, sometimes too careless with chance—which you know about yourself, no?"

Guillermo deflated slightly but nodded agreement. "But in battle my courage helps."

"Yes, Major. You have faults, but you know them." She broadened her smile. "To know your faults is to know wisdom. To control them is to show great strength."

"Theresa, I am not used to women examining my moles."

She shook her head and again placed her hand on his arm. "We must be honest, Major. Now, listen to my respect. Here is my gift to you. I hope you can accept it as sufficient. Will you try?"

Morales stared at her again with his head cocked. "Yes. I want peace between us. We must work together."

"Wisely said, Major Morales. You have the respect of our wonderful General. You have the respect of other officers, and of your men when you are in combat. And you have my respect for what you do best. You are an excellent warrior. It is what you were born for. Major Guillermo Morales, trusted aide to our General Maximo Gomez, I salute you." She sat at attention and saluted.

He sat stolidly for a moment, examining her set, serious face for any sign of sarcasm. Slowly, a wide smile spread across his black-bearded face, and he returned the salute. "Thank you, Captain Theresa Valdez. I now see what Maximo Gomez means about you." He stopped and smirked, well aware of the awe in which she held their General, and comfortable enough in the glow of her praise to tease her. "But now, my esteemed colleague, we must ride, no?"

"So what does our General say about me, Major?"

Guillermo pushed his mount past her pony, started into a canter and shouted back over his shoulder, as if passing along a casual afterthought, "That you are a woman of great courage and great insight to the hearts and minds of men."

Chapter Five

LET US SAVE CUBA, CRIES KING, OF UTAH
Returns Heartsick from a Tour of the Desolated, Distressed Isle
* * * * *
WILL DEMAND INTERVENTION
Blanco Powerless to Stay the Work of Extermination Begun
by Butcher Weyler

Tampa, Fla., January 17—Congressman King arrived here tonight from Cuba, where he has been informing himself about the real state of affairs in order to guide his actions in our National House of Representatives. He said to the World correspondent: "I am in favor of giving Spain a certain time to wind up the war, and if this fails to do it then I am for intervention by the United States. The horror of the conditions of the *reconcentrados* has not been half told. They are still dying by the hundreds in the streets." *The World*, January 17.

* * * * *

No successes on one side or the other can alter the essential fact that the Cubans are struggling for liberty against a tyranny as intolerable as any that history has known. The sympathy of all enlightened minds is with the insurgents, whether in victory or in defeat. Joseph Pulitzer, Editorial: *The World*, January 19.

The Zapata Swamp

Federico sat on his haunches, absent-mindedly stirring the tea that simmered in the small kettle. He looked across the clearing, where his oldest living son, a trusted sergeant and friend of the *Yanqui*, swung slowly in a hammock. Federico was proud of himself for producing such a strong and respected son. His squash patch was doing well. Many strips of meat from the two wild pigs he had trapped were drying over the smoke pit. In these times of trouble all over Cuba, he was still able to feed his family. The sun was shining and his bones did not ache. His wife was a good *bruja*. The *Yanqui* would live to fight again, and Theresa Valdez, who reminded him so much of his lovely little first wife, was a guest in his *bohio*. Today he did not feel too bad about his sixty-seven years.

He plucked the hot pot from the coals and started for the *bohio* just as Major Morales sauntered out. Federico came swiftly to attention and saluted. "I am sorry you cannot stay longer as my guest, Major. It is my honor to serve you."

Morales returned the salute and grinned, pleased to respect this wizened old Negro who had fought so well in the Ten Years War and already given so much to this one. "Thank you, Federico, but I will return in a day or two with our General, who will be pleased to see you again." He glanced at Fidel in the hammock. "Sergeant! It is time."

Fidel rolled gracefully from the hammock, fully awake and ready to ride. At the sound of the command, Oinja and Theresa emerged from the *bohio* and Oinja rushed to her stepson, who gave her a long embrace. "Ah, my son. When will I ever lay eyes on you again?"

"When the saints will it, Mama Oinja. I am pleased for the few days here at home. It is more than many of our *companeros* will ever know."

Oinja shrugged and crossed herself. It was never good to ask too much of the saints, but she willed Fidel to return with the General. "Do not forget to pray, Fidelito."

Fidel kissed her on the forehead and turned to Theresa, who stood smiling at Oinja's side. "I will be in the Sierra de Trinidad, Mama Oinja. Maybe I can visit again before the rainy season."

Theresa embraced Fidel. "Thank you for helping Christopher, Fidel. He is lucky, we are lucky, *Cuba Libre!* is lucky to have such a good *compañero*."

Theresa turned to Guillermo Morales, shook hands and said, "Thank you for your strength, Major, for getting me here safely. Our beloved General is fortunate to have such an aide."

Morales smiled, pleased, and looked around at the members of Federico's family, all of whom seemed to mirror her words. "Thank you, Captain Valdez," he said simply and headed for his horse.

For the first few moments, Federico, Oinja and Theresa stood quietly, staring at the rapidly disappearing sounds. Oinja squared her shoulders and turned toward her husband. "Do you have that tea, old man?" Without waiting for his answer she turned and, Theresa in tow, entered the *bohio*.

"Tea," he said a moment later, as he hurried into the one room shack and smiled cautiously at his wife.

Oinja gestured at a large calabash sitting on the ground and Federico poured in the tea, which she was using as a poultice. The *Yanqui* was lying naked on his stomach. She reached into the calabash, squeezed a sponge slightly and applied it to Christopher's neck and shoulders. His malarial fever had not yet broken. He was still pouring sweat. Lost in delirium, he stood in the parlor next to his little brother, Alex, staring into the long coffin that contained their father. Little Alex gazed into their father's frozen face. Then their father sat up in the coffin, preaching to his boys: "That cavalry charge was the high water mark of the Confederacy. We came up that hill hellbent-for-leather, Stars and Bars rippling in the wind. Proved we were men that day. Yes, sir."

Christopher despised the words, which he had heard a thousand times. He was only fifteen years old, but he had himself spent as many years fighting as had his father, and he believed that his father should shut up, especially since he was dead.

But little Alex listened rapturously. He licked his lollipop faster and faster. Alex was dressed in the miniature uniform of a Confederate General, and his golden curls had turned white in the sunlight that filtered in through the parlor window. Their father had also changed clothes, and was now dressed as the cavalry major he had once been. "Your mother never understood that, boys. Right up to the day she died, bless her saintly soul, she never understood about war, about the ultimate test of manhood, about the comradeship, about the glory. Man at his noblest." Their dead father beamed. His face was years younger, beardless, and sepia-toned, like the photograph he'd had taken of himself in Richmond in 1862.

Their mother's ghost turned around on the piano stool and said, "Man at his noblest? Hmmph! Man at his most irresponsible." She was a young woman, dressed in her wedding gown. "You all ran off to kill Yankees like you was going on a fox hunt. You all left everything to go off chasing that old whore, Glory."

His delirium shifted and now Christopher sat on the edge of the boardwalk in front of the dry goods store his mother had been trying to run alone for as long as he could remember. It was late October, 1867, the day before his seventh birthday. Christopher whittled on a pine board, slicing off small curls, watching them fall into a mud puddle and float around in circles. For almost five years his father had been missing somewhere in west Texas, but he was supposed to come home today; his mother had gotten a wire. He tried to remember his father, but he wasn't really sure he wanted to.

A large grey wagon pulled by four mules stopped on the far side of the street. A tall, filthy, yellow-faced man with a long brown and white beard climbed down from the tailgate and limped across the street to the dry goods store, walked up the two wooden steps that raised the boardwalk above the mud, started to enter the store, then stopped, turned around and said, "You Chris?"

"Yes, sir."

"I'm your pa, boy. Come give me a hug." Christopher obliged, but as soon as the filthy man entered the store, he ran down the street and into the woods, and cried until long after dark.

It was raining now, but it was hot, close. He had dropped his knife somewhere, but he was carrying a long stick and poking in a hole. He was looking for something he'd lost, but it wasn't his knife. Then, off in the distance he heard his mother calling him. No, it was Consuelo. She was laughing and waving her hands. The second crop in the new cane field was in and almost ready for harvest. Soon the *camposinos* would be coming to help them burn the fields and harvest the sugar. But not today; today was a holiday. Christopher and Consuelo ran through the field and tried to hide from each other. Christopher stopped and looked around. "Con-suel-lo. Where are you?" Her head popped up less than ten feet away.

"Boo." She stuck out her tongue and disappeared.

"I'll get you, wench. And when I do, I'll...fix you." He crashed through the cane toward where she had been. But he couldn't find her. He had the stick again, and he was poking through the rubble, over-turning scraps of corrugated iron, pulling apart palm mats. There was a small body under one of the mats.

"No! No! No !" Christopher screamed. "Consuelooooo!"

"Holy Mother of God!" Theresa shuddered and crossed herself, as Federico ran into the shack. Oinja merely grunted and lashed out at her husband, "Bring that other tea, old man. Hurry."

Christopher opened his eyes. His mother, young as a bride, and the old colored maid were looking down at him. He was sick, in his crib, and they were mumbling and shaking their heads. Why are they speak-ing Spanish?

"Christopher, please. Drink some of this tea Federico made for you. It will help your fever. Please," Theresa entreated.

"You drink this tea, Mr. Captain!" Oinja spoke loudly, firmly. Almost against his will, Christopher heard. "You want to get better, you drink this tea. You want to die, don't drink it. Right now!" Like a help-less child, he allowed the big woman to raise his head.

Suddenly his reviving consciousness recognized that he was naked. "My clothes," he mumbled.

"You men are all alike," Oinja laughed. "You all worry about noth-ing. Now drink!" Unlike her Federico, Oinja stood in awe of neither the General nor his officers. She turned her attention to her husband, who stood at the bedside watching Theresa feed Christopher his tea.

"Federico! Don't just stand there like a tree! Fix some soup for your captain. It will be awhile before his chills start. We must feed him something!" She scowled at Federico, who shuffled from the hut and returned to his fire.

"He will sleep for a little while after he eats, but then the chills will start and his mind will return to the night devils. Then you must help him." Oinja looked the city woman in the eye and laughed.

"Well, of course," Theresa smiled, puzzled by Oinja's merriment.

"When those chills start, there be two ways to keep him warm. We pile on all our thin blankets, and you warm him with your body."

"You mean. . ."

"Yes!" the fat woman laughed again. "Take your clothes off and warm him with your body." She's almost as helpless as my Federico, Oinja thought.

Hesitant and feeling an unaccustomed shyness, Theresa glanced around the room. "What about Federico?"

Oinja's black eyes almost popped from her head as she tried to contain her glee. "You care what my old man thinks? He do you no harm, lady. But I'll keep him out." She suppressed her laugh and stared at Theresa, who still seemed uncertain. Oinja knew how the young quatroon served the revolution. She also sensed that Theresa was somehow infatuated with the sick *Yanqui*." Have you been known by this man?" Oinja asked, catching Theresa by surprise.

"No!" Theresa shook her head, shocked, but also feeling a bit guilty. All her life she had fantasized about Christopher and Consuelo and, in weaker and more lonely moments, put herself in her older sister's place. The last time she had been together with Consuelo, her sister had complained that the war was coarsening Christopher, that every time he returned from one of his months long absences he was harder, more distant, and that he no longer seemed to feel joy. Theresa had merely nodded, fully aware of what her years as a Havana prostitute had done to her own ability to feel joy. Christopher had never shown her anything but kindness and understanding; her brother-in-law was one of the very few men for whom Theresa felt respect, let alone sincere affection.

Oinja felt the younger woman's confusion and decided to leave her alone. "All right, lady. You stay here and take care of this man. I'm gonna go and take care of mine—and my other children too." She laughed again and left the *bohio*.

Federico was gone. He had started the soup simmering over the charcoal fire, turned it over to one of his children and walked into the forest. Federico was a strong man, but he did not understand women, especially the tall, heavy-bodied, scar-cheeked woman who had been living with him for the last twenty years and who had presented him with four of his seven children. Federico knew how to survive in the jungles and swamps. He knew how to feed his large family, even in this time of troubles. He had the respect of his oldest living son, Fidel, and that of General Gomez and this *Yanqui* captain. Though the joints of his hands and knees were beginning to stiffen with the creaking sickness, his skinny black body was all sinew and tendon. He could still work twenty hours a day, drill his woman much more often than she was willing, and father sons. But women he did not understand. Federico's grandfather once told Federico that women were the key to understanding the world. The old man had been shipped across the Middle Passage from West Africa to Hispaniola, and then to the auction block at Santiago de Cuba, and knew the old stories. "Women were the first people," he had told Federico. "Woman crawled from the earth womb just as man crawls from the woman womb. Women are older than us. Even a young woman is older than the oldest man, because the secret of the world lives in her belly. It is a secret no man can know."

Federico shook his head. Whatever he had done to offend Oinja, he must do it just about every day, because she was always yelling at him, and treating him like one of the less tractable of their small children. "It's that old Mr. Knower, Mrs. Beknown story all over again," he said aloud, shaking his head. "But I sure can't seem to get underneath what that story's saying. No, sir!" His grandfather had told the story many times and Federico had passed it along to anyone who would listen.

Federico thought of the two women in the cabin, first of Theresa who reminded him of his beloved and gentle Bettita, and then of Oinja. Maybe I am Mr. Beknower, he thought, just as Oinja's deep voice commanded him back to the clearing. He rose from his haunches and walked slowly back toward the cabin, his responsibilities and his wife.

"It is starting," Oinja yelled from the dark interior of the cabin. Theresa had been napping by the fire. She stretched, stood up slowly and smiled at Federico, who grinned sheepishly back. "Theresa!" Oinja called.

Christopher's chills had started with great force; enormous goose-bumps covered his gaunt, yellow body. Though the women quickly covered him with the family's thin blankets, his shaking merely increased.

"Well, Lady?" Oinja grinned at Theresa, shook her head and thought, this woman has too much Spanish pride and not enough African sense. Theresa stared at the vibrating captain, then across the room to where Federico stood leering at her with almost toothless gums. "Federico!" Oinja hissed. "Go outside and watch the children. Now!" She looked back at Theresa. "Do you want to keep this man?"

Theresa blushed at the question. She laughed as she undressed, and asked herself, When did I last blush? At anything? For one short moment, standing naked before the bed, she felt more vulnerable than she had in years. She looked at Oinja, as if to say, Silly, isn't it? I've been to bed with so many men. And yet...

Oinja shook her head and thought, this girl *puta* maybe knows how to fuck Spanish officers and be a good spy. Maybe she knows how to kill Spanish, too, but she has crazy ideas. Theresa laughed again, caught up by the absurdity of her shyness. Oinja joined her, and the two women roared without embarrassment or restraint.

Federico, who was peering into the cabin through one of the innumerable rents in the lashed palm fronds, didn't dare laugh, but he smiled to himself and licked his lips. Ah, little one! She looks so much like Bettita, he thought, and felt a sharp emptiness at the pit of his stomach as he relived the first time his Bettita had come to him more than forty years before. She had been darker than this light-skinned mulatto woman, but she had possessed similar grace and similar small round breasts. He dropped his hand to caress his ancient but still restless *pinga*.

Theresa stopped laughing and climbed under the blankets with her naked, vibrating brother-in-law. Oinja nodded her pleasure and approval, rearranged the blankets, bent over to kiss the younger woman on the top of her head and strode heavily from the cabin.

He doesn't even know I'm in bed with him, Theresa thought, as she tried to wrap her slight frame around the full length of his shivering body. Even as tears came to her eyes, she smiled ruefully. I am no more than his nurse. She felt a wave of anger at the world she lived in and what that world had meant to her life. For a moment the anger shifted to her patient, who had always seen her as nothing but a hurt little girl with the right political sympathies.

Christopher thrashed about on the narrow bed, and she yelled, "Christopher! Lie still!" When he quieted back down, she sobbed silently against his back. She felt guilt for her anger at this crippled man, but clung to him like a lifeline. He was now her only connection to her beloved sister. Lying next to Christopher, trying to pour her warmth into him, she felt again a sharp revulsion at what she did with her body.

In the years between the wars, after the bruja had helped her with the abortion and she had run away to *La Habana*, prostitution had been a job, something that was forbidden by the Church, but something that allowed her a freedom she had never known in the suffocating house of her constantly pawing uncle. But now, three years into a hopeless rebellion against Spain, she yearned to be finished with it. The rest of her hopes she had long abandoned, though sometimes she still dreamed of freedom for her body. "Christopher! Lie still!" she yelled and, sobbing, surrendered to her anger.

* * * *

Christopher heard the voice again, Consuelo's voice calling as from a great distance. "I love you, Consuelo," he whispered raggedly. "I will love you until I die." Christopher's eyes were wide open but caught far back in the past. "Not to worry, my love. We will have other children." He raised his hand, brushed a tear from Theresa's face and continued his delirium.

Consuelo was sleeping now. The doctor turned his fat, white-suited body and nodded at Christopher. "Take the baby away." The doctor kept flapping his hands. "Take it away and bury it."

His fever is coming back, Theresa thought. For a few moments he seemed relaxed and to be falling into a gentle sleep, smiling, as if drifting along in the lap of a pleasant dream.

Christopher and Consuelo were lying on a hillside a week before the wedding. Though Spanish custom forbade it, her mother had allowed her to go for a ride unchaperoned. Consuelo talked about how happy she was while Christopher riveted most of his attention on her small, mother-of-pearl buttons, which he was unfastening. She was lying on her back, staring at the clouds, trying desperately to think of things to talk about. "I feel so sorry for little Theresa. That house with all its crepe and bitterness, that's no place for her. Not any more, not with me gone. And my uncle..." She shivered.

"That's all right," he answered absently. "She can stay with us any time she likes." When he'd finished with the long row of closely spaced buttons, he spread apart the two wings of her dress. He kissed her softly on her full lips, lifted her hips slightly, and slid her petticoats down over her feet. His hand shook as he slid the wide straps of the chemise from her shoulders.

Though she had said or done nothing either to help or to hinder him, Consuelo's fright quickly overcame her desire. She couldn't let this happen, not before their marriage. "Please, Christopher. Don't."

Suddenly Christopher was sweating and his hands were moving over Theresa's body. She threw the blankets to the floor and tried to rise from the bed. When he felt her pulling away, he pulled her back onto the bed and rolled on top of her. "Consuelo," he panted.

"I love you, Consuelo." His mouth was over her breast and his hand was moving up between her thighs. "Please, sweetheart."

But then she was clawing at him and screaming. "Nooo! Christopher! Dooooon't!" He was trying to enter her, but she had become rigid.

Her voice again came to him as from a great distance. But she was here, under him, with him. He ignored the distant voice and the clawing fingers. He called her name, again and again, "Consuelo, Consuelo, Consuelo," and kept trying to enter her.

He had her pinned to the bed. She struggled, terrified. Although his eyes were open, his mind and heart were trapped years back into the past that had blossomed between the wars. "Please, Consuelo. I love you!"

"No! Oh, God, NO! I'm Theresa. Don't!" Although she had been with untold dozens of men, and had made love to them in an endless variety of positions and circumstances, she felt only horror. Her desperation rose from her mouth in one long scream. "No-o-o-o!"

Suddenly Oinja was there with them and rolled Christopher over onto his back. As soon as Theresa found herself free, she saw both Oinja and Federico staring at her bruised nakedness. Red blotches covered her breasts, and she felt a long welt rising on her thigh. Totally disregarding both her nakedness and Federico's intent leer, she knelt on the floor and, rigid and gasping, held to the edge of the cot.

Oinja noticed Federico, picked up the water gourd and threw it at him as hard as she could. "Bring me some water!" she screamed. Within seconds he returned, panting over Theresa with a gourd so full that water sloshed onto his bare feet. "Get out and stay out, old man. And I don't want to catch you peeking through the sides of the *bohío* either." Without giving her dejected man another look, the large woman took the sponge to Theresa's body, much in the same way that she had earlier sponged Christopher's. "It is only the fever, lady. It is nothing. It is the fever. He does not know where he is."

"I know," Theresa stammered. "That's the trouble." But she gradually relaxed, soothed by the older woman's cooing voice and strong hands. For a few minutes she allowed herself to be carried back to her infancy, when her mother used a similar sponge to bathe away her pains.

Again and again the scar-cheeked African dipped the sponge into the calabash, squeezed it half dry, and used it as a tool to caress Theresa's face and body. "It is all right, it is all right," she crooned, as she thought of her own body and what had happened to it over the years. When she sensed Theresa's strength returning, she helped her back into her blouse and skirt, and turned her attention to the sick *Yanqui*, who had fallen into a feverish sleep. She looked up long enough to say, "He will get better fast now. You will see," and frowned as Theresa shrugged indifferently.

As Oinja sponged Christopher, her smile returned. His penis had shrunk from its full-blooded erection of a few minutes before to a shriveled oddity no larger than her thumb. She reached over, lifted the lifeless little member and pointed it at Theresa. "You see, lady. Just like a baby. It runs around all day long, getting into mischief, causing the whole world nothing but miseries. But then it go to sleep and become a little angel."

Late the next day Theresa was alone in the *bohío* with Christopher, bathing his face and chest. Though he was still sweating, his fever had broken and he seemed to be sleeping peacefully. As she thought of her brother-in-law and her feelings for him, Oinja's sharp words came back to her: 'Haven't you been known by this man?' Known? By Christopher?

She bit her lip and studied the pasty, yellowish features of this gaunt man whom she had loved in some way or another since shortly after her twelfth birthday. Known? Hardly. She rinsed the sponge in the water gourd and placed it on Christopher's forehead.

"Theresa?"

She looked into his open grey eyes. The whites were still yellow but focused. She smiled and sponged his cheeks and chin. "Yes, my brother?"

"Is there anything to eat?"

She stopped sponging, looked him in the eye and said, "If you are hungry, my brother, then I will feed you."

Chapter Six

CABINET MEETING EXTRAORDINARY
Spanish Prime Minister is Seeking for a Way Out

* * * *

The developments of the night have been of a more sensational character even than those of the day. After receiving the first message from Gen. Lee earlier in the day, the President summoned his Cabinet immediately. The door was shut against all other visitors. Then Secretary Long hurried to the Navy Department and wired to Admiral Sicard to detach the battle-ship *Maine* from the Squadron of Evolution and send her to Havana. *The World*, January 25.

The Zapata Swamp

Christopher awakened from his long siege weak and depressed, but lucid. He lay on his back and stared at the roof of the cabin where woven palm fronds created intricate patterns. He thought of calling out, but realized that he was safe and that no one expected anything of him. Slowly he relaxed into his pain. His heart took charge and, in the temporary privacy of the *bohio*, his tears welled and flowed. They were still flowing twenty minutes later when Theresa came in to check on him. Lost in his love and grief and regrets, he did not hear her enter.

When he felt a cool hand on his forehead, he half turned. Theresa's face appeared, shimmering through the scrim of his tears. For a brief moment he saw Consuelo and collapsed into hard-wracking sobs. Embarrassed by his lack of control, he turned his back to Theresa who fell on her knees, exploded into her own long suppressed sobs and threw her head and upper body across his back.

Oinja and Federico burst into the *bohio*, took one glance at the grieving in-laws and backed out. For the next hour they sat silently around the fire and listened to the undulating sounds of mourning that poured from their cabin. When the inter-twined sobs and howls finally softened, Federico touched Oinja on the arm. There were tears in his eyes. "I think maybe this will help our *Yanqui* friend to heal," he whispered.

Oinja grasped his hand, placed it between her huge breasts and smiled fondly. "Sometimes, old man, your wisdom shines and reminds me about why I love you."

"Maybe I should take him some soup?"

Oinja shook her head, amused at how quickly her man could turn back into a fool. "No, old man. We will turn his care completely over to Theresa now. It will be good for them both." She smiled to remove any sense of criticism. "Do you not think that is a good idea?" Federico nodded, flashed his broken-tooth and allowed his excited hand to move to the center of Oinja's left breast.

By the next evening Christopher was already recovering his strength. Although he had slept fourteen hours the night before and had taken three long naps during the day, he had also taken two short walks into the jungle. Between Oinja's herb-laced soups and Theresa's tenderness, he could feel the strength pouring back into his body. During this second day of his convalescence, however, an obsession slowly built; he needed to know what had taken place in *El Cajon del Muerto*. He needed the details. But each time he asked, Theresa shook her head hard and said, "No, Christopher. I can't. It is bad enough to go there in my nightmares."

As was almost always true of country folk who slept in cramped quarters, they spent most of their evenings out of doors around the mandala of a small charcoal fire. That evening, after a rich soup laced with smoked snake, Christopher turned to Theresa and said, "Theresa, I must insist. For my peace of mind. I must be able to see Consuelo dead."

"Captain Jackson," Oinja said sternly. "Get her death scene from your mind. Bury her or your grief will bury you."

For the first time he spoke brusquely to her. "I cannot bury her if I cannot see her." He stared across the fire at Theresa, his mouth compressed to a hard straight line. "Tell me, Theresa. It will help you, too."

Federico looked from Oinja, who was shaking her head, to Theresa, who seemed to be taking her lead from Oinja, to Christopher, whose eyes were burning into Theresa's. "Oinja, my esteemed mate, in this thing you are wrong." He pulled a long, red-tipped stick from the fire and whipped it lightly but repeatedly against a flat stone. "The truth often makes weak men weaker; but it always makes strong men stronger." Federico looked at Theresa and Christopher, then nodded at Theresa. "Captain Valdez, I am only a sergeant from the old war, and I know that in my woman's eyes I am often a fool. But I know what I know. You must honor the *Yanqui* with the truth. Share that truth, little sister. It will help your own heart grow stronger. Let us hear the hard truth of *El Cajon del Muerto*."

Theresa nodded almost imperceptibly. "One minute, if you please." She rose from the fire and entered the *bohio*.

When she failed to return after a few minutes, Christopher rose to go after her, but Oinja grabbed his leg by the trousers and shook her head. "Give her the time she needs, Captain." Christopher sat back down and sipped his tea.

When Theresa returned, she sat across from Christopher and well back from the fire with her face in shadow, her jaw set, resolute. "I did not know they were in *El Cajon del Muerto* until it was too late. Like you, Christopher, I thought they would be safe at Aunt Ibeza's house. Even when I heard what the Spanish had done there I did not believe that Consuelo and the girls could possibly be affected. But when I heard…" She stopped a moment, not wanting to speak in this world about horrors that still visited her in the other world of dreams. "Our General decided to liberate the camp. He needed women to go into that place and prepare our people, so I volunteered. It was raining…"

"So Gomez knew that my family was in the camp?"

Theresa shrugged. "Perhaps. I do not know. He knew that there were many other *mambi* families in the camp. The Spanish were already telling the Americans that the camps were all closed, but it was a lie, so our General decided on the raid. I did not see him at that time, but Major Alavero told me of his words: 'It is already too late for too many. Close that place of death.'" She broke down for a moment. "I am sorry, Christopher." When she regained control she added, "That is how I got into the camp." The other *mambises* were quiet, respectful of Theresa's pain. Even Christopher realized that he could not rush her. She would tell the story at her own pace and in her own way.

"To the Spanish who 'collected' our squad, we were just another band of wandering peasants in want of salvation. In the middle of a downpour and shortly before dark, the guards pushed us through the barbed wire that surrounded *El Cajon del Muerto*. When the rest of the group dispersed to search for their families and contacts, I stood by myself and shut my eyes for a moment. The horror was too much for me. And the smell…the smell….Only after taking some deep breaths and strengthening myself against the stench could I open my eyes.

"Hundreds of make-shift shelters crowded around a small hamlet of four adobe houses and half a dozen outbuildings. Though a few inmates had been able to obtain large packing crates or tents and tarps, most of the shelters were no more than thatch-covered burrows and palm frond lean-to's. I found out later that the tiny shelters had been constructed by the camp's first inmates, most of whom had since died of starvation or disease." Theresa stopped to take a breath. "Hundreds of family groups conducted every aspect of their suffering in the open; they squatted or lay in the mud, their only cover a straw hat or filthy blanket. Around the few original buildings dozens of palm trees, all denuded of their fronds, almost touched the low clouds. After eight days of rain the *reconcentrado* was sinking into expanding pools of mud. Despite the presence of several thousand inmates, except for the feeble screams of the sick and mourning, the camp was strangely quiet and still."

"Please, Theresa." Christopher stretched his arm across the small fire and cupped his hand on her knee, as if to give her strength and control. "My family. Please!"

She drew further into herself and stared into the fire pit, remaining quiet for a long time. When she started again she spoke in the third person, in a barely audible monotone, and clinically, as if observing herself and the scene from a great distance. She watched unblinking as a burial team picked a naked boy from the ground. A bent man with a white beard grasped the boy by his shoulders. A black woman wearing a gunny sack grabbed the ankles. They swung the body into a stained sheet. Stopping several times to rest, the couple staggered to the eastern edge of camp and emptied the sheet into a long trench.

It was not just the stillness or obvious despair that immobilized her. More, it was the stenches—death, disease and defecation. Other than a few partially protected open latrines, the Spanish had provided no sanitary facilities. The sickest inmates loosed their bladders and bowels where they lay. Though all but the most recently arrived were in various stages of starvation, it was the diseases, malaria, yellow fever, and particularly cholera, dysentery and typhoid that daily carried away dozens of people.

How many have already died? she wondered, forcing herself to move. She wrapped her ragged shawl around her nose and mouth and set out to explore the maze of mud and inmates. Her immediate need was to find Consuelo and her three daughters. The first person who seemed alert enough to help was a skinny black woman intent on nursing a bloated bellied, orange skinned boy. Puzzled, the woman, who was very young, stared at her. "Theresa?"

She squatted down next to the woman and stroked the head of the little boy, whose huge eyes stared into space. "Please forgive me, lady," she said. "Do we know each other?"

The woman reached out and jerked at Theresa's shawl. "You are Consuelo's little sister. I used to work for the *Yanqui*."

Theresa jerked away. "Who are you?"

"You know me, though I have lost many kilos of good fat. I am Alonzo's little sister. I am Bianca."

Theresa put her arms around the young mother and pulled her close. "Forgive me, Bianca! " She glanced at the little boy, who had shown no interest in her presence. "This is Carlos, no?"

Bianca looked up with dry, exhausted eyes. "He died last week. Now my baby is dying."

From inside her blouse, Theresa pulled one of the dozen small packets of sugar she had smuggled in to maintain her strength. "This may keep him alive another day or two." She watched as the younger woman tore the cane leaf package apart and fed the brown granules of sugar to her little boy, who sucked each sticky bit from her fingers. "Bianca? The *mambises* will raid this place of death. Tell our friends. We will start a riot maybe one hour after dark. We..."

"When? Tonight?" The young mother did not look up from her feeding.

"No. I am sorry for how I said this news. When the weather is right." She stroked Carlos's head and tried not to cry. "Maybe in four or five days."

Bianca looked up and let out a despairing keen. "Ah, Theresa, it will be too late for us."

Theresa glanced at the boy and looked her fellow partisan in the eye. "I think maybe it is already too late, Bianca."

Bianca bent down and kissed her son on the head. "I know," she whispered."

Theresa watched in painful impotence as the mother continued to feed the granules to her son. Finally she asked, "Bianca? Where is Consuelo? And her girls?"

For the first time Bianca's sorrow seemed to embrace Theresa. "I think maybe they are still over by the palm trees, Theresa. Try there. I am sorry. I heard that she was dying. Yesterday I heard that."

"Thank you," Theresa mumbled, as she blinked and turned away. Trying to move as directly as possible, she wove her way through the tiny islands of squalor. The word spread quickly. "Someone is looking for Consuelo Jackson." When she found her sister under a tiny lean-to, she could barely recognize her even though those protecting the shelter said, "That is her, that is Consuelo Jackson. She has the fever, like so many. But she is sleeping now. Maybe she will live a little longer." Consuelo lay flat on her back next to a little girl, who was crying weakly. Ignoring the match-limbed girl, Theresa dropped to her knees in the mud and smoothed the filthy, tangled hair of the strange, sleeping skeleton who resembled only faintly her once beautiful sister. Her skin is so cold, Theresa thought. I hope she doesn't chill. "How long has she been sleeping?" she asked an old woman who had hunkered down near the shelter. The woman wore a huge rain hat of palm fronds that reached from her head almost to the ground, like a tepee with eyes. "She sleep almost since before dark, Lady," the old woman answered in the sing-song dialect of Sancti Spiritus Province. "She don't sleep so much before."

Theresa continued to smooth her sister's hair. Where are the girls? she wondered. Mother of God! Have they died? Elizabeth?" she said to the emaciated little girl who had been named after her father's mother. "Elizabeth?"

The child looked at her with dead, empty eyes. "Mama," she cried. "Mama. Mama."

"Where are your sisters?"

The eyes staring out from the fronds of the tepee moved rapidly from Theresa to Consuelo to Elizabeth and back, as if waiting for the lightning. Her eyes were bright, intense. Finally she whispered, "They die on the last week, Lady. Same day. The fever eat their hearts."

Theresa was no longer listening. Consuelo had not moved, at all. She allowed her hand to drop tentatively down over the cold, dripping face to the nose and mouth. Her shaking hand stopped and her face froze. She fell over on her sister's body, keening, in the high wail of a dying rabbit. "Mother of God! Consuelo! Mother of God!"

The years of hope mixed with frustration, loneliness and self-loathing bubbled over. Oblivious to her surroundings, Theresa rocked back and forth. Elizabeth cried more loudly, and crawled over to try to push Theresa away from her mother. The old woman scurried away to find the burial detail.

By the night of the raid Elizabeth, too, had died, her malnourished body no match for the fevers that swept the *reconcentrados* in huge, irregular waves. A burial detail had tossed the small body into a mass grave and partially covered it with a few shovels of quicklime and mud.

* * * * *

By the time she finished, Theresa's arms were wrapped around her knees. She rocked back and forth and tears flowed down her face. As she rocked, her face moved forward into the flickering light of the fire and back into shadow, back and forth like the contorted mask of a nightmare etched in acid.

Christopher was so trapped by his own loss and guilt that he could not respond to Theresa's pain; he could neither move nor speak. Though she had answered his need for a portrait of Consuelo's death, he lacked the strength to reach out to her. Oinja pulled her wide, tragic eyes from Theresa and glanced at Christopher, who seemed frozen behind a mask of disbelief. She looked at Federico, who stared into the coals, as if in search of a palliative. She shook her head hard, uttered a long howl and moved to Theresa, whom she folded to her bosom. "Oh, little one," she cried in her deep alto. "Oh, my little one."

Oinja's gesture brought Christopher back. The cost of Theresa's numerous sacrifices for *Cuba Libre!* knifed through his mind. Another dam burst and a fresh wave of respect for her washed over him. As he realized the depth of their kinship, his frozen face collapsed to fluid lines of empathy. He pulled himself slowly to his feet, stepped across the fire to Theresa's side and put his hand on Oinja's shoulder. "Oinja, please! Leave us!"

Oinja gave him one sharp look, nodded brusquely and grabbed Federico's hand. The old couple retreated to the *bohio*, where they stood well back in the darkness beyond the doorway and watched. Christopher took Theresa by the upper arms, pulled her half way to her feet and held her to his chest. "I am sorry that you must know so much pain." He wanted to reassure her, but did not know the words, so he rocked her as Oinja had rocked her, and even as he did so he knew that he was rocking himself.

Later that night, long after Federico and his family had fallen asleep, Christopher and Theresa huddled next to each other close to the coals of the diminished fire. At first they were comfortable to be alone together, and to hold off the dreams they both feared. In the last hour, however, the silences had grown uncomfortable. She knew the nightmare of the *reconcentrado* would return. Although still drowning in her own grief, she sensed that only by reaching out to him could she help herself survive. She struggled to find comforting words. "She was my sister. I know how much she loved you, and that you loved her, and the girls." A little later she put her hand over his. "They are with God."

He jerked back, repelled by her sentiment. "They are in the earth. They are dead. Nothing."

"Christopher!" She felt as though he had slapped her.

"We are nothing."

"No! Even for me, that is just too bleak."

"Listen to me, Theresa! The Spanish. We kill them. They kill us. Then more Spanish come, and more. We keep killing them, but they still come. It makes no difference." He turned away, wrapped his arms around his legs, rested his chin on his knees and stared once more into the coals. "It makes no difference, none at all. But I will continue to kill them."

Though she understood and even shared much of his despair, Theresa required hope. She tried again. "What do you think will happen?" she asked.

"Happen? What?"

"Tomorrow, Christopher. Next month. Next year? What is going to happen? To us? To Cuba?"

Christopher stopped poking the fire and shrugged. "To tell you the truth, Theresa, I really don't give a good goddamn."

Again she recoiled, then chided gently, "You say that because of all you have lost. You do not really mean…"

"Yes, I probably do say these things because of my loss." He broke a small bundle of twigs and added them to the fire. "I am sorry." When she failed to respond, he put his hand on her knee. "Theresa. It has been good to share our grief. You have helped me. Thank you. I wish I had more to give, but I am empty. The future is an abyss."

She was shaking her head before he was half-finished. "No, Christopher. We must have hope. I could not have survived my years in *La Habana* without hope. Without hope I would have killed myself long ago."

"Hope for what, Theresa? What can you possibly be hoping for?" She cringed and pulled away.

"Do you have a need to hurt me, Christopher?"

"Of course not," he mumbled. "It is just that...hope is an abstraction without meaning—Like *Cuba Libre!* Consuelo was right about that, wasn't she?"

Theresa shook her head hard. "*Cuba Libre!* is not an abstraction. It is our one best hope for our future, for the future of our children."

Christopher remembered Consuelo's angry disbelief. He chortled bitterly. "Children? What children?"

"They were my family, too. But we have to think of Cuba's children. Even now, lost as we are in our own grief, we have to think of the living and unborn."

"I do not possess such strength, Theresa." After a moment he added, "Consuelo was right. Nothing is worth sacrificing your family. And that is what I did. I sacrificed my family—and yours."

"Consuelo would not see it that way, Christopher. She would understand."

"Oh? You think so? You should have been there the night I left, the night before I sent them off to Cardenas." His voice broke. "She cursed me, Theresa. Our last hours together we spent in bitterness. That night will stay in my dreams"

"I cannot believe that Consuelo would ever, ever curse you."

He shrugged, as if her belief or disbelief was a matter of supreme indifference. "In so many words. She accused me of killing them. And do you know what I sounded like that night? I sounded like you. I paraded my self-righteous little political abstractions and rationalized sending my loved ones to their deaths."

You blind, self-pathetic fool, she thought, but said, "You had no way of knowing!"

He shrugged again, as if to dismiss her arguments as irrelevancies.

"I knew we were tied down in a war that has become hopeless. I knew that she wanted me to take her and the girls back to Georgia—or at least to send her if I wouldn't go."

"You had good reasons for..."

"Goddamnit, Theresa. Shut up!"

She fought to hold back fresh tears and started to her feet, but gritted her teeth and dug a little deeper into the earth with her buttocks. You will not succeed in chasing me away! she told herself. She had dealt with the grief of too many men to be frightened away by her brother-in-law's despairing rant. "So what do you plan to do?" she asked in what she hoped was a reasonable voice.

He bit off a sharp retort, stared at her for a moment and matched her reasonable tone. "I will continue to kill Spaniards. What else is there to do?"

After a long silence during which she searched in vain for words to touch his heart, Theresa let out a sigh that was half sob, rose from the fire and moved to one of the hammocks strung between the palms. "I am sorry, Christopher, sorry for your pain and despair. I will pray to the Virgin that your heart will heal."

"Good night," he mumbled. He continued to stare into the fire, where the shifting shapes of the red and orange coals appeared as the contorted faces of his family screaming at him from an inferno. Even though he could not pull himself from his own despair, he sensed how shabbily he had responded to Theresa's pain, and to her obvious concern for him. He lifted his head and stared into the shadows, where she was swaying lightly in her hammock. "Theresa?"

"Yes?" she said after a small silence.

"I do not mean to hurt you with my black thoughts. I appreciate your friendship and care, much more than I can put into words right now."

Her heart tightened. He sounded so distant, so...removed. "Thank you."

After a moment he tried again. "It's not that I don't feel anything. It's just that my feelings are in turmoil. I deal far better with ideas, Theresa, and yet it is my feelings that are in control. That frightens me. I do not feel in control."

"Thank you for trying to explain. I appreciate your concern, Christopher. Good night."

Chapter Seven

SEC. LONG IS SORRY SPAIN IS SCARED
But if We Didn't Keep Our Ships About Cuba
We'd Have to Lay Them Up

* * * *

REALLY, IT ISN'T UNUSUAL
It Has Just Occurred to Us That We Were Rude in
Not Visiting Cuban Ports Before

* * * *

Washington, February 4—In view of the presence of an unusually strong fleet in southern waters, Sec. Long was asked tonight to give an authorized statement on that feature of the Spanish-American situation. He said: "There should be no hostile significance attached by the Spanish or anyone else to the fact that the battle-ship *Maine* and the cruiser Montgomery are in Cuban waters, or because the North Atlantic Squadron is maneuvering off the Florida coast." *The World*, February 5.

The Zapata Swamp

O inja piled warm ashes around the sides of her black iron pot. She knew she was losing the balancing act between keeping the meal warm and over-cooking it, and she was irritated. "Federico, there is something wrong. I do not care what you say. I can smell it."

Federico stopped bagging charcoal, stood up straight for a moment, placed his hands on his hips and arched his back. "It is only because our General is late. Not to worry so much."

"Your general's lateness may spoil the special dinner I made for him. But that is not what I mean, old man. General Gomez will always manage to take care of himself."

"It is the tension we feel before a battle, Oinja. Our General Gomez is always late. You will see. When he arrives, all will be well."

"It is Theresa who I am worried about. She should not have let the *Yanqui* take her mind back to *El Cajon del Muerto*."

"Maybe so, wife, but when General Gomez arrives, she will be fine. She loves the General like a father she never knew."

Oinja ground her teeth. "General Gomez is not the center of the world, old man. Theresa's problem, her newest problem, is the *Yanqui*. Understand? And the tension between those two has been with us all day. It has nothing to do with your general, old man. It is the tension between a man and a woman."

Federico shook his head and bent over to resume sacking his charcoal. "They are both officers. They know our General ordered them here for a reason, but they do not know what that reason is. And he is late." Federico glanced across the clearing to the *bohio*, where Christopher and Theresa stood a couple of meters apart, helping two of the older children weave new palm fronds into the thin walls. Although both chatted with the children, neither adult seemed aware of the other's existence. Perhaps my woman is right, Federico told himself, finally struck by the silent distance between them.

"I am going to find out what is going on," Oinja announced.

"No, woman. Wait. If they want us to know something, they will tell us. Until then it is not our business."

Oinja sighed and wrapped additional banana leaves around the dishes of black beans, yellow squash, rice and shredded pork she had spiced with her hottest chiles. It was one of General Gomez's favorite dishes, and she silently cursed him for being too late to enjoy the meal at its best. She glanced over at her man, confident that he was wrong but unwilling to fight with him in front of the two officers. "We will see, old man," she muttered.

"We will see, old man," Federico mimicked under his breath, his back to his wife.

Theresa was numb. Despite her long experience with men, she felt Christopher's distance as a prolonged blow. She had tried to show her concern and sympathy and sister-like love. All he seemed capable of was withdrawing into cynicism. He was obviously offended by her attempt to reach out to him, but why? Guilt? It was the only possible explanation. He was reacting to her gift as if she were the devil.

She had tried thrice during the day to talk about what had taken place between them, but all she had gotten were apologies, regrets and a quick change of subject. On the third attempt, he had turned to glare at her, his mouth a straight thin line. "Theresa," he had said. "Hear this! I apologize for afflicting you with my pain last night. You have enough of your own."

"No, Christopher. Please. Much of our pain is the same."

Christopher had chortled. "Thank you, dear sister, but I am afraid my pain is my own."

She had wanted to scream, but had merely nodded, taut-faced, and walked into the jungle to be alone with yet another wound. How could he possibly reject the hours they had spent around the fire, hours that had brought them closer than they had ever been.

Now, in the late afternoon light, she carefully wove another frond through the latticework. Why are they so confused about the life of the heart? she wondered. What is it about men?

Suddenly Federico froze and looked up from his work. "Listen!" he hissed. The squabbling jungle birds had fallen almost silent. Theresa and the two men ran for their rifles and separated, each headed for different sides of the clearing. Oinja and her children continued working , as if nothing has happened. When she was sure everything looked normal, Oinja began the old planting song they used for a code: "If you want to reap the sugar, you got to burn the field." Almost immediately, and from not far into the forest, a cracked but pleasant tenor picked up the refrain.

A few moments later the Supreme Commander of *Cuba Libre!* rode into the camp, Guillermo Morales at his side. Federico, Theresa and Christopher re-entered the clearing and stowed their weapons; the latter two hung back, always slightly awed to be in the radiant presence of the only great leader of *Cuba Libre!* still alive after the deaths of Jose Marti and the Maceo brothers. Federico felt no such timidity and trotted to the head of the General's mount to grab the reins.

"Hello, my old friend." Maximo Gomez beamed and stroked his short white beard, delighted as always to be the guest of Federico, his companion in arms during The Ten Years War. "It is good to be home." His deep-set eyes sparkled.

As the General was intent on repeatedly demonstrating his sympathy for Christopher and Theresa, their reunion began on a dark note. But half way through the best meal any of them had eaten in some time, Maximo Gomez decided that they been sad long enough. "Enough of war and sorrow, my friends." He smiled, and the radiance of his white teeth and open, positive manner seemed to fill the jungle. His penetrating gaze embraced his companions and charged them with his love and concern. "Let us have a story."

All day Christopher had been anticipating the General's arrival. He wanted desperately to know what Gomez had in store for him. But given his own weakness at the moment, he doubted his ability to perform any mission more complex than ambushing Spanish *pendejos.* "General Gomez? Please, could we discuss why you brought us here. I know it must be important for you to have..."

"Tomorrow, Captain Jackson." Gomez opened his palms, and cocked his head sadly, as if to say, Let us relax, It has been a long ride.

The General turned to Federico. "Now, old friend, a story, please."

Federico grinned as he felt his chest swell with pride. "Which story?"

"Let me see. Tell us that old Mr. Beknower story you got from your grandfather."

"Of course, my General. But you have heard that story before. Many times. Would you not prefer a different one?"

Maximo Gomez laughed, which caused others to laugh, as his laugh carried the joy and lust for life of a much younger and far more innocent man. "No, no, no, my good old friend. That is my favorite story in the whole world."

Federico glanced at Oinja. Whenever he told the story, she smiled for days, as if he had spoken wisdom greater than he knew. He did not like to tell the story in front of women; they seemed to understand it far better than he. But he wanted very much to please his old friend. He recounted the story just as he had heard it so many years ago from his grandfather.

"When Mr. Knower had seen seventeen years, his father gave him a beautiful maiden all his own, and young Mr. Knower's *pinga* stood right up and saluted that girl, she was that pretty. And after the first few nights of sleeping with that girl, young Mr. Knower, he's sure he knows all about that girl. He touched her all over, and tasted and smelled her. He entered into her secret place so far he thought he was in the center of the world. And that girl, she now be Mrs. Beknown, she wants him to know her. She did everything she could to get that boy to know her. She opened herself up and made children for him. She talked to him about every single thing she'd done that day, or thought, or heard. She talked him almost deaf she wanted so bad for him to know her."

He stopped and looked around. Of the men only Maximo Gomez was smiling. Guillermo had nodded off and Christopher looked as though he had drawn into himself, away from the story and the clearing to another lifetime. Oinja was already giggling to herself, and Theresa looked fascinated; the start of a smile softened the taut angularity of her tired face.

"Go on!" Gomez ordered with a smile. "We can take it."

Federico nodded. "But Mr. Beknower didn't know that the secrets of the earth lived in her belly, and that he would never know her because he could not know them. He was just too dumb. And Mrs. Beknown, she come to see that he was too dumb to do the only thing she ever really wanted, to be known by her man. And when she figured that out, she never saw him as a man any more.

"Mr. Knower became a mighty chief with twenty wives and whole villages of slaves. All the chiefs and warriors in his country gave him respect. But old Mrs. Beknown always saw him as a little boy. And once his other wives figured out how dumb he was, they too treated him like a little boy. Old Mr. Knower kept finding young girls who wanted to be known, but he never did get that job done right."

The General laughed loud and long, and most of the others laughed with him, either because they enjoyed the tale or because they were pleased to see their leader in such good humor.

Christopher raised his eyes, noticed Oinja and Theresa exchange knowing glances, and smiled ruefully. He caught Theresa's eye for a moment, mouthed. "I am sorry," and dropped his gaze back to the tops of his boots. The General glanced at Christopher's bowed head, arched his brows thoughtfully and shook his head.

Early the next morning Theresa, Christopher and Guillermo Morales joined their general on a bowl-shaped limestone outcropping. They were on the far north side of Federico's clearing. The large white and gold limestone disk angled gently to the southeast and radiated the bright morning sun. At the top of the bowl their leader sat cross-legged, like a khaki-clothed Buddha. His followers sat at his feet, absorbing his every gesture.

Maximo Gomez lifted his finger, as if to reiterate a lesson. "Let us get back to what Theresa told us about her little rendezvous with Amos Jordan. Her excellent information has given me an idea." He turned to Morales and chucked him under the chin. "Do you not agree that we should pay close attention to the information our lovely Chief of Intelligence bestows upon us?"

Although his eyes were blank, Morales nodded in agreement. "Of course, my General. I have nothing but the greatest respect for our captain." He smiled winningly at Theresa, "Is that not so—Captain Valdez?"

Theresa reached across, nodded and patted Guillermo on the arm, as if trying to calm the anxieties of a child. "But of course, my major."

Christopher glanced from Morales to Theresa and back to Morales, who was beaming. What the hell is this all about? he wondered, well aware of Theresa's deep-seated contempt for the brave but arrogant and often reckless major. He glanced at the General, who was beaming as if he had arranged the rapprochement himself.

"Now that we are clear on this little point of—what do you *Yanquis* call it, Christopher? Domestic tranquility? Let us return to our task. Agreed?"

Everyone nodded, pleased by the General's warmth and wisdom, and waited for him to continue. "In addition to what Theresa tells us, I have some other news that is turning my idea into a plan."

"Sir?" Morales had never had much patience with the General's guessing games. What nonsense. Why can't he just come out with it?

Christopher dropped his gaze, self-satisfied by Morales' obvious impatience. "General, do you mean Lee's request for the American fleet?"

Gomez waved a stubby finger in Christopher's face. "In part, Captain. But only part. My news is that Lee has succeeded. McKinley will send at least a ship or two, perhaps more." Before they could react, he held up his hand. "Now! Remember Jordan's real concern?"

Christopher closed his eyes to concentrate and Guillermo Morales shook his head. "General?" Morales asked.

"Ah, my apologies, Guillermo. Sometimes I forget. You are a man of action." He patted Morales on the cheek, as if reassuring a puppy.

He then dropped his playful mood and leaned forward. "Listen! According to Theresa, Jordan is afraid that an American ship might insult the Spanish into an incident. Why is that so? Because he is afraid that an incident might in turn provoke America to declare war.

"General, don't you think the Spanish diplomats are a little too sophisticated for that?" As much as Christopher detested the Spanish, he appreciated their diplomatic oiliness.

Gomez shrugged and sighed. "Unfortunately, yes. Spain will walk across the ocean backwards to avoid war with McKinley. That is precisely why the Spanish will be very nervous about the presence in Havana harbor of an American battleship or two. They know that American public opinion has turned against them—largely because of the human tragedy they concocted with the *reconcentrados*. The Spanish will walk on water. They will come across to the *Yanqui* sailors as sweetness and light. They will fawn like slaves—which will bring out the usual *Yanqui* arrogance. My sources tell me that our Spanish cousins are planning band concerts for the sailors and forcing their fat wives to invite the American officers to dinner."

Gomez smiled at each of his subordinates in turn and again lifted a finger. "The Spanish fear an incident more than they fear the fever."

"Doesn't sound to me like Jordan has much to worry about," Christopher observed.

"Nooooo...not yet. However: A few weeks ago I wired our illustrious Estrada Palma in New York and made a little request of my own. Dr. Palma had a very interesting meeting with our proclaimed friend, Mr. Hearst, and some other influential people. Even Atkins was there, representing you *Yanqui* planters." Gomez grinned at his *Yanqui* captain.

Christopher turned his head and spat. "What was that would-be aristocrat doing in New York?"

"Your Mr. Atkins seems to have the ear of the Wall Street people. The interesting thing is, at least according to Palma's last wire, Atkins has decided to support *Cuba Libre!*"

"General Gomez, at the very best, Atkins doesn't give a damn about anything but his sugar cane and coffee beans."

Gomez nodded curtly. "Of course. The powerful usually commit only to those causes that will preserve and extend their power." He shrugged. "So?"

Guillermo Morales sat quietly, staring at the worn sole of one of his boots. Politics bored him. Killing Spaniards was important. So was a pair of new boots. A nap also would be nice. "General," he reminded patiently. "you were talking about Estrada Palma and the *Yanqui* ship."

"Yes, yes. Thank you, Guillermo. Palma also requested that America send a battleship."

"Why did Dr. Palma do that?" Theresa asked.

Gomez reached over to chuck her under the chin. "Because I asked him to."

"General? Why?"

"One moment, Captain Jackson. Clarity will come. Now: In addition to the ship and Atkins' promise, we will be receiving increased aid from the Wall Streeters. Rifles, munitions, field pieces, medicines, food. Much more aid."

Everyone nodded, pleased.

But within seconds Christopher cleared his throat. "Why the ship, sir?"

"One moment, Christopher. Let us first speak of truth."

"The truth, General?" Morales shook his head.

"Yes, my son. Truth. The truth of our cause and our lives. Let us deal with the hard truths of where we are, what it has cost—and what we might hope to do about it. For an officer, Guillermo, especially for one about to become a colonel, such questions are not academic foolishness. No?"

At the hint of promotion, Morales came to full alert.

"Here is the truth, my friends. After three years of the most vicious war we have ever waged against Spain, we are at stalemate. Truth: They can no longer control the countryside. Truth: Even with all the American aid in the world, we cannot drive them from the cities. Truth: I have always opposed the idea of American intervention. If they enter this war, we may never get rid of them. I have always found even the idea of their presence in our land most frightening.

"However, and this is the most important truth: Unless we can draw the *Yanquis* into the war, we cannot win." His right arm crossed his chest, fingers extended stiffly like a knife or wedge. "Ne-ver!" he added, drawing the word out like a prayer as his hand swept back across his chest at the level of their necks. "Never!"

The Leader squinted hard at Christopher. "Unless we can draw America into our revolution, we will never win. Agreed?"

"Yes, sir!" his followers agreed in unison. The truth was the truth. They had fought the Spanish to stalemate.

"And we all agree on the next truth, too. Don't we?" He waited for a response.

Theresa shook her head. There were tears in her eyes. "We may never win, General. But we will never stop trying."

"Thank you, my daughter. Yes, that is another hard truth. We will never, ever stop trying. What does that mean?" Without waiting for an answer he continued: "Unless we can find a way to win, this war will go on and on and on. And our families…" he stopped and pointed at each of them. "Our families, like mine, like yours, will continue to die, thousands upon thousands of innocents, just as they always have." Christopher exhaled sharply, half gasp, half sob, and rose from his seat to leave.

"Jackson! Sit down!" Gomez commanded. Morales did not even try to conceal a smirk, and Theresa jerked back as if she'd been slapped. She shook her head and muttered, "Sit down, Christopher."

Christopher sat back down and regained control. "I am sorry, General Gomez, but I have not yet mourned sufficiently. Everything you say is true. We already know that. Why...?"

"Mourned sufficiently? Who among us has had the leisure to mourn sufficiently? When we have driven Spain from the island, then—and only then—will we know that luxury."

Theresa spoke up, tremulous but determined. She had never before questioned her leader, at least not to his face. "Sir? Christopher is right. Why...?"

Gomez scrutinized his officers. His sad eyes rested the longest on Christopher's face, and noticed the yellow-tinged eyes and the deep care lines that had etched into the *Yanqui*'s face since their last visit. No! he said to himself and shook his head. Although the Leader empathized with Christopher's recent losses, he reminded himself that such feelings were counter-productive to the task at hand.

"Yes," he continued, almost apologetically. "We all know the truth, my friends. But some truths are easy to forget. We all know this, don't we? As long as our revolution lasts, innocents will continue to die." He made a circle with his hand, as if to include the four of them. "Innocents and not so innocent alike. The war will last until Spain leaves. *Cuba Libre!* lacks sufficient strength to drive Spain out. So everyone will continue to suffer, just as they, just as we, have always suffered.

"Now, my esteemed *companeros*, we will return to the original question." And again he chose Christopher to gaze upon. "I know that you do not want to see more of our brothers and sisters lose what you and Theresa and Guillermo—and I—have all already lost. I know that about you, my friends. But I will promise you this: We will never defeat Spain by ourselves."

Christopher exhaled a long breath and nodded. "I know that, General."

"But you still want to know why I asked our illustrious Dr. Palma to get us a ship?"

"Yes, General. I would."

The Supreme Commander of *Cuba Libre!* stared into Christopher's grey eyes, as if assessing him. "We are going to create an incident," he stated flatly, and stopped talking. Like a white bearded vulture assessing its prey, he moved his head back and forth from officer to officer, and waited. "We will attack that ship."

Christopher was stunned. When Morales caught the drift of Gomez's announcement, he whistled softly. A huge grin spread across his black-bearded face. "And blame it on the Spanish, No?"

"Excellent, Guillermo," Gomez said , slapping Morales on the back. "Sometimes your mind shows an amazing grasp of the possible."

Theresa blinked and nodded. "What an idea! When?"

"As soon as possible." Although Gomez was pleased with Guillermo's obvious response, he was far more interested in Christopher's. He scrutinized the captain's fever-thin face, trying to read his mind. Morales, not usually aware of subtleties, quickly became uncomfortable with the silence and shifted uneasily. Finally the General asked, "Well, Christopher?"

"Well what, sir?" He felt dizzy. The General's statement had unleashed a torrent of conflicting ideas and emotions. McKinley, the recently elected American President, had run on a platform of non-involvement. Any incident sufficiently effective to draw America into the war would have to result from serious damage to American property.

"General, you say they are getting ready to give us increased aid. Won't that suffice?"

The General held his finger up again and nodded, as if in agreement. "You are, of course, absolutely correct, Christopher. They want to help us. Regardless of their outrageously mixed motives, they are on our side. At least for the moment. And certainly our strategy vis a vis our great northern giant must always be one of cooperation and friendship. Otherwise they will eat us."

"Sir? America will, or at least should, become Cuba's closest ally."

The General clenched his jaw and deep vertical lines appeared above his nose. Theresa felt every muscle in her body tighten and Guillermo again smirked, pleased that the *Yanqui* seemed to be acting the fool in front of their General and Theresa. But Gomez leaned forward again, stretched out his arm and placed his hand on Christopher's shoulder. "We are at war, Captain. This is a strategic move. I am the general. You are the captain. I will determine strategy. You will stick to tactics. Is that understood? It is my job to worry about our long term relationship with your northern brothers."

Christopher nodded. "Yes, General Gomez."

Gomez smiled, patted Christopher's shoulder twice and removed his arm. "Be clear about one thing. Each of you! I have no wish to spill *Yanqui* blood, and that will probably not—at least may not—be necessary.

Gomez shifted his position so that his entire body and all his considerable magnetism focused on Christopher. "As you always remind anyone who calls you *Yanqui* to your face, you are Cuban. You have proven yourself too often, have made too many sacrifices for things to be otherwise. Please know and never forget: I respect your commitment just as I respect your sacrifices. Also, my friend, I do appreciate your confusion. So, listen!"

The General waved his right hand wildly, chopping each word for emphasis. "If-we-can-damage-that-battleship, America-will-enter-the-war. Of-that-I-am-absolutely-certain!" For added emphasis, he slapped the rock upon which they were sitting.

"But surely there must be another way, General. If we are found out, we lose everything. There has…"

"Is there? Think, Captain Jackson. When Spain becomes too bold, as with the *reconcentrados*, American public opinion starts yelling 'foul' and clamoring for war. When war fever rises in America, Spain backs down. She makes short-term concessions and promises she has no intention of fulfilling, and then the American press becomes interested in something else, like the Dreyfus trial or the Klondike. Spain understands very well that American public opinion is a confused circle, like a dog chasing its own tail."

"And every turn costs thousands of Cuban lives," Morales added savagely.

"Yes," the General continued. "That is part of the point, but only part. It is not just a matter of trying to balance a couple of hundred possible American casualties against tens upon tens upon tens of thousands of Cubans. Remember, however, what your President Lincoln said during your Civil War. In a letter to someone or other, Lincoln said that if he could save the Union by retaining slavery, he would do it. On the other hand, if he had to abolish slavery to maintain the Union, he would do that. And if maintaining the Union required him to free some men and keep others in bondage, he would do that too. The point he was trying to make, I believe, was that he was out to save his country—regardless of the costs."

"President Lincoln is no hero of mine, sir."

"Of course not. You were raised in a part of the country where his name is still a curse. Yes, but my point is: If I were convinced that I could win independence for Cuba by blowing up my entire army, all of us included, I would immediately give the order." He stopped to take a breath, then asked each officer in turn. "Wouldn't you?"

"Yes!" each of the three agreed.

"For our freedom from Spain—and a quick end to this fifty year long war—one American battleship is not such a high price. Do-you-understand?"

Christopher could not force himself to respond. As he watched the General's hand emphasize each of the last words, chop, chop, chop, he became aware of the sun, which was now hitting him in the eye.

"However serious the damage, the American press will immediately hold Spain responsible. Hearst and Pulitzer will light a bomb that will blow McKinley—and Congress—right off the fence." General Maximo Gomez, Supreme Commander of the ragged, poorly-armed revolutionary army, nodded sagely and smiled at his companions. "So, my friends, that is my reasoning, and that is what we must do. We must create an incident that will bring the northern colossus into our tragic stalemate."

Christopher finally nodded. In such a cauldron, what is one foreign warship? "I see your point, General. You are absolutely correct."

The General beamed and the tension dissipated. "Now, my esteemed friends, the question is, of course, why do I see fit to share all this with you? Why did I bring you from *La Habana*, my daughter? And why, my excellent Captain Jackson, did I drag you all the way back from the *Oriente*?"

When Christopher started to reply, Gomez held up his hand, palm out, to stop him. "It is the three of you who must find the way. Theresa, it is you who must supply our two friends here with information. It will be your last action as commander of our illustrious little bordello. After your success, you will close the house and leave *La Habana*. You will finally leave your life there behind. Understood?" Theresa nodded, impaled happily on this promise.

The General turned to Major Morales. "It is you, Guillermo, my valued aide and associate, who must supply the means, probably in the way of a bomb. Is our old friend the watchmaker still alive?"

Morales was tapping his foot with excitement. "I believe so, my esteemed General. The last I heard."

"Good! See to it! And Guillermo?"

"Yes, my General?"

"You will be in charge of the operation. You will listen, and you will try to act with more wisdom and discretion than you sometimes show. But you will be in charge. Understood?"

Morales squared his shoulders and sat at attention. "Yes, sir!"

Gomez turned again to focus on Christopher. "Now. Captain Jackson. You must find an appropriate situation, and you must develop the means to capitalize on the opportunity."

Christopher looked into the older man's eyes. Though Gomez was smiling, his eyes had narrowed to hard slits. Christopher blinked and nodded, "Yes, sir. I understand," he added, shoving his qualms and confusions to the back of his mind.

Morales smiled, pleased that his *Yanqui* antagonist would do this difficult thing for Cuba.

Maximo Gomez tried to conceal his relief. Since he had applied the stick successfully, he decided to proffer one small carrot. "Christopher, it is not my intention to take large numbers of American lives. If possible, we will not take any. The important thing is to seriously damage their great new ship. If we can do that without taking life, we will. However, it is up to you and Guillermo to find the way."

Christopher nodded. "I will find that way." He still felt caught. What if something goes wrong? Finally, with a great burst of will, he slammed shut the door to his imagination; the possibilities were too numerous. "I am at your service, my General," he said, rising to his feet. "But for now? If we are to leave in the next few days, sir, I really need to rest."

"Certainly, my son. We want you strong." Gomez jumped to his feet and Theresa and Guillermo followed. "But please, my friends. One more moment? I must make three points. First, the three of you are responsible for this action. Guillermo, Theresa, you must help

Christopher in any way possible. He will need things that only you can provide. Second, any help you get from anyone else must be explained as being for other activities. Only the four of us must know who is responsible. Ever! This is an action for which no one will ever be able to take credit. Third..."

"Just a moment, Sir." Christopher stood perfectly still, frozen by the General's last words. "Sir, I had hoped you would not order Theresa back to *La Habana*. She is the only member of her family left."

Theresa flashed her brother-in-law a sharp look of embarrassed rage. "I am not an innocent little girl, Christopher. I, too, am an officer in *Cuba Libre!* I ask for no special concessions. And if I ever think I might need one, I will make the request myself."

"Well said, Captain Valdez." Guillermo smirked, pleased to see her anger directed at Christopher.

"Stop this!" Gomez shook his head and gave a short, sad laugh, as if bemused by the *Yanqui*'s naivete. "Captain Jackson, you are the last member of your family alive. The same is true for me, and for thousands of our brothers and sisters. That is the whole point of—finally— having one desperate opportunity to end this war." Christopher nodded. "Remember what I just said about blowing up my own troops— if it would help free Cuba?" When Christopher again nodded, Gomez added, "Theresa will be able to get you information. She may be useful in other ways, so she will return with you. She, too, is sworn to our desperate but noble cause."

Christopher turned to Theresa and bit out words that obviously came hard. "Forgive me, Theresa. I was out of line."

Gomez continued as if the interruption had not taken place. "Third, if you...when you succeed in damaging the ship, leave *La Habana* immediately and return here for new orders. None of you will be returning to *La Habana* until we win our independence. We will take no chances that anyone might find the opportunity to interrogate you. Understand?

"Now, Christopher. How much time will you need?

Christopher thought for a moment. "If such a thing is possible, I should be able to do it in two weeks, three at the outside."

Gomez nodded. "What I want to do is coordinate your action with all action in western Cuba. Within the next few days, our armed activities will taper off. We will even withdraw our forces from some positions."

"Blood of Christ! General. We have given blood for every meter of ground we control, for every blockhouse...that..."

"Stop, Guillermo. Now!" Gomez waited for Morales to simmer down before continuing. "Sometimes, my friend, you forget who is in charge. And some day, I fear, your choler will get you in trouble. Did you not hear what I just repeated about my willingness to blow up my entire army? Did you not hear that?"

Christopher glanced back and forth at his two superior officers and thought, you're damned right, Maximo. Problem is, he's going to get anyone connected with him in trouble.

"I am sorry, General, sir." Morales mumbled.

"We know from experience that Spain is subservient to America when she thinks she is losing and far more independent, even careless, when she thinks she is winning the war. If Spain is confident, she may make a mistake, as she did with the *reconcentrados.* I would like very much for her to make at least one big mistake, preferably a diplomatic one, before Christopher completes his little task.

He put his arm around Guillermo's shoulder and steered him toward the middle of Federico's clearing. "Yes, my good friend and esteemed colleague, for us to surrender ground entails risk. But blowing up the *Yanqui* battleship is also a risk. So was starting this blood-thirsty little war in the first place." He stopped and drew a breath. "We have been gambling—and losing—thousands of lives, hundreds of thousands of lives, and we have been losing these lives for over half a century now. We are about to gamble a great deal on one throw of the dice."

He removed his hand from Guillermo's shoulder, took one long step ahead of his three followers and turned to face them. He smiled warmly. "And one more little thing: As of this moment, Guillermo, you are now Colonel Morales. Please accept my heartiest congratulations. And you, Christopher, are now Major Jackson."

Morales smiled broadly. To be a colonel! A colonel has first pickings when they burn Loyalist plantations or strip the dead. He thought immediately of his worn boots. "Thank you, sir. I will try to serve as I have always served."

"You are a good soldier, Guillermo, but continue to be aware of your weaknesses. Control you moods, and try, just a little harder please, to control your vanity." Gomez slapped him heartily on the back, as if to soften the cautionary. "Congratulations."

During the exchange Christopher had been thinking along similar lines. Morales always had a hard time being inconspicuous. If their mission were to succeed, and Christopher realized that he would indeed do everything possible to make sure it would, then they would have to play their roles well—and quietly.

Just before falling asleep that evening, Christopher thought: Some honor! Every peasant in the army who led more than a couple of hundred men was a colonel. At least! he added, thinking of the brave but vain Morales. But his smile disappeared when his mind returned to the task at hand.

Chapter Eight

CONGRESS AND CUBA

Spanish Prime Minister is Seeking for a Way Out

* * * *

The Senate is growing impatient in the Cuban matter, and so are the people. Mr. Cannon, of Utah, yesterday introduced a resolution calling upon the President to insist that Spain "shall recognize the independence of the Cuban Republic" by March 4, on pain of having the United States "assert" that independence within ninety days thereafter. This is "hot talk," but it represents the popular feeling.

The brutal butchery called war in Cuba has lasted too long. It is time to stop it with the strong hand. The Spanish pretense of ability to govern the island is a demonstrated absurdity. Injustice, rapine, the murder of helpless women and children, have gone quite as far as an enlightened nation which has assumed the guardianship of human liberty in this hemisphere ought to permit. If the Administration continues its policy of dalliance, Congress may some fine day rise up in its might as the war-making power and proclaim Cuban independence. Patience has worn itself out. Joseph Pulitzer, Editorial: *The World*, January 14.

Havana

Amos Jordan's unwillingness to sign his letter of resignation from the Consular Corps arose at least in part from his love for Cuban evenings. And of late his evening walks along the harbor front had provided the most peaceful moments of his day. Now, as he walked along the broad, palm-lined sidewalk that meandered along the bay, he breathed deeply, savoring the salt breeze. Midway along the seawall he stopped to gaze around the broad sweep of the natural harbor. To his right the rich patterns of the Plaza de Santa Isabella glowed in the late light. The plaza was filled with royal palms and surrounded by the ornate colonial buildings that symbolized Spain's four hundred year presence in the New World. Piled up behind the plaza stood the colored stucco and tiled houses of Havana's small middle class. Behind the houses the rolling hills of *La Habana* stretched away to the south and east. Such a beautiful place, Jordan thought. So beautiful and so deadly.

He turned his head to the left and gazed down and out across the long, narrow bay, where hundreds of brightly painted fishing boats bobbed at their moorings. Across the brown waters of the harbor stood El Morro, the combination fortress and dungeon that brooded over the narrow entrance to the harbor. Sometimes Jordan fancied that he could hear the echoes of screams from the chambers where Major Alvarez and his numerous predecessors extracted information from Spain's enemies, both real and imagined. Even though he knew that such sounds were figments of his imagination, Jordon also knew that, at least in Cuba, torture was still common, even on the eve of the twentieth century.

Only after forcing his attention to dwell for several minutes on the "grim battlements," as he called El Morro, did Jordan allow his vision to wander up channel to Buoy Nine and the huge white battleship that now dominated Havana harbor. Though the harbor also contained three antiquated cruisers of Admiral Cervera's Atlantic Squadron, they were dwarfed and dimmed by the almost new and ultra-modern *USS Maine*. Jordan gazed ambivalently at the great white ship, shook his head and continued on toward the Alhambra, the private club favored by many of the city's foreign residents. Despite his political concerns, Jordan looked forward to a sociable evening with Lt. Commander Smith and a few of the *Maine*'s junior officers.

Christopher Jackson lounged in a high-back chair that commanded an unobstructed view of the main reception room of the Alhambra, through which, according to Theresa, Amos Jordan would soon be walking. Since returning to the capitol a week earlier, he had been scheming to get aboard the *Maine*. Now, with Theresa's help, he thought he had found the key. Although dressed in white linens, like most of the civilians frequenting the Alhambra, and though, like many others, he was reading a newspaper, Christopher felt conspicuous. Slowly, almost too casually, he flipped the pages of the New York World.

Yee-ow! he thought, as he read Joseph Pulitzer's reactions to the presence in Havana of the *Maine*. He smiled, amused. The Americans obviously saw the presence of their great white ship as an act of provocation. He became so engrossed with the editorial and its implications that he almost missed the sight of Amos Jordan limping across the red-tiled reception room and up the broad steps that led to the terraces. So, Christopher thought. She's right.

Jordan paused at the second terrace, disappointed to see that Armand Q. Atkins was with the American officers. Atkins was a pro-Spanish planter who had just returned from a trip to New York to discover that the rebels had again burned his sugar plantation. Jordan had expected to have the group from the *Maine* to himself. He started to turn back, but saw that Lt. Commander Smith had already spotted him.

"Ah, there you are, sir." Smith called. The three younger officers stood to attention, while Atkins rose slowly to his feet and tried to mask his contempt for the diplomat. Smith was tall, lean and tan, with a shock of white hair that matched his dress whites. He smiled brightly, pleased to host an important member of the American Consulate.

"Good evening, gentlemen." Jordan nodded at Atkins and shook hands with Smith, who introduced him to the younger officers. Here are three bullets that look to be from different molds, Jordan thought as he shook hands with the three ensigns. Richard Perkins, whose straight black hair and high cheekbones accentuated his one quarter Cherokee heritage, was a recent Annapolis graduate whose farmer father had commanded a frigate during the Civil War. George Bedford, his blonde hair already thinning, was the scion of a Long Island banker and graduate of Harvard College, "class of '94, sir. Classics." The third ensign, Ephraim Pratt, was a freckle-faced redhead who was pushing thirty and had worked his way up from the ranks.

As Jordan began to discern the difference between these identically dressed and close-cropped "bullets," he found Pratt to be somewhat of a character, partly because he seemed the least affected, but mostly because he claimed to have run away from a polygamous Mormon family to go to sea. "Why?" Jordan asked as their drinks arrived.

"Well, sir, it was either run away or continue to get beaten by my pa."

"Those were the only two alternatives?"

"Well, sir, I reckon I could have maybe killed him and stayed. But at the time it didn't hardly seem worth it." Pratt shrugged. "I probably should have but, hell, I like the Navy. Besides," he added as an afterthought, "there was this girl."

Jordan watched Pratt drain his wine glass. "You're a Mormon and you drink?"

"Yes, sir. Sure do." Pratt beamed. "I'm a fallen man. Once I left Zion there was no stoppin' me. Devil's grabbed me by the short hairs and I'm just sailing along for the ride."

As far as Jordan could tell, Pratt was oblivious to the raised eyebrows and slightly stiffening spines of his fellow officers. But when Atkins snickered, Pratt reddened and wondered if getting cashiered was too stiff a price to pay for flattening the planter's nose.

"Good evening, gentlemen."

Pratt turned his murderous glare to the door. A tall, gaunt civilian smiled at Amos Jordan and approached the table. As Pratt rose again to be introduced, he heard Atkins mutter, "Good Christ! It's Jackson. I thought he was dead."

"Mr. Jackson. It is good to see you," Jordan smiled and limped around the table to shake hands with Christopher. "Here, come and join us." Although he had met Christopher only twice before, Jordan had taken an instant liking to the tall planter, who struck him as much more direct and infinitely less class-conscious than Atkins and most of the other American-Cuban planters, virtually all of whom had fled the South in the first two decades after the Civil War.

"Thank you, Jordan. Don't mind if I do."

The three younger officers were quickly, albeit unintentionally, eliminated from the conversation. And of the three, only Pratt sensed the underlying tensions masked by the polite, concentric conversation. As he greeted Christopher, Armand Atkins donned a solicitous mask. "We were all deeply sorrowed to hear of the loss of your family, Jackson. Please accept my condolences."

Christopher bowed slightly. Thank you for your concern, Atkins."

Jordan reached across the table and touched Christopher's sleeve. "My God, man. I'm sorry to hear..."

Christopher shook his head. "Please."

Atkins continued, ignoring his fellow planter's obvious desire to drop the topic. "You know, just before leaving for New York I heard— through the grapevine—that you'd been shot by the rebels while attempting to defend your cane fields. What happened?"

"Well, as you can see, your vine bore some bad grapes." Though he continued to smile at Atkins, Christopher realized almost as soon as the words were out that his sarcasm had only increased the distance between them.

Atkins smiled back, "By all rights you should be dead. Anyone stupid enough to run around a rebel-infested countryside is courting disaster and deserves whatever he gets, even if you're...he...is just trying to run a plantation."

"I'm flattered by your concern for the state of my intelligence, Atkins, but all my disasters have already occurred. I have little left to lose. Nor, my friend, do I own the means to sit on my duff in Havana waiting for our Spanish "protectors" to re-conquer the countryside."

"You keep going back to that burned out estate of yours and the rebels will cut your duff up into little pieces." Atkins smiled at the image.

"I've had my problems with the damned rebels, " Christopher replied, grimacing at the word. Shut up! he told himself. Be more amenable—or blow this mission. But he could not hold back the charged bitterness of the next sentence. "But, as you may know, I owe the loss of my family—not to the rebels but to our noble Spanish protectors."

Atkins reddened. "I am sorry," he mumbled. "Still, we must remember that the Spanish did not start the war."

Christopher merely raised his eyebrows. The table remained silent until Ensign Perkins, Annapolis, '97, saw the embarrassed pause as his chance to shine. He sat up at attention, glared intently at Christopher and asked, "Have you had trouble with the spics, sir?"

Christopher glanced at Jordan, lifted his shoulders as if to suggest, what do I do? The truth is the truth? and said, "You might say so, Ensign. While 'protecting' my wife and daughters from Maximo Gomez and his cutthroats, the Spanish allowed them to die. Nothing personal, you understand. A couple of hundred thousand people have died in the hundreds of civilian concentration camps."

Perkins' jaw dropped. Other than Ensign Pratt, who mumbled, "Jesus Christ," no one said anything for a very long minute.

Finally Christopher spoke. "Gentlemen, I am sorry. My family is dead, and there is absolutely nothing that any of us can do about it—except perhaps to end this war as quickly as possible." He looked straight at Atkins. "And that is something that even you should agree to, Atkins. It should be clear to all but the most pig-headed loyalists that Spain can no longer win."

Atkins thought of his recent meeting with the New York and Washington power brokers, nodded slightly, and said, "I have, recently, come to the same conclusion." Christopher raised his eyebrows, nodded his acknowledgement of Atkins' surprising statement, which was accompanied by empathetic nods from the three officers. "I would like very much to stand you all to a drink. And I would like to hear the news," Christopher added.

Atkins was not about to ruin the balance of the evening in the company of both Jordan and Jackson. He rose to leave. "I am sorry, gentlemen. Delightful as the company is, I must be on my way. Previous engagement, you know. Sorry." Though the others rose for their farewells to Atkins, Christopher remained seated, drew a deep breath and relaxed. After the second of several drinks, he played his role with greater ease. "Well, gentlemen," he began, as soon as his companions were re-seated. He rose his glass. "Here's to the officers of the *Maine*."

The men raised their glasses and smiled. Suddenly Ensign George Bedford put a few pieces together. "Sir? You're Alex's brother?"

"Yes. I am," he said, unsettled to meet the man Alex had mentioned in his last letter. "You were with my brother at Harvard, were you not?"

"Yes, sir. He was in my dining club. I was President, you know."

"Oh?" Christopher barely concealed a grin. "If you're a friend of Alex's, you've got a lot to recommend you," he said, although given Alex's romanticism and naiveté, Christopher suspected that he was flattering the young ensign. "How is Alex? As good as he sounds in his letters?"

"Sir, he seems less than ecstatic with his job at the War Department. He really wants more action, you know. Promotions there seem to be as slow as they are in the Navy."

Christopher nodded and changed the subject. "Well, gentlemen. Have the Spanish been behaving themselves for you?"

Now that he had established a connection with the planter, Bedford presumed to dominate the conversation. "Fine. Yes, sir. They have been absolutely gracious, and we are having a glorious good time. Couldn't be better."

Amos Jordan winked at Christopher and thought of his own naiveté as a young lieutenant riding out from Washington to the first battle of Bull Run.

"I'm pleased that you're enjoying yourselves." Christopher smiled, while his brooding mind stood at some distance from the amenities floating around the table and pondered the ease with which appearances deceive. He wanted very much to ask Bedford if he'd ever given much thought to the magical powers of duplicity, but Lt. Commander Smith launched a concise sermon that saved him the trouble.

"Ensign Bedford. The Spanish hate us, and they resent very much our presence in their harbor." Smith knew that his high cheekbones, deep tan and pure white hair added to his regal mien. He inhaled deeply and sat very straight. "Our diplomats humiliate them. Our newspapers bully them. From their point of view the presence of the *Maine* is a crude affront to a sovereign nation." He stopped for a second and studied the two civilians to gauge their reaction to his wisdom. Both were nodding their affirmation. "I am surprised, really surprised, that they haven't tried to blow us out of the water." He focused his black eyes on each of his three ensigns in turn. "Accept their hospitality, Ensign Bedford. Smile from ear to ear. But keep your brain cocked."

"Bravo, Commander." Jordan agreed. Bedford turned pink.

Christopher studied the four officers. Maximo Gomez is right, he thought, then said, "Unless Spain defeats the rebels in the next few months, which strikes me as highly unlikely, your American correspondents will declare war all by themselves."

Jordan chuckled. "I had not heard that you'd taken up prophesy during your recent stay in the jungle."

"But he is probably right, you know," Smith added. "That is why we're here."

"Spain's hour has come," Bedford interjected a little too pompously, attempting to win back some of the ground he'd lost in the previous exchange. "*Cuba Libre!* has become a chant throughout America. Our diplomatic corps is exerting tremendous pressure all over Europe. Spain will accede to our demands—without a war."

"God, I hope not," Pratt mumbled.

"Oh?" Christopher asked, responding to both ensigns at once. "My apologies to you in advance, Mr. Jordan. No slight intended. Ensign Bedford, Spain's diplomatic corps has always been more oily, more evasive, more deceptive—hence more effective—than yours."

Jordan's chuckle broke a short silence. "Do not be offended, Gentlemen. Mr. Jackson has hit the nail quite precisely. For example," he continued after a slight pause, "think for a moment about our Major Alvarez, the gracious little man who dined with us aboard your splendid battleship two nights past. Do you know what he does?"

"Yes, sir," Perkins responded, as if answering a classroom question at Annapolis. "He is in the Intelligence Service, which means that he's probably using his charm to check us out."

"Close, Ensign, quite close," Jordan smiled, giving Perkins the pat he seemed so badly to desire. "He is Spain's Inquisitor. I've heard him called 'The Beast.' He has people arrested and thrown into El Morro, that hulking fortress at the entrance to the harbor, or La Punta, that other harbor guardian you can't quite see from here. Most of the people he has thrown into the dungeons are probably innocent of any wrong-doing. Very few re-emerge. The man is hated by all but the most fanatic of the Spanish loyalists and European planters."

Christopher wanted to hug the Vice-Consul.

"If we may get back to the war, Gentlemen," Bedford began, desperate to show his mettle. "We will have to intervene. We need to kick the spics out and annex the island. My father says..."

"Why annexation, young man?" Jordan interrupted.

Lt. Commander Smith came to his ensign's aid. "With all due respect, Mr. Jordan. The answer is obvious—or should be. The Cubans are incapable of governing themselves. Two-thirds of the population is illiterate; half are ex-slaves."

Though Christopher wanted to speak out, he had already said more than enough. "Ah, yes! The White Man's Burden." Jordan shook his head. "We Anglo-Saxons will determine what God wants from the darker, less progressive races of the world. We will determine their best interests—and fulfill them in terms of our own.

"Gentlemen!" The Vice-Consul placed his liver-spotted hands palms down on the white tablecloth and looked around. "Thus far we have resisted the urge to join the great powers in their mad and greedy scramble for colonies. If we intervene in Cuba—and, from what I hear, in the Philippines—and annex either or both, we will establish a precedent whose consequences will haunt us for the next century—at least. Perhaps we should, perhaps we will have to help the Cubans gain their independence. But we should not stay to rule them." Having had his say, Jordan rose to leave. He'd spend the rest of a hopefully less political evening with Theresa, who had recently returned from another family visit. "Gentlemen, I have enjoyed your company. You are good officers and, I am sure, good men. I know that you are looking forward to war and that when—and if—it comes, you will be a credit to yourselves, your service and your country. I will see you at dinner aboard ship.

"Mr. Jackson. I like your views. I hope to see more of you." And with that twisted climax to a series of sentiments not one of the officers completely understood, the veteran of the Battle of the Peach Orchard limped from the terrace.

Almost as soon as the group had sat back down, and assuming incorrectly that the planter was as baffled as he, Lt. Commander Smith turned to Christopher. "I'm afraid that I must apologize for him, Mr. Jackson. He's usually very charming and entertaining."

"He certainly seems worried about the presence here of your splendid ship," Christopher observed. Then he held up a long index finger and tapped his temple as if he had just remembered something of import. "You know, gentlemen, there are rumors, some from fairly reliable sources, that the Spanish may try something.

"So we've heard, Mr. Jackson. So we've heard." Ensign Pratt smiled from ear to ear. "Sir, the *Maine* would like nothing better than to blow the whole Spanish army right off this island."

Although Christopher discounted the hyperbole, he decided that he liked the freckle-faced Westerner. "I hope you're right, Ensign. The *Maine* does indeed look powerful."

Lt.Commander Smith rose to his feet. "Mr. Jackson, we must get back to the ship. Would you like to see her?

"Very much," Christopher said, struggling to conceal the depth of his excitement.

"We would be pleased to have you dine with us. The *Maine* is a real beauty." He glanced at Pratt then back to Christopher. "And she could certainly destroy anything on this island—within range of her guns."

Christopher stood to shake hands with each of the officers. "I would consider it an honor to visit."

"Fine, we're having a group, including our outspoken vice-consul, on Thursday. We'll send a launch. About 1800 hours."

"Thursday sounds good. And…thank you. I have certainly enjoyed our visit."Long after the officers had left, Christopher sat on the terrace and sipped rum, his long, linen-draped legs propped up on the chair earlier occupied by George Bedford. He stared across the harbor where the great white battleship stretched out against the night sky like a brooding ghost. He watched the lights of the ship come on and the lights of dockside Havana gradually dim. An hour later, just before curfew, he rose from his reverie, ambled down the wide sandstone steps of the Alhambra and headed toward the Old City and another night of bad dreams.

Chapter Nine

BLANCO RETURNS TO HAVANA FOILED
He Is Worse Off than Campos Was After His Defeat by Gen. Maceo.

* * * *

NOT A CUBAN CHIEF BRIBED
Famine Continues, Autonomy Fails, Madrid Growls, Havana Protests.

Havana, by way of Key West, February 10—With starvation continuing, autonomy failing, Madrid complaining, Havana protesting and his very subordinates prophesying failure, Gen. Blanco returns to the Governor-General's Palace worse off than Gen. Campos was after the Battle of Coliseo. The entering wedge of American-Foodstuffs—for-Cubans and American ships in Cuban waters—intensifies the helplessness of the situation for Spain. "Autonomy without an American protectorate is worthless," said a member of the Autonomista Cabinet. "American intervention is our only hope." This is a momentous admission. But autonomy really has become a laughingstock with the public.

Starvation goes on the same as ever in all the cities of Cuba except Havana, where it seems to be lessening, at least partly because of the arrival of American food. This week some American supplies were sent to some of the outlying towns, but they are only a drop in the bucket to what is needed. *The World*, February 11.

Havana

As Ensign Bedford led him into the spacious Officers' Mess, Christopher raised his eyebrows with pleasure. "Nice club, Ensign."

"The Navy is both the oldest and the most modern of the services, sir." Bedford felt secure, at home, appreciated. "Our traditions require the best. Fortunately our country believes that we are worth providing for."

"Yes, apparently so." Christopher absorbed the richness of the room as he would absorb a sunset.

"Enjoy yourself, Mr. Jackson. We will be sitting down to dinner in twenty minutes." Bedford excused himself and left.

Christopher accepted a glass of champagne from a tray extended to him by a dignified, blank-faced Negro steward, and gazed around a very exclusive club. Large oriental carpets accented the pecan parquet floor. Oil portraits of naval heroes, each lighted by a small brass lamp, decorated the inlaid walnut walls. Soft light from the chandeliers bathed the Officers' Mess in an orange glow. On the far side of the room Negro stewards in dress whites fussed at large round tables, each sparkling with highly polished crystal and silver. Other stewards glided through the room, appearing silently, almost invisibly, among the officers and their guests at precisely the right time to light a cigar, freshen a drink or polish away an imaginary stain. Still other stewards lined the walls, eyes constantly alert. The officers, both Spanish and American, were in full dress uniform, as were the diplomats, most of whom wore white tails and be-medaled sashes.

Christopher caught his breath, startled to see Major Ignacio Alverez, The Inquisitor, in obviously good humored conversation with Captain Sigsbee, the *Maine*'s commanding officer. How does that greasy little turd get around like this? Christopher wondered. Of course. He's valuable as an intelligence officer precisely because he does get around. Out of the corner of his eye, he observed the fat Spaniard turn his head slightly and take Christopher in. He felt a surge of fear as he realized how vulnerable he was, how naked he felt in the Spaniard's presence. For a long moment his stomach constricted. He knew that he could not, at least for the moment, control his voice, so he continued to stand just within the entrance of the large room. With great effort, he sipped his champagne and admired a setting in which Alvarez moved with apparent ease.

After making a mental note to avoid the intelligence officer as much as possible, and another to remain quiet and soft-spoken regardless, Christopher studied the chemistry of the guests, many of whom were European diplomats and Spanish officers. Something is going on here! What is it? The something, the 'it', was just at the edge of his mind. Something about the mixture, something about the way the Spanish and American officers, all smiles, related to each other.

A hand on his arm snapped his concentration, and he turned to face Amos Jordan, the only diplomat in the room to have arrived in an every-day frock coat. "You seem, ah...pre-occupied, Mr. Jackson. Are you already bored by this brilliant assemblage of roosters?"

Christopher smiled, relieved. "No, more like puzzled. Something is going on between these 'roosters' that I can't quite grasp."

"You can smell it, but you can't quite identify the smell?"

Christopher raised his eyebrows. "Yes, something like that."

"What you smell, Jackson, is a conflicting blend of fear and arrogance." Christopher bowed. "You are very perceptive—for an American diplomat."

Jordan laughed. "Given your comment the other night at the Alhambra, I'll accept that as a compliment."

"It was genuine, but..." Christopher's eyes left Jordan's face for a moment and flitted around the room. "There is something else."

"Ah, yes. Let's see, the specific spice. You are, I am sure, quite used to Spanish arrogance but not..."

Christopher blinked. Yes! Of course! "The Americans are in control of the situation—and know it. The Spanish know it, too."

"Yes, Jackson. Our countrymen are feeling very superior to the Spanish. I am afraid that we want very much to go to war with them."

"Your countrymen, sir. I left Georgia not long after it ceased to be an occupied state not quite destroyed by your General Sherman. Moreover, my family is..." He clenched his jaw, "was Cuban. Other than the brother who works in Washington, I have never had any positive connections to your country."

"I don't quite understand," Jordan replied. "Are you suggesting that you would approve of America going to war with Spain? Or that you would disapprove?"

I must be very, very careful about how I act with this man, Christopher told himself before continuing. "Oh, I'd be happy enough to see America help us get rid of the Spanish."

"I thought as much."

"It's not your country's help I worry about," Christopher continued. "It's her attitude, her sense of destiny. After kicking Spain out, you may decide to stay and...civilize us."

Amos Jordan cocked his head and gave his tall companion a twisted smile. "We will not stay in Cuba," he said slowly through tight lips. "America will not follow that particular primrose path to imperial perdition."

"Good evening, gentlemen." Caught up in his dance with Jordan, Christopher failed to notice Ensign Pratt's approach. "We're about to be seated for dinner. Commander Smith would be pleased to have the two of you join our table." With that, the runaway Mormon turned on his heel and marched to one of the large, linen-covered tables that filled the far side of the Mess. Amos and Christopher exchanged wry smiles and followed.In addition to Jordan, Smith, Bedford and Pratt, the table included The Inquisitor and another Spanish major. Christopher immediately tensed, acutely aware that his ability to carry off his charade depended upon maintaining absolute control over his still-recuperating body, including his tongue. He knew enough about Alvarez to know that the man was always smooth and, precisely because of his smoothness, unusually deceptive. Like the Spaniards at the other tables, however, the two Spanish majors concentrated on their one single care: oozing charm and good humor. It was almost, Christopher realized, as if every Spaniard in the room believed that Spain's only protection from the coming deluge was the personal charm of her public servants.

Amos Jordan was more intrigued by the other half of the brew, the arrogance that emanated, in some cases positively reeked, from the American officers, several of whom seemed unable to mask their contempt with even a veneer of subtlety. Jordan could almost see the wheels turning in the minds of the Americans who were, by and large, taller than their guests, broader-shouldered, lighter-complexioned, more confident and better educated. Few of the Spanish officers in the room spoke acceptable English. That virtually none of the Americans spoke more than a smattering of Spanish was irrelevant. At times during the ensuing conversation, Jordan didn't know whether to laugh or cry. From religion to language to morals to politics, the Americans exuded superiority. The Spanish were obviously eager to please their conquerors-to-be; the Americans condescended to be pleased.

Ignacio Alvarez, however, spoke excellent English. During the main course of beef burgundy, parslied potatoes and steamed asparagus, Major Alvarez managed with some subtlety to turn the conversation against *Cuba Libre!* Lt. Commander Smith took a bite of potato, swallowed and pointed his glistening fork at Major Alvarez. "I've noticed that a high percentage of the island is nigger. In fact, I don't understand how you people distinguish between whites and blacks. Seems to me like just about everyone has some color in them."

"Not everyone, Commander," Alvarez replied. "A better estimate would be about half black and another twenty-five per cent mulatto. But your observation certainly touches a basic Cuban truth. You are a man of some perception."

"My God, Major!" Bedford exclaimed. "The country won't be capable of running itself."

"Very true, Ensign. We have been trying to make the same point, but your countrymen, at least your rather excitable journalists, do not seem to be listening."

Jordan glanced at Christopher, who was thinking of his dead mulatto wife, and whose left hand gripped the chair seat so hard that his knuckles had turned white. What Jordan could not see was the grinding of the planter's will. Why doesn't Jackson say something? Jordan wondered. Certainly the man is capable of putting both Smith and Alvarez in their places. Is he just trying to be a good guest? Then, for no apparent reason, Jordan sensed with the certainty of revelation that Jackson was playing a role. Jordan shook his head, as if to force away an unsettling thought. "I'm not at all sure, Major, that 'color' is the major question here, at least as far as self-governance is concerned. Had Spain re-invested even a small percentage of her profits, say in education, the question would be less relevant."

"Ah, Señor Jordan," Alvarez beamed. "As you should know, and as American Southerners such as Commander Smith must know, education is wasted on ex-slaves. This is a country of ex-slaves." The Inquisitor turned his soft Spaniel eyes to Christopher and asked, "As an immigrant from the old Confederacy and as an estate owner, I am sure you can support my point."

Christopher could barely control his response. "I was married to a mulatto woman, Major. And I come from a southern family that couldn't afford slaves. Moreover, like many of the American-Cuban planters, I have become less than impressed by how Spain is handling this revolution—which has already cost me my entire family." Alvarez glared briefly at Christopher but quickly resumed his mask.

Ensign Pratt, who was sitting on the Inquisitor's left, chose the moment for a bit of malicious mischief. "Gentlemen, Mr. Jackson has struck a chord. I propose a toast to freedom: for all the countries of our hemisphere—including Cuba—and for each and every one of her citizens." He raised his glass and smiled innocently at his table mates. The non-English speaking major raised his glass and smiled back. Alvarez scowled, but raised his glass a few inches off the table. Smith and Christopher barely suppressed their glee at Pratt's bald insult, and George Bedford barely managed to conceal his jealousy. Amos Jordan was appalled by the prank, however; it epitomized the arrogance of the American officers, most of whom already salivated in anticipation of a war they knew they would easily win.

Alvarez mumbled the meaning of the toast to his colleague, who grimaced. Alvarez then drew the long, resigned breath of one who had accepted a heavy cross, and asked, "Ensign Pratt?" He folded his napkin, placed his short forearms on the table and locked his fingers together. "I may speak frankly, no?" Pratt looked around the table, grinned and nodded. "Our countries are not yet at war. My country is trying very hard not to go to war with yours. Still, what will be will be. I, too, am a professional soldier. I, too, follow my orders." Alvarez focused his soft eyes on Pratt's freckled face until the younger man blushed and dropped his gaze.

Although Christopher saw the essential justice in the major's point, he also knew that, like himself, the major was wearing a mask; he was a professional manipulator who, at the moment, was performing his job superbly. Christopher could not help but feel a little sorry for Pratt. For the next few minutes, the table ate in embarrassed silence or, in Pratt's case, not at all. Finally Lt. Commander Smith folded his napkin neatly and, restricting his offer to Christopher and Amos Jordan, asked, "Would you like a tour of the ship? Ensign Pratt would be pleased to escort you while our Spanish guests, Ensign Bedford and I take a turn around the deck."

"Thank you Commander, but I've had the grand tour," Jordan demured. "I think I'd prefer the turn around the deck."

"Mr. Jackson?"

"Yes, I think I would find it interesting," Christopher answered. "But first, excuse me for just a minute."

"Steward?"

A thin, highly polished black steward approached and bowed almost imperceptibly. "Yes, sir?"

"I left a package of cigars on the buffet over there. Would you fetch it, please?" When the steward returned, Christopher passed around the box of panatellas, then asked the steward to start the box around the surrounding tables. As he started to unwrap his own, Ensign Pratt touched his arm.

"I'm sorry, sir. There's no smoking below decks. Coal dust is highly combustible, you know."

"Forgive me, Ensign. I guess I didn't realize that," Christopher said, intrigued, and placed the uncut cigar in his breast pocket. The two men walked out of the Mess and onto the highly polished oak plank deck. "Perhaps I've lived in Cuba too long. What's the problem with coal dust?"

"Well, sir, the dust is suspended particles of coal, which means it'll burn. It can get trapped in flues and vents, like gas, which means it can explode. The *Maine*'s a new ship, and a clean one, but coal dust is still coal dust, and we burn a whole lot of coal—even at anchor. Let's turn in here." Pratt led him down a narrow passageway lined with oblong doors and up a ladder-well to the observation deck. They toured the chart rooms, the gun turrets and Fire Control, the conning tower, and even peeked into the Captain's quarters. Almost everywhere they went in the command areas, young Marine sentries snapped to attention. Nowhere did Christopher detect even a hint of laziness or poor morale. Every brass fixture, every porthole, every deck was polished to at least dull brilliance.

When they finished with the junior officers' quarters, Pratt led him below decks to the hydraulic pump room, where he stopped. "We won't have time to cover the entire below decks area, Mr. Jackson, so we'll proceed forward from here."

Christopher tried to hide his disappointment. "That's fine, Pratt. But tell me, what are we missing?"

"Well, just behind us, almost three stories high, is the engine room. Behind that we've got the steering engine room and the tiller room. Underneath those rooms, there are four storage holds, including three of our magazines."

"Magazines?"

"Yes, sir, areas where we store explosives. For example, there's a room back there for six inch shells, one for small arms ammunition and one for torpedo heads and gun cotton. You'll see what I mean as we move forward, where most of our explosives are stored."

"Sounds interesting," Christopher replied, thinking, Good God! This ship is little more than a munitions storehouse.

In the next ten minutes the two men moved forward through the two huge boiler rooms and the almost as huge hold where coal was stored. As they moved into the forward pump room, Pratt, who had been talking almost non-stop, said something that caused Christopher to listen more carefully. "I never have understood why they put so many different kinds of combustibles in such close proximity. Hell's bells! From here forward almost to the bow, we've got four of our largest magazines plus the torpedo room. And immediately to the rear of all this we've got that damned coal bin we just came over."

Christopher smiled. "Are you suggesting that the designers of the *Maine* didn't know what they were doing?"

Pratt chuckled. "Well, no sir, not exactly. That coal bin is damned well ventilated, but I'll tell you something. My pa had a one-horse coal mine down in southeastern Utah, and that booger used to blow up on him every year or so." As Pratt talked, he guided his guest through the

several small storerooms that sat immediately above the powder magazine and the six inch shell magazine. "Let's climb down here and take a
look. You can see what we've got stored up for Admiral Cervera's navy
and El Morro, comes the day. You're not a secret agent for the Spanish,
are you?" Pratt grinned at his own joke. Something in his boyish glee
reminded Christopher of his little brother.

He responded with the widest, most genuine smile he'd managed in
weeks. "No, Ensign. I'm a lot of things, but a Spanish agent is not one
of them."

As they descended to the starboard side magazines, Christopher
experienced an emotion very close to religious awe. The long room was
cut into aisles of steel and oak racks. Each grooved shelf was lined with
shells for the *Maine*'s 10" guns.

"This ship is fast—at least for a battleship—well-armed, well-
manned. We can take on any ship in Cervera's fleet—with ease."

"I believe it." As they walked through each of the four magazines,
Christopher's spirits drooped. Even if he could, through some minor
miracle, gain entry to the magazines, there seemed to be no place where
he could conceal even a small bomb. And what could one small bomb
accomplish?

Pratt's voice broke into his consciousness: "Mr. Jackson? Sir?"

Christopher glanced up. "I'm sorry. My father was in the Civil war.
Somehow, all these shells, all this stored destruction, well, it brings back
stories he told of Fighting Joe Wheeler."

"Is that right? My Uncle Jeb was at Gettysburg. On the other side,
of course." They ascended a ladder into another storage area. Pratt
mumbled, "This place scares me." The door to the storeroom read
'Paint Locker.' Christopher followed Pratt's pointed hand to see tall
shelves and cabinets full of paints, lacquers and shellacs. He stared at a
six foot tall shelf rack piled with large squares of cheesecloth.

"What's the problem here, Ensign?" he asked, as he took in the
screened duct that ran along the overhead. Coal dust again?"

"That combined with a small room crammed with combustibles."As
they continued on up to the next level, the berthing deck, where the
off-duty watch wallowed in their hammocks, Pratt resumed his story.
"Uncle Jeb used to tell great stories about the war, but my pa said old
Jeb could never lie right. Said he stretched the truth six ways to Sunday

and couldn't even keep his own lies straight from one Sabbath to the next."

"But they were good stories?" Christopher replied absently, his mind still on the paint locker.

"Damn right! Excuse me, sir. Sometimes I forget I'm an officer. Yeh, they were good. Maybe that's why I joined the Navy after I ran away from home. Adventure, glory, good pay. And now that I'm an officer. Hell, things couldn't be better."

Christopher nodded, thinking: He should feel proud of himself. But glory? Christopher recalled the degree to which his younger brother had always been mesmerized by their father's war stories. As Pratt preceded him into the open deck area that led back to the wardroom, Christopher thought of the three years of war he had known in rural Cuba: The sick-sweet smell of burning cane fields; the spindly-legged, bloated bellied children; the fly and land-crab-infested corpses; the seemingly endless butchery. Glory?

Just before re-entering the wardroom, he stopped, placed his hand on the younger man's shoulder and said, "My younger brother, Ensign Bedford's friend, is several years younger than you, but has the same outlook."

"Is he in the army?"

"No, he works as a civilian clerk in the War Department. He never quite managed to get into West Point, so he settled for Harvard."

"Settled for Harvard?" Pratt beamed with pure delight. "Wow! Don't ever put it like that to George Bedford. He'd lay an egg."

"In my letters to my brother—my father cursed him with the highly romantic moniker of Alexander Dumas Jackson—and in my few visits back to the States, I have tried to convince him that blood, mayhem and suffering are anything but beautiful. I have tried to convince him that there is nothing beautiful about a man stoically watching land-crabs or vultures try to haul away fragments of his exposed intestines as he sits dying under a beautiful palm tree. And I have tried to convince him that that there is nothing beautiful about thousands of women and children a month dying of starvation."

"Well, sir, we all know that death and maiming—and deprivation—are possible in war. But there is glory to be won."

"Where? In being able to kill another man before he kills you? In executing orders that wound sleep?"

Pratt shook his head and responded stiffly. "I'm proud to serve my country. And the Navy. I believe in them both."

"We all have to follow somebody's orders," Christopher insisted. "We are all subordinate to commitments that dwarf conscience, and sleep—and the possibility of joy." He shook his head, as if to chase away the cobwebs of depression weaving their sticky tendrils around the edges of his mind. "Let me say one more thing, Ensign. War has swept back and forth across this island for more than half a century. It has destroyed everything, including, as you know, my family. It has, thus far, built nothing—except a large number of Spanish fortunes. In this land, Ensign Pratt, glory is a naive, irrelevant and dangerous abstraction. I know. I have succumbed to it myself. By so succumbing, I contributed to the deaths of my family."

"You and my brother are moved by those old lies because you have listened too long to the distorted memories of old men, old men who are themselves prisoners of a distorted past, who lost their youth at Shiloh and Bull Run, old men who tell their desperate stories to justify their sacrifices, old men who cling frantically to the last shreds of their youthful delusions."

"Do your duty. Do it well, Ensign. But do not confuse war, real war, with glory. It may be exciting; fear often is. But..."

Pratt cocked his head , confused by his guest's sudden intensity. "I'm sorry, sir. But as you can see, everyone's gathering for coffee and brandy."

"I'm sorry, too. Usually I don't go off on rampages like this." Christopher grinned apologetically, as if to belie his mood. "Perhaps I had too much wine for dinner. I certainly have my share of bad dreams."

Sounds more like a bad case of melancholia to me, Pratt thought. Although he liked the tall Southerner, he could certainly be depressing. Totally understandable considering his losses. Still. Pratt felt his own spirits sag.

As they walked into the wardroom to rejoin Lt. Commander Smith, Christopher asked: "I gather from the atmosphere at dinner that America is prepared for war with Spain?"

"Whether America is prepared or not I don't know, sir. But the *Maine* is prepared, and so is the rest of the Navy. We have a new Assistant Secretary of the Navy, Theodore Roosevelt, and he is cracking the whip and getting the navy everything we ask for."

Christopher could not resist a smile. "Spain has at least a hundred thousand troops in Cuba, plus a large if somewhat antiquated fleet."

"Well, of course we can't do it alone. But with some help and three or four weeks? We'll get you your freedom, Mr. Jackson. We'll rid Cuba of Spain once and for all. That's a promise." Ephraim Pratt, runaway Mormon from the Wild West, stuck out his hand for Christopher to shake. He stood at his full height of 5'-11", as solemn as a Manhattan magnate committing the assets of his bank to a foreign government.

Christopher shook his hand with equal solemnity. "I believe you will, Ensign. I believe you will."

Chapter Ten

A SLANDERER OF OUR WOMEN
Spanish Prime Minister is Seeking for a Way Out

* * * *

Dupuy de Lome, the Spanish Ambassador to Washington, has been dismissed and sent packing back to Spain. In a private letter intercepted by the Cuban Junta and passed on to Washington, De Lome called the PRESIDENT a small politician catering to the popular sentiment.

Right. He deserved dismissal for that offense.

But what about his much more grievous offense? Years ago, as the World showed yesterday, he published a book in which he insulted American womanhood as it has never been insulted before, even by an arrant Englishman. He suggested in terms too plain to be misunderstood that American women were dissolute before marriage and after, and that after marriage they earned in disreputable ways the money they spent in foreign travel and the like.

But in spite of this infamous libel upon American womanhood, the Cleveland Administration and its successor, the McKinley Administration, accepted this jaunty slanderer of American womanhood as persona grata. It was not till he called Mr. McKinley names that a demand was made for his recall. Why? Joseph Pulitzer, Editorial: *The World*, February 11.

Havana

J oseph Rabinsky was a nervous and easily frightened, sixty year old mouse, and looked the part. Scarcely five feet tall, he was tubercularly thin and cursed with the pale green complexion of a sick man who seldom ventured into the sun. Only when he was working were his hands steady. Rabinsky's few acquaintances joked that he had never managed to decide whether he wanted to be a watchmaker or a junk dealer. Over the years Joseph had crammed every available inch of space with racks of used clothes and wooden boxes full of household goods and bric-a-brac. He had lined the walls to the ceiling with used books, the musty odor of which permeated the shop. One narrow aisle meandered from the front door of his narrow shop to the small counter and workbench in the rear.

Joseph spent long hours bent over his work and barely managed to look up even when a customer appeared. If the customer required service, he found his way to the rear of the store and asked for it. Otherwise, Joseph attended to the minute and beautiful precision of his watches. Although his various infirmities were obvious to anyone who came within a block of him, Joseph's strengths were apparent only to those who knew him well. He was afraid of everything, all the time, yet he was also incredibly brave. He shrank from most people and from most facets of life, yet had managed over the years to forge an iron will.

As a boy of eleven standing in front of a synagogue in western Siberia, he watched a Cossack split his father's head with a cavalry saber. A week later the remnants of his family began a five thousand mile, eight month trek to Hamburg. The refugees fled Siberia and one of Nicholas I's numerous pogroms in late spring amidst swarms of mosquitoes, and traveled the last two months through one of the worst winters northern

Europe had seen in a generation. By the time they arrived in Hamburg in early January, one of Joseph's young cousins had died, and both Joseph and his mother had developed bad cases of consumption.

After long stays in Hamburg and Madrid, Joseph finally migrated to Cuba where he lived in a three room flat above his shop and quickly learned to hate the Spanish, who proved to be very different as rulers of a colony than as subjects in their native land. Within a year Joseph became involved in the various rebellions that led to the Ten Years War. Although he lived in great fear of being betrayed by his gentile colleagues, he continued to work for *Cuba Libre!* even after the end of the war. When he finally married, he chose, or rather was chosen by, the mother of two small children, the bitter widow of a close friend.

Rachael Eisenberg Sandoval Rabinsky was almost ten years younger than her husband, whom she married because of rather than despite his infirmities. Since her first husband had died because of his involvement in *Cuba Libre!*, Rachael was determined to find a man so weak and spineless that he could not possibly be involved in what she called the "lunatics' lunacy." She had been fooled by her first husband, a quiet, unassuming physician. She would not be fooled again, or so she thought. She knew that Joseph liked her children and that they liked him, so she seduced the "rabbit," as she was fond of calling him behind his back, and smothered him with rich food and physical attention, none of which affected his appearance. She felt secure in her knowledge that he was too shy, too afraid of people and life ever to threaten her security.

Joseph, of course, had never mentioned his involvement in the revolution. Rachael fed him and told him what to think. As far as she was concerned, he could not possibly be happier. But Joseph could have been much happier. He loved his stepdaughter and her brother. He loved working on his watches, and he loved music. Otherwise, he hated the world and everything in it, including Rachael.

When Guillermo Morales entered Joseph's shop late in the afternoon of February eleventh, Joseph recognized him immediately and broke into a sweat. His hands, unselfconsciously under control for hours, shook so hard he had to put down the watch he'd been concentrating upon. Morales had entered the store four times in the last three years, and each time had ordered Joseph to build a small, easily conceal able device to blow people apart. And each time Joseph had complied, always at great cost to the equanimity he tried so hard to maintain.

"Major Morales," he managed to mumble at his visitor's feet.

"Hello, my good friend. I see you are hard at work as usual." Morales smiled benevolently at the frail jeweler, who refused to look up. Morales watched the sweat popping from Joseph's head and wondered, how many curses can a man acquire and still retain his manhood? "You are very good at what you do. An artist, I think."

"May I be of service?"

"Of service?" Morales replied innocently. "My friends and I do have a little something for you to do, but I also came to enquire after your family, and to share my joy with you."

"My family is well. What cause do you have for joy? Have we won our independance? It seems to me that I saw Spanish troops in the street today, still laughing."

"Ah, my friend, you are so right. My joy is very small. Still, allow me to share it with you."

Joseph finally looked up. "Very well."

Morales blinked. He felt like an insect under the intense gaze of giant, distorted eyes staring through twin magnifying glasses. "I...uh... am now Colonel Morales." He drew himself up to his full height of almost 5'9" and expanded his barrel chest. "Our Leader has done me a great honor."

"If Maximo Gomez promoted you, you must deserve it. Congratulations, Colonel." Joseph cleared his throat. "What do you need?"

Morales deflated and frowned. "We need another bomb."

"What kind of bomb do you want this time? What for?"

"Ah, Joseph." Morales wagged his finger and shook his head. "You do not want to know what it is for. But I can tell you what we need."

"Very well." Joseph did not really want to know the 'what for.' One of his recurring fears was that some day the Spanish would capture and torture him, and that he would break.

"I need a bomb, as powerful as you can make it but small enough to fit inside a cigar box, and it must have an unmarked timer set for six hours." He thought for a moment, suddenly unsure of Christopher's intentions. He smiled. "No, set it for four hours. That will be better."

Joseph nodded. "When do you want it?"

Morales thought for a moment. Christopher said that he would visit the *Maine* at least one more time before trying to plant the bomb. "I will pick it up Wednesday afternoon."

Long after the colonel's departure Joseph sat behind his counter and stared glumly at the disassembled watch. For a man with a price on his head Morales took too many risks—which placed his more cautious allies in unnecessary peril. Joseph finally shook his head, shivered and returned to the delicate and safe precision of his watches.

That evening he was even more preoccupied than usual. Judith, his twenty-eight year old stepdaughter, tried several times to talk about Don Quixote, which they had both read, but Joseph could not pull his mind away from Morales's visit. As if to make the conversation even more difficult, Rachael contributed an almost non-stop screed of repetitious complaints: The price of food was too high, and too scarce. The curfew was a bother. The Spanish troops were becoming increasingly outrageous. On and on.

Finally despairing of the conversation, Judith turned her hazel eyes to her stepfather and said, "I think I'd like to go to the Alhambra and listen to David. Will you walk with me, Father?"

"Certainly. You cannot go alone." Even though he knew the answer before he asked, Joseph turned to Rachael. "Would you like to come along, dear?"

"No, you two go!" Rachael almost spat, without raising her eyes from her stitching. As they prepared to leave, she increased the speed of her rocking. When the short old man and the tall young woman leaned down to kiss her bent and rigid head, they could hear her teeth grinding.

They walked slowly toward the harbor, each lost in thought. Neither Judith nor Joseph understood Rachael's unrelenting bitterness, which seemed to intensify by the month. Each other they understood very well, for Joseph had instilled in both his stepchildren his love for books and music. He was proud of them, loved their company and worried about them incessantly.

Judith finally broke the silence. "What do you think will happen, Papa?"

"I don't know, Judith. I think that we will some day win this war.

Some day we will live in peace, and not worry about such things as soldiers, and curfews, and...body searches."

At 5'7" Judith Sandoval was a head taller than most Cuban women and many men. She was a full-bodied, quietly beautiful woman who towered over her stepfather. The soldiers at the checkpoints loved to run their hands over her body. Despite her contempt for the "little, crucifix-covered boys," as she called them, Judith never resisted. Like most other Cuban women, she stared straight ahead and waited for the "lice to stop crawling."

"Papa?" After thinking about his response to her question, she decided to try again. "That is not what I mean."

"Oh?"

"I mean, what is going to happen to me? I am almost twenty-eight. I do not want to stay at home forever. David has his job in the orchestra, but there is nothing for me to do, and...no one for me to marry."

Joseph smiled up at his stepdaughter. What was there for her in Cuba? Although David had not been admitted to the university because of his religion, he was reading law and would, perhaps, be able to practice someday—when and if Spain left. But Judith? Though she was talented, energetic and beautiful, he knew that unless she managed to find a husband, she would spend her life in her brother's house, a maiden aunt children would grow up avoiding.

"You are still young, my little dove. Things may get better." Though he knew how flat the hope sounded to her, he could think of nothing else to say, and they walked on in silence.

They entered a small public garden and took their usual seat on a wooden bench just below the walled terraces of the Alhambra, where they could hear the music almost as well as the rich and influential members of the club. They sat quietly, listening to a Mozart sonata and gazing out over the harbor at the fishing fleet and the great white battleship.

Joseph smiled and bobbed his pale, goggled head to the rhythm of the music. Who could she marry? Most of the small Jewish community, refugees from successive waves of European anti-semitism, had left Cuba at the start of the new war. Joseph, too, had wanted to emigrate to America, but Rachael still refused. Not until he had been forced to accept the finality of her obstinacy did Joseph succumb to the temptation to rejoin *Cuba Libre!* He was determined that the two young people he had raised would some day live in a free Cuba. At the same time, he knew that the revolution had waxed and waned for fifty years, and that it could well continue for fifty more.

"Have you thought of leaving Cuba?" he finally blurted. "Of maybe going to New York?"

"I've thought of many things, Papa, but I will never leave as long as you...I will never leave you."

"You are being very foolish." He wanted to say more, but at that moment David's cello rose above the other instruments. They listened intently, carried away by the purity of sound and sorrowful feelings that swept over them and, for the moment, washed away their fears. The yellow, orange and magenta sky, the harbor and the music embraced the two in a moment of radiance.

When centrifugal force reasserted itself and the shards again fell apart, Joseph murmured, "These moments with you and David are what I live for." Judith squeezed his hand.

An hour later as they walked back down the cobblestone avenue that ran along the harbor, Joseph experienced a long moment of fright. Moving toward them in a white suit and Panama hat was Guillermo Morales. The strutting colonel seemed as casual as any loyalist gentleman out for an evening stroll. The man's a fool, a danger, Joseph thought, as he glared silently at Morales. Another man walked with him, a tall European with a gaunt face.

Morales didn't seem at all surprised to see Joseph. He bowed, said "Good evening, sir," allowed his eyes to run slowly along Judith's body, and continued on. The man with him was not quite so casual. He could not take his eyes from Judith, who met his gaze directly and openly.

Christopher almost tripped over his feet as he craned his neck to watch the beautiful woman and the shrunken man continue on. "Who was that?"

"That, Jackson, is the Jew who is building our little bomb."

"Good God!" Christopher stopped, turned fully around and stared at the oddly matched couple. For a moment he concentrated on the bent, bobbing back of the little man walking away from him, then asked as casually as possible, "Who is the woman?"

"Judith Sandoval, his step-daughter. She is very desirable, no? Like fruit so ripe it is about to fall from the vine into your waiting hand."

"Yes, she is that." But it's not just her form or face, Christopher thought. What was it? Radiance? Pride? Self-assurance? She held her head high and walked as if she were very strong. "She is not demure," he said, "like most Spanish women."

"I don't know much about her." Morales shrugged. "But they are not Spanish. They are Jews. Still, sometimes I dream of the moist warmth between her thighs."

"She doesn't look like any Jewess I've ever seen." Memories of a drive through New York's Lower East Side flashed across Christopher's mind: throngs of black-garbed, half-starved refugees, the Jews of Eastern Europe, he'd been told. He shuddered as he remembered the stink of the densely packed streets, where seemingly endless crowds of black-clad people cooked cabbage soup, shopped and screamed at each other.

"Christopher!" Morales smiled wickedly. "Be careful. They say that strong-willed young women turn into very hard old bitches."

"I was just asking about her, Guillermo. She is an unusually striking woman."

Morales laughed. "Good thing Theresa is not with us to hear those words."

"What is that supposed to mean?"

Morales shrugged. "She would be jealous, of course."

Christopher stopped and faced his colonel. "I don't believe I like what you're implying, Morales. She was my wife's sister." Although Christopher recognized the defensiveness of his tone, he continued, "I love her like a sister."

Morales smirked. "That may be, but that is not how Theresa loves you."

Christopher's jaw tightened. "I do not mean to be insubordinate, Colonel, but your filthy mind is hardly capable of insight to members of my family."

Morales slammed his fist into Christopher's shoulder. "Watch your mouth!"

Shocked by the blow, Christopher glanced around just as a two-man patrol emerged from the shadows and approached them. "You goddamned fool!" Christopher muttered. "I will do the talking," he ordered, as if he were the superior officer.

"Good evening, gentlemen," the soldiers began, almost in unison.

"Good evening, officers," Christopher responded.

"Please produce your identification cards," the older soldier ordered.

"Certainly. What seems to be the problem?"

Morales could not restrain himself. "You people are paid to stop criminals and arrest revolutionary scum—not to stop gentlemen on the street." He glared contemptuously at the two soldiers, who ignored the statement and carefully examined the papers handed to them first by Christopher and then, albeit reluctantly, by Morales.

"So you are a planter, Sir? From Matanzas Province? And you are a *Yanqui*?"

"That is correct."

"And what brings you to *La Habana*?"

"The shit morsel rebels burned my estate. I am here until you brave Spaniards end their filthy little try for independance."

The soldier handed back Christopher's papers. "That is proving to be a difficult job, sir," he replied as he turned to Morales.

"You—a cattleman from Camaguey?"

"Yes, Private. Is that not what my papers say?"

The soldier carefully examined Guillermo's face, committing it to memory. "Yes, of course, sir. But papers can be made to say anything. It is best for us to be careful." He snapped to attention, clicked his heels, glared at Guillermo, but handed back the papers. "Why did you hit this man with your fist?"

"It is a matter of honor, soldier, and as such is none of your business."

The younger soldier moved his Mauser to port arms and took a step forward, ready to club this rude civilian. The older soldier shook his head and smiled disarmingly, although he could feel his dislike for this haughty, dark-bearded bully rise in his throat like bile. "Ah, but you are mistaken, sir. When it comes to the safety of these streets, I am afraid that everything is my business. Would you care to dispute this little fact?" The soldier smiled again, half hoping that this unpleasant man would take his unpleasantness just one step further.

Morales gained control over his anger and backed off just as Christopher intervened. "Please let me apologize for my colleague, young man." He pulled his wallet from inside his coat and held out a hundred peseta note. "My friend and I have been drinking. And we have been arguing about the presence in our harbor of this *Yanqui* ship."

The two soldiers stared at the note, which more than surpassed the salary both earned in a month.

"What is the nature of your argument? if I may be so bold," the older soldier asked, allowing his eyes to flit for a second toward Morales.

"I was telling my colleague here that the North Americans mean no disrespect for our Spanish Protectors. This ship is no more than a courtesy visit. He disagrees."

"I would like to hear your 'colleague' speak for himself. Mr…" The soldier glanced again at Guillermo's papers. "Mr. Bienavides?"

Now fully in control of his simmering anti-Spanish rage, Morales smiled at the soldier. "Mr. Jackson tells the truth. We are very good friends, but I hit him because sometimes he speaks like a fool and sometimes I have trouble controlling my anger.

"That *Yanqui* ship is an insult to our Spanish friends. It is but one more example of arrogance. They are trying to provoke us, do you not agree?"

Both soldiers nodded, and the younger one spoke for the first time. "That is true, Roberto. Remember, our lieutenant said the same thing just yesterday."

The older soldier plucked the bill from Christopher's hand and smiled. "You should listen more closely to your friend, Mr. Jackson. Good evening, Gentlemen."

When the soldiers had returned to their place of observation in the shadows of a narrow street and the two *mambises* had walked around the graceful bend of the avenue, Guillermo allowed his anger to focus on Christopher. "You think I am a fool because I am brave and refuse to hide from these *pendejos*. Perhaps, that is true, Jackson. I would rather be on the battlefield than skulking around like a cowardly spy. I do not understand how you and Theresa and the other *putas* manage all this smiling hypocrisy."

"Do not refer to Theresa as a *puta*, Colonel. Our Leader has great respect for her."

"I have made my peace with Theresa, Major. And I, too, respect her. But I am not blind. Nor, like you, do I pretend to be. Two facts. One you know but refuse to think about, the other you refuse to know. One, Theresa fucks for a good cause—unlike before the war when she just fucked for money. But regardless of why she does it, Theresa is a *puta*. Two, she does not love you like you love her. She loves you like a woman loves a man."

"Goddamnit! Morales. How many times do I have to tell you..."

Morales balled up his fist but immediately regained control. "Theresa wants you, Jackson. Everyone sees that. The next time you see them—if we leave this mission alive—ask Federico or Oinja. Even their big ox of a son, Fidel, knows it. Everybody knows that Theresa has eyes only for you. And now that Consuelo is dead, there is nothing to stop her from going after you."

"That would be close to incest," Christopher responded mildly, aware that Morales was speaking truths he had not wanted to admit.

Guillermo laughed. "There is precedent. Read the Bible."

Later that night, just before falling asleep, Judith relived the evening. The music and twilight, the walk with her beloved Papa, all had been perfect. Even her mother had softened a little by the time they had returned home, and promised to walk with them the next time they went. Judith thought of the direct, questioning gaze of the tall man she'd seen with her Papa's acquaintance. When she'd asked about him, Papa had almost yelled, "I do not know. Do not ask." Judith was sure her Papa was involved in the revolution, and respected that involvement. And she knew it was the one matter they would never discuss.

But what about the tall man? she wondered. What was it about those bold but entreating eyes? What did he want? What was he asking? Maybe it was nothing. Maybe it was just that his eyes were not undressing her like the other man, the barrel-chested, insolent one who had entered Papa's shop earlier in the day.

Chapter Eleven

GEN. BOOTH FOR PEACE
Salvation Army Chief Says War Over Cuba Would
Aggravate Suffering
* * * *

THE NEXT OUTBREAK OF ANTI AUTONOMY SPANISH
LOYALISTS LIKELY TO BE DIRECTED AGAINST AMERICANS
* * * *

Pittsburgh, February 13—All good men must deplore the terrible condition of affairs in Cuba. But to widen the area of suffering by another war would, it seems to me, aggravate the evil a thousand times over, seeing that it would only involve a much larger multitude in greater suffering. William T. Booth, in a telegram to Joseph Pulitzer. *The World*, February 11.

Havana

Christopher crossed to the window of his small second story room and stared down into the intersection where a six man Spanish patrol searched the lines of homeless refugees trying to enter Habana Viejo, the Old City. Privates guarded each of the narrow converging streets. In the middle of the intersection, two corporals stood a few feet apart, facing each other. Individual peasants, most on foot but some pulling carts, passed slowly between the two corporals. Anyone wanting to enter the market area had to run their gauntlet. The corporals searched every third or fourth person and every cart. They were particularly conscientious with the younger women, none of whom dared to complain. Rather, each woman stood quietly and stared straight ahead as Spanish lice infested their bodies.

Then something happened that helped Christopher resolve his last few doubts about the wisdom of drawing America into the war. One of the corporals discovered a bulge between the breasts of a middle-aged Negro. He shouted an order and all four privates pointed their Mausers at the woman and her teen-age son. The second corporal reached out and, with one violent jerk, ripped the woman's dirty cotton blouse almost completely off and snatched a small bag from between her pendulous breasts. The boy took one startled look at his terrified mother and moved two steps toward the corporal. Before he could take a third, one of the privates ran up behind and rammed the butt of his rifle against the boy's skull.

Christopher had heard the sound before, the slightly hollow thwak of a melon being cracked, and knew the boy was dead. The half-naked mother took two steps toward her son and stopped, frozen. Two privates grabbed the boy's ankles and pulled him from the intersection. The mother followed, fell to her knees, raised her fists to the sky and howled.

The peasants standing in the long line continued to look straight ahead, as if nothing had happened. The corporals resumed their searching, although with more self-restraint. The mother's deep wail ebbed and flowed as her head and upper body bobbed up and down over the corpse.

Christopher leaned his forehead against the wall and closed his eyes. The croaking skeletons of the refugees he had met on the trail popped into his vision. He shuddered at Theresa's image of Consuelo at the moment of her death, and that of Elizabeth, who had been so vivacious and fun-loving as a little girl, and of his other two daughters, who had died days earlier. He sat down on the edge of the narrow bed and allowed his face to drop into his hands. "How many more times?" he moaned. "How many more years?"

As Theresa's words came back to him, the scene on the street below catalyzed all the horrors he had seen in three years of war, "They are dead, Christopher. They are all dead." He thought of his general's prophecy that the war would go on forever, and then he thought of the great white battleship and its crew of a few hundred. "It will be a small price," he hissed.

Christopher flopped back on the bed, stared at the ceiling and envisioned the explosion of the ship, the white-suited bodies floating in the harbor, and the screams of the maimed and dying. Ephraim Pratt's smiling, freckled face rose into view. The face detached itself from the body, separating into smaller and smaller pieces as it rose. The face was no longer smiling, nor was it Pratt's face. The face was Alex's, and it was cursing him as it, too, blew apart.

He rose again to his feet and returned to the window. But it will not be necessary to harm the crew, he told himself, acutely aware that on this point he disagreed with his immediate superior. Morales wanted to create the maximum possible impact, which meant the maximum possible rage.

Christopher sat back on the edge of his bed and finished a half liter of rum. He fell onto his back, stared at the ceiling and tried not to think of his life. By 3:00 in the morning he had been in a fitful sleep for less than an hour. Someone in the far distance was knocking on his door, but he could not make himself care, even when the knocking became louder and more intense, and even though he knew it was Morales. Whether from rum or concentration or depression, Christopher could not force his body back to the task at hand.

Morales finally burst into the room, crashed through Christopher's apathy and dragged him from his bed. "You drunken bastard. You're going to cost us our mission."

Morales was yelling at him. What? Still lost in his pain, Christopher could not force himself to deal with his melodramatic and arrogant superior.

Morales slapped him hard, twice. "Do you realize the stakes? DO YOU?"

At the second slap, Christopher broke through his wall of preoccupation and pushed Morales away. "Yes, Goddamnit! "

"What's going to happen if you fail? You miserable drunk!"

"I am not drunk, Colonel. So calm down." Christopher grasped Morales by the shoulders and pushed him down into the room's one chair. "I have been drinking, yes, but I am not drunk. What are you so on edge about? I'm the one who has to plant that fucking bomb. And what are you doing running around town hours after curfew?"

Morales relaxed a little. Jackson was right; he was on edge. And Jackson's exposure would be extreme. "Yes, I am nervous."

"Christ almighty, Guillermo. You know I drink at night when I can't sleep. But have you ever seen me drunk?" Christopher glared at Morales, who stiffened again and glared back at him. "Have you?"

"No, but ever since your wife died..."

"Yes?" Christopher tensed.

"You drink too damn much, and you drink much more than someone should who's just recovering from the fever, and your drinking has increased since this *Maine* business started. Are you trying to kill yourself?"

Morales asked the question so seriously and with so much parental concern that Christopher laughed, and with the laughter the tension between the two men broke.

"I'm not going to kill myself, and I'm not going to drink another drop until tomorrow night, until it's over. And then, if you don't mind, Colonel Morales, I'm going to drink myself into oblivion."

Morales nodded. "Just make sure you close down Theresa's operation and get her and yourself out of Havana before you drown yourself."

Christopher nodded, and the two men sat quietly for a moment, embarrassed by what had just taken place between them. Christopher finally broke the silence. "Guillermo?" Morales looked up from his worn boots. "This mission the General has given us? It is hard for me. You know that."

Morales nodded. "Yes, I see that." He rose to his feet and placed an arm around Christopher's shoulder. "That is why you are a good soldier, my friend. You understand the implications of your actions." The colonel continued to himself: But I am glad I had Joseph set the timer two hours early, my confused friend, because I know you will do something foolish, like try to save the crew. "Yes, this *Maine* thing is hard for you. But you will do well, perhaps even better than you think."

"Perhaps. Perhaps, but I don't have to like what I am doing."

"No, a good soldier seldom does. That's..." At a noise from the street, Morales became absolutely still. Christopher walked to the window and lifted one of the venetian blinds. Below them, a six-man patrol was breaking into two man units, apparently one unit for each of the three cheap hotels that stood together like abandoned spinsters.

"Are they looking for you?" Christopher whispered.

Guillermo admitted with unaccustomed candor, "It is possible. It was just a matter of time before someone recognized me."

"You fool," Christopher spat. "If you didn't insist on strutting around Havana like a newly rich peasant..." He pulled open a door that revealed narrow steps and Morales entered the passage.

"Christopher...?"

"What?"

"If you don't see me by 11:00 tomorrow morning, then you will have to get the bomb from the Jew. Do you remember what I told you about his shop?" Christopher nodded. "Good. Go with God."

"You too, Guillermo. You too."

"And...not to worry. If they are on to me, I will not let them take me alive."

Christopher nodded and closed the narrow door that led to the roof. He sniffed deeply to make sure the room still stank of rum, rumpled his bed-clothes and climbed in under the blanket. "You too, Guillermo."

He had been in bed for at least five minutes before the soldiers pounded on the door. He waited until the second string of hard knocks had subsided before yelling out drunkenly in English, "Go away, Rosa. I'm too tired. Go home."

"Guardia Civil, Señor. Por favor."

"Yes. One moment. I am coming." He opened the door and stepped back, as if surprised from a stupor. One of the soldiers stood in the doorway while the other glanced around the room and looked under the bed.

"Are you alone, sir?"

"Yes. I wasn't, but she had to go. You know how it is, Comrade. What with the curfew and…"

"Yes, I know," the soldier responded curtly. "Where does that door lead?"

"That? I don't know, Captain. Maybe to the roof?"

"I am a corporal. Salazar! Inspect the roof." The second soldier moved into the room, jerked open the door and clambered up the narrow flight of stairs. After several minutes the private returned and shook his head at the corporal, who was inspecting Christopher's papers. "You have been in Cuba a long time."

"Yes, Corporal. I am a permanent resident, a planter. At least I plant when the sons of whore rebels are not burning my fields and trying to kill me."

"You will get to return to your fields, sir. The rebel gangs have been very quiet the last two weeks. Perhaps we have them on the run. Good night. Or maybe good morning is better, no?" The two soldiers backed from the room and shut the door behind them.

Christopher collapsed again on his back and remembered the conversation he and Morales had had the day before. "What if something happens to you, Colonel? The way you run around the city, it amazes me that no one has spotted you."

Morales had laughed. "No one is going to catch me, Jackson. I am the image of carefulness. Not to worry."

"Yes, sir, Colonel." Christopher smiled, aware that he enjoyed calling the vain man by his new and exalted rank. "But you know, Colonel, even though my disguise as a planter is far more credible than yours, I leave this room only in the evening, and only when I must."

"So? I will return to my room, but first I go to see a certain young lady."

Christopher shook his head and tried to relax into sleep. One more day, Guillermo, he told himself. Please stay off the streets just one more day. Then you can get your vain little ass shot off. Even though Christopher finally succeeded in pushing Morales out of his mind, he could not sleep. Rather, he pored over his plans, and tried to anticipate what might go wrong. Theresa was the key. She must arouse Pratt's interest and distract his attention long enough for Chrisopher to plant the bomb. She would have to play her role very well.

Although he was uncomfortable using her, he could see no other choice. She, too, was an officer in *Cuba Libre!* and she, too, was under orders. Moreover, she had far fewer compunctions about their mission than did he, and he knew it.

How about the watchmaker? The man has seen me once, briefly, in Guillermo's company. Will he remember me? Will he trust me? And what about Judith? Although he knew he was allowing his mind to wander, he envisioned the erect and obviously proud woman who had looked him directly in the eye, almost as if she had been a man. Will I see her? He shook his head and mumbled, "What's left of my soul is married to *Cuba Libre!* Almost immediately, however, he thought of Theresa, and of the ties that bound them together. Though he saw her as his little sister, Christopher's short fantasy about Judith had caused a pang of guilt. Finally he drifted on the verge of a sleep he would not quite realize, and both Judith and Theresa receded before a sharp memory of Consuelo.

* * * * *

They were in the cane fields, just before harvest. She had snuck up on him while he was inspecting the rows and calculating how many cutters he would need to hire, and for how long. She had risen from the cane like a mermaid from the sea, naked beneath her unbuttoned blouse, her long hair wrapped around her like a veil.

"Come on, old man. You work so hard you will not be any good for me." He looked up from the columns of figures, enchanted as always by her compelling vitality. She danced around him as she slowly removed her dress. She had removed her shift before leaving the house and had packed a lunch and bottle of wine, all calculated to lure him from the work that was already carving a double crease between his eyes.

"Just a minute, my little dove. Let me finish this."

But she was unfastening his belt and humming the old rebel marching song he'd taught her.

"Ah, to hell with it," he muttered gleefully, dropping his notebook to the ground. Consuelo fell to her knees and Christopher held his hands gently at the back of her neck and ran his fingers through her curly black hair.

"Do you love me?" She looked up at him, a playful smile on her full lips.

"Yes, Ma'am. I surely do."

"Good! If you'd answered differently, I was going to bite off your head. Maybe I still will." She cupped his testicles in her hands and squeezed softly. He stood mesmerized, stroking the back of her head. This woman, he thought. This woman! He had never before met anyone who took such obvious delight in breathing, or who was as excited about as many things: books, cooking, making love, sunsets, horses, talking. Whatever Consuelo did, she did completely. Even her sleep was total.

"Jesus, Consuelo." She had kissed the head of his penis, dropped her open mouth over his erection and bitten down just hard enough to make him yell. Suddenly she let go and fell back against a row of cane. "You look so...f-f-funny," she giggled. He saw himself through her eyes: a tall man standing rigidly before her, his hands groping air, his trousers down around his ankles, his locked knees quivering, his face an open book of tragi-comic vulnerability. "Sweetheart," he laughed. "I guess you're right."

She rose from her knees and pretended to run away. He took one step after her and fell, cursing his hobbled ankles. She laughed and circled around. Rather than trying to move to his feet, he turned and lurched at her until she allowed herself to be captured.

As she stood before him, still pretending to push him away, he cupped her buttocks in his hands, buried his face in her breasts, kissed each dark, erect nipple and, almost out of control, moaned, "Consuelo. Love of my life. Consuelo." It was now her turn to hold his head in her hands, which she did with great tenderness. She sank to the earth, gently pushed him over onto his back, and bent down to kiss him.

Even as they made love she maintained control, relishing one of her frequent rushes of assertiveness. Each time he became too strong for her, or began to surrender to his urgency, she whispered, "No," softly but firmly. But when she knew he could wait no longer, she pressed herself hard against him and surrendered to the spasm welling up from deep inside her. At the moment of climax, each was wrapped in cells of separate ecstasy, each almost oblivious to the other. But as their spirits floated to earth, they came back together and caressed each other.

"Christopher."

"Mmmm?" He lay on his back, watching the afternoon clouds move in from the east. He was at peace, in total harmony with the earth and sky and Consuelo. He turned dreamily toward her excited face.

"Put your hand down here." She took his hand and placed it on her smooth, slightly rounded abdomen. He moved his hand in slow circles, barely touching her skin, wondering at the almost electric tension between his warm hand and her cool belly. But he soon thought of her sex and allowed his fingers to drop lower.

"No, wait a minute." She pulled his searching fingers back up to her belly and left her hand on top of his. "Don't you feel anything?"

"I feel your heart singing in your stomach. It sings, 'Beware all ye mortals who enter here.'" She laughed and he felt her stomach muscles tighten.

"No, you fool." She was still giggling. "It says, 'Listen to me, old man. I am your son. I will be coming to see you soon.' Can't you hear him?"

Christopher laughed and bent over to run his tongue across her navel, just as her meaning struck. He kissed her belly very gently and said, "I love you, Consuelo. And I will love our son."

She smiled, pleased but not quite ready to abandon her role. "Master, you won't beat me too hard if it's only a girl?" She had taken on the semi-whining manner of an ex-slave, allowing for a moment her African heritage to overcome her European. While he looked quizzically up at her, she stuck out her tongue and said, "I love you, too, you silly man."

But even as Consuelo smiled, Theresa's grief-stricken face rose up to replace Consuelo's. "She is dead, Christopher. They are all dead."

Chapter Twelve

"CUBA A TOMB," SAYS HAWTHORNE
*Journal's Commissioner Continues His Description of Harrowing
Scenes on the Island*

* * * * *

**THE NEXT OUTBREAK OF ANTI AUTONOMY SPANISH
LOYALISTS LIKELY TO BE DIRECTED AGAINST AMERICANS**

* * * * *

Havana Harbor via Key West, Febuary 15—In the courtyard of the orphanage were seated about forty children trying solemnly to concentrate on a lesson being taught by an emaciated young woman of about twenty.

All around these starving but more fortunate children sprawled the forms of the even less well-nourished. All these latter children could do was endure for a few more hours or days the pangs of gnawing hunger, and then sink noiselessly into nothingness. Many of them were afflicted with the diseases that accompany starvation. Their feet and legs were swollen with dropsy, their skin was foul and sore with eruptions, and their eyes were being extinguished by ophthalmia. They had no strength to brush away the flies that were settling on them.

The whole place was strangely silent; so many children and no noise. As I walked slowly past the little rooms, I felt as though this place were a catacomb or a tomb peopled with lifeless effigies of humanity. Julian Hawthorne: *The New York Journal*, February 15.

Havana, February 15

E arly in the afternoon, almost two hours after Morales had failed to appear, Christopher turned into the Calle de Balboa and approached Joseph Rabinsky's shop. He walked confidently, almost arrogantly, a prosperous-looking planter whose only care seemed to be making money. Just before entering the shop, however, he glanced casually around.

When he walked through the door he was jarred slightly by the ringing camel bells, and even more by the green visor and two shining orbs of glass that jerked up, stared at him briefly from the end of the tunnel-like aisle, then dropped back down to their work. Almost overpowered by the combined odors of mildewed clothes and musty books, Christopher threaded his way down the aisle and came to a hesitant stop in front of the counter. His confidence had evaporated.

"You are the *Yanqui*?" Rabinsky asked without again raising his eyes.

"Yes. I am an associate of Guillermo Morales."

"Where is the revolution's newest and brashest colonel? Has he been caught?"

"I don't know. He has probably been recognized."

"Then he will be caught, won't he? And if he is caught and if he talks, that will be the end for all of us. Is that not so?" Joseph raised his huge, frail head from the dis-assembled watch and for one fleeting second looked Christopher in the eye, then dropped his gaze back to the workbench.

Christopher noticed that the man's hands were shaking. "Not necessarily," he said lamely, disconcerted as much by the size of the man's green eyes behind his magnifying lense glasses as by the directness of his questions. "I have come for the bomb. Morales said it would be ready." Joseph's hands returned to their work. "Did you hear me?" Christopher spoke flatly, sharply. The sweating gnome made him nervous.

Though Joseph refused to look up, Christopher could tell that he had ceased even pretending to work on the watch. "I am sorry," Joseph finally said. "It is not ready."

"What do you mean? Christ! old man, you've had damn near a week." Christopher felt his knees go slightly weak. Everything hinged on the bomb.

Joseph looked up. "I am sorry," he whispered. "Morales gave me some instructions about portability. They are difficult. You will have to come back."

"Let me see it." Joseph continued to sit, his shaking right hand still holding the tiny screwdriver. "Let me see the goat-fucking bomb!"

Joseph knew that the *Yanqui* was not going to leave until he had what he wanted. He rose, moved his bent body to the right wall, removed a few musty books that he had converted to a storage box, and put his hands on the bomb. "Please. Come over here." Christopher walked over to stand above the watchmaker, who held three small packages. "Morales told me that this bomb will serve as a fuse to set off a fire and a far larger blast."

Christopher nodded. "That is the theory."

"It is possible. Little bombs have served before as the fuse to far bigger ones. He also ordered me to make the bomb so that it could be taken from a cigar box and transferred to another container. What size? The same as the cigar box?"

"No, flatter. And forget about the cigar box. Do you have some white cheese-cloth?"

Joseph shrugged. "It can be had."

"Good! I need the package to fit this." Christopher opened his loosely fitting linen jacket to reveal a large pocket he had sewn in below the left breast. "It must not look lumpy."

Joseph scrutinized the make-shift pocket and said, "Come back at 2:00.

The tall *Yanqui* looked at him sharply, grunted assent and turned and stalked from the shop. Joseph was very relieved to see him go.

PART I: VIVA CUBA LIBRE!

* * * *

An hour later Judith was sitting just behind the wrought iron grill-work of the second floor window that looked out over the narrow street. She was turning the collar on David's white shirt and thinking dark thoughts. She had seen the *Yanqui* enter and leave the shop, and she knew that the errand Papa had sent her on was connected to the *Yanqui*. Though she knew that men like the *Yanqui* and Morales were not really customers, she had never voiced her suspicions. She knew that Joseph was desperate to protect his family, and that only through his total silence could he possibly succeed in doing so.

She jerked alert. At the end of the street a man in a white suit struggled with a two man patrol. Evidently the patrol was in the process of arresting the man who, even from a distance, seemed familiar. Suddenly the man kicked out in several directions, broke away and dashed down the middle of the narrow street in a perfectly straight line. Almost immediately other soldiers appeared, and a short, fat officer pointed at the runaway. Slowly, as if at half speed, the soldiers raised their Mausers and fired. Judith gasped. It was the bearded man she had seen with the *Yanqui*, and he was not running to the shop but by it, without so much as glancing in its direction. He made no attempt to dodge the bullets, but ran straight down the street past the shop. Judith noticed that he was smiling, as if he knew precisely what he was doing, almost as if, unbeknown to the soldiers, he was using them.

He stumbled once, and Judith noticed that there were round red spots on his back and leg. He rose, wobbling, to his feet and started to run again, not nearly as fast but in a line that was almost as straight. The rifles continued to fire until, fifteen or twenty meters beyond the shop, he fell to the cobblestones and lay perfectly still.

Rachael appeared next to her, yelling the same question over and over. "My God, Judith! What's happening? My God, Judith! What's happening?"

"I don't know," Judith lied. "Stay here. Whatever happens, stay here!" Making a split-second decision, she pushed her mother gently aside and ran across the room to the stairs that led down to the shop.

Joseph was bent over his watch, trying to block out the noisy announcement that his world might be grinding to a halt. He looked up at Judith and tried to smile until he noticed the fear and knowledge that lurked just beneath the surface of her eyes. He felt the world stop completely and said, "Yes, Judith, I know."

He became very calm, very direct. "It is time. I have been expecting them for years. If soldiers enter the shop, I want you to be upstairs with your mother. Tell her nothing. Do not even tell her what I know you suspect. She will hate me soon enough."

Although she was almost in control of her voice, Judith could not control the tears that exploded from her eyes and streamed down her cheeks. She knew that there was nothing she could say, nothing, really, that even needed to be said. They had always been closer than any of the words that had passed between them. "I will never see you again, Papa." She reached down and stroked his sweating head.

"No. There will be nothing else. Now! Go to your mother."

As she started up the stairs she heard the camel bells. Joseph turned slightly, hissed, "Trust the *Yanqui*!" and returned for the final time to his work.

She heard the camel bells ring again. Since the soldiers could not see her where she stood behind the curtain at the top of the stairs, Judith watched the fat little officer lead his men single file down the aisle. The officer's pistol was pointed at Joseph, who did not bother to raise his head.

"Are you the Jew, Joseph Rabinsky?"

Head still bowed, Joseph's eyes took in the khaki tunic and brass buttons of the officer's uniform. He noticed that though the buttons were polished, they had been polished carelessly and were green around the edges. "I am Joseph Rabinsky. And, yes, I am a Jew."

For the first time in years he felt no fear, no dread. He looked up at the officer's round, smiling face. Joseph was slightly surprised to see that the officer was a major, until he remembered who this major probably was. He again began to shiver.

"You are under arrest, Jew, for treason." the major smiled.

"Oh?"

"His Majesty believes you are one of the terrorist bandits who are trying to destroy Cuba."

"His Majesty is eight years old and does not know I exist.

The officer frowned. "I, Major Alvarez, would like the pleasure of your company." Joseph felt his knees buckle and hoped he would die quickly. Not only did he not want to betray Maximo Gomez and *Cuba Libre!*, he also did not want to betray the memory of his friend, Aaron Sandoval, Rachael's first husband, who had died so many years before, and without revealing his secrets. Joseph stood silently as one of the soldiers tied his hands behind his back. As soon as the soldier finished, the major spun him around. "Upstairs!"

"No-o-o-o!" Joseph screamed, as a wave of terror swept over him. "That is my family. Please!" But the squad was already pushing him up the stairs. "Rachael! Judith! RUN!" he screamed, just as the major's pistol slammed against the back of his head. One of the soldiers grabbed his limp body by the coat collar and dragged him up the steps.

They were met at the top by Rachael who screamed curses at her unconscious husband. When the lead soldier tried to grab her, she ran to the rear door, to the outside steps that led down to a small patio and the alley. When she saw the grinning soldier Alvarez had posted at the top of the landing, she slammed the door in his face and ran around the room in tight circles, screaming, "Joseph, you betrayed me!" at full volume. Judith stood in the corner of the small living room, horrified as much by her mother's performance as by the disintegration of their lives. Even the soldiers were immobilized for one short moment, amazed by the skinny old woman careening around the room like a headless chicken.

"Shut her up!" Alvarez shouted to no one in particular. When none of his soldiers looked like he was about to move, the major raised his pistol and shot Rachael just below the right eye. The explosion reverberated through the room, followed by total silence.

Judith saw the angry glint in the major's eyes, the pistol rising slowly toward her mother, her mother's mouth opening and closing, again and again. As slow as the actions seemed to her, however, they were far swifter than her reaction. She tried to open her mouth to protest, but no sound came out. She tried to raise her hand to stop the major, but her mother was already dead, sitting spraddle-legged against the wall, before Judith could move.

Then, without knowing quite how, Judith was on the floor and staring into a ring of sweaty, leering faces. She had fainted. She felt the hands, hundreds of smelly hands, moving over her naked body. Men sat on her spread-eagled legs, which had lost their feeling. She felt the hard movements as one of the men moved inside her. His sweat splashed into her eyes and mouth. The scream that welled up from her stomach was cut short by a fist that slammed against her temple.

When she regained consciousness the engorged faces and sweaty, seldom-washed bodies had disappeared. At first she could hear nothing but the ticking of the three clocks from below. As the world filtered back in, it occurred to her that the street was noisier than usual, and more excited.

After awhile Judith rose up on one arm. Her dead mother stared at her. She looked down at the blood and semen drying on her stomach and thighs. Just before passing out again, she vomited hard, first on herself and then, again and again, on the worn, flowered carpeting.

Later, trying to avoid her mother's fixed eyes, Judith crawled over to the small kitchen sink, pulled herself up by the ledge, poured water into the shallow zinc basin, grabbed a towel and started to clean her body. She tried to ignore the dull throb in her temple where the soldier had hit her. Then sensing a sharper pain, she put her fingers to her mouth. She had bitten through her lower lip.

A quarter of an hour later she was still scrubbing her body, so preoccupied with removing the filth from her skin that she failed to hear the footsteps moving quietly up the outside stairs. When the door squeaked open, however, she whirled around, dropped the wet towel and tried to back away. A pair of shocked grey eyes stared at her.

* * * * *

During the interval between his first and second visit to Joseph's shop, Christopher had returned to his room, which he examined carefully after packing his one valise. He then walked across the Parque Central to the Hotel *Inglaterre* to check the valise with the porter. He and Theresa would be leaving town immediately after their visit to the *Maine*. They would not be returning to the Old City.

While walking slowly back to Joseph's shop, Christopher concentrated on the problems that he hoped he'd solved. Theresa must play her part well, he told himself, aware that her performance was beyond his control. If Pratt, or anyone else, saw through her acting, all would be lost. Could she do it? He smiled. Probably.

Christopher felt less secure about the warning he'd prepared for the crew of the *Maine*. According to Morales the bomb would explode six hours after he connected the wires. If he wired the bomb at 5:30 or so, just before he and Theresa went aboard, and if they left the ship around 8:00, the American consulate would have until after 11:30 to warn the crew.

He turned into the Calle de Balboa, so preoccupied with plans for the coming evening that he almost failed to notice the excitement that hummed through the narrow street. "What's happening, sir?" he asked one of the shopkeepers, a large round man wearing a dirty green apron.

"The guard came. They shot a man right there," the round man replied, pointing at a brown spot down the street. "They say the dead man was a colonel of the *insurrectos*."

"Blood of Christ!" Christopher exclaimed. "Are the *insurrectos* so close as that?"

The shopkeeper shrugged and gave Christopher an overtly suspicious glance. Who is this tall man with the accent? he wondered. A spy for the Spanish pigs? "I think it had something to do with the old Jew watchmaker. There was shooting in his shop, too. Afterwards they took the Jew away. The Jew's son was entering the shop as they left. They took him away, too."

Christopher could barely maintain control. Though he was bothered by Morales's death—and he had no doubt that the man shot in the street was Morales—he was stunned by the arrest of the watchmaker. "These are troubled times for Cuba, no?" he replied as casually as he could.

"Yes, for some people," the shopkeeper answered, his voice guarded and neutral. He could detect Christopher's uneasiness. "We should all mind our own business perhaps."

Christopher nodded, as if already thinking of something else, and continued on down the street past Joseph's shop. Without looking directly at the storefront, he could see that the Spanish had not bothered to post a guard. Counting his steps as he went, he walked down to the corner of the long street and turned the corner.

Almost as soon as he was around the corner, his jaunty self-confidence disappeared. His head spun. His mind had ceased to function. He leaned against a wall, hyper-ventilating. For the next few minutes he concentrated on his breathing. In, out, in, out, in, out....After getting to the point where he could take a series of deep breaths, hold them and then let them out slowly, he stood a little straighter and tried to think.

Too bad about Guillermo. The fool! How was he betrayed? What do they know? What does his death mean? Christopher forced his mind to move slowly, methodically. How long can the watchmaker last in El Morro before he talks? Is the bomb ready? Is it still there in the wall?

He noticed that he was sweating and that, despite the heat of the afternoon, he felt chilled. Not now, he thought, willing his body to stay strong. Do the Spanish suspect anything about the *Maine?* Will they question Rabinsky immediately? How much time do I have before I'm arrested? Christopher's imagination took him in wider and wider circles. He shook his head again. No! Think!

He turned down the alley and counted the steps that should lead him to Joseph's rear patio. As he walked he told himself that the Spanish probably would not begin a serious examination of the watchmaker until at least the next day, by which time both Christopher and Theresa would be long gone. Just before picking the locked gate into Joseph's patio, he drew a breath of relief: Joseph had no idea what the bomb was for. At least according to Morales.

Somewhat reassured, Christopher quietly climbed the stairs that led to Joseph's quarters. When he opened the door and saw the naked woman, he stood for a second and stared. Even when she turned to face him and dropped her towel, he kept staring, lost in an unexpected world. Although he was acutely aware of the pale fullness of her body, he was hypnotized by her badly bruised face and wild hazel eyes. They burned into his, wide-open, horror-filled.

As soon as he realized what he was doing, Christopher averted his face and said, "I am sorry, Lady. Forgive me." When he saw the dead woman sprawled against the wall, he recoiled sharply and felt another knot of rage in his stomach. His head still averted from Judith, he said, "I must come in." His eyes focused on the stairs that led down to the shop.

Judith said nothing and remained next to the sink. Her right hand continued to move up and down her thighs as if she still held the towel.

Her huge eyes follow him as he stepped over Rachael's extended legs and walked across the room.

He recoiled from the sight of the dead woman with the grotesque hole beneath her right eye and was at the bottom of the stairs before he realized that the wild-eyed mute was Judith Sandoval, the erect and confident woman he had seen at the harbor. "My God!" he muttered. His earlier vision of Judith faded; he would never be able to forget the mute, wild brutishness of her frightened eyes.

Christopher shook his head, as if to free it from everything he had seen and heard since turning into the Calle de Balboa. He walked to the right wall, searched carefully for the correct shelf and removed the package the watchmaker had prepared for him.

He took the package to the work bench and inspected its contents: Two sticks of dynamite wrapped securely in a fuse, a small, pre-set timer, a detonator and two pairs of copper wires. The old man had painted the tips of one set red and those of the other green. All Christopher had to do was twine the wires together—and deliver the package. He repacked the flat package in its cheesecloth wrapping, and placed it in his large, make-shift pocket. I sure hope this old man knew what he was doing, he thought, and started back up the stairs. How can I help? he wondered. How do I even go about approaching her?

Before reaching the top of the stairs he stopped to listen. Nothing. He waited a full minute then cleared his throat. Still nothing. He did not want to re-enter the room but knew he must; there was no other safe way out of the shop. He finally cleared his throat again. "Lady?" Nothing. "Judith? May I come up?"

He heard a dry, hoarse whisper. "Yes." He paused for another few seconds and moved up the last stair. He did not see her until he was completely into the room. In his absence she had donned a robe and found a gun. He looked straight into the barrel of an old pistol and stared into Judith's slightly narrowed eyes.

Part of the wildness had left her face, but the intense loathing that replaced it was just as intense and a lot more personal. Christopher started to take a step toward her but stopped dead when her finger tightened on the trigger. The two stood and looked at each other, and Christopher knew that he was at least as afraid of her as she was of him.

"I did not come to hurt you, Miss," he stammered. Silence. "I was an…associate of your step-father." Nothing. Judith's expression did not change, nor did the position of the pistol. At the moment Christopher's mind was empty of everything but his great need to get away from this place of death and from this mad woman. "Perhaps your step-father mentioned me? I am the *Yanqui*"

"He was my father."

"What?" Christopher was as startled by what she said as he was by the sound of her voice.

"He was my father. Joseph was my father."

Although she sounded as though her mind was working at the level of a child's, he decided to grasp the thread and pull her back into the world. "I think your father would want you to listen to me, and I think we should leave this place. The Spanish will be back."

"This is where I live."

Although she seemed to be returning to the world, he knew that he could not stand in front of her pistol much longer. "You stay then. I have to leave."

"My father said I should trust the *Yanqui*." She spoke haltingly, but not without connection. "You are one of those whose job it is to kill Spaniards?"

He nodded. "It is my only joy." The pistol dropped slowly from before his nose. "You are lucky to be alive," he said without conviction.

"I want to kill Spaniards," she replied. Then she was in his arms, her body wracked by huge, convulsive sobs. He sat down with her on the top stair and held her like a child, stroking her tangled hair and whispering, "There, there. It will be all right. We will take care of you," just as his mother had whispered so often when he was small.

What am I saying? one part of his mind asked. I should get out of here. But the rest of his mind did not care. The compassion that had risen from some long-buried cistern pushed both his desire and his self-disgust back into the darkness of his blood. This woman's life was destroyed because her father had committed himself to the revolution, and because of the arrogant carelessness of Guillermo Morales. Although Christopher had never before assumed personal responsibility for the innocent victims of *Cuba Libre!* he felt responsible for this one. He was thankful that Judith could not see his tears.

Gradually her great sobs slowed and softened, and after awhile he said, "We must go." She nodded meekly, rose shakily to her feet and crossed to her small room to dress.

But the sound of rustling cloth suddenly stopped. "I can't go. I must wait for David, for my brother."

"Oh, my God!" Christopher muttered, remembering the words of the round shopkeeper. What do I do now? "Judith?"

Perhaps it was his tone. A tremulous "Yes?" followed another short silence.

"David was arrested with your father. They are together." Again, silence. He wanted to say something positive, to comfort her, but he knew that any word of hope would be a lie. "He, too, will soon be dead, Judith." After an interminably long minute he added, "The soldiers were from El Morro." He thought of the Spaniel-eyed major he had met aboard the *Maine*. Somehow, somewhere, Christopher swore silently, I am going to kill that smiling little bastard with my bare hands.

He found it increasingly difficult to deal with Judith's continued silence. He walked over and rearranged the old woman's body so she looked less grotesque. A few minutes later Judith walked out, dressed simply in a black worsted dress and a floppy, wide-brimmed straw hat. Her bruised face was still drained, chalk-white, but set. She knelt for a moment by her mother, who was now lying flat on the floor, her eyes closed. When Judith looked back up, her eyes expressed her thanks.

As she rose she asked, "The revolution needs money?"

"Always."

"My father has money we can take. He would approve. Wait here." She stepped down the stairs, moved a row of books a shelf higher than the one where Christopher found the bomb, and extracted a small metal box from where it rested against a somewhat larger one. She looked at the larger one for a second, shook her head, replaced the books and returned up the stairs. "This is for killing Spaniards," she said and hand-ed Christopher the box.

* * * * *

"This is not a whorehouse, Theresa" Christopher declared with great force, "and you know it! The four women who live here travel only in the best company." Though Theresa was right about the Casa de Ponce de Leon, he hated the self-disgust in her voice. It was as if Judith's presence in the house was a mirror in which Theresa stared at the squalor of her years as a whore for *Cuba Libre!* He did not want to cause Theresa more pain, but this young woman needed help, and she had become one of them. "Theresa, I need to keep Judith here until we leave. And I need your help. Right now!"

Theresa blinked. He spoke as her commanding officer, which he was. She must not allow her feelings to interfere with their job. "Bring her up." As he started to leave the room, she could not keep from asking, "Are you in love with her?"

"No," he said softly. "I am not." He noticed the open longing in her face, the anticipation of final rejection and the rush of relief that followed his answer. Does she know that I know? he wondered as he walked down to the lobby to fetch Judith.

After introducing the two women and waiting a few minutes to make sure that Theresa would behave herself, he returned to the lobby to wait. Though he knew that Theresa would not object to him sitting in her room while she dressed, he was not about to do it with Judith present.

As he descended to the lobby, however, he was greeted by a rude shock: Standing at Parade Rest in the lobby was a Spanish corporal. Christopher nodded at the corporal and sat down to read the American newspaper he usually carried as a prop.

Whose bodyguard is he? Christopher wondered. Then he remembered that Alvarez, the Inquisitor, was one of Isabella's regulars. He remembered his vow to kill the man and decided to engage the corporal in conversation. He smiled, winked and said, "Officers get to have all the fun, no?"

The corporal smiled back. "Not always, sir. My major is a very generous man. Each month when he visits here, when he finishes with his whore, he allows me to have my pleasure with her." The corporal puffed out his chest slightly. "He even stays in the room to observe her actions, and to make sure, of course, that she shows me a good time."

Chee-rist! Christopher swore to himself. "Tell me, Corporal. Your major, is he not Ignacio Alvarez? my friend from El Morro?"

The soldier, who knew his major would not be down for at least an hour, smiled even more broadly, took a seat and accepted the cigar that Christopher proffered. "Ah, I am glad you know my major. Isn't he outstanding?" Without waiting for a response, the soldier continued. "I think sometimes if we had more men like the major, we would have stopped these sons of whore revolutionaries years ago."

"Maybe so, maybe so," Christopher answered thoughtfully. "He is the best I know at ferreting out traitors and extracting any useful information. Wouldn't you say?"

"Yes, yes, sir. Very true. Just today, for example, this very day, we killed Guillermo Morales and…"

"Who was he?" Christopher asked as he dipped his cigar against the rim of the ash tray.

"Morales? A rebel colonel, that's who! We thought he was a major on Gomez's staff, but he has been telling everyone in Havana that he is a colonel. So?" The corporal shrugged.

"Sounds to me like the man's a fool."

"Was, sir. Was. We shot him just before we arrested a Jew. Unfortunately, he tried to get away, and we had to kill him before we had a chance to question him."

"Who? The Jew?"

"No, no, no." The corporal squinted and looked at Christopher as if the tall civilian were dense. "No. Morales. We have the Jew in El Morro with his son."

"Oh? They are traitors also?"

The corporal shrugged, as if to suggest that he didn't know, but then brightened as he thought of what the next day would probably bring. "We will not know until tomorrow, but we will know." He laughed as he remembered that Alvarez had promised him the nail pincers. "Unless…"

The soldier's face fell and Christopher thought, The man should have been an actor. He has a different face for each minute. "Unless what?"

"Well, I…uh…hit him kind of hard in the back of the head when we arrested him, and…we are not yet sure that he will live."

"That would be a shame, Corporal, but then again, what will be will be."

Just as the corporal started to answer, he glanced at the stairs, leapt to his feet and leered. Christopher turned and saw Theresa, clad only in her short thin chemise, standing seductively on the stairway.

"Good evening, Señor Bienevides," she said, her voice dripping with honey. "I am ready to receive you now."

What in Hell's name is going on? Christopher wondered, as he winked companionably at the leering soldier and followed Theresa up the stairs.

* * * * *

Almost as soon as Christopher had left Theresa's room, she asked, for want of something better to say, "How old are you, Judith?"

"Almost twenty-seven. How old are you?" Judith was not the least bit interested in Theresa's age or, for that matter, anything else about her. She wanted nothing more than to be alone, anywhere, with her grief. But she was capable of great strength, and knew that the present required strength. She sensed that this mulatto woman who so obviously resented her presence was also a woman of strength.

Theresa was amused by Judith's response. "Almost twenty-five," she replied. She was less pleased by Judith's next question, and even less pleased by her response to it.

"Are you the *Yanqui*'s mistress?"

"No, I am not his mistress!" Theresa fired back, "I am a whore for *Cuba Libre!* I sleep with Spanish officers and diplomats and other important men, and pass their words and their gold to my colleagues." Theresa was confused. Why had she felt compelled to state such truths? And to state them in such a rough way? She looked away from her mirror and over to Judith. The young Jewish woman was staring at her with obvious revulsion and rubbing her hands up and down her thighs, as if trying to rub away some deep stain.

Theresa felt deeply ashamed, not because she 'fucked for the cause,' as she so frequently told herself, but because of her coarseness with this young woman who had not yet returned from her own descent into hell. Theresa looked at herself in the mirror with some of the same revulsion she saw in Judith's eyes, then turned to the younger woman and said, "I am very, very sorry, Judith. Please forgive me." After a slight pause she added, "I have no women friends. I do not know how to act around you. I do not know how to act around any other woman—except when I'm in public, on stage."

Though Judith said nothing, her eyes softened a little and her hands stopped their rubbing.

Mother of God! Theresa thought. What is happening to my strength? I never tell people what I feel. But she would have poured forth her entire life to the younger woman had not someone knocked frantically on her door. "I think maybe we can help each other, you and I," she said before she opened the door.

"Theresa! Thank God!" An elegant, long-boned black woman pushed her way into the room. "Quick! It's Isabella. We must do something. Please, Theresa. Please!"

Theresa slapped the hysterical woman across the cheek. "Calm down, Angelina." Instantly her voice softened and she caressed the face she had just slapped. "What is wrong, Angelina?"

"The Beast is hurting her. I can hear the moans through my wall. But I think he must have her gagged, because…"

What timing! Theresa thought. "Stay here. Both of you. Christopher will know what to do."

"Alvarez' guard is downstairs, Theresa."

Theresa nodded, then shed her robe and left the room naked but for her chemise.

As soon as she managed to pull Christopher away from the major's bodyguard and get him to her room, Theresa explained the situation.

Christopher, aware of her urgency, asked, "Where is your pistol?"

Theresa hurried to her wardrobe, reached under the bottom shelf and handed the weapon over. "We will have to do something about the bodyguard," Christopher said. "If he gets away, everything, and I do mean everything, is lost." He turned to Judith. "We are going to kill two of the men who killed your mother and raped you. Can you help us?"

"Yes!"

Christopher peered into her narrowed eyes and nodded. "Theresa, as soon as we're finished, get everyone out of here. Gomez ordered you to close down; we'll just close—for good, Theresa—a few hours early."

"Yes!" Theresa exclaimed. "Thank you, Virgin Mother."

Christopher turned to Angelina. "You and Judith take care of the corporal. Come, Theresa."

As soon as Christopher and Theresa left the room, Angelina looked disdainfully at Judith and asked, "This corporal who helped to kill your mother and rape you, can you kill him?"

"Yes!" Judith hissed. "He is the Philistine, the enemy of Israel."

Angelina gave Judith a puzzled glance, handed her a knife, and said, "Hide behind the door. I will do the rest." She walked out the door, opened her silk wrapper so that her large breasts were almost completely exposed, and descended the stairs to the lobby. "Corporal?"

The soldier again leapt to his feet, allowing the half-finished cigar to drop to the floor. "Lady, how may I serve thee?" His eyes were riveted to her breasts, which led him like a false beacon to his death.

"Major Alvarez has arranged for you to join him in Paradise. Come with me, please." Angelina turned on her heel and ascended the steps, confident that the corporal would follow the swaying curves of her buttocks. She walked through the open door, sat down on the bed, opened her wrapper completely and held out her arms to the corporal.

The corporal walked through the door, mesmerized. He unhooked his holster and dropped it to the floor, said, "Ah, sweet sister," then looked around to his right, puzzled. Something had happened to his neck. He turned just in time to see the second sweep of Judith's knife, which plunged into his chest.

"Pig!" Judith cried. "Pig!" The soldier felt the blood spouting from his neck and knew that he was moving too slowly. He put up an arm to protect himself and tried to marshall his rapidly disappearing powers of concentration. Why was this woman doing this?

He was on the floor, still puzzled, still moving his weak hands ineffectually as the knife rose and fell, rose and fell in his chest and stomach and groin. The other woman was on top of him with a pillow. He wanted to scream, but even before the pillow descended to cover his face, he knew it was too late. The last words he heard, his final rites, were "Pig! Pig! Pig!"

* * * * *

"Now!" Theresa whispered, as she saw the corporal disappear. Christopher nodded and kicked in the thin door. He entered the room, his pistol leveled at the Inquisitor's head, and gasped.

Isabella was lying face down on the bed, moaning into the gag

Alvarez had stuffed into her mouth. He had tied her arms and legs to the bed posts. Both of them were naked and Alvarez was sitting astride his victim's thighs, his surprised face smeared with a thin patina of blood. Isabella's back, buttocks and thighs were covered with dozens of bloody bites. She turned her gagged head toward the door and the miracle that stood there in the form of Christopher and Theresa.

"Move, slime," Christopher stated flatly.

Though Major Alvarez's eyes moved covertly to the small dresser where he had placed his holster on top of his sloppily piled uniform, he smiled back at Christopher as if they were long-separated brothers. "Mr. Jackson," he purred. "I really didn't expect to see you until this evening."

"I'll bet," Christopher grunted, as he moved toward the bed. "I said MOVE! Get off her." He slammed the barrel of Theresa's pistol against the Inquisitor's forehead and watched him fall to the floor. Even though blood gushed from a huge gash in his head, Alvarez still smiled. "Theresa, untie Isabella."

"I should have moved faster," Alvarez said from the floor. His tone was conversational, as if they were discussing the weather. "You were seen with that idiot, Morales, two nights ago. I was planning to get to you tonight or tomorrow, but I have been busy with other things." Without warning, he yelled, "Martinez!" at the top of his lungs.

It was Christopher's turn to smile. He walked over to where Alvarez was sitting on the floor, said, "I don't think your bodyguard will be of much use to you," then swung the pistol with all his might, destroying Alvarez's frozen smile and most of the face behind it.

"Is he dead?" Theresa asked. She had untied Isabella and helped her to a sitting position. Isabella clutched a sheet in front of her and peered, still in shock, at the bloody pulp that had been the Inquisitor's face.

Christopher looked at Alvarez' hairy, heaving chest, and shook his head. "Not yet, but . . ." He grabbed a bloody pillow from the bed, placed it over the pistol and prepared to administer the coup de grace.

"Please, Major!" Isabella was off the bed, still clutching her covering. She placed her hand on the pillow. "Please!" Her eyes blazed. Christopher shrugged, handed her the pistol and watched as she lowered the pillow-covered pistol to the Inquisitor's raw mouth and pulled the trigger.

Within ten minutes, the occupants of the Casa de Ponce de Leon had packed their bags and, one by one, left the house, never to return. Theresa, the last to leave, posted a long-prepared quarantine sign that read, 'Danger! CHOLERA-CHOLERA-CHOLERA.' For three years the four prostitutes and their chaperon had supplied bits and pieces of priceless information to *Cuba Libre!*. In the process they had passed along tens of thousands of pesos, most of which bought arms, ammunition and medicine. Although they had suffered countless indignities and numerous instances of physical pain, they knew that hundreds of thousands of others, *insurrectos* and civilians alike, had suffered far worse.

When Christopher, Theresa and Judith arrived in the room he had reserved at the *Inglaterre*, he turned to Theresa and asked, "Can you go through with this as we've planned?"

Theresa did not hesitate, though she was frightened and exhausted by what they had just done. "Of course, Christopher. What other choices have we?"

Christopher nodded. "You have half an hour for a bath. We will leave for the *Maine* at 5:30."

Chapter Thirteen

SPAIN REFUSES TO APOLOGIZE, ARMS SIX MERCHANT SHIPS;
WE ORDER SHOT AND SHELL

Madrid, Febuary 14—Work has begun in Cadiz for arming as fast cruisers six ships belonging to the Spanish Transatlantic Company Line. The steamer Ciudad de Cadiz, which will escort to Havana the squadrons of torpedo boat chasers, will be armed with ten guns. Startling news today of threatened trouble between Spain and the United States. The situation is extremely critical.

* * * * *

UNITED STATES FLEET ASSEMBLES NEAR KEY WEST
ORDERS ARE PLACED FOR ALL KINDS OF PROJECTILES,
AND CONGRESS CALLS UPON THE ADMINISTRATION
FOR INFORMATION ABOUT CUBA

Biggest Filibustering Expedition of the War Gets Away with Millions of Cartridges—President McKinley Expected to Announce Action to be taken by the United States. *The New York Journal,* February 15.

* * * * *

OFFICERS OF BATTLESHIP MAINE ENTERTAINING
*Our Sailors Grim and Ready for War, But Insist on Being
Good Hosts*

Havana, Febuary 15 — The battleship *Maine,* presently anchored at buoy Nine in Havana Harbor, is spic and span and ready for any eventuality. The officers of the *Maine* have been entertained at the Spanish clubs by sundry government officials, who are very formal but quite courteous. Captain Sigsbee and his officers, who are just as formal, have been wining the Spanish officials and officers aboard the *Maine. The World,* February 15.

Havana

Ensign Ephraim Pratt was used to falling in love, often and easily. The freckle-faced Mormon had fled the mountain kingdom of Utah because ardor for the Bishop's oldest daughter had over-powered his fear for his own skin. Had he been less prone to fall for every attractive face that returned his warm smile, Pratt might have questioned Theresa's flattering attention. But he was already swept away in a world of fantasy: The images dancing before his eyes sprang from old tales of Negro women and savage sexual appetites.

Theresa sat on his right and Jackson on his left. On Theresa's right sat a Spanish colonel who spent the dinner hour monopolizing Lt. Commander Smith's attention. Although Ensign Bedford had glanced covertly at Theresa every time he'd had the chance, she had ignored him. And even though the tall planter had exchanged minor pleasantries with her during the evening, he was rambling on about the intricacies of growing, harvesting and refining sugar cane to George Bedford, who sat on his left. For all practical purposes, Pratt had the delicious Theresa to himself.

"Are you enjoying the crepes, Miss Valdez?"

"Ah, but of course. Everything ees very deeleecious." She smiled her thanks, as if giving him the entire credit for such a sumptuous feast. "Deed you eat like thees in Oo-tah?"

Pratt laughed and tried to ignore Bedford's malevolent glare. "No, ma'am. I sure didn't. For one thing, we didn't have the fixin's to make things like this. And besides..."

"Pratt. I really doubt that our guest wants to listen to another of your illiterate Mormon yarns. Perhaps Miss Valdez would prefer to discuss less quaint primitivisms."

Christopher smiled into his napkin and waited to see how Theresa would respond.

"Please excuse me, Ensign….Oh, I am veree sorry but I seem to have lost your name. Maybe…" She smiled sheepishly.

"Bedford. George Bedford, Harvard, '95." Bedford drew himself erect in his chair and thought, Finally! I have her attention.

"Oh, thank you. Eet ees good of you to remind me," Theresa replied with enchanting innocence. "Now thees Harbert ninety-seex I don't know. Ees that part of your *llamo*, your, er…name? Or ees that maybee your house street *numero?*"

Theresa pushed sweetly on. "What I want to say, Mr. Beebfart, ees that I find thees storees of Mr. Pratt's to be tres charmant, and I also find Mr. Pratt to be tres charmant."

Watch it! Theresa, Christopher thought. Don't over-play your hand. While he listened to Pratt's story, he watched Bedford's hands. The young New Yorker had returned to rigid control. Slowly and carefully, he finished the last two bites of his dessert, folded his napkin with elaborate attention to precise creases, waited for his adversary across the table to come to a natural break in his tall tale, then excused himself politely and left.

After the interruption of his adversary's exit, Ephraim Pratt smiled joyously and talked on. "Besides that, my old man kept Ma in such a state that she couldn't keep her mind on her cookin' much. He was a polygamous circuit-rider who'd trot from one of his one mule ranches to the next, usually in an advanced state of religious and sexual frenzy.

"He'd come around once, maybe twice a month. A couple days before he was supposed ta show, Ma'd start gettin' edgy. When she saw the old man climbin' up the wash on his little mustang, her lips'd turn thin and white, and her whole body'd tighten up like a strung bow. She wouldn't be good fer much but cryin' fer a good week after he left on his rounds. Then fer a couple days she'd be kinda cheery. She'd do some cooking—but nothing like this, you understand—and play with the little ones. But then after a couple days, she'd start ponderin' my old man and then she'd start movin' over towards bein' edgy again."

Theresa was so moved by the story that she dropped her napkin. She and Pratt bent over at the same time to pick it up. Their heads touched and her hand brushed lightly along Pratt's thigh.

He felt his father's powers move within him. More than anything in the world he wanted an excuse to again touch or be touched by her. In the next minute she asked two questions. The first took him halfway to heaven; the second moved him at least a quarter of the way back to earth.

"Chreestopher said you might geeve me a tour of the sheep. Would that be good for a woman to do?"

Pratt nodded, beaming. "Miss Valdez, it would by my pleasure."

"Are you coming, Chreestopher?" she asked, still smiling at Pratt with her large, vulnerable eyes. Jackson nodded amiably and rose from the table.

Why does he want to come? Pratt wondered. Damn it! He's seen the blasted ship already. But Pratt nodded and started from the Mess, Theresa at his side and Christopher in tow. When she took his arm and smiled gratefully up at him, Pratt knew elation and all but forgot they had a chaperone.

Her arm in Pratt's, Theresa walked along the polished hardwood deck and reviewed Christopher's instructions. Within seconds of entering the paint locker, a stop which she must instigate, she would develop a headache. While in the Paint Locker she must distract this amusing fool long enough for Christopher to plant the bomb.

As they moved out of Navy Stores and approached the Paint Locker, Pratt concluded another tall tale. "So while my old man was in the cabin performin' his sacred duty with my Ma on that worn out old sack of corn shuck that passed fer a mattress, I climbed aboard his mustang and lit out fer San Diego and the United States Navy."

Theresa laughed and looked up admiringly. "Excuse me, Ephreem. Ees eet good that I call you Ephreem?"

"Sure enough. Can I call you Theresa?" When she smiled, Pratt turned to Christopher, who was still walking to their rear, and raised his eyebrows, as though asking her father's consent.

Christopher laughed and said, "Just call me Christopher."

"Ephreem? What's een thees room here?" She stopped and turned her head back toward the Paint Locker.

"That? That, sweet Theresa, is one helluva mess. Paints, shellacs, thinners, you know, stuff like that."

"Oh, good! My father painted the houses. I love thees smell." She started to pull the latch, but Pratt stepped in ahead of her, bowed, smiled and jerked open the heavy metal hatch.

"I hate the smell," Christopher complained. "I'll wait out here." But as soon as the love-birds turned down the first aisle, he stepped inside the locker. Since he had twisted the timing wires together just before coming aboard ship, Christopher required only a few seconds of the long minute Theresa provided. With one hand he lifted the pile of light, cheesecloth swipes. With the other he extracted the cheesecloth-wrapped package from his inside pocket and inserted it toward the bottom of the pile.

Almost as soon as she rounded the corner of the aisle, Theresa fell to the floor. "Jumpin Jehohvah! Theresa? What happened?" Pratt leaned over, his concerned eyes riveted to her legs, which were exposed to view.

"My ankle. I tweested eet, just a leetle beet, I think." She tried to rise, then held out her arm for assistance. When the enchanted ensign managed to get her to her feet, she was standing six inches away and looking up into his blue eyes. He bent down and received the most open, totally inviting kiss he would ever know. Her arm dropped down to the open V at the top of his buttocks. For a brief second she pushed herself against his glory.

"Not yet, Ephreem. Please!" She was panting. "We must wait a leettle. My heart, she ees too excited. See?" She took a deep breath, as if to control the chaos he had created in her blood, grabbed his hand in both of hers and placed it between her breasts. "Can you feel how eet ees beating so hard?"

"Yes! Yes, I can, sweet Theresa. I love you!"

"No, sweet man. Eet ees too fast for love. Please! We must go." And she led him out into the passageway, where Christopher waited.

Half an hour later, just as they stepped ashore from the launch, Christopher said, "That was a superb performance, Theresa. You were perfect."

She smiled. "I really do like him, Christopher. He does have a certain charm."

He felt something like jealousy, shook his head and said, "I'll meet you and Judith at the stable in fifteen minutes. Be ready to ride."

Theresa nodded and reached up to touch his shoulder. "Christopher?"

"We can talk later, Theresa."

"Christopher?" Her voice was insistent, entreating.

"What?"

"You are sure that your warning will work and that none of those young men will be hurt?"

He had been wondering the same thing. According to Morales, the bomb was set for six hours. "No, Theresa, I am not sure. But I have prepared a warning. There should be plenty of time for them to evacuate the ship."

"What if they do not leave the ship, Christopher?"

He shrugged, feigning a stoic acceptance he did not feel. "Well, I guess it depends on what kind of chaos an explosion in the paint locker can trigger. It may not damage much, though hopefully at least enough for our purposes. Given the right—or maybe wrong—circumstances, the ship could end up blowing apart. We shall see."

"Yes." She looked worried, but nodded curtly and headed back toward the hotel.

He watched until she had turned a corner, then followed her in the direction of the Ingleterre and the American Consulate. When he was two blocks from the hotel, Christopher looked around for a likely messenger. A young boy, his arms and legs so emaciated that they could pass for broomsticks, walked in Christopher's direction. When the latter whistled, the boy stopped and looked. "Hey, little man, do you want to make ten pesetas?" The boy stopped and stared at him so long that Christopher repeated the question.

Miguel was immediately suspicious. He had been on his own since his mother's death the year before, and had survived only by learning quickly. One of the first lessons was, Trust no one, especially if he called you 'friend' or 'little man.' Still, ten pesetas was a lot of money for someone who had eaten nothing but bits of garbage for three days. "What must I do?" Miguel struck what he thought to be his toughest pose.

"Deliver this message." Christopher took the note from his pocket and held it out like a bill of sale. "Do you know where the American Consulate is?"

"In the rich man's hotel, no?"

Christopher nodded. "Deliver this message to the guard on the second floor of the hotel."

"What else?"

"Nothing else. But it is very important that you deliver the message. Can you do that?"

"But, of course, sir. I am not stupid."

Christopher grunted and handed Miguel the note, printed in Spanish, which read: "Officer of the Day, American Consulate, Havana. The Spanish have planted a submarine bomb under the hull of the battleship *Maine*. The bomb will detonate the night of February 15." No signature, no alias, no instructions as to what should be done. Christopher fished two five peseta notes from his pocket and handed them to Miguel. "I want your note delivered by 9:00 tonight. "Is that a problem?"

"So I have time to eat first, no?"

Christopher nodded. "Here's another five pesetas for food. Just do not forget."

Miguel nodded solemnly. "I am your man, sir. Do not worry!"

After watching the boy turn around the corner to the night market, Christopher headed for the stables. A few minutes later he stopped and listened to a distant clock toll 8:30 P.M.

When Miguel arrived at the night market, the first smell he sensed was that of cooking garlic. Within the next twenty minutes he ate two large plates of rice, beans and pimento, each plate topped with a deep-fried snapper. As soon as he was stuffed, he realized how tired he was. After a long nap curled up in an alley, he remembered his promise to the rich man.

He was half way back to the hotel when the first blast riveted him in his tracks. Like so many other people that night, Miguel's first reaction was wonder. As soon as he heard the second blast, he turned and ran toward the harbor.

* * * * *

"Danged nice evening," Ensign Pratt thought out loud as he paced slowly back and forth across the forward deck. He stared across the harbor and conjured up before his unfocused eyes the sensuous face of Theresa Valdez, with whom, he was sure, he was madly in love. What a wonderful listener, he thought. With her gazing into my eyes I could spin yarns to eternity and back. Pratt lifted his sleeve and savored the perfume that clung faintly to his dress whites. He could still sense the glow that had poured over him when they had come together in the Paint Locker, their hungry mouths seeking each other, and her breasts and loins pressed against his body.

But even as he savored the moment, a thought black as a coiled snake rose to trouble his reverie. The warm glow cooled. There was something wrong with the whole incident. He leaned against the railing, stared into the still, brown waters of the harbor, and tried to reconstruct the evening, this time from a more objective point of view.

Jackson had brought Theresa aboard about 17:30 hours. Why had he brought her along? Sure she was his sister-in-law—or so they both said. But almost from the moment of stepping aboard ship, Jackson had, consciously or not, planted Theresa where Pratt would be sure to engage her in conversation. Why? Had the planter been trying to set him up for his own amusement?

And what about the tour they'd taken after dinner? If Jackson was sufficiently sensitive to drop a few steps behind so Pratt and Theresa could enjoy each other's attentions in semi-privacy, why hadn't he been sensitive enough to stay in the wardroom and let them take the tour alone? Why had he wanted to go along? Was he that interested in the *Maine*?

He thought of Theresa's eyes as she had descended the gangplank to the waiting launch, her face staring up at his for one last meeting. What was it he had seen in those huge chocolate orbs? Sadness? Regret? Suddenly his mother's face came into focus. Why? Her skin was taut, her lips a hard, thin line across her hatchet face. His father was coming, and she was already drawing away from a world that she dreaded. Pratt had seen the same tautness of apprehension on Christopher's face. What was he dreading?

The pieces wouldn't quite fit together, so he shook his head to clear the dark mood. His mind drifted back to Theresa, the sense of her breasts pressed against him and the softness of her lips. He raised his arm again and breathed deeply of the perfume that clung like a desperate memory to his linen sleeve. He sniffed again, gazed dreamily toward Havana and smiled the last smile of his life.

He heard or, rather, felt a muffled explosion somewhere deep within the ship. A few seconds later he heard a huge blast. The deck beneath his feet leaped sharply. Had he not been holding onto the railing he would have been thrown overboard. He turned instinctively and started for the closest ladder well and his duty station. In the seconds between the first major blast and the second, two jumbled thoughts crashed together: Was he that interested in the *Maine*? The Paint Locker.

By the time the second blast blew the great white ship apart, Ensign Pratt had already reached the ladder well and leaped down the first few steps. One tentacle of the second blast shot up the ladder well, tore off his legs below the knee and blew him into the harbor. In the fraction of a second that separated him from his past and the epiphany that was cascading over him, he saw Theresa's eyes, very knowing, very sad. She was standing in the launch and looking up at him, waving good-bye.

* * * *

When the *Maine* blew apart at 9:40, Theresa, Judith and Christopher had barely crossed the *Rio Almanderes* and into the countryside that swept from the hills of *La Habana*. They had covered less than five miles of their long trip to the east.

"What was that?" Judith asked after the second blast.

"I don't know," Christopher answered truthfully and spurred his mount to a canter. Though he tried to appear indifferent to the blasts, he was worried. Certainly it was not the *Maine*. He pulled out his pocket watch. Not even 10:00. The bomb should not go off for at least another hour and a half. But perhaps the watchmaker had made a mistake. Maybe he had misunderstood Guillermo's instructions. Or maybe Morales…He shivered.

If it was the *Maine*, Christopher knew that his warning may not have been sufficient. Not that he gave a tinker's damn about America. He loved the red clay of Georgia, which he sometimes missed. He loved his brother, Alex, and he loved the principles that had evolved from the American Revolution, which he wanted for his adopted home. As was the case with many southern expatriates, however, toward the United States he had never felt love or loyalty. The sailors aboard the *Maine* were a different matter.

Upon leaving the Alhambra that evening, Amos Jordan ambled along the seawall wondering what, if anything, he had missed by not dining aboard the *Maine*. He was looking directly at the great white battleship when the first explosion seemed to lift it out of the water. Since there was no immediate sign of smoke or fire, Jordan was not sure he should believe what his senses had just told him.

In the long seconds that separated the second and much larger blast from the first, the world stopped; everyone along the seawall halted, as if caught in mid-stride. The only sound to be heard during that long slice of silence was the cawing of gulls as they rose angrily from their perches on the guano-covered rocks.

Before the frozen spectators could even begin to register what had taken place, the second and third blasts blew the ship apart. Much of the ship's stern and super-structure exploded in different directions, and blew white-clad sailors into the sky before they fell back into what was already a cauldron or into the dark waters. The forward half of the *Maine* rose ten feet out of the water then settled back as an unrecognizable mass of contorted steel. The entire harbor lighted up to one brilliant flash and then subsided to an uneven glow, as smoke and flame and secondary explosions rose from the forward magazines and boilers.

Amos Jordan was staggered by the blasts, and by the probable consequences of the *Maine's* destruction, which swept over him as a great psychic after-shock. He fell to his knees and rested his forehead on the top of the sea wall. Increasing numbers of shouting people ran toward the landing where small boats were already heading for the great, smoking wreck of a ship. Jordan remained glued to the sea wall for a long time, and many of the less frantic passers-by assumed he was praying for the dead. They lowered their voices and crossed themselves. What was flashing through Jordan's mind, however, was not prayer but despair. Whatever—or whoever—had caused the destruction of the *Maine*, the results would be the same: The work of all the diplomats of Madrid and Washington, the concern of most European powers trying to keep America out of the war—all had come to naught. Even in his wildest dreams, Jordan could not have anticipated such a total reversal of the optimism he had begun to nurture earlier in the afternoon. Despite a series of incredibly stupid moves on the part of the Spanish ambassador to Washington, the "Cuban Problem" seemed to be stumbling toward resolution. The sinking of the *Maine* could not have come at a worse time.

After close to ten minutes of paralysis, Jordan rose to his feet and limped toward the landing, where several hundred people had already gathered. He pushed his way slowly through the crowd to where the bodies were being sorted. With the arrival of the first boat load of charred and bloody sailors, the crowd fell into a buzzing silence, huddled in small, whispering groups or withdrew into their own thoughts. The landing and seawall slowly filled with these shocked witnesses, random filings pulled toward the harbor by the irresistible magnet of disaster. Although most of them were far less aware than Amos Jordan of the probable consequences, many sensed that they were part of a major event. Whether Loyalist or revolutionary, Spaniard, Cuban or expatriate, they sensed that this night would change their lives.

Horse-drawn ambulances from both the private and the military hospitals filed slowly by the head of the landing. As the rescue boats pulled in, volunteers lifted the bodies and placed them in two rows, one for the still living and one for the dead. Within a few hours it would be apparent that well over two hundred sailors and marines had lost their lives.

A few survivors seemed to be untouched by the blast, and those who could pitched in to help. A few others, lost in shock, wandered aimlessly around the landing until someone led them like blind children to one of the waiting ambulances. Amos Jordan made no attempt to help with the wounded. Rather, he stood between the double row of bodies and the rotating ambulances and examined the faces of the dead and wounded, searching for acquaintances. He felt a deep need to relate to the concrete, personal and particular elements of the nightmare unfolding before his eyes. Jordan had always been forced by his job to think in terms of the macrocosmic, of national and international cause and effect. But at this moment he was rooted to the microcosmic, to the here and now, to the particular, individual consequences of abstract political movements.

Among the dead, the living and the maimed, Jordan recognized Lt. Commander Smith, who had either drowned or been killed by the concussion. His body was intact and nowhere was there a sign of blood. One of the stewards limped by, his black face covered with blood that bubbled from a ragged gash on the head. Jordan nodded to Ensign Perkins who, apparently unharmed, moved busily back and forth through the bodies, encouraging the conscious and helping to identify the more seriously wounded. Jordan gazed briefly at the body of Ensign George Bedford, his dead face contorted by intense pain, the bones of his twisted body jutting out at unnatural angles.

"Oh, no! Jesus! It's Pratt." Ensign Perkins stood beside the litter, tears running down his face. Jordan walked over and put his arm around Perkins' shoulder as a Spanish soldier and two civilians placed a writhing body on a stretcher and carried it toward the waiting line of ambulances. Jordan looked down at the stretcher and felt his knees buckle. Though the nameplate on the tunic read, "Pratt, Ephraim L., Ensign," the freckles and smile had disappeared, as had much of both legs. A deep channel of blood and pus slashed across the middle of what had been Pratt's face. From his round, open mouth one continuous scream rose up in crescendo, fell back to a guttural moan, then rose again, up and down, up and down, like a gross parody of a Jewish cantor at prayer. Even as the ambulance jerked and pulled away, the entirely self-conscious song of despair knifed through the hushed crowd.

Part II

REMEMBER THE *MAINE!*

Chapter Fourteen

U.S.S MAINE BLOWN UP IN HAVANA HARBOR
Destruction of the War Ship Maine Was the Work of an Enemy
* * * * *

ASSISTANT SECRETARY ROOSEVELT CONVINCED THE
EXPLOSION OF THE WAR SHIP WAS NOT AN ACCIDENT
* * * * *

The Journal Offers $50,000 Reward for the Conviction of the Criminals
Who Sent 258 American Sailors to their Death. Naval Officers Unanimous
That the Ship Was Destroyed on Purpose.

The suspicion that the *Maine* was deliberately blown up grows
stronger every hour. Not a single fact to the contrary has been produced.
Captain Sigsbee, of the *Maine*, and Consul General Lee both urge that
public opinion be suspended until they have completed their investigation.
They are taking the course of tactful men who are convinced that there
has been a treachery. *The New York Journal*, February 16.
* * * * *

HEARD OF A PLOT TO BLOW UP THE *MAINE*

New York, Febuary 17—Dr. C.E. Pendleton arrived here yesterday from
Key West....Dr. Pendleton had been in Havana a few days only when
the story of the Maine having her guns leveled at Morro Castle began to
be circulated and discussed by the frequenters of the cafes. The rumor
naturally created excitement.

The sympathizers with the insurgents were open in their boasts that
the United States had at last awakened to the gravity of the situation and
was ready to act upon the slightest provocation.

On the other hand, the Spaniards were by no means reticent in their
threats and defiance. They did not hesitate to say that if the Americans
were not careful their fate would be a matter of history in a very few days.

Washington, D.C.

Though his alarm clock had gone off and another annoying storm was beating an irregular tattoo on his bedroom window, Alex fought to stay asleep. The last thing he wanted was to face one more in an endless stream of days shuffling papers at the War Department. Rather, he wanted to continue to dream of Charlotte and his desire for her. Just the night before, in a break from the dancing, he had maneuvered her into a side hall, kissed her cheeks and neck, then allowed his lips to move down to the swell of her bosom, half expecting to get slapped in the process. But Charlotte stared at him through emerald green eyes, smiled archly and said, "I rather liked that, Alex. Do it again," which he did.

Now, lying in bed and listening to the rain, Alex felt his blood swelling. While he wasn't at all sure that he was in love with Charlotte, he knew he desired her, and not only for her beauty and spirit. Her father, Richard Boggs was one of the richest men in Washington, and Charlotte was his only heir. If Alex could land her, the War Department could go hang.

Suddenly there was a loud, officious knock on his door. Alex leaped from his bed, donned his worn cotton robe and opened the door. Mrs. Crofts, his landlady, glared at his unkempt appearance, held out a tray that contained a pot of coffee, a small plate of rolls and *The World*. "Looks like war, if you ask me, Mr. Jackson," and with that pronouncement, she turned and stalked down the narrow hallway to her own rooms. What was that all about? Alex wondered, shaking his head. He placed the tray on the library table that took up a quarter of the space in his small parlor, sat down, poured himself a cup of coffee and opened the paper. "Oh, my God!" he whispered. Leaving his coffee to cool, Alex scanned the headlines and following articles then focused on the initial list of casualties.

"Oh, my God! Bedford!" He felt a hollowness in his stomach as he remembered his old classmate at Harvard.

Half an hour later, shaved, bathed but only half dressed and still lost in thought, Alex gazed through the steamed over parlor window at the gusts of rain. After a long while he lifted his hand, started to wipe away the mist, paused, then used his index finger to print: George Bedford/ Harvard, 1894/ Ensign, U.S.N./ b. 1873, d. Feb. 15, 1898/ In the service of his God, his race, and his flag.

Alex turned back to the table and his abandoned breakfast. A letter from George lay on top of the newspaper, the front page of which blazed with six inch high letters: *USS MAINE* EXPLODES IN HAVANA HARBOR. He picked up the letter with one hand, absently nibbled on a cold roll from the other and stared at the headline. "Impossible," he said aloud. "It's just not possible." Alex knew, however, that it was very possible. He sat down in his one chair and read the letter one more time.

Havana, February 9, 1898
Aboard the USS Maine

My dear Alex:
Your first reaction must be one of wonder. 'Why is George Bedford writing to me?' You may even be trying to remember, 'Who is George Bedford?' but I think not. I know we weren't close at Harvard, but we were in the same club, and we seem to have gotten on well enough. So.

I've met your brother! First at the Alhambra, a local club for the better sort of Cubans, and once since as our guest aboard the Maine. Because you once mentioned that he only wrote you every year or two, I thought you might like to know how he is. Mr. Jackson was rather pleased when I mentioned that I'd known you at school.

I'm sorry to say that he's had a rather hard time of it. Not only have the rebels burned his plantation. Worse, far worse. his wife and daughters recently died in one of Butcher Weyler's re-concentration villages. I'm sorry to be the bearer of such tidings, Alex, but I thought you ought to know.

Alex laid the letter aside for a moment as his heart went out to Christopher. While he had never met any of Christopher's daughters, had never even seen a photograph of them, he retained a sharp image of Consuelo, the petite, beautiful mulatto Christopher had introduced him to on one of his infrequent visits to the States. Though Alex had been somewhat disconcerted by Consuelo's racial background, he quickly found himself enchanted by her vitality and enthusiasm. And though initially bothered by the social implications of their inter-racial marriage, he quickly realized that approval or disapproval was not his prerogative. Well before their short visit to Cambridge ended, Alex found himself delighting in their obvious love for each other and his older brother's happiness. While Alex could not imagine Consuelo dead, he could very easily imagine the impact of her death on Christopher. What will he do without her, and without their children? Alex wondered. How will he continue on? What will he do with his life?

He walked into the room that served as both bedroom and study. It included a small writing desk and a shelf of books that featured the romantic and heroic novels of Charles Kingsley and Sir Walter Scott. He chose a blue and white striped cravat from his tie rack, fashioned a careful four-in-hand knot, donned his one tweed frock coat and stepped in front of the mirror mounted above his dresser to check the results. Alex stood just under six feet in height. A former running back on Harvard's football team, he was lean but muscular and graceful. He stared into the mirror, admired his full head of wavy blonde hair and the set of his grey eyes, practiced the smile he loved to flash when he sought to charm, which was often, and prepared to leave his small, two room lodgings for his job at the War Department. On his way through the parlor, he stopped, picked up George Bedford's letter and continued reading.

> *On a far different topic: I'll be glad when war comes, Alex, as it surely must. Promotions are awfully slow in peacetime. One of our lieutenants has spent fourteen years in his present rank and is almost forty. A good war with Spain will change all of that. It will give us younger men a chance to show our mettle.*
>
> *Unfortunately, the Spanish are exceedingly well behaved. We've been invited to concerts and balls. They keep their hot-eyed women pretty much out of reach, though I can't fault them for that. Other than the scarcity of available women, however, society here is rather pleasant. The Spanish are afraid of us and are being decent.*

I've seen some of the families of the rebels, or mambises *as they call themselves. Most of them are coloreds and mulattoes! Did you know that? They're ragged and half-starved. We visited one of the re-concentration towns on an inspection tour. It was a beastly sight! Many of the people were just lying in the dirt. They're only half-dressed and very primitive in their responses. Several of the women were trying to nurse their children and had their breasts exposed to public view. If these are the people who are behind the revolution, I fear for Cuba.*

The people show precious little evidence of ambition or resourcefulness. I sincerely doubt their ability to govern themselves. If we help them gain their freedom from Spain, we shall be here a long time. But then that's part of our responsibility as white men, isn't it?

That's about all from the Pearl of the Antilles. Your brother promises that he'll write soon. When the war begins, maybe you can obtain a commission and come on over. It should prove to be a glorious good time. Until then, I remain...

Alex stared again at the headlines of *The World*, felt a surge of determination and allowed Bedford's letter to drop to the floor. Within a minute he had left his lodgings and was rushing excitedly toward his office.

"Alexander Jackson would like a word with you, sir."

"Jackson? Jackson? The young Harvard man working in Procurement? Tell him to come on up." Despite his affable response to the clerk's announcement, John Alger, Secretary of War, was wary. Since shortly after midnight when the news came in from Havana, everyone in the world had been trying to see him, had been bombarding him with questions he couldn't answer and demands that he didn't even begin to know how to meet. Alger stroked his short white beard, glanced around the sumptuous corner office he had been occupying in the short month since his appointment by the newly elected President McKinley, and tried to place Jackson. What does that young whippersnapper want of me? Alger wondered, pulling out his watch to check the time. Still an hour to lunch, and he must be the tenth person who's been to see me today. What do they all expect me to do?

The Secretary of War groaned as he looked around at his desk, which was piled with telegrams, memos, lists, and bound documents. Where do I begin? he wondered, running his hands through his thinning salt and pepper hair. He knew he should be doing something, but what? There was just too much happening, and all of it far too quickly. Earlier that morning he had actually dictated a couple of letters and approved some reports. Now, however, he just sat behind his desk, feeling suffocated under the mountain of paper and visitors crushing down upon him. Alger was acutely aware of one reality: Unlike the Navy Department, which Theodore Roosevelt had succeeded in reorganizing in a matter of weeks, the War Department was a disaster. The Navy might very well be able to take on Spain and win major battles. The Army, however, was an organizational and logistical mess—short on men, short on modern weapons and munitions and, at least at the moment, capable of little more than chasing recalcitrant bands of savages around the western desert.

The clerk thrust his head inside the door. "Jackson's here, sir." Shortly after the head disappeared, Alex walked in.

"Good morning, General Alger. How are you, sir?"

"Fine Jackson, just fine. As you can see from my desk, it's a busy day. But we all have to gird our loins for the coming battle, eh?" Secretary Alger beamed benevolently. "Sit down, young man. Sit down. I hope you haven't been sent up here by that old reprobate, Lewis, to get money, because I don't have any to give. Congress is going to be as parsimonious as a Scot."

"No sir. I came up here on my own hook."

"You did, eh?" Alger relaxed slightly and began shuffling importantly through a file of meaningless lists that some clerk or other had placed on his desk. Alger knew that he couldn't do much for anyone at the moment. The sinking of the *Maine* had plunged all of Washington, and the War Department in particular, into a chaos from which he didn't expect ever to emerge. The Secretary hated requests for favors almost as much as he hated the need to make decisions and issue orders. He hated this generation of young fops who seemed so sure of themselves and so sure of America's destiny. At times he felt like screaming at them, but he was too good a politician for that. Alger's charm and political usefulness to the Republican Party had won him his appointment as McKinley's Secretary of War. And his charm would, he hoped, pull him through. In the meantime, however...He looked up at Jackson and smiled, "So, young man, what might I be able to do for you?

"Sir, I would like to obtain a commission in the army. I want to go to Cuba. I had a friend on the *Maine* and I'd like, well, I'd like to avenge his murder." During his short speech Alex looked the Secretary in the eye, but as soon as he finished, he heard his own breathlessness, like that of a child quoting a hope list to Santa Claus. He lowered his gaze.

"What makes you so sure there's going to be a war?" The Secretary watched Jackson carefully, pleased to note that he had scored a point. A sharp wave of surprise washed across the young man's face.

"Well, sir, they sank the *Maine* and..."

"We think the Spanish sunk the *Maine*. But we don't know that for a fact, do we?" All morning long, Alger thought, I've been pinned to the wall by salvoes of paper. Ah, but it feels good to be on the offensive.

Alex was startled by the Secretary's response. He knew the Spanish had blown up the *Maine*. Hell, the whole country knew it by now. Everyone in the War Department, hell, everyone in Washington, was running around like the capitol had been invaded. What in blue blazes is the old windbag talking about? "Sir? I don't understand. Surely there's going to be..."

"Surely there's going to be what? A war? Why is everyone in this damned place so hot and heavy about war? You all think that's the way to paradise?" The Secretary leaped to his feet with what he hoped to be taken as the spontaneity of righteous indignation. The gesture was marred, however. In the process of leaping, he managed to knock a foot high pile of documents from his desk. As he bent down to pick them up, Alex scrambled over to help. For the next few minutes the Secretary of War and the young clerk crawled around the office on their hands and knees, gleaning bureaucratic corn from the stubble field of Alger's oriental carpet.

Finally reseated behind his piled desk, the old politician decided to take a more educational approach. "Young man," he began confidentially, "you're probably right. There will be a war. Not because there should be one, however, and certainly not because we're ready to fight one. Congress wants a war because the people want a war, because the loudest demagogues want a war. So war it will probably be."

The Secretary again rose from his chair, this time in a more stately and considered fashion, and paced around the room. Alex craned his neck back and forth, twisting his body half out of his chair as he tried to follow Alger's movements.

"You work for Lewis in Procurement, right?"

"Yes, sir."

"How many procurement specialists—buyers, book-keepers, the like—do you think we have in the Army?"

"Twenty, maybe thirty."

"That really know what they're doing?"

"I don't know, sir, maybe half that. At most! I've been in the Department for almost four years now. I can't say that I'm very impressed by either the motivation or the energy displayed by most of my fellow bureaucrats. Other than Lewis himself, there's not one man in Procurement who was here when we last fought a war."

"Precisely. Most of you, like most of us, are political appointees. You got your job because you knew somebody and because that somebody, hopefully, was willing to exercise a little bit of blind faith."

"Well, General, I did graduate cum laude from Harvard. I'm a quick study and I take my responsibilities seriously." Even though they bore me half to death, he added silently.

"Surely you are. Surely you do." For a moment the Secretary felt like patting the young man on the head, just as he patted his collie when the affectionate animal seemed particularly eager to please, but he immediately thought better of it and continued his pacing. "If we have a war, and if you stay with us, you'll learn even faster. You'll have to. We all will. When this hypothetical war is finished we may have a modern, efficient, well-organized army. But right now we're a mess."

"Sir! America is the greatest country in the world. There are countries that look stronger, that have larger armies and navies, but they're on the downslide, sir. They're morally bankrupt. We're on the ascendant."

"Yes, we're on 'the ascendant,' as you so grandiloquently describe it, but I'm not quite sure what anybody's moral bankruptcy has to do with the question." Secretary Alger stared at Jackson as if he were a character in a Fourth of July tableau. My God! he thought. Is this the kind of naive romantic our colleges are producing? I must think about cutting back on my annual dole to Yale.

When Alex started stammering, Alger shook his head. "Hmmmph! God, destiny and morality may all be on our side, but that doesn't, in and of itself, guarantee world stature—especially among the powers you've just described as morally bankrupt." He glared into Jackson's wide and slightly shocked grey eyes, and decided to try still a different tack. "Do you know how many men we have on active duty in the Army?"

"About twenty-five thousand, sir,"

"Very good. Do you know how long it's been since anything as large as a brigade stood formation?"

Alex shook his head. "No, sir."

"Not since the War of the Rebellion. Not for more than thirty years. Less than two thousand men now on active duty have seen combat, and most of that was spent chasing half-starved squaws out the other side of Kansas City somewhere. And not very recently at that. Except for a few ragged Apaches in Arizona Territory, the savages have been quiet for years."

"Are you suggesting, sir, that we can't lick the Spanish?" Alex's tone mirrored his continued shock. He would not have believed such words could come from the Secretary of War, and from a general who had distinguished himself in the Army of the Potomac.

Secretary Alger pulled out his watch. "No, that's not what I'm suggesting. I'll put it to you as simply as I can, and then you, both of us, must get back to work. The machinery for making war is rusty, extremely rusty. Except for landing some marines at Veracruz during the Mexican War, we have no experience shipping troops by sea, or in affecting a landing. Getting people to fight is no problem. Getting the money to fight is no problem—providing, of course, that the size of Congress's appropriation proves to be at least half the size of its mouth. But getting arms and ammunition is a problem. Getting medicine and canned food is a problem. Getting trains and ships to haul men and guns and supplies is a problem. Getting generals to lead glorious charges is not a problem. Getting people who can coordinate them and keep them supplied is. That, young man, is the problem."

The Secretary stood up for the third and final time. "If you want to go off and chase chivalric rainbows, quit this office right now and go. If you want to charge after glory like those dead idiots in Tennyson's poem, go over to the Navy Department and talk to Roosevelt. He's certainly damned determined that he's going."

Alex stood up, disappointed and more than a little angry.

"Just a minute, young man. I'm not quite finished. If you want to make a contribution to this war you're so damned cock-sure we're going to have, stay here with me. Stay here at the War Department and try to get a handle on things. Cannon fodder's going to be a lot easier to come by than intelligent civil servants. However, if you decide that you just can't pass up this once-in-a-lifetime chance for military immortality, go ahead. But as far as I'm concerned at least, if you go, it will damned sure be without a military commission! Now let's get back to work."

The Secretary sat back down, bent over and shuffled through his papers. He looked at the titles of some, half-glanced at others, but signed all. He was still fuming when his chief clerk stuck his head in the door and announced the arrival of his luncheon appointment.

* * * * *

Alex couldn't believe his eyes. The outer office of the Assistant Secretary of the Navy looked like the hunting lodge of some Teutonic baron. Every square inch of wall space was hung with the trappings of western masculinity: photographs of Roosevelt branding cows and lassoing steers, standing in front of a lake holding a huge string of trout, standing with one foot propped on the neck of a downed elk, smoking a peace-pipe with half a dozen domesticated Indians, and sitting in front of a chuck wagon with cowboy cronies. Roosevelt was the center of each picture, and in each his chest protruded manfully. Sandwiched in between all the photographs were two paintings by Frederick Remington, the romantic illustrator who worked for Hearst at the *Journal*. Above the photographs and paintings, horns and antlers of every description jutted from the wall. Though Alex felt awed by the display, he knew instantly that he would like Roosevelt.

"May I help you?"

Alex shifted his focus from the wall. From behind a small desk across the room, a middle-aged woman wearing a starched cotton blouse, a narrow black tie and a pair of spectacles, stared at him. Though obviously amused, she was not surprised by such a reaction to her beloved Roosevelt's reception room.

"Uh, yes, ma'am. I'd like to see the Assistant Secretary, Mr. Roosevelt."

"May I have your name? sir."

"Jackson, Ma'am. Alexander Dumas Jackson."

"Was your father the Count of Monte Cristo?"

Oh, Jesus! Alex thought. Another one. "No, he was a Confederate cavalry major. Dumas was his favorite author. Is Mr. Roosevelt available?"

"What's your business?"

"I'm with the War Department. Procurement." Alex had come to talk about fighting, not procurement, but he knew he had to get into Roosevelt's presence before he could talk about anything.

"Mr. Roosevelt is conferring with some army and naval officers at the moment. I'll see if they care to be disturbed."

"That's all right, I'm in no hurry." But she was gone. Head erect and back ram-rod straight, she marched into the inner-sanctum without knocking and was on her way back before he could think what to do next, or what to say if she told him to go on in, which she did.

Alex took a deep breath and walked into the large, rustically decorated office as though he were a man of some importance. An army major, a navy captain, a commodore and Roosevelt were studying a huge wall-map of Cuba. Roosevelt stood on a bearskin rug, his right foot on the set, snarling head. He talked in a jovial, but intense voice, and whacked the map with a yardstick as he talked.

"So, as you say, Winnie, Havana harbor has a narrow mouth and Santiago harbor has a narrow mouth. So we blockade the harbors. Then what?"

"Well, Theodore, it's not going to take much to stop up the harbors, or, for that matter, to blockade the entire island. If we're lucky, we might even bottle up a part of Admiral Cervera's fleet. If we can accomplish most of that and patrol constantly around the island, Spain will have a difficult time re-supplying her army." Commodore Winfield Scott Schley saw Alex standing just inside the door and stopped talking.

Roosevelt whacked the map twice more, exclaimed, "Yes, Winnie. We can do that," and strode briskly over to Alex, hand out-stretched. "Theodore Roosevelt. What can I do for you?"

"My name is Alexander Jackson. I'm from Procurement over at the War Department.

"Well, fancy that. What is a clerk from the War Department doing over here at Navy?" Then, nodding briefly as if just struck by an idea, and without waiting for Alex to reply, Roosevelt said, "Alex. I'd like to introduce you to some of my friends. Gentlemen, you heard who this young man is. Alexander…?"

"Alexander Jackson, sir."

"Yes. Alex. From Procurement. This is Commodore Winfield Scott Schley. Captain Scott Mahon. And this soldier over here is Major Leonard Wood, the 'fighting surgeon.'" The three men, who ranged in age from their mid-forties to mid-sixties, nodded and shook his hand. All three seemed more distant than Roosevelt, more aware of their positions and dignity. "Excuse us just a second, Alex. We'll be right with you." Roosevelt smiled and turned his back.

Of the three officers, Alex was most intrigued by the relatively young major, Leonard Wood, whose name he had heard and whose face was vaguely familiar. Wood had won the Congressional Medal of Honor fighting a renegade Apache called Geronimo. Tall, blonde and, like Roosevelt, still in his thirties, Wood seemed to breathe efficiency. He lacked Roosevelt's charisma but shared his friend's love of energy and organization, as well his impatience with laziness and mediocrity. Although a medical doctor and a member of the Surgeon General's staff, Wood had devoted more energy, talent and interest to killing savages than to healing soldiers. Alex knew that the major also served the new President as his personal surgeon.

All three of the men looked their roles. All were tall and thin. Schley and Mahon wore beautifully cultivated mustaches, gold braid and rows of campaign ribbons. Wood was more austere but just as authoritative. Clean-shaven and dressed in his blue cavalry uniform, his chest sported but one ribbon, the white stars on blue field of the Congressional Medal of Honor. Alex felt like a frumpy dude in his fancy cravat, soft-collared shirt and velvet-lined, tweed Prince Albert. And he felt very much at a disadvantage. He was less intimidated by Roosevelt, who seemed more affable and less stern.

The four men standing in front of the map were discussing congressional appropriations. Because Alex could hear every word, he felt like an ignored wart, conspicuous and useless. "Alger and I asked the old man to request a hundred million from Congress," Roosevelt said, "but we'll be lucky if he asks for half that, and he'll probably take a month even getting the request ready."

"I think you're being a little too hard on the President," Schley said.

"Wait and see, Winnie. If I were President, I'd have had a war message down to the Congress two hours ago. That gutless windbag doesn't even know what he's going to do, much less how or when. Those oily spics have insulted the dignity of this country, and all McKinley can do is sit over there in his oval office and wring his fat hands."

"Slow down, Theodore," Wood interrupted. "We've had the news about the *Maine* for less than twenty-four hours. Maybe we're getting just a bit ahead of ourselves. Besides, we can push all we want, but you should know by now that the President doesn't budge easily. Keep the pressure on. Have Hearst keep it on. In the meantime, until war comes, and come it will, let's concentrate on our job. Let's get ready for it."

The two naval officers choroused their assent. Roosevelt looked like he wanted to stamp his foot. Instead, he whipped the yardstick against his leg and glared at the map. Wood continued. "And let's not offend this young man's ears with negative talk about the President."

At the mention of the young man, Roosevelt's tone and appearance changed instantly. He turned back to Alex. "Procurement, right? Which branch?"

"Army, Sir."

Roosevelt and Wood exchanged glances. "Alex here may be just what the doctor ordered. Right, Doctor?" Wood frowned at the pleasantry he'd heard at least a hundred times. "Come over here and sit down. Let's do some serious talking."

Just as Alex was about to accept the invitation, Commodore Schley interrupted. He was the oldest of the group, the most formal and, as Alex was soon to discover, both a political ally and a social outsider. "I have a few chores before returning to my ship. Wire me if...anything develops. A pleasure meeting you, Jackson," he concluded without warmth, and left the room. Alex sensed the slight but immediate relaxation of the other men.

"He's certainly old school," Wood said.

"Yes, he is, Leonard," Mahon replied. "However, he's probably the most brilliant and daring commander in the Navy, and he's definitely an expansionist. He's already cabled Dewey at Hong Kong with some of our suggestions for an attack on Manila."

"True, but any man who doesn't like football must have something wrong," Roosevelt quipped, turning to Alex. "You like football?"

"Yes, sir. I played two years at Harvard. "

"Well, bully for you." Both Roosevelt and Wood grinned. Mahon smiled too, though slightly more cynically, as if to say, 'Here we go again.'

"Wood and I are both Harvard men, you know. Say, we're going to go out and throw a ball around for a while during the lunch hour. Care to join us? I knew there was something about you I liked."

"Yes, SIR! I'd love to," Alex said, and then turned to beam at Wood. "I knew I'd seen your face somewhere before, Major. Weren't you once President of the Debating Society? Your portrait's on the dining room wall."

"That's me," Wood smiled. "So you were a debater too…"

The conversation bounced merrily along between the three good old boys for another five minutes, with Captain Mahon, who had not had the good taste to graduate from Harvard, joshing all three. Then, without warning, Roosevelt decided to get back to business.

"All right, Alex. Why did Lewis send you over here?"

"He didn't, Mr. Roosevelt. I came over here on my own hook, and I…didn't…come over here to talk about procurement."

"Aha!" Mahon interjected. "Another plot by another devious Harvard man. Don't you Boston boys know anything about honor?" Alex thought Mahon was kidding, but he wasn't sure. "Why are you here?"

Alex took a deep breath and then gushed: "Rumor has it that you're determined to go to Cuba. So am I. I think war with Spain will be a glorious adventure. It will add to our possessions, guarantee our stature among the first rank of European powers. We should have driven Spain from the New World decades ago. I had a friend on the *Maine*. I want to do my share. I don't want to miss…"

"Stop!" Roosevelt held up his hands in mock surrender. "We're not the enemy. There's no need to talk us to death."

"That's all right, Teddy. He's for real." Mahon grinned mischievously. "He's a Havvud man all right."

"So, you think I'm going to Cuba and you think I can help you to go along? Question: What can you do to help me?" Roosevelt eyed Alex speculatively. "Are you a leader of men? Were you captain of any teams at school? Were you president of anything? Have you been in charge of anything?"

"Well, no...I guess I haven't. But I graduated cum laude, and I've received two promotions in the four years since I've been in Procurement."

"But you're not really able to offer much, are you?" Roosevelt quarried good-naturedly.

"Now wait a minute, Theodore," Major Wood cautioned. "Alex here might have quite a bit to offer. If your plans for a volunteer cavalry regiment materialize..."

"Doggone it, Lenny. I've told you already. Don't worry. We'll get that regiment together if I have to wrestle McKinley and Alger at the same time with one hand tied behind my back." Roosevelt struck a fighter's pose and grimaced at Wood, who ignored him and continued.

"If our plans materialize, we're going to be fighting the regular army and every National Guard unit and every other volunteer outfit—for supplies, for ammunition, for everything, right? Remember what you said when Alex here first came in? 'He may be just what the doctor ordered.'"

Roosevelt pondered Wood's remarks for a moment and then chuckled. "Yep, you're right, Lenny. Come on. Let's go play some football," he said, placing his arm around Alex's shoulder and giving it a manful squeeze.

Chapter Fifteen

AMERICAN WOMEN READY TO GIVE UP HUSBANDS, SONS AND
SWEETHEARTS TO DEFEND THE NATION'S HONOR
*Love of Country and Reverence for the "Old Flag" Outweigh the
Devotion Which Binds Man and Wife and True! Lovers*

* * * *

WIDOWS WOULD HAVE THEIR SONS GO TO BATTLE TO
UPHOLD THE NATION'S HONOR

World correspondents in leading cities in America were instructed yesterday to obtain the views of representative women on the relations between the United States and Spain, and learn from them whether, should war be declared, they would be willing to send their loved ones to the front. The following opinions were obtained:

Washington, April 20—Mrs. M.A. Gatewood, No. 1314 Ninth St., NW. I am a widow and have but one son, my sole support. Should the honor and protection of our country require him to go to the war, I should send him forth most willingly, believing that "He without whose will not even a sparrow falls" will care for both him and me.

New Orleans, April 21—Mrs. J. Pinckney, No. 258 Carondeiet Street. I have plenty of national pride and patriotism. I believe that in the South the love of country is as intense as in any part of the Union. I believe the mothers of the South would send their sons and husbands to fight for the Union just as willingly as they sent them to fight for the Confederacy.

Richmond, Va., April 20—Miss Carolyn Martin. Let every American woman remember and heed the words of the women of Sparta. Let the God-given spark of patriotism glow till family ties—aye, and tender ties—are shriveled by the heat. Let them say, to brother and lover alike, "Take thy shield: return with it—or on it.!" *The World*, April 21.

Arlington, Virginia

At eighteen, Charlotte Boggs was aware of her youth, her wealth and her position. Though she was naive, inexperienced and much taken with the glitter of her social world, Charlotte was more intelligent than anyone but her doting father realized. She knew that her beauty was, at best, perishable capital, and that her intelligence was hardly a marketable commodity. Rather than trying to dazzle company with her wit, she summarized what others said, always laughed at other's witticisms, and nodded knowingly or frowned severely whenever she felt such expressions to be appropriate. Charlotte concentrated on the two qualities men seemed to want from their women: looking pretty and encouraging suitors to talk about themselves. Though she often wished that they would at least occasionally listen seriously to what she had to say, Charlotte had become quite expert, she thought, at the two things she had been raised to think men thought they wanted.

Although Charlotte felt that Alex would propose to her this evening, she was not about to leave anything to chance. She sat down at her dressing table, glared into the mirror and frowned. She wanted to be at her most attractive best for her father's party, but as often as she pinched her cheeks, she could not get the color to stay. Finally, mildly disgusted, she dipped her index finger into a small pot of rouge, dabbed a bit on each cheek, rubbed vigorously, grabbed a handkerchief and rubbed some more until she thought she'd obliterated the evidence. Charlotte was not pleased with her complexion, which she perceived to be her worst feature. As usual, however, she was determined to do all she could with her various gifts. She searched her face one more time.

Finally smiling, she ran her tongue slowly over her lips. My teeth are one of my best assets, she thought. My teeth and my bosom. She pulled down hard on her tightly cinched, whale-bone corset and exposed

another half inch of pale, firm flesh. After patting her red curls and cursing the unruliness of her hair, she stood up and practised her various
poses. Well, she thought, staring critically into the mirror, guess I'm
ready for Alex—and Father.

Mr. Boggs had finally come around to accepting Alex as a suitor,
which had taken some serious conniving on her part. The stage was
now set. The two men had been getting on much better the past few
weeks, ever since her father discovered that Alex was working well with
Roosevelt. At the end of Alex's last visit, her father had invited him into
the library for cigars and brandy. Still, whether her father would allow
Alex to ask for her hand remained an open question.

Charlotte left her dressing room and glided down the winding stairs
to the salon. To add to her scant five feet, she wore her red curls piled
and twisted atop her head. She had lightly powdered her face, arms and
exposed bosom to hide the sheen that would develop during the course
of the evening. Charlotte knew that her green taffeta dress and single
sapphire necklace complemented perfectly her red hair and cream complexion. Now safely away from her critical mirror, she felt very beautiful
and very sure of herself.

Richard Boggs had invited twenty more-or-less important people
to dinner, and many of the guests had already arrived. As she swept
gracefully down the stairs, like Dolly Madison, she thought, Charlotte
relished the short hush that fell over the room. While women's eyes were
sometimes critically, albeit jealously, perceptive, her effect on men, particularly older men, was always the same, and she loved it. She moved
smoothly from group to group, listening to the conversation, exchanging pleasantries and searching for Alex.

Everyone was talking of the war and what was likely to come of it.
After two months of trying to avoid the issue, the President had finally
prepared his war message and was sure to send it down to the Congress
within the next day or two. And of Congress's response no one had
even the least doubt. The Naval Board of Inquiry had determined, to
everyone's not at all surprised satisfaction, that Spain had torpedoed the
Maine. From the war, bound to be short and glorious, America would
emerge with an empire.

One of the guests was the British military attache, a thin, stiff colonel in his mid-forties who stuttered slightly when he got excited, which

he tried not to do. Colonel Harrington-Smythe had spent most of his career in India and held strong opinions about the superiority of Anglo-Saxon civilization.

At calmer moments during the preceding years, many members of his audiences tended to be somewhat critical of his arrogance and outspoken snobbism, even though they also tended to share his views. In the electric atmosphere of a capital girding for war against Catholic Spain, however, many greeted the opinions of men like Harrington-Smythe with sagacious, agreeable and self-congratulatory nods. Certainly the white race was superior to the dark. Any examination of the progress made by the peoples of northern Europe and America, as compared to the almost willful backwardness of other countries, demonstrated that. Even in Europe it was possible to make distinctions between the northern, Protestant countries and the southern, Catholic countries. In the long crusade of those carrying the White Man's Burden, the drive to bring progress and enlightenment to the darker and duller races of the globe, the lion's share of the burden would have to be carried by the Protestants, for they best understood the principles behind the dynamo of industrial progress, and how to apply them.

"I suppose the only sporting thing you can do after defeating Spain is to annex her former colonies." Harrington-Smythe was in his glory. He stood gracefully, his left arm perched on the mantle, his right hand swishing a half-empty glass of sherry. That he cut an elegant figure in his red and blue Horse Guards' uniform, he was smugly aware.

"I mean, those people certainly aren't capable of governing themselves, are they? I've been to Cuba and Puerto Rico. The natives are mostly niggers and illiterate peasants. They're no more capable of self-government than the wogs of India."

Harrington-Smythe stopped to sip his sherry, allowing a brief look of ecstasy to pass over his face. He was a man of exquisite refinement and believed he should allow his sensitivity to show; women appreciated such displays of subtlety. He allowed his eyes to dwell for a fraction of a second on Charlotte's ample bosom and rise slowly to sweep across her face. Her eyes were wide open, as if she were listening to a prophet, and her bosom heaved with feigned excitement. My God, but I'd like to bed the little vixen, he thought, continuing his lecture on intellectual and moral superiority.

Charlotte felt pressure on her elbow and turned around to meet her father and Alex. She smiled up at Alex with open admiration. He was growing a mustache, which was coming in slightly less blonde than his wavy hair. He'd been spending most of his spare time riding in the parks and shooting at the rifle range, and his office pallor had given way to a deep tan which, added to his grey eyes and new mustache, created quite a dashing combination. Charlotte was pleased with him. Not that she really wanted to marry him. I mean, after all, she was fond of telling herself, he doesn't have any money or any real position. But he excited her, partly because of how he affected her physically, but also because he seemed to actually listen to her and to at least consider her opinions. Whether to marry him or not was a decision for later, after he came back from the war. For the moment she knew only that she wanted to spend as much time with him as she could, and to be far closer to him physically than propriety would allow. She thought it would be exciting to be engaged to him, and was sure he'd ask her.

Alex's fingers caressed the inside of her wrist and a slight thrill raced along her legs and back. Rather than speaking, Alex just smiled slightly and gazed down into her light green eyes. He was listening to Harrington-Smythe, and found himself agreeing with almost everything the man said.

Charlotte's father was less impressed. Richard Boggs was almost seventy years old. After spending much of his life acquiring a fortune in Washington real estate, he had traded some of his money for the socially acceptable but sexually frigid daughter of the senior senator from Virginia. Other than social position, he had gained nothing from the marriage—except Charlotte, who was one of his two consuming loves; the other was making money.

Boggs had learned early in his career that the self-serving intellectualizing of men like Harrington-Smythe was no more than pompous nonsense. Chauvinistically-inspired moral principles, especially when voiced by mindless snobs, were so much drivel. The only valid reason for going to Cuba was economic gain. Americans had invested in Cuba, and were eager to invest much more. Spain had already had sufficient time to demonstrate her inability to maintain order. Therefore, America should replace Spain as controller of the island. It was that simple.

Boggs grabbed Alex's arm and pulled him away from Harrington-

Smythe's attentive audience. Alex and Charlotte exchanged suitably disappointed looks, then Charlotte turned back to the tall Britisher and Alex accompanied Mr. Boggs onto the veranda.

"Cigar, young man?"

"Yes, sir. Don't mind if I do."

The two men carefully unwrapped their cigars, which had been grown in Cuba and wrapped in Tampa. They paid careful obeisance to each step of the time-honored ritual: They sniffed their cigars, held them out at arm's length for general inspection, bit off the ends, took initial puffs and exhaled with consummate satisfaction. After the obligatory moment of silence, during which each man relished the synthesis of the moment, the azalea scented evening, the cigars and themselves, Mr. Boggs cleared his throat and spoke. "What do you think of Harrington-Smythe?"

"You mean, do I like him?"

Boggs shook his head impatiently. Of course not. You couldn't possibly like him. The man's an ass. What do you think of his opinions?"

"Well, I...I think he's right. I think that the Anglo-Saxon race is the most civilized in history, and that we have much to give to the rest of the world, if it will only let us. I think we're more capable of governing Cuba than the Spanish are, even though they are white men, after a fashion. I certainly think we're more capable of governing the natives than they are of governing themselves. And we should. It's in their best interests."

"The white man's burden, eh? Grab the natives by their loin clothes and baptize them with the great blessings of our superior civilization?" My God, Boggs thought, the boy's an incurably naive romantic. Maybe a trip to Cuba and a little stint of warfare will do him some good.

"Well, yes, sir, something like that. Of course, we're not just concerned with the natives. Belgium, the Netherlands, France, Britain and Germany, all the powers, are expanding like crazy. They've already carved up most of Africa, and they're going to carve up China before we get there, if we let them. This is our chance to get some colonies before it's too late. We need raw materials and markets, too. It's in our best interests to drive the Spaniard from Cuba."

"You bet your sweet tooth it is, boy. Cuba's in our back yard. Ruled by Spain the island's damn near worthless. Ruled by her own niggers she's absolutely worthless. Ruled by us she's no longer in our back-yard;

she's in our hip pocket. America's a great country because of her size, her capital and her industrial might. You believe that?"

"Yes, sir. Yes I do."

"You'd better. All that nonsense Harrington-Smythe spouts is so much bull piz." The old man got more excited as he talked. He paced up and down the veranda waving his cigar. Its glowing tip moved in wide circles. "You can spout all the noble sentiments you want, boy—as long as you don't believe them. And you sure as hell don't want to believe other men's flowery words, or to assume that their noble ideals have one damned thing to do with the way they conduct their lives."

Richard Boggs stopped his pacing and leaned out over the veranda railing to spit. Alex disagreed with the old man, but privately. He's right about national self-interest as far as money matters are concerned, Alex thought. But he's wrong about men. Most people are like my father— basically decent people who want to do what's right. "I suppose you're right, sir," he ventured. "I guess I never thought about it that way."

"Most people your age haven't." This is about enough philosophical nonsense for one evening, Boggs decided, and launched into different territory. "How's your relationship with Roosevelt?"

Alex was a bit taken aback. Relationship, sir? Alex shrugged. "We're hardly on the same social level. I'm in charge of getting his regiment of volunteers supplied with the best logistics available. I believe he and Major Wood appreciate my work. I feel incredibly lucky to be working for him, sir. Theodore Roosevelt is the most powerful man I have ever met. He's absolutely inspiring. What he's managed to do at the Navy Department in less than a year is almost unbelievable."

Boggs nodded thoughtfully. "I agree with that assessment, Alex. He's also a comer politically. You've made an excellent connection. Continue to nurture it."

"Don't worry. I know…"

"On a far different topic, young man." Boggs paused for a moment and stared into Alex's eyes. "Are you in love with Charlotte?"

"Yes, Mr. Boggs, I am."

Boggs examined Alex closely. He liked the way the younger man stood—erect, poised, since hooking up with Roosevelt seemingly more confident of himself and his abilities. And he liked the way Alex met his gaze, direct, unflinching. That Alex was ambitious and that he was attracted to Charlotte, at least in part because of her money, didn't bother the old man at all. What he cared about was Alex's character and strength and determination and, most of all, his ability to make Charlotte happy. "Do you think she loves you?"

Alex blinked, thought for a moment and nodded what he thought was the truth. "She hasn't said so in so many words, sir, but then neither have I. But yes. Yes, I believe Charlotte does love me. And for what it's worth, I also believe that she respects me."

Again, Boggs nodded. "She does, and she's a far better judge of character than any of her previous beaus ever understood. Whatever you do, son, never underestimate my daughter's intelligence. She saw your potential before I did, perhaps even before you did." But not before Roosevelt apparently did, Boggs added to himself.

Alex took a deep breath and decided to take the initiative. "I was hoping we'd get a chance to talk tonight. I'd like your permission to ask her hand in marriage." While Alex was not really sure that he was in love with Charlotte, he was very sure he wanted to marry her. She was pretty, pleasant, rich, well-connected and physically magnetic. When, after a silence of more than a minute, Boggs had not responded, Alex cleared his throat and spoke again. "May I ask her?"

The old man narrowed his eyes, as if attempting to peer down to the depths of Alex's soul. "Yes. You may ask her. And good luck to you. But if you ever do anything to hurt her, I'll have you hunted down and hanged."

"I wouldn't dream of hurting her, Mr. Boggs. I love her," which was at least partly true. Alex had never intentionally hurt anyone. He was vain, egocentric, naive and ambitious, but he was usually considerate and he loved to please others, particularly his superiors. He could not even understand meanness, much less exercise it intentionally. If he frequently dealt in half-truths and occasional outright lies, it was only because he was to the manor born: He'd grown up on his father's tall tales and evasions, and had always assumed, even at Harvard and since, that imagination and glibness were a brace of tools indispensable to getting on in the world.

The two men remained awkwardly silent for a few more minutes, each lost in his own thoughts. When they heard the dinner bell tinkling through the reception and drawing rooms, they quickly finished their cigars. Just before they joined the guests pairing off to enter the dining room, Mr. Boggs placed his hand on Alex's shoulder and said, "I believe you do love Charlotte. I also believe she loves you."

Richard Boggs smiled and turned away. Yes, she loves you, he thought. Today. Maybe for a few months. She may be swept away by your dash and charm, but she'll never marry you. Boggs believed that he knew his daughter quite well. Though barely eighteen, Charlotte had been engaged twice since her sixteenth birthday and, after a few giddy months, had found sufficient reason to break each one. Boggs believed his daughter to be willful, but loveable, intelligent, but flighty, and not about to settle into the dull routine of marriage. There were too many potential beaus to settle down with one, or so Boggs thought. The old man nodded at a congressman's wife who had extended her arm and, smiling with a great sense of self-satisfaction, squired her into the dining room.

* * * * *

It was almost midnight. Except for those guests, including Alex, who had been invited to sleep over, everyone had left. He and Charlotte were standing on the verandah, holding hands, basking in each other's company and inhaling the spring scents of frangipani and azaleas that wafted up from the garden. Neither had spoken for several minutes. Finally, Alex took a deep breath, put his hands on Charlotte's hips, pulled her close and kissed her tenderly on the lips. "Char, I want to spend my life with you. Will you marry me?"

Even though she thrilled at the proposal, Charlotte arched her eyebrows in pretended surprise, leaned back, remained silent for what seemed to Alex to be a very long time, then played the inquisitor. "So, Mr. Alexander Dumas Jackson, why should I marry you? Or, to put it more like my father would, why should *I* marry *you*?"

Why indeed? Alex thought she was playing with him, but wasn't quite sure. "Because I think I appreciate who you are, rather than how you want to appear to most men. Because I want nothing quite so much as to care for you, to nurture and treasure you. Because I really do believe that I can make you happy."

She gave a short nod, less than satisfied with his response. Does he think I'm a cat, to be kept and stroked? "How about desire? Most men do, you know."

"Oh, my God. Desire you? Do you really doubt...?"

Without waiting for him to finish, she stuck her finger in her mouth, ran it slowly around her lips, then pushed it into his mouth. "Be quiet."

His erection was immediate and hard. He pulled her close, kissed both her eyes and cheeks, dropped his face to her neck, where he breathed deeply of her lilac scent, and moved to her mouth, which was open and yearning. He knew that she was toying with him and he couldn't have been happier, that is until she pulled back, looked him straight in the eye and asked, this time with no trace of humor or irony, "Haven't you forgotten something?"

His mind was on her body and how it would look and feel stripped of her party gown. "Excuse me?"

"Isn't there something else you'd like to say to me, Mr. Jackson, something one often connects to marriage proposals?"

Alex blinked, confused as much by her tone as her words. "Char, I know I don't have money or position. In that way I'm not much of a match. But I have some real strengths and plenty of ambition. I know I can make you proud of me."

"I'm already proud of you, Alex. Father and I agree on your worth as a man. Even though you are a bit of a fool. How do you feel about me?"

"Why, I think the world of you, Char. You're the most beautiful, interesting and desirable woman I've ever known." Then, almost as an afterthought, he added, "I love you!"

"Do you now?"

"Char, I love you to distraction. My love for you starts at the pit of my stomach, moves through my heart and sometimes almost overpowers me to the point where I can think of little else."

"That sounds more like desire. Do you really love me? Me?"

Though he was confused by the question and a distinction he didn't quite grasp, Alex was sure that he wanted her, and that he wanted her for life, but for once he knew that his accustomed glibness could backfire. He struggled for the truth as he understood it. He stood back, placed his palms along her cheeks, looked into her green eyes and repeated her question. "Do I love you? Yes, dear, dear Char. I love you. I love who you are as a woman, as a person, as a partner. I love your quiet intelligence, which you too often hide. I love your ability to see into the hearts and motives of others, including me. I love your wit. I love—and respect—your strength and independence, though I often sense that it separates you from most of your empty-headed peers. And, yes, I love you physically too. Just thinking of your bare skin can drive me dizzy. I love you. I want you. I need you. I believe I can enrich your life. I know you can enrich…"

She stepped close, put both arms around him and stopped the flow with a long, deep kiss. When she pulled away to catch her breath, Alex continued his flow of verbal assurance. She shook her head, returned to the kiss and pushed the length of her body against his and moved her breasts back and forth slowly across his chest. "Mr. Jackson, do you remember those kisses at the ball in January when you kissed my bosom and I asked you to do it again?" Though he was busy nibbling on her ear and caressing her bare shoulders, he nodded. "Do it again!" she commanded. "Do it again."

"Oh, God, Char. I love you so much." He bent down and covered the exposed halves of her breasts with kisses, continuing until she placed her hands behind his head, pulled him even closer and whispered, "I accept. I will marry you. I love you, Alex—and desire you. But please, right now, stop. We must stop."

* * * * *

Alex was having trouble falling asleep. The evening raced back and forth across the fertile fields of his imagination. Charlotte loved him! She'd promised to marry him as soon as he returned from Cuba. He found her physical passion to be almost overwhelming. He was confused as to whether she was more experienced at such matters than he'd imagined, or just incredibly natural and spontaneous. Just before kissing him, Charlotte had run her tongue over her lips and then over his. While they were kissing, she'd slowly opened her mouth and allowed his tongue to enter her. She'd bitten down on it, quickly, gently, repeatedly. He could feel his erection straining against his trousers and against her abdomen. He knew she had to be aware of it and of what she was doing to him, but she didn't seem to care. At least she hadn't stopped.

He'd wanted very much to pull down the top of her gown and kiss her naked breasts, but hadn't. And as much as he'd wanted to caress other parts of her body, he didn't. Rather, he'd kept his hands locked discreetly together toward the bottom of her whale bone stiffened back. After her acceptance, they had kissed again for a long time, and it was Alex who finally pulled away, afraid that someone, her father for instance, would discover them.

Now, lying in bed, luxuriating under the soft eiderdown, he gloried in the new life that seemed to be stretching out before him and congratulated himself for not taking advantage—or at least not trying to take advantage—of Charlotte's obvious passion. The man must be the stronger, he thought, especially if the man claims to be a gentleman. He smiled to himself, brim full of self-satisfaction. He loved the feel of the silk sheets and the weightless luxury of the quilt that covered the four-poster. He stretched out his legs until his feet pushed against the bottom of the comforter and drifted into a deep sleep.

"Alex. Wake up." He turned over and grunted. "Alex?"

He opened his eyes and looked up. Charlotte was bending over him and frowning.

Before waking him she'd opened the drapes to let in the moon-light. As soon as she saw that he was awake, she erased the frown, ran her slightly pointed tongue over her lips and smiled sweetly. "I couldn't sleep, sweetheart. I'm so excited, and so wildly in love with you. Can I just sit close to you for a few minutes?"

Alex was dumbfounded. "Are you crazy, Char? Your father would kill me." He looked toward the door, half expecting to see the old man silhouetted in the hall light, horse whip in hand. But the door was shut. He noticed that Charlotte had even turned the key in the lock. "Good Lord, sweetheart. What are you doing?"

"I just want to be close to you, just for a little while. Please?" She stood in the half light looking more like a little girl than a woman, her long white nightgown concealing almost completely the ample curves of her body.

"Sure, sweetheart. I'm sorry. It's just...well...you caught me by surprise. Come, sit down by me, right here." He rose up on one elbow, patted the top of the coverlet, and smiled.

"Uh-uh!" Charlotte shook her head, pulled the sheet and comforter half way back, and slid into bed beside him. "I'll get cold if I don't stay covered." She put her arms around his chest, cuddled up against him, and purred like a freshly fed kitten.

Oh my God! What do I do now? Alex wondered. He knew what he should do. As a gentleman, he should insist that she leave, regardless of her proclaimed wishes. That's what he should do. That's what he wanted to do, but…he could feel her body against his, separated only by her silk nightgown and his cotton nightshirt. When he felt an erection swelling he turned onto his stomach, but it didn't help. She stretched out her body and pushed against him. He became acutely conscious of two things, her breasts pushing softly against his arm, and the now throbbing erection he was trying to bury in the mattress.

"I'm awfully excited about our being engaged, aren't you? I think it's terribly romantic," she whispered into his ear. I hope the war lasts a long time, she was thinking; our engagement can go on and on. She was sure that Alex would be a hero, maybe even get wounded. Nothing too serious, of course. He was too dashing for that. She would be very proud of him. "I think you're awfully handsome, Alex. Do you think I'm even a little bit pretty?"

She knew that she was pretty and Alex knew that she knew, but there was only one possible response. He turned back onto his side, caressed her face and hair with his hand and said, "I think you're beautiful, sweetheart. You're the most beautiful girl I've ever seen." He felt her thigh move slightly against his erection and decided to surrender. His last resistant thought was: We need to get married as soon as possible, hopefully before I leave Washington. Then he found himself kissing her.

Charlotte immediately fell onto her back and withdrew slightly, responding more passively to his kisses. She knew that she had probably already gone too far, and that it was up to her to maintain control.

Alex bent over and covered her face and neck with kisses. He felt his hands molding her breasts and moving down her belly toward the warmth. Her thighs opened slightly and he massaged her, just as the Boston whore had instructed him on that sticky October night five years earlier. He tried not to think of his own erection.

His fingers felt the moisture soak through her gown. She could remain passive no longer and whispered his name. Her thighs were opening and closing, and he could feel her arms and hands on his body, trying to pull him closer. Suddenly he broke the hold, stood up on his knees and jerked his nightshirt over his head.

"Alex! I'm a virgin," she gasped. But Alex was already beyond the point of no return. All he could see was her full white body. The silk gown was up around her neck and seemed to separate her head and voice from what was really important. The disembodied voice entreated, but from a distance. He heard the voice calling, "Alex, please, Alex," but it didn't register; it had nothing to do with them. Circe had cast her spell, had turned him into a swine.

Even as he entered her, she continued to entreat him, but he felt her arms around him and her body moving under him. And then, before it even occurred to him to assert a little self-control, the blood over-powered him and he erupted. His body shook violently once and then subsided to a series of increasingly minor after-tremors. He was still, depleted, adrift in space. His body collapsed upon hers like a blanket of rubber lead. Little more than a minute had passed from the first instant of ecstatic penetration to the much longer nirvana of sexual exhaustion.

Charlotte was not sure what had happened. Her body still moved, still sought to surround and hold, still hungered to be known. She felt him erupt, then felt his ardent elasticity melt. It was as if she had been climbing a mountain, about to reach the summit, about to break through the final ring of mist into the sunlight. A strange exultation had been rising from deep within her body. But just as she started up out of the mist, the sun disappeared, the summit fell away. She was alone, deserted.

She tried to get closer to him, but she could feel his distance. She felt like crying, but instead said, "I love you." Even as she made the declaration she realized that she was stronger than Alex, superior to him in some new way that she didn't understand. Without warning he had weakened, become somehow vulnerable, dependent. I wonder if it's always like this, she thought. It was as though she and Alex had been arm wrestling and he had allowed her to win, and all too quickly. She didn't know quite what to make of it. She heard him say, "I love you too, Charlotte," but his words now lacked passion, seemed somehow distant, hollow. She heard something in his voice she didn't want to hear, though she could not have said what.

Suddenly, she became acutely conscious of his weight on her breasts. She moved slightly and felt him leave her. She immediately became conscious of two sensations: She felt open, exposed, more vulnerable than she had ever been in her protected life; and she felt his juices seeping from her. "It's st...sticky," she whimpered.

"I know, sweetheart. I'm...sorry." Alex crept from the bed, found a handkerchief and returned. Overcome by his own shame—at what he had allowed them to do, at how poorly he had performed, and at her obvious disappointment—he felt that he would not be able to touch her again, ever. He just wanted her to leave so he could be alone with his self-disgust and depression. He started to hand her the handkerchief but immediately thought better of it. For an instant he thought he understood her, what kind of mischievous, romantic impulse must have drawn her to his room, what kind of fear and rejection she must be feeling at this moment, and what a weak, spineless villain he must be. He crawled across the bed, kissed her gently on the cheeks and lips, slowly and tenderly wiped her still open vagina, dabbed at the stain on the sheet, then allowed the monogrammed handkerchief to sink to the floor.

He could feel her body stiffen and knew that she was crying. He pulled the comforter over them, took her stiffening body in his arms and rocked back and forth. Neither of them said a word. Though she wasn't sobbing, he felt the tears pouring down her cheeks. Every once in a while he whispered, "Sssshhh" and stroked her hair. The crying stopped after awhile and the two lovers lay quietly, awkwardly holding each other, increasingly embarrassed by the way their still naked bodies were touching.

"I love you, Charlotte," Alex whispered. "I love you with all my heart and soul." Though he was still not quite sure what he meant by that, he knew that the words comforted both of them, and that he felt for her a tenderness and protectiveness he had never before experienced. When she turned her tear-streaked face to his, he repeated the sentiment, again and again.

Even after Charlotte returned to her room, Alex found it difficult to fall asleep. He was ashamed about what they—what he—had done. They weren't married, and probably wouldn't be for months. What if she panicked and reported the affair to her father? Alex cringed. What if she became pregnant? He gritted his teeth, clutched the sheet with both hands and cursed himself. I should have been stronger. The man's responsibility, always, is to be stronger.

Still, the more he thought about it, the more he was able to transfer the responsibility for what had happened to Charlotte. "She started it," he said aloud, like a school boy explaining his bloody nose to his teacher.

His mind stopped, locked onto an ominous possibility. If she's pregnant, I won't be able to go to Cuba. Alex sat up in bed, shivering with dread. He thought of Christopher, whom he hadn't seen for three years and from whom he heard so seldom. Christopher had been more like a father than a brother, especially since their Pa had died. Alex wanted to go to Cuba more than anything in the world, even more than he wanted to marry Charlotte, despite her position, wealth and connections.

It was not only Christopher that pulled him to Cuba, however. Cuba was a land of adventure, mystery, enchantment. It was the place where he would finally prove himself, where he would meet some kind of ultimate test and pass it, just as Christopher must have. He thought of Roosevelt and his affable but aggressive magnetism. Teddy was the most powerful and persuasive man Alex had ever met, and Alex was both flattered and excited to be a part of his "team." As a member of Roosevelt's regiment of volunteers, he would help avenge the destruction of the *Maine*. He would help bring America to new power and prestige in a world where both were counted in terms of the number of colonial possessions a country befriended. At least as important, he would, by passing the nebulous and imaginary test he had set for himself, prove his great potential to Roosevelt and assure his career in government service.

"I just hope I can at least see Cuba before she has to...before she knows." He tried to set up a timetable. It'll probably be a few more days before Congress declares war. After that it would take him at least a month to sort out and coordinate the shipment of the supplies he'd been wrangling for "Teddy's Terrors" as the regiment was already being called. How long will training take? How long to travel by train to Florida and ship to Cuba? At least two months? God! but I hope I haven't shot myself in the foot.

Alex fell asleep dreaming that he was back in Georgia. He was a little boy again, trying to board the train and leave town. The train was going north, where the streets were paved, where there was money and a future. His father had told him about the North, where everyone was rich and powerful. He tried to climb aboard but something kept pulling at his leg. He finally looked down and saw the heavy iron chain. It led down the street through a mud puddle and around the corner of his mother's store into a dark alley. At the end of the alley he saw that the chain was attached to a baby carriage. Charlotte stood behind the carriage. She was holding a baby and smiling. He noticed that she was pregnant. But then he wasn't in the alley anymore. He was in the ocean, swimming for Cuba. Christopher stood on the Cuban side of the ocean yelling, "Come on, boy. Come on! You can make it." But Charlotte was standing on the Florida side. He couldn't see her, but he knew she was throwing a net to catch him. He felt the net settle around his head and shoulders. He tried to swim on, but he was caught. He couldn't see Christopher any longer. All he could see were the ropes of the net.

Chapter Sixteen

WAR WITH SPAIN!
*Congress and President in Absolute Accord. Spain's Insults
Answered. America Will Fight*

Washington, April 25— The Congress and Administration yesterday sent a formal declaration of war to the Spanish Charge d' Affairs. Citing Spain's own declaration of the 23rd., Washington claims the country is ready and willing to eject Spain from the New World.

* * * *

PACIFIC FLEET LEAVES HONG KONG
Adm. Dewey and Pacific Fleet Head for Philippines?

New York via cable from Hong Kong, April 25—After close to two months of waiting for an order he knew would come, Adm. Dewey steamed from Hong Kong harbor and headed into the China Sea. While his destination has not been confirmed, the rumors are that he intends to engage the Spanish fleet somewhere in the Philippines. *The New York Journal*, April 26.

Sancti Spiritus Province

Calixto Garcia, General of the Eastern army, walked back to the spot where the signal sergeant was watching the advancing Spanish troops through his field glasses. "How long before the lead company reaches Major Jackson's position?"

"Five to ten minutes, General. It is as you say. Look." General Garcia stared through the glasses. The lead Spanish company of about two hundred men had divided itself into four skirmish lines, each of which was spread across less than a hundred meters of the long valley. Each line was no more than twenty-five meters behind its predecessor.

"They are too close together," the general said. "They are like sheep; they are always too close together." He looked along the base of the woods and knew he had been right: This company had no cavalry to protect its flanks. Its members were judas goats. The general swept his glasses to his right. Several hundred meters to the west, the rest of the battalion of Spanish infantry moved up the valley in closed skirmish lines, each platoon closely bunched. "My God, but I wish I had one or two Gatling guns, Miguel."

Though only a sergeant, Miguel had been thinking the same thing. He nodded then pointed at the forest on the south side of the valley. General Garcia nodded. "Yes, perhaps one troop of cavalry is with that battalion. It will be of no help to the lead company. And if our scouts are correct, we know that the Spanish have no cavalry on the north side." He turned his glasses down the valley, which meandered through the hills like a dying river. He saw no evidence that the Spanish had provided any back up for the battalion. He smiled. As usual, the Spanish were overly confident that their plan would work; they had no idea that, for once, they were outnumbered. Garcia's trap would make short work of the battalion, just as it would make short work of the judas goats.

The only unknown was the Spanish cavalry. If the Spanish stumbled on the Cuban cavalry in the woods, the element of surprise would be lost. And if they managed to maneuver behind the *Yanqui*'s position? He shrugged. Even though Garcia had the element of surprise in his favor, battles created their own momentum—and their own surprises. Once the melee began, he could continue to give orders, but no one would heed them. Centrifugal forces would pull everything apart. Company commanders would gradually lose control over their platoons. Platoon leaders would yell themselves hoarse trying to direct the movements of squads. Only squad leaders would have any chance of controlling the movements of more than three or four men. Once the battle was joined, each unit commander would be on his own, reacting to the immediacy of each situation as it arose. Ultimately victory or defeat would hinge on the ability of the squad leaders of both sides to stay alive and in charge. Garcia shrugged again, confident that he had done all that he could. He took out his package of French cigarettes, extracted one and sat back to wait.

"What time is it, General?"

Calixto Garcia pulled out his watch. "About 11:15." Before returning the watch to his pocket, he turned it over and stared reflectively at the inscription: "For Pedro on the occasion of his confirmation April 22, 1886—Mother and Father." Twelve years tomorrow, he thought; Pedro has already been dead more than a year. But even as the old general thought of his youngest son, he knew he must move his mind in other directions. Otherwise, he would begin to think of the thousands of *mambises* he had ordered to their deaths, and of the families who survived to mourn their passing. In that direction lies madness, he thought, forcing his concentration back to the valley that stretched out beneath him.

Although Christopher had given each of his commanders explicit orders not to fire at the approaching company of Spaniards, he was far from sure that his battalion of irregulars, including more than a hundred women, could be that closely disciplined. He held his breath again and again as he watched the leading line of Spanish skirmishers approach the well-concealed trench his troops had cut across the valley. His soldiers knew what was supposed to happen, and that, for this initial battle, they had nothing to do but lie low and watch. Every person in the quarter mile long, eight hundred troop line concentrated on two things: the approaching company of skirmishers, now less than two hundred meters from the trench, and the forest on the north side of the valley where elements of General Abajo's cavalry were waiting to charge.

A long gasp swept along the line as Abajo's cavalry swept from the forest in four waves of one hundred each. They rode at a gallop, heads low, machetes poised. The first wave had covered almost fifty meters before the surprised Spanish infantry began to react.

* * * * *

"Blood of the devil, piss-drinking country. What a place to die!"

"Hey, Ricardo, I know what you mean. Maybe we have been in Purgatory all these years and didn't even know it. Hey?" Ponce laughed nervously and looked around the valley. Ponce's platoon formed the leading skirmish line of judas goats. He was very much afraid, but tried not to show it. If the Cubans are here, like everybody says, he and his friends were all dead men.

Ponce had known for a long time that he would never leave this fever-infested land. Nobody left, except officers, who came to get rich, and sometimes did. The enlisted men, the conscripts, would always be here. When they died of the fever or were killed by the rebels, they were buried here. None of them would ever return to the golden hills of Spain. The women with dancing eyes and the slopes of ripening grapes were receding phantoms that could be grasped only in wine-rich dreams.

But even though he knew he would never leave Cuba alive, Ponce also knew that he was not ready to die. Even here in this bug and fever-infested land, life could be good for an hour or two. Sometimes the food was not so bad, and the Cuban rum turned him into a giant. Sometimes they patrolled for days without even seeing a Cuban. And on warm evenings he could sit on the barracks roof, cleaning his rifle, watching the sun set in the western hills, listening to the music float through the air from the distant cafes. Evenings in barracks were his favorite hours. It seemed, somehow, that when he sat on the roof everything was peaceful and in focus. The sounds and smells of the evening blended with the colors of the setting sun and washed over him in waves of harmony.

Ponce no longer dreamed of becoming a rich shepherd, or even of owning his own flock of goats. He knew that he would never again see his brothers and that he would never have a wife or children. During his three years in Cuba he had received two letters, one written by the village priest when his mother died, and another, a year later, when his aunt wrote to tell him that Antonia had married another man. Since that letter he had pushed any thought of "tomorrow" from his mind. When he left his barracks on patrol, he prayed for but one thing: to live long enough to see his beloved sunset. Usually he felt that he would return alive to the barracks, but today he felt differently. The general had brought many men to this valley, and many guns. Rumor had it that they were going to attack and destroy rebel headquarters. But everyone knew the rebels had spies everywhere, and that the army could not even drill without the rebel high command knowing when and where. They had all agreed that the rebels would know about this large force moving toward them.

"Hey, Ricardo. How far to the enemy camp?"

"How in Christ's blood should I know? You think I look like an officer? Ask Gonzalez. He's the son of a whore sergeant."

But the sergeant couldn't speak. He just shook his head angrily and motioned Ponce to get back in place. The sergeant, too, knew that he was a dead man, and was whiling away the last moments of his life counting "Hail Marys." His only concern was in seeing how many he could count before the first bullet was fired. The rebels must be close. Ponce shivered, then had a happier thought. The rebels know we are coming! Maybe they also know how big our army is. They don't have good weapons. Maybe they have decided to leave this camp of theirs and move to a safer place.

Ponce smiled and decided to share his idea with Ricardo. But he was distracted by a strange movement in the grass eighty or ninety meters ahead of him, and the sun was shining on something. What was it? All morning the men had moved their eyes constantly back and forth across the lush grasses of the valley and along the base of the heavily forested ridges that paralleled the valley. What was he seeing? His eyes were tired from the constant strain, but...yes, there it was again.

"Sergeant, I think I saw something..." His voice trailed off as he heard Ricardo's gasp. Ponce turned to his left to see what was happening. He could not believe his eyes. Hundreds of rebel horsemen were pouring from the forest.

"Mary, Mother of God!" Ricardo yelled, dropping his rifle. He ran toward the forest on the opposite side of the valley. Ponce heard the sergeant yell, "Wheel left! Fire at Will!" Just before he responded to the order, Ponce saw Ricardo run by the lieutenant, who raised his pistol and shot the would-be deserter in the head. Ricardo leaped to his right and slammed into the grass. It was as if the boy had decided to turn right in mid-stride and had executed the movement without turning his body.

Ponce turned back to the onrushing cavalry. He fell to one knee, raised his Mauser and aimed at one of the riders. Every one in the company was firing at the horsemen. Already some of the rebels were falling from their mounts. Ponce pulled the trigger, aimed at another rider and pulled the trigger again. Nothing. He had forgotten to re-cock the bolt-action rifle. "Blood of Christ!" he swore. He carefully squeezed the trigger and was pleased to see the rider, a fat Negro, fly from his saddle.

By the time he had emptied the first magazine of eight rounds, he was sure he had hit at least two men. But that was not enough, he knew. As he reloaded, Ponce noticed that the line of horsemen had already swept over and mowed down half of his company. The riders were taking heavy casualties, but there were so many of them that they destroyed everything and everyone they rode over.

None of the rebels seemed to have any rifles. They rode low on their horses, machetes poised, and yelled their frightening battle cry, "Ma-che-te! Ma-che-te!"

The first wave of riders was almost upon him. He shot once more and hit a huge sorrel in the chest. The horse fell and catapulted its rider over its neck. The rebel, a pale, curly-headed boy of thirteen or fourteen, landed on his feet at a dead run. The boy was running straight at him, machete raised and crying "ma-che-te!" in a high, squeaky voice. Just as Ponce pulled the trigger, he noticed the boy's eyes, and that the boy was at least as frightened as he was.

The first wave of riders was beyond him now, but there was a second wave behind it and, apparently, a third behind the second. He tried to fire at a rider who was almost on top of him, but the horse rushed over him and knocked him unconscious.

When Ponce came to, the riders were gone. He started to rise from the grass but couldn't, so he crawled on his hands and knees toward the forest from which the riders had come. He knew that the battle wasn't over. The rest of his battalion was only a few hundred meters to the rear and would be moving forward at quick time. Ponce did not want to be still in the field when the battle repeated itself. But after crawling only a few meters, he had to rest.

Christopher saw some of the Spanish break and run, a couple of whom were shot by their own officers. He smiled grimly as he thought of what would happen to those few deserters who managed to make it to the far side of the valley, where another five hundred mounted *mambises* waited for the second stage of the battle.

The first stage ended quickly. From the time the four hundred horsemen flowed from the forest on the south side of the valley to the time they flowed back into the forest on the north side, not much more than five minutes had elapsed. The *mambises* had mowed through the ripe crop of Spaniards like mounted scythes. With the exception of thirty or forty wounded and a few who were probably playing dead, the entire company was destroyed. By the time the fourth and final wave of horsemen swept across the field, the firing had completely stopped. The final wave moved at a canter, swinging machetes at anything Spanish still moving. If the rebel wounded were capable of climbing up behind, they were picked up; if not, they were left to lie with the Spanish. By the time the fourth wave had crossed three fourths of the valley, they broke into a mad gallop. Leading elements of the advancing Spanish battalion had advanced to within four hundred meters and were firing at the Cubans.

Christopher shook his head, wiped the sweat from his eyes, and turned to Fidel. "Now it's our turn. Pass the reminder: No one is to fire until the front line is within fifty meters. I'll fire first. Each shot is to be aimed at a man's chest." He turned to Theresa and repeated the order.

The long trench that dissected the valley was shaped like a shallow V. Christopher and his lieutenants stood at the point of the V, the legs of which opened to the west, as if to embrace the Spaniards. It had taken the rebels almost a week to build the trench, which was a meter deep, two meters wide at the bottom and three meters wide at the top. Christopher's troops leaned against the slope and rested their rifles on the parapet, which they had disguised with sod.

The open V would allow them to inter-lock their firepower. The troops extending from the point out the first two hundred yards along the legs of the V would fire straight down the valley. The rest of the rebels would fire at right angles to the legs of the open V.

Christopher glanced at Judith, who was unarmed except for a Spanish dagger she carried in a sheath strapped to her thigh. She had learned rapidly, at least partly because of her hatred for the Spanish soldiers. She was still plagued by nightmares about the incidents surrounding the deaths of her family and her own rape, and she was still silent most of the time. However, though she talked little, even to Theresa and Christopher, she had come to trust them. "What are our chances?" she asked.

"It depends upon what you mean, Judith. Our chances, those of us here in the trench, are excellent. The chances of our army winning this battle? I don't know. What will be, will be."

In some ways the second stage of the battle—and of General Garcia's plan—succeeded even better than the first. Within a few seconds of Christopher's first shot, all eight hundred of his troops had fired once; within the first minute most had fired several times. The Spaniards suffered more than two hundred deaths and three hundred wounded before they could figure out what was happening. The Spanish survivors knelt or lay in the grass and fired back at targets that were only fractionally visible. After the initial fusillades, the *mambises* fired only at targets of opportunity.

It's a goddamn turkey shoot, Christopher thought. As far as he could tell, virtually none of his people had even been wounded. "What happened to that squadron of Spanish cavalry?" he asked Fidel. Even as he shrugged ignorance, the rifle fire on their left increased dramatically. "Oh, my God!" Christopher said, shifting his attention. The Spanish cavalry had out-flanked them and emerged from the forest at their rear. They were about to over-run the far left leg of the V.

"Shift your fire!" he yelled, pointing to the left. "Shift your fire! Shift your fire!" Gradually, too slowly, almost as if they were half asleep, more and more of the rebels noticed what was happening and turned their weapons to the south. The *mambises* at the far end of the trench were obviously in serious trouble. A few leaped from the trench and were immediately cut down.

At that moment another two hundred of Abajo's cavalry charged from the forest and attacked the by now disorganized Spanish horsemen from the rear. At the same time four hundred rebels who had earlier ridden across the valley galloped back. Since the Spaniards were concentrating their fire on those rebels attempting to flee from the trench, they were oblivious to the new attack until the four hundred rebel horsemen were among them.

Three fourths of a kilometer up the valley the second troop of Spanish cavalry broke from their concealment and rushed toward the battle. Before they had ridden half the distance, however, they were distracted by the final two hundred of Abajo's south squadron, who dashed out of the forest to meet them. And as the Spanish turned to meet their new challenge, Abajo administered his coup de grace. The north squadron, reinforced by the troops who had earlier decimated the Spanish judas goats, rode down from the ridge and into the valley.

Within half an hour the second phase of the battle was over and the field secure. Just as General Abajo rode up to receive Christopher's report, the first Spanish artillery shells came in, landing more than a half mile beyond the trench.

"They're not usually that far off," Christopher said.

"They're firing blind. We caught their spotters." General Abajo had a hard time standing still. Though his horse was well-trained, the smell of blood had made him unusually skittish. "Hold still, you whore!" Abajo screamed. In a slightly lower voice he asked Christopher, "How's your flank?"

"I don't know, General. Fidel hasn't gotten back yet. But perhaps as many as thirty dead, another thirty or forty badly wounded. How about your cavalry?"

"Could have been worse. When we reached the far side of the valley after the first charge, we counted. We left fifty-three men on the field, but they're not all dead. In the clash with the Spanish cavalry attacking your left flank, we lost maybe twenty killed. On this final sweep maybe another forty or so. Altogether no more than one hundred and fifty dead and about the same number too badly wounded to ride."

"We'll get your badly wounded to the field hospital, sir."

"Good. By the way, Major, we need some of these rifles and ammunition."

"Certainly, sir. That's why we're cleaning up the battlefield."

Every able-bodied man and woman had left the trench to finish off the Spanish wounded, carry the Cuban wounded from the field, and scavenge arms, boots and ammunition. Federico was enjoying himself immensely. He was sure his presence had kept his Fidelito from harm during the battle, and he was just as sure that he had shot at least four Spaniards. And now, as he walked through the battlefield, listening to the moans of the wounded, he concentrated on finding Spaniards to kill. Other people could care for the wounded and gather the weapons. His job was to be God's messenger, to bring quick and merciful death to the Spanish wounded. He walked from body to body; if one moved he slashed the head or neck with his machete.

He didn't see the Spanish pistol lift from the grass to blow his head apart until it was too late. He heard Fidel yell, "Paaaa-pi!" and turned around just as the pistol exploded less than a meter away. Fidel was leaping toward him, his face contorted with the fear that comes from absolute knowledge, but Federico was already dead before Fidel leaped upon the man who had fired the pistol and split him almost in two with one blow of his machete.

* * * * *

Ponce had regained consciousness during the middle of the big battle. He knew he had fought his war. He wanted to live and to return to Spain. He had been lying on his stomach, glued to the ground, crying. He couldn't help it, just as he couldn't help thinking about Spain. His head hurt, ants crawled all over his face, and he wanted to go home. Most of all, he wanted to watch the sunset one more time. He knew what was going on around him; like their Spanish teachers, the Cubans systematically killed and stripped their enemy wounded.

Maybe, he thought. Maybe if I join the rebels they will let me live. That's it. I'll become a Cuban . I will help them win their war. It wasn't much of a hope, but it was all he could muster. Ponce now knew what he had to do. He had to find some way of gaining temporary safety so he could talk to the Cuban soldiers before they could cut off his head. He would take a hostage. Yes! Then they would have to listen to him, and they would be able to see how sincere he was.

A woman walked by. Her man's boots were almost covered by a long skirt. She is probably looking for Cuban wounded. He bolted from the ground, knife in hand, and grabbed the woman around the neck, almost breaking it in the process. He pushed the knife against her left breast and yelled at the top of his lungs, "I will kill her. Listen to me! I will kill her!"

Not again. Please, God, not again. Judith's neck hurt and she could hardly breathe. She twisted hard and the point penetrated her skin.

"Don't move! I don't want to hurt you," a high, broken voice yelled in her ear. And then, louder, hysterically, "Listen to me! Please!"

Theresa, Fidel and an increasingly large group of *mambises* gathered around in a wide circle. Several had wanted to rush the soldier or, even simpler, shoot him when his head was clear of Judith's. But Fidel yelled for them all to stand still and do nothing. "What do you want?" he asked as calmly as possible.

"I want to live!" Ponce screamed. He was breathing very rapidly and moving around in little backward circles so they couldn't rush him from behind. "Please, I want to live!"

"We all want to live." Fidel thought of his slightly confused, but almost always smiling father, who was lying on his back, faceless, some forty meters away. "If you *pendejos* would go home, we'd all live in peace."

"Don't! Don't!" Ponce screamed. "I don't want preaching. I just want to live."

It's the same stench, Judith thought. She felt herself becoming sick at her stomach. Her knees turned rubbery as she relived the horror that had taken place in the little room above Joseph's shop. She forgot the pain in her neck and breast. The stench was worse. Garlic and months of accumulated body odors rose from the sweaty jacket of the frightened Spaniard. Judith wanted to yell, "Help me!" but all that came out was a squeak. She could barely breathe, let alone yell. Then she saw Christopher, and her despair and sense of helplessness subsided slightly. Her hatred for the Spaniard and his stench gradually over-powered her fear, and she stopped struggling.

Christopher whispered to Fidel for a moment and then addressed the Spaniard. "So you want to live. What do you propose we do with you?"

"Let me join your army. Please? I am a good soldier. I know how to obey orders. I don't want to fight you." Ponce had to stop for breath. He tried to take deeper breaths, to assert more control over himself, but he couldn't. He realized that he had emptied his bowels. The stench embarrassed him.

"How do we know that you're not trying to trick us? Maybe you'll run away and tell your general all about us, no?"

"No, sir! I'm only a private. I hate the army. They brought me here to be killed. They're never going to let me go home."

Christopher decided to believe him and consulted briefly with Fidel and the rest of his lieutenants. "All right. You can join us. And live. What's your name?"

"Ponce Salazar, General." Ponce's voice dropped a decibel or two, and Judith felt his grip relax slightly. He couldn't, she thought. How could Christopher take such a stinking, repulsive creature into our ranks? She did not know that she had been fighting alongside a number of ex-Spanish soldiers ever since her flight from *La Habana*.

"All right, Ponce. Release the woman. You can join our army."

Ponce was elated. His desperate gamble had paid off. "I'm sorry, Miss," he said to Judith as he released her. He would have to find some way of making it up to her. He smiled sheepishly when she turned to glare at him. Her neck was raw and there was blood on her blouse. "Please forgive me, Madonna. I was very scared; I did not want to hurt you."

But Judith wasn't paying any attention. She had turned her back and was bent over, doing something with her skirt. Ponce heard the tall leader yell, "No, Judith!" Then she was on him. She was large; he wasn't. She had him on his back. He had never seen such eyes. He watched the dagger rise up, catch the glint of the sun and descend into his chest. He could do nothing but watch. The dagger rose again, but this time it didn't reflect the sun; it was dripping something. I wonder what that is? he thought, as the knife plunged again into his chest. He was still conscious when some hurtling force knocked the screaming woman off his stomach, and then the light rushed away.

"Goddamnit, Judith! I gave the man my word." After knocking her from the bleeding soldier, Christopher twisted the dagger from her tightly clenched hand and slapped her face so hard that the blood gushed from her nose.

"But he's a filthy Spaniard," Judith screamed. "He could have been one of the men who killed Joseph and . . ." Her voice trailed off.

"He could have been, but I doubt it. And, you should know, there are many Spaniards fighting with us. Many of them have killed Cubans, but that is in the past. They are with us now."

Christopher rose from the ground, glanced down at Judith, who was now sobbing, and walked away. He stopped, turned his head and yelled, "You will be responsible for seeing that this man lives." As Christopher hurried back to the trench, he cursed Judith's presence among them. While there were times when he was pleased that the tall, sadly beautiful woman was in camp, he knew that his deeply felt sense of personal responsibility for her well-being distracted him from his other responsibilities, as well as from his more personal preoccupations.

Again and again in subsequent weeks, he had gone over his plans for the *Maine*. What possibly could have gone wrong? Why had the bomb gone off two hours earlier than he and Morales had agreed? Was Judith's father responsible? Had the man really known what he was doing? But his focus always returned to Guillermo Morales who had made no secret of his desire to create maximum havoc.

Even though these questions and others floated back and forth across his consciousness like stinking flotsam, his concern for Judith kept them from becoming an obsession. And this same concern had kept him away from the bottle. If she were a problem—and she frequently was—she was also a tonic, a balm, capable of drawing the poison from his swollen mind. But as he walked away from the scene of the battle, his mind shut down and he allowed himself the luxury of solitary rage.

Judith walked along beside the litter that carried Ponce back to the field hospital. He looked harmless now, very frail and vulnerable. He still stank of sweat, garlic and feces, but he didn't really smell much different than the Cubans, especially the seriously wounded. And, other than the grass and blood-stained Spanish uniform, he didn't look any different than the numerous Cubans of Spanish decent. She looked down and noticed that his eyes were open, staring at her. He was trying to speak.

"Stop. He wants to say something." The bearers were more than willing to stop. They were walking east, along the edge of the valley, and had already covered more than half a kilometer since leaving the battlefield. One of the bearers had once been a Spanish soldier himself and had volunteered to help carry Ponce.

Judith bent down to see what the Spaniard wanted.

"I'm sorry, Miss. I didn't want to hurt you. I was scared."

Judith could barely hear his words, but she understood the look on his face and felt sorry for him. "I, too, am sorry. I hope you get well. I'm sorry I stabbed you." The soldier smiled and closed his eyes. Judith nodded to the bearers, who lifted the litter and fell back into the long procession of stretchers carrying the more seriously wounded.

After walking another two hundred meters, the bearer who had been a Spanish soldier motioned to his partner to set the litter down. As all the bearers did who needed a rest, they stepped to the side of the trail to allow the slowly moving line of human carnage to pass them by. With the exception of a few women and old men who had been detailed to help, the wounded were required to care for themselves. The walking wounded helped each other, and carried the litters of those who couldn't walk. Other than bandages and native herbs, and a small amount of morphine captured from the Spanish, the procession was without medicine. It was not without lamentation. Many of the women who had followed their men into battle now followed their bodies home. They did not mourn silently, and their long, keening howls of anguish and fear rose and fell along the evacuation corridor as an irregular chorus of despair.

"Good. He is sleeping now," Judith said. "He will not notice the bumps."

The Spanish bearer peered at Ponce, then reached down to touch his face. "No, Miss. He is dead."

The other bearer took out a partially smoked cigar and began chewing on it. "That is too bad, but now we can help some of our own people. Let's roll him into the bushes."

"No!" The Spanish bearer replied angrily. "We will carry him back and bury him properly. He was going to be one of us."

"But he was not one of us, not really, not yet. He fought against us in this battle." The second bearer jabbed his un-lit cigar at the first and glared. "You Spanish. Yeck!"

They are like little children, Judith thought. She felt sorrow for the dead soldier, which confused her. She was also worried about Christopher. What would he think? He had made her responsible for getting the man back to the hospital alive, and she had failed. But she also knew that worrying about one dead Spaniard would help nobody.

"Place his body in the bushes," she said. "He was my responsibility and he is dead. We must help the living."

Silently the two men, one frowning and one smiling, lifted the limp body, carried it ten feet into the jungle, and placed it in a thick forest of small ferns. Judith motioned two men, one of whom himself should have been carried, to deposit on the litter the half-dead man they were supporting between them. Without saying a word or changing a facial expression, the two men placed their companion on the litter and walked on.

Chapter Seventeen

PRESIDENT REQUESTS VOLUNTEERS FOR ARMY
National Guards Called Up

* * * *

THOUSANDS PREPARED TO ANSWER THE CALL

TEDDY ROOSEVELT TO FORM CAVALRY REGIMENT

Washington, April 27 — President McKinley today sent forth a call to patriotism. In addition to the Army and the state National Guards, war with Spain will require at least 30,000 volunteers. President assures Congress that United States will win the war easily, and that many times the number of volunteers needed will be forthcoming.

The World has also learned that Theodore Roosevelt, the Assistant Secretary of the Navy, is ready to resign his post and lead a regiment of cowboys and indian fighters to Cuba. *The World*, April 27.

Santa Fe, New Mexico Territory

M iguel Otero, Governor of New Mexico Territory, was elated. Finally! He'd show Joseph Pulitzer what New Mexicans were made of. If Pulitzer insisted on doubting the loyalty of the good Hispanic population of the Territory, then he'd furnish proof that would force Pulitzer to eat his words. "We'll see who's loyal," he muttered, scanning the original of the telegram he'd sent earlier in the week:

Governor's Mansion
Santa Fe, New Mexico Terr.
April 24, 1898
The Honorable Russel A. Alger,
Secretary of War Washington, D.C.

You will remember, sir, that almost two weeks ago, in anticipation of hostilities with Spain, I offered a regiment of volunteer cavalry from this territory. Now that war has begun, I would like to reiterate same—a full regiment of experienced horsemen, almost all of whom are of Spanish descent.

It has now been a half century since the Treaty of Guadalupe Hidalgo. I assure you that few if any of our citizens harbor any animosity toward the American government. As you know, many of our citizens of Spanish descent served honorably in the Civil War and again in the Indian Wars. Most consider themselves loyal citizens of the United States. Many would like to demonstrate their loyalty by performing their patriotic duty on the battlefield.

I assure you that our citizens view the criminal destruction of the Maine with the same sense of outrage as you Easterners. We ask only a chance to demonstrate our loyalty. Please advise, as I remain your humble and obedient servant,

Miguel Otero, Governor
New Mexico Territory

Otero was still lost in thought when his aide brought in Alger's answer. Though New Mexico would not be "required" to send a regiment, a battalion of good men would be appreciated. "The four territories (New Mexico, Oklahoma, Indian and Arizona) will supply a battalion each to form the First United States Cavalry Regiment, U.S. Volunteers, with Leonard Wood as Colonel and Theodore Roosevelt as Lt. Colonel. The New Mexico contingent should be ready to leave for training in San Antonio, Texas by May 5."

Holy Mother! Otero thought. We're in. Not a regiment, but still... He immediately summoned his aides. "We will have a public rally," he told them. "At 2:00 this afternoon in the plaza. New Mexico will be joining the war. Pass the word. I want a crowd!" As soon as his aides scurried out, he started to compose his remarks.

By 1:45 Governor Otero was ready. In addition to writing a short but stirring speech, he'd cabled a request for volunteers to Albuquerque, Las Cruces and Farmington. But just as he was donning his frock coat and preparing to cross the street to the plaza, he received another cable, this one from Roosevelt, outlining his needs. The Assistant Secretary of the Navy had nothing to say, one way or another, about Otero's offer for Spanish sir-named troopers. He had plenty to say about his other 'requirements.' Roosevelt wanted "the best possible examples" of those types who had been most responsible "for extending the enlightening mantle of civilization to the wild and barbarous territories of the West." Otero winced at that particular innuendo, but he understood the prejudice; he'd been co-existing with Anglo chauvinism for years. New Mexico was to be included in the war. That was all that mattered.

Governor Otero walked through the outer rooms of the three hundred year-old governor's palace, out across the veranda and into the plaza, where he was greeted simultaneously by a great cheer and a swirl of dust.

"Make way fer the guv! Make way fer the guv!"

Otero glanced up at a huge, red-bearded stranger wearing leather pants and a filthy, flowered vest. Amused, Otero followed the stranger, who was pushing his way through the jostling, exuberant crowd toward the band rotunda. "Make way fer the guv!" As soon as he was safe on the rotunda, Otero turned to shake the giant's hand. "Thank you, young man. Who are you?"

The red beard grabbed the soft, white hand of the Governor and almost crushed it with his enthusiasm. "Pike, Guv. William Pike. Happy as hell ta meech ya. I hate Spics as much as the rest of ya and I'm happy fer this war."

Otero felt his face turning red and dropped the affable idiot's hand as soon as he could get it away. Either Pike doesn't recognize me as being a 'spic' or doesn't know what he's saying, or both, he thought. He shook his head once, put a huge smile on his face, looked out over the crowd and raised his hands for silence.

"Ladies and Gentlemen." He again smiled at the mob that packed the plaza. The mob wasn't quieting down, so he flapped his short arms. "Please!" he yelled, still smiling. Something's wrong here, he thought. What is it? What is it? Then one part of the truth dawned on him. Where are the women? In the hundreds of faces spread before him he could spot only a score or so of women, most of whom were probably saloon girls. "Gentlemen! Gentlemen, please!" Perhaps it's the unruliness of the crowd, he told himself.

Suddenly the affable red-beard was on the rotunda next to him, yelling at the crowd, many of whom were jumping up and down, waving the special edition of the Santa Fe New Mexican that read "WAR WITH SPAIN" in six inch headlines. "Quiet! Damn ye!" Pike roared at the crowd. The crowd just laughed and yelled good-naturedly back. Today was War Day, a time for drinking and celebrating, a welcome break in the blustery, dusty weather that plagued Santa Fe every spring. "Quiet! Damn ye!" Pike repeated. "The guv wants ta speak."

"Damn yer own self," a heckler yelled back. "Who the hell do ya think YE are?"

"Hey, Shitheel! Whatcha runnin fer? Governess?" yelled another. Those around the second speaker laughed, then drew back, quieted. The big red-beard looked as though he were about to leap off the rotunda and into their midst. But the little governor grabbed the giant's arm and held on.

"Get back up here, you fool. Do you want to start a riot?"

Confused, Pike stood back and looked down into the Governor's steady black eyes. People, especially little people, especially little people standing within range of one of his rock-sized fists, didn't call Big Bill Pike "fool." But the Governor stared back and the crowd began to quiet.

"I came over here to address the good citizens of New Mexico, not to preside over a free-for-all. Sit down and behave yourself."

Otero's words stabbed into the giant, who retreated a step, as if trying to escape the little man's words and basilisk eyes. Then a huge grin spread across Pike's face. He bowed elaborately and sat down on the edge of the rotunda, an over-size boy who had decided to obey his demanding father.

The mob roared its approval. By taming his would-be benefactor, Otero had gained the mob's respect—and attention.

"Ladies and Gentlemen," the governor began, "WE ARE AT WAR!" Otero raised his small but tightly balled fists above his head. The mob roared. "WE ARE GOING TO CUBA!" Another roar of approval. "WE ARE GOING TO AVENGE THE *Maine* !" Still another roar. Otero stalked back and forth across the band rotunda like a bantam rooster. He was in charge. He allowed his prepared speech to flutter to the ground.

"America is girding for war. Even now American boys are being recruited to sail across the sea and crush the Spanish oppressor. America is setting sail for Cuba. Will New Mexico be left behind?"

"NO!" the crowd roared.

"America is getting ready to strike a blow for freedom. She has balled her fists in righteous indignation." Otero again balled his fists and raised his arms straight up. "Do we have fists?"

"Hell, yes!"

"All across this great land patriotic Americans are preparing to fight for the freedom of an oppressed people. Are we prepared to fight?"

"Hell, yes!"

"Are we, the citizens of New Mexico, loyal citizens?"

"Hell, yes! Hell, yes! Hell, yes!" The crowd, caught up in the spirit, chanted in unison. Otero looked to his right. Pike, the huge red-beard, was standing slightly to his rear, conducting the crowd's response with his huge arms like a Sunday School choir director. The Governor smiled. Hell, this is more fun than a political campaign. A shadow still lurked at the edge of his mind, but he couldn't be bothered, at least not right now. The prayer meeting was going too well.

"Are we New Mexicans—Hispanic and Anglo—prepared to fight?"

"Hell, yes! Hell, yes! Hell, yes!"

"To give our all for freedom and justice?"

"Hell, yes!"

"Are we going to win this war?"

" Hell, yes! HELL, Yes! "

"Good ! I knew that would be your answer. I have here," He plucked Secretary Alger's cable from his pocket, "a cable from the Secretary of WAR."

Prolonged cheer.

"The Army is recruiting a regiment of volunteer cavalry—cowboys, prospectors, trappers, lawmen. Washington expects the Territory to provide one battalion of mounted cavalry for the Cuban war. Can we do it?"

Pandemonium.

The Governor nodded his head vigorously. "Yes, my fellow New Mexicans. We can and we shall. Recruiting will begin the day after tomorrow. Washington wants men who can ride and shoot, who are in good shape, who are between eighteen and forty-five years of age. They want the best, and we've got the best! Right?"

"Hell, yes! "

"Are we going to win?" Otero again raised his fists straight up. He couldn't remember when he'd enjoyed himself more.

"HELL, YES! HELL, YES! HELL, YES!"

As he stepped from the rotunda, the friendly giant stepped down behind him. The chanting crowd parted like the Red Sea and the unlikely pair, the conservatively dressed bantam rooster and the lumbering bear, passed smilingly through. When the Governor reached the door of the Palace, he stopped and turned. "Thanks for your help, Mr...?"

"Pike, Guv. William Pike. And I want ta go ter Cuber."

"Can you ride and shoot?" Otero looked closely at the giant for the first time. Pike was almost 6'6" tall and must have weighed 250 pounds. Otero was 5'4" and weighed 140. Pike was duded up like a gambler who'd been camping in the same clothes for the better part of a decade: The neck of a once white cotton shirt was stained black with sweat and grit. His flowered vest was covered with the evidence of hundreds of nights around the fire: Beans, coffee, grease and wine combined to almost obliterate the original floral pattern. The Governor noted that Pike not only looked like a bear; he smelled like one.

"Yessir, Guv. I sure can ride 'n shoot. I was in the Injun wars and fought against Geronimo. Yessir."

"Good, I'm sure you'll be accepted. And...thanks for your help." Otero smiled and entered the Palace.

William Pike stood for a moment and stared at the solid oak door that had just shut in his face. His slow brain couldn't quite figure out why the Guv had left and why he hadn't been invited in to chew the rag for a while.

"Uppity spic son-of-a-bitch!" he muttered at the door. "Think yer too good ter offer a drink ter William Pike?" He turned and shuffled down the veranda-covered street, a slightly angry hulk of rising odors and bruised feelings.

Before he'd covered twenty yards, however, Pike spotted an old drinking partner. His hurt and confusion evaporated like a mid-summer mist. "Hey, Shorty!" he yelled at a six foot tall bean-pole that had duded itself up like Billy the Kid. "Wait up. I'll buy yer a drink." Grinning from ear to ear, he shuffled into the dusty street to greet his long lost friend.

Governor Otero sat behind his desk and tried to work. Though there was much to do, he couldn't concentrate. What was wrong? He knew the speech had been successful, and that New Mexico would have no difficulty recruiting a battalion of good men for the cavalry regiment. So what was wrong? He shuffled aimlessly through the papers filed on his desk. His eyes slowly focused on a copy of the cable he'd sent to Secretary Alger and centered on one clause, "a full regiment of experienced horsemen, almost all of whom are of Spanish descent." Almost all of whom are of Spanish descent. Are of Spanish descent. Spanish descent.

"No, I can't believe it." He felt himself sinking deeper into his cowhide-covered chair. He stared at the cable. That's it; that's what's wrong. He could feel the onset of fatigue as the perception leaped into clear focus: The cheering, drinking mob that had responded so enthusiastically to his call was a gringo mob. He forced his mind to wander back across the crowd of shouting, up-turned faces. Where were the New Mexicans of Spanish descent? Where were the settled and responsible citizens of Santa Fe? They had not been present. Of that he was certain. The mob had been composed of the drifting, legend-seeking emigres from the crowded eastern cities of Anglo-America and the riff-raff cowboys and sheepherders that the news of possible war had drawn like flies. The crowd had been composed of cowboys, mineral prospectors, retired soldiers, and the people who leeched from them: store-keepers, gamblers, barmen and hotel-keepers, the people who had been flocking into the Southwest for fifty years, ignorant of its traditions but eager to grab some of its riches, and always eager to change the unanticipated humdrum of their work in the "wild west" for any distraction that promised glory, excitement or unearned riches.

Otero felt his dream disintegrate. He saw with sharp if belated clarity that his regiment of "Spanish descent" had been an illusion. Far too many of his fellow *Hispanos* were still smarting from the terms of the Gadsden Purchase and the treaty of *Guadalupe-Hildalgo*. They resented the endless and growing presence of these stinking purveyors of Anglo-Saxon civilization who were so unabashedly contemptuous of Spanish language, religion and customs. Otero knew that the battalion he was preparing would be composed of Anglos rather than *Hispanos*.

In his moment of clarity, Otero also realized that, given the racial tensions in the Territory, the Anglo officers who controlled the National Guard would be unwilling to accept more than a token number of *Hispano* volunteers even if, by some miracle, a few stepped forward. Ten days later he was to nod his head in sad confirmation. Of the four hundred and ten men he put on the trains to San Antonio, there were three *Hispanos*, Captain Maxwell Luna, the romantic scion of an old Albuquerque family; Pedro Morales, a private from Bernalillo; and Michael Archuletta, a half-Irish private from the northern wastelands of the San Juan. All the rest were Anglo.

Governor Otero sighed and pushed his chair back from the desk. Well, he'd done all he could. He'd done his job, and no one in Washington would be able to fault him; nor would anyone in the Territory. Still, it would be nice if...He spent the rest of the afternoon staring at the wall and dreaming of his battalion of Hispanic-Americans charging through the jungles of Cuba, freeing their Cuban cousins and demonstrating in heroic battles their loyalty to the great United States.

Chapter Eighteen

CUBANS WIN A BATTLE AT MARIEL

* * * * *

On Board the Journal Dispatch Boat Anita, off Havana, May 5 — The first consignment of arms and ammunition supplied to the Cuban insurgents by the United States Government reached them yesterday, but it took a fight to get them ashore.

The tug Leyden carried the munitions of war, and also a party of insurgents under General Acosta, and five scouts under Captain Dorst, of the Fourth United States Cavalry. The Leyden first landed Acosta and his men near Mariel, thirty-three miles west of Havana. Acosta's mission was to find a rebel column and bring it to the beach next day to receive Uncle Sam's guns and cartridges.

The landing of the tug's cargo was in progress when a troop of 200 Spanish cavalry attacked Acosta's men. It was a pretty even thing for half an hour, but Acosta's men, fighting from cover, at last managed to drive the Spaniards away. *The New York Journal*, May 7.

Northern New Mexico Territory

M ichael Archuletta froze. She was calling his name, whispering to him from her pallet on the dirt floor of their hogan. He turned from the small, pot-bellied stove and glided to her side where he knelt and gazed into the brown eyes staring up at him. He took the damp cloth from her forehead, rinsed it in a pail of water and slowly bathed her face. "I love you, Sky Woman." He whispered the words with the intensity of a shaman casting away the darkness.

"I am dying," she stated simply, frowning at her husband as if worried he would do something silly. "You find another woman to care for you."

Michael said nothing but shook his head slowly back and forth and continued bathing her face. "Sky Woman..." he finally stammered, but found himself unable to go on. "Don't..."

She reached over and touched his lean, dark cheek and smiled into his green eyes. "It is time, my husband. There is nothing to be done." Her face was serene, and the worry lines above her nose had faded away.

As Sky Woman sank more deeply into her serenity, Archuletta became more agitated. He moved nervously back and forth between the stove and her pallet, freshening the tea that she no longer even pretended to drink. He wandered around their cramped hogan, searching the rough shelves, his small library of two dozen books, his saddle-bags and her army chest for some herb or talisman to arrest the spirit that was trying to flee her torn body. But even as he stumbled around the circular room, he kept his head turned almost constantly in her direction, as if afraid that her spirit would slip away during his desperate search for help.

She lay perfectly still, following his actions with her eyes. After awhile he gave up looking for magic and returned to her side. He would try to hold onto her with his eyes and his will, which was considerable. He sat by her side for a long time, his eyes locked with hers, his hand covering her out-stretched palm. As he stared into her eyes, he thought of the sadness that had always been there, and of the deep, uncommon knowledge that had always seemed to haunt even her most joyous moments.

Even at the squaw dance where they'd first met, he'd been struck by the sweet sadness of her smile, the tragic knowledge that seemed to glow within the depths of her eyes. In many ways Sky Woman was a light and lyrical person. She loved to ride, to sing, and to make love, just as she loved her husband, her parents and all the members of her clan. Whatever was responsible for her "depths," as he called it, she never seemed depressed. She listened well and loved to help others, especially the old ones. Whatever it was that caused the sadness behind her smile also enhanced her love of the moment. Sky Woman had always embraced life, though with less serenity than she now seemed to embrace death.

Michael started from his reverie. Though the serene smile still clung to her face, he had, somehow, allowed the light to leave her eyes. He wanted very much to cry, but found he couldn't. He caressed her cheek then rose stiffly to his feet, poured himself a cup of the still simmering tea and hunkered down by the stove. He sipped his tea and stared at his dead wife. The flickering light from the kerosene lantern resting on the earth floor by her pallet played across his face and across her dead eyes, which still stared softly into his.

A little later he filled a bucket with fresh spring water and washed her bruised and torn body. Then, as he stared again at the wounds the two gringos had made with their knives, the tears finally came. After the tears passed, he took her small bottle of store perfume and rubbed it over her body, then bent down to kiss her mouth and inhale the "Lilacs of Spring." With unaccustomed awkwardness he dressed her in her full, green cotton skirt, purple velveteen blouse and doeskin moccasins. He transferred to his own finger her turquoise ring.

Suddenly overcome with sadness and rage, he threw the tin cup to the ground, stuffed his saddlebags with his clothes and threw them out the door, poured kerosene over the interior of the hogan, lit a twig from the stove, and walked out the door, tossing the burning twig onto the floor. He dragged his neighing horse to a small hill, pulled a pint of whiskey from his saddlebags, and hunkered down to stare at the blaze.

By dawn nothing was left but a mound of ashes and a thin column of white smoke that spiraled straight up in the still air. During the two hours it had taken the fire to consume itself and Sky Woman, Michael had sipped slowly from the bottle and thought about his Irish mother. She had come from Dublin to New York to El Paso to work as governess for a rich merchant. The year before Michael's birth she had tired of the merchant's attentions and the insults of his wife. At the first opportunity she had stolen her employer's household money and ridden four hundred miles north to the Colorado-New Mexico frontier. The man she chose to accompany her on her long trek was an *Hispano* sheepherder who had wandered back through El Paso after a three month visit to relatives in Ciudad Juarez.

By the time Michael was three, she had turned the sheepherder into an insecure rancher who grazed sheep along a thousand acres of bottom land that meandered for miles along the Navajo River. But when Michael was nine the Denver owner of the land tried to evict the family through legal means. When that failed he hired drifters to shoot Michael's father.

Michael Archuletta stayed with his mother until her death. Or, rather, she followed him from one ranch to another and one flock of sheep to the next, seven ranches in twelve years. She gave her son her love for books, her pride and her fierce love of independence. He supported her, loved her, and inhaled her hatred for the "Americans," who had cheated, insulted and degraded her ever since her arrival at Ellis Island. She had nothing to do with the "American" shopkeepers of, Aztec, Durango and Pagosa Springs, the settlements that formed the boundaries of her and her son's nomad existence. She and Michael were despised by the local shopkeepers, who thought she was crazy and knew that he was dangerous. Their only friends were the *Hispano* and Navajo sheepherders with whom they summered in the high meadows of the San Juan and La Plata mountains and with whom they wintered in the one room log shacks and hogans of northern New Mexico.

When his mother died, Michael took a long trip with a Navajo friend to the Chuska Mountains of northwestern New Mexico. On that trip he attended a squaw dance and met the sad-eyed but smiling young woman known as Sky Woman. Two months later he rode back to the Chuskas with presents for her family and returned to the Colorado border country with Sky Woman and a hundred sheep. The couple lived on the northeastern fringe of the Navajo reservation, tending their sheep and trying to ignore the increasing numbers of Americans who were moving across their country. They lived alone with their few horses and dogs, their sheep and the respect of the various herders who passed through from time to time.

Though he was aware of the pale rosiness of early dawn, Archuletta continued to stare toward the mound of smoking ashes that marked the site of the hogan. When he drained the final drops of whiskey and threw the bottle into the ashes, the small explosion of the super-heated glass snapped him from his revery. He saddled his horse and, just as the sun rose above the sharp-peaked San Juan mountains, rode off toward Aztec.

He did not bother to report his wife's murder or to seek information from any of the Americans who inhabited the region. Rather, he went to the hogan of a friend, received a promise to tend the flock, "even for many years," and rode on a zig-zag pattern that took him to many of the Navajo hogans and *Hispano* cabins of the northern plateau. He passed on the description of the two men that Sky Woman had given him, asked if anyone had seen them and, when his listeners shook their heads, turned and rode on.

He had ridden almost to Two Grey Buttes when he encountered an old Navajo woman herding a small flock. She was on foot, scurrying back and forth behind the bleating goats, assisted by a mangy dog who looked too old to breathe, let alone herd.

"Hello, Auntie," he said in Navajo. "You and your brave dog have really got those dumb goats going."

"Aiee! Mister. Nobody will help me. Those goats are like my children. They're going to run away and leave old Granny to die in the sun. My old man's run away to Durango to drink the Americans' poison. Nobody wants to help Granny any more."

"Hey, Auntie. You know the world changes. I know your troubles because troubles ride with me. Two Americans committed filth upon my wife. Then they tore her with their knives. Her spirit has left me to ride with the wind."

"The Americans have always been trouble for us, just as you New Mexicans were before them."

"My wife was of the people, Auntie."

"I am sorry to hear of her death," the old woman replied without emotion. "It was worse when I was young. You should have been at *Basque Redondo* with the heartless American, Kit Carson. After he led us on the Long Walk, he had us living in gopher holes for four years. We lived with death. Now you know. We will always live with death."

"Auntie, I am looking for the two Americans who did this thing to my wife. What stories have you heard?"

"I know many stories. I have many more stories than goats. You still need a strong wife. You come and live with me and keep me warm at night and I'll tell you many stories."

The old woman giggled at the thought, but when the young man failed to react, she looked sharply up at him and spoke bluntly. "What did the Americans look like?"

"One was tall and thin; the other was shorter, but also thin. They both had dark beards and hair. They smelled like bears. The taller man was a blue eyes."

"Aiee! young man. Is that all you can say? All Americans smell like bears. They never clean their bodies."

"I did not see them. My wife was dying when she told me about them."

"Hmmph! Maybe I have a story for you. Last night before the first star, I met three of our people. They were going to the trading post. I asked them if they had any stories. They told me they had met two Americans who were heading south to Santa Fe. The two Americans bought some lamb's meat from our people and rode on. They didn't want to talk, especially the tall man. Such rudeness. What are Americans like if they have no time for stories? Maybe these men were the evil ones who deprived you of your woman. Only people without stories would do such a thing, no?"

"Did your people find out anything else?"

"Aiee!" The old woman slapped her head. "The shorter man who talked a little said they were going to Santa Fe to be soldiers. The Americans are getting ready to start a new war against somebody. Our people said that the blue eyes became angry with the other man for talking so much."

"Thank you, Auntie. You remembered well." Michael Archuletta remounted and turned south-east toward Santa Fe.

"Hey, Mister. You come back sometime at night and I'll tell you some good stories," she cackled, smiling up at the rider.

"Hey, Auntie. Maybe I will. Someday. Maybe I will. May grass always flow with your goats." The old woman watched him ride away. When he finally turned around a hill and out of sight, she called her dog, slapped the closest nanny with her stick and continued her meandering search for grass.

Chapter Nineteen

NEW PLAN FOR ANNEXING HAWAII
Resolution Before Congress for Bringing Islands Into the Union

* * * * *

Washington, May 8—Representative Newlands, of Nevada, has introduced a joint resolution for the annexation of Hawaii. It provides for the confirmation of the cession by the Hawaii Republic of all rights of sovereignty over the Islands and their dependencies. *The World*, May 8.

Santa Fe, New Mexico Territory

"How many more miles to Santa Fe?"

The conductor glanced down at the fancy dude with a look of amused annoyance. "This here's Pecos comin' up. Last stop. Ain't but thirty miles er so inta Santa Fe. Where ya headed that yer in sech a hurry?"

"I'm joining the Volunteer Cavalry," Alex answered, smiling proudly.

"Heh!" The conductor stared at the dude for a few seconds, shrugged his shoulders and limped on down the aisle, shaking his head. This dude don't look any more savvy than the rest of them, he thought. The conductor had seen several eastern swells coming through to join the cowboy cavalry, most of whom looked too dandified to sit a horse, let alone ride one. One thing he couldn't figure out, though. Most of the eastern dudes coming west so they could go east to Cuba were big men. They averaged four or five inches in height more than the cowboys, trappers and miners who had spent their youths scrounging a living from the Great American Desert. Their limbs were straight, their complexions clear. They were larger of frame and less wiry than the native Westerners with whom they would be serving, and most of them seemed to still have all their teeth.

As he thought of the difference between these large, well-to-do Easterners and the dried-up men with whom he'd spent his life, the conductor rediscovered with thunderous clarity something he'd always known. Money makes a difference. The conductor thought of his seven brothers and sisters, three of whom had died of diphtheria. He thought of his own three children, one of whom had died of typhus. He thought of his wife, twenty years younger than himself but looking fully as old. The conductor wondered if this passenger—or any of the other fancy dudes coming west—had ever known suffering or tasted the certainty of inevitable defeat. And he wondered why men like these were abandoning their lives of comfort to fight in a war that didn't concern them.

As he stared at the slowly passing red rock and pinon, Alexander Dumas Jackson asked the same question. Why had he left the sophistication of the Capital, the promise of his budding career as a bureaucrat, and the smooth splendor of Charlotte's skin? All for a dried out, dusty and uncomfortable trip into this geographical and cultural desert? And why was he planning to travel to an even more backward and barbaric island off the tip of Key West? He shook his head and smiled. He knew perfectly well why he had come. He was bored with his job; he desired adventure and the possibility of glory; he wanted, most of all, to see Christopher.

Alex focused on the pinon and juniper that covered the south slope of the *Sangre de Cristo* mountains. The gnarled trees seemed to be fighting their way from the arid soil, like so many of the passengers on the train. He shook his head again. He didn't really mind the discomforts of the trip, and he knew he'd be fine as soon as he got a hot bath and a good night's sleep in a real bed.

"This here's Pecos," the conductor yelled from the rear of the car. "Won't be here fer long." Alex looked out toward the Pecos "station," little more than a huge box that opened toward the tracks. A lone man, dressed in ragged buckskins, picked up a bedroll and started for the train. My gosh, Alex thought. He looks like something out of the old West.

A moment later the man approached from the rear and threw his dusty bedroll down next to Alex's highly polished boots. "Howdy, pilgrim. Mind if I set? Them's pinon trees. Good fire wood. Nuts er a real treat."

Alex turned from the window, which was beginning to steam over with his warm breath. The apparition smiled at him through a filthy beard and bad teeth.

"No, I mean, yes. Sit down." Alex immediately regretted his manners. He was almost overwhelmed by the worst stench he could remember experiencing.

"Sorry about the smell. Don't bother me none. Guess 'cause I'm used to 'er. But folks always kinda shies away when I'm around. And they always try ter stay upwind. It's the bear fat. Keeps the varmints off real good."

"Oh," Alex ventured, mesmerized by both the smell and the hazel eyes that, contrary to all other aspects of the mountain man's appearance, stared innocently at the younger man's befuddlement. "Seems strong enough to work."

The apparition exploded in laughter, bent over, slapped his thighs, stomped his feet and clapped his hands. "You said it, pilgrim. Yessir. It sure do work. Where ya headed?"

"Santa Fe."

"Is that a fact? So 'm I. Whaccha gonna do in Santer Fe?"

"Join the Volunteer Cavalry that's going to Cuba." Alex was disconcerted by the directness of the apparition's questions. He'd heard that Westerners were more taciturn.

"Is that a fact?" The apparition slapped his thigh again, sending a small cloud of dust into the air and a small pile of mud crumbs onto the floor. "I knew it, Mr....Sorry, didn't getcher name."

"Jackson, Alexander Jackson. And what..."

"Thought it was somethin' like that. Well, Alex." The apparition sat up straight, placed both hands flat on his knees and smiled benevolently, as if preparing to bestow some great blessing upon his listener. "Had a dream last night and knew this mornin' that I was gonna meet a new friend, and that we was gonna do a spell of travelin'. I'm fixin' ter go ter Cuber, too. How do ya like them apples?"

Alex wasn't sure. He was both fascinated with and repelled by the man's directness. He wasn't at all sure he wanted to encourage it. But since he didn't know what else to do, he answered politely. "I'm glad to hear that you're going. It should be a good romp."

"A good romp?" The Westerner stared blankly at Alex for a long second then blinked twice. "Yessiree, ole buddy, that's a fact. My name's Marty Mason. Friends call me Mountain Man Mason."

"Have you always been?"

"A mountain man? Nope. Don't know that I rightly am now. Been out three years, from Lowell, Massachusetts. Useter work in a shoe factory but I couldn't stand 'er. Went ter Chicager fer awhile, but that weren't no better. Like ter read dime novels?" Alex shook his head, bemused. "I do. Love 'em. Thas where I got the idear ter move west."

As Mountain Man Mason babbled on, Alex pondered the foul-smelling bundle of incongruities that had, apparently, adopted him.

Though Alex had given a lot of thought to his own participation in the regiment, the picture he would cut in his uniform, and the democratic decision of his fellow college men to enlist as "regular fellows," he had given no thought at all to the other regular fellows of the west with whom he would be eating, sleeping and fighting. Slightly discomfited, he wondered what the rest of his new companions would be like. As he listened to Mountain Man, he nodded occasionally and gazed from the window of the slowly moving train.

"You ain't really listenin' ter me, are ye?" Mountain Man asked. "Yer kinda wonderin' about me, ain't ya?" Then, without waiting for an answer, which he didn't seem to expect, he rushed on. "That's all right. Them folks as don't call me Mountain Man call me Rapid Mouth. I do like ter talk, an thas a fact. Been storin' up some, too. Been over in Mora County livin' with the Mex's eight er nine months. Doin' a little pros- pecting. Didn't get off ten words a day, 'cept ter myself. Damn Mex's don't know no English. Been part of this country fer fifty years 'n still don't speak English."

Alex thought he saw an opening and leaped in. "I understand that Spanish is the native language for most of the older residents of New Mexico. Have you learned any of it?"

Mountain Man looked at Alex as if the latter were crazy. "Learnt any Mex? Hell, no. What'd I wanter do that fer? I'm a white man. Them spics wanter live in America, they gonna have ter learn English, an thas a fact, Bub. There's a pile a white men around who know Mex fer one reason er another, but ain't too many brags on the fact."

"Well, it seems to me," Alex started, but his weak rejoinder was swept away by the foul smelling torrent of Mountain Man's interrupted autobiography.

"Don't like Mex's too much, but I can live with 'em. Know damn near everybody in the area, an thas a fact. You can check. Hell, one time I was doin' some work in the La Platas, over near Durango. Went ter town fer some goods an ran inter Bill Pike an four other fellers. 'Fore we finished, knew everyone in town, 'cludin' the sheriff and jailer."

Alex chuckled. Mountain Man was at least interesting, harmless background noise that seemed to complement the flat-roofed mud houses the train was rolling by.

So this is Santa Fe, he thought. Other than the pinon and juniper trees, everything was reddish brown—the houses, walls and streets, even the people, or so it seemed.

"Well, pilgrim, this here's it. Ya gotter place ta hang yer hat?"

"I'm supposed to have accommodations at the Territorial House. How about yourself?"

"Too pricey fer me. I'll jes camp out on the plaza. If they boot me, I'll check in above the Teamster's Bar. Soft women 'n hard beds, if ye receive my meanin." Mountain Man was standing even before the train pulled into the station. He grabbed his bedroll, loped half way down the aisle, then turned to shout back, "See yer later, pilgrim. Be over tonight with some a the boys ta show ye the sights."

He was gone before Alex could protest. All Alex wanted was a long bath, a hot meal and a soft bed. The last thing he needed was to traipse around the bars of Santa Fe with three or four stinking primitives.

* * * * *

Alex stared at the mob milling around the small bar. Other than a few Mexican and Indian women, who made their way through continuous gauntlets of pinching and squeezing to keep the tables supplied with beer and tequila, almost all the occupants of the bar were white men, most of whom were celebrating both their freedom and their new, vague sense of being a part of something larger than themselves. Most of the would-be recruits crowding the bar shared more traits with Alex than he would have cared to admit. Some were married, but most were not. Though several, like Mountain Man and his friends, were anachronisms, misfits born a half century late and half a pickled mind short, most of the warrior wannabes were hard-working cowboys, miners and store clerks who were deserting the unfulfilling regimens of their work-a-day worlds. A few sought glory; all sought excitement. And excitement was coming early, especially for Alex.

Shortly after he'd stretched out in his feather bed at the Territorial House, Mountain Man and two of his friends had crashed into the room and virtually forced him to accompany them on their rounds. Now, sitting around a table in the Mercator Bar, he was still too petrified by the incident to relax, let alone enter into the spirit of the occasion. This just is not happening, he repeated to himself. Civilized people just don't act this way.

"What's this?" he asked, as Bill Pike, the giant red beard, plunked a bottle of golden liquid down in the middle of the table. The red beard just grinned, took a handful of limes from a bag, and sliced them into quarters with a huge clasp knife.

"Tequila," Shorty spat.

"What Shorty means," Mountain Man elaborated, "is this here poison's the most fierce good fer fun tonic that the good Lord put here fer our considerable enjoyment. It's Mexican firewater, 'n it's good. Thas a fact."

"Only good thing about the spics is their booze and their women," Shorty added in his clipped, hard syllables. "Try it."

"Watch," Bill Pike commanded, grinning. He licked the back of his hand, poured a small pile of salt on the wet spot, squeezed on some juice from the lime, took a deep pull from the bottle of tequila, licked the gooey collage from the back of his hand, puckered and broke again into his almost continual smile.

"See, ain't that easy?" Mountain Man asked. Alex thought he was going to throw up; it was the most disgusting thing he'd ever seen. Still, he knew that he had to go along. His new friends had made it absolutely clear that they had adopted him and that, Goddamnit, he was going to learn to act like a man.

After his third Tequila Macho, as Bill Pike called their straight tequila concoction, Alex discovered that he was enjoying himself. In fact, he thought, as he listened to one tall tale after another, he couldn't remember when he'd had a better time. These men were the salt of the earth.

For the last ten minutes, he hadn't uttered a word. He just sat in his chair, chin propped on his elbows, watching the roaring crowd and listening to Rapid Mouth and Big Bill Pike brag about adventures that, he was sure, the two had concocted from whole cloth for his exclusive entertainment.

Shorty, who was tall and beanpole thin, with glacially blue eyes, said little. Though he laughed cynically at some of his friends' stories, he spent most of his attention glaring around the room.

"How come ya bein so goddamned quiet?" Pike barked, almost knocking Shorty out of his chair with a friendly punch. "Ya gotta sour stomach er somethin?"

"You just leave me alone, you over-grown puppy. I'm just fine sittin' here listenin' to you and Ding-bat Mason fartin' through your mouths so as to impress this here dude. Ain't no call for me ta break wind, too."

"Now that just ain't like you, Shorty," Rapid Mouth said. "If it ain't a sour stomach, must be some trouble. Ya have some trouble up north last week? One a them Naverjos catch ya screwin' one a their wives?"

Rapid Mouth's laugh was cut short by Shorty's fist, which slammed across his nose and sent him to the floor. Shorty leaped from the chair and glared down at his victim. "Listen here, you smart-assed sheep-fuck-er, What I do up north ain't none of yer fuckin' business."

At the mention of "Navajo" a dark-skinned man in sheepskin pants and velveteen shirt had turned his entire attention to the fight, the fifth or sixth that had broken out that night. Although he said nothing during the short-lived fracas, Michael Archuletta looked at Shorty very carefully and listened even more carefully to the man's words.

"I'm sorry, Shorty," Rapid Mouth mumbled from the floor. "It's jes that I know how ya likes them Navajo women, 'n I thought that maybe ye'd found yerself some trouble." Shorty fell to his knees, straddled Rapid Mouth and swung at his head with both fists.

Shorty knew that everyone in the cantina was listening, but he couldn't control himself. "I told ya, sheep fucker," Shorty hissed. "Keep your foul smellin' mouth out of my business. I didn't have no fuckin' trouble with anyone. At least til I got here."

Bill Pike took one long look around the room, picked up a half full bottle of tequila, and thoughtfully smashed it against the side of Shorty's head, which ended the altercation and sent the gawkers back to their tables. Pike picked Shorty up and propped him, still unconscious, in his chair. After another long minute, Marty, alias Mountain Man, alias Rapid Mouth Mason, picked himself up out of the sawdust and spit, and sat back down. Even though his nose was dripping slowly onto the table, he called for another bottle of tequila, licked the back of his hand, and recommenced his bout with the Mexican white lightning.

Alex sat frozen. Each vignette was more improbable than its predecessor. In the most improbable scene of all, Bill Pike, Rapid Mouth, Alex and, eventually, Shorty sat quietly around the table and concentrated upon becoming blind drunk. No one said a word about the battle, and soon the three old friends were laughing and cussing at each other as if it had never taken place.

Finally, after considerable, albeit muddled thought, Alex cleared his throat three times, pushed his chair back, stood up from the table and prepared to speak. The words squeaked from his anesthetized mouth. As he spoke, his three new friends stared at him with vague curiosity, as if watching a chipmunk stand upon its hind legs to speak. "Gentlemen... It's been...long days. Gotta go to bed now. Sorry." Without further ado, the young refugee from Georgia, via Harvard and the War Department, turned toward the door and marched in a perfectly straight line out into the plaza, where he promptly collapsed and vomited on the steps of the band rotunda.

Back inside the cantina the three anachronisms were discussing Cuba. Shorty could not believe that his two friends were serious about joining up, even though he'd ridden to Santa Fe with the same idea in mind. "Goddamn, Rapid Mouth. You been runnin' from bosses yer whole fuckin' life, and yer going ta join the fuckin' army?"

"Well, ole buddy," Mountain Man replied, his nose still leaking slowly onto the table, "prospectin' ain't what she used ter be, 'n I'm gettin' fed up not havin' nobody ter talk to, 'cept sheep and Mex's."

Bill Pike placed his huge paw on Mountain Man's shoulder. "Shit, Rapid Mouth, you jes wanna go'n kill some o' them spics from Spain. You ain't foolin' nobody."

"Yep, thas a fact," Mountain Man admitted, grinning. "I c'n think of worse ways ta spend a couple months, 'specially since we'll get money and grub fer doin' it, an be doin' ole Uncle Sam a good turn ta boot."

Pike turned to Shorty. "Sure do sound good ta me. Why doncha come along? Hell, we'll be back in a couple a months, an' with some money saved."

"Wouldn't pass it up for the world, though can't say as I'm much for Army life."

"Dee-lighted!" Mountain Man pounded the table, which made his nose bleed more profusely. "I hear them Cuban gals is real hot tamales. The women's warm 'n the rum runs free."

Shorty nodded, smiling at Rapid Mouth's nose. "Yep, sounds good. Came down from Pagosa half thinkin' I might. I ain't too hot on goin' back up north fer a spell." A cloud seemed to pass across Shorty's vision.

He shook his head, shivered briefly, and prepared to sip-lick another tequila. "But let's hit the hay. The dude's right. It's gettin' late"

Shorty's two friends were so pleased he'd decided to go to Cuba with them that they completely missed the brief spasm that had changed Shorty's mood. Michael Archuletta, who had been covertly watching Shorty's every gesture, missed nothing. After the three anachronisms left, Michael turned back to the bar and stared into the bottom of his whiskey glass. At first he saw only the distorted reflection of his own dark face. But after swirling the last quarter inch of whiskey for a while, other faces began to appear. First Sky Woman's: laughing at him the first time he'd tried to make fry bread; gazing softly up into his face at the Teec Nos Pos squaw dance; imploring him in a way he didn't understand when he found her naked and dying on the path to the river. He saw the flames rising from the hogan and Shorty's hate-twisted face as he straddled Mountain Man's body and swung his balled fists insanely at the man's head. Finally, and for a long time, he saw Sky Woman's face as she stared at him in the moments of her death.

Chapter Twenty

AMERICAN TROOPS TO OCCUPY THE PHILIPPINES AS
FORETOLD BY THE JOURNAL

* * * * *

Washington, May 9—The Journal's exclusive publication of the plans for
the occupation of the Philippine Islands was fully verified today. 10,000
troops are to be rushed to Manila. Acting Rear-Admiral Dewey will
remain in command of the approaches to the city of Manila until relieved
by General Merriam, who will sail from San Francisco with the first
detachment of troops. *The New York Journal*, May 10.

Santa Fe

Alex stood on the platform between two of the cars and waved at the screaming crowd. A few of the onlookers had lapsed into silence, as if intuiting the deaths from malaria, yellow fever and bullets that awaited many of the young adventurers. But the mounting hysteria of the rest of the crowd drowned out the small islands of silence. America was on the move.

Young women wearing their prettiest dresses and sashes of red, white and blue bunting walked along the track, passing box lunches through the windows to the brave troopers. A young woman with soft brown eyes approached Alex and handed him a lunch. As he accepted it and smiled his thanks, he felt the coolness of her fingers as they brushed across his outstretched hand. She looked up at him for a moment, slightly puzzled and totally vulnerable.

"What's your name?" Alex asked, smitten by the depths of her eyes.

"Mary Ellen Evans," she stammered. "What's yours?"

"Alexander Du...Alex. Alex Jackson. What's your address?"

"Fourteen Canyon Road. Are you going to write to me?"

"I sure am," Alex assured her, a little too loudly, simultaneously sensing the envy of the surrounding troopers and slight pangs of guilt as he remembered another young woman to whom he had made a similar promise in Washington ten days earlier.

The train pulled slowly from the station. They were still holding the box lunch between them and he was still touching her cool fingers. "May I kiss you?" he asked. She looked quickly to her right and left and lifted her chin, eyes closed and lips slightly puckered. Alex leaned down from the platform and kissed her once, coolly, and then a second time, more warmly.

He cursed the train as it built up momentum and pulled away from the young woman. Mary Ellen Easton? Eakins? Edons? Alex panicked as he realized that he had already forgotten her name, but he was too embarrassed by his carelessness to ask again, so he just stood between the cars and waved as she receded into the distance, a solitary figure surrounded by a howling crowd, a diminishing patriot dressed in white and draped with bunting who stood quietly, both hands hanging at her sides, watching the train jerk away toward the east.

When he could no longer see the station, Alex elbowed his way into the car and, ignoring the calls of Bill Pike and Rapid Mouth, found a seat next to a quiet, dark-complexioned man with whom, apparently, no one was anxious to sit. Alex was still thinking of the young woman, the excitement of the momentary flirtation and the Washington fiancée he had just betrayed, or at least wanted to. Not until the train had almost reached Pecos Pass did he realize that silence had descended on the car like a mantle of fog.

The recruits were subdued, lost in thought. They had left the bands, the liquor and the pretty girls at the station, and were headed east, toward six weeks of training at San Antonio, another long train ride to Florida, and a boat trip to Cuba. The new volunteers were still excited and determined. Now that they had time to think, however, their great adventure seemed a little more complicated than it had when the liquor, the kisses and the patriotic slogans flowed freely to the stirring bars of the "Battle Hymn of the Republic."

Alex sat quietly all the way to Las Vegas. The man next to him didn't seem to want to talk, which satisfied Alex just fine. Not until an hour after the train had stopped for the Las Vegas contingent did Alex attempt to meet his seat mate. Other than discovering that the man's name was Michael Archuletta, however, Alex could get nothing from him. The man showed no interest in making friends.

Later that evening, when Archuletta seemed to be responding to the sunset that stretched across the New Mexico plains, Alex tried again. "That sure is a bee-ootiful sunset," he exclaimed appreciatively, trying to emulate the casual western drawl he had been listening to for the past week.

"What's that?" Archuletta replied, roused from a memory where Sky Woman was fixing their evening meal during a similar sunset.

"The sunset. It sure is bee-ootiful."

"Yes," Archuletta snapped, nodding his head and turning from the window, as if Alex's statement had broken a spell. "Do you always talk like that?" He glanced at Alex and watched him turn red. After a minute of embarrassed silence, the sheepherder rose from his seat and walked to the other end of the car.

Alex felt shrunken and confused. He knew that his words had offended the man, but not how or why. When Archuletta finally returned from the platform between the cars, where he had stood quietly gazing west toward the sunset, Alex decided to try one more time. "I'm sorry," he said simply, looking straight into Archuletta's eyes. When the man failed to respond, Alex turned away and concentrated on the fading light. The horizon, a line of the southernmost *Sangre de Cristo* mountains, waned from grey to black. The jagged line scored a sky that had faded from magenta to indigo.

"Jackson?" Alex turned from the window to find Archuletta eyeing him with speculative interest. Alex said nothing. He started to smile but thought better of it. Rather, as had the sheepherder earlier, he merely nodded his head. "Moments that are beautiful don't need words. Words don't add much to what is already clear. If the moment is already perfect, words wound the peace." Archuletta smiled slightly, shut his eyes and pretended to fall asleep.

After spending half an hour trying to decode the sheepherder's statement, which struck Alex as some strange form of sermon, he sank back into the corner of the seat and drifted in and out of a restless sleep. Alex dreamed of his father, who was already old and listless when Alex was born. The old man hardly ever worked, and never without complaint. He was too tired, too incapacitated by his war wounds, and too contemptuous of the shopkeeper's role assigned to him by his hard-faced wife, whose frugality and determination had kept the family together, both during the war years and after.

In Alex's dreams the old man was always talking and Alex was always listening. The old man swept across cannon devastated hills on a bay gelding, sword arm slashing at foul-mouthed Yankees, many of whom were runaway slaves trying to destroy the South and defile its women. In the dreams Alex always rode behind his father; he, too, flashed a sword. He helped his father with "the only work man was fit for," and his father praised him for his bravery. They always rode up hill, out of the forest and toward the light. The Yankees were always on foot, always seemed to be little more than blue-coated bushes and roots that sprang from the creepers and tried to pull them from the prancing gelding. All the time they were charging up the hill, his father never stopped talking, just as he never stopped flashing his sword. And Alex never stopped listening to the long tales of heroic deeds performed by brave and honorable men.

But this time Alex's dream changed in mid-course. He and his father weren't on the hill any longer; they were in the store. Little Alex was sorting spools of thread and stacking them on the glass counter. It was August and his chin was dripping sweat onto the counter, which he kept wiping with his handkerchief, glancing nervously toward his father to see if the old man had noticed. But the old man was talking to two of his cronies, one of whom kept dipping into the cracker barrel, stuffing his mouth, and nodding his perfectly bald, glistening head in sage agreement with everything the other two were saying.

His father was doing most of the talking and combing his long salt and pepper beard with his fingers. The men had gone out on patrol the night before and destroyed one of the black devils who had done something awful to a white woman. Alex didn't understand what the men were talking about, except that they had done something very brave and important. Christopher had said that the war had been over for twelve years and that the Yankees had finally all gone home, but Alex knew that his older brother was wrong. Their father said that the war would go on forever, and that the Yankees and niggers were in cahoots. Little Alex stood behind the counter, slowly moving his handkerchief in perfect circles on the polished glass.

Alex was afraid of his father, who always made him work and never praised him. But the boy was also proud of the old man and wanted desperately to please him. He couldn't wait to grow up and help his father protect the county against the black devils who were really Yankees in disguise.

Suddenly, Christopher was standing next to him. His brother's eyes looked as though they were going to pop from his head. He was mumbling, "The old bastard killed George, the old bastard killed George," over and over, as if it were a chant. Alex didn't understand what Christopher was talking about, though he knew George. Was George a secret Yankee? Had the old man been forced to fight against him? Alex watched his older brother turn and leave the store. He felt like crying because Christopher hadn't paid any attention to him, but as soon as Christopher's plaid shirt disappeared, Alex returned to polishing the counter. His father was still talking.

Then Michael Archuletta was standing at his side. Alex pulled on Archuletta's arm, just as he had pulled on Christopher's, but the man also ignored him. He seemed intent upon listening to the three veterans discuss their adventures of the night before. Then Archuletta spit into the cracker barrel, looked down at Alex and said, "Those are termites pretending to be men. Will you ever grow up, little termite?" Then he disappeared and little Alex was again polishing the sweat-stained counter.

Alex awoke with a jerk and stared at Archuletta, who was sleeping next to him. My God! I'm sweating, he thought, staring at his hands. He pulled a large red handkerchief from his pocket and wiped his face and hands. It took him a moment to figure out where he was. Never before had he dreamed about the store. Nor did he remember such an incident, though some nudge in the back of his mind told him that it had occurred. What was Archuletta doing in the dream? And what did he mean about termites? Certainly the dream dealt with more than just talking too much. He knew that he talked too much, especially when he was nervous, or trying to impress someone, which was often the same thing. But in the dream he had said nothing; only his father had spoken.

Alex stared covertly across the seat at Archuletta. What is there about this man? Why is he so different? Is it just that he's Mexican, or at least part Mexican? Why is he the only Mexican in the outfit? Everyone else seems to be going to Cuba because they think it will be an adventure. Why is he going?

As the train sped southeast across the plains, Alex kept worrying. He couldn't make any more sense of Archuletta's presence in the dream than he could of the incident. He and Christopher had never discussed it, just as they had never discussed anything else relating to the old man since his death. Alex grew up knowing that his brother had always hated their father. There was much they would have to talk about when he got to Cuba. After an hour or so of sleeplessness, during which he stared, sightless, out the window, he fell into a deep sleep, disturbed only by erotic dreams of the girl at the Santa Fe station.

Chapter Twenty-One

LEE WILL OCCUPY PALACE IN HAVANA, AND WILL BE MILITARY DICTATOR IN CUBA

* * * *

Washington, May 9—Major General Fitzhugh Lee will be the first military governor of Cuba. He was at the War Department today consulting Secretary Alger and General Miles. For the next two weeks he will act as the official advisor of Secretary Alger. When Havana is taken General Lee will...assume the temporary dictatorship of the island until a republican and stable form of government is established by the Cubans. *The World*, May 10.

The Bay of Banes, Northern Oriente Province

Christopher raised his field glasses and scanned their position. They had left their headquarters and field hospital two kilometers back in the jungle. The balance of their two hundred man unit stretched across two long hills and a connecting ridge. Christopher and eighty of his *mambises* huddled in a hastily dug trench that snaked along the vine-covered top of the ridge.

From the sea to their north, a Spanish coastal patrol slammed three-inch shells into their position. Less than a quarter mile away, well-concealed Spanish soldiers sniped at the least movement. The rebels could still retreat down their ridges to the north toward the beach; otherwise, they were pinned to their trenches.

Christopher turned to Fidel, Cuba Libre's newest captain, who was still out of breath from running up the hill from the beach. "How are we doing?"

The huge black son of Federico and Oinja grunted and pointed out into the bay where the South Carolina filibuster, Jessie Anne, was burning. "We have the supplies on the beach, but they can't help us much down there. We have to get rid of that Spanish gunboat."

Christopher shook his head. "Not as long as the Spanish hold the other ridge." He hunkered down further into the trench to think. Their mounted column and hundred pack mules had traveled light in order to intercept the American supply boat at the scheduled time. Because they traveled light, without their two pack howitzers, they had been able to cross eastern Cuba from south to north in less than three days. Had they covered the ground any less rapidly, they would have missed the Jessie Anne, or failed to unload the supplies before she was discovered by the Spanish gunboat that was now shelling them. "If we only had our artillery," Christopher muttered, cursing the need for haste that had cost them their howitzers.

"We aren't going to have any artillery, Colonel, so…"

"No, and there's not a damn thing we can do about the gunboat, is there?" Fidel's stoicism often irritated Christopher.

"No. So…"

"So let's concentrate on these pubic lice Spanish infantry. We have to deal with them regardless of what that damned gunboat does." Christopher picked up his field glasses and slowly re-scanned their position—the two hills, the crescent shaped connecting ridge, and a heavily jungled slope that fell away from the ridge to the bay. A Spanish company of a couple hundred occupied the long ridge to the south. Unfortunately, the Spanish positions were higher than their own. The Cubans had withdrawn into the loose semi-circle that surrounded their large *ramada* of horses and mules and their precious supplies, which Fidel's company had pulled from the burning Jessie Anne. In addition to better tactical position, the Spanish had the gunboat and much more ammunition; they were slowly wearing the Cubans down.

Christopher sighed and lowered his field glasses. There was one hope, and it was beyond his control. Still…"Fidel. Take forty men back through the jungle and around to the rear of that Spanish-infested hill. Form a wedge and take the hill. I'll give you half an hour to get into position, then we'll concentrate our fire on their position. Understood?"

Fidel nodded. Like Christopher, he knew that most of them would die assaulting the hill, even if they succeeded in taking it. He also realized that they would all die and their re-supply mission fail if they continued where they were. "Yes, Colonel. A half hour will do very well. We will then wait for you to mass your fire."

Christopher clapped Fidel on the back and sent him scurrying down the north side of the hill where, except for the fire coming from the gunboat, he and his men would be relatively well-protected as they crawled along the beach, then south to the Spanish rear.

Christopher shook his head and thought, Great plan—if. If. If. If. He looked along the trench and blinked. Keeping his head well below the top of the parapet, he crawled to the peasant family that huddled together at the end of the trench. The couple and their teen-age son were good fighters—when they had weapons. But without them the family would only get in the way.

"Pablo. Take your wife and son. All three of you. Go back and help Judith with the wounded." Pablo glared at Christopher, silently protesting the slur to his manhood. Christopher let out a tired breath and put his arm around the old peasant's shoulder. "I am sorry, my friend, that I don't have weapons for you. When we get those supplies off the beach, you will have the first shiny new rifles to come from their nest in the crates."

"Very well, my Colonel." The peasant nodded somberly at his family, who followed him down the back of the hill and along the jungle trail to the makeshift hospital.

For the next ten minutes Christopher used his field glasses to scan both his own position and that of the Spaniards. From time to time he tapped one of the men huddled with him in the trench and used him as a runner to carry a message down the exposed connecting ridge and up the hill to their other flank.

Though they had been able to bring two crates of ammunition from the beach before the Spanish gunboat sent them to the hills, they still had to ration their rounds. His *mambises* had started the battle with an average of ten rounds apiece. No one was allowed to fire, except at a target of clear opportunity. Even so, most of his troops had fewer than half a dozen rounds left. If the Spanish launched a frontal assault, which he doubted they had the courage to do, the Cubans would be over-run after the second or third feint. If, however, the Spanish officers were smart, they had only to wait patiently, keep the Cubans pinned down, expose themselves only often enough to draw the Cubans' fire, and wait for them to run out of ammunition. The Spanish gunboat would easily keep the Cubans from the supplies waiting on the beach.

"You! What's your name?" Christopher was looking at a boy of thirteen who had been with him less than a week.

"Francisco, sir. May I be of service?" The boy was pleased to be picked by his colonel.

"You see that man without a hat?" Christopher pointed to the western edge of the ridge line, where a skinny mulatto shook his fist at one of his troops.

"Yes, sir. Lieutenant Martinez. No?"

Christopher nodded. "Go to him. Quickly!" Christopher pulled out his pocket watch. 'Tell him this: In twenty-five minutes he is to have his troops start pouring fire slowly and carefully into the Spanish position. Do you understand?" The boy nodded and departed. "Hurry!" Christopher yelled at the boy's back.

Christopher drew a deep breath, lit a small cigar and watched the boy run. Maybe this will work, he told himself, aware that if it didn't he would have lost a third of his men, his best friend, and perhaps the battle. What have I forgotten? For a moment he drew on his cigar and stared blankly into the bottom of the trench.

Just as Francisco made it across the unprotected ridge and started up the hill, a Spanish sniper shot him. He lay in the sun screaming, his legs twitching. Another shot hit him in the back. Through his field glasses Christopher could see the little spurt of dust rise from the boy's shirt. "Runner!" Christopher yelled. The last of his messengers approached, a peasant girl in her early twenties, with black eyes and a badly pock-marked face. She was dressed in the same filthy white shirt and equally filthy white duck trousers worn by male Cuban peasants and most of the *mambises*.

"Yes, sir?" She looked him directly in the eyes and nervously wiped her sweating hands on her trousers. She, too, had seen the boy fall and knew that she would have to follow him. Her name was Juanita, and she tried very hard not to show her fear. Christopher shook his head, pondered for the thousandth time the bravery and sacrifice of the Cuban women, and asked: "You know what to say? Where to go?"

"I have ears. I heard. But I must go quickly. Please."

Christopher nodded and she left. "Yes, little one, you must go quickly," he whispered, as she ran in a zig-zag pattern down the hill to the open ridge. "You must go quickly or your fear will overcome you." He watched the girl run past the now still body of the previous runner.

Juanita zigged and zagged, trying desperately to outrun and out-dodge the Spanish bullets. She heard them buzzing by her head like angry hornets and striking the ground in front of her. She felt very cold in the back of her neck, like she had felt as a small girl when lost in the jungle. "Mother of God, sweet baby Jesus, Mother of God," she prayed over and over. She was running up the hill now. Thirty meters. Twenty meters.

Something was wrong. She hadn't felt anything but a little tug on her hip, but her face was in the grass. "I've got to move," she screamed.

"I've got to!" She thought she was whispering, but the men on the hill had turned around and two of them were running down to her. She shut her eyes, bit her lip against the pain, and squirmed up toward them.

Juanita felt the men jerk her up by her armpits and opened her eyes just before they reached the trench at the top of the ridge. Something hit her ankle very hard. The man on her left let go of her arm and fell away. She stumbled, but the other man pulled her over the parapet. She thrashed around in the bottom of the trench, moaning, trying to remember what it was she was supposed to say to these men, and listening to their voices.

"How is it with Ernesto?" one of the men asked in a Havana accent.

"I think that our Ernesto just became a hero," another man answered in a deep voice. "The back of his head is missing."

Juanita tried again to remember what had made her leave her trench on the other hill. "Please! No, Captain! No!" An old man was bending over her and pulling down her trousers. At first she thought he was wounded, because of the bandage wrapped around his head, but as her vision cleared she saw that he was a medic, and that his eyes were filled with tenderness rather than lust.

"Eee—iii! little sister." He had rolled her over on her side to examine the wound, which was bleeding badly. "I think it is only a flesh wound, but you will not sit easily on your horse for a long time."

She could feel the old medic probing around her buttock with his fingers. Then she noticed that a few of the soldiers were glancing covertly at her nakedness, and she screamed, "You sons of whore bastards!" But her screams worsened her pain. "You shameless fucking warts," she whispered as the men, shamed, turned away.

The medic finished bandaging her, pulled her rough canvas trousers back into place, and laid her in the bottom of the trench.

"I am sorry, little sister," he said, "but we can't move you back to the hospital until after the battle."

"Hey, Papa Mendoza. Is this all our *Yanqui* colonel has left for runners?" The lieutenant was bending over her. "Hey, pretty-eyed fighter. Why did the *Yanqui* send you?"

Juanita looked up at Lieutenant Martinez, a pale-faced mulatto city dweller, who was even younger than she. She struggled for a moment and said, "The colonel wants you…to mass your fire on the Spanish hill. Aim directly at the trenches. Captain Fidel will attack them from the rear. Maybe twenty minutes."

"We have little ammunition left, three-four rounds per man. We have been waiting."

At that moment a series of deep booms sounded out in the water. The young lieutenant, a former law student, put his field glasses to his eyes and scanned the bay. His smile became very wide. He dropped his glasses, excited, and turned to the wounded runner. "Thank you, pretty eyes," he said, kissing her on the forehead, and then he was gone.

Juanita smiled, then grimaced as she felt the wound in her foot begin to throb. "Papa Mendoza?" The old medic turned back to her. "My left foot. I think it too is shot."

Mendoza saw the blood staining the bottom of her pants leg, lifted the cuff just above the ankle, and gasped. The Spanish bullet had entered her ankle, shattered the beautifully delicate bones, and exited crazily through the top of her foot. The old man knew that the foot would have to be sawn off above the ankle. Only Judith can do this, he thought. Only the Jewish Angel will have the strength. "Yes, little sister," he said softly, as he applied a tourniquet just below her knee. "Your foot has been shot."

Christopher blinked. Something was firing fairly large shells at the Spanish gun boat which, in turn, was returning the fire as rapidly as her crew could reload her three inch gun. Since he could see very little of the bay itself, Christopher swept his field glasses along the jungle skyline on either side of the bay. Finally he spotted a single plume of smoke rising over the jungle to the northeast. "God damn!" he shouted. "That's got to be an American boat. Though he couldn't see the ship, no other conclusion was possible. The Cubans didn't have a navy, and when the Americans had declared war on Spain they had blockaded the island.

Christopher was looking directly at the Spanish gunboat when its stern exploded in flames, and he continued to watch as the boat's twenty man crew and small contingent of soldiers leaped into the water and swam for the beach.

"Ramon, quick! Get over to Captain Valdez's platoon. Have her go to the beach and round up the Spanish rats who are leaving that ship." The man took off down the north side of the hill at a running crouch.

Most of the crew from the American gunboat stood around the beach and exchanged smiles and handshakes with their Cuban allies. Since few of the Cubans spoke any English and none of the sailors spoke any Spanish, the ability of the new allies to display their mutual good will was somewhat limited.

The Americans were both intrigued and bothered by what they had found on the beach. Except for a lieutenant J.G. who had spent time in Havana a year earlier, none of the men had been to Cuba, and none had met even one representative of the Cuban Liberation Army. Here before them, scurrying around the beach, was a full battalion of Cubans. They looked like an army of beggars, tramps and runaway slaves. Many seemed either too young or too old to fight, and several were women. They were filthy, ragged and skinny. Most of them, including their American colonel, positively stank.

The sailors wandered the battlefield to stare at the Spanish dead, most of whom were well-dressed, relatively clean, fairly young, and very…white. It dawned on the sailors that the outstanding characteristic of the Cuban army was not its raggedness, filth or malnourishment; its salient characteristic was its blackness. Far more than half of this battalion were niggers. Even this filthy but attractive young captain Valdez was mulatto, or at most a quatroon. The sailors began to wonder why, other than the sinking of the *Maine*, they were in Cuba. Were these scum the courageous freedom fighters they had read about in the papers?

The sailors were particularly intrigued by the gaunt, deeply tanned colonel, who said he was from Georgia and had lived in Cuba for twelve years. The man claimed, rather outrageously, that he was no longer an American, but a Cuban.

"But, Colonel," an incredulous boatswain's mate asked. "Aren't you all fightin' for the privilege of bein' annexed to the good ole U.S. of A.?"

"No, young man," Christopher replied a little sternly. "We're fighting for independence, for the right to determine our own destiny, just as you Americans did at Concord and Yorktown."

"Uh, Colonel?" one of the junior officers asked, with what he thought was great tact. "How many of your soldiers can, uh, read and write?"

Christopher saw where the ensign was coming from and frowned.

"Of this group? Maybe five or ten percent. In all of Cuba, maybe twenty percent."

The ensign looked around at his friends, smirked broadly and turned away.

"Ensign!" Christopher hissed. The young man spun back around as if attached to Christopher by an invisible wire. "The population of this land has dropped from a little more than one and a half million to far less than a million in less than three years. In that time at least two hundred thousand people—including my own family—have starved to death. Most of these soldiers you seem so contemptuous of have been living on roots for three days. There aren't a hundred schools in the entire country—and never have been. The only university has been closed for more than two years." He wanted to go on with his litany but, instead, clamped his mouth shut and glared around at the circle of silent sailors.

The commander of the gunboat was embarrassed by the attitude of his men and wanted to change the subject. "What would have happened had we not shown up?"

"One moment, Commander. I have one more thing I want to say to this young man." Christopher turned back to the ensign. "I was born and raised in Georgia. I know how many, how most, Americans feel about Negroes, and that's at least one reason why so many of us Cubans are suspicious of your motives, and apprehensive about the help your great country is giving us. Even though we need that help very, very badly. If we aren't careful, and you aren't careful, you will swallow us."

Partially purged of his anger, Christopher turned back to the gunboat's commanding officer. "To answer your question, Commander, if you hadn't come along, the Spaniards would have swallowed us. Thanks for your assistance." Christopher nodded at the lieutenant commander, who struck him as being both a good officer and a decent man.

"Do you know your losses, Colonel? Is there anything else we can do to help?"

Christopher turned to Theresa, who answered in English, "Seventeen dead, maybe eighteen. One ees meesing. Judith says there are maybe seventy wounded, twelve to feefteen serious. Maybe two or three more will die before thee dawn."

"Do you have any morphine or laudanum?" Christopher asked. "We never have enough to dull their pain."

"Lieutenant Crookston'.'

The lieutenant J.G., who had been to Havana, stared at Theresa, whom he was sure he recognized. "Sir?"

"Take two men and go aboard the ship. Keep a few supplies back for our own use, then bring the medicine chest back here and turn it over to the Cubans."

"Hot damn ! I knew I knew that nigger woman."

The two sailors looked at the lieutenant in surprise. All the way to the ship and most of the way back he had been unusually quiet, as if trying to figure something out. "Which nigger woman, sir," one of the sailors asked. "There's several of ' em. "

"The pretty mulatto, the one that's a captain," the officer explained. "She's a fuckin' whore."

"Yeh? no kidding," the other sailor exclaimed. "How do ya know, sir?" The two sailors looked at each other and grinned.

"Well, I..." The officer caught himself. Why the hell am I talking like this to enlisted men? Me and my goddamn mouth. I'm always doing this to myself. "I saw her in a café in Havana with my commanding officer. She specializes in big shots."

"We're a long way from Havana, sir. Are you sure she's the same one?" the first sailor asked, trying to hide his grin. "Most niggers kinda look alike."

"She's the same one. She hasn't even bothered to change her name, but I don't have the foggiest what she's doin' here with this raggedy-assed outfit. Last time I saw her she was decked out like the Queen of Sheba."

"How was she, Lieutenant?" the second man asked.

His masculine prowess appealed to, the big-mouthed lieutenant J.G. gave up even the pretense of being circumspect, or of maintaining any distance from the two enlisted men. " That one wouldn't even look at a lieutenant, but the whore I had was incredible. She wouldn't do anything...you know, anything exotic, but she sure did a great job with the basics."

The two sailors couldn't take their eyes off Theresa when they got back to the beach. They lugged the medicine chest over and placed it at her feet. "Where do you want this here chest, Captain, Ma'am?" the first sailor asked, trying to keep the leer out of his voice.

"At thee hospeetal," Theresa replied in her lilting Cuban accent. "Please follow me." She turned and started along a path that meandered along the beach before turning into the jungle where it narrowed. The two sailors picked up the chest, grinned at each other, and followed her into the early evening gloom of the thick foliage.

Within a quarter of an hour the two sailors were sweating profusely. They had had to stop to rest several times, much to the obvious and barely suppressed contempt of the mulatto woman they were planning to proposition. Shortly after their next rest, however, they broke into a clearing. The battalion "hospital" was little more than a series of palm-thatched lean-tos, each partially sheltering two or three of the more seriously wounded. Four medics, supervised by Judith Sandoval, hovered over a long makeshift table. An old woman held a kerosene lamp above the table with one hand while trying with the other to attach it to a large tri-pod.

Neither sailor had ever been in the presence of trauma cases. By the time their shore party had arrived at the battle scene, all the seriously wounded had been evacuated. All they had seen were the twisted corpses of the Spanish soldiers and sailors that littered the beach. They were prepared for neither the gore nor the seemingly inhuman sounds that gurgled from many of the seriously wounded.

"Hello, Judith," Theresa murmured, switching back to Spanish. "How does it go?"

Judith lifted her face from the softly moaning body spread out on the rough table, and wiped the sweat from her face with her free arm. "As always, sister. It would go better with more medicine, especially morphine."

"Voila!" Theresa exclaimed in her best French accent, and pointed at the medicine chest. "See what these two strong *Yanquis* have brought you," she added in English. The two sailors, oblivious to the irony in her voice, looked at each other and winked. They had scored a point with the nigger whore and were on their way.

Judith glanced at the sailors and nodded at the chest. "Antonio, Pancho. Bring that chest here and open it." Two of the medics stepped away from the table to get the chest, and the first sailor almost fainted. The tall, fair-skinned, heavy-breasted medic hadn't stepped away from the table because she was busy suturing a leg that was missing a foot.

The bloody, mangled foot still rested, sole down, on the table.

"Jesus!" the first sailor whispered. "Let's get out of here!" He grabbed the first sailor by the arm and turned toward the jungle.

"One moment, please!" Theresa commanded. "Please to wait for me or you weel become lost." The two sailors stopped, turned and hunkered down to wait for their beautiful guide. They stared at the ground and whispered, occasionally raising their eyes to look at their lieutenant's nigger whore.

Ten minutes later Judith and Theresa finished their conversation and gave each other a long, affectionate hug. Theresa started toward the two sailors, stared at them intently for a second, then turned back and said a few more words to Judith. Judith merely nodded and glowered at the Americans.

* * * *

"Hey, Stevie. I figure we're almost half-way between the hospital and the beach. What d'ya think?" the first sailor asked.

"I'd say that's about right, Stevie responded, and started puffing a little more noticeably. He was already coursing rivers of sweat. He looked at Theresa's back, said "Whew!" as dramatically as he could, and sat down. "I'm beat. Gotta take five."

The first sailor leaned against the royal palm, said, "Good idea," and hung his head, watching Theresa out of the corner of his eye. She sure is dirty. Don't look like no high class Havana whore to me, he thought. "Hey, Theresa. Slow down!" he yelled.

Theresa knew the sailors had stopped, but she didn't want to get too close to them. She had dealt with enough men to know exactly what these two were thinking. She turned, walked back a few steps, and stopped almost ten meters from the sailors. "My name ees not Theresa, sailor. My name ees Capitan Valdez." You sons of dogs, she thought. Do you think I'm stupid. If you even try to touch me, I'll cut off your little *pingas*.

"Ah, Capitan! The man called Stevie bowed. "We been told ALL about you. Right, Slim?"

Slim nodded. "Yessiree, nigger lady whore Capitan. We have a friend who says you like fuckee-fuckee," he said slowly, epitomizing the countless legions of condescending morons who, when talking to the very old, the very young, and foreigners, raise their voices and resort to baby talk. "We," he continued, pointing to himself and Stevie, "have twenty dollars. You want, yes?" He plucked from his pocket the twenty dollar gold piece he had won shooting craps and waved it in front of her face, as if he were holding a cookie up in front of a five year old.

"I want? NO!" Theresa screamed, losing control. She charged across the short patch of ground separating herself from Slim and went for his eyes.

Many of her compatriots knew she had been a whore. They also knew how well she had served the revolution, and in how many ways. No one had ever insulted her so openly, or presumed so much. Even during the years in Havana, only one old Spanish colonel had ever insulted her, or mistreated her in any way.

In Slim's insult, which combined the "fuckee-fuckee" with the waving coin, Theresa sensed in one intense moment all the shame and degradation experienced by the ten peseta street whore every night of her life. Perhaps another time she would have shrugged off the insult and put more distance between herself and her insulters. Still another time she would have laughed it off. But this evening? In the past three days she had eaten virtually nothing. She had been fighting for almost twenty hours without so much as a catnap, and she was so tired that her usually elaborate control mechanisms simply slipped out of gear.

She sprang at Slim without thinking about her life, or her motives or, for that matter, even about her rage. Slim was ready for her. By the time she had taken the three long steps and actually leaped at Slim's eyes, his one hundred and seventy-five pounds were poised to meet her ninety-five.

Slim grabbed her arms and held her just long enough for Stevie to double up his fist and slam it into her cheek. Though the blow failed to knock her out, it stunned and temporarily blinded her.

"This is gonna…hafta be mighty…fuckin' fast," Slim said between pants, and shoved the gold piece into her shirt pocket. That she would point them out to her colonel, or that it was even theoretically—let alone legally—possible to rape a prostitute occurred to neither of them. She was a whore and a nigger, and they were paying for what they were taking. Who could possibly object?

Within the first minute after wrestling Theresa to the ground, Slim had tied her hands behind her back and gagged her with a long strand of the bitter tasting vecunda vine that grew in the jungle like cobwebs. While Stevie undid and yanked down her trousers, Slim carefully unbuttoned her shirt. He didn't want to rip her thin and filth-caked blouse—not because he was worried about evidence of violation, but rather because, years ago, his pauper mother had taught him never to destroy intentionally anything that might be of any conceivable use to someone else. As he unbuttoned the blouse, he noticed that it had been sewn and re-sawn, and that the dainty stitching resembled that of his mother. He stared briefly at Theresa's small, firm breasts, then propped himself up on one arm and tried, with his other, to undo the numerous buttons of his once white bell bottom trousers.

"These here Cuban niggers are even lower than ours," Stevie muttered. "Shee-it! They don't even wear nothin' underneath." He had pulled her trousers completely down and off one leg, and was running his hand back and forth between her sweating thighs.

Slim didn't respond. He was concentrating so hard on trying to do two things at once that his partner's voice sounded as if it were coming from miles away.

Stevie sat up straight, his knees pressed down against Theresa's splayed legs. While staring into her pubis he ripped away the square bib that covered the front of his bell bottoms.

Theresa opened her eyes. Though she couldn't scream and still couldn't focus clearly, she knew exactly what was happening to her. She threw her head back and forth, tried to kick her feet, moaned as loudly as she could, and chewed on the vines that cut into her mouth and gums.

Time stood still. Simultaneously, she could taste every strand and hair of the green vine and the hundreds of places it was rubbing against her mouth and cheeks; feel every violated cell of her bruised thighs as the big man's pointed knees pressed into her; and hear every wheezy decibel of the two sailors' a-rhythmical and cacophonous gasping. But that was all she could hear, that and her own moans, each of which started deep in the pit of her stomach, rose up through her lungs with increasingly desperate power, and exploded feebly against the vine wall that blocked her mouth.

When her eyes came back into focus, the man whose knees were stabbing her thighs rolled off so that he could get his pants down. She tried to kick him, but he merely looked at her with glassy eyes, frowned slightly, and rolled back on. Theresa tried to buck. He was holding his erect penis which, like a geyser just beginning to peak through the ground, was starting to bubble.

Then she saw something else, something tall and white. It was Judith, who stood behind the two men, holding a machete. She stood very still, as if frozen in place.

Why is she just standing there? Theresa wondered. Why doesn't she move? "Please, Judith! Help me!" she screamed at the top of her lungs. "Please help me!" Again, all that seeped through the wall of vine was a series of inarticulate moans. The man now bent over her was about to enter. Suddenly the other man, who had been slobbering on her breasts, raised his head. He, too, had seen something. His face contorted, his eyes opened wide, and his open mouth became a huge, soundless "O".

* * * *

Judith could not believe that she was still functioning. In addition to treating more than sixty minor wounds, she and her assistants had operated, after a fashion, on fourteen seriously wounded soldiers, eleven men and three women, four of whom had died on the operating table. She knew that more would die during the night, and that still others would die on the long march back to the *Sierra Maestra*.

She realized that part of her fatigue sprang from her many failures; well over half of her serious cases died during or after surgery. She lacked the equipment, she lacked the anesthetics and disinfectants, and she lacked skill. Everything she had learned she had gleaned from the two doctors and half dozen medical students who tried to provide medical services for the Army of Eastern Cuba. Judith knew that she killed almost as many soldiers as she saved, and that her soldiers knew it. But they also knew that most of the men and women she did manage to save would have died without her.

Judith was a strange woman, the soldiers thought. She was taller than most of them, and larger boned, a beautiful but quiet woman who said little, had nothing to do with the men of the regiment—except Christopher and Fidel—but whose compassion for the wounded was becoming legendary. Throughout eastern Cuba she was known as the

Jewish Angel. The people knew that she was from *La Habana*, and that all the men of her family—her father, her step-father, and her brother—were heroes of the revolution. The legend also said that she had attacked a Spanish prisoner at the Battle of Sancti Spiritus, had been ordered to care for the man, and that he had died. No one had since seen her fire a rifle or lift a machete.

Judith finished wrapping a superficial head wound and returned to check on Juanita, the woman whose foot she had amputated. The young girl was still resting quietly. Thank God for the American morphine, Judith thought, as she strapped on her machete and pistol. She took another quick look around the hospital and, as she had promised, hurried after Theresa, who had been gone for almost ten minutes. She knew that Theresa had not wanted to enter the jungle with the two sailors in the first place, and that she was even more apprehensive about returning to the beach with them now that they weren't burdened with the medicine chest.

* * * * *

What are those sounds? she wondered, slowing her long stride to listen. Could it be…? She pulled her machete from its scabbard and moved ahead slowly. There! What's that? She moved around a turn in the faint trail and halted directly behind the sailor who knelt between Theresa's splayed and struggling thighs.

The other man was bending over Theresa's breasts. Then she saw Theresa's eyes, bulging, imploring. She heard Theresa's moans. Though she didn't understand the words, she felt them. She felt her machete arm rise above her head, as though she were about to lead a charge. She saw the machete's target only out of the corner of her eye. She was staring at Theresa. But it wasn't Theresa any longer. It was her, Judith, lying on the ground, semi-conscious, trying to scream for help. The two men were Spanish soldiers, and the jungle had become her old home above Joseph's shop. Where were the other soldiers? She must watch for them. Oh, my God! Help me! Help me! Her mouth was opening and closing, but no sounds came out.

Then the machete, which had pulled itself above her head so long ago, fell from the sky and sliced into the first man between his neck and his right shoulder. She could feel the strength of the blade's pull as it bit deeper and deeper into the man. She could hear her voice now. She was yelling, "Help me! Help, Judith!" at the top of her lungs. And she was now in control of the blade. She tore it from the man, who tried to stand up and then fell to the ground, where he flopped like a torn, beached carp. The second man stared at her. His eyes had grown large and his mouth had fallen open. Once again Judith saw the Spanish soldiers who had raped her and murdered her family. She was lying on the floor of the room, helpless, only vaguely aware of what was going to happen to her. "Help, Judith!" she screamed, and moved the machete from her extreme right to her left with as much force as she could muster. The blade was an extension of her fear and hatred. She felt her whole body coil and concentrate its swinging, unwinding force along the leading edge of the machete. The blade sliced into the side of the man's uplifted head just above the ear.

Almost immediately she dropped the machete. "It's all right, Judith," she cried. "You will be all right now." Tears pouring down her face, she pushed the man from Judith, who was covered with blood. Tenderly she pulled the vine gag from her mouth. "It will be all right, Judith."

But it wasn't Judith who was lying there, staring at her, gasping for breath. It was Theresa, her friend, her sister. "I killed them. KILLED! KILLED!" Judith screamed, becoming even more confused. She looked at Theresa and then at the two men, one of whom was still moving. "Help me, Theresa. I must save him. He must not die. Christopher said I was responsible for him."

"Jesus and Maria," Theresa gasped. "My friend. Please!" She rose to her knees and tried to pull Judith away from the mortally wounded sailor. "JUDITH ! STOP!" she screamed.

Theresa's voice reached her and she blinked, suddenly present. Judith stared at the gored shoulder of the first man, saw that her hands were going through the motions of sewing the gaping wound shut, and recoiled in horror. She wiped her bloody hands on the sailor's white covered back and collapsed next to her friend. "After I attacked that… Spaniard at Sancti Spiritus, I…" She stopped for a moment, still gasping. "I swore I would never again…kill anybody. And now…"

"Where were you?" Theresa asked. "I thought you were going to be right behind me." She took Judith in her arms and held her.

"I was. I WAS! I was right behind you, maybe two or three minutes."

"Oh, Jesus! My sister, it was forever."

"No!" Judith sat up and looked Theresa in the eye. "Listen. I know. When the soldiers raped me. Listen! I have known the minutes that last a thousand years." The two women pulled apart as they heard someone running their way.

"Mother of God protect us! What in the name of the saints has happened here?" Fidel stood in the trail, machete poised, his eyes moving from face to face and body to body. Judith pulled away and stood up to face the huge Negro while Theresa covered her nakedness.

When the women finished explaining what had happened, Fidel looked closely at the first man. "Your blade cut very deep, Judith. This man is bleeding to death." Without a pause he lifted his arm and crashed the hilt of his machete into the top of the sailor's head.

"No!" Judith yelled. "I could have saved him. I..." Fidel dropped the machete, grabbed Judith, held her very close, and patted the back of her head.

"No, Judith. No, my little one, no." His bass voice was very soft. "The man had almost bled to death." Fidel held her for a long time while Theresa slowly redressed. "Theresa," Fidel finally said, when she moved around in front of him. "We have a very big problem."

"Yes," she gasped. " I know." She nodded her head and spat at the two corpses. "What is to be done?"

"I will take care of it," Fidel said, absently. He was thinking about Judith and how good she felt next to him. He knew of her strength, her dedication to the wounded, her compassion for those who were maimed and dying. Like many of the Cuban soldiers, he had admired her from afar and had felt her distance, her need to be left alone. But now her need seemed otherwise. She was weak, vulnerable, in need of warmth and solace. Fidel could feel his strength both pouring into and surrendering to her.

"Fidel?" Theresa's tone and eyes were questioning, a little alarmed by his pre-occupation. "Fidelito? How are you going to take care of it?"

He pulled his face away from Judith's hair. "Go to the stream. Wash your bodies and your clothes. Return to the hospital, and stay there! Do not return to the beach until you get word from me or Christopher. You know nothing about what happened to these pendejos They were last seen leaving the hospital to return to the beach." He looked carefully at Theresa, who nodded, her face set, resolute. He placed his hand under Judith's chin and lifted her face. She still looked wild, out of control. He replaced her head against his chest and appealed with his eyes to Theresa.

Despite her recent ordeal, Theresa smiled. Fidelito was falling in love, and with the least likely prospect in the army. The semi-literate black peasant and the sophisticated urban Jew would be an impossible pair. "This crazy war does crazy things," she said thinly, and Fidel knew precisely what she meant. "I will see to it, Fidelito. She will be all right with me."

"Judith, you will be all right?" he asked.

She looked up at him, saw something in his eyes that she had never seen before and rose slowly to her feet with the help of his extended hand. "Yes, Fidel. I will be fine. In a while. I didn't realize...I didn't think I would ever again lose my mind...like this. But when I saw Theresa..."

"Do not worry, Madonna." Fidel wanted to take her back into his arms, but managed to suppress the more obvious signs of his welling affection. "It is over now." He nodded to Theresa, who gazed back and forth between Fidel and Judith.

Fidel watched the two women until they disappeared into the jungle and then turned to the two corpses.

* * * * *

"Ah, here comes my captain now, Commander. He'll know where your men are." Fidel had loped out of the jungle like a man who had seen the darkness. He stopped at the first group of soldiers, waved his arms wildly, then moved immediately to another group. The first group picked up their rifles and moved warily into the jungle.

What kind of show is he putting on? Christopher wondered. By nature Fidel was quiet and calm, his movements always smooth and efficient. Christopher had never seen the giant move his arms wildly—except when he was pantomiming one of his father's stories.

"My God! What's happened?" the American officer yelled, running towards Fidel. "Where are my men?"

What the hell is wrong? Christopher wondered, walking after the commander, who had grabbed Fidel by the shoulder.

"Where are my men? My hombres?" the commander demanded. But Fidel just kept up his excited chatter and waved wildly toward the jungle. Goddamn darkies, the American thought. How the hell can you run an army with niggers as officers?"

He was about to repeat his question when Christopher queried, *"Que pasa?"*

As Christopher listened to Fidel's involved story about an attack by *guerilleros*, Cuban guerillas loyal to Spain, he saw that Fidel was playing some kind of very serious game. He turned to the officer, who was almost beside himself with impatience.

"What's the darky saying? What's the darky saying?"

Christopher jerked his head around and said, flatly, "This 'darky' is a captain in the Cuban Army of Liberation." He listened a moment, took a deep breath and added, "Your men are dead, Commander. They were ambushed by a group of Spanish loyalists who specialize in murdering women, children and prisoners. I'm sorry."

The commander could not believe what he was hearing. Such things just did not happen, at least not in the Navy. "Where are they?" he asked.

"My captain has sent some of our men to bring out their bodies. They're cut up pretty bad. They were killed by machetes."

"My God! What kind of people would do such a thing?"

"People who have been fighting their neighbors for too many years." Christopher pulled his gaze from the commander's. America has much to learn in Cuba, he thought. She has been away from war for too long.

Chapter Twenty-Two

MCKINLEY AND HIS CABINET DECIDE ON A NEW
COLONIAL POLICY FOR THE UNITED STATES

* * * * *

Washington, May 11—The United States has entered upon a new era. She intends to discard the principles enunciated by the fathers of our country. She will pursue a colonial policy similar to that of England. The American flag will not be hauled down in the Philippines. When the Stars and Stripes wave over *Porto Rico* they will remain. *The New York Journal*, May 11.

San Antonio

When Michael and Alex finally jumped down from the train into the swirling South Texas dust, they fell into rough formation with the men who had been sharing their coach. Miles Wilkinson, a short, barrel-chested sergeant who had fought with Colonel Leonard Wood against Geronimo, walked along the line of tired, dirty men, all of whom were still in civilian clothes, and assigned them to their billets: "You three men, "K" Troop, First squad. Move it out, right Goddamn Now!" at which point the three men grabbed their gear and headed for the squad tents.

As a group of two assigned to 2nd squad, "L" Troop, Michael Archuletta and Alex exchanged glances and "moved it." Alex was pleased to be assigned to the same squad as his quiet friend. Archuletta, too, was pleased. After three days on the train he had decided that the gringo dude had possibilities, and that his attitudes were, by and large, the result of ignorance rather than arrogance.

As soon as they entered the squad tent, the two men discovered that they were outsiders. The other ten men of the squad were gathered around two footlockers where two poker games were in studied progress. No one looked up, other than from the surreptitious corner of an eye. No one greeted them, and when Alex bellowed, "Howdy friends. I'm Alex Jackson and this here's Michael Archuletta. We've been assigned to 2nd squad," no one responded. Alex stood frozen in the doorway until Archuletta tapped him on the shoulder and pointed to an empty double bunk. The two recruits walked over and silently unpacked their gear.

"I smell shit," one of the poker players muttered.

"Naw, Luke," a second man corrected, interrupting the giggle that flowed around the two tables. "That ain't shit. That there's sheep yer smellin'."

"Tha's what I said, Dumbass. I smell shit." Another giggle, louder than the first. As soon as the interchange began, Alex stood up from his unpacking and smiled good-naturedly at the poker players. Archuletta stiffened and continued to unpack.

"You fellas both been chawin too much terbacca," a third player continued. A man of middle height, wide shoulders and a balding, perfectly flat face, he leaned back in his camp chair, stuck his square thumbs between his faded green suspenders and filthy undershirt, and stared straight at the back of the sheepherder's neck. "That there terbacca will plug yer nostrils every time. That ain't sheep ya smell, Luke. That's Mexican."

"That's what I said, Henry. I smell shit."

Other than Henry's hard, sharp laugh, the tent turned perfectly still. The wide smile faded from Alex's face. For the first time in years he knew physical fear and felt himself shrinking into an invisible corner.

Though the world inside the tent had turned claustrophobic, the world outside was alive, vibrant. A train whistled, a sergeant yelled insults at recruits on the far side of the drill field, and a tent flap slapped in a sudden, dusty gust.

In sharp contrast to the signals and expectations sent up by Alex's clanging intuition, Archuletta merely stood up, stretched, smiled at his would-be tormentors, mused aloud in an even, conversational tone: "I wonder if you gringo assholes are as big as your mouths," and started to walk from the tent, only to run into Sergeant Wilkinson, who stood in the doorway scowling at the poker players.

"Well, well, well," he began. "So you brave cowboys 'er feelin' frisky, are ye? Tell ya what. There's two box-cars of supplies that needs unloadin'. Instead of breakin' wind in this stuffy little tent, why don'cha all get up off yer ignorant fat asses and go break wind outdoors where no one has ta smell yer farts?"

"C'mon, Miles," Luke wheedled, glaring at Archuletta. "Hell, Wilkinson, we didn't mean nothin'."

"My name is Sergeant Wilkinson, Shitheel. I ain't jest yer foreman now. We're in the army, 'n these here pilgrims is yer squad-mates. HEAR?"

The poker players all nodded, some angrily, some cynically, a couple amazed at the distance old Miles was putting between them. But they all nodded.

"Good! Now get yer asses out into the sunshine and unload them boxcars!" When the men had filed sullenly out of the tent, Wilkinson glared at the new arrivals for a moment, as if appraising their worth, then turned and strode from the tent.

As soon as the sergeant had left, Alex exploded. "Chrimanetly, Michael. What's wrong with those guys? We're supposed to be on the same side." He knew perfectly well what was wrong, but couldn't admit it. As a boy growing up in rural Georgia he had seen the same anger and resentment, the same hatred flare into insult and violence. He was shocked—not because he had assumed that Westerners were without prejudice, but, rather, because they were all on the same crusade, all comrades on a patriotic and selfless campaign to avenge murdered Americans and free an oppressed people.

Michael Archuletta looked at Alex and shook his head, as if reading the younger man's mind. "Men fight for many reasons, Jackson." He sat down on the unmade bunk, stared at the floor for a minute, and added: "Sometimes it's hard to kill people, at least as many as you'd like. In war you can kill all you want. It may not be the people you really want to kill." The sheepherder shrugged. "But maybe killing Spaniards is almost as good as killing Mexicans." He lay back on the straw pallet, pulled his hat over his eyes and blocked out the world.

The next day a thirty man Ivy League contingent arrived with Roosevelt from New York. That night Alex went to look them up, anxious to spend an hour or two with 'his own kind.' He found six of his peers gathered around a portable poker table, complete with green felt, a bar and a Negro valet, all set up in Private Jones' squad tent. Sitting around the table were the ex-stars of several football and rowing teams. All six were wealthy and, with the exception of Randy Williams, all were members of New York's prestigious Knickerbocker Club. Williams, a Beacon Hill Brahmin, belonged to the even more prestigious Somerset Club.

"Good evening, Alex. Good to see you again. How do you like the army?" Randolph Williams snapped his fingers at the Negro valet and pointed to Alex, who was pulling a camp chair up to the poker table. The greeting was cool and casual, as if the two had parted two hours rather than two weeks earlier.

"I don't know, Randy. The men are not...what I expected."

"That's what David said. Right, David?"

But David Vandervoort didn't answer. Up until the moment of Alex's entrance, two of the poker players had been kidding him mercilessly. As the only non-athlete in the group, he realized that Alexander Dumas Jackson would almost immediately become the fresh butt of their stale humor, he might have stayed around, if only to empathize with his old roommate from Harvard. He had had enough. Just as Alex prepared to make himself at home, Vandervoort threw in his tenth straight hand, rose from the table with the barest nod of courtesy, and left the tent. No one seemed bothered by his departure.

Though David Vandervoort was as rich as any of them, and though he came from a more powerful family, he was, after all, a Jew. None of his friends ever alluded directly to his religion or culture, but several of them, including Randy Williams, kidded him about any number of personal characteristics: his almost incessant reading of novels; his tendency toward portliness; his shyness and naivete, which effectively concealed a brilliant and sensitive mind. Though David Vandervoort had graduated from Harvard summa cum laude, in any crowd larger than two, he was totally inconspicuous.

"What's wrong with David?" Alex asked, as he moved into the man's still warm chair. When the Negro valet brought him a whiskey and some smoked pheasant, he nodded his thanks and settled down to watch the game.

Jonathan Somers raised his slightly hooded eyes, flashed a dazzling smile and said, "Old David's got his kike blood up. He's lost a small bit of his weekly allowance and gone home to mope. Are you going to play?" He was well aware that Alex had no money, other than what he earned.

Before Alex could respond, Donald Wilcox, a tall, ex-Harvard halfback, launched into a reprimand: "That was most definitely not spoken like a gentleman, Somers. David Vandervoort is one of the most intelligent and generous men in my acquaintance. I'm really rather disappointed in you, old fellow."

The object of the sermonette reddened and shuffled the cards, concentrating on his hands. Every second or third riffle a card or two sprayed from his fingers. Several of the other players barely concealed their amusement, as their glinting eyes followed Somers' compulsive shuffling.

"Are you in, Alex?" Somers repeated.

"What are the stakes?" Alex asked, fumbling for his money.

"Five, ten and two bits, three raises maximum."

"Sure. I'll play a few hands." Alex had fifteen dollars clenched in his fist, all the money he had in Texas. He placed the bills on the table and asked for chips as Somers dealt a hand of Five Card Stud.

"Jesus, Alex. Is that all the chips you're going to buy?" Somers looked at Alex with patronizing interest, a smile covering his still wounded pride. He had just put someone else into a face-losing corner.

"I'm sorry, Somers. I thought you meant five, ten or twenty five cents. I don't have enough...on me, at the moment...to play." Alex fumbled the money back into his pocket and pushed his chair away from the table. For the second time in as many days he felt completely alone, almost as alone as when, years before as a small boy, he had watched Christopher shoulder his pack, wave, turn away, and walk down the dusty road that led out of town and to the state university.

Though Alex was so mortified by his own stupidity that he wanted to follow David out the door, he forced himself to remain. Once again, for the thousandth time since his first day at Harvard eight years earlier, he was the poor southerner, the hardworking country boy committing all his tiny inheritance to one roll of the academic dice. However hard he tried, on the football field or in the dining halls, his genteel poverty had kept him on the outside, a smiling, semi-excluded spectator. Like David Copperfield, with whom he identified, Alex had pressed his nose against the frosted window pane and smiled at the table piled with the fragrant and steaming perquisites of money and power. The people on the other side of the pane were happy and well-dressed. Even as they carved and consumed all the tasty viands of position, they waved at him and smiled their good will. They were inviting him to come in and sit down with them. But he could never find the key that unlocked the door.

From across a great chasm of two feet, the distance he had pushed his chair from the table, Alex observed the variety of responses to his discomfiture. One or two of the players were obviously amused. A couple smiled sympathetically, albeit condescendingly. Only Donald Wilcox revealed even a trace of anger at what had just occurred, and he had decided to remain quiet. Though he had chastised Somers for his treatment of Vandervoort, and even though he liked Alex, with whom he had played football, he did not feel compelled to intercede. While Wilcox found Alex to be cheerful and industrious, he saw in the Southerner a streak of ambition, particularly social ambition, that the members of the group had always found distasteful. Like his friends and parents, Wilcox believed that one was born into a particular class. Certain of the more subtle graces and refinements came either with birth or not at all.

Not that the lack of inherited money and position should stand as obstacles to success—whether commercial or social. Of course not. The Rockefellers, Morgans and Carnegies had demonstrated otherwise. It was just that such epitomes of American opportunity never quite managed to rid themselves of their strong odor of assertive avarice. It took at least a couple of generations for the edges to soften, for the more subtle appreciations of wealth and refinement to develop.

Donald Wilcox prided himself on his democratic and liberal attitudes. He believed that all men were created equal, and that no man, certainly no white man, should be denied the opportunity to progress as far as his talents and industry could carry him. Still, even in America, there existed definite advantages to being born rich, Anglo-Saxon and Protestant. For one thing, one didn't sweat as much. Nor did one have to scheme and maneuver for the possible chance to move an eye-blink closer to a higher rung on the ladder. Such a necessity had been fulfilled by a grand-parent or, preferably, a great, great grandparent. Consequently, one could devote one's position and wealth to more subtle movements up the evolutionary ladder.

Wilcox thought that Alex sweated too much, that he was too anxious to be liked and accepted, too concerned for doing the "right" thing, too devoted to appearance. All the group had noticed that, just as they had noticed the faint odor of ambition that accompanied him when invited into their homes to meet their parents and sisters. Alex always looked good, of course. He was, as far as his meager inheritance would allow, the glass of fashion. His manners were perfect, his speech flawless. Always.

Indeed, wherever Alex found himself, whether with a Beacon Hill matron or a Cambridge whore, he easily adopted his speech, costume and mannerisms to his surroundings. Like a chameleon, he was an expert at protective coloration. He hoped that appearance could, eventually, become the magic charm that conjured up reality.

At the moment, however, Alex felt the reality all too heavily. He sat slightly outside the circle and watched large amounts of money change hands. Though most of the pots far exceeded the monthly salary he had earned at the War Department, winners and losers alike reacted to the pots with almost total indifference, other than the expressions of amazement or disgust for the hands themselves.

Alex was even more intrigued and slightly bothered by the tone of the conversation.

"Did you fellows see that book Teddy is reading?" Jones asked the group as a whole, as he stood up to stretch.

"It's Colonel Roosevelt," Somers smiled, pleased to get in a shot. He is the second in command, you know. I'll see your five."

"You'd best not call him Teddy to his face. He hates it. Your five and ten more. Let's see. That the last raise?" Wilcox looked away from Jonathan Somers toward Roger Jones, ex-captain of the Yale Crew, a short but powerfully built blonde with very long arms.

"Yeh, that's it, and I'm out." Jones folded his cards, drained his glass and beckoned to the Negro valet who was, as usual, listening carefully to the nuances of his rich white employer and his equally rich white friends. "Another whiskey, Johnny. Please." Jones smiled good-naturedly at the old Negro who had accompanied the senior Jones to the battles of Bull Run, Shiloh and Richmond. When Johnny returned with the whiskey, Jones smiled again and continued the conversation.

"I think Roosevelt sees this war as one magnificent opportunity. Image is all important."

"The war shouldn't hurt that ambition," Alex interjected, half dreaming of what it would be like to accompany his hero to Albany.

"I don't really think of it as ambition, Alex, old man," Randy Williams stated evenly. "Rather, I see it more as a desire to serve." He looked around the table and laid down his cards. "Three queens." The remaining players threw in their hands.

"Beats three jacks," Somers murmured, shaking his head. Though he was holding only two small pairs, he believed in over-stating his case, even with a losing bluff. "Say, Boy. Bring me another whiskey, and some pheasant, too, if you don't mind."

Why, Alex asked himself as his friends began another hand, why do Somers and the rest make me feel as if I'd just uttered an obscenity when I use the term 'ambition'? which is what it is. Why do they ignore Somers' condescending "boy" when it's used so inaccurately?

"What about the book you said our lieutenant colonel was reading?" Private Jones, Yale, Crew, '94, glanced at his cards and winked knowingly at Private Wilcox, Harvard, Football, '95. "He does read, you know."

Alex was appalled. If he'd made such a flippant reference to Roosevelt, his fellow Ivy Leaguers would have considered the remark tasteless. But Wilcox smiled, asked for two more cards, and continued: "I went over to Headquarters to let him know we'd all gotten settled."

"Which he already knew, Don," Somers said, smiling wickedly. The Roosevelts and the Wilcox's were old friends and shared neighboring summer homes on Long Island. The ex-halfback's pride in the relationship between the two families was his Achilles heel and provided the opportunity for much good-natured ribbing.

"Well . . .yes. But I didn't know that, and…back to the book. He was reading a new one, *The Superiority of the Anglo Saxon Peoples*, and was as excited as hell."

"Is our superiority supposed to be news?" Somers asked, smiling at Alex, who was thinking of Archuletta.

"Superiority is a strong word, bound to be misunderstood by some," Wilcox replied, smiling at his friends. "That's not what our colonel found so intriguing."

"Well?" Jones demanded. "Are you going to keep us on tender hooks all night?" He had invited the group in to play poker, not to engage in abstract philosophical speculation.

Wilcox was flustered. He was just making conversation. Though he knew what he had to say was no big deal, he plunged on: "Well, the book documents the superiority of British and American institutions, which are the result of inherent character, moral restraint and organizational ability. The interesting thing to me is that the book was not written by an Anglo-Saxon—but by a Frenchman."

"Hmmmph! Let's play cards," Jones interjected.

Randy Williams puffed himself up and said, "It does one good to hear such learned discourse from a Frenchie; he must be unusually perceptive." The group chuckled and the game resumed.

During the discussion of Roosevelt's reading material, Alex's mind flowed back and forth between Christopher and Michael. Nagging doubts, problems, questions, kept edging into his mind—pulsing rhythms that had begun in Santa Fe. He could not yet put a finger on the exact nature of what was bothering him; he wasn't even sure he wanted to. But it—whatever IT was—was becoming stronger, harder to push back into his nether consciousness.

"Speaking of natural superiority, Donald," Randy Williams said with just a touch of self-irony, "since you're on such close terms with Roosevelt, when do you think we'll get to Cuba so we can demonstrate some of our Anglo-Saxon talents?"

"I don't know," Wilcox replied, flustered at not having anything significant to report after making so much of his two minute chat with their hero. "I forgot to ask."

Alex saw his chance to insinuate himself more closely into the group. He cleared his throat a bit too noisily and began in a tone that struck almost everyone in the tent, himself included, as rather too self-important. "When we were making our preparations in Washington, the whole matter was discussed at length." He knew he sounded pompous, but he couldn't stop himself. "Several people, including General Shafter, suggested we hold off the invasion until August, but . . .

"August!" Jones and Williams shouted simultaneously, and Jones added, "Hell! That's four months away. I didn't sign on to make a career of the army."

"None of us did," Wilcox said. "What do you mean, Alex, by 'but'?"

"Yes . . ." Before Alex could continue, however, a hearty voice from the door stole his anemic thunder.

"Say, you fellows really want to get to Cuba. Don't you think the Spaniards will wait?" Roosevelt stood in the doorway, resplendent in his brand new khaki uniform, complete with Lieutenant colonel insignia and Australian bush hat.

Everyone in the tent leaped to attention, partly because Roosevelt was second in command; partly because he was their hero, the man who had conceived and pushed through the idea of a volunteer cavalry regiment composed of cowboys and college athletes, but mostly because the barrel-chested, near-sighted Long Islander radiated more energy, self-confidence and force than any other man they would ever meet.

Despite the wealth and social position of their own families, the members of the group sensed in Roosevelt the epitome of the new American dynamo that was finally asserting itself in world politics, Even more than Colonel Leonard Wood, their Medal of Honor winning commanding officer, who was to become Governor-General of occupied Cuba, Roosevelt epitomized the personality behind the two major expansionist slogans of empire-hungry America: "Manifest Destiny" and "The White Man's Burden."

Theodore Roosevelt often struck thoughtful observers as a comic opera parody of the charismatic leader. He was a jingoist, an expansionist and a blustering, intimidating bully. He was also, however, a strong-willed, articulate, decisive proponent of his beliefs. He commanded incredible loyalty from his followers, most of whom were fellow expansionists clamoring for America's pre-ordained place in the sun. To a man, the Ivy League contingent of the Rough Riders was composed of just such followers, devout practitioners of the Gospel of the Anglo-Saxon Church in general, and the American Synod in particular.

"At ease, men. At ease." Roosevelt walked into the tent, straddled a chair and placed his round smiling face on his arms, which were already crossed on the chair's back. He studied each of the six men, all of whom he had recruited personally, and relished their sense of excitement and awe. "Alex, old man. What were you telling the boys here? About going to Cuba?" Roosevelt looked straight at Alex, who sensed a reprimand that he didn't feel he deserved.

"Sir? I was just going to tell the fellows that some of the cautious types, like General Shafter, didn't want us to go to Cuba until Fall, but that..."

"You know better than to listen to those yellow-livered curs, Alex." He deserted Alex immediately, shifting his head and shoulders to exclude him from the conversation. Like Jones and Williams, Roosevelt had not allowed Alex to finish his statement.

"Starting tomorrow there's going to be a lot of distance between us. You agreed to enlist as privates and you'll be treated as privates, though I expect many if not all of you to earn promotions before we leave San Antonio, certainly before we leave Cuba. You have all the qualities of these Westerners I'm so fond of. At least as important, you also have good educations and the habit of leadership.

"However, men, you're going to have to earn what you get, and you're going to have to set an example in everything you do. If you let your guard drop for one moment, the cowboys will make you the laughing stocks of the camp."

Roosevelt looked around the tent with a pugnacious flash of military sternness. "Roger, I want you to send your valet home, as well as this fancy poker table. Randy, get rid of your personal cook. All of you will eat in the enlisted men's Mess, and you will limit your personal kits to Army issue. All of you. Understood?" The lieutenant colonel of volunteers looked at each of the men with what he judged to be the appropriate mixture of authority and good fellowship.

"Yes, SIR!" chorused the assembly of sophisticated scions.

"Fine! Now that we know where we stand, let's get back to Alex's little story about us not going to Cuba. How about a drink, boy?" He turned to the valet he had just exiled back to Manhattan and held up two fingers.

"Sir?" Alex ventured timorously. Roosevelt turned to him with benevolent disinterest, as if he were about to listen to a cute but essentially boring five year old. "Sir. Just as you came in I was about to tell the fellows that you'd managed to win the day, that we'd be shipping out as soon as we finish training."

"Good. Good. I'm glad you understand that, Alex." Roosevelt turned back to the poker table. "There are those—unfortunately in high circles—who believe that the best young men in America, the best raw material for a cavalry regiment the world has ever seen can't stand up to the rainy season and a little malaria and yellow fever. I let them know, in no uncertain terms, that we wouldn't be in Cuba long enough for the mosquitoes to bite us," Appreciative laughter from the group. "let alone infect us." Roosevelt allowed himself to react to the second laugh with a broad smile. He lifted his whiskey glass in a toast: "Here's to the greatest country, the greatest people, and the greatest fighting men on the bully planet."

"Hear! Hear!" The group was on its feet, glasses raised in enthusiastic toast.

"Colonel Roosevelt?" Though just disenfranchised from his valet and poker table, Private Jones couldn't contain his excitement. "When will we be going to Cuba?"

"Three weeks, maybe four. We figure three weeks of training is more than enough for an outfit that can ride and shoot like we can. And before any of you ask how long we'll be there, let me pass on what I told Bill Hearst the other day: It'll take us anywhere from thirty minutes to thirty days to kick Spain out of Cuba, maybe a week more to decide how we'll rule the bloody island once we've won her."

* * * * *

"How'd the poker game go?" Archuletta asked. "Did you win or lose?"

"So so," Alex began. However, discovering immediately that he could not or at least did not want to play games with the sheepherder, he blurted out: "I didn't play. I found out I couldn't afford it, so I just watched."

When Archuletta failed to respond, Alex undressed and climbed into the top bunk, prepared to stare at the tent frame until he fell asleep. From below Archuletta asked one more question: "Why do men who have everything want to fight Spain?"

Alex answered only after a long pause. "Honor, duty, patriotism. Their fathers went to war, or at least had the chance. Now it's their turn. They're prepared to do their duty." Though these were the motives they had all talked about, Alex knew that each of the dudes had his own reason for joining the expedition. For many the flight from boredom had been sufficient. For himself? Christopher? The chance to better himself? His father's oft-told stories of serving with Joe Wheeler?

"Michael. Why did you enlist? You and Gonzalez are the only Mexicans in the entire regiment—except Captain Luna, who's as well-educated and established as any of my dude friends." Silence. After whispering "Michael?" one more time, Alex assumed that the sheepherder had gone to sleep, and tried to follow suit.

Sleep was a long time coming, however. He was worried about what seemed to be a slight deterioration of his relationship with Roosevelt. I guess I shouldn't have left a week early for Santa Fe, he told himself. Roosevelt had wanted him to stay and double-check all the requisitions; he wanted no foul-ups in the supply system. Alex had finally convinced his hero to let him leave a week early, and that everything was in control. He knew that Roosevelt would have preferred him to stay, however, and that the man did not like disagreements of any kind.

Alex also sensed that the week in Santa Fe had, in some indefinable way, widened the gap between himself and the wealthy Ivy Leaguers whose friendships he so badly wanted. When he looked through their eyes, he saw himself making little mistakes, minor offences he didn't even understand, much less intend.

What had happened on the trip west? Or during the week in Santa Fe with Mountain Man Mason and his friends? Or on the three day train ride with the half-Irish, half-Mexican sheepherder? Or, for that matter, to the easy magnanimity of his eastern friends when they found themselves on the bottom rung of a military—hence highly structured—society? Though the last possibility barely flashed across his mind, he sensed that his fellow graduates were undergoing vague but important changes just as rapidly as he was, and that the direction of his changes differed from that of theirs.

His random thoughts shifted from the present to the past and back again, back and forth like beads on a wind-blown string. Later, in his dreams, the shards of the kaleidoscope refused to stay put. When he awoke early the next morning, his mind was as troubled as it had been the preceding evening. Why did Somers and Wilcox say "I smell shit" when I entered the tent? he wondered. Almost as soon as he asked himself the question, Alex realized that his mind wasn't working right. It wasn't the Ivy Leaguers, it was the Arizona cowboys, Henry and Luke, who had talked about shit. And they had directed the remark to Michael rather than to him. Why did he want to attribute the remark, if only briefly, to his eastern friends?

And why were these rich sons of powerful men so eager to go to war? Why was Archuletta? As was usually the case, Archuletta's question had set his mind racing. It did not settle down until he fell again into the world of dream, and into the soft arms of Charlotte, who had come to Havana to see him decorated and promoted to captain for leading a desperate charge up a steep hill occupied by thousands of screaming Spaniards.

Chapter Twenty-Three

PORTO RICO BOMBARDED!
Sampson's Great Guns Crumble the Rock Bastions of
San Juan's Old Morro

* * * * *

AGAIN THE AMERICAN FLEET COMES OUT OF THE STORM OF
SHOT AND SHELL UNINJURED

St. Thomas, May 12—Admiral Sampson has hammered the forts of San Juan de Puerto Rico to powder. Again American marksmanship has shown its deadly efficiency against Spanish fortifications. Once more victory has been won without the loss of a single American ship or the life of a single American hero. San Juan is at Sampson's mercy, just as Manila is at Dewey's. *The New York Journal*, May 12.

* * * * *

COLONEL JOHN JACOB ASTOR ASKS THE PRESIDENT TO
GIVE HIM ACTIVE SERVICE IN THE FIELD
Astor Wants to Serve with Roosevelt, Wood and the
Rough Riders

* * * * *

UNCLE SAM'S GALLOPING REGIMENT OF
"ROUGH RIDERS"
The Most Remarkable Cavalry Troop in All History
Roosevelt, Wood to Lead Cow-Punchers and Fifth Ave. Dudes

San Antonio, May 14—The troopers of the First United States Volunteer Cavalry, or Rough Riders, that have been thronging into this city during the past week are a wild and picturesque lot.

Serving Uncle Sam may be only half as exciting as keeping the rustler off his range, but the cow-puncher has joined because the country has called him. *The New York Journal*, May 14.

San Antonio

At least once a day Archuletta slapped Alex in the face with a wall of verbal ice water. One afternoon during the second week of training the two bunkmates were rubbing down their horses after a three hour session of mounted drill. As was often the case, Alex mused aloud about his brother, and about how much he looked forward to their reunion in Cuba.

"How do you know your brother will want to see you?"

Alex stopped brushing his sorrel mare and looked across her back at Michael, who was staring at him. "What do you mean?"

"What will you say to each other?"

"He's my brother!" Alex didn't know if he was more puzzled or angered by the directness of the question. "We'll talk about what we've been doing."

"Cuba and Spain have been at war for some time now. What has your brother been doing in the war?"

Alex realized with a jolt that he didn't know. Until he had received George Bedford's letter ten short weeks earlier, he had assumed that Christopher was busy tending his sugar plantation, surrounded by his family and domestic bliss. But now? "I don't know. He hasn't mentioned anything about the war."

"What does he say in his letters?"

"Well, he doesn't write very much." Alex replaced the stiff brush he'd been using on his mare and turned his back on Archuletta.

After a silence the sheepherder asked, more gently, "Have you wondered what side he is on? In the war?" Alex could think of nothing to say, but suddenly felt even more alone.

During their weeks in San Antonio, Alex worked hard, forced himself to achieve, to excel at every aspect of camp life, just as he had always worked hard, whether at getting into Harvard after failing to win an appointment to West Point; nearly killing himself to make the Harvard football team; or single-handedly ramming every single one of Roosevelt's requisitions through Procurement. Virtually all the eastern dudes prided themselves on their horsemanship and marksmanship, while Alex excelled in both areas. It was in the drudgery of camp routine and the study of cavalry troop tactics, however, that he easily surpassed most of the recruits, whether cowboy or dude. By the end of the third week he had demonstrated his ability both to lead troops and follow orders.

Because several hundred men had just arrived from the Oklahoma and Indian Territories, everyone gossiped about the possibilities of promotion. Bucky O'Neill had already been promoted to Lieutenant, but everyone in camp agreed that Bucky's promotion had been deserved. Not only was O'Neill a college graduate—a seldom violated criterion—he had been an Arizona Ranger and, more recently, Sheriff of Prescott, Arizona Territory. O'Neill could discuss rustling and roping with the cowboys and Zola's novels with the dudes.

The word was that more promotions would be forthcoming. The ambitious counted on several more commissions and a whole feast of promotions to corporal and sergeant. Most of the dudes were hopeful, but none was more anxious than Alex. The army was his chance.

Though he excelled as a soldier, however, Alex saw himself as a social failure. The problems had begun almost as he left the train at the San Antonio Fairgrounds, at the moment he had accompanied Archuletta into the tent that housed 2nd Squad, "L" Troop. For two months he had been fantasizing about his embryonic companionship with the other Ivy League graduates, almost forty of whom had come west to test their manliness. He also counted on his blossoming connection with Teddy Roosevelt, whose coat-tails provided a sure, albeit mercurial path to success, equally significant were his friendships with the western cowboys and the untutored, democratic protoplasm of the raw but dynamic West. Within the first week of training, however, he had become disillusioned about all three expectations.

Despite his partial disillusionment, however, Alex knew he was making progress. The men of his squad still didn't embrace him as a friend, and never would, but they came to respect both his sweat and his emerging talents. By the third and final week of training, many of the men had also altered their attitude toward Michael Archuletta, who forced the cowboys to respect him, at least in their own way: "He's a pretty good soldier even if he ain't nothin' but a dirty mex sheepherder."

The more Alex immersed himself in his training, the more estranged he became from his eastern friends. He possessed neither the means to keep up with them in the evening nor the patience to continue hanging around like a semi-accepted lap dog. Nor, with the exception of David Vandervoort, who was in his troop, did any of his fellow graduates take the trouble to seek him out.

One evening toward the end of their final week at the San Antonio Fairgrounds, Michael and Alex sat in front of their tents cleaning their newly-issued Krag-Jorgenson rifles. There had been a small thunder shower just after dinner; the air was cool, clean, free of the dust that had plagued them for days. Both men were content to sit quietly, their hands occupied by the kind of routine tasks that free the mind to dream. Alex was thinking of Charlotte, who was caught up in the social whirl that accompanied the war fever.

Her irregular letters, including the sweetly-scented one that had arrived that afternoon, prattled on about the war, about the excitement of Dewey's great victory in the Philippines, about the tens of thousands of volunteers preparing to invade Puerto Rico and Cuba, but mostly about the scads of heavenly parties she had been attending. Many of their male friends had been awarded commissions in the various volunteer regiments that were forming, and they all looked so gallant in their beautiful uniforms.

Whenever she spoke of "their male friends" in her letters, Alex felt a double twinge: first because the woman he thought he loved and knew he wanted to marry could—and would—speak so gaily about all the young lieutenants in their circle, most of whom, he was sure, were political appointees; second because the "male friends" had sufficient connections to have commissions bestowed upon them as some sort of *droit de signeur* confirmation right—and he didn't.

Alex had not told Archuletta about his fiancee, and that omission bothered him. Even though his bunk mate had told him virtually nothing about his life, and never volunteered any personal information, Alex had revealed much of his past to the sheepherder, had reeled out episode upon episode of his early years in Georgia with a gray ghost of a mother he could barely remember; a bitter, Negro chasing father who ignored him; and an older hero brother who had taught and protected him, deserted him, and then from afar helped with his college expenses. He had rambled on about his years at Harvard and his months at the War Department, especially, the two hectic months when he had been working so closely with Roosevelt to garner the best supplies for the regiment. He had discussed his reasons for enlisting: his anger at the destruction of the *Maine* and the murder of George Bedford, his wish to see Christopher, and his dream of advancing his career by performing well in Cuba.

In all the hours of conversation between the two men, both of whom were outcasts of a sort, Alex had revealed and Michael absorbed. The sheepherder listened carefully, asked questions, some of them awkwardly direct, and commented rarely. It was the directness of the questions that most bothered Alex, as if Michael were implying, however subtly, that Alex didn't really know what he was doing, or who he was, or what he wanted. Thus his reluctance to discuss his increasingly confused feelings for Charlotte.

Now, sitting next to Archuletta in the rich San Antonio twilight, Alex felt particularly alone. The beautiful evening only seemed to emphasize the strange malaise of confusion creeping over him. He looked down at the rifle bolt he was holding and wondered, briefly if he would really have to kill anyone. They were always talking about killing Spaniards, but he wondered about the difference between abstract Spaniards and one garlic breathing soldier.

"What are you thinking about?" Archuletta had finished cleaning his rifle and was staring at him.

"I was wondering if I could kill somebody. I don't know."

"The first time may be hard. It gets easier. Why do you wonder?"

"I've always dreamed of war and glory. My old man hardly talked of anything else, except maybe lynching darkies. I've always dreamed of leading desperate charges, maybe getting wounded and wearing a blood-stained bandage around my head, maybe even getting killed." Alex finished reassembling his new rifle, walked into the tent to replace the weapon in its rack, reappeared and leaned against the wooden door frame.

Archuletta hadn't moved. He cradled the polished rifle in his hands and stared at the now fading twilight.

"Somehow, in my dreams, I always push the enemy off the hill," Alex continued. "They fire their rifles or they retreat. Some of them turn and run. Some of them fall down, dead I guess. But I never actually, personally, kill anybody."

Michael Archuletta looked over at Alex. "A few of these men have lynched rustlers and bank robbers. A few have shot up sheepherders' camps. Some fought in the last of the Indian wars. Maybe some of these men, but probably not all that many, know the difference between killing Spaniards and killing Spaniards."

Alex stared down at the sheepherder, waiting for an elaboration that was not forthcoming. He was about to ask "What do you mean?" when William Pike and Mountain Man Mason charged around the corner of the tent.

"Howdy, Alex!" Pike boomed, bearing down on Alex as if prepared either to run him over or give him a bear hug. "Where ya been keepin' yerself? Huh? Howdy, Archuletta. Screwed any good ewes lately?"

Michael stood, every nerve alert to what might happen next, but Pike just laughed and tried to embrace the man he had just insulted. Archuletta backed away, disconcerted in a way Alex had never before observed. Pike pulled back, his eyes hard and blank for a moment. Then, "Shee-it, Mex, I don't mean nothin'. Yer Alex's friend, and thas fine. Yer a pretty good soldier fer a mex, and thas fine, too. C'mon. We're headin' out fer town. There's a dance, and we're goin'. All of us. You too, Mex."

Relieved to have been jerked so loudly away from his preoccupation with self, Alex turned to Archuletta. "Come on. Let's go. It sounds like fun."

Archuletta shook his head. "You go ahead. I've never been to a dance in my life—except squaw dances with the *Dine*, with the Navajo. I'll be staying here." He glanced at William Pike, thinking the man looked ridiculous without his beard. Pike owned a large, wedge-shaped head that began as a broad, low forehead scarred by a deep crease and ended in a tiny chin that receded almost to the point of invisibility.

Mountain Man stared back at Archuletta for a moment and then spat a glob of black juice from the corner of his mouth. Here they'd gone out of their way to treat the Mex like a real human being, and the dumbass didn't even have enough sense to appreciate what his betters were offering. "That's jes fine. You stay if ya want. We're goin'. And thas a fact. Soon's we pick up Shorty we're fer gittin' GONE!" He turned and started to walk away.

As soon as he heard Shorty's name, Archuletta decided to brave the insults of Anglo San Antonio and the unreliability of Alex's friends. "I think I will come along. I haven't been out of this place since we arrived."

Maybe the man's starting to relax a little, Alex thought, as the two of them followed Mountain Man and Bill Pike toward Shorty's squad tent on the far side of the parade ground.

The dance, to which the Rough Riders had been explicitly uninvited, took place in Exhibition Hall at the south end of the fairgrounds. It was sponsored by the Elks and attended by virtually the entire second tier, that is, the Anglo tier, of San Antonio society. The sponsors had uninvited the soldiers of the cowboy regiment with a sign posted outside the entrance—NO SOLDIERS ADMITTED—which absolutely guaranteed that at least a few would show.

Not that the Elks didn't admire the soldiers. No one was more patriotic or more vociferous in their support of the war than the Benevolent and Protective Order of the Elks. But the place for soldiers was in Cuba, where they could spit in the eye of Spain, strike the chains from a down-trodden people, and show the world what America was made of. Unfortunately, such hardy specimens of Americana did not mix well with the local gentry, especially the wives and daughters, whose sensitivities would almost certainly be offended by the course language and primitive behavior of the heroes.

The five troopers immediately drew the attention of almost everyone present. Alex noticed three things: a flow of hostility from the men and most of the older women; the perceptible winding down of the conversation; and a lovely brunette of maybe seventeen or eighteen who reminded him for a moment of the girl he'd kissed at the Santa Fe station.

As the five new arrivals made their way to the bar—Bill Pike and Mountain Man as noisily as possible—Michael Archuletta felt a deep burn at the back of his neck; he sensed that everyone in the room was staring directly at him, and that they didn't like what they saw. He also noticed that the band was playing more frantically, as if to ward off the inevitable.

Mountain Man Mason, 146 pounds of psychopathic joy, downed four straight, non-stop shots of B.P.O.E. whiskey and headed for the dance floor. Alex thought that he should try to stop him, but his attention was pulled away by a group of five business-like citizens moving in his direction. Three of the group were deeply tanned, in their thirties or forties, and looked out of place in their Sunday attire. The fourth was a young, pale-faced man who limped slightly and kept his right hand concealed in his pocket. The fifth was also young, but harder looking, with slightly crossed brown eyes and a deputy sheriff's badge peeking out from behind the lapel of his frock coat.

One of the three older men was definitely in charge and even more definitely upset. "You men aren't wanted here. Please leave."

"We ain't hurtin' nothin'," Shorty whined, his eyes darting from face to face and his mind racing to the skinning knife he carried in his sleeve.

The deputy sheriff took a step forward, jutting his star out a little more conspicuously as he moved. "Now why don't y'all just sashay back ta yer tents like good sojurs! We don't want no trouble."

"Hey, mister," Bill Pike interjected good-naturedly, "we don't want no trouble neither. We jes lookin' fer a good time."

"If you're not lookin' for trouble, mister, why'd you bring this greaser along?" The older man was talking to Pike but looking at Archuletta. "You know god-damned good and well not to bring greasers into white society."

Nobody said anything for a moment. Archuletta stood perfectly still, his hatred under tight control as he stared calmly at the white-headed speaker. Finally, Alex cleared his throat and blustered: "Please accept my apologies, sir. Like my friend here says, we're just trying to have a good time. We are most definitely not looking for trouble." Shorty and Bill Pike looked at him as if he were insane, but Alex plunged on, talking even faster. "We've been cooped up on that dusty parade ground for almost three weeks. We just want to have a quiet evening. Why don't we just finish these drinks so nothing is wasted and be on our way?"

More silence. Like his friends, the five locals stared at him like he was loco. Then, without warning, the pale-faced man with the limp moved forward and pulled a derringer from his coat pocket. "You filthy fuckin' scum, shut yer shit-eatin' mouths and get this filthy fuckin' spic out of here—right now this same fuckin' minute. You HEAR?"

Alex and his friends started immediately for the door. Their five antagonists stood and watched, the pale-faced man with the derringer glowering, the other four grinning. Each of the four khaki-clad heroes retreated for a different reason, but they retreated at once. Alex thought about what would happen to any possible promotion were he to get involved in a barroom brawl. Bill and Shorty were perfectly willing to fight, but not when the opposition had the edge. They were used to having the edge, and were acutely aware of its advantages. Archuletta swallowed a rage he had felt most of his life, but he looked passively at the five and backed away. He had not abandoned the plateaus and canyons of northern New Mexico to get killed in a brawl, or hung later for starting it.

When the four soldiers were almost at the door, they heard an angry scream. Mountain Man had talked the young brunette into a dance and, while dancing, had thrust his thigh between her legs and clutched her buttock with his left hand. He hadn't stopped to think that perhaps the young debutante wasn't used to that sort of embrace. Before he had moved two steps in his favorite dance, the brunette screamed.

The deputy turned from the group he was seeing to the door; dashed across the dance floor, jerking his .45 from his dinner jacket-covered holster as he ran; spun Mountain Man away from the brunette; and encouraged the two pound pistol to etch a perfect arc through the hushed air and land in the middle of Mountain Man's demented head. The last thing Martin, alias Mountain Man, alias Rapid Mouth, Mason remembered was being jerked around to face an enraged man with crossed eyes.

* * * * *

The four soldiers sat at a small table in a cantina three blocks from the fairgrounds. Except for Pike, who was already half drunk, they had been slowly sipping *cerveza*. While none of the four was having a good time, none was anxious to leave. Even Alex was more content to stay where he was than to return to camp.

"God damn! God damn! God DAMN!" Bill Pike was inconsolable. "He's the best friend I ever had. And they're gonna kill 'im. God damn!"

"Oh, bullshit! Bill," Shorty interrupted. They ain't gonna kill him. Hell, dumbfuck, Marty's a white man. They just gonna throw 'im in jail.

Now if it was ol' Mex here?" Shorty put his arm around Archuletta, who gritted his teeth. "If it hadda been ol' Mex, they'd a killed 'im sure. That right, Mex?" Archuletta nodded. "Sure they would," Shorty repeated. But ol' Rapid Mouth? Hell's bells, he's gonna be okay."

"God damn it. God damn it!" Pike again broke the silence that engulfed the depressed group.

"What's the matter, you fat-ass, red-headed buffalo? You gonna mope about Rapid Mouth all night?" Shorty was getting disgusted. Mountain Man Mason was going to jail, and that was that.

"Who said anything about good ol' Rapid Mouth? Shee-it, ol' buddy. It's jes that my crease is actin' up again. God damn!" He rubbed the long purple indentation that slanted across the left side of his forehead, then chugged another *cerveza*. "I'll jes have me a few more a these here, 'n I'll be good as new."

"You have a few more of those Mexican beers and your head'll come right off," Archuletta warned, smiling at the possibility.

"Say, Bill, how'd you get that crease on your head?" Alex knew that you didn't ask Westerners, especially self-proclaimed anachronisms, how they did, or got, or came to anything, but since he now felt a common bond, he plunged right in.

Bill Pike merely groaned, chugged another beer and shook his head.

Shorty laughed, hard and mean. "So you want ta know how Bill got his crease, huh?" He laughed again. "Ya know. Folks used ta call him 'Creaser,' but they learnt real fast not to, unless they wanted to fight some. Right, Bill?" Pike nodded and consumed still another beer. "Yeah, really made him madder 'n hell. Folks was always slippin' and sayin' 'Greaser' instead of 'Creaser.' Sorry, Mex. No offense."

Archuletta took another sip from his bottle, mildly curious as to how the red head had received the scar. "What's the story, Pike?"

William Pike buried his throbbing head in his hands and mumbled, "I use ta work in this here coal mine up in Colorado. I had this here whore in town. She jest about cleaned my plow with my own Winchester 'cause I damn near bit the nipple off a her tit 'cause a scorpion bit me on the ass."

"Huh?" Alex said.

"He ain't lyin', dude," Shorty added. "That ninety pound whore whacked him with his own 30-30. She took that nine pound barrel 'n jes slammed it across his head like it was a flyswatter slappin' flies."

While the subject of the tale cradled his throbbing head, Alex and Archuletta listened to a far-fetched story about William Pike's love life. According to Shorty, every Saturday he road his mule into town, settled it down in the corral across from the new Strater Hotel, and ambled down to the two story, clap-board whorehouse that stood across from the train station.

Pike had a girl upstairs named Josephine, whose companionship he paid $2.00 for a full hour every Saturday he had the money. Even more than making love to Josephine, he loved to nurse her, to suckle contentedly away and dream of the mother who had died of diphtheria before he was weaned.

One dusty Saturday in July of 1894, Big Bill was nursing away after making love in less than a minute, which was a record, even for Bill. But while he was lost in his hour of purchased paradise, a small, tan scorpion crawled up the heat register, scudded across the floor of Josephine's room and pulled itself up the leg of the bed. Whether the scorpion was mad, or hungry, or just plain amorous was never determined; Durango old-timers still argued the possibilities. But with no warning whatsoever, the scorpion crawled across the damp sheet and plunged its barbed tail into the left cheek of Big Bill's sweating posterior.

Upon the sudden and unsweet instant of having his butt stung by the scorpion, Bill clamped down desperately upon the nipple of his hired lover's left tit, which caused said nipple to almost separate from its heretofore secure foundation. Poor Josephine leaped from the bed, grabbed the barrel of Bill's 30-30 from where it was standing against the wall, swung it around her head three times and wiped out the first seven years of his life, including the oral fixation, with the frontier equivalent of a pre-frontal lobotomy.

Then, her nipple hanging from a literal thread, Josephine donned her green cotton wrapper and ran down the rear stairs of the whore house, up the middle of the dusty, shocked-still street, and into the office of old Doc Young.

Old Doc suffered from Parkinson's Disease and always shook when he got excited, and he always got excited in front of a semi-naked woman, even at eighty-two quaking years of age. After listening three times to her shouted demand, "Don't just stand there, you vibrating old fart, fix me, goddamnit, fix me!" Doc led her to a table and sewed the afflicted member back to its moorings. The repair job was prolonged unnecessarily by Josephine, who never ceased cussing and squirming.

The half dozen men and boys who, tongues hanging out, had followed Josephine up the street, quickly multiplied into a crowd of jumping jacks. It was the largest crowd Durango had seen since Bobby Thompson had been hung a year earlier for stealing three horses and shooting Larry Jones in the head for trying to stop him. Everyone in the crowd was jumping up and down, struggling to look over the half curtains and into Doc Young's office.

About the time Old Doc finished his erratic embroidery, Big Bill woke up and decided, despite the blood pouring into his eyes, that he'd best put some space between himself and Josephine. By the time she had climbed back up the stairs, preceded by a buggy whip she held in front of her like a scepter, and followed by half the men and all the half-grown boys in town, Bill Pike had been gone so long that the dust had ceased rattling.

By the time Shorty had finished his story, Michael Archuletta was grinning from ear to ear. For the first time in a long time, he had laughed out loud. Alex had laughed too, during the narration, but he wasn't sure he should have. Pike moaned, holding his head.

Archuletta, believing that Shorty's guard was down, asked casually, "I hear that's pretty good country up around the Colorado-New Mexico border. That so?"

"Yessir, Mex. Sure is." Shorty agreed, waltzing blithely into the sheepherder's trap. "Hell, I was jest there last month. Me 'n a friend was doin' some prospectin' up in the San Juans. Came down the river through Pagosa 'n over inta Navajo country. Damn nice. Rode from mid-winter inta spring in less than a week. Damn nice ride. Even caught ourselves some Navajo nookie."

"Damn! Wish I'd been there for that," Archuletta said. "How'd you manage to pull that off?"

Alex had never heard Michael swear . Nor had he ever seen on his bunkmate's face anything resembling such an eager, voyeuristic glow. Something was going on between the two men that Alex didn't understand, and he suspected that Shorty didn't understand it either.

"We rode over a rise down ta the river. Damned if there wasn't a naked squaw bathin' in one of the pools. Brown as a berry, pretty as a picture, 'n scared as any doe I ever seen."

"No shit?" Archuletta interrupted. "What'd she do? Just lie down in the grass and spread her legs?" An almost maniacal glow lit his face.

Shorty was coming down from his narrative high and sensed that the eastern dude was taking exception to the incident, and maybe he shouldn't go much further. "Well, no. 'tweren't all that easy. But...well, we had to rough her up just a little. Navajo squaws really like ta screw, but sometimes...they don' wanna...'fess up." Shorty mumbled the last few words and looked suspiciously around at his audience. Pike was snoring and Alex looked like he was about to lose his dinner. But Archuletta was still grinning and nodding his head.

"Here, Shorty. How about another *cerveza*?" Archuletta clapped him on the back and handed him a beer. "You sure do tell a good story. I can see the whole thing. Yes, sir, makes me feel just like I was there." The sheepherder lifted his own bottle and toasted the storyteller.

* * * * *

At reveille, hung over, still fully dressed and dreading the razzing he was sure to get from his tent-mates, Alex climbed gingerly from his bunk to the floor. But the troopers were more subdued than usual. One made a half-joking but vaguely deferential comment about folks too lazy to undress before hitting the sack; no one else ventured more than a smirk. What's up? Alex wondered.

At morning formation he found it difficult to remain erect on his mare. His head pounded and his squeamish stomach rebelled at the mare's slightest movement. Though it was not yet June, heat waves bounced from the hard-packed clay of the parade ground. The reviewing officers sat their mounts with the sun at their backs. The 1,200 troops facing them and squinting directly into the light could make out nothing but silhouettes. They had been waiting almost twenty minutes for something to happen. Except for the swish of horse tails warding off flies, and the occasional whinny that ran up and down the lines of mounted cavalry, the parade ground was silent.

Suddenly, there was a commotion in the headquarters area, and the embryonic regiment's two illustrious leaders, Colonel Leonard Wood and Lt. Colonel Theodore Roosevelt, trotted out to join the reviewing officers. A low rumble of anticipation flowed along the mounted ranks, cut short almost immediately by the regimental Sergeant Major's call, "A-tennn-SHUN!" The Adjutant separated from the reviewing line and trotted twenty paces toward the troops. He was a silhouette that emerged from the sun to become first a centaur and then a blue and khaki major on a black horse.

Alex could not get his brain to function. What was happening? What had he missed? What wild rumors had circulated after the five of them had taken off for the dance?

The Adjutant handed the Sergeant Major a list. After a short conversation, the Sergeant Major turned his horse back toward the troopers. "The following men have been promoted to non-commissioned officer. When your name and new rank have been called, ride front and center." The Sergeant Major looked around, waiting to quell any ripple of conversation. But the men knew better. They sat perfectly still. Only their lower halves, their mounts, moved at all. "Anderson, D. Corporal. Archuletta, M. Corporal. Cox, R. Sergeant. Eaton, C. Corporal..."

When he heard Michael's name, Alex glanced quickly to his left. Archuletta was staring straight ahead. As Alex listened to the long list of alphabetized names and realized that his was not among them, he hid his disappointment by listening for the names of his friends: "Jones...Morgan...Somers...Williams...Vandervoort." Jesus, he thought. Even poor old David Vandervoort had made it to corporal. While quite a few of the Ivy Leaguers hadn't made the promotion list, of his small group, only he and Wilcox had been passed over.

Though he had worked hard and, he thought, excelled at shooting, riding and leadership, Alex knew that Archuletta was a better man; the Mexican would make an outstanding non-commissioned officer. But what about Don Wilcox? The man was an excellent soldier and the best natural leader in camp. Alex knew that he had fallen at least slightly from Roosevelt's favor, but what the hell had Don done? He tried to concentrate on Wilcox's problem, and the problems of the three or four other men in the regiment who, he was absolutely sure, deserved promotion. He could feel tears at the corner of his eyes, and concentrated on his friends in a less than successful attempt to evade his own disappointment.

Something was going on in front of him. The Adjutant and Sergeant Major had finished shaking hands and exchanging salutes with the new noncommissioned officers. Rather than calling for a group salute to the reviewing officers, however, the Adjutant pulled a second list from his tunic, consulted it briefly, and then called out: "The following men have been promoted to second lieutenant. When your name is called, proceed forward ten paces beyond this rank: Jackson, A., Meeker, J., O'Donnell, R., Peterson, C., Wilcox, D."

The hush was broken by a slight rumple of surprise. Rumor had omitted a couple of names, Meeker and Peterson, but the other three had been a total surprise only to those men, like Alex, who had returned to camp long after taps. As he rode forward, his head still pounding, Alex fought both to control his aching body and to suppress the tears of pride and happiness that threatened his military composure.

He felt his mare separate herself from the long lines of privates and move through and beyond the thin line of new corporals and sergeants. In the shortest and most glorious ride he was ever to make, Alex merged with the other officer designees and came to a halt in front of the smiling Adjutant. Then Wood and Roosevelt rode out of the sun to meet them. Each of the new officers shook hands with and saluted the major, the lieutenant colonel and the colonel.

"Well, Alex," Roosevelt grinned, shaking Alex's hand and then holding onto it until Alex felt compelled to pull it away. "Did you ever think, the day you stood on my bear-skin rug over at the Navy Department, that you'd be an officer in the best cavalry regiment in the WORLD?"

"No, sir," Alex lied, unwilling to explain the long series of events, real and fantasized, that had led him to this moment.

"Hummph," Roosevelt responded, smiling even more. "I find that a little hard to imagine. I saw, even in February, that—with the right encouragement—you'd be a dandy officer. Isn't that so, Leonard?" he asked, looking to his left toward Leonard Wood, who listened impassively to the conversation, his face revealing a slight expression of distaste. Alex shook hands with his sometime hero, saluted, looking straight ahead, and waited for his commanding officer to come into view.

Leonard Wood's comments were brief and to the point. "I've been watching you, Jackson, closer than you may know. You've worked hard. I'm betting that you'll make an excellent officer, despite your romantic notions. Don't disappoint me. "

"I won't, sir. Thank you, sir."

The colonel moved out of his line of vision, and Alex found himself staring at the heat waves shimmering from the adobe wall on the east side of the parade ground.

Later that morning, as he moved his gear from the squad tent to the troop officers' tent, Henry and Luke approached him and saluted. "We're sorry we gave you such a hard time, lootenant. It's jes that we ain't useter sleepin' with Mexicans and . . ."

"And dudes?" Alex grinned, suddenly reveling in warm feelings of superiority, condescension and generosity.

"Yessir," Luke continued. "But we think ya'll make a dang good officer. It's jes that ya didn't seem ta fit with us, sir."

"Thank you, men. Thank you," the new lieutenant replied, in a resonant military tone guaranteed, albeit unintentionally, to increase the gulf between them. "What do you think of Archuletta's promotion to corporal?"

"Jes fine with us, sir," Henry answered, lying in his flustered teeth.

"Now that ain't so, Henry, an' you know it," Luke broke in. "Sir, the men don't like it. At all! Except for Captain Max Luna—'n he's so white he don't count—Archuletta's the only spic left in the outfit. But the men talked 'er over, 'n we figure the colonels knows what they're doin'. And, damnit, Archuletta is a right good sojer."

"Good. Make sure he's treated with respect! He is a good soldier." Having given his first order, Alex saluted the cowboys, shouldered his gear and marched from the tent. Almost immediately he passed Michael, who merely saluted, nodded, and continued on. Alex almost stopped him but thought better of it. Yes, Michael is a good soldier, he thought; he's a better soldier than I'll ever be.

Seeing Michael reminded Alex of the preceding evening. He shivered as he thought of the near brawl in the dance hall, and how close he had come to blowing the promotion even before he'd received it. At least now he wouldn't be tempted to dash out on drunken sprees with wild-eyed privates.

Just before he entered the troop officers' tent, he placed his gear on the ground, straightened his tunic and wiped the toes of his dusty boots on the back of his pant legs. Best foot forward, he thought.

Captain Alain Thomas looked up from his field desk and casually returned Alex's salute. "Sit down, Lieutenant. How about a cup of coffee?" Alex nodded and the captain got up to pour. Thomas didn't know what to make of the eastern college boys who had joined the regiment; he certainly didn't know what to make of Alexander Dumas Jackson. He and the other new officers, all but one of whom were Ivy Leaguers, were good enough soldiers. But they weren't that good. Goddamn politicians were going to screw up the entire war if the old-timers, like himself, didn't keep their eyes open.

"Jackson, you're going to be third officer. Primary responsibility will be second and third squads."

"Yes, SIR."

"On Colonel Roosevelt's express command, you will also be the regiment's deputy supply officer. In that capacity you'll work through Lieutenant Fred Nelson at Regimental Headquarters. Understood?"

"Yes, sir."

"I understand you've had some supply experience already, on a somewhat larger scale?" Alex nodded. "Good. I expect this troop to be the best supplied troop in the regiment. Always! Put your gear on the bunk in the corner. That will be all."

The tired captain stood, followed by Alex, who had barely touched his coffee. The captain thought for a moment and added, "Give Lieutenant Nelson all the help you can. The man's an idiot. He's why we didn't have enough tents until the end of the first week and enough knives and forks until the second." Captain Thomas returned Alex's salute and left the tent.

"God damn son of a polluted fucking porcupine bitch," Alex mumbled, sounding for the first time like one of his colorful friends. "Supply officer. God damn! I don't need that."

PART II: REMEMBER THE *MAINE!*

* * * *

The remaining days at Exhibition Hall Barracks were hectic. Alex divided his daylight hours between drilling his troops and helping Lieutenant Fred Nelson sort out the rest of the regiment's supplies. He spent his evenings studying troop and squadron tactics. He drilled his troops regularly and well, and enjoyed it. He hated his work with Nelson. Scrounging for supplies reminded him too much and too often of the weeks he had spent in Washington as Teddy's "go-fer." He worked with his troops until mid-afternoon, worked with Fred Nelson until dusk, then retreated to his tent to study and dream.

In part, his incessant reading of cavalry tactics was a reaction to his duties as supply officer. But his studying was also a continuation of his fantasies. Alex had already become an officer, had overcome what he took to be the most difficult hurdle. That he would be a success he had no doubt. He would lead glorious charges, win medals and promotions, and go on to a brilliant career as a professional soldier. Charlotte would make an excellent general's wife. She had the looks, the charm—and the money. Alex was not only a dreamer, however. He knew that a successful career required more than a field promotion and a charming wife, so he studied and dreamed and studied some more.

The most demanding part of his day was the hours he spent with Lieutenant Fred Nelson at Regimental Supply. Nelson was a thirty-year old, over-weight National Guard officer from Saint Louis. "Freddy," as he was called by the enlisted men who worked for him, was probably the most enthusiastically incompetent officer in the regiment.

He was continuously distracted, even in mid-sentence, and lived in mortal fear that someone would ask him to do something that one of his supply clerks couldn't manage. First had been the problem of the squad tents. They hadn't come and hadn't come, and there wasn't a damn thing he could do about it. Nor about the knives and forks, even though Roosevelt went into a towering rage every time he saw the troopers eating with their fingers. Now the problem was khaki tunics. The regiment had been supplied with khaki-colored cotton trousers and blue wool tunics. Even in May the troopers were sweltering in the deep blue wool. Though Roosevelt had been raging at the War Department for at least two weeks, the regiment was still wearing wool tunics.

The first time Alex entered the Quartermaster's tent, Roosevelt was screaming at a visibly cringing Freddy. "Nelson, you lily-livered incompetent, you either get us those cotton shirts—and the machetes, and the smokeless cartridges—NOW, or I'm going to bust your stammering little ass to private."

Silence.

"DO YOU HEAR ME?"

"Yes, s-s-sir," Freddy stuttered, looking as though he were going to collapse.

Suddenly Roosevelt turned on Alex. "I don't know why Wood, why I decided to promote you after you abandoned your job early in Washington. If you'd stayed where you were supposed to for just one more week, maybe two, these foul-ups would not have happened. So, Alex, I'm making you responsible for those cotton tunics. You hear?"

"Yes, sir," Alex clipped back, cursing Roosevelt, cursing Freddy, and cursing the fate that had taken him into the War Department in the first place. Roosevelt turned on his heel and swaggered out into the sun.

Alex watched him go. "So it was Wood who promoted me—and not you," he whispered under his breath. "You chest-pounding, influence peddling, loud-mouthed bully."

"I hope he gets s-sun stroke!" Freddy hissed.

Alex couldn't help nodding his head in agreement. "When I left Washington, all the requisitions were filled out, all started in the proper channels, all well on their way. I had promises from everyone. What the hell was I supposed to do? Pick up every piece of equipment and carry it to San Antonio?"

Freddy's face lit up. Maybe he finally had an ally, someone who knew there was nothing to be done, that it was all too terribly confusing. Or, even better, maybe this young lieutenant was his fairy godfather and could perform miracles. He wrung his hands, smiled and asked, "Who are y-y-you? "

For the next few days Alex did perform miracles, which is to say he monopolized the telegraph: to track down an errant box car that had carried their cotton tunics to Albuquerque; to find another box car loaded with machetes in Chicago and given priority clearance to San Antonio; and to have half a million smokeless cartridges for their Krag-Jorgenson rifles shipped straight to Tampa in a clearly marked box car.

He talked Captain Thomas into assigning Corporal Archuletta to him as an assistant, and used the sheepherder to keep Freddy on his toes. Alex used his knowledge of procurement to create an inventory and disbursement system. He established procedures for Freddy and his clerks to follow, and he left Archuletta to make sure they did.

Michael had two responsibilities, which he carried out with the same quiet diligence that marked all of his activities in the regiment: He made sure that Freddy and his men followed Alex's procedures, and he made sure that "L" Troop got the best of everything that came through Freddy's hands, and that they got it first. The sheepherder used one weapon: terror. With Freddy a little terror went a long way.

When he told Freddy that he was going to pull the chestnuts out of the fire and that Freddy was going to get the credit, Alex laid down some conditions, the most important of which were 1) Alex would make every single decision, 2) Freddy would see that the decisions were executed, and 3) in Alex's absence, Freddy would submit to Archuletta's judgment. Before introducing Michael to Freddy, Alex gave the sheepherder explicit instructions as to what to do and how to act. Archuletta was more than pleased to follow his new orders.

Alex had hinted to the supply officer that the swarthy, green-eyed corporal had once killed a man with a knife, and that Roosevelt had personally recruited him to sneak behind enemy lines to cut throats. Freddy was immediately and permanently terrified.

One afternoon, Freddy turned to Michael, who was watching him fill out reports, and asked, "How did you k-kill those men?"

"What men?" Michael asked, momentarily puzzled.

"Lieutenant Jackson s-said that you k-k-killed somebody, and that's why Roosevelt t-took you."

"Oh, those men. You want to know how I killed them, sir? Why?"

"Well, C-c-corporal. It's not important. I was just c-curious, that's all."

"I don't mind telling you, Lieutenant," Michael smiled. "I cut off their peckers and watched them bleed to death."

Freddy blanched and clutched his crotch with both hands. "I once had my p-p-penis bitten by a c-carp," he stammered miserably. "It took me several m-months to recover. And I c-c-can tell you, it wasn't very f-funny. I'm still very pr-pr-protective of my p-penis"

Alex and Michael stared at him.

The next evening, Alex brought up the issue of Freddy's protectiveness as he and Michael were walking the picket line. "Did you know that Freddy wears a whale bone penis protector?"

"*Que vaya!*" Michael exclaimed, dropping into Spanish for only the third or fourth time since joining the regiment. "What craziness!"

"We were taking showers and I saw him slip it off. I asked him what it was, and then I made him show it to me." Alex was grinning broadly. "Do you know what scrimshaw art is?"

Michael shook his head.

"In New England carvers engrave on whale bone, usually intricate designs. Freddy's got this thin little cup he wears strapped around his waist, like a long thimble. He keeps his penis in the cup."

Michael grinned and shook his head. "You gringos are all crazy. You know that? How can crazy people expect to run the world?"

Alex merely laughed and placed his hand on Michael's shoulder. He was pleased with himself: pleased with the job he was doing as a troop officer, pleased with his decision to put his half-Irish, half-Mexican friend in charge of Freddy, most of all pleased with the apparent trust and friendship of this man who had come to him from the northern wilderness of New Mexico. In fact, Alex was feeling so good at the moment, so pleased with himself, the world, and the fading magenta sunset, that both the war and his own elaborate fantasies seemed worlds away.

"You gringos are crazy, you know," Michael continued on a more serious note. You...we don't have any business going to Cuba."

"We've got all the business in the world," Alex replied "The Spaniards blew up the *Maine*. A friend of mine was killed in that explosion. And we've been sitting back and watching Spain cannibalize that island forever. Don't you think...?"

"That's only half the steak, Alex. Do you think Roosevelt and Wood and all those senators you talk about are taking us to war to 'free' a bunch of Cuban revolutionaries?"

Goddamn it, Michael, Alex thought. Here we go again. "Well, sometimes it takes a catalyst, like the *Maine*, before our actions catch up with our ideals."

"Perhaps." Michael was not convinced, but decided not to pursue the subject.

PART II: REMEMBER THE *MAINE!*

"Michael, why did you enlist?" It was Alex's turn to ask a direct question, one he had been saving for weeks.

"Because I wanted to get away from my sheep for awhile, and...I wanted to do something else. I thought that enlisting would give me the chance to do the something else."

The two men walked back to the tent rows in silence. Michael had considered telling Alex the whole story. However, years ago his mother had told him, "You can be friends with a man without feeling responsible for him. But if you share with each other the important secrets, you are tied together."

Alex, too, was lost in thought, scarcely aware of the lanterns being lighted inside the long lines of tents, or of the glow that transfused the canvas and silhouetted the hundreds of soldiers cleaning their rifles and polishing their gear. Usually, Alex relished this part of the evening. This was his period of calm before he tackled his books. He felt in harmony, a part of the whole, radiant with the glow of the regiment's potential. On this particular evening, however, he was pre-occupied. Once again, Michael's questions had disturbed his equanimity.

Why were they going to Cuba? Alex knew that the question was more complicated than avenging Spain's destruction of the *Maine*, Not for him perhaps. He was sure of his reasons and saw no contradiction thus no irony in the yoking of his ambitions for a successful career with the Cuban insurrectionists' fight for freedom. He believed all the noble and altruistic sentiments sweeping the country about America's motives for declaring war on Spain. He believed, but...questions like those posed by Michael bothered him; they attacked from nowhere and disturbed the current of his self-confidence.

Chapter Twenty-Four

A SHORT WAR IF POSSIBLE; A LONG ONE IF NECESSARY
ABOVE ALL A DECISIVE AND VICTORIOUS ONE
All Power Is in the President's Hands

* * * *

What did the American people expect when President McKinley gave Spain forty-eight hours to get out of Cuba? That the whole naval and military strength of the United States would at once be put forth to enforce the order, that Cuba would be freed and the *reconcentrados* saved from starvation within a few days, or a few weeks at most?

The people have been disappointed. More than a month has passed since America declared war, and Spain is still in Cuba, stronger to resist us than when war was declared.

The President has asked for everything, and everything has been given to him. All the power is his, and so is all the responsibility. To that responsibility he will be held.

The American people can do nothing but wait. If behind the wall of secrecy there are brains and courage all will be well. If not, then no man can say how much more weariness and humiliation and loss of national prestige will have to be endured. William Randolph Hearst, Editorial: *The New York Journal*, May 25.

San Antonio to Tampa

I t was late afternoon and they had been loading gear and horses since dawn. All along the track soldiers hung onto their haltered horses, waiting to shove, lead or cajole them aboard the slatted cattle cars that would carry them to Tampa. The colonels had divided the transfer to Florida into five sections, five separate trains to carry the twelve hundred men, fourteen hundred horses and two hundred pack mules. The fifth and final train was all but loaded, and the first four were already long gone.

Michael was exhausted. He had been chasing Freddy and his supply clerks all day long. It was their job to load the regimental supplies, a task Freddy had already botched. The National Guard officer had put two hundred McClellan saddles on a train carrying pilgrims and farm implements to El Paso, which lay in a direction roughly opposite to that of Tampa. Fortunately, Alex had been able to wire ahead; the saddles were now resting on the platform at Danes, Texas; whether or not they would reach Tampa in time for embarkation to Cuba was, of course, impossible to say. The rest of the day had gone better. But now, as he sauntered down the platform to re-check Freddy's latest efforts, Michael realized how tired he was—tired of Freddy's incompetence, tired of being a nurse-maid, and tired of a day that had gone on so long that more mistakes were bound to occur.

Suddenly a commotion broke out two cars down the track. What's that idiot done now? Michael wondered as he ran down the platform. But Freddy had done nothing. He was standing quietly aside, mouth agape, an innocent spectator absorbed in the pageant unfolding before him.

Michael shoved his way through the crowd of gawking, applauding cowboy soldiers. Four muleskinners, all but one fairly small, were putting on quite a show. Actually the mules were the ones putting on the show; the skinners were the supporting cast. The skinners were attempting to load twenty mules aboard a cattle car, but were having one helluva time doing it. Some of the horses were difficult; the mules were next to impossible. The four skinners knew what they were doing, however, and were slowly getting the job done, though not without an occasional kick from one of the better marksmen among the mules.

Suddenly someone yelled "A-ten-shun!" and the action froze—except for the mules, who didn't recognize the chain of command, and chose the distraction to deliver half a dozen joyful kicks to the legs and thighs of the skinners, who seemed torn between the call to authority and the more natural call of self-preservation.

It was Roosevelt, impatient to leave. The fourth section of the train had been gone for more than an hour. As second in command of the regiment, he had been detailed to bring up the rear, and was determined "to get this tragi-comic excuse for a freak show on the bloody road NOW!" He strutted through the ramrod straight crowd and glared at the skinners, who were being pulled around the platform by the frolicking mules.

"How long have you poor excuses for horsemen been allowing these mules to get the best of you?"

"Sir? We knows what we's doin', sir. Jes takes a mite a time 'n patience." The speaker was Runt McGinty, scarce five feet tall but the best skinner in the regiment.

"You what?" Roosevelt took one step forward, whacking his riding crop along his leggings. McGinty couldn't answer, however. He was busy being dragged down the platform by his favorite mule and had been obliged to turn his backside to Roosevelt. The lieutenant colonel gritted his teeth, turned toward Captain Thomas and said, in the most even tone he could muster: "I want those mules aboard in ten minutes. Period!" and stalked back to the caboose, his headquarters for the three day journey that would take five.

Captain Thomas rushed up to the frustrated and cursing skinners and yelled, "How much help do you need? We need ta GIT!"

"We don't need no help, Cap'n. We jes need ta be left alone." McGinty's mule, taking full advantage of another target of opportunity, kicked out at the captain with both hind hooves.

"Goddamnit, McGinty," the captain yelled, scurrying back out of the line of fire, "whether you think you need it or not, you're gonna get help right blinkin' now." The captain dashed into the crowd of amused spectators: "You. You. You…and you! Git over there and help out!" He had selected the four largest men on the platform, not one of whom, including Bill Pike, knew anything about mules.

"Oh, shit," McGinty muttered under his breath. "Now we're gonna have fun." The four volunteered soldiers, all of whom were bigger than smarter, were not at all anxious to be heroes. However, they huddled for a moment, decided that valor was the better part of wisdom, and launched a broadside attack on the mule closest to the leading ramp, knocking it off its legs and breaking its right forelock.

"You dumbass, overgrown sons of dumbass bitches. You jes cost me one mule. Get yer dumbass fuckin' asses outa here, or I'll shoot ya."

"McGinty!" the captain roared, confused by what had just happened. "They will help you, or your ass is mud. Hear?"

McGinty nodded grimly and started giving directions. "Pike, you and them other clumsy assholes git up front, 'n stay there. All I wan'cha ta do is pull on them halters. Ya hear?" The four giants nodded, shuffled around to the top of the ramp, and started pulling mules aboard the squeaking cattle car. Within ten minutes all but three of the now hysterically kicking mules were aboard.

"See, McGinty," one of the giants yelled from the cattle car, bending over to give the mule skinner the jeer. See what a little muscle 'll do? Hee hee!"

McGinty just nodded his dour round head and mumbled. "Ya'd better watch yer ass, Hogan. This here detail ain't over 'til the last o' them sons o' burro fuckers is . . ." As if waiting for the appropriate cue, the last mule to be hauled aboard honed in on McGinty's unspoken wish. Demonstrating superb coordination the eighteen hand tall mule caught Hogan in his protruding posterior with both rear hooves. The cheering crowd watched the giant ascend from the cattle car at a forty-five degree angle, execute simultaneously a perfect arc and a near perfect backward somersault, and dive head first into the platform, to wild applause.

"Alright, Hogan, you dumbass clown," Pike yelled, bent nearly double with laughter, "You've had yer fun. Let's git fer done." More laughter. But Hogan refused to get up and return to work. He even refused to move. "Hogan!" Pike yelled. "C'mon!"

McGinty, who stood close to Hogan's landing site, turned white, and the part of the crowd closest to the prone Irishman stopped cheering. McGinty walked over, looked down at Hogan's face, and announced reverently, "He's dead, Pike. Gotta broken neck."

* * * * *

They had been on the road almost three hours, rolling through the pine forests of east Texas. The men in the car were quiet. Many had seen violent death before—on stampedes, in mine cave-ins, at public hangings, etc. Some had been members of posses or Indian fighters. Regardless, Hogan's death had sobered them all. The first Rough Rider casualty of the war had occurred unexpectedly, in the midst of a holiday atmosphere, just as they were finally leaving for the long-promised Cuban picnic. Many of the volunteer soldiers now understood something they had always known but almost forgotten: Even American soldiers are mortal.

Lieutenant Alexander Dumas Jackson shared facing seats with Michael Archuletta and David Vandervoort, the bad luck poker player from Manhattan who had left the game early the second evening in San Antonio. They had invited Freddy to share their seat, knowing full well that he would spend as much of the journey as possible in the water closet from which he would emerge only after being yelled at repeatedly by whichever soldier got tired of hopping up and down in anticipation of a relieved bladder. Alex and Michael were trying to nap, exhausted from the ordeal of managing Freddy for nine straight hours.

Corporal David Vandervoort was reading *War and Peace*, humming under his breath and stroking his thin brown moustache. Vandervoort was another brand of dreamer, a bookworm who was happiest when buried in a novel. He read every time he had a spare thirty seconds, carried thirty pounds of excess baggage—all of it books—even kept thin books tucked inside his tunic.

Many of the less literate Westerners razzed him every time they got a chance. That is they razzed him until Lieutenant Bucky O'Neill, former Arizona Ranger and Sheriff of Prescott, offered to fight anyone who took exception to reading. Bucky's passion was French novels, especially Zola and Stendahl. He was also as macho a western, rugged, non-conforming individualist as any cowboy in the outfit, and everyone knew it.

David was lost in the novel. He had become Pierre, and was moving through the brilliant fog of Saint Petersburg society, watching the Imperial Russian Officer Corps dance away the last hours of its existence.

At that moment two cowboy soldiers came crashing down the aisle, dragging a huge crate of sandwiches and yelling, "Soo-ee, soo-ee, sooo-EE!" The hog call broke the spell of gloom. Soldiers snapped from their naps and reveries, laughing at the hog-callers. David Vandervoort was put off by the disturbance, but not too put off to ignore the food; he dropped his novel and grabbed six sandwiches. "My Lord," he uttered in amazement. "This is supper? Each of the sandwiches consisted of two pieces of hard tack and a thin slice of corned beef. "It would certainly be nice to sit down to dinner at Del Monico's about now."

From across the seat Alex laughed. "That it would." He had been there once, four years before, just after George Bedford had graduated. Bedford's parents had taken them to dinner, the most expensive he'd ever heard of, let alone eaten. Alex looked down at his hard tack sandwich, took one chewy bite and mumbled, "It's not so bad. I'm sure it'll get worse."

"That's another problem with you gringos," Michael interjected. "You eat too much beef. Maybe that's why your brains have all gone mushy." He wolfed down his first sandwich in three unmasticated bites.

After fighting their way through the tough sandwiches, Alex and Michael talked, joined only occasionally by David, who looked up from his book every twenty minutes or so to see if the world was still spinning.

"If the cartridges just get to Tampa, we'll be ready," Alex thought aloud. During the past week he had worried more about the supply problem than about "L" Troop. He knew the other officers would worry about the troop; there was no one else to worry about the supplies.

"How about the spurs, Alex?" Archuletta asked.

Alex grunted. "Don't remind me. I don't even want to think about those silly spurs."

David looked up. "Spurs? Are we going to be issued spurs?" He glanced from Michael's broad grin to Alex's grimace. "When?"

"That's what Roosevelt wants to know," Michael continued. "He wired the War Department personally, asking them—ordering them—to send the regiment's spurs on the next train. He also yelled at our lieutenant friend here for messing up his priorities and worrying more about machetes than spurs. Right, Alex?" Alex merely grunted and stared out the window. "You should have seen the answer we got back from Major Gleeson at the War Department."

"What answer?" Alex asked, jerking his head away from the moon that now peeked above the pine forests . "You didn't say anything about an answer."

"Well, there's a copy in the files. I took the answer straight over to Roosevelt. Want to know what it said?"

"You know damned good and well I do."

"Good. Do you want to know what it said, David?" David nodded, enjoying Michael's game. Alex, however, wanted to strangle him. "Major Gleeson said, quote: "About your spurs: I thought you'd win those on the battlefield.""

After a moment of silence, Alex said, "Jesus! Gleeson said that to Roosevelt?" Michael nodded, grinning, looking more like a leprechaun with a suntan than a squaw-man sheepherder. "And you took the message to him? And delivered it personally?"

"Yes, sir, Lieutenant. I surely did, just like I was ordered to. The colonel told me to bring him any news about the spurs immediately, so I did. You know me, sir. I always follow my orders. Sacred duty and all that."

David kept his head moving back and forth as he followed the conversation between the Harvard graduate and the self-taught son of an Irish chambermaid and a Mexican tumbleweed. He wasn't sure he understood the relationship between the two men, but found it much more interesting to observe and to participate in than the bland intellectual abstractions and social chitchat of the Group. David was particularly intrigued by Alex, whom he had known only slightly until they became roommates during their last year at Harvard. The man had grown, seemed more...substantial...in some vague way, more sure of himself, even now when he was the passive but willing straight man in another man's game.

"All right, Michael. What did the colonel do?" Alex stretched his legs out on the seat next to David, clasped his hands behind his head and squinted at the sheepherder.

"Nothing."

"Nothing?"

"Nothing, at least at first. Then he turned red and his hand started shaking. It sounded kind of like he was cussing under his breath. Except I know colonels don't cuss. They don't, do they, sir?"

Alex bit his lip to keep from cracking a smile. David, however, had already succumbed, and cackled at a vision of their stern hero turning apoplectic at the jibe from Washington.

A few minutes later Alex mused, "We probably will have to win those spurs, won't we?"

Michael stopped smiling. "We probably will."

"At least we've got the horses to win them with," David added. Like every other man of the regiment, whether cowboy or dude, he had been raised around horses, rode well, and loved the movement of a strong, well-fed mount, "There's never been a regiment with such horses."

"At least that we've ever seen," Alex replied, thinking of the great cavalry squadrons led by the likes of Jeb Stuart and Crazy Horse.

"They're good horses, David. Damned good horses. Now!"

"What's that supposed to mean?" Alex asked, bothered as much by Archuletta's tone as by his substance.

"You ever see a horse after three days in a cattle car? In the summer?"

David blinked. "But we're going to feed and water them twice a day. And exercise them."

"That's right, David. That's why we're taking three days," Alex replied.

"At least three days," David corrected.

"That's because we only have rations for three days. There's no way we're actually going to get there in three." Michael thought for a moment before adding, "You wait, Alex. Those horses are going to melt away before we hit Tampa."

* * * * *

By the end of the third day they had gotten only as far as central Alabama, and it looked as though the three days would stretch to five. Though the trains rolled east all night every night, they rolled very little during the day. The weather had begun hot and humid, but as they rolled across the Deep South, both humidity and temperature increased. As uncomfortable as the men were, everyone—officers and privates alike—worried more about their horses than themselves, and with good cause. All of the horses and mules were losing weight, many were sick, and a dozen had already died. The trains stopped twice a day, early morning and early evening, to feed, water and exercise the horses. Each stop consumed from two to four hours. Not a single town along the way was equipped to handle the huge herd, even when divided among five trains. Each stop became more frustrating than the last.

In central Alabama the patriotic citizens of the town supplied a long line of watering troughs by running hoses from the fire station. Since it was important that the horses be watered, fed and exercised simultaneously, all the action took place on Main Street. Mindful of the digestive inefficiency of horses, several of the citizens had suggested that the horse station be set up on the stretch of empty land leading north from the town. However, these few unpatriotic souls were over-ruled by the local merchants, the women's clubs and the fraternal organizations, all of whom wanted the action to take place where a) everyone could see the parade, b) the ladies could pass out their box lunches to the soldiers, and c) the soldiers could spend their money, if any, without inconvenience.

The solid citizens should have listened. Not a single soldier had received so much as a penny since enlisting. Except for the dudes, everyone was flat broke. Moreover, the soldiers were too busy caring for their sick mules and horses to accept box lunches; all they could do was blow kisses and wink, so the good women were forced to take their mountain of fried chicken aboard the train. All was not lost, however. At least those who wanted to see a parade weren't disappointed. The horses were amazing. They seemed to eat and defecate simultaneously; their stomachs were too distempered for even the more rudimentary digestive processes that horses are known for. Never had so many innocent bystanders seen so many horses eat so little and shit so much. By the time the soldiers of the fifth train had finished walking almost three hundred mules and horses up and down the street, the entire, once-dusty road ran ankle deep. The street was as green as grass and richer than a two-holer during a flu epidemic.

As the train rocked on across Alabama, Roosevelt worried more and more about the horses. Since he was in frequent telegraphic contact with Colonel Leonard Wood in the lead train, he knew that the problem with the horses was not unique to his section. He also knew, however, that without the horses the regiment was nothing—twelve hundred dismounted and disgruntled cowboys, totally ignorant of infantry tactics. The former Assistant Secretary of the Navy cursed the vagaries of the weather, cursed the Quartermaster General's Corps, cursed the overburdened, but patriotic Southerners for their logistics inadequacies, and cursed the decision to haul their horseflesh across the entire deep South in the summertime. That he and Wood and the other eager beavers had pushed hard for a summer invasion of Cuba—and were, therefore, responsible for the horse-killing trek—did not occur to him. The war was there, now. It was going to be won, now. And the Rough Riders were going to get there, now!

Roosevelt was a man of action. Throughout the short war he operated on the principle that if he turned his back for more than a fraction of a second, Spain would pull the plug and abandon Cuba without firing a shot. He also operated on the principle that if he relaxed his frontal attack on McKinley and the War Department for more than two consecutive seconds, the Navy and the Regular Army would win the war without him. Most important to his sense of self, Roosevelt operated on the principle that his sponsorship of the regiment was one of the great gambles of his life. If any one of a thousand possible things went seriously wrong, not only would he not win glory in Cuba, he would also be the laughing stock of Washington and New York, if not of the entire country. As a man of action denied all other alternatives, he acted in the only way open to him: He called a meeting and invited the nine officers aboard the train to attend. "Gentlemen," he began. "We've got problems with the horses."

The nine officers glanced around at each other. Since the worsening condition of the horses and mules had been the greatest single topic of conversation for a day-and-a-half, no one was particularly startled by their commanding officer's announcement. "Do all of you, do any of you realize what will happen to our regiment if we lose our horses? Or even a large part of them?"

They nodded as one. Alex looked his sometime hero directly in the eye. "The question is, Colonel, what can we do about it?" Michael had been right, as usual. The regiment had two choices: slow down and give the horses more exercise, or lose half of them before they arrived in Tampa.

"I'm not sure about what to do. That's why I called this meeting." Two or three of the more cynical officers seemed amused by Roosevelt's apparent lack of confidence. Their smirks were premature, however. The man had weaknesses certainly, weaknesses that had become increasingly apparent to those, including Alex, who worked under him. He was always ready to accept the glory that followed success, seldom willing to accept the blame that accompanies failure. He did not know a tenth as much about conducting wars as he thought he did. He was generous with his friends, petty and vindictive toward his enemies, condescending and bullying to both. He was all these things and more, both good and bad. But stupid he was not. Despite gargantuan impatience with the slowness of their progress toward Tampa and Cuba, Roosevelt knew that he needed the horses. He also knew very well what he had to do to save them. His statement was a gambit, a hope that he could elicit from his junior officers a better suggestion than the one he had conceived.

"We've got to get the horses more room in the cattle cars," Lieutenant Wilcox offered, "which means finding more cattle cars."

"And more exercise, and more often," Captain Thomas added.

Roosevelt nodded. He removed his pince-nez and squinted thoughtfully at Wilcox. "We'll not find any more cattle cars, gentlemen. Each of the four trains ahead of us has scrounged through every depot we've passed "

"Then we've got to get them more exercise, sir, and more often," Alex reiterated, supporting the suggestion of his Troop commander. He knew that he was not the only man in the room who had dreamed big about Cuba and its opportunities. With the possible exception of Freddy, who was only pretending to listen, every man in the car had dreamed major dreams about his contribution to the war effort, and of the war's contribution to his future. Each time one of the officers saw one of the panting horses struggle from the over-crowded cattle cars, his dreams of glory receded further into the mists.

Roosevelt replaced his polished spectacles and leaped to his feet. "Of course you're right, Alex. I was hoping someone would come up with a suggestion that wouldn't cost us so bloody much time, but..." He paced up and down the narrow aisle of the private car. "It'll slow us down another three or four hours a day. Starting today we'll add one more stop. But, please, let's try to keep it under three hours." The officers nodded their heads in agreement.

"Colonel?" Roosevelt looked down at Captain Alain Thomas, Alex's Troop commander, and nodded. "Sir, what are we going to do about these uncooperative, disorganized and incompetent Johnny Rebs? Each town we stop in is more fouled up than the last."

Alex felt himself losing his temper. Although he knew he had no business contradicting his Troop commander, he was about to leap into the breach when Roosevelt took the step for him. Roosevelt puffed out his pigeon chest in what he took to be a legitimate display of righteous indignation: "Captain Thomas! I would like to tell you something. I am going to tell you very carefully, and I am only going to tell you once. Do you understand?"

Thomas was mortified. The colonel was talking to him as to a ten year old truant who'd been caught peeking into the bedroom of the girl next door. "Yes, sir," he mumbled, staring at the floor and silently cursing both Roosevelt and the assembled lieutenants, each of whom was so embarrassed by Thomas' gaff and Roosevelt's tone that he was looking anywhere but at the action.

Roosevelt glared at Thomas, swept his eyes around the room, saw that every head was bowed, as if in prayer, snorted twice and began: "First, CAPTAIN Thomas, they're not Johnny Rebs. The war's been over about as long as you've been alive, CAPTAIN, and these people are bully good citizens of the United States. Do you understand?" Thomas nodded.

"Second, SIR! Not one of these towns had more than two days notice to prepare for us. At least a third of them have had to service three out of the five trains. Because our own schedule is so fouled up, we've had to change schedules several times, and some of these towns have had to prepare water, feed—and fried chicken—in little more than half a day.

They're kind of like us, CAPTAIN, doing the best bloody job they can under very difficult circumstances."

Roosevelt thought he was finished, but he had one more thought. "Speaking of chicken, CAPTAIN, I noticed last night that you've been enjoying your share. You know damned good and well that we're paying these towns for the feed and water for the horses, but that we're not paying for the box lunches. These 'uncooperative Johnny Rebs', as you call them, have plied us with so much food, so much southern hospitality, that we still have much of our three day ration of hard tack and corned beef.

"The next time you, any of you, bite into a piece of fried chicken or a piece of pecan pie, you think of that Johnny Reb in a dress who slaved over a cook stove to prepare it for you." Roosevelt exhaled a long sigh, his bullying tirade subsided and his normal voice took over: "That will be all, gentlemen."

As the train pulled into the last town in eastern Alabama, David Vandervoort looked over at Alex and said, "You know, my friend, it will probably take much more than our little excursion to Cuba to heal the wounds left over from the Civil War."

Michael opened his eyes and looked at David appreciatively. He had been tempted to pass the New Yorker off as a slightly over-weight book worm, but was coming to see in the man a shy thoughtfulness that very few of his peers even sensed, let alone appreciated. Michael smiled to himself: Here I've dismissed him as a book worm because he loves books, and I've always gobbled up every book I've ever been able to get my hands on, at least…until…He bit his lip and glanced over at Alex, who was staring at him.

After a moment Michael said, "About these southern patriots, Alex."

"Yes, as I was saying a while ago, I grew up around people who cursed the uniform we're wearing. We see a lot of stars and stripes in the stations we've been moving through. And the people mean it; they're pleased about this war and the chance to show their patriotism. But if you go into their homes and schools and public buildings, you'll see the stars and bars, the old Confederate flag, damn near everywhere. They're excited about being Americans right now, but when the excitement's over, they'll settle back down. Down here the old war, and the eleven year occupation by Federal troops that followed it, still festers."

Michael nodded. He was not thinking of the Old South, however. He was thinking of his wife's people, the Navajo, who had been rounded up by Kit Carson the year the Civil War began. Carson had force-marched the Navajo Nation from Canyon de Chelly in northern Arizona to Fort Sumner in southeastern New Mexico, where the Navajo had been forced for the next four years to live—and die—like prairie dogs. No matter how many times they waved the American flag, no matter how many Navajo men leaped at the chance to run off and fight American wars, they would never forget, or allow their children to forget their experiences during and after the American Civil War. "You don't conquer people and occupy their country without feeding bitterness," Michael stated.

"No," Alex agreed, "but it doesn't take folks long to get excited about going to war again. You know, this part of the country was pretty badly torn up during the War, but...look at those faces, and those flags."

The train was pulling to a stop alongside the station platform. A band was playing, of all things, "The Battle Hymn of the Republic." The hymn drew an enchanted smile from David, who had closed his book in order to watch the crowd, and in order to make sure he got one of the box lunches that would shortly be held up to the window by some young lady or other. The members of the large and enthusiastic crowd, most of them under fifty years of age, held up banners that read, "Remember the *Maine*" and "Kick em, Teddy's Terrors." The troopers had been glowing under similar banners, bands and enthusiasm across the entire South, and had come to expect it. Since they had been told that they would only be in this station for ten minutes, most of the soldiers didn't even bother to leave their seats.

"Where are the old folks?" David asked. All along the route he had noticed that something was different about the crowds they had encountered since entering southeast Texas, but only now did he figure out what. The crowds contained very few older women, and even fewer old men.

"Most of the men died young," Alex responded, suddenly more depressed than he had been for months. "And many of those who survived haven't had all that much to live for." He thought of his dead father and his father's cronies, prematurely old men who lived as if their hearts and minds had been permanently frozen since Lee's surrender at Appomattox Courthouse.

His memories and impressions heightened by the vague ideas that had haunted him since Roosevelt's attack on Captain Thomas, Alex looked closely for the first time at the older women. The younger women were part of the screaming, applauding crowd. The older women were part of the background. Dressed in black, they stood quietly, mutely watching the trains full of exuberant soldiers pass by. He tried to remember the bitter, used-up, silent watchfulness of his mother, who had died so many years earlier, and who had always seemed so insubstantial, so ghost-like. Watching the old women standing at the rear of the platform, protected from the sun by the over-hanging roof of the station, Alex realized with great force what had consumed and finally killed his mother. Christopher had come to the same conclusion years earlier, which was the major reason for his life-long hatred of their father. The older boy had often tried to communicate to his younger brother what he felt and why. But Alex hadn't understood. Alex hadn't even really listened. He had been too young, too caught up in the old man's glorious fabrications, too mesmerized by the emerging myths of the antebellum South.

Well, he thought, still watching the old women, almost all of whom were dressed in the black dresses they had been wearing for at least 33 years. Boys may succumb to myths, but perhaps grown men can transcend them.... He realized that Michael was talking to him.

"Those old women don't seem too excited about all us happy warriors," Michael stated, as if reading Alex's mind.

"No...they don't. They've lost too much." Alex saw his mother's face in the gaunt faces along the wall. He felt tears coming to his eyes and, ashamed, pulled his hat over his eyes and pretended to fall asleep.

Michael sensed what was wrong with Alex and looked out the window, concentrating on the old faces. Each of the women stood absolutely alone, though most of them were standing in a group. It was as if their black dresses insulated them from the joy and innocence and folly of their children and grandchildren, or, as was often the case, their nieces and nephews. They are the only ones who remember, Michael thought, craning his neck as the train pulled from the station and prepared to cut across a corner of Georgia to Tallahassee.

Chapter Twenty-Five

SPAIN ALMOST READY TO ASK FOR PEACE
Minister of Marine Declares the Cabinet Will Do Its Best to Obtain It "Honorably"

* * * *

Madrid, May 27—The Madrid correspondent of the Daily Mail says, "The political outlook is brighter and the Ministerialists believe that a Cabinet crisis can be averted. Captain Anoun, Minister of Marine, declared in the Cortes today that when an opportunity presented itself the Cabinet would not fail to do its best to bring about an honorable peace." *The New York Journal*, May 27.

* * * *

"I HAVE FOUND THE ENEMY"— SCHLEY NOW FOR A BATTLE AT SANTIAGO

Washington, May 30—Commodore Schley has cabled that he has seen the enemy in Santiago Harbor.

Secretary Long tonight received a cipher cable-gram from Commodore Schley, announcing officially that Admiral Cervera is in Santiago with his formidable squadron of four fast-armored cruisers and two torpedo boat destroyers.

When enough of the message had been deciphered to make it clear that Secretary Long's convictions on the subject had been proved correct, the Navy Department in the neighborhood of the Navigation Bureau became a blaze of light and messengers were hastily dispatched to President McKinley, Secretary Long, Secretary Alger and General Miles. *The New York Journal*, May 30.

The Eastern Edge of the Sierra Maestra

General Calixto Garcia studied Christopher the same way he had studied legal documents years ago at the University of Salamanca. After a short silence, during which he drummed the fingers of both hands on the edge of his desk, Garcia pushed back his chair. "Your encounter with the American gunboat is just one more piece of evidence that the blockade is working. I am told that no supplies or reinforcements have come from Spain for almost a month."

Christopher nodded. "If the Americans continue to send arms and ammunition, sir, we will win, eventually. Their blockade will make it much easier."

"I'm afraid our big neighbor to the north is planning to send much more than a fleet of ships," Garcia stated flatly, rising to his feet and striding to a map of Santiago de Cuba.

"That is the news you were speaking of, sir?"

"Yes." Garcia gave Christopher a short but hard, appraising look and jerked his head back to the map. "Come here so you can see what we must do. For some reason that only God can fathom," Garcia began, "Admiral Cervera has sailed his entire fleet into Santiago Harbor. For reasons even a fool could fathom, the Americans want to keep him there. If they can, they will sink his fleet right there." He jabbed his finger at the narrow-necked bay that lay southwest of Santiago de Cuba. "In the next few days the Americans are going to try to sink one of their own ships in the narrow neck of the harbor, which should keep Cervera pretty well bottled up."

"Sounds good, General. If Cervera decides to sail out and fight, he must pass the sunken ship in single file—if at all. The American battleships and cruisers will pick them off one by one."

"That's right, Colonel. Cervera is already all but checkmated. But

I'm afraid that this absolutely splendid gift is not the big—and possibly frightening—news."

Christopher looked at the map and waited. Finally he said, "Sir?" and pulled the general back from one of his reveries.

"As many of us feared, your countrymen are planning a land invasion of Cuba. I'm afraid it will prove much easier to get them off their ships than to get them back on."

"They're not my countrymen, General Garcia. I am a Cuban. My three daughters were born of a Cuban woman. They are buried with her on Cuban soil."

"Please forgive me," Garcia mumbled. "I know you are Cuban. I just like to tease you now and then." The general was embarrassed. It was easy to make fun of the *Yanqui*'s defensiveness, but to forget the sacrifices the man had already made for *Cuba Libre!* was inexcusable.

"Now let me show you what will probably happen and what will probably be required of us. The American army will land somewhere along this coast." He used his finger to draw a line along the southeastern coast from the middle of the *Sierra Maestra* on the west to Guantanamo Bay on the east. "We won't know exactly when—or where—for another week or so. But wherever they land, and it will be on the south coast of Oriente Province, we will have to help."

"To what degree, Sir?"

"To a considerable degree. The Americans will require a blocking force of almost twenty thousand."

Christopher registered his shock and disapproval. "But, General! That could lead to a disaster. We've never massed that many of our troops in one place. We don't have the ammunition for a battle that big. We . . ."

"We will do everything the Americans ask," Garcia interrupted. "We have no choice!" he added emphatically. "If we go along with the Americans, we can win this war within a month or two. We can win *Cuba Libre!* and rid our land of the killing and dying. Hopefully, forever," he added softly.

"And what about the American army? And about all the Washington politicians who want to pull us ashore once they have us hooked?"

"Look, COLONEL!" Garcia almost hissed. "We take our chances. This is what we will do. We sucked America into this war and we are now deprived of choice. Our only alternative is to cooperate—and pray. We can only hope that they will leave us to determine our own destiny. Be that as it may, Colonel Jackson, we are now playing by their rules. DO YOU UNDERSTAND?"

"Yes, sir!" Christopher replied, drawing himself to attention.

"Relax, Colonel," the general added after taking in and exhaling a deep breath. "I'm not mad at you. I'm just frustrated. I'm not any happier about having an American army in Cuba than you are. However…" He stopped a second to consider the wisdom of his remarks. "The provisional government—including Maximo Gomez—has decided to work with the Americans. We soldiers have sworn to follow the government's orders. And we shall. Regardless of what we may think of those orders. General Gomez and I decided long ago that too many countries of this hemisphere are ruled by the military. If such a thing ever happens in Cuba, I don't want to live to see it." The general plunked back down in his chair and stared at the ceiling, where two spiders were competing to see which could weave the most intricate web.

"What do you want of me and my men, General?"

Calixto Garcia was writing on a piece of soiled stationary. He looked up with an expression that seemed to say, Oh, yes. There was something else, wasn't there? "I want very little of your men—until the land invasion actually commences. You will leave your battalion here, under the command of Major Ruiz."

"But, sir, I . . ." Christopher protested, but caught himself and stopped. He had dropped his gaze to the floor. When he raised it back to the general, he noticed that the old firebrand was smiling.

"I think you will enjoy what I have in mind for you. At least, you should enjoy the second assignment. Come back over to the map for a moment. You will notice that from this hill," Garcia began, pointing to a hill less than a kilometer west-northwest of the harbor, "you have a good view of the bay. You also have a good view of El Morro fortress on the east side of the harbor, and of these eastern hills overlooking both the harbor and San Juan. These hills here are called El Caney and San Juan Ridge." He squinted at the map and pointed to a series of fortified ridges that overlooked the harbor from the northeast. "You will notice that these two ridges, especially El Caney, look right down into the throat of the city of San Juan, no?"

Christopher nodded. "It also looks as though this hill over here to the west of the harbor has an excellent view of the ocean."

"Precisely. While you were up north getting that beautiful shipment of arms, a young naval lieutenant from the American squadron came to consult with me about the invasions. I tried to tell this young man that the Americans should not plan to land before October. The American soldiers, like the Spanish, will be very vulnerable to malaria and yellow fever."

"Yes, sir. As hard as various fevers have been on us, they've played hell with the Spanish."

"How are your own bouts with malaria?"

"I think I'm out of the woods, General. At least for a while." Christopher smiled and knocked on the top of the wooden desk. "What did the lieutenant say?"

"That General Miles and the Secretary of War have already calculated all the odds. Despite the fever, they will invade sometime in early June."

"They do not realize what they are doing to their soldiers."

"No. They most certainly do not. Be that as it may. Still…Your job, Colonel, is to give the *Yanquis* some important information."

"Sir?"

"That is the first part of your mission. You will take your two captain friends, Theresa and Fidel and half a dozen of our most Spanish looking men and women. You will make your way, without fighting the Spanish, to this hill." The general pointed to the first hill that sat west of the harbor. "If that hill is taken, find someplace else that will give you the power to observe both the harbor and the ocean. You will use the people with you—as you see fit—to move in and out of San Juan and Santiago, and perhaps these two hamlets on the east side of the harbor," he concluded, pointing at Siboney and Daiquiri. "Choose only soldiers who listen well, and who are among those upon whom little is lost. Understand?"

"Yes, sir. Do I report to you or the *Yanquis*?"

"The *Yanquis*. Find out everything you possibly can that will help them make a successful landing. I want to know everything going on in the towns, in the surrounding hills, and on the beach. But first I want the *Yanquis* to know it. Whether we like it or not, and regardless of how we get along later, today the United States is our ally."

Christopher nodded. "How do I contact them?"

"You'll know when they seal the harbor. At dawn on the next day, a launch will pick you up right here." The general pointed at a small, sheltered beach five miles west of the harbor."

"You said that my assignment was a double one.

"I've covered both. You get the information. You deliver it to the *Yanquis*. Then you come home and deliver the same information to me. AND." General Garcia stopped for a second before repeating, "AND you will bring me specific information as to when and where the *Yanquis* will land, and anything else of import you can glean from your visit to their flagship. What are their plans and intentions?"

Christopher nodded and saluted. "We will leave first thing in the morning, sir."

* * * *

The evening of their second day at the observation post, Theresa joined Christopher at the fire ring, where he was making careful notes and waiting for the final patrol to return from San Juan. "Where are Judith and Fidel?" she asked. "It seems that they are getting very close."

Christopher shrugged. They work well together."

"Work well together?" she mimicked. "I think they are falling in love."

Christopher raised his eyebrows. "They are very different. Do you think they can make a life together after the war?"

"After the war?" Theresa laughed. "What difference does it make? The war has always been with us. There will never be an after."

He shrugged. "Two, three months more. And then . . ."

She realized that, for the first time, he was looking at her with an open and obvious yearning. Whether for peace or for her she could not tell.

At that moment a scout walked into the clearing. Christopher blinked and turned away. "So, Sergeant?" Christopher asked. What did you see on the road?"

"Ah, Colonel. That is hard to say," the sergeant replied. "Miguel, he says there are twenty, but I only count nineteen. I think maybe Carlos is right. He counted twenty-one twice. But it is very hard to say for sure." The sergeant smiled and shrugged his shoulders.

"Salazar! If I could get your brains to work half as well as your mouth, I'd have half a sergeant." Theresa put her hand on Christopher's arm, which calmed him slightly. "Please tell me roughly what you saw."

"But certainly, Colonel. I try very hard to be a good soldier. I know I talk too much. Even when I was still pissing the bed at night, my sainted mother, Jesus bless her . . ." The sergeant stopped talking just long enough to cross himself. "...used to tell me to keep my mouth shut or I would never get anything to eat except mosquitoes and fireflies."

"Sergeant," Theresa interrupted, aware that Christopher was about to explode. "The colonel and I would like very much for you to tell us—in as few words as possible—what you saw. Can you do that for us? Please?"

"Yes, Captain Valdez. But of course." Aware that he really had been talking too much, Salazar came directly to the point. "About twenty men, led by a lieutenant. The patrol was mounted, on mules, I think, but I'm not sure. They had the color of...mules. They were moving north, towards Holguin and away from our position here on the hill. Unless they change course, we are clear. And if they do change course there is nothing they will attempt without help, no?"

Theresa wasn't so sure, but she didn't want to risk allowing the sergeant to lose control of his mouth again. She didn't think Christopher could take the noise without saying something he would later regret. "Thank you for your report, sergeant. Your information is very useful. Please return to your patrol." She returned the pleased sergeant's salute with a warm smile. As soon as the man had left, she asked, "How long would it take that patrol to reach San Juan?"

"I was just thinking the same thing," Christopher answered, smiling back at her.

"What has gotten into you? You suddenly find the Spanish army and the possibility of discovery to be humorous?"

"No, not really," he replied, tightening his facial muscles to their usual granite mask. "I was just . . ." He stopped. What the hell has gotten into me this morning? he wondered.

"Come on, Christopher," Theresa prompted, suddenly enjoying herself. "You just what?" Men are so funny, she thought. They're always trying so hard to kill the little boy in them. Sometimes they succeed, but usually not. Usually they just think they have. "You were just what?" she repeated.

"Just thinking about two things, two beautiful things, Theresa: your gentle patience with that blabbering sergeant, and your…insights. Have you ever noticed how often we have been thinking the same things?"

You donkey, she thought. We have been thinking the same things since I was a little girl and you were courting Consuelo "Yes, Christopher. I have noticed."

They sat in silence while Theresa pondered her love for a man who had lost so much and found it so difficult to touch his own heart. For the first time since their stay in the Zapata Swamp with Oinja, Theresa felt a surge of hope, and for the first time since her surrender to Guillermo Morales so many years before, she felt desire move as a slow shock wave from the pit of her stomach to her groin and out along her nerve endings. She was aware of a raw, powerful hunger she had all but forgotten.

* * * *

If there is to be a naval battle, Christopher told himself, we have the best seats in the house. For almost a week now, they had taken turns sneaking out to the point where, concealed by creepers, they could look down on the close-necked harbor, to Cervera's fleet, self-corked at their buoys; and out to sea, where Commodore Schley's squadron patrolled, eager for Cervera to come out and fight.

"How will we know when the *Yanquis* plan to seal the harbor?" Fidel asked as he handed Christopher the field glasses.

"We'll sure as hell hear it, whether we're able to see it or not. And we'll not want to miss the show. Come on. Let's go eat." The two friends slid down the rock out-cropping and trotted back into the jungle. Ten minutes later they moved into their camp, a small clearing for cooking and four almost invisible trails that led to sleeping areas.

"Santa Barbara!" Fidel exclaimed. "What is that?"

"I don't know, but it sure smells better than sweet potato stew."

"It is a goat, no?" Fidel smiled at Sergeant Salazar, the non-stop talker, who was slowly turning the wood spit. Like the rest of Christopher's small squad, he was dressed as a civilian.

Salazar smiled, revealing a mouth of blackened or missing teeth. "Yes, Captain, she is a goat. We caught her in the jungle. Just this morning, on our way back from Santiago. She is very tough and will be very stringy, but she is a goat."

Later that evening, after the rest of their group had headed out on reconnaissance patrol or returned to their pallets, the three officers and Judith sat, quietly content, around the smokeless fire of charcoal, enjoying the silence and each other. The evening was dry and clear. For the first time in a week, for an entire day no rain had fallen. The only sounds to be heard were the natural sounds of the jungle night. Their stomachs were more pleasantly full than they had been for a week. They were warm and dry and together. Now, as they sat around the circle, the war seemed miles, even years, away.

They had known other moments of respite, of stasis, of peace. Though such hours came rarely, sometimes weeks or even months apart, when such a time came, it was recognized and cherished: a moment during a rest stop along the trail when a soldier leans against a palm tree and scratches his back, purring like a cat. Or during a night patrol a soldier takes shelter from the almost incessant rain under a rock overhang, lights the stump of an old cigar and mindlessly contemplates the rapidly changing patterns of the puddles. Sometimes, as on this night, a group sits around a circle of fire-warmed stones and listens to a song or a story, or just sits.

During the past hour the four friends had swapped a few stories. Judith had sung an old Russian folk song she had learned from her stepfather, and Fidel had, to Judith's delight, told Federico's story about Mr. Knower and Mrs. Beknown. Both Christopher and Theresa had remained quiet, content to bask in the warmth.

Judith glowed with a sense of wholeness she had never before known. Though she had been close to Joseph Rabinsky, her nervous stepfather, and to David, her dreamy violinist brother, she had never even imagined what she was now experiencing. Since the deaths of her family, she had trusted only one man, Major, now Colonel Christopher Jackson. Even though she trusted Christopher, however, she was unable to touch him, could never warm to his tight-lipped and unemotional efficiency. But in those few comforting moments in Fidel's arms at the Bay of Banes, she had sensed a refuge of strength and warmth, secure protection against the knowledge of what her horror and her machete had wrought. And then, in the succeeding days, Fidel's strength and tenderness had eaten into her heart. Now, surrounded by the only family she possessed, Judith decided to make a move. Her foot was already resting against Fidel's, and she felt his awareness. She reached out and placed her palm on the top of his thigh and sensed his body go rigid.

Instantly aware of what was going on, Theresa felt a rush of joy for Judith; she was deciding to live again. Christopher focused on the dirt at his feet, oblivious to what was passing between their friends.

"Christopher, what is worrying you?" Theresa finally asked, after covertly watching his sad, set face for a long time. She placed a hand on his and squeezed.

He raised his eyes from the coals. "Do I seem bothered?"

She laughed and turned toward Fidel, who was savoring the sensation of his hand resting on Judith's and of hers still squeezing the top of his large thigh, and of her bare foot resting against his own.

"You know, Fidelito," Theresa said, smiling at them. "There should be another chapter to that story."

"Yes?" Fidel raised his heavy black eyebrows. Judith intuited what was coming and bit her lip to keep from laughing.

"Yes," Theresa continued. "You men, listen. Old Mr. Knower, he puff himself up with pride because he thinks he so smart. He think he see everything. He leads great armies. He eats more than a giant." She giggled and, simultaneously, poked both Fidel and Christopher in the stomach, which caused even Christopher to grin and tap her hand. "He sees so far and worries so much, he even figure out that old Father Sun he comes up every day in the east and goes down every night in the west." Everyone laughed, though Fidel felt a strong tug of emotion as he remembered his father's voice and mannerisms. Federico was a very good father, he thought, as he listened to Theresa imitate the old man.

"But old Mr. Beknower, he's really so dumb and so blind he don't even know it. His eyes be so sharp he can see an army on the far side of a mountain, but he be so blind he can't see the sadness in his own face. He be so smart he can read the stars, but he be too dumb to read his own heart."

"What are you trying to say, Theresa?" Christopher asked, both amused and bothered by the dialect story, which emphasized her own African heritage. "You trying to tell me something?"

His three friends just looked at him and grinned. "Now old Mrs. Beknown," Theresa continued, ignoring him, "she can't see through the mountains or read the stars. Somehow that just not something she wants to worry about. She too busy smelling the wind and listening to the plants grow. She too busy," and here her voice softened and became slightly more serious, "tasting her man's sighs and trying to help him read his heart."

The four were silent for a moment, then Christopher raised his eyes and looked directly into Theresa's. The glowing light from the coals seemed to focus and concentrate all the hurt, bitterness and loneliness he had been storing up since the terrible night at Oinja's when he had arisen from a malarial stupor to discover that he was alone in the world. His words came out far sharper than he intended. "I am not your man, Theresa. And you are not my woman."

Theresa shut her eyes tightly for a moment and then rose to her feet. "I know I am not your woman, Christopher. Your scarred heart won't let you love. But you have always been my man." She turned and walked into the jungle darkness.

Christopher sat very still, dumbfounded. Thousands of little memories—words, touches, gestures—rose out of the blackness of his mind and assaulted him with a storm of contradictory emotions.

"Colonel Jackson, you are a real schmuck!" Judith declared, rising from the fire to follow Theresa.

"What?" he asked, stung by her tone. Judith had never before reproached him about anything.

"Certainly you aren't totally unaware of Theresa's feelings for you?" she asked.

"No. I suspected, I guess," he lied, remembering Theresa's tendernesses when he had come to her at Federico and Oinja's *bohio*. Ever since that night, he had forced himself to ignore or misread her unwavering loyalty. "But I don't know what to do with her...feelings."

"Why don't you try to open your arms and accept them, Mr. Beknower?" Judith fired back, more as an order than as a question, and disappeared into the night.

Christopher looked at the glowing coals, glared at Fidel, looked back at the coals and asked, "What's a 'schmuck'?"

"I don't know, but you sure must be one. I've never seen Judith that mad before. At least not with a friend."

"Maybe so. Maybe I am." After a moment Christopher added halfheartedly, "What do you think, Fidel?"

Fidel took a deep breath and pasted a smile on his face, as if to soften his truth. "Colonel Jackson, my one old friend, I think you are even dumber than Mr. Beknower. I think maybe some old African woman made up Mr. Beknower after meeting some dumb *Yanqui* who looked at the world and saw that it was simple, but didn't understand what he'd seen, so he decided to make it more complicated, so he could have something to worry about."

"So you think I should love Theresa? Just like that?"

"I think you should open up your cold heart to the warm sun. Then whatever will be, will be."

"But she is Consuelo's sister."

"That is true. So? When Consuelo died, all the light went out of Theresa's world, and she had no one to love—except you. You are all the light she has, and you keep it buried deep inside, like a frightened seed locked away from the sun—and from life. I think maybe you are afraid of that seed, my friend, because maybe you know, maybe you know that if you allow this beautiful little woman to touch you, this little seed will sprout." Fidel looked away in the direction taken by Theresa and Judith.

"Even if we could...get together," Christopher wondered aloud, "what would happen to us after the war?"

Fidel bent almost double with deep yet bitter laughter. When he finally stopped, he said, "You may be long dead before the war is over. You better live now. Anyhow, what is there to worry about? You own good land. You think I worry about such things? I am an African peasant, a former slave. Other than my job as your foreman, I own nothing. Judith is white and reads books. Yet, we are coming to love each other. Now! Now! My good friend. Now! We will see about tomorrow, tomorrow." Even as he preached his truth, however, Fidel felt the darkness at the back of his mind. What would happen then?

Long after midnight, after tossing sleeplessly for hours on his hammock, Christopher rose and quietly covered the fifteen paces that separated him from Theresa. She was curled up in her hammock like a little girl. He stood for some time and stared down, unaware that she was wide awake. He started to reach down and stroke her hair, thought better of it, and turned away.

"Christopher," she whispered. Something in her voice reminded him poignantly of that night, so many life times ago, when he had gone to her with that awful need to hold and be held by another human being. He turned back, took the two steps to Theresa's hammock and fell on his knees. In one long, great sigh his heart opened as an explosion of wracked sobs.

Theresa rolled from her hammock to the ground. She took the tall, crumpled man in her thin arms and rocked back and forth. Knowing there was no need to speak, she poured her love and strength into his shaking frame and, simultaneously, felt great exhilaration: She knew! Her strength and love could drive the poisons from Christopher's long shriveled heart.

After a long time of silent holding, she realized that his hands had become restless. His left hand moved down her back to cup her buttock and his body spasmed. She immediately responded by putting her arm around his neck and pulling his mouth against the curve of her neck. "I have loved you for so long," she whispered. Then their hands and lips were everywhere. "Here, my love. Lie on your back," she said. She undid the front of his trousers, stood up briefly to strip away her canvas pants and shirt and, naked against the waning moon, straddled his thighs. When he started to turn over, she said, "No, Christopher. I need to take you. Please, just surrender to me. Let me take you."

For a long second he thought of the many men she had known and of her professional skills. He thought of Guillermo Morales and Amos Jordan and all the nameless, faceless others to whom she had sold herself. Then his vision cleared and saw what was so apparent to their friends: She loved him. "I need your strength," he said, and surrendered his heart and body.

Late the next night the friends again surrounded the fire. For the second day in a row the weather had been good. However, the breeze had picked up from the southeast; they knew the rains would begin again by the next day. Christopher reached over and took Theresa's hand, responding to her smile with the shy warmth of an adolescent boy surrendering to a form of tenderness he cannot quite understand.

"Christopher?" Theresa asked, after they'd sat hand in hand for a few minutes. He arched his eyebrows as if to say 'yes', and waited. "Christopher?" she repeated. "Last night I asked you what you were worried about. I still want to know. Is it the *Yanquis?*"

"No. As General Garcia made crystal clear, what the Americans do now is beyond our control."

"If not Cuba, what?" Theresa continued, determined to get at the source of Christopher's recurring periods of preoccupation.

"It is not the future, Little One. It is the past that holds my mind." He halted almost in mid-sentence, aware that, for the first time, he had addressed her by a term of endearment.

Theresa noticed also, and warmed, even as she asked, half dreading the answer: "Is it Consuelo? Is it the sister we will both always love? And whose memory will...tie us together?"

"No, Little One." He stopped for a second, savoring the softening in her eyes, her response to his voice. His fingers tingled, as if they had just touched her lips "But I think maybe you are right, Mrs. Beknown. Our love for Consuelo, and the memory of her love for us will bind us together. My problem is, I don't want to go aboard that ship tomorrow, or the next day, or ever."

"That's what's been bothering you?" Judith asked. "We thought that it was—"

"Something important? No, Judith, just my little fear, or maybe guilt. It seems to me sometimes that fear and guilt are two sides of the same coin."

"It is the *Maine*!" Theresa stated, both relieved and saddened. "You are still more of a *Yanqui* sometimes than you like to admit, no?" She stroked his cheek and brushed a piece of ash from his forehead.

"Perhaps," he responded, nodding his head. "I didn't like the idea of destroying that ship. I never believed that our little "incident" would trigger a charnel house. And I have hated myself . . ."

"Destroying the *Maine* was necessary, Christopher." Theresa metamorphosed to her lover's spiritual advisor; she was wiser, more pragmatic, an outside and acute observer. "No one connected with that explosion will ever be able to take credit for it. But it was absolutely necessary!"

"So I've been told." He gave a short, bitter laugh.

"Listen to me! Remember what General Gomez said in the swamp? The war could have gone on another two or three years. Remember? Remember what you said to me just last night? Because of what you did—what I helped you with—the war might finally end."

"And the men on the ship, Theresa? I knew some of those men."

"Christopher, my long love, you know what both General Gomez and General Garcia would say to that: 'In wartime it is often necessary for a commander to send thousands of men, his own men, to certain death.' Besides, we both know, or at least have every reason to believe, that the premature explosion was Guillermo's little contribution."

Christopher shrugged, indifferent to her logic. Rather than even attempting to explain the complicated web of guilt that tied him to the hulk rusting in Havana harbor, he rose to his feet and left the fire.

"Mother of God, Christopher!" Theresa yelled. "Don't run away from me. I need you."

Now I have ruined it, she thought. My mouth is too big and my tongue too sharp. She walked out into the jungle in a direction opposite to that taken by her would-be lover.

The argument had triggered great insecurity in Judith. She felt a need to be alone with Fidel. She took his huge hand and placed it on her thigh, using her hand to push his back and forth along the rough fabric of her long cotton skirt. "Do you want me, Fidelito?"

"Yes, Madonna. Shall we walk?"

"Yes!" She felt a deep flush rise from her chest to cover her neck and face.

"I have a better idea," he grinned, and picked her up as if she were a doll and carried her up slope to their observation post.

As she lay flat on her back on the stone, which still radiated the heat it had stored during a full day's exposure to the cloudless sky, Judith relished the warmth rising through her. I have been through so much in the last few months, she thought. I have lost so much. We all have. "But I have also found much," she said aloud, as Fidel's fingers finished unbuttoning her shirt. Beneath her deeply tanned neck her breasts were very full and milk white. She lifted her hips and watched Fidel's eyes as he removed her skirt and bent over to kiss her stomach just below the navel.

"You are my life, Fidelito," she whispered.

The huge, semi-literate son of a runaway slave lay down on the warm rock and took into his arms the sophisticated stepdaughter of the Jewish watchmaker. *Cuba Libre!* had torn both of them violently from a world that existed only in grey shards of memory and could never be re-created. They were united in their dedication to the present, and to the concrete physical reality of their hours together. They were Mr. Beknower and Mrs. Beknown, an aroused and yearning woman opening her vulnerable and secret self, actively surrendering to the hard, directional force of her mate; and a desperately hungry man who yearned for nothing more than to escape into a mysterious world of nirvana. Mr. Beknower focused all his energy and all his love on possessing and knowing this woman who so mindlessly and effortlessly led him into the brief, but radiant cosmos, of sexual climax. In his quest, which began as a tender exploration, but climaxed as a frenzied plunge toward the core of everything, Mr. Beknower transcended his self. And in doing so, he was totally possessed by Mrs. Beknown, whose world surrounded him, and whose strength both used and transformed his vulnerability.

Fidel sprawled on his right side, totally spent, defenseless, content, his mind drifting freely. Judith held herself tightly against him. Their bodies formed a serpentine bas-relief, a composition in black and white carved from the underlying limestone.

As she drifted back to earth, Judith felt the hard force still throbbing inside her, even as it began, erratically, to diminish and withdraw into its own world. In that brief but brilliant flash of reality a woman sometimes senses, she felt herself losing him. She pushed harder, willing her muscles to expand and contract, striving desperately to hold on. She knew, like all women know at such moments, that she was the stronger, the more enduring. He had overcome her only to surrender to her.

Judith kissed Fidel tenderly, as if he were a child. Every muscle in his body had gone slack. Though he had drawn away from her and was drifting in his own world, she kept touching him. Her muscles were still taut, her nerve endings still ecstatic. She felt herself move lightly on his body and concentrated on the thin layer of electricity between her fingertip and his skin.

"Don't," he said. "That tickles."

Judith didn't answer, but smiled and kept moving, trying to touch him as lightly as possible.

"Please, Madonna. I can't." He moved slightly away from her. "Being touched like that afterwards gives me the shivers." He kissed her forehead, with great tenderness but without desire.

Is it always like this? she wondered. Will he slip away? Later? Like he is slipping away from me now? "Fidelito?" she whispered, her voice carrying a note of subdued urgency.

"Hhmmmmnn?" he answered drowsily, his mind still on the far side of the moon.

"After the war is over? What will we do? What will happen to us?" She ran her fingers, lightly, teasingly, over his abdomen, as if to counter the urgency behind her question. Still, she could feel him tense and pull away.

"I've told you, Judith. I don't think about that. I can deal with nothing but this day and this hour. Here with you."

"Or in battle, or eating, or drinking rum, or whatever you happen to be doing at the moment." She hated the tone of her voice and apologized. "I'm sorry, Fidelito. I come from a people who plan every move, who give almost as much thought to the future as they do to the past."

"I am also sorry, my little Jewish angel. I am sorry that I am not that way. My family didn't plan for the future; they just lived as they could, and as well as they could."

She pulled closer, suddenly afraid of the future. "Things will be different for us, Fidelito. After the war we…I have some money, or at least I think I do. My stepfather had money hidden at the shop that I didn't take with us. Maybe we can return to *La Habana* and re-open the shop." She kissed him on the chest.

As her breasts brushed across his chest, he felt new arousal. "I am a field man, a peasant, and I always will be. Right now I am honored as a captain in the Army of *Cuba Libre!* If Christopher lives, I will help him rebuild. If not, then I am nothing but a field hand who has learned to read." He sat up and put his arms around her.

"Then we will buy some land, Fidelito. Next to Christopher. That way we will always be close to our friends."

"Let us not talk about them, Madonna, or about what may happen in the far distance. Come to me. Now! Let us push the world away. Now!"

At that moment the sky lit up with one, two, then dozens of explosions. Called abruptly back to earth, Judith clung to Fidel as he pulled awkwardly but gently away. In the flashes of light from the harbor Fidel saw that her tortured face was covered with tears, as if he had already abandoned her. Even as she slid from the rock, he leaned over and tried to brush the tears away with his full lips. He inhaled the white glow of her nakedness as it disappeared beneath her worn blouse and skirt.

For some reason that she didn't understand, and depressed by their post-coital conversation, Judith was now embarrassed by her naked-ness and, once dressed, even more embarrassed by his. It is as if, she thought later, we laid down to make love in one world and rose to find ourselves in another. Without another word they ran back to camp. The explosions continued to light up the warm night air. The American bombardment had begun.

Chapter Twenty-Six

THE WAR MUST BE FOUGHT OUT

* * * *

Doubtless President McKinley will be glad when the war is finished, but he cannot be supposed to wish for its conclusion until we have wrested Cuba and Porto Rico from the enemy, and shown the world that we know how to conduct a war when one is thrust upon us. Were peace to come now, our only substantial victory would be that of Dewey in Manila.

Peace is desirable, but it must be a conquered peace, proving the military power of the United States and demonstrating that we are not a great, unwieldy mass such as China was revealed to be by her war with little Japan. William Randolph Hearst, Editorial: *The New York Journal*, June 3.

Santiago Harbor

When the second bombardment of the harbor began, Christopher was sitting on the rock he used as an observation post. Theresa sat at his side holding his hand. She had walked up half an hour earlier, determined not to probe or question, or even to speak. Rather, she sat down next to him and gazed at the moonlight playing on the decks and turrets of the American warships.

Finally, he reached out and touched her hand. "I'm sorry, Theresa. The *Maine* is, for me, a very confusing memory."

"I, too, am sorry. Sometimes I think I have a very big mouth."

"That is the truth, Little One," he replied, kissing her cheek. "Even when you were a little teenage brat, even then you had a big mouth. Sometimes your hard words are bitter to swallow—but good for the patient."

The first explosions drew them from themselves to the ocean, where two long lines of warships steamed back and forth a thousand yards from the narrow mouth of Santiago harbor. Cervera, the Spanish admiral, apparently had no intention of coming out to engage the American fleet; he had pulled his ships back and clustered them against the extreme north end of the harbor. Nor did the Americans seem particularly interested in the bottled-up fleet of antique warships. Rather than shelling the harbor itself, the long grey ships were shelling the fortifications that straddled the east and west approaches, El Morro on the east and Socapa on the west.

"What is going to happen down there, Christopher?" Theresa asked, just as Fidel, Judith and their group of "civilian" agents crawled out on the point to join them.

Christopher nodded to the new arrivals and then explained what, according to General Garcia, the American commodore had in mind.

"After twenty minutes or so, someone, probably some gallant young fool in search of a promotion, is going to sail into the mouth of the harbor and sink his own ship. The idea is to put a cork into the bottle, into the mouth of the harbor, and make it very difficult for the Spanish fleet to run away."

"Or even to come out and fight—if they dare, no?" Fidel was excited, pleased both to be an uninvolved spectator at the greatest fireworks display he had ever seen, and to be yanked away from what was rapidly developing into an uncomfortable situation with Judith.

"The Spanish will not come out and fight. I don't know what Cervera is thinking of, or what weird orders he's following, but that fleet has lost its chance to fight, just as it's about to lose its chance to flee."

A few minutes later, just as the moon appeared from behind a thin strata of cirrus clouds, a small ship steamed around the headland and aimed straight for the harbor.

"Christopher? What will happen if the Spanish spot that little ship?" Judith asked, fascinated by the apparent daring of its crew.

"Hah! Even I know the answer to that question, Madonna," Fidel replied, slightly irked that Judith always directed her questions to her savior rather than to her lover. "If the Spanish see the ship, they will try to sink it."

"Those sailors better pray to their saints that the moon goes back behind the clouds," Theresa said.

Christopher grunted assent. "It's not just the moon, Theresa. That bombardment is also shedding a lot of flash light." He passed his field glasses to Fidel. "Follow the prow of the ship almost due northwest, where the entrance is the narrowest." Fidel swung the glasses slowly, stopped and nodded. "I think that is where they will try to scuttle their little ship," Christopher continued. "If they can sink it broadside, they will all but block the harbor." He grinned. There were times, he realized, when he was proud of his ex-countrymen.

"After they sink their ship, then what?" Theresa wondered aloud.

"What do you mean? I just told you."

"No. What about the crew? What will happen to them? It is almost as light as day on the water. That is a very bright moon."

Christopher thought for a moment. "If they're not picked up by their brothers, then, I don't know."

PART II: REMEMBER THE *MAINE*!

* * * *

Richard P. Hobson, Lieutenant, U.S.N., stood at the wheel of the collier, *USS Merrimack*, and tried to keep his mind on his watch. But however hard he tried, his eyes kept lifting to the faces of the two crew members with whom he shared the wheelhouse. The men's faces were streaming sweat, even though it was almost 2:00 A.M. Like himself, each member of his seven man crew was a volunteer. Each had decided, in a rash moment, that this assignment provided the chance to gain great glory. Each had been told that there was little chance they would live through the mission. Until the last few minutes, however, none, including Hobson, really understood what such words meant.

Lieutenant Hobson looked down at his watch, which he held in his palm. If I drop this watch and break it the old man will never forgive me, he told himself. He'll roll over in his grave and curse me from hell. The watch was elaborately engraved. When anyone opened the cover to see the time, there was a tiny click, followed by the first two bars of "The Star Spangled Banner." Hobson placed the watch on the sill to the rear of the wheel. It will be safe there, he thought. At least I can't drop it. He took out a handkerchief and wiped his face. "Say, Kelly. This is quite a bombardment," he stated jovially to the boatswain's mate standing at his side. "Did ja ever see anything like this before?"

"N-no, sir," the young man replied. "Not even on the Fourth of July."

"That's all for us, Kelly. Just so we can run in and have ourselves some fun blowing up government property." He chuckled, drawing an apprehensive stare from Kelly and Seaman Charette, who were even more afraid than he was, and didn't have to hide it.

"They're sure puttin' out a helluva lotta fire power, Lieutenant," Kelly said, as reverently as the altar boy he had been just four short years earlier. "That's mighty considerate of the admiral to shoot off all them guns just fer us. But I sure do hope he don't fergit to come'n get us when we're sittin' in the water freezin' our whatnots."

Hobson looked at the man. "He won't forget!" I hope, I hope, I hope.

"Time!" he screamed suddenly, as if yelling to someone half a mile away. He yelled down the tube to Phillips, the engineer's mate. "How's it look?"

A voice drifted back up the tube. "Steams up, Skipper."

"All right, let's have at it, men. Full speed ahead" He flipped the lever so hard that it rang against its brass barrier, but the ship's movement forward was far short of a leap They had loaded the old collier with as much ballast as it could possibly carry, in hopes that, once it was scuttled, the collier would stay in its place across the mouth of the harbor.

The ship slowly picked up speed. "Take the wheel, Kelly, and keep it dead on. I'm going to take one last look around." Hobson skipped down the ladder well to the main deck and ran forward to where Seaman Murphy was taking soundings. "What's the mark?" Hobson yelled.

"Forty, Sir, and coming down," Murphy yelled back. Christ all mighty, I'm not deaf! he wanted to say, but Hobson had already disappeared. "Goddamn! Down to thirty-five."

Within five minutes Hobson was back in the wheelhouse, scanning the port and starboard horizons for the nearest juts of land. Even with binoculars it would be difficult to locate the precise point between the two lips of the mouth. At least the unwelcome moonlight was good for something. He hoped to sink the *Merrimack* in less than twenty fathoms. If he could, and if he could locate the right place to sink it, and if the ballast sufficed to hold it in place, then they would have succeeded; the Spanish fleet would be contained. "It sure would be nice to be there for the parade," he said, then looked around and grinned at his two assistants.

Suddenly a shell exploded off to port, less than fifty yards from the bow. "Hey, Skipper, they've seen us," Murphy yelled.

"Well, do tell!" Kelly spat out sarcastically. "Murphy's got eyes."

"Belay that, Kelly! I'm trying to concentrate," Hobson screamed. "Why the hell doesn't the *Oregon* silence those damned guns?" Nobody bothered to answer him, and he continued to sweep his glasses across the harbor, looking for the tiny peninsula that marked the mouth.

Another shell exploded, this one about one hundred yards off to starboard. "They ain't much fer gunners," Charette yelled.

"Shit, they're close enough fer me," Kelly croaked.

"You men, SHUT UP!" Hobson yelled. "Kelly, get your smart mouth forward and get the sounding from Murphy. This looks close."

"God! I hope so, Skipper." Kelly leaped down the ladder and was back in less than a minute. "Twenty-two fathoms."

Hobson took one more sweep with his glasses, drummed his fingers on the wheel and yelled, "This is it, men!" just a little more dramatically than he'd intended. Calm down, Hobson old boy, he told himself, and managed to speak somewhat more normally into the speaking tube. "All right, Murphy. Stop engines. We're here." He turned to Kelly. "Get some help and drop every anchor we've got. Charette! Take the wheel."

Hobson immediately left the wheelhouse and headed for the forward cargo hatch. A round from El Morro landed twenty yards from their bow. He leaned into the cargo hatch and screamed, "Clauson! Montague!"

"Sir?" came back a disembodied voice from the black pit.

"You ready?"

"Yessir. We got seven charges rigged. Is it time?"

"You bet your bell bottoms it's time. Light the fuse and get your asses up here. "

"Aye, aye, SIR!"

Hobson turned around and looked for Kelly, who was standing at his left side and peering down into the hold. "Oh, there you are. Are we anchored?"

"Yes, sir. We got seven anchors planted. We're hooked. "

Hobson was already running. "Good !" he yelled over his shoulder. He climbed back up to the wheel house and shouted into the tube, "Murphy, get your men up on deck. It's time to go home."

"Aye, aye, sir!" Murphy screamed back. "Be right there."

Three minutes later the eight volunteers were seated on the ship's stern, listening for the muffled explosions that should, if all went well, blow the bottom out of the *Merrimack*. Suddenly, they felt the deck jump beneath their feet. A large billow of orange and black smoke rose slowly from the forward hatch.

"Where the hell is Cadet Powell and that launch?" Charette yelled. "We gotta get off this thing "

"I don't know," Hobson answered, "but we can't stay here much longer. Board the life boat." Less than a minute after they pulled away from the rapidly settling ship, a Spanish round tore the wheel house from the deck.

"Pull harder, damnit!" Hobson yelled, as the men rowed frantically and unevenly from the burning ship. "Those bastards have enough moonlight to get our range, and they've got it." Where the hell is Powell and that launch, he wondered, and yelled, "Head for the ocean."

The boat turned slowly and headed out to sea, but the men had rowed less than twenty yards when a round from Socapa fortress sent up a geyser thirty yards in front of them. Terrified, the sailors changed directions and headed off at a forty degree angle.

"Where's that fucking Powell?" Kelly screamed. "They're gonna get us. They're gonna get us!" No one bothered to answer.

Most of the guns of the El Morro and Scopa fortresses were trained either on the *Merrimack* or on something else, perhaps the rescue launch, farther out at sea. But every few minutes a round from Scopa headed their way and forced them gradually back toward the *Merrimack*. Finally, when the sailors were about to collapse over their oars in a terrified, exhausted stupor, the *Merrimack* exploded and the guns aimed in her direction stopped firing.

"Head back for the *Merrimack*, men, and put your backs into it." The men looked at him as if he was crazy, and no one moved. "Do it!" he screamed. "It's our only chance." The explosion had ripped the collier from its moorings. The wreck had drifted onto a submerged shoal, where it only partially blocked the channel, but enough of the twisted hulk remained above water to give the men some cover.

They climbed under a huge, contorted piece of metal sheeting, well aware that they would not be protected from anything even remotely close to a direct hit. Apparently, however, the Spanish had decided not to bother with them; the bay contained more interesting prey.

"It's the launch," Seaman Dugan yelled. "See! There it is." The rescue launch was zig-zagging back and forth across the entrance to the harbor, trying, systematically, to search the outer reaches of the harbor for the *Merrimack*'s life boat.

"Where's the boat?" Hobson yelled. "We're going to have to row out to her."

The eight men looked around. After a long silence Montague mumbled, "It's gone, Skipper. I guess no one tied it up when we came back aboard." His quiet comment was followed by an even longer silence. Unless the launch steamed right up to them, the rescue crew couldn't possibly see them, or hear them above the noise of the launch's engines.

Twice during the next two hours the rescue launch passed within fifty yards of the wreck. The eight men yelled at the top of their lungs, but to no avail. Each time, someone aboard the launch shined a spotlight across the wreck, but no one aboard the launch saw or heard anything. Shortly after dawn, after dodging Spanish guns for almost three hours, the launch left the bay and steamed back to the fleet.

"Why didn't they see us?" Kelly asked, looking around at his companions, two of whom were stretched out, sobbing, along one of the rails.

"I don't know," Hobson answered in a hoarse whisper, "but I don't think we're going to die. This mess hasn't sunk, at all, in more than an hour, and the Spanish have silenced their guns."

* * * * *

"Look, Christopher. Over there." Judith pointed toward the Spanish fleet. A large barge was sailing out from the most protected part of the harbor toward the wreck of the *Merrimack.* "What's going on?"

Christopher took the field glasses from Fidel and examined the barge, which was flying a white flag. "My God!" he exclaimed, handing the glasses back to Fidel. "Look at the wreck, on the left side, just above the water line."

Fidel looked carefully, nodded, and passed the glasses along to Theresa. "How many, do you think?"

After a moment Theresa shrugged. "Five or six, maybe more. I wonder if the Spanish lice have spotted them."

"I'm sure that's where the barge is headed," Christopher said. "Here, let me see those glasses again. I think that's Cervera's personal barge. The big brave admiral is coming out himself to capture those sailors."

The Cubans watched as the barge pulled up alongside the wreck of the *Merrimack* and snatched eight white-clad figures from the hulk. A few minutes later a small launch, also sporting a white flag, pulled away from the far side of the barge and headed straight out toward the American fleet.

"Why are they doing that?" Judith asked, amazed that a small Spanish boat would dare to sail out toward the double line of large grey ships.

"Probably to do a little gloating and to inform the American admiral that his heroes have been captured," Christopher replied.

"What's there to gloat about?" Judith asked. "Didn't General Garcia say that the American ship would be sunk to block the harbor? And isn't the harbor blocked?"

Christopher moved his field glasses carefully back and forth between the wreck and the narrow channels on either side of it. "Perhaps not, but no more than one ship at a time is going to get through, and that one is going to have to proceed very, very carefully."

* * * *

Four hours later Christopher sat awkwardly in the stern of the launch carrying him to Admiral Sampson's flagship. He felt uncomfortable with the sailors, who couldn't keep their eyes off him. I guess I am a sight, he admitted to himself, looking down at the freshly washed but heavily patched khaki officer's tunic, which he wore over white duck, peasant trousers.

It was not just the worn, makeshift uniform that intrigued the sailors, however. When they had been told that they would be picking up a Cuban colonel from General Garcia's staff, they had expected to find someone who looked like a colonel. Instead, they had been met on the beach by a tiny band of armed but ragged peasants and this English-speaking scarecrow.

As he walked up the gangway, Christopher thought of his visits aboard the *Maine* and of Ephraim Pratt. The flagship seemed very similar to the *Maine*, and his discomfort increased when he returned the salute of the young Officer of the Deck.

Within minutes he found himself seated in the wardroom with a glass of iced tea in his hand, surrounded by half a dozen ranking officers, all of whom eyed him with curiosity. After several minutes of polite silence, Admiral Sampson plunged immediately into the question at hand: "Could you see what took place in the small hours of this morning?"

"Yes, sir," Christopher replied, and narrated as simply but thoroughly as possible what he and his party had seen in the harbor. He concluded with Admiral Cervera's capture of the eight sailors, and then waited.

Sampson grunted and walked to a large map of the harbor. "Colonel, could you locate the exact whereabouts of the *Merrimack*?"

Christopher walked over, studied the map carefully and moved the felt silhouette of the ship a few degrees to the southwest. He looked at his work then changed the position slightly. "I believe this is correct, Admiral."

Again Sampson grunted. "Not what we had hoped for, gentlemen, but if Cervera chooses to run for it, he'll have to come out in a single file of sitting ducks." Without changing tone the admiral proceeded directly to the next question. "What were your people able to find out about Santiago and its environs?"

Christopher pulled an oil-skin package from inside his tunic, opened it, and handed the admiral four sheets of stained wrapping paper, each one covered with neat rows of descriptions and figures.

"Good," Sampson grunted twice. After the third grunt he handed the sheets to Commodore Schley, the second in command of the fleet and his personal rival.

"All right, Colonel Jackson," Sampson said, walking back to his map. "I'll show you what we have in mind. You show me how, if at all, your rag-tag army can be of use." The admiral smiled, and his staff laughed, politely (they thought) but pointedly. "Later this month, hopefully by the 15th, we plan to land about 15,000 troops somewhere along this coast, with another 50,000 to follow. Our object will be to capture the harbor, the Spanish fleet—if it's still there—and Santiago itself. This will give us a harbor and a departure base for a second landing at Havana—if the war lasts that long."

Again his staff laughed, as if to imply that with America in the war the conflict would be over in a week.

Trying to control his anger, Christopher spoke out. "Admiral Sampson, I've told you about Spanish strength. Granted, more than 100,000 men, a third of the Spanish army, are sick during this time of year. Still, there are at least 30,000 healthy troops in and around Santiago de Cuba. They are well-supplied."

"Not so, Colonel!" Commodore Schley looked at him intently, as if to say, What in the hell is an American like you doing in the Cuban Army? "The Spanish in Cuba have received no supplies from Spain for more than a month. What's more, they're not going to get any. Your own figures indicate that food is running short in Santiago. We'll starve them out."

"Commodore!" Christopher barely managed to contain his sense of outrage. "People have been starving in Santiago—and elsewhere in Cuba—for more almost three years, but that hasn't stopped the Spanish Army. You may indeed finish this war quickly, but it won't be because you succeed in landing 15,000 men—or 50,000 men on this beach." He whacked the map with his hand. "If you win that easily, it will be because Madrid will have decided not to fight."

"That's a rather subtle distinction, Colonel Jackson," the admiral interrupted. "Please sit down and have another glass of iced tea. It's very good tea; The *Oregon* brought it from the west coast. Came all the way from Hong Kong."

After a rather strained interlude, Admiral Sampson continued, amazed that a few years in Cuba could strip away a man's sense of humor as well as his manners. "Where does your General Garcia think we should land our troops?"

"And why?" Schley added, disliking the need to cooperate with the Cuban insurgents. For three years the Cubans had been trying to evict the Spanish, but they had botched things so badly that America had been forced to enter the war. The Commodore believed that America could whip Spain easily, without an iota of help from these filthy and ineffectual revolutionaries.

"Yes, sir," Christopher answered, back in control and prepared to do his job as efficiently as possible. Pointing to the two small hamlets on the beach east of the harbor, Daiqueri and Siboney, Christopher explained and justified Calixto Garcia's advice to the Americans. During the next half hour he pinpointed every Spanish fortification in the area, and whether or not it could be reached by naval gunfire.

When he had finished, Sampson grunted twice and Schley nodded, commenting to himself: At least these peasants aren't led by fools.

Christopher continued, "Your Secretary of War and your General Miles have asked us for quite a lot during the invasion. We are prepared to do everything possible to cooperate with you." Even though we would prefer that you send us supplies and keep your glory-seeking soldiers at home, he added to himself, as he looked around the cabin at the arrogant and patronizing officers. "We will provide troops, probably about 12,000, to block Spanish reinforcements from coming into the Santiago area from Holguin, Guantanamo and Bayamo."

"Very good, Colonel. If you can, in fact, accomplish this blocking maneuver, we can handle the fighting quite easily."

Christopher turned to his new antagonist, Captain Blodgett. "Washington has asked us to do just a little more, Captain, and we intend to do it. Hundreds of thousands of Cubans have died in the last three years. We, too, would like the war to end as quickly as possible."

"Fair enough, Colonel," Admiral Sampson interjected. "Please continue."

"Many of the guns and fortifications on the west side of the harbor are protected from your naval gunfire. We will supply a 7,000-man division to neutralize the west side. If you capture the heights above San Juan with those guns still in place, they'll blow you to smithereens." Most of the officers nodded. Yes, that would be very useful. "We will also make sure you meet no organized resistance during your landing, and we will provide guides to the interior. All we ask here is that you refrain from bombarding the beaches. Our soldiers will already be in position." He stopped and looked around the room.

"Very well, Colonel Jackson, I'm satisfied," Sampson said, drumming his fingers along his belly.

"Colonel, what do you mean by no 'organized resistance'?" Schley was more impressed with the colonel than he had wanted to be. Still, there was something...

"The Spanish loyalists, many of whom hate the idea of autonomy, will have snipers in the jungle. Many of them will still be there when you land."

"But there will be no organized resistance?" Schley asked.

"No, sir. Unless you fail to lift your bombardment in time, in which case we will fight you. I don't want my men blown up by your shells."

The admiral groaned to his feet and everyone else in the room stood. "Two questions, Colonel. What other information do you have that you may have...forgotten? And what can we do to make your job easier?"

Christopher thought for a moment. "Three things," he said. "The Spanish fleet is very low on coal." The standing officers nodded and smiled; Christopher's information confirmed what they already suspected. "And as far as your helping us is concerned, if you could send a barge with all the arms and ammunition you can spare, we'd appreciate it."

Admiral Sampson looked around at his staff, all of whom seemed to be sharing his ebullience. "Two problems, Colonel. We don't have enough to help you, and we can't land anything on the side of the harbor now occupied by your men. The submerged mangrove forests would rip us apart."

Sampson noticed the shadow of disappointed anger flit across Christopher's face, and hastened to add: "But we can do better than that." Walking back to his map board, he pulled down a second map, this one of extreme eastern Cuba. "If you can have a pickup party here, off the eastern point of Guantanamo Bay, one week from tonight, we will see that you get several thousand rifles and at least a million rounds of ammunition. Can you do it?"

"Admiral, for such a shipment General Garcia would move the entire island to Key West."

"That won't be necessary, Jackson," Commodore Schley said, amused at the idea of having the illiterate and impoverished island any closer to the States than it already was. What was it about this Colonel Jackson? Something in the eyes perhaps? Or in the accent. "You mentioned three things that we could do to help you, Colonel. What is the third thing?"

"My soldiers have had little to eat. Two days ago we shared a skinny goat; other than that we've been living on plantains and boiled yams." Though he felt a little sheepish, he plunged right on. "Could you spare some soup for my men? And maybe a little bread?"

Ten minutes later Commodore Schley and Christopher stood by the gangway watching Negro stewards lower a huge roast beef, a ten gallon container of soup and six dozen loaves of bread to the waiting launch, which bobbed forty feet below them.

The Commodore snapped his fingers as his memory jogged the pieces into place. "What did you do before the revolution?"

"I was a sugar planter, sir. I raised crops and...a family."

Schley nodded and smiled. "I met a young man in Washington with an impossibly romantic name: Alexander Dumas Jackson. Any relation?"

"My brother. I haven't heard from him since...is he still in Washington?"

"He's probably in Tampa by now," Schley replied. "Or at least on the way. Joe Wheeler managed to wrangle command of the cavalry division your brother is in."

Christopher felt a hollowness at the pit of his stomach. "Sir. I'm not sure I follow you."

"Your brother is one of Theodore Roosevelt's aides. Unless I'm mistaken, he is in Roosevelt's cavalry regiment."

Christopher could not believe what he was hearing. Though he hadn't heard from Alex for a long time, and though he was too preoccupied to often worry about him, Christopher had assumed that the Harvard degree would keep the romantic fool out of harm's way.

"My brother...coming to Cuba?" he asked, still incredulous.

"He enlisted after the *Maine*," Schley continued, "and he was lucky to be accepted. I remember the day I met him in Roosevelt's office in the Navy Department. Alex mentioned his reasons for wanting to go to Cuba. You were one of them, Colonel."

"What were his other reasons?"

"Apparently one of your brother's good friends from Harvard was killed on the *Maine*."

"Oh, my God!" Christopher whispered involuntarily, remembering as if it were yesterday his conversation with George Bedford.

Five minutes later, Christopher was in the launch, steaming back to his Cuban friends. Cradled between his legs was the food he had scrounged from the Admiral's Mess. He had looked forward with great anticipation, with glee almost, to the expressions on the faces of his group when he walked ashore with his presents. But now he sat like a stone in the stern of the bouncing launch, oblivious to his presents. Christopher could think only of his baby brother, a small, crying boy who was waving to him, begging him to turn around and return home.

Chapter Twenty-Seven

ACTION IN CUBA AT LAST

* * * * *

At last something is being done. Schley has been turned loose upon the defenses of Santiago, and if he has not already reduced them and made his way to the fleet hiding behind, he will do it before long.

* * * * *

BOLD DASH INTO SANTIAGO HARBOR CONTEMPLATED
The Forts and Mines Will Be First Destroyed
AMERICAN SHIPS MUST ENTER THE HARBOR
IN SINGLE FILE
The New York Journal, June 2.

* * * * *

THIS WAR'S GREAT LESSON

The ultra-conservatives, the timid, the dull have raised their chorus of protest against every territorial gain made by the Republic. The Louisiana Purchase, the buying of Florida, the annexation of Texas, the acquisition of California, each in turn alarmed the same kinds of people who are now perturbed by the prospect of additions to our domain as a result of the Spanish war. William Randolph Hearst, Editorial: *The New York Journal,* June 2.

Tampa, Florida

In grey twilight the train carrying the last troops of the First United States Volunteer Cavalry came to its final halt at Ybor City, eight miles north of the Tampa camp. The dispirited troopers gazed through a light drizzle at shacks filled with Negroes and mulattoes, most of whom were Cuban cigar wrappers. The ragged spectators watched silently as the troopers pulled sick horses and mules from the cars. Though the troopers were relieved, finally, to be at their last interim station, they were strangely cowed by the spectators. Every crowd along the way had welcomed them warmly. This thin band of Cubans stared at them with passive hostility.

As the horses stumbled quietly from their cattle cars, a net of depression settled over the entire regiment, entwining everyone and everything in its invisible shrouds. Nothing, it was turning out, was as they had anticipated. They had expected to be fed a hot meal when they detrained, but there was no food waiting, hot or cold. They had expected to be met with sufficient transport for their supplies. They were met by no one other than the ragged knots of tired looking Cubans. Supply trains were backed up for miles, and only one railroad track led to the piers. Had they not been able to requisition the few wagons to be found in the shanty town, they would have been unable to truck even a small part of their supplies to camp.

Each soldier knew, without orders, what he must do. Whatever their prejudices as a group or their weaknesses as individuals, they were horsemen. Without so much as a grumble, they shouldered their sixty pound packs and nine pound rifles, strapped on their machetes, .44 revolvers and cartridge belts, picked up the halter of at least one sick animal, and headed south in a mile long line that trudged toward Tampa Bay. Only seven of the horses had died during the last stage of the journey, but five more would not survive the eight-mile trek through soft sand. As if to accent the mood, the intermittent drizzle changed to a torrential downpour.

The camp itself was squalid. Formerly the drill field for the Sixth Cavalry, its western boundary began less than a quarter mile behind the Tampa Bay Hotel and provided the best breeding ground in the entire area for mosquitoes. Designed for fewer than 6,000 soldiers, the camp was packed with several times that number. Because Generals Miles and Shafter were convinced that the gathering army would be embarking immediately for Cuba, they had made virtually no effort to set up proper sanitary facilities. Latrines were too shallow and too close to the cook tents; the men picketed their horses too close to where they slept and ate; few of the regiments made even token efforts to keep their areas clean. By the time the first wave of the invasion departed on June 7, more than a hundred men had come down with malaria and twice that number with dysentery. And by the time the army finally abandoned the camp in September, more men had died of yellow fever, typhus and dysentery than were killed in Cuba by Spanish bullets.

During their time in camp, Alex's single greatest frustration continued to be Freddy, who seemed less and less competent as the hour of embarkation drew near. But once Alex made up his mind as to what he had to do, Freddy's transformation proved to be relatively easy. Their second afternoon in camp, Alex was sitting behind his small field desk in the supply tent, studying Freddy, who kept moving and restacking the loose piles of paper that cluttered his desk. After shaking his head three times, as if trying to put the devil behind him, Alex jerked Freddy's camp chair out from under him, leaped on the surprised and prostrate first lieutenant and punched him in the face.

Alex dropped his fists to his sides and glowered down at Freddy, who had covered his face with his hands and was now peeking at Alex through slightly opened fingers. "Wh-why d-d-did you do that?" he whined.

"Because you needed it, Lieutenant Anderson. You're absolutely worthless—and getting worse." After a moment of listening to Freddy's raw hyperventilation, and watching a trickle of blood seep out from between the man's splayed fingers, Alex rose to his feet and extended his hand to his victim. In that moment his reactions changed from rage to shame.

"I don't know what to say, Fredd…Lieutenant." Alex could feel the start of his own tears. "I was more upset with things, and with you, than I knew. I'm sorry. I guess I just lost my head."

Freddy rose to his feet and daubed at his bloody nose and broken lower lip. He had stopped crying. Suddenly he raised his head and launched his autobiography. "That's okay. I've never been hit before, by anyone. I was never even s-spanked by my f-f-father. I…"

He dropped into his chair and folded his arms around himself. "I was s-sent to military school at f-f-fourteen, after being s-s-seduced by my g-governess's widowed sister. Then I was sent to V.M.I. When I g-graduated, my f-f-f-father bought me a commission in the National Guard." He stopped for a moment and then concentrated years of bitterness and impotence into the next, stutter-free sentence. "I've hated…every . . fucking minute of the…whole…fucking…thing, every waking minute since I was sent away from home."

"I'm sorry, Lieutenant," Alex whispered. He had never seen such an air of total defeat. Even his own father had masked failure with nostalgic war stories and had turned his frustrations into the venom of the lynch-happy Night Riders who preceded the formation of the Klan.

"I know I've done an awful job as Supply Officer. And I know that you and Michael laugh at me. But this is all I c-c-can do. I c-can't c-c-command men in battle. I'd be too f-f-frightened."

Alex saw an opening and jumped blindly in with both feet: "If that's true, Freddy, if you really feel that way, then you'd better get with it." He hesitated a fraction of a second and then plunged on. "Colonel Roosevelt believes that our ability to be supplied will make or break us in Cuba. As you know, he's been…less than satisfied with your work. Word is, you're going to be transferred to one of the line troops and I'm going to take your place."

"You've g-g-got to be j-joking!" Freddy insisted, terrified. "I wouldn't l-last t-t-ten minutes with a t-troop."

"I agree." Alex placed his hands on Freddy's shoulders and looked him in the eye. "And I sure as hell don't want to get stuck with this job. I want to be with my troops, not in charge of a mule train. But there's not one damn thing I can do about it; it's up to you, Freddy. Totally up to you. You know what needs to be done, and you can get the job done—if you want to. If not…?" He drew his index finger across Freddy's throat.

Freddy nodded, first weakly and then more decisively. One well-aimed punch had somehow broken through to pools of untapped determination. Finally, he looked Alex in the eye and said: "I'll be b-better. I'll do a better job."

My God, Alex thought. I think he will. "Don't try, Fred. Do it!" he said, as he turned on his heel and stalked from the tent.

Freddy looked around the tent two or three times, spent the next half hour drawing up and reviewing lists, then, after taking several deep breaths and letting them out, like a swimmer preparing to race, he bawled out with all the authority he could muster, "Adams! McNichols! Galway! Draper! Get in here right n-now!"

That evening Freddy cautiously, but willfully, sat with some of the other officers at supper. He added little to the conversation; mostly he listened to Alex and Lieutenant Wilcox swap stories about their college days. But when he got back to his quarters, he felt a slight glow of achievement, and just the faintest, embryonic sense of belonging. As he sat on the edge of his cot rubbing medicinal cream onto his split lip, Freddy thought of the two incidents that had inspired his parents to send him off to boarding school. For the first time in years the memory brought a giggle to his lips.

As a boy, Freddy lived with his parents and grandfather in a large house in St. Louis. He had one whole wing of the house to himself, a governess, a fish pond and a tree house, the latter built for rather than by him. His grandfather had built the mansion after making a fortune brokering freight on the Mississippi and Missouri. Long since retired and grown bored, the old man spent half his time chasing the women servants, much to the consternation of Freddy's parents—who were still fighting desperately to add a modicum of grace and social standing to the still new mansion the old man had built as a joke. His grandfather spent the rest of his time chortling over the *nouveau riche* airs of his children and trying unsuccessfully to turn Freddy into a rebel.

Partly because he was fascinated with the mechanism and partly because he knew it would infuriate Freddy's mother—whom he despised—the old man brought back from Italy a bronze fountain, a statue of a cherub with a tiny little penis that sprayed a thin trickle of water. The old man installed the fountain in the fishpond next to

Freddy's tree house, filled the pond with carp, and gave the assemblage to Freddy on his twelfth birthday.

On hot summer nights when he couldn't stand lying in a pool of sweat any longer, Freddy would climb from his narrow bed and go out to sit in the cool waters of the carp pond, where he would often fall asleep. Unfortunately, for the long-term health of the carp, he experienced his first wet dream in the pond, and woke to the pleasurable sensation of the carp nuzzling the salts that seeped from his freshly flushed phallus.

As soon as he mastered the system, Freddy masturbated nightly in the carp pond. He felt strong, some would say untoward, affection for the amorous carp, that is until almost a year later. The week before his thirteenth birthday, Daisy, a huge orange carp, got carried away and took a pea-sized nibble. Freddy shot from the pond, dashed into the house, grabbed his cricket bat, dashed back to the pond and, like Samson swinging the jawbone of an ass, tore into the innocent carp. By the time he'd calmed down, he'd massacred the carp, and the pond was so red that the little cherub fountain peed pink for the next week. Freddy's grandfather was so delighted with the incident that he repeatedly interrupted the boring chit-chat of his son's dinner parties to tell the story, and to swear that the Italian gyp artist who'd sold him the fountain had seen him coming and sold him a cherub with a ruptured kidney.

Freddy's parents reacted to the incident with something less than absolute delight. At that early stage in his career, Freddy demonstrated the well-developed naiveté that would pursue him all the days of his life: He found that he couldn't lie, and told his parents the entire story. His mother banned him from the dining room for a month and insisted that her husband forbid the boy ever again to so much as touch "his filthy little thing." They thought about sending him to boarding school, but the old man threatened to disown them, so they suspended the action until after Freddy's second major crime, which was followed shortly by the old man's timely death.

Whenever they were unhappy with Freddy's behavior, his parents resorted to separation rather than confrontation. The latter created short-term unpleasantness; the former swept long-term problems under the psychic rug.

* * * * *

Freddy sat on his flea-infested cot in the mosquito- infested tent in the middle of a fever-infested bog and giggled again. Later that night, just before falling asleep with the exhausted knowledge of a job well begun, Freddy cried for his grandfather, the only person he had ever loved and the only person who had ever shown him any affection. As he fell asleep, the image of his grandfather and the image of Second Lieutenant Alexander Dumas Jackson blurred together in his dreams. He looked up to Alex, more than he would ever be able to say, or show. Somehow Alex's blow had demonstrated that somebody, finally, cared enough for him to knock him out of his ennui. Maybe he should tell Alex about the carp pond. Since his grandfather had enjoyed it, maybe Alex would. No, on second thought he wasn't sure that he wanted to admit to anyone, particularly Alex, that he used to masturbate, or, for that matter, that he still did. Maybe he could tell Alex about Mrs. Bridgett, his governess's sister. Yes, surely Alex would find that story amusing. Early in the morn- ing Freddy had another dream, in which he excelled at his job as supply officer and won Alex's friendship.

* * * * *

That same evening Alex and Michael leaned against the fence that separated the camp from the ginger bread-bedecked Tampa Bay Hotel, whose lights brightened the entire area. The hotel had been taken over as headquarters by the General Staff, as well as by Hearst's army of war correspondents and several society types who had sailed down in their yachts to bid the happy warriors a properly patriotic bon voyage.

Though the two friends talked from time to time, they were content to listen to the music that came to them from the hotel, courtesy of a tantalizing if short-lived breeze. After one long period of silence, during which each man seemed satisfied to drift in random thoughts, Alex tried to explain to Michael what was probably going on in the hotel's large dance hall, the perimeters of which were usually crowded with one-lung northerners trying to prolong their rasping lives. He tried to explain the dancing, the protocol of arrivals and departures, the jockeying for position at the dinner table, and the desperately contrived witticisms that passed for civilized conversation.

Despite Alex's explanations, Michael seemed to understand only vaguely why wealthy and powerful people enjoyed—or at least endured—such frivolity. "Like I told you before," Michael said, smiling and shaking his head, "you gringos eat too much beef."

Alex grinned with ambivalence. Not only did the activities at the hotel not excite him the way they once would have, they also seemed to produce sounds that emanated from a different word, a world that was distant, irrelevant and dying, just as the century was dying.

Unaware that he would be dancing with his fiancée on the polished and irrelevant parquet floors of that same hotel two nights later, he tried, vainly, to picture himself there with Charlotte. What would they talk about? What could they talk about? Other than Ron Wilcox and David Vandervoort, he no longer even attempted to mix with the members of the Group. He had realized, finally, that as far as the Group was concerned, he had never been much more than a tolerated and occasionally charming hanger-on. He did not possess the means to keep up with them; he could only leech from their good-natured if condescending beneficence, as he had since his first year at Harvard. Nor did he any longer possess even the desire to be a part of their lives. Or so he at least thought.

As he leaned on the fence and gazed at the lights of the hotel, Alex realized that he did not really know what he wanted to do with his life, except to go to Cuba, win a little glory, and see Christopher. He was no longer even sure about the glory. Idleness, the frustration of waiting and the insects had already sent more than a score of troopers to the medical tents with dysentery, malaria and yellow fever. Depression hung over the camp like a malevolent fog.

After a long period of silence, Alex chuckled to himself and said, "I clobbered Freddy today."

"Oh?"

"I kicked his chair out from under him. When he was flat on his back I . . ." Alex halted for a moment, staring at the brightly lit hotel and ignoring his friend's eyes. "I fell on top of him and punched him."

Although surprised initially, as Alex continued his story Michael found himself nodding. When Alex concluded, the sheepherder thought for a moment and said, "Don't worry about Freddy. You did him a favor. What's more, I bet he knows you did him a favor."

"Yeh, I'm sure," Alex replied sarcastically and continued to gaze at the hotel.

Michael stared at Alex for a moment, and asked, "Have I ever told you about my wife?"

Alex snapped immediately from his reverie. "No. I didn't know you had one."

"Seven years ago tonight I married a young Navajo. Her name was Sky Woman. She was nineteen years old, tall and graceful, with eyes as deep as night and a laugh that made things grow."

"Was?"

"She's dead," Michael stated, simply. "She was the most beautiful part of my life. And when she died, something in me . . ." He didn't finish the statement. Rather, he looked at Alex and asked, "Shall I tell you about her?" Alex nodded, touched by Michael's first real confidence.

"I met her at a dance, maybe a dance more like that one across the way than I thought," he said, gesturing toward the hotel. "Everything was very formal. There was, what did you call it? Protocol? Ceremony is very important with the *Dine*, the People, as they call themselves. Perhaps even more important than with your society friends over there."

For the next half hour the widower talked about his wife and the years they'd spent together. He said nothing about her death, and Alex, though curious, didn't ask. Rather, Michael concentrated on their life at sheep camp, the weeks they'd spent with Sky Woman's large and extended family, their attendance at the squaw dances, goat roasts and sings that provided the focus of community activity with the Navajo people. Alex was entranced by a life totally foreign to anything he had ever experienced. And as he listened he began, for the first time, to understand some of the apparent contradictions in Michael's character. All he had known before was that the man's Irish mother was an avid reader, and that Michael had read deeply in philosophy, history and Shakespeare during the long winters at sheep camp. Though Alex and the rest of the Ivy League graduates were all readers, and all of them read more systematically than Michael, the sheepherder had always seemed more attentive, more observant, more intuitively perceptive than either Alex or any of the Group. Why was that?

As Michael explained his life among the Navajo, Alex sensed that Navajo values and customs had mixed well with his love of reading. Perhaps, Alex mused, like many who speak three languages fluently, Michael possessed qualities of observation that altered both the variety and the quality of his insights.

Michael didn't feel entirely comfortable sharing so much of his life, but it was the anniversary of his marriage. Inspired by the music from the hotel, and affected by the gloom that had descended upon them since their arrival in this filthy camp, he responded to his need to be known. As the two friends walked back to their quarters, Michael realized that his motives and goals were becoming muddy, confused. He had always been susceptible to new influences and ideas. He not only read books; he absorbed and used them. He had integrated much of the Irish-Catholic lore taught him by his mother, and much of the rural New Mexico lore taught him by his Hispanic father. He learned from his parents, from books, and from his years with Sky Woman and her people. And now he was learning from this gringo army he had joined.

Though Michael liked little of what he saw, and believed that these gringos really were crazy, he found that he had become interested in their world; he wanted to know more about what made them tick. More important—and more troubling—he was discovering that his interest in the gringos, their vanities, their illusions and their wars, was only a symptom. He had, however unintentionally, again become interested in life. Killing Shorty was still the focal point of his existence, his only real goal, but every now and again, and increasingly often, he surprised and annoyed himself by thinking of the future. After killing Shorty, what? Where? And with whom? Ever since the night of Sky Woman's death in April, his only ambition was to kill her murderers. Beyond that single act, the future was an abyss, which was the way he preferred it; it allowed him to focus his energy and hatred. But now, he realized, revenge was not enough.

* * * *

Two nights later Alex found himself walking toward the wide steps of the Tampa Bay Hotel, feeling both annoyed with him self and very much out of place. Three hours earlier Roosevelt had called him to Headquarters and greeted him with a big smile.

"Howdy, Alex. You will never guess what I have."

"Good afternoon, Colonel. How are you, sir?" Alex was immediately suspicious. Roosevelt was flashing his bon vivant smile. Why? What does he want? Alex decided that he should smile. "I give up, sir. What do you have?"

"This is for you, old sport. From your future father-in-law." Still grinning, Roosevelt handed Alex an engraved invitation. Alex tore open the envelope and glanced at the invitation, which was for drinks, a buffet dinner and dance that same evening. Scrawled on the back of the card was a short note. "Charlotte and I are looking forward to a good visit, as we're both quite proud of you. Meet us in our suite at 8:00. Warm regards, Richard Boggs, Esquire."

Alex looked up at Roosevelt, mumbled, "Sir, I don't have anything to wear." Then turned red at the inanity of his response.

Roosevelt laughed good-naturedly. He knew that Boggs had no real objection to Alex as a son-in-law and, more importantly, that Boggs might one day become a valuable supporter of his political ambitions. Roosevelt had almost let his chagrin over Alex's early departure from Washington damage a possibly important connection. But it wasn't too late. Besides, there was every reason in the world to treat Alex with a little more respect. He deserved it, and getting Alex back on his side could certainly do no harm. He placed his arm on Alex's shoulder and propelled him out of the tent into the middle of the long regimental street. With one arm still draped over the young lieutenant's shoulder, Roosevelt said, "Look around you, Alex." He swept his free arm melodramatically down the street. "What do you see?"

"Sir?" Alex looked, carefully. "Well-ordered tents, men carefully checking and packing their gear. A cavalry regiment to which I am very proud to belong."

"You better believe it, Bub." Roosevelt puffed out his chest. "Now, what do you see elsewhere in this flea-bitten camp?"

Alex sighed. "Poorly laid out camp sites, insufficient segregation of men and horses, poorly located and carelessly dug latrines. A bunch of undisciplined National Guard and volunteer troops paying no attention to sanitation in a swampy camp where such attention is mandatory." Alex looked at Roosevelt and perceived that he was right on target.

"But you don't see those conditions in our regiment, do you, Alex?"

"No, sir. You and Colonel Wood have given excellent orders, and they're being followed." And that's the truth, Alex thought.

"Who do you think has the best equipment—of all the troops going to Cuba? The best troops and the most practical uniforms?"

"We do," Alex affirmed, again recognizing the talent and diligence of the two commanding officers. "Our Krag-Jorgensons are the only modern—and only smokeless—rifles in either corps. With our .44 pistols and 18" machetes we're ready for jungle warfare. And our uniforms are practical, sir. Even though they aren't very dashing."

"True, they're not. But they're the badge of this regiment. They're certainly distinctive, and when we get into battle we'll be the envy of every wool-covered, dye-sweating one of those dashing blue boys." Roosevelt looked keenly at Alex and then concluded: "This is the uniform of the First United States Volunteer Cavalry Regiment, the Rough Riders as we're coming to be called. Because of people I know and strings I have pulled, we've received—already received—more attention from the press—than all the rest of the regiments and divisions put together. This is a dashing uniform, red bandanna and all. It's dashing because it's ours, because of who is wearing it, Alex. It's dashing because we are wearing it." Then, after a slight pause, "You get my point?"

"Yes, sir!" And he did. He just hoped that Charlotte would recognize the uniform for what it was.

As he left the colonel's tent, he blushed at his unfairness to Charlotte, not because she wouldn't be disappointed in his uniform. As far as he could tell, she judged everything and everyone in terms of appearance; she probably always would. What prompted his embarrassment was the realization that he, too, still based his own judgments on appearances. Who the hell was he to jump on Charlotte because she probably wouldn't like his uniform? Who was he to criticize her superficiality? After all, he had asked her to marry him primarily because of her wealth and connections, certainly more for those reasons than for any deep love he bore her.

Now, walking across the veranda and into the huge lobby of the hotel, Alex was still annoyed with his own hypocrisy. And he was still annoyed with Teddy who, he suspected, was buttering back up to him because of Boggs. Most of all, he was annoyed for having accepted the invitation. Even though he thought he understood his motives for engaging himself to Charlotte, however, the motives were still sufficiently powerful to propel him through the lobby and up the stairs to the suite occupied by Richard Boggs and his daughter.

Before knocking on the polished door he stopped to look at himself in the full-length mirror that stood against the opposite wall, guarded by a brace of potted palm trees. His boots, belt buckle and second lieutenant bars positively glowed. His cotton khaki uniform was freshly creased. He nodded, straightened slightly, and concentrated on his face. Well, he thought, I certainly don't look much like the dandified procurement clerk Charlotte fell in love with. His dark blonde hair was clipped very short up the sides and back, and was no more than two inches long on top. Like an easter egg dipped in sienna, the lower two thirds of his face and head were deep reddish brown; the top third, starting just above the eyes, was still office-pallor white, where the sun's effects ended and his hat began. The deep tan under-scored the hardened grayness of his eyes, accented by a few white wrinkles that came from squinting into the sun. He wasn't sure what effect he would have on Charlotte and her father, but he knew he had changed since the last time he had sat in their drawing room sipping sherry.

Richard Boggs answered the door. As the two men shook hands, Alex noticed Charlotte standing by the window on the far side of the room. Her green eyes were questioning.

"Come in, son. Come on in." Boggs stepped aside and made a mock bow. Alex was pleased to discover that the older man was as sardonic and hard-bitten as ever. Two months earlier, Alex had been a little intimidated by Charlotte's father and in disagreement with at least some of his opinions. As the evening progressed, he discovered that he liked the man very much and even agreed with more of his opinions.

"Charlotte. I believe you know this young…cowboy." Boggs smiled and pushed Alex toward the window as Charlotte, who let out a small but appropriate gasp, fell into his arms.

Alex was not prepared for the feelings that rushed over him. Hunger and warmth radiated from the pit of his loins to his toes and fingers. He held her for a long moment, savoring her smell and warmth. He kissed her lightly on the lips then held her at arms length and gazed into her eyes. "It's been a long time, Char...sweetheart. I've missed you."

"I've missed you too, Alex, and I've really been looking forward to seeing you before you leave. I saw Colonel Roosevelt earlier this evening, and I couldn't believe he'd come to our little party dressed that way. And when I kidded him about it, he gave me a funny look, like he was remembering something. But then he explained, and I think your uniforms are just marvelous. They're very practical, aren't they?"

"Yes, Char. They are that," he grinned.

"Now I want you to tell me all about your training and the new friends you've made and everything you've been doing. And then I'll tell you all about the parties I've been to and all the exciting conversations about Cuba. I've even met some sugar planters who are really interesting. I'll tell you all about it, but first I want to hear about you."

Her eyes scanned his face, as if searching for something, and Alex's initial distaste for the non-stop outburst gave way to more empathic emotions. What he saw in her eyes and hadn't recognized in her voice was nervous desperation. She obviously wanted to please him, but not sure how, she resorted to one of her skills with men: get them to talk about themselves. "Well, Char, it's a long, complicated story," he said, squeezing her hands.

"Come on, lovebirds!" Boggs interrupted. "You can do your billing and cooing later tonight. We've got a party to host and people to see. Alex, you stay close to me. There are people I want you to meet."

"Yes, sir," Alex agreed, still looking into Charlotte's face, which seemed to be relaxing and softening. He gave her his arm and followed Boggs out the door. Alex had mixed feelings about spending the evening at the side of an influence peddler like Boggs. He wanted to be with Charlotte, to try and share with her his new life, his thoughts, and his friends—particularly Michael Archuletta. He wasn't sure she could understand. He was pleased to discover, however, that what she felt did matter to him. At the same time, Boggs and his vaunted connections intrigued him. Even though the possibility of "making connections" didn't thrill him the way it once had, he knew that it certainly wouldn't do any harm to meet a few people. He also wanted to hear the latest rumors about Cuba.

As they swept into the large ballroom, however, Alex discovered that he felt very much out of place—not only because of his khaki uniform, which contrasted so sharply with the deep blue wool of the dress uniforms of the Regular Army officers and the white linen suits of the civilians. It was more than the uniform. He felt that he had moved too quickly from one world into another, from the real world of disciplined troops madly preparing for war, to a fantasy world of fancy uniforms, beautiful gowns and elegant posturing.

The three of them halted for a moment just inside the high arch and waited to be announced. As the six man Negro orchestra tuned up, the assembled host of patriotic and important people milled around the long table heaped with platter after platter of rich food. A small group of important looking, silver haired men, two civilians and two generals, one enormously fat, detached themselves from their other companions and ambled over to greet their host.

"Good evening, Mr. Boggs," three of the four men said simultaneously.

"Miss Boggs, how are you this evening?" the fat general added, after quickly and critically taking in Alex's uniform. None of the four bothered to greet him.

"Evening, Gentlemen." Boggs looked around, grabbed Alex by the arm and propelled him forward. "Alex, I would like you to meet some of my very good friends. Gentlemen, my future son-in-law, Lieutenant Alexander Jackson. Alex, Senator Hanna, Senator Platt, General Wheeler and General Shafter."

Alex shook hands with the four personages, who smiled politely, uttered an amenity or two, and returned to their conversation. Only General Wheeler showed any real interest in him. "So yer one of Teddy's boys, eh?" Wheeler asked. "Yer regiment's jes been assigned to mah division, and ah'm glad ta have you all with me." Wheeler's eyes sparkled. Currently a congressman from Alabama, Joe Wheeler had taken leave from the House to assume command of the cavalry division. Wheeler was an ex-cavalry general and hero of the Confederacy who was in his mid-sixties, slight but sinewy. He sported an unfashionably long white beard. "Where ya-all from, son?"

"Georgia, Sir," Alex responded proudly. My father was a major in your command. William Jackson?"

"Jackson? Jackson . . ." A slight frown crossed the old general's face as he remembered the major, a brave but unreliable braggart who would have lost his post had he not been wounded and captured by the Yankees. Wheeler smiled. "Ah, yes, ah do remember the man, a danged brave officer. You should feel right proud."

"Thank you, General. I do. My pa talked of little else but that cavalry squadron until the day he died." Alex wanted to pursue the conversation, but Charlotte was tugging at his arm, trying to get him out on the dance floor.

Reluctantly, he excused himself from the group and waltzed his beautiful fiancée around the room. He noticed that he and Charlotte were probably the youngest people on the floor. Most of the dancers were either politicians or general grade officers who danced their matronly women stiffly around the ballroom. Few of the dancers were talking; few seemed to be enjoying themselves. The Negro orchestra was doing a passable job with the waltzes, but most of the dancers seemed indifferent, as though they were moving through some sort of obligatory ritual. The two lovers said little, though both had much that they wanted to say. Charlotte contented herself, at first, by smiling up at Alex and squeezing his hand. Alex, in turn, tried to keep from staring at her décolletage and, instead, gazed deeply into her eyes.

"What are you thinking, Alex?"

Her question startled him. It was as if she were reading his mind. He felt caught. He allowed his gaze again to wander down over her creamy neck and half-exposed breasts. God but she's desirable, he thought.

"Please, Alex. What are you thinking about? I really want to know."

He noticed that her bosom was turning pink from embarrassment, so he raised his eyes and said: "I'm sorry, Char. I was thinking about how much I love you. And I was thinking of…making love to you." He regretted the words as soon as he had uttered them: What's gotten into me? Why did I say that?

But his words seemed to delight her. She nuzzled her head against his shoulder for a moment and said, "I love you too, Alex. I really do!" which added considerably to his confusion. For the past six weeks he had been shedding one skin and developing another. He had been shedding, albeit unconsciously, the skin of the connection-seeking charmer and opportunist. He had been forming a new and stronger identity, one where he was beginning to recognize and depend upon his own talents and energies. For the first time in his life, his studies at Harvard excepted, he was relying more heavily on discipline, energy and intelligence than on personality and glibness. He had discovered that he liked himself. That is, mostly. At the moment, he wasn't so sure.

Charlotte was looking at him strangely again, and he realized that he had lost the rhythm of the waltz. This perturbed her. Most of the men she danced with concentrated every bit of their attention on these few cherished moments. Her fiancée, however, with whom she hadn't danced for almost two long months, seemed lost in some faraway place. She was not flattered.

He decided to plunge right in. Maybe she'd understand; maybe she wouldn't. "Charlotte, I'm confused about some things, about my feelings toward…a lot of things."

She looked at him just a bit critically. For the first time this evening he seemed to be speaking to her rather than down to her. She cocked her head.

"I'm not sure exactly what's been happening to me since I joined the regiment. Maybe I'm…This sounds awfully silly, but maybe I'm growing up."

"What kinds of things?" Finally! she said to herself. He's starting to recognize that I'm here.

"Washington seems a long ways away. Even tonight seems a long ways away."

"That's silly. How can where you are seem far away?"

"I'm preoccupied with my men, with learning a new job, with what may or may not happen in Cuba. I've met one or two men who've altered my views on a few subjects. Maybe," he chuckled. "Maybe I'm starting to take one or two of my old philosophy professors a little more seriously. I seem to be questioning things more."

"Is that always wise?"

Alex looked at her closely. "No, Charlotte. Maybe it isn't. But asking questions is a new experience for me. Even a little heady. I'm willing to take the chance."

"Even if...even if the answers pull us apart?"

"Sweetheart, I don't know that that's going to happen. I just know that some things seem more...strange...than they used to."

The dance ended and, as they started back toward her father's group, Charlotte stopped and turned Alex towards her. "Thank you," she said, with strong feeling. "Thank you for talking to me like you just did. Like I'm real, and worthy of understanding."

"Charlotte, Sweetheart. You are very, very real." They squeezed hands and rejoined the group, which was still arguing about Cuba and how America could best annex her. "Can we talk again? Later tonight?"

Charlotte nodded, feeling both relief and a surge of confidence.

"Ah, there you are, children." Boggs broke away from the group and put his arms around the two truants. "Come here, Alex. You haven't met Jordan yet. Charlotte, you're not interested in any of this men's talk. Why don't you go and visit around with some of our guests? Play hostess for awhile?"

Though she was incensed, she said, "Yes, Daddy." With a rueful glance at Alex, she swayed gracefully off to perform her duties as hostess to a powerful father.

The men turned their backs on Charlotte and plunged back into the business of the real world. "Alex, you ran off before you could meet my old friend from the Grand Army of the Potomac. This dour looking fellow is Amos Jordan, our Vice-Consul at Havana. Amos, Lieutenant Alexander Jackson."

Jordan bowed slightly, shook Alex's proffered hand, and looked at him very carefully. "You are Christopher Jackson's brother?"

"Y-yes, sir," Alex stuttered. "How did you know?"

"I know your brother. Not well, but we've met on several occasions. Did you know that he's a major in the Cuban Army of Liberation?"

"No, sir." Alex was again taken aback. "I thought he was a sugar planter."

"Good Lord, Alex!" Boggs interjected. "You mean your brother's one of those rebels we're going to have to deal with when this thing's all over?" Hanna and Shafter snickered.

"That's no laughin' matter, folks." Georgia's "Fighting Joe" Wheeler gave the two men a hard look. "That army o' peasants has fought Spain to a stand-still fer three loooong years. And it hasn't been fer want o' tryin' on Spain's part."

Jordan ignored Hanna and Shafter and glanced at Wheeler, against whom he'd fought thirty-five years earlier. Looking back at Alex, he continued their conversation. "You know he lost his family?"

Alex nodded. "Yes. Yes, I know."

"Like many other Cubans your brother has lost everything, probably, including his health. He hasn't planted a crop in three years. Nobody has, which is the major reason the island's starving." Amos Jordan wanted to say more to this young officer, who knew so little about Cuba, or even, apparently, about his own brother. Obviously, young Jackson was attached to Boggs through Charlotte, which meant that he was probably as enthusiastic about annexing Cuba—and Puerto Rico and Guam and the Philippines—as these other hell-bent-for-leather imperialists. Apparently, the young man embraced everything his older brother detested.

"I'm sorry...I only knew that he had lost his family," Alex stammered. He remembered Christopher's beautiful wife, whom he had met but once, shortly after their marriage. He felt a sharp pang of emptiness, as if he could reach out and touch his brother's sadness.

Jordan softened a little, aware of the younger man's pain and sensing that it wasn't really fair of him to use Alex as a scapegoat for his rage against chest-thumping expansionists like Boggs and Hanna. "Well, Lieutenant, there's a lot about your brother and his activities with the Cuban revolution that I've learned only recently, and a lot more, I'm sure, that I'll never know. However . . ." He turned back to his earlier adversaries, with whom he'd been arguing during Alex's tour around the dance floor. "I know a lot about Cuba, and how she ticks. She will never, willingly, allow herself to be annexed to the United States. If, Senator Hanna, your amendment succeeds in the Senate, your name will become a curse for unborn generations of Cubans. And if you succeed in annexing Puerto Rico and the Philippines—which you probably will—a few of you may live long enough to regret it."

With the exception of Richard Boggs and Alex, everyone in the group hoped that the fiery little man would stalk out of the room. Amos Jordan had no intention of leaving, however. Given the right opportunity, he was prepared to address the entire assemblage. Despite his strong disagreement with Jordan—and they disagreed on just about everything—Richard Boggs liked and appreciated his old Civil War buddy. The man had strange notions and stranger loyalties, but he always let you know exactly where he stood, and Boggs didn't know many people like that. Jordan was becoming even more of a nigger lover than he'd been in his youth, and he seemed to enjoy challenging the expansionists, but he could sure as hell get energy flowing.

Suddenly, the group started to break up. Jordan had outfaced them all. Since he had decided to stay, the important personages decided to leave. Hanna, Platt, Shafter and Wheeler shook hands solemnly with their host and Alex. And they shook hands with Jordan, despite their private assessments of the man. As they walked away in separate directions, however, both Platt and Hanna took mental notes to have McKinley replace him in Havana after the war. That Jordan had already submitted his resignation was not yet public knowledge.

"Well, Amos, you old firebrand, you sure scattered those quail." Boggs enjoyed his guests' discomfiture, even though he knew they were right and Amos was wrong. Jordan was less amused. He knew that he could not reach these men, just as he hadn't been able to reach John Hay, the Secretary of State. He also knew that unless someone reached them, they would plunge the country into a morass of foreign entanglements that could determine America's history for the next century. "I'm not out to scatter quail, Richard, or to put on a sideshow. I simply want to make you understand that entering this war is a mistake. And staying in Cuba afterwards—or in Puerto Rico or the Philippines—will be a greater mistake. This country was never meant to be an imperial power."

"Amos, you're a dear friend, but on that point we'll always disagree. We have too much to give the lesser races of the world. Our guidance will be good for them. And for us. Excuse me for a minute, will you?" Boggs turned and sought out some of the matrons who had been spending the evening clustered around the punch bowl.

"Yes, we have much to offer the world," Jordan muttered. "But by precept, by example. Not by conquest."

"Sir?" Alex asked, disconcerted to find himself alone with this slight man who had bowled him over.

Jordan looked at him closely. "Young man, walk in fear of pious sentiments and smiling offers of friendship. Every time I hear politicians talk about the 'White Man's Burden', I wonder what we're looking for: tin? copper? coffee? tobacco? Washington stinks of greed and hubris so damned much it's enough to gag a mule-sized maggot."

"Sir? About my brother. Could you give me some more details?"

"Yes, but let's get a drink first, maybe get a breath of fresh air." Jordan shook his head, as if to clear his mind. "I have a lot of respect for your brother. He's trying to cope in a world that not one person in this room can even slightly comprehend."

* * * * *

Everyone had left, either to their suites, back to camp or back to their yachts. Boggs, aware that the lovers wanted some time alone, had retired discreetly to his bedroom. Charlotte and Alex were swinging on the suite's veranda. Neither had said anything since her father's departure ten minutes earlier. Each was lost in thought, content for the moment to dream to the rhythm of the lightly squeaking swing. "You want to hear something funny?" Charlotte finally ventured, as she stroked the back of his neck with her left thumb and forefinger. "Hmmnnh?" Alex purred, acutely aware of her warmth next to him, and the white line of light surf that ebbed back and forth in the gulf moonlight.

"When I was getting dressed this evening, and thinking about the party and the war and everything, I fancied I was Becky Sharp getting ready for the big ball the night before Waterloo. Isn't that hilarious?"

"No, not really," Alex responded, trying to remember the details of *Vanity Fair* and the conniving, ambitious woman who clawed charmingly through its pages. "If there's a Becky here, it's me, Char. I'm the one whose motives should be suspect, not you."

"That's not what I mean, Alex. I was thinking of the excitement. Everyone in this country, at least everyone in Washington, would love to have been here tonight to send the troops off in style."

"There were no troops here tonight, Charlotte, and damn few of the officers below the rank of colonel. This party wasn't for the soldiers. But come to think of it, neither was that fancy dress ball that preceded Waterloo."

Charlotte withdrew her hand and returned it to her lap. She was merely attempting to make light-hearted fun of herself; she didn't need a sermon from her lover.

"I'm sorry, Char. Maybe tonight was our little Vanity Fair. But you're no Becky Sharp. You don't possess sufficient avarice." Alex bent over and kissed her lightly on the mouth, remembering the electric touch of her fingers on the back of his neck. He moved his lips to her cheek, the side of her neck, her throat and along the exposed contours of her breasts. She ran her fingers across his face, ruffled his hair and giggled. He raised his head, ran a finger around her lips and said, "And you're a heck of a lot more affectionate." After another moment of silence, willing himself to deny the erection that pushed against the front of his trousers, he plunged into the topic that had bothered him since discovering that she was in Tampa. "Charlotte? Why do you love me?" He felt her stiffen slightly and pull away from him.

"I don't know, Alex. At least I didn't, before this evening." She grabbed his hand and stroked it. He noticed that suddenly her palm was sweaty.

"But now you think you do?"

She nodded and lapsed into silence for a moment, as if searching for the appropriate words. Then: "I've always seen you as different from all my other beaus, different, I guess, from any man I've ever known."

"Good opening, sweetheart. Every man wants to hear that."

"And every woman!" she rebutted with an undertone of bitterness that caught him by surprise. "Please don't interrupt me. I'm trying to say what I feel. I'm not attempting, for maybe the first time ever, to flatter anyone. Please. Listen to me." Charlotte's voice contained a note of entreaty mixed with determination that touched Alex and compelled his entire attention.

"I know that you're interested in me, at least partly, because of my father's…money." The last word came hard for her, and she blushed as she uttered it. When she sensed that he was going to contradict her, she squeezed his hand firmly and plunged ahead. "I know most men are. Just as I know that I'm physically attractive, and that most men want me.

"I've always sensed something else in you, Alex. You've always seemed naturally kind, and interested in people. Your humor has never been at other people's expense. I know you're ambitious, but you always struck me as the kind of man who refused to sit back and just wait for fortune. I guess what I'm saying is that you always seemed—and do seem—to have substance. And you've never taken advantage of me, at least not that I know of." She remembered the night she had entered his bedroom and smiled. "Though I delight in the memory of taking advantage of you."

Alex laughed. "I've always wondered about that." He leaned over and kissed the smooth swell of her breast, which the whalebone corset and green taffeta dress barely managed to contain. She put her arm around his head and, for a brief moment, held him against her heart.

"I knew that I wanted to marry you," he continued, "but I'm not, I wasn't sure, that I loved you or, if I did, why I did. I've never had money, or influence. At Harvard and since, I've frequently felt some kind of quiet rage. Men with no more brains or education than I have seem to succeed automatically—because of their fathers' wealth, influence, or both."

"And you were attracted to me because of my money?" Charlotte was smiling, which bewildered him.

"Yes. In part because of your money."

"And the rest?"

"Because you are, in fact, beautiful. You're the most beautiful woman I've ever known. And the most desirable," he added, and bestowed a light kiss on each of her breasts."

"I've always believed that you felt that way." Charlotte smiled and kissed him on the nose. She was very critical of much of her face and body. Though she knew that she was attractive and could be seductive, she had never considered herself beautiful. "But I'm not, not really. Maybe you love me more than you know."

Alex disregarded her last statement. He was thinking of the conversation itself, and of their conversation on the dance floor earlier in the evening. "Do you realize this is the first time we've ever really talked?" he asked.

"Maybe you never considered I was worth talking to?" Her smile was more teasing than it had been earlier, touched with just a shade of mockery.

"I've never thought about it either way," he lied, "though I guess I have felt that you prattle on just a bit, every now and then."

"That's true. I do prattle, especially when I'm nervous. Or..." She bit her lip.

"Or what?"

"Or when I sense that it's expected of me," she said, with the same underlying tone of bitterness she'd used moments before. She rose from the swing and stepped to the railing, her back to him, her face jutted out toward the bay, as if trying to hear or smell something she had always imagined but never quite captured. If she were wrong about Alex, she would scare him away, lose him forever. If she were right, however, maybe, just maybe..."I've been taught all my life to be as attractive as God's gifts, a dressmaker, and my own wits could make me. I've been taught, by my father, my governess, and by the teachers at my finishing school, to be a good listener, to laugh appreciatively at anything a man says, regardless of how inane, or to nod demurely with the appropriate amount of awe when a man makes a political point, even if I think it's completely outrageous. I've been taught to be decorative and charming. I can play the piano and speak French. I know how to entertain. But I've never been expected to be able to think, or to have an opinion of my own—much less dare to venture one. No one has ever really wondered—or cared—if I understood what was going on around me—my father included. He's just always expected me to listen to men, to prattle about the empty-headed activities of his sweet but empty-headed daughter and her equally sweet and empty-headed friends."

The increasing vehemence of her remarks jolted Alex. She was like a volcano that had been heating up for years and then, without warning, had erupted. For the second time in just a few minutes he thought of the conversation they had had on the dance floor. "That's how I've always seen you, Charlotte. At least until..."

"Until when? she asked, whirling from the bay to face him, tears streaming down her face.

"Until earlier this evening, when we were dancing. Until then I was becoming sure that I didn't love you, that there wasn't really a heck of a lot inside you to love. I didn't realize until it was too late that you're somebody I can talk with, someone I could actually enjoy spending my life with."

"Why too late?"

Alex still sat in the swing, paralyzed, both hands flat on his knees.

"Why too late?" she repeated. While he was sitting, helpless, staring at her, she used the sleeves of her dress to wipe the tears from her face, like a little girl.

"I've as much as admitted that I was interested in your money. Maybe, in some ways, I still am. In the last few hours I've recognized that maybe I have loved you. No! I think, maybe tonight I really started, for the first time, to really love you, to want you, to want more than..."

"You say the nicest things," she interrupted. "When you're pushed hard enough. Tonight you talked to me, and I loved it. Come inside and make love to me. I'll love that too." She laughed and put her arms around him. "At least I loved it before when I seduced you. I wanted you so much that night. Now I want you even more."

"Charlotte, my love, you are absolutely shameless." He rose and took her hand.

Chapter Twenty-Eight

SPANISH SAY THEY SUNK THE *MERRIMACK*
* * * * *

EIGHT PRISONERS TAKEN — LIVES LOST IN
WRECK UNKNOWN
*Merrimack Was A Collier Supposed To Have Been
Manned by Volunteers.*
The New York Journal, June 4.
* * * * *

THE HERO OF SANTIAGO.
Like the splendid suicide of Somers in the harbor of Tripoli, like the self-regardless devotion with which Cushing drove his launch over the boom around the *Albermerle*, was the dash of the *Merrimack* into the shadow of death at Santiago. It was an exploit that will take its place among the eternal glories of the American Navy. William Randolph Hearst, Editorial: *The New York Journal*, June 5.

Tampa

Michael dashed back to his tent from the evening meal, if meal it could be called. Half the men in his squad hadn't even bothered to brave the storm for the beans, hard tack, embalmed beef and watery coffee that was their usual evening fare. For what seemed like the hundredth time that day, Michael stripped off his soaked hat and dripping poncho.

The storm had rolled in from the Gulf shortly after dawn and continued throughout the day, varying only in intensity. During the long squalls the rain speared in almost horizontally, peppering any soldier who, intent on some long postponed errand or latrine call, braved its ferocity. When the squalls ceased, the rain fell straight down, transforming the marshy camp to a morass of mud and horse droppings. Even the flies and mosquitoes stayed under cover. The officers made no attempt to drill their troops, who spent the day confined to their tents, talking quietly about their pasts, cleaning their already spotless weapons, and sleeping.

Michael had just rolled a cigarette, stretched out on his bunk and fallen into a Sky Woman revery when the regimental bugler blew Assembly. "Now What?" he muttered, dragging deeply on the tightly rolled cigarette. Even though most of the other twelve men of the squad rose to don their boots and ponchos, Michael continued to lie on his bunk, taking an occasional drag from his smoke and staring at the top of the tent.

It had been a long day. He had made two trips to the hospital with Alex, three trips to the Supply Depot, and had returned from checking on their horses just before chow call. The two men in their troop who had contracted Yellow Fever would live, but they would not go to Cuba. All was as well as could be expected at the supply depot, where Freddy was arranging their supplies for shipment. And most of the horses were in good shape, though three were shaking seriously and seemed to have developed an equine fever.

Now, with the chores of the day behind him, Corporal Archuletta wanted only to lie perfectly still and re-live the last time he and Sky Woman had gone down to the river to bathe and lie in the sun. He needed to see her laughing face and rich, stream-glistening skin. He needed to romp with her in the same shallow pool she had been bathing in the day Shorty and his friend had ridden over the ridge to rip her apart. He needed to dream of the past, of the years when his heart still sang.

When the bugle sounded again, he rose from his reverie, kicked the last sleeping private from his bunk and prepared to dash out into the rain one more time. Why do those crazy gringos want to call the regiment to Assembly in the middle of a storm? he wondered.

Slowly the regiment assembled on or, rather, in the drill field, which now resembled a shallow lake. When the officers finally streamed from their quarters to take their places at the heads of the various troops, Michael marched up to Alex, saluted, and asked, "What's happening, Lieutenant?"

"Beats me, Michael. Maybe the colonels are worried about the horses."

Michael nodded, only too aware of the degree to which their success in Cuba depended upon healthy mounts. "I don't know what else we can do, Lieutenant. We've rubbed those horses down five different times today. They're fed, watered and rested. All we can do now is hope that that weird fever doesn't spread."

Alex shrugged. "Other than concern for the horses, I have no idea what could bring the brass out into the rain."

"Maybe we're getting ready to ship out. I've heard rumors."

Alex nodded, hoping that Michael's intuition was working. "As far as I'm concerned, we can't leave this disease factory too fast."

Suddenly the rain stopped, the clouds started to break apart, and the men's spirits lightened. When Colonel Wood, Lt. Colonel Roosevelt and Major Brodie splashed from their quarters and plowed through the mud to their respective positions, the men were all waiting at attention. They had shaken off their heavy sullenness and were anxious to hear the news.

Wood strode forward, his flat face set hard. He looked grimly up and down the long lines of troops, shouted "At ease!" and, after pacing back and forth for a moment, started to speak. "I have news, men, and most of it is bad. I will not mince words." He looked again along the lines of expectant volunteers, excellent horsemen and marksmen all, each eager, for whatever reasons, to ship to Cuba.

"For some of you, for more than a third of you, there is no good news. We have been told that we will be allowed to take to Cuba only eight troops, just under seven hundred men." He stopped for a moment and allowed the deep groan that rolled along the line like distant canon fire to subside. "We assume, and we have been reassured, that the four troops forced to stay behind will come over later as reinforcements." He looked at the troop standing in front of him. A few eyes were darting back and forth, but most of the men stood in stony silence, waiting to see where the axe would chop.

"We have selected, for reasons I shan't go into, we have chosen the following troops to stay behind: Troop C, Troop H, Troop I, and Troop M." The troop standing directly in front of him was Troop H, whose officers and men stared at him in shocked, unbelieving silence. Wood noticed that tears had formed in the eyes of Lieutenant Randy Williams and ran freely from the cheeks of at least two privates. Wood tightened his jaw and fought back the tears welling in his own eyes. Williams had turned out to be as excellent at leading soldiers as he had been at leading the football team at Harvard. Williams and his men, in fact all the men of the four deleted troops, had trained just as hard as the men of the other eight. Of that fact there would never be any question. Little did the colonel know that the four troops assigned to stay in Tampa would undergo risks every much as great as those undertaken by their brothers in Cuba.

"There is no way I can soften the blow for you men," Wood continued, looking straight at Williams. "You have trained hard and served honorably. I wish that you could accompany us, but I know that you will serve here as well as if you were with us, and that when you are finally called to join us in Cuba, you will be as ready as you now are to answer the call.

"As for the rest of you!" Colonel Leonard Wood again moved his gaze slowly up and down the line. The four troops whose adventures had been canceled already stood out sharply from the other eight. "It breaks my heart to have to tell you this, but even for those of us leaving for Cuba, the news is bad; indeed, I doubt that it could be worse." He paused, took a deep breath, and barked out news so thunderous that no one believed him. At first. "We must leave our horses behind. Except for staff officers, we will have no horses in Cuba. The two divisions of the cavalry corps will serve in Cuba as infantry. I am sorry, men. Dreadfully sorry."

The men swallowed the news in absolute silence. The breeze freshened, and the men's ponchos began to flap around their legs. For more than a minute the silence continued. Like the men of his command, Wood stood still, his mind pouring over the activities of the last two months. Never had a regiment been recruited and trained so quickly. Never had a regiment developed such esprit de corps so charged with anticipation, and never, so far as he knew, had such a regiment received such a lethal double blow to its hopes and talents.

Hearing Roosevelt clear his throat, Wood snapped from his revery and back to the unpleasant job at hand. The troopers waited. How many axes did the colonel have left to drop?

"We will be going to Cuba as infantry," Wood repeated. "In our attempts to have these orders reversed, Colonel Roosevelt and I have left no stone unturned. Regardless, our horses—along with many of our best men—will remain here!" he said for the third time, as if still unable to believe his own words. "We have been told that there is not sufficient transport to get the horses—or even all the men—to Cuba." Leonard Wood turned to confer with his lieutenant colonel. "Theodore, why don't you give them the good news? What there is of it."

Roosevelt nodded and stepped forward. "Officers and men of the First United States Volunteer Cavalry, as Colonel Wood just said, the die is cast. We will follow our fate. Those of us scheduled to proceed to Cuba will do so immediately. We are scheduled to board ship at 0700 hours tomorrow morning. We will commence to break camp immediately. Those men detailed to stay in Tampa are ordered to help us in every way possible." He stepped back next to Wood, who immediately yelled, "Sergeant Major, dismiss the formation!"

By 0300 hours on June 8, the seven hundred men of the reduced regiment had been sitting or lying by the railroad track for almost an hour. The rain had started again, and the soaking wet troops lay in the mud and sand, their backs propped against their packs. In less than six hours they had struck their tents, packed their gear and moved everything the regiment owned to a deserted siding two miles from the camp. Half an hour later they had moved again, dispiritedly packing their gear to another track, two miles further from the port of Tampa. Now they waited and moaned, eight troops of dismounted and demoralized automatons, many of whom were cursing the day they had first heard of Cuba and the *Maine*.

Finally, they heard a train hooting in the distance, chugging towards them from the direction of the port, apparently coming along their track.

"Lieutenant Jackson!" Colonel Wood yelled.

Alex, who was sitting on his pack less than ten yards away, snapped to attention. "Sir!"

"Make sure that train stops." Wood walked over, grabbed Alex by the shoulder, glared at him for a second, and added, a little less harshly, "If we are not at the pier by 0700, we may get left. Understand?"

"Understood, Colonel. Absolutely! We'll stop it, sir." Alex ran down the line, yelling "Archuletta! Corporal Archuletta!" When the sheepherder materialized out of the rain, Alex said, "Get your squad. We're going to stop that train."

"Yessir," Michael grinned. "I'll get my squad and a few more to boot."

Five minutes later, Alex, two other lieutenants and fifty men stood down track from the rest of the regiment. Three men straddled the rails and waved lanterns.

"Michael. When that train even looks like it might slow down, I want your squad aboard her. Stop the train even if you have to threaten the engineer." Michael nodded, pleased, finally, to be doing something. Just then Roosevelt strode up, pounding his fist into his open palm and looking like he wanted to eat bear. When Alex explained the plan Roosevelt clapped him on the back. "Bully for you, Alex. When your corporal jumps aboard, I'm jumping too. I'll talk that engine pusher out of his train."

A few minutes later, as the train slowed, the engineer stuck his grizzled head out from the engine cab at a forty-five degree angle and yelled "Get off my goddamn tracks, idjits. Ya wanna git run over?"

"We need this train!" Roosevelt yelled in his most authoritarian voice.

"This ain't no goddamn troop train, idjit. Get off mah goddamned tracks."

"What kind of train is it?" Roosevelt challenged.

"This ain't nothin' but an empty goddamned coal train, idjit. Now git!"

"Stand pat!" Roosevelt growled at the men straddling the track. The three soldiers stiffened and continued to wave their lanterns, and the train continued to slow.

"Git outa mah way, Goddamnit. I gotta git anotha load o' coal fo' them ships o'er yondah." The engineer waved his arm vaguely but angrily in the direction of the port.

Lieutenant Colonel Roosevelt had made his decision. He ran down the track, grabbed the hand bar and pulled himself aboard the engine, followed a few seconds later by Corporal Archuletta and four members of his squad. The empty train immediately began to screech and rattle to a halt, perfectly positioned in the middle of the regiment.

Alex and the two other lieutenants shoved aboard the engine, pushing three privates out of the way as they did so. Within minutes Colonel Wood, Major Brodie and two captains had crowded aboard. Thirteen Rough Riders confronted one tired old man who had already put in sixteen straight hours shuttling coal to the Tampa port. The old man could feel Roosevelt's big chest pushed against him, and he could see a double image of his coal-streaked, stubble field face reflected in the lenses of Roosevelt's spectacles. He could not help but inhale the raw onions that Roosevelt ate like apples and exhaled with every blustering breath.

"Take us to the port," Roosevelt commanded.

"Ah can't. Ah gotta git more coal. 'N git outa mah goddamned cab!"

"No, sir!" Roosevelt responded. "We need wheels, and you, my friend, are it."

"Ah ain't yo friend, mistah, and ah ain't got nothin' but empty coal cars. They ain't no good fer haulin' folks," the engineer whined. Then, changing tone, he yelled, "Git off mah engine. This is mah PLACE!"

Roosevelt ignored him, though some of the other members of the Wild Bunch began to fidgit. "We're going to Cuba, NOW! And we need this train right BLOODY NOW!" Roosevelt was used to having his way, immediately, without argument, and was becoming perturbed with this scrawny old man who acted as if he owned the engine.

But the scrawny old man, who had never heard of Roosevelt, was also getting perturbed. No one came aboard his engine and told him what to do. He knew he had to surrender to the hundreds of men who surrounded his train, but these men were going to get out of his cab, damn it. "All right, all right, Mistah Robber soljer. Ah'll take you all to the port. BUT GET OFF MAH GODDAMN ENGINE! Or ahm walkin' home, raht NOW!" The old man shook with exhausted rage. The Tampa area was the most confused mess he had ever seen anywhere. Trains were backed up on sidings as far as three states north. More than a thousand box cars full of necessary supplies were a thousand miles from Tampa. Everyone connected with the railroad had been working around the clock. His wife was sick with the ague. On top of everything else, the goddamned army wants to steal his train. "Git! Goddamnit! GIT!" Without uttering another word, the banditos in khaki climbed down from the engine and started loading their troops and supplies into the coal cars. Forty minutes later the train backed slowly down the track to the Tampa piers.

During the hour-long ride Alex sat on his haunches and tried, in vain, to keep his uniform free of coal dust and the pool of black water on the floor of the coal car. Had he not been sure that Charlotte would be at the pier to send him off, he would have leaned into the grime like everyone else. For the eight hours since the morale shattering assembly, Alex had been too busy to think about the discoveries that caromed across the back burner of his brain. He tried to concentrate on Charlotte and on the unexpected qualities she had revealed. He tried to push the catastrophe of the horses to the back of his mind and dwell instead on the wonderful smoothness and vibrancy of her body. But Charlotte's body kept slipping away. Instead he saw the picket lines of well-trained and well-fed horses, the sweating flanks of his mare, and the squad and squadron tactics performed by cowboy centaurs. He tried to remember and dwell upon the difficult but frank and revealing conversation he and Charlotte had shared on the hotel veranda.

But like everyone else in the regiment, Alex felt crushed by the double blow that had descended upon them the preceding evening. Since most of the enlisted men had lived hard lives and were already disillusioned, however, they took the disappointment in stride and just became a bit more cynical. For Alex and a few others, the loss was more traumatic. These men had been raised on a diet of Scott, Dumas, Kingsley and Kipling. They saw themselves as the last of the Romantic heroes, and their regiment as the answer to just about every dream and delusion they had ever nurtured. Two such men deserted from the regiment at Tampa. A third shot himself in the foot and was furloughed back to his Long Island estate.

Upon receiving the news that they would be horseless in Cuba, Alex had seen his already cracked and splintered delusions fall almost completely away. Like the other dreamers in the regiment, he felt crushed, betrayed. At first the discovery of his new and sharply intensified love for Charlotte both complicated and heightened the depth of his disillusionment. As he rocked along in the sooty coal car carrying him to the pier, however, Alex discovered that he still possessed dreams and goals: A future with Charlotte, finally shining above the clouds of guilt and doubt; the meeting with Christopher, whose image more than anything else beckoned him to Cuba; and the knowledge that he was becoming an efficient officer who could still win honor and advancement in Cuba—albeit, without a horse.

The train backed slowly through a confusing maze of box cars and warehouses, slowed to a stop, started up again, backed another hundred yards, and came to a grinding halt a quarter of a mile from the closest pier. The order to unload drifted back from car to car, and the soaking wet, soot-covered soldiers began silently to unload themselves and their supplies. "Lieutenant Jackson!" A soldier ran through the milling soldiers calling his name.

"Right here, Private. What do you need?"

"Colonel Roosevelt wants you, sir. And he wants that Mexican corporal that was on the train with you, and twenty-five men." Alex nodded, saluted the private and went to get his troops. What now? he wondered.

* * * *

"Look, Humphreys."

"Colonel Humphreys to you, Roosevelt. I'm a full colonel in the Regular Army, not one of your suck ass clerks in the Navy Department. If you want to talk to me, use my rank."

Alex could hear Roosevelt's teeth grinding, but he knew the man well enough by now to know that he would get what he came for, regardless of what he had to say or do. Determination, bluster and, at times, diplomacy had gotten the regiment created. Such qualities had gotten it the best equipment of any regiment that would see action in Cuba, had gotten it assigned to Cuba in the first place, and gotten it moved to the pier—albeit by coal train. Roosevelt's teeth might grind, but he would play any game required—and win.

"Look, Colonel Humphreys," Roosevelt tried again, his voice and manner more subdued. "My regiment needs a transport. We need to get to Cuba. We've been assigned a role in the first landing force."

"I'm perfectly aware of what your assignment is—and of your predicament." Slightly mollified, Colonel Humphreys decided to be pleasant. Now that he had put Roosevelt on the defensive, he decided that it wouldn't hurt to help him, if possible. After all, the man was connected. "You must understand my predicament, Colonel Roosevelt. As Harbor Master, I have to load 15,000 men and their supplies onto a fleet of rotting transports that can't possibly take more than 10,000." He pointed at the clipboard he was carrying. "These regiments have been assigned to these ships. I am sorry, Colonel, but there is no ship opposite your regiment."

"Then, by damn! We'll bloody well take one," Roosevelt blustered.

"That is, of course, always a possibility," Humphreys replied, smiling benignly. "Not every ship is...ah...physically occupied as of yet."

"Which ones are not yet 'physically occupied,' sir? Show me one! Please," he added as an afterthought.

"The *Yucatan* has been assigned to two Regular Army regiments."

"But they're not aboard yet? Are they?"

Humphreys shook his head.

"Where is it, Colonel Humphreys, sir? Where is the *Yucatan*?"

Humphreys pointed at an antiquated merchant transport sitting more than half a mile out in the bay.

"Thank you, sir. I won't forget this most subtle form of assistance." Roosevelt saluted and dragged his men away and out of Humphrey's hearing. "Alex, you and ten men come with me. We're going to capture us a ship, just like we captured us a train." The ex-Assistant Secretary of the Navy showed his teeth and transformed himself into a pigeon-chest-ed, khaki-clad, be-spectacled Captain Kidd. Alex and Michael smiled at each other, as if to say, This is going to be even better than the train.

"Yes, sir!" Alex grinned, saluting smartly, so intrigued with the adventure that both Charlotte and his lost mare subsided back into the murky pool of his unconscious. Even the intermittent showers became no more than an atmospheric prop for their anticipated theatrics.

"Archuletta. You get your posterior back to Colonel Wood at top speed. Except for one troop to guard our gear, I want the regiment right here. Immediately!" Roosevelt made an X with his coal-dust-encrusted boot on the concrete pier. "Right here! Right bloody NOW!"

"Yes, sir!" Archuletta didn't stay even long enough to salute.

"All right, Alex old sport. We're back on the playing field at Harvard. It's fourth down in the fourth quarter of the Yale game. We've got thirty yards to go, and we're trailing 6-0. What are we gonna do?" Roosevelt bent over like he was calling signals. He spit on his palms and rubbed them together.

Although Alex felt a little silly, he was having a good time. "Well, Teddy," he began, realizing immediately that he had never used the nickname that Roosevelt allowed only his closest friends. "Sir, we sure as hell ain't punting. How about an end run?"

"Good idea, Bub. Let's get the show on the road." Like a band of mufti-colored buccaneers out to purge the *Spanish Main*, they comman-deered a launch and headed for the unsuspecting *Yucatan*. A little over an hour later, the old transport pulled up alongside the pier.

Shortly after the last troop boarded, two infantry regiments marched up under the command of a brigadier general. "What the hell's going on here?" the general yelled up at the Rough Riders. "What are you doing aboard this ship? Who in thunderation's in charge?" The general could not quite believe his eyes. Instead of facing an empty ship, he was facing several hundred soot-faced volunteers, most of whom grinned down at him, and a couple of whom jumped up and down and pointed at him with uninhibited glee.

"Colonel Leonard Wood, sir. First United States Volunteers. May I be of service?" Still as besmirched with coal dust as his men, Wood leaned over the railing and saluted smartly.

"What are you doing on this ship, Colonel? This is our ship?"

"My sincere apologies for the confusion, General. This ship has been assigned to us," Wood exaggerated.

"Get your men off that ship this minute, or you're going to get it," the general yelled, succumbing to petulant frustration.

My God! The man sounds like my mother scolding me for forgetting a chore. "General, the *Yucatan* is ours. As you can see, we are in possession."

"Come down off that boat, Colonel, or we'll take it by force. We're entitled." The general stamped his foot, much to the delight of the Rough Riders.

"I am sorry, General. We are aboard and aboard we will stay. You will have to find another ship." The general glared at Wood for another moment, conferred with his staff, had one of his majors shout, "About Face!" and marched away at the tail of a long, dispirited column. The Rough Riders broke into a loud jeer which they would have continued until long after the defeated blue coats disappeared from sight had not Leonard Wood, a little shaken by his success, called the regiment to attention.

Though the men stood quietly, even the rigor mortis of attention could not deprive them of their smiles, or of their unexpected and much needed elan. They would never forget their horses or the comrades they had been forced to leave behind. But they were once again a unit—proud, confident, expectant. Whatever else happened, or to whom, they were on their way to Cuba. "Gumption and guts!" Roosevelt muttered, smiling broadly at the idea of commandeering a train and hijacking a ship.

"What?" Wood glanced from the retreating infantry column to Roosevelt, who stood at his side.

"Gumption and guts, Leonard. That's what we've got that these blue bellies don't."

Wood nodded, smiling slightly. "That's right, Theodore. Gumption and guts, and Yankee initiative." The two colonels had already put in a sleepless but productive twenty-four hours and would work twelve more before the regiment completed the process of shipping and storing its small mountain of equipment. They were doing a good job, and knew it.

When the regiment boarded the Yucatan at shortly after 0800 hours, the weather had been so overcast that the men had been unable to make out the frenzied activity that consumed the port. By 11:00 A.M., however, the storm had swept back into the Gulf. The colorful chaos of loading too many men on too few ships with vastly inadequate logistical support came into panoramic focus for the first time. Alex had known that the embarkation would be chaotic; it had to be. Since their tragi-comic departure from San Antonio everything had become increasingly worse. The attempt to embark 15,000 troops from an under-sized and inadequately staffed port, which was serviced by a totally antiquated railroad, was the most comically chaotic mess Alex, or anyone else aboard the Yucatan, had ever seen. As he would too soon discover, however, the debarkation off the coast of Santiago de Cuba would be far more confusing, and infinitely less comical.

Alex spent the day standing at the top of the gangway. During the long process of transferring their supplies aboard the ship, he and Freddy exercised divided responsibilities. Freddy remained at the railroad track and supervised the order of transport; Alex remained on board and supervised the stowage. Because of his vantage point at the top of the gangway, he could both check off supplies as they came aboard and observe the chaos on the pier. More than two dozen transports were vying for berths along the two small piers of Tampa Port. Apparently, no one had even attempted to create an orderly plan of embarkation. Officers had drawn their regiments up in semi-ordered formations, which waited hours to board transports that were still standing a mile or more out in the Gulf. Other regiments struggled vainly to get close enough to the piers to load transports that had been tied up and waiting for hours. A few of the commanders, following the rumored lead of the Rough Riders, stole position on the piers and attempted to commandeer any available ship.

Because of the inadequate port facilities, several regiments were never able to find their supplies. Since few supply officers or shippers had bothered to make out bills of lading, officers moved from box car to box car, shooting the locks off the sealed cars and rummaging the contents for anything that might prove useful. Several regiments missed finding large portions of their ammunition, uniforms and medicine. One regiment of Missouri volunteers was still without boots when it landed in Cuba.

Enough regiments found enough of their supplies, however, to wreak havoc on the piers. Lines of mules, soldier-porters and pressed-into-service Cuban exiles swarmed over the single track and the piers like long lines of industrious albeit confused ants. The hundreds of porters constantly broke through the lines of waiting regiments and cursed through crowds of milling reporters and civilian spectator-patriots. Since it required at least six to eight hours to load a regiment and its gear, the two piers gradually filled with piles of supplies. In the meantime, more and more regiments were detraining and seeking at least a place to stand. The three bands, one military and two civilian, gradually found themselves pressed back against a warehouse wall where they continued to bleat out their notes of support, only to be drowned out by the curses of the porters and the braying of the mules.

For most of the day Alex watched supplies move up the gang-plank and kept an eye out for Charlotte. He enjoyed the spectacle immensely, partly because he was far enough removed from the chaos to obtain some cosmic distance, and partly because he, his fellow volunteers and most of their gear were safely aboard. Late in the afternoon, the moment he glimpsed Charlotte alighting from an open buggy, he turned his clipboard over to Michael, requested permission to go ashore and dashed down the gangway into the maelstrom of cursing soldiers.

"We weren't able to get a carriage until just an hour ago," Charlotte's father yelled at him. "Your goddamn generals and colonels and reporters 'borrowed' them all. I've had this goddamned buggy reserved for days, and one of your generals stole it." Boggs would have preferred to scream at the general, but Second Lieutenant Alexander Dumas Jackson would have to do.

Though he wanted to laugh at the silliness of Boggs' rage, Alex said, "I'm sorry, sir, but I'm not the man who borrowed your buggy," and looked Richard Boggs straight in the eye.

"No...no, I reckon as how you're not." Boggs stared back at Alex and immediately lowered his voice. "No, young man. You may be in impertinent pup, but at least you're not a general." He grinned.

Charlotte said nothing during the exchange. She stood with one hand on the carriage, the other clutching her parasol, her head turning slowly back and forth between her father and her lover. Finally, she looked straight at Alex and slowly ran her tongue over her lips. Two nights earlier she had discovered that the gesture drove Alex mad.

"Good afternoon, Lieutenant Jackson," she said, in rather distant, mock-formal tones. She had rehearsed an entire, tantalizingly formal charade, which she had planned to act out for him on the pier. By the time they had finally recovered their carriage, however, she was afraid she would miss him all together. Now, facing him before a backdrop of sweating, yelling soldiers, she found it difficult to maintain the taunting aloofness she had rehearsed so well. Alex merely grinned and opened his coal-stained arms, into which she immediately fell.

"You'll write me, won't you?" she asked. "Every day?"

"Yes, my love. And you me?" She buried her face in his chest. Neither felt any need to talk, especially with her father standing five feet away, fidgeting nervously from one foot to the other. They had already done their talking, made their important discoveries and exchanged their promises.

The whistle of the *Yucatan* blew one long blast. Alex squeezed Charlotte tightly then held her away at arms length, trying to pump his heart into his eyes and then pour it from his into hers. "I...love...you!" he said, simply but with great force. Charlotte said nothing. Her sophisticated, well-rehearsed composure had slipped totally away. Her eyes were full of tears, and she nodded, imploringly, again and again.

"I expect great things of you, Alex," Boggs stated, shaking hands firmly. "Do your duty well and your future will be made, at least as far as I'm concerned."

Though Alex knew that his future father-in-law's words were no idle promise, he merely grinned, bowed, and said: "Sir, I joined up because I've always dreamed of..." He started to share with the cynical businessman his dreams of glorious charges, but caught himself, partly because he didn't think that Boggs would appreciate them, partly because, somehow, the old dreams had become less clear, as if they were receding into a cold mist. "I've always dreamed of trying a little harder than the next fellow—and succeeding."

"Good man! We'll see you when you get back from Cuba, maybe before. It's been damned near a score of years since I've been to the island."

"Yes, sir," Alex replied. He gave Charlotte one last hug and disappeared into the crowd.

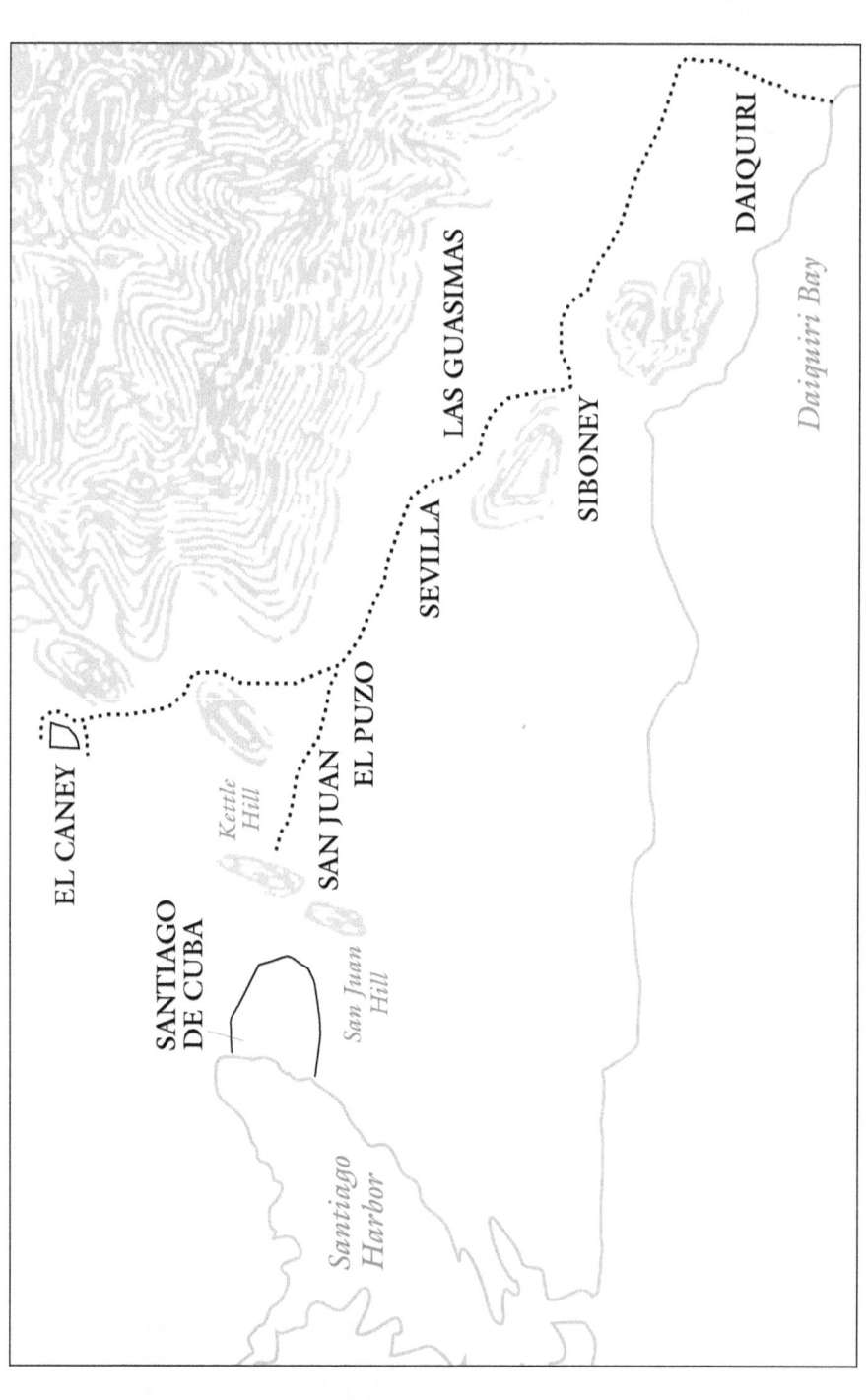

Part III

A PYRRHIC VICTORY

Chapter Twenty-Nine

ENTIRE ARMY LANDED UNDER FIRE
Sixteen Thousand Men Disembark at Daiqueri

* * * * *

Washington, June 22—President McKinley was notified at a quarter to twelve o'clock tonight that General Shafter and his army of 16,000 men were landed on Cuban soil.

General Shafter's message stated that aside from a heavy skirmish fire there was no opposition offered by the Spanish troops. Tonight the troops are sleeping on Cuban soil. *The New York Journal*, June 23.

* * * * *

ALL WE SEIZE FROM SPAIN WE WILL KEEP
Here Is the New Colonial Policy which Will Be Acted on
by the Administration

Washington, June 23—In view of the many false theories existent relative to the President's colonial policy, the following statement from a high authority as to the aims and purposes of the Administration will prove of great interest.

First, the Administration intends to establish a protectorate over Cuba—a species of protectorate which involves the retention of a competent military force upon the island, and the constant supervising of the Cuban Government as it is established by the military authorities of the United States. *The New York Journal*, June 24.

Daiqueri, Cuba

Seated in the stern of his skiff, Christopher watched his six soldiers as they manned the unfamiliar oars. They had raised their single sail, but the breeze had yet to stir. As Christopher studied his rowers, he tried to recount what he knew of each man's life before the war, and wondered how many of them would survive the coming battles. When they finally entered the channel, he pulled out his watch, studied it with furrowed brow, as if his will could advance either its hands or his speed, then looked east where the low grey sky was brightening to magenta.

By the time he had returned to his skiff, it was almost dawn. This last conference with General Garcia had lasted even longer than usual, though the news had been all good. Three Cuban divisions had cut and blockaded the three major roads leading to Santiago de Cuba; a fourth had silenced the fortifications on the west side of the harbor. Christopher's battalion had taken the beaches between Siboney and Daiqueri, where the Americans planned to land. With the naval bombardment scheduled to start at any moment, he felt a vague but desperate need to return to his *mambises*, who were camped in and around a small fort, waiting to guide the Americans into the interior. Other than for snipers, the American landing would be unopposed.

As the small skiff moved across the outer harbor, Christopher turned his mind to the larger implications of the battle to come, which would involve more than sixty thousand troops, American, Cuban and Spanish. It would be the largest battle ever fought on Cuban soil—and probably the most decisive.

Suddenly, without warning, scores of almost simultaneous thunderclaps split the silence, jerking Christopher from his reverie. He blinked twice, shook his head and lifted his eyes to his startled companions.

"It has begun!" Jorge said. Everyone looked at him and nodded.

Each of the *mambises* knew they were about to experience a campaign more intense and prolonged than any they had known. Just as Christopher's impatience with their progress along the coast was about to snap, the breeze freshened.

"A good omen, Colonel. No?"

"Yes, Juan. It may rain all day, but perhaps this breeze tells us that the sun will shine on our cause." Christopher smiled at his rowers and tried to communicate an enthusiasm he did not feel. How long would the battle take? A week? A month? Even a week-long battle would be longer than anything the Cuban Army of Liberation had ever seen, and would require battle discipline it had never been required to develop.

They sailed around a headland and spotted the fort they had captured from the Spanish a few days earlier. "Colonel Jackson! Look! Toward the fort!" Ramon, the asthmatic, had turned even paler than usual.

"Jesus Suffering Christ!" Christopher whispered. "Get this whore of a boat beached!" Though on the seaward side of the light surf, Christopher, stood up in the stern. The surf caught the boat and almost threw it up to the beach. Even before it touched bottom, Christopher leaped into the waist deep water and struggled to shore. "Fidel!" he gasped, running for the fort. "Fidel!" The yell disappeared in the crescendos of the naval guns. All along the coast large fragments of palms and mangroves leaped into the air. Smoke and dust rose from one corner of the fort. All Christopher could hear were the deep gasps of his lungs. Soldiers dashed in different directions, hid behind trees or sprinted from their campsites toward the fort. In what he would always remember as slow motion, Christopher tore along the sandy path and pushed through the entrance, still yelling, "Fidel! Fidel!"

"Over here, Colonel," Judith's alto voice screamed from the blackness of one of the fort's small rooms. "Fidelito is in here." Judith had already established her aid station in the fort's largest room, expecting to help with the American wounded. Now, with the help of Peg-leg Juanita, two helpers and a kerosene lamp, she was tending her own wounded.

"Here I am," boomed Fidel's voice from the corner. "I have a little bee sting."

Christopher didn't even bother to acknowledge Fidel's comment, though he felt a flash of partial relief. "What in the hell are all these people doing in here?" he screamed. The room was so crowded with wounded that he could barely make his way through to where Fidel was standing. He stared at Fidel, whose smile faded, and ran back into the open yard of the fort to discover more wounded and at least two dead. Some of the wounded screamed in pain and fright as shells continued to explode. Others sat and stared passively into the distance.

I've got to get these people out of here, Christopher thought, just as a shell exploded on a parapet, sending a hail of shrapnel and stone into the bodies of the huddled wounded. He turned and dashed back into the aid station.

"Fidel, you ignorant bastard!" Christopher screamed. "See what you've done? This place is a goddamned primary target. Without giving his second in command a chance to explain, Christopher screamed even louder. "Where's a flag?" Fidel looked at him in hurt, angry silence. "Where's the fucking FLAG, Fidel?"

Fidel shook his head, as if to clear it. His arm was throbbing, and he was weak from the loss of blood. Who cared about the captured Spanish flag? Still confused by his pain and Christopher's unaccustomed criticism, he turned away and started ushering the walking wounded out of the fort.

"FIDEL!" Christopher was beside himself with rage. Maybe his father had been right about the niggers. Fidel was acting like his head was carved from mahogany. "Where is the Cuban flag?"

Fidel willed his pain into the noisy background and cleared his head. He knew what Christopher wanted, and why. "Mario! Go to the east trench. Get the flag from Lieutenant Rubio. Hurry!" The short, fat private cradled his wounded right hand in his left and scurried from the fort.

Christopher shook his head, raced past the confused runner and returned in less than five minutes with their flag. Within three minutes of the time the flag reached the top of the halyard, the one-sided battle ended. The American fire lifted from the beach and shifted inland.

Christopher collapsed at the foot of the wall below the flag, held his head in his hands, and cried, "Those arrogant bastards, those arrogant fucking bastards" over and over in English. During the half hour-long bombardment, the Americans had managed to kill seven soldiers and wound twenty-three others, four of whom would be dead before evening. The Battle for Santiago de Cuba had gotten off to a calamitous start.

* * * * *

Though it was still too dark to make out any details, Alex could see the outline of the low hills that rose almost directly behind the beach, and the tall shadow of the *Sierra Maestra* that stretched away to the northwest. Mesmerized by the naval bombardment of Daiqueri Beach, he leaned against the rail, raised his hand to his forehead and shielded his eyes from the light rain. There didn't seem to be any Spanish activity; at least no one was returning the American gunfire. Except for a small, apparently abandoned fort, the beach showed few signs of ever having been occupied. Other than the incredible racket, the bombardment seemed to be accomplishing little, unless the admiral had attached strategic importance to decimating the thick groves of beach palms.

As the dawn brightened, the wall of black-green mottled to a variety of lighter shades. From blankets of fog lying in the low spots in the jungle, a fine mist rose like a scrim, and the contours of the hills behind the beach emerged into hazy relief.

"What do you think of Cuba?"

Alex turned to face David Vandervoort. "It looks a bit massive, particularly in the early dawn. If it weren't for our gunfire, it would be quite peaceful."

"It's been a long time since Cuba was peaceful." Vandervoort paused for a moment. "But it is massive. Those mountains over there?" He took the pipe from his mouth and pointed to the *Sierra Maestra*. "Some of those peaks tower over 5,000 feet—starting pretty close to sea level."

"That's right. You've been here, haven't you?"

"A couple of times. My father has holdings in Cuba. My first trip down was right after my bar mitzvah."

"I keep forgetting you're Jewish, you going to Harvard and all."

David laughed. "Sometimes we forget we're Jews. 'We are Vandervoorts,' my father is fond of saying. We came from Holland, and we've been in America for well over two hundred years. We don't look, or talk, or even think like those wretches from Russia and Poland who swarm through the Lower East Side. Still, we are Jews. Or, at least ,Mother is. She's taken all the responsibility for our religious training. Father just...works. Other than money and power, he's interested in very little." David re-lit his pipe and leaned over the rail to stare at the orange and black explosions on the beach.

"Sometimes you amaze me," Alex said. David shook his head. "I thought just about anyone with any sense was interested in power and money."

David exhaled a puff of aromatic smoke. "My father would agree. He thinks that anyone who reads as much as I do is a fool, even if the reader is a rabbi."

Alex shook his head and changed the subject. "What's going on over there?" he wondered, pointing at the small fort, where someone was running up a flag.

"I don't know, Alex. I have trouble seeing that far. What's it look like?"

"Some kind of flag. Two horizontal stripes, one red, one gold."

"Is there a star in the middle?"

"Yeh, I think so. It's too far to tell."

"Well, if there is, that's the Cuban flag, that is, the flag of the Cuban Provisional Republic."

Alex was somewhat taken aback. "I didn't realize they had a government. I think of the Cubans as little bands of men running around ambushing Spaniards. For some reason it never struck me that they'd be organized."

Michael Archuletta joined them at the rail. "Have you been watching that flag?" he asked, without bothering to greet either of his two friends. "It must have been a signal. Look!" Shells were no longer falling near the fort. The Navy had lifted its gunfire from the beach to concentrate on the interior.

"David thinks that may be the Cuban flag, Michael. Maybe the Cubans just took the fort, though we haven't seen any activity along the beach."

"Maybe the Cubans have been there all along," Michael replied. The three Rough Riders stared at the fort for another few seconds, then turned from the rail and went below for breakfast. Though the landing was upper-most in the minds of each, none of the three wanted to discuss it.

Shortly after 9:00 A.M. runners notified the officers of the regiment to attend a meeting on the fantail of the Yucatan. When Michael arrived with the summons, Alex and Freddy were down in the hold checking on their supplies and equipment.

"All right, Michael," Alex yelled back at his corporal, who had leaned over the hatch to pass along the message. "We'll be there in about five minutes." A few minutes later Alex and Freddy slapped the dust from their uniforms and moved across the deck to join their fellow officers. "I think we'll be okay," Freddy said, "if we c-can get even half this stuff off the s-ship."

"Yeh, if," Alex nodded. "This whole operation is based on 'if.'" Alex was pre-occupied. Since Freddy seemed, finally, to be taking charge of the supplies, Alex had been able to spend most of his two weeks aboard the Yucatan studying infantry tactics, about which no one had any expertise.

No elements of the Army had dealt with infantry tactics since the Civil War. Almost as crucial, no large unit of the U.S. military had been involved in an amphibious assault since a brigade of Marines stormed Veracruz a half century earlier. Before it even began, the American invasion of Cuba almost breached on the shoals of inter-service jealousy. Though General Shafter had declined an offer from the Navy to assist with the actual landing, neither he nor his staff possessed even the most rudimentary sense of what such a landing would require. Had the Navy not taken over during the early hours of the assault, Shafter's invasion would have floundered. Even by the time Wood and Roosevelt called their staff meeting at 9:00, returning sailors had passed the word that the landing was a mess. The wind had picked up, and boats were over-turning and being abandoned; dozens of men had drowned.

Alex and Freddy arrived at the fantail to find their fellow officers sinking into depression. Several were scanning the beach with their field glasses and shaking their heads. Someone yelled attention, and the nineteen officers of the regiment leaped to their feet. General "Fighting Joe" Wheeler, a legendary hero of the Confederacy, strode through their ranks, preceded by Major Brodie, Lieutenant Colonel Roosevelt and Colonel Wood.

PART III: A PYRRHIC VICTORY

"At ease, Gentlemen. Sit down if you will." Leonard Wood spoke to his officers in a quiet voice. Slim, intense, quietly forceful, he was a good complement to his louder and more boisterous second in command. "Though infantry we have become, we are still assigned to the Cavalry Division, which will be composed of two brigades. Our brigade will be commanded by General Young, a good friend. The brigade will consist of ourselves, the First Regular Cavalry, and the Ninth Colored Cavalry." He paused for a moment as a rumble of discontent passed through the staff.

"I know how many of you feel about serving with Coloreds; I also know how many of our troopers feel about it. However, your feelings are completely unwarranted. The Ninth Regiment—and the Tenth, which will serve with the Second Brigade—are the "Buffalo Soldiers" who won so much fame during the Indian Wars; many of the men are veterans of those campaigns. I served with them in the campaigns against Geronimo. Moreover, the Coloreds are, of course, led by white officers. They are totally reliable."

Wood scanned the eyes of his officers. He knew that several would not be reassured by his words. He also suspected that, regardless of what their private sentiments might be, each of his officers would cooperate with their sister regiment.

"I would like now to introduce you to Major General Wheeler." The officers stood and applauded. To a man, they were as excited about the leadership of the division as they were about the leadership of the regiment.

"Gentlemen, Ah'm proud to be your commanding general," Wheeler began, fingering his salt and pepper beard and sweeping his squinting gaze across the faces of the officers. "Our orders are to proceed ashore as soon as possible, which oughta be in about thirty minutes. Your brigade, that is to say, General Young's brigade, will land first." The General stopped for a moment while the officers applauded.

"Tomorrow morning at day-break your brigade will march to Siboney. From there you must, repeat must, make camp further inland than General Lawton's infantry division." The old Confederate stopped, smiled, and rubbed his palms together as if he were a banker who had just made a large loan at a usurious rate.

"General Lawton's infantry has been assigned ta lead the attack inta the interior. Now hear this, boys. Ah think the cavalry should have that honor. So, on the morning of the twenty-fifth, your brigade will head for Santiago. Your guides will be from *Cuba Libre!*, folks from the Cuban Army of Liberation. We—not the infantry—will draw first blood."

The junior officers applauded; Wood and Roosevelt beamed. This was precisely the kind of leadership they had anticipated from Wheeler. The execution of such an end run would generate headlines for the Rough Riders, horses or no. "Despite the lack of champagne, gentlemen," Wheeler concluded, "I propose a toast: To the officers! May the war last till each of us is dead, wounded or promoted!" The potential heroes leaped to their feet. "Hear! Hear!"

An hour later Alex and fifteen of his troopers were in a landing craft being rowed ashore by sailors. Though he was as excited as anyone else about 'drawing first blood,' he was worried. "Michael, do you remember what the cargo officer said this morning? About how long it would take to get all our supplies ashore?"

"Yeh, he said it would take about a week, and that..."

"And that General Shafter had coordinated the attack to begin after all the initial supplies had been landed. Right?"

"Yeh."

"If Wheeler is serious about upstaging the infantry and starting a division-wide attack in three days, what's he—what are we going to do for supplies? What are we going to do for food, ammunition and medicine?"

Rather than answering, Michael held onto the gunwale of the bobbing lifeboat and glowered at the sea. Though Alex had lost much of his naiveté and several of his delusions since his arrival in Santa Fe less than two short months before, he was still propelled by the heroic dreams of his childhood. Now, for the first time, the two sides of his personality—as well as the two halves of his official responsibilities—clashed in direct conflict: The dreamer and assistant Troop commander was thrilled by Wheeler's daring and insubordination, and by the opportunity to win early glory. The practical, down-to-earth procurement clerk and assistant supply officer was appalled by a plan so flagrantly oblivious to logistical realities. To this side of Alex it seemed that "Fighting Joe" Wheeler's thirst for geriatric glory completely disregarded the welfare of the division and assumed, naively, that the logistics mess would become no worse than it already was. Alex resolved to talk to Roosevelt as soon as they landed, though he doubted that the man would even stop long enough to listen: Both Roosevelt and Wood were at least as desperate for glory as the old Confederate.

The landing was a minor catastrophe. As they approached the pier, Michael nudged Alex and swung his finger in a wide arc from right to left. Hundreds of longboats and lighters from dozens of ships converged on the single, short pier at Daiqueri. As the oar-propelled boats moved toward the pier, they were forced to dodge the all but empty boats returning to the ships for another cargo. Then they had to dodge each other as the coxswain's of each craft jockeyed for position. Finally, they had to thread their way through the scores of boats that had been rowed ashore by the soldiers themselves and then abandoned.

As his boat made for the pier, it seemed to Alex that they were fighting their way through a Saragossa sea of bobbing, sinking and splintering hulks. The boats were so tightly packed around the pier that it seemed possible to just walk across them to the land.

At that moment Alex's boat collided with a boat carrying fifteen soldiers of the Ninth Colored Cavalry. The prow of the boat carrying the Negro soldiers rode up over the prow of Alex's boat, almost crushing Private Allen, and then capsized, throwing its occupants into the ocean.

"Stop rowing!" Michael yelled, galvanized into action before Alex could recover from the horror of seeing the fully loaded soldiers disappear beneath the swells. The men immediately shipped their oars and waited. Somehow, most of the Buffalo soldiers managed to slip from their packs and cartridge belts. Within the first two minutes after the collision, the Rough Riders pulled eleven of their Negro brothers from the sea. For another few minutes that seemed like hours, the men aboard the boats stared down into the green swells and waited for someone or something to float to the surface. Then someone from one of the other boats . yelled, "Let's get this show on the road. Them niggers sunk like stones." Though Michael couldn't see him, he recognized Shorty's voice.

"All right, let's go," Alex commanded, and the boat recommenced its trip to the little pier.

Chapter Thirty

ROOSEVELT'S ROUGH RIDERS AMBUSHED
Many Killed and Wounded by the Spanish
CHARGE AND ROUT ENEMY FROM THE BUSH
*New York's Society Youths in the First Wild and
Deadly Dash of the War*

* * * *

ROOSEVELT HIMSELF LED THE CHARGE IN THE FACE
OF A WITHERING FIRE FROM THE ENEMY
The New York Journal, June 25.

* * * *

ROOSEVELT TELLS OF THE HEROISM OF HIS TROOPERS
Spanish Fire, He Says, Was Accurate and Fearfully Heavy

* * * *

Daiqueri, June 26—"There must have been nearly 1,500 Spanish troops to the front and sides of us," said Lieutenant-Colonel Roosevelt today when discussing the fight. "They held the ridges with rifle pits and machine guns and hid a body of men in ambush in the thick jungle at the sides of the road. Our advance guard struck the men in ambush and drove them out. But they lost Captain Thomas, Lieutenant Mitchell and about fifteen men killed and wounded." *The New York Journal*, June 27.

Sibonney

M ichael awoke long before dawn and stared up through the palm fronds of his lean-to, oblivious to both the fronds and the stars, which were gradually disappearing into the grey soup of pre-dawn. Rather, he stared into Sky Woman's drained but composed face. She was talking to him, and he was straining to catch her fading voice. He had no trouble seeing her face, or even touching her. At times, when the wind was right, he believed that he could still smell the scent of her sage scrubbed skin. Her voice, however, had become more difficult. She still talked to him, just as she had been talking to him almost every night since her death. But her voice grew fainter night by night, as if it were being swept down the canyons by the winds of time and distance.

As he lay on his back, his head propped against his pack, Michael strained to catch the wisps of her fading voice: "Why do…men do such…things…no, Michael, no…you will become…like them…you will kill your spirit."

You will kill your spirit. Much of the lore he had inherited from both his Irish mother and his Mexican father insisted that he listen to dreams and voices. And gradually his need to know, to discover, had begun to battle his need for vengeance. He still knew that he would kill Shorty, but not before he had satisfied Sky Woman's question, "Why do men do such things?"

Michael rose quietly to his feet and walked over to check his gear. He knew that within minutes the watch would be making his rounds to wake the men, and to remind each of them to be as quiet as possible. General Lawton's infantry division was camped less than a mile to their rear. Since Joe Wheeler was pushing through his decision to disobey General Shafter's orders, the members of the cavalry division had gone to sleep knowing that they would be sneaking north before daybreak.

As soon as he saw the watch begin to wake the troops, Michael pitched in. After waking the officers, he woke his fellow non-coms and then started back to his lean-to.

"Hey, Mex. Is it time ta go?"

Michael walked over to the voice and discovered Big Bill Pike staring up at him. "Morning, Pike." He hunkered down beside the big redhead. "You set for a little action?"

"You betch yer sweet brown ass, Mex. We're gonna ball us some o' them dago spics."

"Great, Pike. In the meantime, why don't you get Shorty and the rest of the boys up and about?"

Four hours later and several miles inland, the regiment was moving single file up a winding jungle trail. Captain Thomas's "L" Troop was at point. The eighty-eight officers and men of the troop were strung out over several hundred yards of densely forested terrain. Already the heat and humidity were exacting their toll. Unaccustomed to carrying heavy packs, the dismounted troopers were discarding what they perceived to be the less necessary parts of their gear, including shelter halves, ponchos, spare clothes and even the less savory parts of their food rations. Already two troopers had collapsed from heat exhaustion and had been left alongside the trail, which meandered back and forth along the south-sloping hill.

Alex could seldom see more than eight or ten of his men at any one time. Nor could he or anyone else see more than a few feet into the jungle. Since the trail ran close to the ridge line, he could occasionally look across the valley to the left, where the Buffalo Soldiers hiked along a parallel trail. Other than the few sounds and even fewer glimpses they caught of the Ninth Cavalry, it was as if "L" Troop was alone in the jungle. Though Alex knew that the rest of the regiment stretched somewhere out behind them, they had had no contact for more than an hour.

Alex could feel the sweat coursing down his back and arms, and knew that the intense heat and humidity were only partly responsible. He felt very alone and afraid—not afraid of the enemy as much as afraid of what he and his two squads would do when they encountered the Spanish. Would he be able to remember all the things he had worked so diligently to master in San Antonio? Would he have the presence of mind to lead his men well?

They came out of the jungle onto a small bluff that over-looked a wide ravine. On the far side of the ravine he could see the other cavalry brigade, almost a mile distant, as its members moved through occasional open spaces in the jungle. The distant soldiers seemed to be scurrying through the clearings like frantic ants. He could hear the distant 'pop, pop' of rifle fire and realized that the troops of the Second Brigade were involved in a battle.

"That's funny, Lootenant." Alex looked around to his right. Shorty was sprawled out on his stomach a few yards away, staring at the distant battle. "I hear lotsa shots, but the only smokes I see is from our boys."

"The Spanish Mausers fire smokeless cartridges, Ninny," Pike replied caustically. "You ain't never gonna see any of their smokes. Ain't that right, Lieutenant?" Pike beamed at Alex, like a small boy waiting for a pat on the head.

"That's right, Bill. And aren't you glad that our Krag-Jorgensons fire smokeless, too? Most everyone else is firing black powder." Alex thanked Roosevelt's foresight. The Rough Riders were the one regiment in the invading force to be equipped with modern rifles. They, at least, would be able to fight the Spanish on equal terms. As for most of the rest of the invading force? Every round fired from their ancient Sharps, Remingtons and Winchesters would send out a puff of tell-tale black smoke.

Suddenly, a firefight broke out a few hundred yards to their front, at about the place where Captain Thomas and the two leading squads ought to be.

"Corporal Archuletta!" Alex yelled toward the rear, where Michael was bringing up the fourth squad. His men passed the word back down the trail, like a canyon echo, "Archuletta! Archuletta! Archuletta!"

When Michael appeared a few minutes later, tense and out of breath, Alex jerked his head towards the front. "Get up to Captain Thomas. He's with Lieutenant Mitchell at point. Find out what, if anything, we're to do."

With a curt nod Michael turned and trotted up the winding path. After the first minute, ill at ease with the loneliness of the unfamiliar trail, he began to run. Other than the firing, which seemed to be increasing, Michael could hear only the slap slap of his boots on the trail and the squawks of the alarmed jungle birds. He heard a volley of shots to his right front. The volley was followed immediately by a ragged fusillade that came from his left and not very far ahead. That sounds like our Krags, he thought, as he ran around a bend in the trail and almost tripped over four men flat on their stomachs in the middle of the trail.

"What's happening, Dugan?" Michael asked, confused and out of breath. Dugan lifted his mud-covered face and stared dumbly at the corporal. "What's going on, Dugan?" Michael yelled, hoping to get through with more volume. By that time two of the three other men had turned to face him, one of them red with embarrassment. "All right, Allen. What in the hell's going on?" Michael asked, giving up on Dugan.

"Gee, I don't know, Corporal. We saw a couple of straw hats in the jungle. Somebody up front said, 'Hey, wouldja look at that?' then there was this volley of shots..." Allen's voice trailed off and stopped.

"And?"

"We just hit the ground, Corporal. We couldn't see nothin' ta fire at, and them spics was whackin' away at us. Hell, there wasn't nothin' we could do."

It occurred to Michael that he shouldn't be standing up, so he hunkered down next to Allen. "How about the rest of the men? Where's Captain Thomas?"

"I don't know, Corporal. I guess they're up the trail where all the racket's comin' from. Jimmy Morton here hit the ground as soon as the first shots was fired," Allen continued, pointing at the one man who still lay face down in the trail. "He's an old injun fighter. The rest of us was scared when we left camp this mornin' and old Jimmy said, 'you boys jes stick with me. We'll do jes fine.' Ain't that right, Jimmy? And when old Jimmy..."

Michael blocked out the rest of the babble. He rose to his feet, tried to decide whether or not to force the four men to accompany him, and kicked Morton, who still refused to acknowledge his presence. As he bent over to jerk the man to his feet, Michael felt a chill run up his back. He rolled the man over and stared into his dead, mud-covered face. There was a small, black hole almost in the exact middle of Private Morton's forehead.

"At least Morton hit the ground with a reason," Michael whispered, standing up. He turned to the other three men, who stared at the corpse. "Let's go. You don't want to stay here."

"But Corporal. What about the buzzards?" Dugan asked.

"I'm sorry. We don't have time to bury him. Not now." Without another word, the three troopers picked up their rifles and chased after Michael, who was already running up the trail toward the firefight.

The Spanish seemed to be firing from two sides; regular, precision volleys came from both the right and the left sides of the trail. Straight ahead and much closer, he could hear the irregular volleys of the Americans. He turned another bend in the trail and stumbled into the first two squads of "L" Troop. The thirty-six men and two officers were lying, squatting or kneeling in a tight half circle. A few men guarded the south, or open, end of the circle; the rest peered into the dense foliage, firing only occasionally.

"Where's Captain Thomas?" Michael yelled.

"Over there, Archuletta. Deader than shit." Sergeant Evans, a short, sinewy bronco buster from New Mexico, ran over in a crouch and squatted down next to Michael. He pointed to the body of the troop commander, which was stretched out on its back under a bush, hands folded over its chest, its face covered by a bullet-riddled slouch hat. "Glad to see you, Mex. Things here ain't worth a shit. Cap'n got it in the head first thing. They got us pinned down and we can't see a fuckin' thing."

"How many casualties?" Michael looked around the position, intrigued by the troop lieutenant, who moved jerkily from trooper to trooper. The men seemed to be holding up well. No one was firing wildly. Since they could see nothing but jungle, they listened to the direction of the Spanish volleys and then fired immediately in that direction.

"Other than the captain, no dead, but we've got three wounded, one bad. The lieutenant's keepin' us all pretty much under cover, but I think he's wacko." Sergeant Evans nodded at Lieutenant Mitchell. "Where's Lieutenant Jackson and the other two squads?"

"Not too far back. They'll be coming," Michael said, unable to move his eyes from the frantic lieutenant. Mitchell didn't seem able to stay in one place for more than a few seconds. He was up and down, bobbing and weaving, rushing from one of his men to another. "Your lieutenant's going to get his ass shot off, Sergeant," Michael observed, amazed by the officer's nervous energy.

"Yeh, I know." Both men crouched lower as a shower of leaves and twigs dropped on their heads. "I been trying ta tell him, but..." Evans shrugged his shoulders. "He's been a lieutenant for ten years. Just missed the last of the Indian wars, and I think he's been cursing his youth ever since. I think his spokes are comin' loose." Evans glared at the frantic officer and shook his head. "Say, Mex, I'm really enjoyin' this chit-chat, but would ya mind an awful lot gettin' Lieutenant Jackson and them other two squads up here? I really am scared kinda shitless by what's happenin' to old Mitchell over there."

Just as Michael nodded and turned back toward the trail, Alex and the rest of "L" Troop bolted into the clearing and hit the ground. Sergeant Evans gave a quick report and pointed at the hyperactive lieutenant, who had failed to register the sudden appearance of thirty-eight men and another officer.

Though Alex listened, he couldn't take his eyes or ears away from Lieutenant Mitchell, who was bobbing and weaving in their direction.

"Choose your targets carefully, men," Mitchell said. He patted each trooper on the top of his head and bounced on down the line. "Choose each target carefully, men. That's good. That's good. Husband your ammunition." Another pat, another smile, and then he was facing Alex. "Choose your targets carefully. Oh! Hi, Alex. We're trying to conserve our ammunition. Good to see you."

Alex was dumbfounded by the man's appearance. He seemed to be sane, and yet...what was it? The light in his eyes? The awful, set smile that contorted his face? The hectic obsession with movement? "Get down, Lieutenant!" Alex ordered, as if addressing a private. "We've got to figure a way to get at those Spaniards."

"I can't do that, Alex. I've got to reassure the men. I've got to set an example. Besides, the Captain is figuring it out." Mitchell turned to go, impatient to keep moving.

"Mitchell!" Alex screamed. "Captain Thomas is dead! We have to figure out what to do."

Mitchell gave him a funny look, his head cocked to one side. "Oh, no, Alex. The Captain looks like he's resting, but he's thinking. He'll come up with something." He leaped to his feet and continued his rounds. "Choose your targets carefully, men."

Alex turned to Michael and Sergeant Evans. "It's up to us," he said, wracking his brain for an idea. "What the hell do you do when pinned down by an invisible enemy?"

"No, Sir!" Evans said, shaking his head vehemently. "It's not up to us, Lieutenant. It's up to you!" Evans bridled slightly as he sensed Archuletta's contempt. Goddamn uppity spic, he thought. What does he want me to do?

After an initial moment of panic, Alex recalled his training. He had to act before the pinned down men broke and ran. He had to act, and hope that the rest of the regiment reached them soon.

"All right, Sergeant. Corporal. We're here." He drew a small semi-circle in the dirt. "The Spanish seem to be here and here, to the north-east and the north-west." He drew a wide arc above the semi-circle, from west to north to east. "We're going to form an open 'V' skirmish line, with the point of the 'V' facing north. Evans, you fan your men to the right. Archuletta, you fan yours to the left. Move out on your stomachs. Each of you leave two men with me for runners."

The two non-coms stared at him. After thinking hard for a long moment, Alex continued. "I want you to spread your men out, at least five yards apart. When they're in position I want you to move them slowly forward, on their stomachs! And I want them to move toward the Spanish. Understood?"

The two non-coms nodded grimly. They knew that it would be difficult to get the men spread out, even more difficult to keep them spread out. They also realized that if any of the men were killed or seriously wounded, their bodies would be very difficult to find after the battle. Without voicing any of the doubts they may have had, however, the two men moved their troops into position. Each man moved through the wet, clinging jungle on his belly, his rifle cradled across his bent elbows.

Sergeant Evans crawled out first, leading his two squads off to the north-east, prepared to drop one man off every five yards as the lieutenant had ordered. As he moved, he tried to look up through the dark green canopy at the sky. Here and there he could see small patches of blue. Even then, however, he usually saw grey. The clouds were building for an afternoon shower.

Alex turned to his remaining troops, three lightly wounded and the two runners. "Keep up an erratic, slow fire, and keep it at least four feet above the ground. We want the Spanish to think we're all still here, but we sure as hell don't want to hit our own boys." The men nodded, assumed sitting positions behind trees, and commenced firing.

Michael moved off to the north-west with his two squads, then doubled back briefly to see Alex. "I have never had a real friend before, other than my wife." Though his face was dead-pan, he stuck out his hand for a stunned Alex to shake. The sheepherder looked intently at his Harvard educated officer friend for a brief second or two, then disappeared into the jungle.

Alex felt open, vulnerable. He shook his head, looked around the clearing and made firm eye contact with the few remaining soldiers. The mad lieutenant now squatted by the side of the Captain's body, as if waiting for new orders or a kind word.

The lieutenant bent over suddenly, lifted Captain Thomas's battered hat, and stared at his shattered face. He looked over at Alex, as if seeking confirmation for what he had just discovered, replaced the hat and stood up. Almost immediately a volley of bullets cracked through the clearing and Mitchell fell to his knees, his arms folded across his chest like a young girl trying to conceal her breasts.

Horrified, two of the soldiers lay down their rifles and stared at Mitchell. "Keep firing, Goddamnit!" Alex screamed. Maintaining his crouch, he zig-zagged to where Mitchell was kneeling.

Blood seeped rapidly through the man's splayed fingers, and he frowned at Alex, as if the latter were responsible. "My father lives in Kent, Ohio now," Mitchell said, desperate to explain something. "He moved there three years ago after my mother died." Mitchell looked at Captain Thomas's body, then back at Alex, who pressed him down on his back and pried his crossed arms away from the wound.

"I think the captain is dead. He has holes in his face. And I have holes in my chest, don't I?" Mitchell looked down at his red-splotched hands and giggled. "My father said there would be days like this." Still smiling slyly, as if playing a joke, Lieutenant Mitchell collapsed.

Alex placed the man's head in his lap, pulled out a field dressing, opened the man's tunic, and went to work on the bullet holes. Not until he was finished with the dressing did he realize that Mitchell was dead. For a few seconds that seemed like an hour, Alex gazed at the man's chest. He then looked at the body of Captain Thomas, back at Mitchell, and back again to the Captain. It occurred to him that he was now in command of "L" Troop.

Alex jerked himself alert, saw that his runners were staring at him, and moved carefully over to their position behind a clump of three royal palms.

"Sir? Is the lieutenant dead?" Robinson asked. When Alex nodded, Robinson added, "Are we all going to die here?"

"What are you talking about, Private? Just keep low. I don't know what happened to the captain, but I saw Lieutenant Mitchell get it. He stood straight up."

"No, Sir," Robinson wheedled. "I don't think that makes any difference. They know we're here." Suddenly the private started to cry. "We've got to get out of here, Lieutenant. They're going to kill us all."

Without giving a thought to what he was doing, or why, Alex lost patience with the private. He wanted to concentrate on the two branches of his 'V," on Evans and Archuletta and their men. He didn't have time to argue chances of survival with a terrified soldier. He coiled his arm and knocked Private Robinson off his haunches. When the man stayed on his back and started to wriggle away like an over-turned snake, Alex grabbed his ankle and pulled him back. "Robinson, I'm going to give you one chance to demonstrate that you're a good soldier. If you louse up, every man in this outfit will know what a chickenshit son of a bitch you are. You hear?" He was now holding Robinson by the belt buckle.

Robinson nodded and started to sit up, but a volley of Spanish bullets hit the palm fronds above their heads, sending down a sharp rain of slivers. Robinson put both hands over his face and tried to turn over. Alex rolled him back and said, very quietly, "Robinson, I want you to find Major Brodie or one of the colonels. I want the rest of the outfit up here—right now! I want you to RUN all the way back down that trail until you find Brodie or Wood or Roosevelt. You HEAR?" Without waiting for an answer, Alex pulled out his .44 revolver, cocked it, and aimed between Robinson's startled eyes. The private nodded vigorously and was still nodding ten seconds later when he turned the first bend in the trail. He ran in a crouch, his head tucked down almost to his navel.

"I don't think you'll have any more trouble with Andy, sir. He's a good man. He really is." Alex looked around and glared at the speaker, a tall, thin, half-breed Cherokee from Oklahoma Territory. The man calmly returned his stare and Alex finally softened his look. "Maybe you're right, Bates. I hope so."

Suddenly the left wing of the skirmish line opened up with their Krags. A few seconds later the right wing followed suit. After listening for a moment Alex said, "All right, boys. Cease fire. We don't want to confuse things more. Bates! Move it out. Get to Sergeant Evans. His men are to continue forward as fast as they can crawl. Put on pressure. Oliver!" He turned to a soldier with a bandaged head. "Are you strong enough? Can you get to Corporal Archuletta with the same message?"

Oliver nodded. "Yes, sir."

As soon as the two men started their zig-zag routes, Alex looked around. The two dead officers were lying on their backs in the middle of the clearing. The wounded men were well-concealed behind a large pile of humus, the two less seriously wounded tending a third, who seemed to have lapsed into a coma. Alex's final runner squatted next to him, his head moving back and forth from right to left with such rapidity that Alex could hear the man's neck bones go click-click-click. The Spanish volleys had become less regular, more frantic.

"Yessir, Lootenant, I'm with ya." Luke Adamson, the private who had been so insulting to Alex and Michael during their first evening in San Antonio, was chewing a large wad of tobacco. He sent a long stream of the juice in the direction of the Spanish volleys, plopped down on his stomach and crawled forward with the same nonchalance he had displayed on the drill field. Alex couldn't help smiling. Luke wasn't even waiting for him to lead the way. Either that man's not even half as afraid as I am, Alex thought, or he's one helluva fine actor. Alex zig-zagged across the clearing, took up a position five yards to the left of Private Adamson and plunked himself down in the ripe mud.

Corporal Archuletta's wing of the skirmish line seemed to be firing more steadily, more assuredly. Michael's's troopers must be able to see the Spanish, Alex thought, as he crawled through the underbrush, right elbow, left leg, left elbow, right leg, his .44 pistol waving its long nose to the right and left as he crawled. Those dagos must be pretty confused, he thought. They're the ones who are used to having the advantage of smokeless cartridges. Alex jerked his head to the right as Sergeant Evans' east wing started firing almost non-stop. Evans' troops were whooping and hollering, as if out on a cattle drive.

PART III: A PYRRHIC VICTORY

"Let's go, Luke!" Alex yelled, rising to his feet. He looked over at the private, who was grinning. Alex grinned back, though he felt slightly unsteady on his feet. Then he started yelling, more to reinforce his own wobbly courage than to scare the enemy. Running in a sharp crouch, he moved through the jungle from tree to tree, more or less in the direction of the Spanish Mausers, whose sharp crack was higher, somehow more intense, than the sound of the American Krags.

Although he had no intention of getting to the Spanish before the rest of his command, Alex's adrenalin propelled him into the Spanish clearing before he knew where he was. He stared straight into the face of a shocked Spanish soldier and backed immediately into the protection of the trees without even firing his pistol.

The Spaniard stood in the clearing for a fraction of a second longer and then started back to the protection of a fallen log. Alex's tobacco-chewing private raised his rifle, waited for the frightened Spaniard to lift his leg to climb over the log, aimed at a spot high between the man's shoulder blades and pulled the trigger. The man's arms jerked out and his body flew into a long trench and crashed down upon the surprised heads of several Spanish defenders.

Alex heard his troopers yelling to the right and left. Luke yelled, "Kill the spic fuckers! Kill the spic fuckers!"

Alex discovered that he was shaking uncontrollably. Why hadn't he fired at the soldier? He looked around and discovered three more of the long Spanish trenches, each protected on the south side by fallen palm logs. He also saw numerous shadows, as men from his skirmish lines flitted from tree to tree, slowly outflanking the Spanish positions.

"Enfilade!" he yelled, first to his right and then to his left. His men picked up the command. "Enfilade!" More and more of his men concentrated on out-flanking the Spanish trenches. They soon found protected positions that allowed them to fire down into the trenches, which forced the defenders to keep their heads down and allowed even more of the Rough Riders to get into position.

Within ten minutes the battle, or at least its initial stage, was all but over. The surviving Spanish tried to retreat from what were proving to be mass graves. First singly, then in groups, they leaped from their log-reinforced trenches and disappeared up slope into the jungle.

When he thought that the last Spaniard had left the trench in front of him, Alex skirted carefully around to the right and, pistol held out in front of him like a shield, leapt down into the trench. Three Spanish soldiers huddled in the mud at the bottom of the trench. Each had been shot in the head. Alex felt a sharp chill run down his back and raised his eyes. A Spanish officer sat against the far end of the trench, scarcely ten feet away. Blood coursed down a deep crease along the side of his head and dripped onto his blue and white jacket. The man stared at Alex. He held a pistol, which rested between his legs.

For what seemed like a very long time the two officers stared at each other. Alex heard the shots of the Krags and Mausers off to his right and left, the cries and shrieks of the indignant jungle birds and the dry scuttle of the land crabs as they scurried toward an unexpected feast. He heard the heavy beat of the vultures' wings as the huge, red-faced, Cuban scavengers settled down on trees and bushes a few yards away, patiently waiting. And he heard the labored breathing of the Spanish officer, who continued to lock eyes with him, and the soft grunts of one of the wounded Spanish defenders lying at his feet in the bottom of the trench.

Alex had thought all three of the men dead, and the grunts so shocked him that he allowed his eyes to fall away from the Spanish officer's. Almost instantly he felt a sharp tug in his left side and heard a loud explosion. He looked up, saw that the officer's pistol pointed shakily in his direction, and then jerked back as the top of the man's head disappeared. He felt himself sinking slowly onto the ground and noticed that his pistol had gone off.

"Nice shot, Lieutenant. You blew that spic fucker apart." Private Adamson plopped down next to him and let loose a thin stream of tobacco juice at the Spanish corpses. "Yessir, Lieutenant, that surely was nice. Say?" His voice rose slightly as he noticed that Alex was wounded. "You okay?"

Alex glanced at him uncomprehendingly, looked back down at his pistol and over at the dead officer, the remnant of whose face was almost solid red. Alex leaned over, vomited on one of the trench's defenders, and fell over on his right side in a dead faint.

Chapter Thirty-One

ROOSEVELT'S ROUGH RIDERS IN ACTION
They Fought Like Fiends Among the Cuban Hills—1,000 of Them Against 2,000 Spaniards. But They drove the Dons to Where They Died—Not Without Loss to Our Gallant Troopers.

* * * *

WHAT ELSE COULD HAPPEN IN SO FIERCE A FIGHT?
Living and dead covered themselves with glory. That glory will be vividly reflected and will shine out for as all—and for all time—from the fascinating pages of our magnificent PHOTOGRAPHIC Military and Naval HISTORY of the WAR. (issued weekly.) These are the men that make history. This is the History that they make. 10c per copy. Advertisement for the War Supplement: *The New York Journal*, June 27.

Las Guasimas

"What the bloody hell happened here?" Roosevelt asked, as he rode into the clearing, pistol in hand, followed by several hundred of his dismounted cavalry. The late-comers milled around the battle site, stared at the thirty-odd Spanish corpses, and questioned the members of "L" Troop, most of whom were lying exhausted on the ground.

Archuletta looked up and away from his patient. "Christ almighty, Michael," Alex cursed. "Loosen it just a bit; my ribs aren't going to fall out."

Michael whispered, "Stop whining. The boss man has come to see your heroism." Roosevelt seemed to be having trouble with Little Texas, one of but four Rough Rider horses to make it out of Tampa.

"What'd you do? What happened here?" Roosevelt repeated, glaring down at Alex, who refused to meet his eyes.

"Lieutenant Jackson formed a wedge-shaped skirmish line and we broke up a Spanish ambush," Michael reported.

"Where's Captain Thomas? Where's Mitchell? I want their reports."

Alex finally looked up and glared at Roosevelt. "They're dead, Colonel. Otherwise, I'm sure they'd be here to report." Then, turning abruptly away from Roosevelt, Alex asked Archuletta, "Have you sent back search parties to look for dead and wounded?"

"Sergeant Evans is taking care of it, sir"

Though upset because he was too late for the action, and because Lieutenant Jackson seemed withdrawn to the point of disrespect, Roosevelt decided to be magnanimous. "Bully good job, Lieutenant Jackson. Yessiree. Bully good job!" He turned to two civilians who had ridden up beside him. "Ah, there you are. Come over here and meet a genuine hero, gentlemen. Alex, meet the press."

Alex and Michael exchanged amazed glances. They knew that at least a hundred war correspondents had sailed down from Key West, and they knew that the four best known newspapermen in the country, Frederick Remington, Richard Harding Davis, Edward Marshall and William Randolph Hearst, had sailed down on Hearst's private yacht. But neither of the two soldiers had really expected to see reporters on the front lines. Something about their presence defied reality.

"Gentlemen, "Roosevelt continued. "I'd like to introduce you to Lieutenant Alexander Dumas Jackson, Harvard, '94. Because of his bravery and presence of mind, the lieutenant here has just won command of "L" Troop. Alex, this is Edward Marshall. Alex shook hands with a tall man in a black and white rain coat whose gaze kept falling to his bandaged ribs. "And this fellow over here, who's an old Cuba hand and also the best-known correspondent in America, is Richard Harding Davis." Alex shook hands with Davis, who was wearing high-laced boots, khakis and a safari hat. He noticed that Davis was perfectly calm and totally alert. Alex had the feeling that the famous man was inhaling every detail of what was going on around him. The reporters quizzed Alex about the attack, interviewed two of the privates, then rode away with Roosevelt, who went looking for General Young, the brigade commander.

Why Roosevelt was in such haste to find the brigade commander became apparent almost immediately. Fighting Joe Wheeler had ordered The First Brigade to move up to Las Guasimas. The two white regiments, the First Regular Cavalry and the Rough Riders, would lead the assault. The Ninth Colored Cavalry would follow in reserve. After capturing the large blockhouse at Las Guasimas, they were to link up with the Second Brigade at the Sevilla Road. From there the entire division would push forward to the heights above San Juan City. Should the plan succeed, Joe Wheeler would verify and refurbish his legend. Equally important, as far as the old warrior was concerned, he would succeed in embarrassing General Lawton, commander of the infantry division.

PART III: A PYRRHIC VICTORY

* * * * *

Alex's "L" Troop moved forward near the eastern end of a long, ragged line. He knew that "A" Troop was somewhere to his right, that "K" Troop was somewhere to his left, and that a troop of Buffalo Soldiers was somewhere to his rear. As far as his senses could tell, however, "L" Troop was proceeding forward alone. There was no grand plan, no over-all strategy, no discernible purpose to their movements. He and his already exhausted troopers seemed to be totally alone in the up-sloping jungle. He was confident of their existence solely because his runners kept in constant contact with each squad.

Alex heard a sharp noise, started, and turned to his left. One of the Negro troopers of the Ninth Cavalry was staring at him. Chee-rist! Alex thought. We're moving so slowly that we've been over-run by our own reserves. At least we've got reinforcements for whatever happens.

His small shot of euphoria did not last long. Like the rest of the American Army—the Rough Riders excepted—the Ninth Cavalry was supplied with old Remingtons and Springfields, rifles which fired black-smoke cartridges. As the Negro troopers began to inter-mix with the Rough Riders, the Spanish sharpshooters discovered that they finally had clear targets. Alex heard a man yell on his right, then another, and still another. Cursing the jungle and the black-smoke cartridges, he tried to fix the location of the cries. Since Wood and Roosevelt had ordered that no one stop to help the wounded, it was imperative that everyone remember where they had been when someone was hit. But everything looked alike: bamboo interspersed with palms interspersed with jack pines interspersed with vicuna vines interspersed with hedge-like bushes interspersed with hedges of long-thorned bougainvillea.

The further into the jungle he pushed and the more pained cries he heard, the more afraid Alex became, sensing the green wall of loneliness that surrounded each wounded and dying man. With each step the pain in his side and the nausea became worse. Only terror kept him moving forward, feeding his will to survive. He knew that land crabs and vultures waited to devour the helpless.

A sharp thud and an even sharper expulsion of breath pulled Alex momentarily from the fog of his pain and concentration. The Negro soldier on his left had collapsed, holding his stomach with both hands, and stared at him. Avoiding the man's imploring eyes and without speaking a word, Alex handed the soldier his canteen, turned away, and continued on.

Almost immediately the land began to open up and Alex found himself at the edge of a huge clearing that continued for several hundred yards up-slope toward the summit. The Spaniards had fortified several buildings of what appeared to be an old ranch, and had dug long trenches into the down-slope side of the buildings. Although Alex could not yet see any of his troopers, he yelled to his right and then his left. "Do not leave cover. Stay in the trees. Do not leave cover!" As soon as he knew that he had made it through the jungle, Alex regained his self-control. His pain remained, but the terror fell away.

Within fifteen minutes the entire brigade hovered at the edge of the jungle, stretched out in a half mile long line poised to assault the ranch. During the brief time it took the brigade to re-group, the troopers rested and traded pot shots with entrenched Spaniards.

Alex heard a command, flowing from the left as troopers passed along the word. "Troop commanders to the left, pronto." Alex turned command of the troop over to Sergeant Evans and walked the quarter mile to Wood's make-shift command post, which swarmed with officers and war correspondents. Almost as soon as Alex arrived, Generals Young and Wheeler joined the melee. Now virtually the entire division, almost 5,000 men, was poised to take the Sevilla Road, which would lead them to the high ridges over-looking the harbor and the city of San Juan.

General Wheeler was in a hurry. The successful advance he had unleashed before dawn was a direct violation of the orders issued by General Shafter. Not only had he usurped the position assigned to Lawton's infantry; he had also launched his attack a good five days earlier than Shafter had planned. Wheeler felt that if he could accomplish his objective, Shafter would be unable to complain. He also knew that as soon as Shafter, or one of Shafter's aides, caught up with him, the show would be over. He would have to dig in and wait for the rest of the invasion force to catch up. The old Confederate was absolutely sure of one thing: the faster he and his dismounted cavalry division moved, the more difficult it would be for anyone from the rear to catch him. If they couldn't catch up with him, they sure as hell couldn't order him to stop.

The officers crowded around him, sheltered by the large umbrella of a towering cianna tree. Wheeler began describing his plan even before the last of the officers arrived. "General Young's First Brigade: You folks are gonna charge those trenches and buildings. You'll move up this here slope just like you moved through the jungle. Rough Riders on the right flank, First Cav. on the left, Ninth Coloreds in reserve. One big difference, though. We crept through the jungle. Had to, I guess. But when you and your boys leave the jungle and start up through this here clearing, I want you to run every step of the way. Don't stop fer nothin'. We don't know how heavily them blockhouses are defended, and we don't know what, if anything, is on the far side of that there ridge behind the blockhouses. We do know this. The quicker you can get yerselves across that there clearing and take the position, the sooner the Spanish will stop shooting at you. Get mah meaning?"

"Yes, sir!"

"When you get to them block houses, don't even slow down. You tell your boys they can do all the breathin' they want once they get over the top of that ridge. Got it?"

The assembled officers nodded and chorused, "Yes, sir!"

"Fine, boys. I appreciate your enthusiasm. Now, the Second Brigade, under my direct command, is going to leap-frog the ridge about a half mile to the right and go straight to that valley on the map that dissects the Sevilla Road. From there we'll be poised to go after San Juan Ridge. We'll have position on Lawton's infantry, in case they ever decide to stop playin' on the beach and come up here. And we're sure as hell gonna have position on the spics, right?"

The officers nodded and, after receiving a few tactical orders, returned to their fairly well rested troops. Fifteen minutes later, to the accompaniment of bugles and a chorus of ragged battle cries, the First Brigade charged out of the jungle and into the upland clearing. The rest of the battle was anti-climactic. Seldom had so many gotten so worked up to overcome so few. Though a few Americans fell during the assault on the buildings, which turned out to be an abandoned distillery rather than a fort, by the time the assaulting force had covered a third of the distance, the two hundred Spanish defenders decided to give up; they were out of their trenches, out of the buildings and over the hill into the jungle long before the swiftest of the American soldiers reached the distillery. Within twenty minutes the battle of Las Guasimas was over.

Roosevelt, who had led the charge, was exultant. He paced Little Texas back and forth within full view of any Spanish sharpshooters that might still be lurking about. He gave command upon contradictory command to his troops, who were digging in on the north side of the ridge and preparing to support Joe Wheeler's advance on the Sevilla Road. He paraded his correspondents around the area, drew maps of the entire day's action, and explained in exhaustive detail the part the Rough Riders had played. He praised every trooper he saw, and assured each of them that they were part of the best cavalry regiment the world had ever seen, and that they would have been even better had they been able to bring their horses. Since Colonel Wood was at Brigade head-quarters conferring with General Young, Roosevelt was free to praise his men and, indirectly, Wood and himself, to the sky.

As far as the correspondents—and the American public—were concerned, the entire battle had been a Rough Rider action. By the next day America would discover that she had a new hero, Teddy Roosevelt. From that day forward, Roosevelt and the Rough Riders would dominate the headlines and capture the imagination of the reading public. Within two days more correspondents covered the seven hundred man half-regiment of Rough Riders than the balance of the 25,000 man invading force combined.

Rather than bragging about his recent victory and polishing his image, Alex felt that Roosevelt should be sending search parties back into the jungle to search for the dead and wounded. When he suggested as much to Captain Rob Church, the regimental surgeon, another Harvard alumnus, Church, in disbelief that the order had not already been given, instantly sent a hundred man search party back into the jungle.

Michael Archuletta tried to follow Alex's directions to the Negro trooper some seventy or eighty yards back. After a fifteen minute search he found the man's body—not because of the clarity of Alex's directions as much as by the raucous noise of the vultures. The trooper had bled to death, and his body was already being pecked at by a dozen land crabs and three huge vultures.

As soon as he found a litter party to carry the corpse back to Las Guasimas, Michael roamed back and forth along the skirmish line, re-checking areas already searched and helping to carry the dead and seriously wounded to the trail.

PART III: A PYRRHIC VICTORY

"Corporal Archuletta!" someone called in an obvious fright. Michael crashed through the underbrush toward a disembodied, hysterical voice some twenty or thirty yards away. When he arrived at the source, the private behind the voice merely pointed and continued to crush land crabs with his rifle butt. One of the Rough Riders, whose face was unrecognizable, was lying on his back, his body twisted almost into a knot. A dead vulture, its neck broken, lay beside him; the body of a second was still clutched in his hands. Neither soldier spoke as they pulled the dead man's hands from the vulture's neck.

By the time the search party returned to the buildings at Las Guasimas, the long, summer twilight had already begun. Threatening clouds had retreated higher into the *Sierra Maestra* and the suffocating humidity had lightened. As the exhausted units reorganized, one consequence of their mad dash through the jungle became obvious, and those troopers who had abandoned parts of their equipment understood what they had done. One flaw of General Wheeler's insubordinate advance was his complete disregard for logistics. Much of what the division needed to supply the troops remained aboard ship. There was no back-up, no extra tents or clothing or food or even ammunition, and very little in the way of medical supplies or equipment closer than the beachhead, now half a day away. Troopers piled their wounded companions into springless ox carts and sent them on the bone jarring journey back down the rutted trail. Other than applying field dressings, there was nothing the medical staff could do for the wounded, even less than they could do for the troopers suffering from heat exhaustion or the onset of yellow fever.

Each man had been issued a two day ration of canned beef and hardtack. Almost immediately the famished troopers discovered that they were on short rations, and would stay on short rations for at least three more days. Some of those who had abandoned parts of their kits along the trail were able to beg a piece of hard tack or a piece of embalmed beef from a friend; others went without. Those who had abandoned ponchos and shelter halves had no protection from the afternoon rains that were to plague their advance, and a number of those who developed malarial or yellow fevers first suffered hypothermia from constant soakings.

While the surviving members of his squad worried about food,

Michael was more than content to spend a few minutes alone. He walked slowly back along the trail that led from Las Guasimas towards the beach at *Siboney.*

Before he had covered fifty yards he heard horses galloping down the trail and stepped aside just as large party of horsemen, led by General Wheeler, almost knocked him aside. The general yanked his horse to a halt, glared at the startled corporal, and asked, "You—Cuban?"

"Sir?"

"You a Cuban, young man? You look like a Cuban. What's yer name?" The general eyed him suspiciously, obviously upset.

"No, sir. Corporal Michael Archuletta, sir." Michael felt vaguely uneasy. The general's feelings were obvious: If you're dark-complex-ioned you're suspect. "So yer not Cuban, ay? Good. From what I've seen today, the Cuban army's nothin' but a band of scavengers. You know what I saw today, Corporal?"

"Sir?"

"I saw a bunch of General Garcia's so-called soldiers scrounging along the beach and along all the trails leading inland. Everything our men lost or threw away those scavengers is walkin' away with.

"Can't figure out how such ragamuffins fought the spics to a stand-still. Glad to hear yer not Cuban." Wheeler scratched his beard, nodded sternly at the dark-skinned corporal and cantered up the trail.

* * * *

By late evening the Rough Riders had settled into their camp at Las Guasimas. In addition to establishing their headquarters in the largest of the distillery buildings, Wood and Roosevelt had created comfortable quarters for the increasing number of war correspondents, whom the two colonels treated as their equals. Though Edward Marshall had been sent back to the beach with a bullet in his spine, Frederick Remington and four other correspondents had taken his place. And when Joe Wheeler returned that evening to discover the special relationship between the press and the Rough Riders, he decided to establish his own headquarters at Las Guasimas. Wheeler's decision completed the transition of the buildings from deserted distillery to Spanish fort to a crowded and noisy juxtaposition of division headquarters and press club.

By the time Alex returned from the regimental aid station, General Wheeler and his staff had just finished moving into the best half of the main building.

"Ah, there you are, Alex." Roosevelt stood up so fast that he knocked over the camp table, spilling coffee all over General Wheeler's brand new tunic. "Sorry, General," he smiled, more amused than penitent, "but this is the young officer we've been waiting to hear from. His troop led the attack. Come on over here, Alex. How do you feel?"

"I'll be fine, Colonel. Just a little . . ."

"Good. Good. You met General Wheeler at the Tampa Bay Hotel, I believe? We want a full report. Your troop, "L" Troop of the First United States Volunteer Cavalry," Roosevelt emphasized loudly enough for all the correspondents to hear, "your troop drew first blood. Bully good, Alex. Bully good. Our cowboy cavalry demonstrated its mettle against a well-armed and determined enemy."

At first Alex wasn't sure whether Roosevelt wanted to make a speech for the benefit of the press or to hear a battle report, though he noticed that the correspondents were closing in on the officers like a pack of dogs after a bitch in heat. He also noticed that the closer the press got to the circle the more enthusiastic and charismatic Roosevelt became.

"All right, Lieutenant." Roosevelt drew himself up to his full, barrel-chested height and beamed with cherubic radiance. Leonard Wood remained seated, pleased with the attention the regiment was getting, but slightly contemptuous of the ease with which his good friend was able to charm the press.

Wheeler stood close to Roosevelt, as if to emphasize both to the press and to his constituents in Alabama that he was the general commanding this brave bunch of frontiersmen; that he was the brilliant and daring strategist who had ordered—and won—a victory at least a week before the rest of the army was planning even to move from the beach-head.

Alex took a seat next to Leonard Wood and began his report. Even as he talked, however, he envisioned the Spanish officer with whom he had exchanged shots. Though the top of the man's head was missing, he was smiling at Alex, as if to ask, 'Why, my friend? What have we done to each other?' Alex shook his head and stared around at the smiling faces of the staff officers and the correspondents. Out of a corner of his eye he could see Remington, who was seated on a camp school, sketching the scene on a large tablet of newsprint.

"We should never have marched up that trail in single file, sir. We walked into one ambush after another." Alex looked around, taken aback by the startled and angry reactions of Wheeler and the colonels. The reporters scribbled furiously. Christ almighty! Alex thought. These people say they want to know what happened.

"Captain Thomas was with Lieutenant Mitchell at point," he continued. "By the time I arrived, the Captain was dead. The men were clustered behind a few palm trees, shooting at the air. All the Spanish seem to have rifles that fire smokeless cartridges. We couldn't see anything. Because of the way the jungle seems to absorb and deflect sound, it was difficult even to get a precise sense of their positions."

Alex stopped for a moment, looked accusingly at Joe Wheeler, and thought of the Procurement Office at the War Department, of America's total unpreparedness for the war, and of the incredible logistics foul-ups that had begun to surface as early as late February. He bit his lip as he thought of his own hard-charging naivete and shook his head again. Alex wanted out of the building. His side hurt and he was exhausted. He wanted to lie down, to sleep. He looked around at his deflated and stern-faced superiors, none of whom made a move either to shut him up or to hurry him along. The press waited, pencils poised.

"Once we spread out in a skirmish line things got better. In fact, my gut feeling is that the Spaniards are putting up almost token resistance, almost as if they're more concerned with—I don't know—not so much concerned with winning as with losing honorably."

"Don't let the Spaniards fool you, Alex," Roosevelt warned. "You won because you—because the Rough Riders—fought hard and well. Besides, you know bloody well you can't trust a spic. They've been pulling the wool over our eyes in Washington and Madrid for years. They're surely capable of pulling the wool over our eyes in Cuba."

Alex hesitated, unsure of how to respond. At that moment, however, he was saved by a commotion that started at the door and immediately swept away the balance of his report.

David Vandervoort rushed into the room and saluted. Not sure about which of the senior officers he should focus upon, he moved his eyes back and forth between the three and spent at least half of the time looking at and talking to the wall. "The infantry division is moving up, sir. General Lawton just rode into the clearing. He's on his way here, and he looks madder than hops."

Vandervoort was nervous. He had run to headquarters with the news more from loyalty to his colonels than from any desire to be present when the confrontation between Wheeler and Lawton took place. Once inside, however, he quickly discovered that he was trapped; there was nowhere to go. Lawton was in the door before anyone present in the room could even react to David's news.

General Lawton stood in the doorway and glared at Wheeler and Roosevelt. "Wheeler," he began without preamble, "if I were General Shafter, you'd be relieved of your command, court-martialed, and your geriatric rebel ass sent howling back to the wilds of Alabama."

"Now you jest wait a minute, you Yankee noodle. Me and my folks here had the intestinal fortitude to take the initiative, jest like we did thirty-five years ago." Wheeler puffed up his chest and moved toward Lawton.

With the exception of Alex, who remained seated, all of Wheeler's staff followed him, as did the entire corps of correspondents. "Lawton, you cautious, ward-room commander. If you'd a had the guts to move up off that beach, you coulda been here instead a me. And stop shakin' yer head like a goddamned life-denyin' priest. We came here ta kick spic asses, didn't we? Well that's what this old hoss has been doin'. If Shafter don't like the fact that I'm kickin' Spanish ass, then he can stand there and vibrate off a couple hundred a them excess pounds he hauls around." Wheeler was so mad he was spitting.

Lawton didn't back down. A West Point graduate and career officer who had spent better than forty years in the Army, he continued to block the doorway and stare contemptuously at his old adversary, at the room full of amateur glory-seekers, and at the leach-like correspondents, who scribbled furiously. "Wheeler, you're not the only glory seeker in Cuba. And neither are your play colonels here. I, too, would like a little glory. It's part of the reason all of us are here.

"But you know something, Congressman Wheeler? You know one of the real distinctions between a professional officer and political string pullers like you and Roosevelt? A professional follows orders. A professional may not like his orders, but by damn! he follows them.

"General Shafter may not cut much of a military figure, Wheeler, and he may not be a legend. And, yes, you insubordinate Confederate ass, he is a couple of hundred pounds overweight. However, he just happens to be in command of this invasion, and he just happened to give all of us—including you, you unreconstructed rebel adolescent—a direct order: We were all to wait on the beach until our supplies got here. General Shafter's orders are to be obeyed—even by you and your regiments of cowboys and niggers."

Despite the moral support of his large band of officers, all of whom confronted one steely-eyed infantry general, Wheeler backed down. He had won a victory, the first land victory of the war. He had also violated a direct order, and knew it. "Lawton, you know damned good and well it may take a week to get them supplies landed. Hell, man, I'm gettin' on in years. I may not live a week."

"Well, General. You should have given some thought to that before you traded your influence for a commission." Despite his frustration at being upstaged by his old nemesis, Lawton could not help but smile. This little bit of horn locking in front of the press was proving to be by far the best part of a bad day.

"Besides, Lem," Wheeler continued in what he meant to be conciliatory tones, "by the time those supplies get here, the spics may have been gone fer a week." Wheeler looked nervously around at Roosevelt and Wood, who dutifully nodded their support.

"Good Lord, Wheeler!" Lawton exhaled a long breath of disgusted resignation. "Where the hell do you think they're going to go? General Garcia has every road leading in and out of Santiago blockaded. Admiral Sampson's got the whole blinking island blockaded. The Spaniards are going to have to fight somewhere—or surrender, in which case we've won the shortest war in American history."

"Goddamnit, Lem. I don't want them ta surrender. I want them ta fight! I didn't pull every goddamn string it's possible ta pull in Washington—and neither did Teddy here—jest ta sail down here for a two or three day outing." Wheeler was starting to counter-attack. He stalked back and forth in front of Lawton, an aging bantam rooster preparing to spit in the face of a chicken hawk.

But the more Wheeler protested and gestured, the more contemptuous Lawton became. "I know all about your string-pulling, Joseph.

And I know all about Teddy's." He glared at the shocked but excited correspondents. Without bothering to look at Roosevelt, whom he despised, Lawton spat: "He has even less respect for the chain of command than you do, Joseph. Teddy has a pipeline to every important office in Washington. And if you think all these grease-faced leaches with note pads are here to cover your exploits, Congressman, you've got another think coming." Without so much as a glance at Roosevelt or Wood, Lawton turned and stalked out the door. He was back in three seconds.

"General Shafter has ordered me to place my division a mile and a half in front of yours, across the Sevilla Road. Both of us are to stay put until we are fully re-supplied, which, as you know, could take close to a week. Now, if either you or your cowboys and niggers attempt to out-flank me again, I'll shoot you. Do you understand that, Wheeler?" Without waiting for an answer, he spun about on his heel, almost crashed into the sill, and left for good.

After a very long silence, during which everyone, including the press, breathed very quietly, Wood finally said, "Evidently Shafter's not sufficiently mad—in either sense of the word—to order us back to the beach."

"Or to have us give our positions back to the spics," Roosevelt added. Then, possibly for the benefit of the press, he turned back to Alex and raised his voice, "These men have performed valiantly today, in the best tradition of the American citizen-soldier," He patted Alex benevolently on the shoulder. "This day's action by the Rough Riders will shorten the war. And you can quote me on that, Gentlemen."

"Because of their actions we are one long step closer to victory over Spain. Their praises should be sung to the sky." On that glorious note Roosevelt turned and marched from the building, pursued by the entire corps of correspondents.

Alex wanted to cover his head, which pounded with pain and confusion. He could not even begin to sort out the events and impressions that had bombarded him during the long day.

"Goddamnit! I wanted to say something to that Yankee idiot before he ran off with his tail between his legs." Wheeler marched up to where Alex and David Vandervoort were sitting. Though David jumped immediately to attention, Alex continued to sit; he held his aching head in his hands and concentrated on not thinking about his throbbing ribs, or of the disfigured head of the Spanish officer he had shot, or of the old general, his father's life-long hero, who stood three feet away, yelling at full volume.

"And as far as General Garcia and his bare-assed army of niggers are concerned, they ain't worth the powder it'd take ta blew them up!"

Alex realized that 'Fighting Joe' wasn't yelling at him; rather, he was yelling at General Lawton, who was well out of range.

"Did I tell you about what I saw on the beach today? One of General Garcia's divisions, led by some half-nigger mongrel name of Costillo, was out trash picking. Those people ain't soldiers; they're scavengers, and they're gonna be totally unreliable."

Silence. After a full minute, Alex opened his eyes and discovered that the old Confederate had disappeared. He turned to David, who was still mesmerized by the sideshow he had stumbled into. "You okay, David?"

David stared at him for a moment, then shook his head hard. "Let's get out of here, Alex, before one of those lunatics comes back.

Chapter Thirty-Two

SHAFTER MUST STRIKE NOW OR AID WILL
REACH SANTIAGO
General Pando and 8,000 Men Rapidly Nearing the Beleaguered City—
Miles Expects the Stronghold to Fall Within Forty-eight Hours

* * * * *

Washington, June 29 — The dispatch sent to the Journal early this morning and containing information that General Shafter would proceed at once to take Santiago without waiting for reinforcements was confirmed as to its accuracy today.

As a matter of fact, there is the strongest reason for believing that the Department urged General Shafter to move promptly, because it is believed that grave danger menaces General Shafter and his command.

The Spanish troops in Santiago province are much more numerous than was originally thought, and Pando, with his 8,000 men, it is believed, is much closer to Santiago than the Cuban agents and spies thought possible. *The New York Journal,* June 30.

Sibonney

C hristopher whacked away at the jungle with his machete. Though General Garcia had ordered him to rejoin General Costillo's division supporting the Americans at Daiqueri and *Siboney*, Christopher hated both—whack—the idea of joining Costillo's—whack—division and the—whack—idea of fighting alongside the—whack—Americans. He wanted to continue fighting as he had for so many—whack—months and years, with Cubans against the—whack—Spaniards. Ever since his battalion had been bombarded by the—whack—American—whack—navy seven days earlier, he had wanted to stay as far away from the—whack—fucking—whack Yankees as possible.

"Christopher?" He stopped his slashing and looked at Theresa's face which, like his own, streamed with filthy sweat. "How much further to the beach?"

He shifted his eyes and glanced at the foremost group of the hundred soldiers he'd been allowed to bring along, many of whom had recently been discharged from the hospital. Turning from his men back to Theresa, he shrugged his shoulders and said, "I don't know. Early this afternoon sometime. Maybe another hour to the beach. Soon enough, Little One." He reached over and stroked some of the sweat and grime from her forehead and cheeks.

A wave of sadness swept over him. She looks so frail, so worn, he thought. If Cuba is a woman, Theresa could be her statue. She has given everything—except her life. She has received nothing. Even Consuelo had a few years of happiness. He turned again to the almost impenetrable vines. Whack. Whack. The machete was becoming too heavy to lift. He would let one of his men lead the way. But only in a minute, after he had regained control.

Was it all, finally, about over? And would it all, finally, be worth the horror and suffering and cruelty and sacrifice? He thought again of Theresa, of the lines forming around her deep-set eyes, of the ragged tunic and duck trousers that made her look as though she were twelve going on fifty, and of the long-term malnutrition that was already beginning to attack her skin and teeth. Yes, Theresa was a fit symbol for Cuba. But she was also his. He wanted nothing more, he now knew, than to protect her and love her. He wanted to give her children as he and Consuelo had given each other children. And he wanted to see those children grow as Cuba would grow—free, strong, self-sufficient. He drew a deep breath, sheathed his machete, and stood at the side of the trail, motioning the men behind him to continue on.

"You should not be working so hard when the fever is trying to come back." Theresa poured some water from her canteen onto her threadbare, green, polka-dot bandana and used it to wash his forehead.

"I know," he answered, trying to smile away his depression. "Theresa, remember when I gave you this bandana?

"Yes, Christopher, I remember." She rinsed the large, faded piece of once bright silk. "In February, when we left Havana after...executing that beast and..." She shivered violently. "It was less than five months ago, but it seems like years." She held the square of silk up to the light, carefully inspecting the large worn spots, where the threads were separating.

"It has been a lifetime, Theresa." He rose to his feet. "Let's go. The sooner we get to the east side of the harbor and find Costillo, the sooner we can rest."

Theresa nodded. "And wash."

* * * * *

"I can't even find our supply depot, so how do you expect me to find Freddy?" Michael folded his arms, as if daring Alex to criticize him.

"I don't expect anything as far as Freddy's concerned, but he couldn't have just disappeared."

"Maybe he's not off the *Yucatan* yet."

"Shee-it!" Alex ignored Michael's cynical suggestion and started down the beach in a new direction. He shouldered his way through the throngs of soldiers, both American and Cuban, through the increasing numbers of starving refugees who had appeared from nowhere, and through the growing mountains of equipment. Since the regiment had already received a small trickle of supplies, logic told him that Freddy had to be on the beach somewhere.

"Lieutenant Jackson!" Alex stopped and turned around. David Vandervoort stood next to Michael, who was still standing in the middle of the beach with his arms crossed. David was beckoning to Alex, and Michael was shaking his head in disbelief.

"I've found him," David said as soon as Alex was close enough for him to drop the formal, military address the three friends reserved for public consumption. "He has the supplies stored around the bend, about one hundred yards in from the beach."

"Christ almighty!" Alex exclaimed. "Why'd he do that? We may never have found him "

"He said he could guard the supplies a lot more easily if they were off the beach," David said. "You know, keep them away from the other regiments—and away from the Cubans."

Neither David nor Michael could help grinning at the conflicting emotions that crossed Alex's face. And Michael, who had regained his usually even temper, said, "It is a good idea, and we'd better let him know it."

Alex nodded. Though he was getting tired of treating Freddy like a hurt twelve-year old, the man had managed to shape up. "Yep, you're right, Michael. As usual," he added, a little chagrined to have his friend tell him something he should have already known. "Let's go see him."

The trio threaded their way back through the milling crowd and piled supplies. Suddenly, Alex stopped and pointed at a group of Cuban soldiers, who were wearing blue U.S. Army tunics, most of which didn't fit, and carrying U.S. blanket rolls. "What the hell do they think they're doing?" He dashed over to the group of Cubans, whirled a huge Negro around, and looked into eyes that blazed up immediately with open rage. "Where did you get this?" Alex yelled. He pointed at the blue wool coat with sergeant's stripes the man was carrying over his arm. The rest of the Cubans, including three women, gathered around the huge Negro, whose left hand was wrapped in a filthy bandage.

"Maybe he doesn't speak English," Michael suggested, glancing uneasily from Alex to David to the Cuban and back again.

Only Alex seemed not to notice the situation he had placed them in.

Though he detested the chore, he was preoccupied with the regiment's supplies and resentful of every hour he had to spend away from "L" Troop. The Cuban scavengers were the proverbial last straw. Ignoring his friends, he glared at the Cubans, grabbed at the blue wool tunic, jerked it hard three times and repeated, "Where did you get this?"

Michael stepped forward, smiled at the Negro and said in Spanish, "My lieutenant would like to know, sir, how you and your friends came by these uniforms and packs."

Fidel grinned broadly, a signal his companions immediately imitated. "The soldiers of your General Lawton threw them away four or five days ago. They were too hot. We do not have very much. We never throw anything away. At night, in the winter, when it is cold, these beautiful wool coats will be our friends. Is that not so?" Fidel could not keep his eyes from Alex's face. What was there about this *Yanqui?*

Michael nodded and translated for Alex, who shook his head. "Do you believe him?"

"Yes, but I'll ask who he is and the name of his outfit." Without waiting for Alex's approval, he turned back to Fidel. "My name is Corporal Michael Archuletta. This is my officer, Lieutenant Jackson. May I have the pleasure of your name and rank?"

"My name is Fidel Federico. I am a captain in the Cuban Army of Liberation." He drew himself up proudly, looked hard at Alex, and became very excited. "My officer is also Jackson. The eyes. They are the same. You are Christopher's baby brother." Without waiting for Michael to translate, he grabbed Alex in a bear hug and yelled, "Christopher's brother, Christopher's brother."

"Stop! He is wounded," Michael yelled.

Even as Alex screamed, however, Fidel felt his own pain in his wounded hand. As soon as Fidel put him down, Alex dropped to the ground, holding his ribs, and rocked back and forth in a barely controlled moan.

"He knows your brother," Michael said, bending over to touch Alex's shoulder. "This man is a captain, believe it or not, and he is in your brother's outfit."

Alex continued to rock back and forth but nodded at Michael's words. Finally he looked up, smiled weakly at Fidel, and asked, "Where is he?"

When Michael finished translating, a tall, lightly tanned woman moved to Fidel's side. "My name is Judith Sandoval-Rabinsky," she said in English, sticking her hand out, first to Alex and then to his two friends. "I, too, am a friend of your brother. He saved my life." Noticing the confused looks passing back and forth between the *Yanquis*, she smiled archly and added: "Yes, I am a Jew, but I am also, like your brother, a Cuban. All my family have died in the revolution."

"All?" was all Alex could get out. The woman was wildly beautiful, a black-haired amazon.

Michael was even more impressed, not because she was Jewish, or strangely out of place with this band of Negro and mulatto revolutionaries, but rather because, for the first time since Sky Woman's death, he saw something in a woman's face and heard something in her voice that made his mouth run dry.

Judith nodded her head several times. "Yes, brother of our friend, all."

Amos Jordan's words at the Tampa Bay Hotel rushed back to Alex's mind, registering more strongly and far more painfully than they had originally. "And my brother's family. I have heard that they too..."

"Yes," Judith assented quietly, in a tone that made her seem at least twenty years his senior. "Only Theresa is left."

"Who's she?"

"Theresa is many people. She is the younger sister of Christopher's dead wife. She is a captain in the army of Cuba Libre. She is a woman who has made unbelievable sacrifices for our revolution." She touched Fidel's arm and looked up at him with eyes that revealed her heart.

Without realizing just how or why, Michael felt his stomach tighten.

"She is also Christopher's companion. It is she who has kept his soul from dying."

Throughout the exchange, Fidel glanced back and forth between his Judith and their new friend. He understood the sense if not the words of what was passing between the two. Christopher will be pleased, he thought. Maybe he will forgive me for forgetting about the flag during that bad day on the beach. The incident at the small fortress still stood between them, a tender, invisible barrier that neither of them mentioned.

"I'm sorry to ask again," Alex asked. "But you didn't tell me where I can find Christopher." Suddenly his eyes lit up, he snapped his fingers, said "Come!" and marched rapidly up the beach, beckoning the entire party to follow him.

"Here!" David said. "Off to the right." Alex merely nodded and turned away from the beach. A dozen yards from the supply dump, Alex halted and waited for the rest of the group to gather around. One of the three men in front of the supply tents ducked inside. A moment later Freddy charged toward them. "Well? Judith. Where can I find Christopher?"

"He should be here later this afternoon," Judith said, puzzled by Alex's flight down the beach. A panting, wild-eyed officer charged toward Alex, then stood patiently, but imploringly at Alex's side, like an old dog that has sniffed out its master in a crowd.

"Christopher has been fighting on the other side of the harbor," Judith continued. "All of us are part of his battalion. Your navy killed and wounded many on the first day of the battle. I stayed with these men so that they could get your better medicine."

"You're a nurse?" Michael interrupted, all the more intrigued. Among his wife's people, the *Dineh*, healers were highly respected.

"Not really," Judith answered. "But I am all that we have."

Christopher will be here soon, Alex thought. Finally. He turned to Freddy, who was yearning to be noticed. "Break open enough supplies for these people to have a good meal tonight." Ignoring Freddy's look of disapproval, Alex turned back to Judith. "How many men will Christopher be bringing with him?"

"I don't know how many will still be alive. They have been fighting hard all week. Maybe a hundred."

Alex raised his eyebrows. General Wheeler had given him the impression that the Cubans hadn't been doing any fighting at all, and that they were spending all their time scavenging and stealing. He turned back to Freddy. "Give this woman and her soldiers enough food for a hundred good suppers."

"B-b-but..." Freddy was shocked. He had gotten the regiment's supplies ashore and found an excellent area for the supply depot, had, in short, done the best job of his career. Throughout the entire three days since completing the transfer of supplies from the Yucatan, he had fantasized about how pleased Alex would be with his work. But now? Not a word of thanks. Not a single 'well-done, Lieutenant.' Nothing but an insane request to give their carefully hoarded food to this amazon and her band of niggers. "N-no!" he finally blurted. "I'm s-senior to you, and I w-w-won't do it."

"Lieutenant Nelson," Alex said more carefully. "These people are our allies. They're from my brother's outfit, and they're very hungry. We can spare the food."

"No! G-goddamnit. I g-got these supplies here." He stamped his foot and pointed to the ground. "These s-supplies are not for any d-dago niggers, and they're n-not f-f-for any other r-regiment. They're for the Rough Riders."

"Lieutenant Nelson?"

Freddy looked at Archuletta, who was glaring at him. He could feel himself backing down. Even though he knew he was right, Freddy had used all his energy and all his small capacity for rebellion to put up even this token battle. He looked Michael in the eye for a second or two and then stared at the ground.

"If you don't follow Lieutenant Jackson's request right this minute, I'm going to tell the entire regiment about that piece of scrimshaw whalebone you wear around a particular part of your body."

Freddy felt betrayed. Archuletta's blow found its mark. He turned from the group without another word and slipped back into his headquarters tent.

Twenty minutes later, the Cubans were laden down with more than enough food for a good feast. As they started to move back to the beach, Alex shook hands with Fidel and Judith. "Tell Christopher I'll spend the night here. Tomorrow afternoon I'll have to get back to Las Guasimas, because..." He started to mention the planned offensive against San Juan but thought better of it. That would be taking too big a chance.

"Yes, we know, Lieutenant." Judith smiled thinly. We, too, are a part of your attack."

Alex blushed. "I'm sorry. I..."

"No, no, no. We Cubans know what your leaders think of us, and we know that we don't look like much. But we have been fighting the Spaniards a long time. Thank you for the food."

Alex nodded and watched the Cubans file away toward the beach and their rendezvous with his brother. I wonder if they really can fight? he thought, shaking his head. In addition to the other two women, he had noticed among the rag-tag group an old man and two young boys. Despite their leanness, their rags, and the apparent peculiarities of their recruiting and supply systems, however, Alex could not help feeling a certain awe for these people whose revolution he and his countrymen had come to win.

Still bemused by his first encounter with Cubans, he found Freddy inside his tent. "We can make at least two trips by night-fall," he said, as he ducked his head under the flap. "We've got fifty mules left, and I want them moving back and forth every daylight hour."

"We're way ahead of you, Lieutenant." Michael said from his perch atop one of the packing crates. "David's already headed back down to the beach to bring up the supply train. And Lieutenant Anderson here has everything marked and sorted. Our supplies are ready to roll. "

Alex glanced over at Freddy, who was lying on his back, but Freddy refused to look at him or in any way acknowledge his presence. "I'm sorry," Alex said. "I got carried away out there. But that is my brother's outfit, and they are hungry."

"And what about our troops?" Freddy snapped, swinging his feet back to the floor. "Don't you th-think they're hungry?"

"No, I don't," Alex answered evenly. "At the moment at least, hunger is not one of our problems. The line finally has plenty of chow, thanks to your efficiency, Fred."

What in the hell have I started? Alex asked himself. And how in the hell am I going to get out of it? He looked over at Michael, who was sitting on his crossed legs, like a contented Buddha. He clearly had no intention of interfering.

"Fred, I'm truly sorry," Alex repeated. No response. Gritting his teeth, he strode over to Freddy's bunk and sat down next to him. After several minutes of strained silence, he put his arm around Freddy's shoulder. "I was so shocked to hear about my brother that I forgot to compliment you on a job well done. Before we ran into the Cubans, we were talking about what an outstanding job you are doing with the supplies. Isn't that right, Michael?"

Alex glared at Michael, who said, "Truth, Freddy. I don't even think much about cutting your throat anymore."

"But you w-w-w-w-ere going to tell about my wh-whale bone," he screamed at Michael. "That was a d-dirty t-t-t-trick!"

Alex saw tears springing to Freddy's eyes and realized that he was coming unhinged again. "Fred! Goddamnit!" He jerked Freddy to his feet and glared at him. "I said, we are proud of you! I'm proud of you. YOU ARE DOING A DAMNED GOOD JOB! All right?"

Freddy stared back, bug-eyed. Finally he nodded. Alex released him, patted him on the back and added, in a more conversational voice, "I said I was sorry. And I am." He sat back down on the bunk and after a very long moment, Freddy sat down beside him.

"I just didn't w-want to give our supplies to those d-dago niggers, Alex. You d-don't have any idea how hard it was to g-get them off the ship and l-l-landed—and collected here."

Alex nodded. " I think I do, Fred. You may be the only person on this entire beach who knows what in the hell he's doing. This has probably been your outstanding achievement in the war, if not in your career."

"Do you really th-think so?" Freddy asked, his innocent face glowing.

Alex knew that this particular battle was over. He nodded his head in strong affirmation.

"I guess I was d-d-disappointed. I b-built up this picture of what you'd say when you s-saw the supplies, how p-pleased you'd be. Then you just m-marched in with those d-d-d-d-dago niggers and ignored m-m-me." He stopped for a second and then blurted, "I thought we'd have a p-party this evening, just the f-four of us. I even brought p-presents."

"What?" Alex looked at Michael, who stared at the ceiling of the tent. "I'm sorry. I didn't mean to ruin anything. Let's have the party anyhow. I'm sure David and Michael and I will really enjoy it. Right, Michael?"

"Truth, Fred. I don't think I've ever been to a real, honest-to-God party before."

* * * * *

Shortly after Christopher arrived in camp, Fidel approached to make his report. Christopher grimaced when he saw his friend's still bandaged hand. He could not forget what he had said, nor the look on Fidel's face when the meaning behind the insult had registered. Christopher knew that the morning of the American shelling had driven an invisible wedge between them, and that the wedge would be difficult to extract.

But now Fidel was grinning. "I have met your brother. He is here. He is on the beach."

Christopher was stunned. Just that morning he and Theresa had been talking about Alex. The American commodore had been right. Though he felt a new weight descend upon him, Christopher put his arm on Fidel's shoulder. "Come, walk with me, my friend. Walk with me and tell me what you have seen, and how you have been."

An hour later the two men were still sitting beneath a royal palm on a small rise that looked south over the beach to the ocean. Almost a mile out in the bay the American ships hovered on the darkening sea like grey ghosts.

Each man was lost in his own thoughts, and neither had spoken for almost a quarter of an hour. Christopher was content to watch the lights of the ships blink on one by one. Despite a minor attack of the fever, he felt healthier and more content than he had in months. Though he was close to exhaustion, both physically and spiritually, he knew he was more than holding his own with his equally malnourished and exhausted troops. Theresa's love was a balm, and it was working. And for the moment there was rest, quiet, a beautiful sunset, and the lights blinking on in the bay.

Whatever was to happen during the remaining weeks of the war, Christopher felt that he and Fidel had patched over at least the surface of a serious rift. If he was both angered and saddened that his romantic fool of a baby brother had come to Cuba, at least the anger would have to wait. In the meantime, he liked hearing what Fidel had told him about Alex's generosity. The war was nearly finished and no harm would come to his brother. Like many of the Cuban officers, he felt that had the Spanish been serious about fighting off an American invasion, they would have opposed the American landing far more vigorously. They certainly possessed the capacity.

For the first time in the six months since Consuelo's death, he gave thought to the future, to his cane fields, to the consuming and productive work that might finally be. Perhaps Alex will stay in Cuba and work the fields with us, he mused.

"We had better return, Colonel. Like the Spaniards, the *Yanquis* shoot anything that moves after dark."

Christopher started to rise, but thought of something he wanted to say and sat back down. He placed his hand on his captain's knee. "Fidelito, I am pleased to hear news of my brother. But I would also like to hear about yourself, about your hand, about how you have been this past week. How goes it with you, my friend?"

"I am well, except for this *Yanqui* flea bite." He held up his hand. "I have a good woman and a good friend. This evening I had a good meal, donated by my good friend's good brother. What else is there?"

"The war will be over soon. Very soon."

"Yes, I have sensed that to be the truth."

Something about Fidel's flat, emotionless tone bothered Christopher. "What will you do? You will return with me to the land, no? And help me re-build?"

"I try not to think about after the war. "But, yes, I would like that. I have always been happy with you, Christopher."

"And Judith?"

A shadow passed across Fidel's eyes. "She wants for me to return with her to Havana. To live there, maybe to reopen her father's...shop."

After a pause, Christopher said, "Perhaps one of you will change." He hated the note of falseness that had crept into his voice, and was aware that Fidel had also heard it.

"Yes, perhaps one of us will change." Shaking off the well-intentioned lies, Fidel rose to his feet.

Chapter Thirty-Three

HOBSON'S FIRST MESSAGE FROM A SPANISH PRISON

* * * *

Greensboro, Ala., June 29—Judge Hobson received this morning the following telegram from his son, Richard Pearson Hobson, the hero who sank the *Merrimack* at the mouth of Santiago Harbor, and who is now a prisoner. "Santiago, June 28.—My health continues good. Feel no uneasiness about me." This was the first news the anxious parents had received from their son. *The New York Journal*, June 30.

Sibonney

"Where are you going, Michael?" Alex asked. He sat back from the fire and rubbed his aching ribs.

"Making the rounds once more to see how our mules and skinners are doing before Fred gets his party going."

"That's f-fine, Michael," Freddy purred. "Just d-don't be gone too long, or you'll m-m-miss out."

David didn't bother to look up. His bespectacled head was so close to the kerosene lantern that the heat should have singed his hair, but he was happily immersed in Whitman's *Leaves of Grass* and oblivious to everything else going on around him.

Michael walked from the warm glow of the fire into the damp night. He stood quietly for a moment, accustoming his eyes to the darkness. As he watched the hazy moon rise above the *Sierra Maestra*, he thought of the clarity of New Mexico nights and the depth of the sky. Sky Woman's face floated before him.

Maybe tonight. Maybe tomorrow night, but soon. Then your spirit can rest. As he made the promise, Sky Woman's beautiful face and laughing eyes came into sharper focus. He waited in the darkness and allowed the pangs of a great hunger to rise up from the pit of his stomach. "I miss you!" he whispered to the sky.

"I miss you!" floated to him as a soundless echo, a light breeze that called him back to the present. Suddenly, her face appeared to him, awash with pain. A terrible memory took hold of him. "They staked me out!" she cried. "They spread my legs as far apart as they could. Then they touched me with their filthy hands." She leaned over and vomited onto the floor of the hogan. "When they finished with me, the shorter man stuck his knife inside me and twisted...and twisted...and twisted."

Once she had told him this, her face was very still and composed, but her eyes glowed with sadness. He knew she was dying, and that he could do nothing—except watch and wait and curse the men who had done this thing to her.

"Sonefabitchin' land crab!" A voice cursed from a distance of fifteen or twenty yards, but it seemed to rush up on Michael and explode right in his ear. Sky Woman's face and voice disintegrated, just as their life together had disintegrated.

Shaken by the memory, Michael stood still a bit longer and focused on the sounds of a large and eager army. Here and there a few soldiers were still preparing their evening meal. Others strolled along the beach, clearly outlined in the soft light of the almost full moon. Men were stretched out on the ground, their backs propped against their packs. Many were smoking. From what seemed to be a great distance, Michael could hear a guitar and the plaintive lyrics of "The Streets of Laredo." Suddenly, a bat swooped from the jungle and cut across his line of vision. He heard the bat's high-pitched screee-ee, and the vision of thousands of men at rest fell away like the shards of a shattered vase. Michael shivered and walked onto the small encampment of Rough Rider mules and skinners.

"Evenin', Mex," Big Bill Pike boomed in his deepest glad-to-see-you voice. "How ya be?"

"Fine, Bill. How are you and the rest of the men doing?" Michael looked around the large circle and nodded or waved to each of the men. When he had completed his greetings, he frowned slightly. The men were passing around a huge, wicker-covered jug of Baccardi. "How much of that Cuban fire water do you have, Bill?"

"Oh, that's all, Mex, jes the one. We bought er off a nigger refugee fer one U.S. of A. buck. These here Cubans may be as ratty lookin' a bunch o' coons and half coons as ever I seen, but they's sure as hell friendly. Ain't that right, boys?"

Several of the troopers nodded and grinned. "Yep, thas right, Billy Boy. That is fer sure a real fact."

"Yessir, Mex," Big Bill continued. "These here coons is jes like the coons I useter trap in the Rockies, 'fore the bottom fell outa the egg-suckin' market. They steal ya blind, but they'll also sell ya anything they got, which ain't much."

"Bill, we're starting the next supply train up the hill at 0600 hours. Captain Jackson wants these men ready to go. On time. Is that clear?" Michael looked around the circle one more time.

"Yeh, Corporal Mex, it's clear," Pike muttered, suddenly less affable. "Shee-it, man, it ain't but a gallon er so."

"Where's Shorty?" Michael asked. Big Bill grinned and some of the other men giggled. As if waiting for his cue, Shorty sauntered back into the clearing, pulling along behind him a mulatto girl.

"Howdy, Mex," Shorty said, walking up to the fire. He and the girl stopped in front of Pike and Archuletta. "You wanna turn, Mex? She'll do anything you want fer half a buck and some food. If ya jes wanna fuck her, she'll do it fer the food." Shorty dropped his hand and grabbed the girl's buttocks. The girl grinned, uncomprehendingly, rocking from one foot to the other.

"No thanks, Shorty," Michael managed to say. "What does she do with the food she's getting from you men?" The girl's skinny arms and legs were covered with open sores.

"Hell, Mex," Pike answered. "We don't know what she does with the food. She must have family er kids er somethin'. She jes takes the food somewhere an' comes right back fer another screwin'."

"I've got the guard roster," Michael interrupted, anxious to change the subject before he lost control. "Anderson, Chip." He glanced at the tall Swede, a storekeeper from Albuquerque. "You're up from 2200 'til 0200. Shorty?" He looked Shorty straight in the eye. "You've got the duty from 0200 'til 0600. Wake the men at 0600."

"Shee-it, Mex," Shorty whined. "That ain't fair. I been screwin' this here gal for the last half hour and I gotta work tomorrow."

"Then you'd better get to bed and get some rest." Michael raised his voice to make sure that everyone in the circle heard his next words. "I checked the roster, my friend. Every man here has had the duty since you have. Your turn!" He turned to the other skinners who, the Swede excepted, nodded their heads in obvious approval of Archuletta's sense of justice.

"All right," Michael continued. "Swede. Shorty. I want you to station yourselves by the tall palm tree just at the jungle side of our picket line. Every fifteen minutes take a stroll around our perimeter. Understood?"

Shorty and the Swede nodded. Michael glared at the two men for a moment and walked out of the circle into the night. When he was less than twenty yards from the fire he stopped and listened to Shorty's indignant outburst: "That goddamn, sheep-fuckin' greaser. Who the hell does he think he is? Teddy must have his head so far up his ass that his shoulders is gotta be hurtin'. Whoever heard a puttin' a fuckin' Mexican, dago spic bastard in charge a white folk?" Michael noticed that only a couple of the voices around the fire growled assent to Shorty's words. Michael smiled. You'll get yours, Son of Shit, he thought, pleased with his plan. Swede was a famous insomniac who never fell asleep on guard duty, which meant that Shorty would be awakened for his shift. Shorty was notorious for being able to fall asleep anywhere.

* * * *

"G-gee, Michael. We've been w-waiting for you."

"Sorry, Fred. I had to post the guard."

Alex looked up from where he was cleaning his pistol. "Who'd you choose?"

"The Swede and Shorty."

"Shorty? He's totally worthless. I can't believe you chose him and Pike for this supply detail." He stared at Michael, trying for the hundredth time to determine what made his friend tick.

Though he could feel the sweat breaking out on his palms, Michael turned to Alex and said, "I brought most of my squad, just as David brought most of his. I don't trust either of those grubbers enough to leave them alone." After a short pause, he forced a smiled and added, "Besides, they're your friends."

"That's so much, bullshit, Michael, and you know it. I thought they were colorful, you know, real Westerners, when I arrived in Santa Fe. Besides, they adopted me so forcefully that..." He glared at Michael, who was smiling at his defensiveness.

"Where's David?" Michael asked, changing the subject.

"He'll be back in a minute," Freddy replied. "He went to the l-l-latrine." Freddy sat at his field desk, hovering over a small pile of brown, paper-wrapped, rectangular packages.

"All right, let's get this show on the road," David said, as he ducked under the tent flap. The lantern glinted on his glasses and turned them into two gold coins.

"G-good! Good! Good!" Freddy repeated, rubbing his hands together. "Pull your chairs up around my d-desk." As soon as his three grinning friends and sometime tormentors complied, he continued. "When I was getting our supplies unloaded, I f-found a few things j-j-j-just lying around." He grinned sheepishly, obviously pleased with himself. "So I l-l-liberated them."

Alex laughed. "Let's see what you've got, Fred."

"Presents," Freddy giggled. "Here's one for you, Alex, and one for you, David, and one for you, M-m-michael." He was almost apologetic as he handed the sheepherder his gift, not because gift was in any way inferior to the others, but because he was still half afraid of the man, whose temperament struck him as unreliable. "P-please open them."

"Christmas in June," David said. "And I'm not even a Christian." He unwrapped his package and discovered a leather-bound volume of Dickens' *Bleak House*, a two inch thick tome with gold leaf on the pages. "Well, I'll be. Fred, this is a beautiful gift. I wish I had something to give in return."

"No!" Freddy shook his head. "You already have g-given me something. I've never had any f-f-friends before."

David felt tears coming to his eyes, and turned away to leaf through his Dickens. "What did you get, Michael?"

Michael held out his present, a copy of Plato's *Dialogues*, also leather-bound. "Thank you," he said, lifting the beautiful book in his hand. "This book is very appropriate, and you are very thoughtful." Almost immediately he started to chuckle, as did the others.

"That's the most stilted statement I've ever heard you make, Michael," Alex said. "You sound like one of my professors at Harvard."

David poked Michael in the ribs and winked at Alex. "What do you expect from someone who actually enjoys philosophy?"

"Now just a second, David," Alex replied. "You know damn good and well that I took a lot of philosophy at Harvard."

"That's right, old sport. But if I remember correctly, you didn't actually enjoy it. You didn't read philosophy in your spare time, Alex. You read military biographies. Right?"

"Open your p-present, Alex." Freddy could barely contain himself as he watched Alex unwrap his gift. "D-do you like it?"

"Jesus H. Christ!" Alex exclaimed. "You bet I do, Fred. You bet I do." He passed around the leather-bound copy of Plutarch's *Lives of the Noble Greeks and Romans.* "This book is very appropriate," he said, mimicking Michael and drawing another laugh from the group.

"Freddy, old buddy?" Freddy looked over at David, who had suddenly become somber. "Where did you get these beautiful books?"

"I t-told you. I l-l-l-liberated them from the *Yucatan.*" He took a step backwards and rolled his eyes from one friend to another.

"You stole them?" David asked, his eyes twinkling but his face set in firm control. "Isn't that a sin for you Christians?"

Freddy was catching on. Pretending not to have noticed David's eyes, he stammered back, "N-nope. That's part of the Law of Moses. That law only applies to J-Jews. It's just that not all Christians have c-caught on yet."

Alex and Michael clapped, delighted with Freddy's spirit. He's come a long way, Alex thought, as he remembered the cowering mass of protoplasm he had first encountered in San Antonio. Only occasionally now, did Freddy revert back to those early days of total incompetence.

Freddy bent over his desk magician-like, and jerked open a large drawer. He pulled out a roast duck packed in ice, spread his hands and said, "*V-v-voila!*" Fucking stuttering, he thought, as he bent over another drawer. This time he pulled the act off to his complete and immense satisfaction. He whipped out a bottle of Napoleon brandy and placed it gently on the desk. "*Et voila,*" he whispered.

"Where in the hell did you get these?" Alex exclaimed.

Freddy refused to answer. Rather, he beamed his over-flowing sense of good will and said, " Now, let's have a p-party."

An hour later the four were leaning back in their chairs, feet propped atop Freddy's desk. They were full, at least partially drunk, and all but Michael totally content.

"This is one fine evening," Alex said. "The best dinner and the best evening I've had since before joining the regiment." Charlotte's lovely face and flawless body appeared in the front of his mind. For a brief moment he succumbed to sharp pangs of loneliness and lust.

Momentarily struck by the shabby military clutter that filled the brown canvas tent, Alex shrugged and pulled himself back to Freddy's party.

Freddy looked around at Michael and David, who nodded their assent. "It's almost p-perfect. If I c-could just stop stuttering."

"Try pebbles," Alex said. "That's what Demosthenes did. Talked with his mouth full of pebbles all the time. It helped him get rid of his stammer."

"That's right," David said. "Only problem: Nobody could understand a word he said." Everyone laughed.

"Fred?" David continued. "Have you always stuttered?"

"No. Just since I was f-fourteen-and-a-half."

"Is that right?" Alex asked. Do you know why? Is it linked to that whale-bone penis protector you wear all the time?"

"N-n-n-no!" He shook his head, as if to emphasize the non-connection of the two phenomena. "But yes, I think I d-d-do know why I s-started."

"I'd rather hear about the whale-bone penis protector," David said, hugely curious.

"I d-d-d-don't want to t-talk about that."

"But you're willing to tell us about how you started stuttering?" David pushed the quarter-full bottle-of brandy back to Freddy, who took a long sip, opened his mouth, and drew the air in across his brandy-coated tongue. Tears blinded his eyes. "Wow! That stuff is p-potent. S-sure, I'll tell you about that. D-doesn't everybody l-like to t-talk about the time they were seduced by an older w-w-woman?"

Alex dropped his feet from the desk to the ground with a thud. "You're kidding! That caused you to stutter?"

Freddy nodded. "I think so. Th-that and my p-parents." He looked around and noticed that, perhaps for the first time since he had met the three, he had their total attention. "Her name was Mrs. Bridgett. Bridgett C-c-conners. She was my g-governess's s-sister, but she wasn't at all like my g-g-governess."

"And she seduced you?" David asked.

Freddy nodded. "I d-don't know what else you'd c-call it. When my p-parents found out they f-f-fired her, and sent me off to b-boarding school. They never l-l-let me come home. I don't think they ever really l-l-loved me."

In the silence that followed, Alex thought of his own childhood, and of his relationship with his older brother hero, his protector and, in many ways, his father. "You know, " he finally said, "all the time I was growing up, I thought my father loved me, but now I'm not so sure."

"I thought your father died when you were still small," David said.

"True, but I grew up on memories of him holding me on his knee and telling me war stories. Even as a toddler, I'd follow him around and listen to his tall tales about the good old days when he and Joe Wheeler chased Yankees."

"Our J-Joe Wheeler?" Freddy raised his head in disbelief, distracted from his grief.

"Haven't I mentioned it? Yeh, Wheeler was a general even then, and my pa served with him. That's all, I mean absolutely all, the old man ever talked about."

"Pass that brandy," David said. "We may have a greater need to get maudlin tomorrow—after the battle. And why are you so quiet, Michael? This is supposed to be a party. You okay?"

Archuletta shrugged. " I'm sorry, friends, he said in a rare moment of candor. "Tonight my heart is with my dead wife."

Chapter Thirty-Four

ANOTHER REPORTED FIGHT AT SANTIAGO
Madrid Hears We Were Repulsed

*President Received Dispatches at Midnight and Reports of an
Engagement Are Circulated in Washington*
OFFICIALS DENY, HOWEVER, THAT THERE WAS A BATTLE
* * * * *

RUMOR THAT GERMAN MARINES ARE IN MANILA
Story Discredited....Our Government Alert
The New York Journal, July 1.

Sibonney, June 30

Though he had been in his hammock for almost four hours, Christopher had managed sleep only in the ragged spaces between nightmares. He wiped the sweat from his forehead and repeated the lie: It must be the fever. But he knew that this minor malarial bout was not the problem. Sometimes he didn't know which was worse, the Gordian knot of his muscle-tensing thoughts or the inter-woven horrors of his dreams. After hours of tossing and turning in the hammock, thought and nightmare had merged. He stood in front of their low adobe house. Consuelo held him tightly, sobbing between words. He was holding the reins of his horse, anxious to mount and be gone. Two of his men waited for him at the end of the lane. It was early in the war and he was leaving them for the first time. "I love our daughters, and I will stay here and care for them." She raised her eyes and looked fiercely into his. "But my spirit goes with you. I am more Amazon than house-maid."

He pressed her against his breast and said, "I know, my African dove. You should have been a Valkari. Know you are with me all the days of my journey."

"It will be a long one, Christopher. The Spaniard has already shown that he will not go home easily."

He could feel the steel in her. Then she pulled away from him and receded into the mists. He tried to follow her, but his horse pulled him toward the road, his waiting friends, and the war. "Consuelo," he called. Nothing. He could barely see her. She raised her hand in farewell.

"Consuelo!"

"I am sorry, Christopher. She is dead. They are all dead." He looked around. The mist had changed to rain. People were screaming and running past him. He shook his head, but the bedlam wouldn't cease. People with huge heads and skeleton bodies were crawling or being

carried through the rain. Suddenly Theresa stood before him, looking almost as thin as one of the skeletons. Her huge black eyes, which
looked so much like Consuelo's, stared at him. Her eyes had sunk deep
into her skull and they seemed to have lost their light. As he looked into
them, he thought he could see Consuelo. She was still waving, but she
was not alone. Their three daughters were also waving. All four faces
were sad, immobile, and they receded further and further into Theresa's
deep-set eyes.

"Consuelo!" He yelled at the top of his lungs. "Please!"

"She is dead, Christopher. They are all dead."

He stared at Theresa. Why was she saying such things? Why did she
look like that? Without realizing what he was doing, he balled his fist
and knocked her down. She lay in the mud and stared vacantly up at him
through the rain.

"Christopher!"

He felt someone shaking his shoulder. "Christopher!" He opened
his eyes and looked up. Theresa was standing over him. Although he
could see little but her white cotton shirt in the overcast night, he knew
it was Theresa rather than Consuelo who was shaking him awake. She
stood quietly at his side, the faint outline of a ghost.

Neither of them said anything for a moment. He reached out and
took her hand into both of his, just as his mother had taken his hand
between hers so many years and lives before. After a while he climbed
from the hammock, and led Theresa up a trail and into a clearing littered with large flat stones.

"The guards," she whispered frantically. "If the American guards
see us out, they will shoot us."

"We're not that close to their lines. Come!" They moved slowly in
the hazed over moonlight. Finally, Christopher felt a rock that was both
flat and free of land crabs. He sat, pulling Theresa down next to him. He
had not released her hand and, once seated, he brought her palm to his
lips and kissed it with far more sadness than passion.

Theresa said nothing, just sat and waited for him to continue.

"In my dream, Consuelo told me that you have always loved me."

Theresa smiled. "Did you need a dream to tell you that?"

He pulled her closer to massage her neck and upper back. No,
I didn't, and yes, I have known for a long time." He stopped for a

moment and listened to her breathing, which had become ragged. She was struggling to hold back tears. He dropped his hand from her back and sat quietly, not touching her.

After awhile he laughed and shook his head. "I just saw something with a little more clarity than usual."

"Oh?"

"Ever since my family—our family—died, you have been taking care of me, Theresa. You have given me everything you have. I have given you nothing."

"Is that what you see, Christopher?"

He nodded. "I always thought it was the other way around, that it was me taking care of my little sister-in-law. But we are more deeply connected. When I think of after the war, I think of us together, and that thought makes me happy."

Her hand came to life and squeezed his. "What are you saying? That you want me?"

" I am saying, if we live, I want our lives to be together. I want us to have children together, and grandchildren."

Theresa tried to suppress the great joy rising in her heart. "Tell me this, Christopher. "Is it me you want? Or am I as close as you can get to Consuelo?"

"I-I'm not sure," he whispered. "You have, in many ways, kept me alive. The few full moments I have known since Consuelo's death, I have known with you. I do not know what else I can say."

Theresa knew he was being truthful. She also knew that, however difficult life with him might be, she wanted only him. But she could not be a substitute Consuelo. She would not be a shadow. "Tell me something else."

"I think you too can make my soul sing."

Theresa squinted through the pre-dawn darkness. If I can just see his eyes, she thought. "I want very much for these things you are saying to be true. I want very, very much for you to love me. But why must you tell me these things now? Why not wait until after the war? It will not be much longer."

"Yes, miracle of miracles. But we are going into a huge battle, Theresa, larger than any we have ever seen. The day after tomorrow will begin the end for Spain."

"No, Christopher, my...almost...love. The tomorrow of the battle is now one day away. And maybe it will bring the beginning for Cuba, no?"

"Yes. My mind now is moving beyond the war, to the land. I keep thinking about the good work that lies before us, of planting and cutting cane—rather than cutting and planting bodies. It has been... so...fucking...long." She squeezed his hand, then stood and placed her arms around him, pulling his head forward against her breasts. "When I think of the hacienda and of the cane now, Theresa, it is always with you."

She leaned against his shoulder. You just want another strong arm to wield a machete in your fields, and a strong mulatto girl to spread her legs for you when your sap is ready to flow." She smiled, teasing him, and the two of them relaxed against each other, satisfied for the moment to feel their mutual strength and to listen to each other's breathing, a steady counter-point against the pre-dawn sounds of the jungle.

* * * * *

Michael could feel the slow passing of time just as acutely as he could feel the long-coiled tautness of his muscles, just as he could feel the sweat that poured from his body. He knew that it was time to act. That it was somewhere between 3:00 and 4:00 A.M. Everyone else in the tent had been asleep for at least three hours.

Is Shorty asleep? He wondered for the hundredth time. Is he asleep? Will I be able to find him? He tried to envision Sky Woman as he had found her that distant evening when he had returned from sheep camp.

Several times a year they had traveled the ninety miles to her parents' home in the Chuska Mountains, and once or twice a year they had attended dances and ceremonials. During the ebb and flow of the seasons, however, it was mostly just their sheep, horses, dog, and the two of them. Each was accustomed to days or even weeks of being alone. When they were together they spoke very little, communicating as much by looks and gestures as by words. In the long evenings around the small, pot-bellied stove that stood in the middle of the hogan, Michael would mend and polish his gear, or reread his few books. Sky Woman would card or spin her wool, or sit and daydream. He had encouraged her to read, but as a small girl she had been forced to leave her family and attend the Indian Agent's boarding school, which was a prison. She hated the school and hated books. And even as the happy wife of the Mexican-Irish sheepherder, she sometimes resented the books that seemed, so often, to come between them. She knew about their spells: When he was immersed in them, he was away and not in her world. Still, she knew that his love for her was stronger; it was of the earth. And he always returned to her.

Michael started. Someone outside the tent had cried out. He listened intently but nothing followed. I must get going, he thought, and slowly moved his feet from his bunk to the floor. His legs were heavy, reluctant to move. He realized that his once fierce passion to kill Shorty had settled into reluctant but bitter determination. When he had left the ashes of the hogan to commence his quest, his motivations had been simple and one-directional: to find the two men and kill them—as slowly and painfully as possible. In the intervening months, however, he had entered a variety of unfamiliar worlds, and been caught up in a strange new life. From an army-cluttered beachhead in southeastern Cuba, Sky Woman and his original impetus for vengeance were thousands of miles and at least one lifetime away.

As he picked up his pistol belt and lariat, a great sadness dragged at the pit of his stomach. With a slight shudder of self-disgust he realized that life and the future—regardless of how vague and unknown it seemed—were far more important than he would have thought even a few weeks earlier.

He moved through the camp quickly. Though the mule skinners were camped less than a five minute walk from the supply dump, Michael spent almost half an hour covering the distance. When he reached the jungle he stopped for a moment, alternately blessing and cursing the moon. Even in the thin cloud cover every shadow seemed alive. For more than ten minutes he moved at a snail's pace on his hands and knees. He had been sweating all night, but as he reached the jungle and stood up, he realized that he was soaking wet. He felt almost ethereal. After resting a moment, he moved west, erect this time, his hands sweeping slowly back and forth in front of his wide open, but now unseeing eyes, his feet moving cautiously in small circles before planting themselves on the spongy earth. A few feet, then a few yards. Every few minutes he stopped to listen, sometimes to the sounds of the night jungle, more often to the rapid shallowness of his own breathing.

When he reached the small clearing where he had posted Shorty, he stood quietly for a long time and listened for the sound he had been hunting: the slightly erratic and highly distinctive snore of his victim, who seemed to be no more than ten feet away. The light was clearer here. Once again on his hands and knees, he moved toward Shorty's snore. When he was within striking distance and could see the man sitting, head bent, at the base of the royal palm, he stopped and froze. The snoring had stopped; he realized that Shorty's eyes were open. "Who's there?" Shorty stammered, jolted awake by the same sharp senses that had kept him alive during his years in the Colorado mountains. Slowly, he pulled his pistol from its holster. "Wh-h-ho the fuck's there?" he repeated in a low hiss.

"Corporal Archuletta," Michael said, "Wake up, Shorty."

"Jesus Christ, Mex. You damn near scared the livin' shit right out o' me. What the hell ya think yer doin', sneakin' up on a guy like that? I'm already awake. Whacha doin'? Checkin' up on me?" Though he was still rattled and not yet totally oriented, Shorty managed to get the appropriate amount of wounded outrage into his voice.

"Lower your voice, Shorty. You're going to wake the whole camp," Michael hissed. "And what's your pistol out for, Private? Are you planning to shoot me?"

"Hell no, Mex. Not me." But as he replaced his pistol, Shorty thought, You sheep-fuckin' chile-eater. I'll get you yet.

Keeping his left side to Shorty, who just might have better than average night vision, Michael slid his own pistol from his holster. "We can't afford to take any chances." Just as he finished the sentence, Michael slammed the barrel of his .44 across the top of Shorty's head.

The man regained consciousness to find himself gagged and bound to the palm tree. Archuletta sat cross-legged in front of him, honing a knife on a small stone. Shorty tried to speak through his gag, but the cloth cut into his lips. "Wha-gh you do-ugh?"

Michael grimaced. "You want to know what's happening, don't you?" He realized that he hadn't known what he would tell Shorty; the words just flowed from his stomach and heart. Sky Woman appeared before him as she had earlier that evening. She was lying in the mud at the edge of the river, naked and still, covered with cuts and bruises. Michael talked, softly but with speed and intensity.

"You and a friend rode down to the San Juan River in April. A Navajo woman was bathing in the river." As he spoke, Sky Woman's image became clearer, larger, more insistent. He felt Shorty's knife probing and twisting between his thighs. Blood and filth crept down his body. His own sweat metamorphosed to a warm, sticky blend of Shorty's semen and Sky Woman's blood. He almost gagged at the fetid blackness crawling over him like a suffocating tide.

I must do this thing, he told himself, and sliced away Shorty's shirt. He removed the terrified man's belt, cut away the front of his trousers and jerked them roughly down around his knees. Then he carved "*Yanqui cabron*" on Shorty's heaving chest.

"The Navajo woman was my wife. You raped her. Then you cut her all over. Then you...stuck your knife up inside her. And turned. And turned. And..." Michael felt the bitter tears on his cheeks mixing with sweat. Sky Woman's hand reached out to reassure him.

He forced himself back under control, stuck the tip of his knife inside Shorty's nostril and, with his free hand, jerked the gag down far enough for the man to answer his question. "Don't move, *Cabron*, or you lose your nose." Though Shorty was blubbering and wanted to scream, the pain in his nose was far greater than the pain in his chest; he tried very hard to remain still. "Where is the man who was with you?"

"D-dead," Shorty gurgled. Michael twisted the knife point slightly. "Where is he? And who is he?" Shorty started to shake his head but immediately regretted the movement. "He's dead. I swear. He died of snake bite...on the...way to...Santa...Fe. And he's...the one who...did your wife, not me. I just...watched.."

"No! No, you're wrong, *Cabron*." Michael shook his head as though denying a friend's assertion that it would be a hot day. "Sky Woman described you. Exactly. She is with me now." He pushed the gag back into place and said, "I am going to kill you. I am going to cut you up and leave you to bleed to death and feed you to the crabs."

Staring straight into Shorty's horrified eyes, Michael dropped his knife down between the man's legs and cut. He felt the blood spurting over his fingers and turned away for a moment to gag. When he turned back, he realized that Shorty's moans were vibrating out through the open pores of his body, and that they could be heard. He opened Shorty's veins, first the thighs, then the wrists. The man was staring at him still, his mind seeking to comprehend the horror that consumed them both. Sky Woman's image was behind him, in front of him, all around him. He had felt her presence as a force that drove him toward the completion of the act he had initiated on that distant dawn when he had burned her body and their hogan. But now her image had become thinner, more distant. The insistent look on her face had dissolved to a horrified grimace, and disappeared.

He was alone with Shorty who was gurgling and gasping, and trying desperately to kick his feet, which Michael was sitting on. Michael heard his own breathing, shallow but explosive. He felt a form of despair he had never known. It began slowly, as Sky Woman's ghost receded, and progressed as a series of waves, each one more terrible than the last.

"I must leave this place of death," he said aloud, talking to Shorty's semi-conscious form as if they were both victims of a nameless demon. Michael cut the ropes holding Shorty to the tree and watched him fall forward. He turned the man over on his back and removed the gag.

"Please..." Shorty whispered.

Michael stared into the sightless eyes and cut Shorty's throat.

Chapter Thirty-Five

SPANISH ARMY IS IN CONFUSION

* * * *

Daqueri, June 30—One look at Santiago from the heights shows the utter confusion of the Spanish army and the hopelessness of their attempting to resist the invaders.

No man who has gone over this trail [from the Sevilla Road]; no man who was not at the terrible downpour of rain which drenched our army to the skin this afternoon, can understand the suffering of our troops and the heroism with which they bore it.

Cavalrymen and infantrymen toiled hour after hour through jungles of poisonous vines and high grass that cut like rough edges. The blistering tropical sunlight makes the skyline of distant hills shimmer. From the stagnant pools strange gray mists float upward, and vultures with outstretched wings look greedily down from above the vegetation.

Thousands of gigantic land crabs, splotched with yellow and red, wriggle and twist themselves along the sides of the road with leprous white claws clicking viciously—a ghastly, dreadful sight to young soldiers fresh from New York, Boston and Detroit. James Creelman: *The New York Journal*, July 1.

Sibonney

"Well, Goddamnit, Michael, this does not smell right. Why would a Spanish *guerillero* take the trouble? Why not just cut the man's throat and be done with it?"

"I don't know, Alex. I'm not sure that it matters. The man is dead." Michael looked Alex straight in the eye and added, "If we had to lose a man on this detail, I can't think of one we'd miss less."

"You never did trust Shorty, did you? Even in San Antonio?" Alex disliked Michael's intermittent cynicism, which today struck him as callousness, despite his own similar assessment of Shorty.

Michael got up from the rock they were sharing. "I can't say that I'm sorry he's dead. What time is it?"

Alex stared at Michael for a moment, then pulled out his watch. "Almost 2:00."

"We'd better get going, sir."

They walked back to the beach in silence. While they made their final check of the area, Michael stayed as far from Alex as possible, and as busy as possible. It wasn't Alex's questions that bothered him. The *guerilleros*, who were known for their viciousness, had tortured and killed other lone sentries and stragglers. What bothered Michael was his own strong urge to tell Alex everything, to explain how he had killed Shorty, and why. Perhaps I still will, he thought. But not now.

When the fifty-mule supply train finally departed the staging area, weaving its way through the mangroves and up the steeply winding jungle trail, Michael stayed at the head of the column with Freddy. Alex and David brought up the rear. Alex shifted his neck continually from one side of the trail to the other. Shorty's mutilated body still floated in front of him. If one *guerillero* can sneak into a camp and kill a guard, he thought, it is certainly possible for a company of such wretches to ambush a mule train.

Suddenly, he crashed into the mule in front of him. The entire train had stopped and bunched up. "What's happening?" he asked.

David looked up from his copy of *Leaves of Grass*, glanced vaguely around the jungle, and recommenced reading.

"Vandervoort!" Alex yelled. "Get up front and find out what's going on!"

David tucked his book inside his tunic, and kicked his mule into a trot. By the time he had crowded halfway up to the front, however, the word was already drifting back: "Lieutenant Jackson to the front! Lieutenant Jackson to the front!" Rather than riding back for Alex, who would get the word faster than he could bring it, David sat and waited placidly for his commanding officer so they could ride to the front of the line together.

But when he rode up alongside, Alex protested, "No, David. One of us must be at the rear. And leave your book stashed."

When Alex arrived at the front of the train, he yelled, "What's wrong now?" and scanned Freddy's face. Rather than answering, Freddy nodded to his right, where Fidel stood at the edge of the jungle. Alex immediately recognized the Cuban captain, nodded an awkward *"Buenos tardes, Amigo,"* and turned to Michael for an explanation.

"He wants you to go with him to see your brother. Now!"

Alex was thrilled, but also reluctant to leave the mule train. For the second time that day he felt like the old Alex, who always waited for a more forceful personality to determine his actions. He wanted to follow the Cuban into the jungle, but was reluctant to abandon his post.

"Captain Federico says that General Shafter has insisted on segregation of the American and Cuban forces." Michael's tone was even, noncommittal. "He considers the Cubans to be unreliable, and doesn't want them crossing our lines."

"I hadn't heard that. They're our allies." Alex spoke to Michael but looked straight at Fidel.

"Yes, they're our allies, but we've taken command. The word is out, Lieutenant: No one trusts the Cubans."

Alex nodded. Much as he hated to admit it—especially considering that Christopher was a colonel in the Cuban army—he suspected that the generals were right. The Cuban army certainly seemed unimpressive in its composition and outfitting. Still, for whatever reason, Christopher had put his trust in just such men. Alex made up his mind. "I will go with the Cuban, but I want you to come along, Michael. If we get into any kind of trouble, I want someone around who can speak Spanish."

Michael was more than happy to join Alex. He needed a distraction. The long ride up into the steep mountain jungle had given him too much time to dwell on Shorty and Sky Woman. He hadn't expected the despair he was feeling, a losing battle to tear his mind away from the disintegration of his life. He knew that his act of vengeance had, somehow, erased Sky Woman's image from the forefront of his mind. In killing Shorty he had killed the last remnants of his old life. He knew that he would never return to New Mexico.

By the time they rode over a heavily forested ridge and into the Cubans' camp, Alex had been seeing faces in the trees for at least fifteen minutes.

"*Su hermano esta aqui*," Fidel said, smiling at Alex.

"Your brother is here," Michael translated. They rode toward a loose grouping of campfire rings and hammocks. The camp was small and seemed to contain fewer than a hundred men and a dozen women. As had been the case in the other bivouac areas they had passed through, there was little activity. Most of the soldiers swung in their hammocks or squatted against the trees. Even those sitting around dead campfires or performing needed chores seemed listless, drained of energy.

As the two *Yanquis* and their escort rode deeper into the camp, however, numbers of Cubans got up and followed them toward Christopher's headquarters, a large campfire ring around which half a dozen men and women rose to meet them.

" They're here, Christopher" Theresa cried. Christopher raised his eyes from the map and stared at the two soldiers accompanying Fidel, struggling to control the emotions that filled his head. He had heard reports of the Rough Riders and their khaki uniforms, which were far more practical than the blue wool uniforms worn by the rest of the American army. He looks good, Christopher thought, as he walked out to greet the dismounting Americans. God! but he looks good.

The knot at the pit of Alex's stomach constricted and rose into his chest. His palms were so sweaty that the mule's reins seemed to be melting. Which one was Christopher? At first the circle of scarecrows seemed to all look alike, though some were black and a couple were women. The tallest of the scarecrows stared at him with great intensity. Alex snapped his head back and met Christopher's hard, grey gaze. But it wasn't Christopher's face or body. It couldn't be. The gaunt and graying man detached himself from the circle and walked toward him. Alex dismounted, started to walk, decided to wait, then walked again, faster, toward the scarecrow.

" Little brother."

"Christopher." Alex took one step forward and stretched out his hand. Confused both by the formality of his gesture and the harsh apparition that stood before him, he withdrew his hand and fell into his older brother's open arms.

Suddenly, Christopher stepped back, tightened his fist and slammed it against his brother's shoulder. "What the hell are you doing in the army?"

Michael stepped forward as if to intervene, but stopped and helped Alex regain his balance. Alex rubbed his shoulder and leaned on Michael. He didn't have to ask what had enraged Christopher. "I wanted to see you. I didn't know you were a part of this revolution. And I didn't know about…" He stopped. That will wait, he thought.

"I swore to Ma, I'd keep you out of the army, Alex."

"I'm my own man now, Christopher. And we've been apart a long time. Still rubbing his shoulder, Alex redirected the conversation. "Christopher, this is my friend, Michael Archuletta. Michael, my brother, Christopher." He stepped aside as the two men shook hands and measured each other.

For reasons Christopher couldn't have explained, he knew he was looking at a man without illusions, and was drawn immediately to the New Mexican sheepherder. This man has lost much, he thought, shaking hands firmly with Michael. "Come into our camp and rest," he said, and motioned the two visitors toward the campfire. "We will share our good Cuban coffee with you."

As they approached the campfire, Michael noticed that Fidel had rejoined the group and was standing next to the woman called Judith. Two of the Cubans left the fire ring as the two Americans approached, but a slight, large-eyed mulatto woman remained, crouching to stir the coals under the large calabash of boiling coffee. Michael nodded as Christopher introduced them to Theresa, who gave him one hard, welcoming glance and then shifted her attention to Alex. Michael realized that he was having a hard time keeping his eyes away from Judith. In what strange ways has she suffered to look so strong? he wondered. He forced his attention back to Theresa, who was talking.

"I wel-come Chreestopher's brother to thees our camp. You and you (she nodded again to Michael) are so very wel-come."

So this is Theresa, Alex thought, smiling back at her, confused by both her appearance and his own reactions. Obviously, she was beautiful, but 'My God! She's a nigger wench,' some part of Alex's father screamed at him. Alex shook his head and rammed the thought back into the far corner of his unconscious.

He smiled at Theresa and looked back at Christopher, who was filling one cup and two small gourds with thick black coffee. "I met Amos Jordan in Tampa. He told me about your wife and children. I wish I had known. You never wrote much, even in school when you were sending me bank drafts."

Christopher handed Alex the tin cup. "You're the guest of honor, brother. That's why you get the cup." Only after passing out the rest of the coffee did Christopher add, "Amos Jordan is a good man." He thought of the evenings they had spent together drinking at the Alhambra in Havana, and of their conversations about Cuban aspirations and American intervention. Suddenly Ephraim Pratt's face, then George Bedford's, rose before him like threatening ghosts. Christopher grimaced and shivered; he had managed to keep the *Maine* from his mind for days. With great will, he pushed back into the cave the dark suggestion that his actions aboard the *Maine* might one day lead to Alex's death. "What happened to Jordan?"

"When America declared war on Spain, Jordan and the rest of the American civil servants were evacuated," Alex replied. "He's retiring, I believe, and planning to return to New England."

Christopher was silent, feeling again the strain of their reunion. Their mother's face appeared before him. "I'm glad to see you, little brother. But I'm not glad to see you in the army. I didn't send you to Harvard for...this!" He flicked Alex's lieutenant's insignia.

"I wanted to see you, Chris. I haven't even heard from you for almost three years." Alex felt like a small boy again, being corrected or coerced by his older brother, who was determined to counteract the influence of their father. He looked his brother in the eye. "The last year or two I didn't know if you were sick, or injured, or dead. What kind of brother does that?"

Christopher winced. Then put his arm around his brother's shoulder. "I was planning to send for you as soon as we won our independence. It has not been an easy war, Alex."

"Why couldn't you have written to me about the death of your family? Why didn't you send for me?"

Christopher scowled. "As you may have figured out after a week on the island, this isn't much of a place for visitors."

"Christopher. You didn't even tell me. Not one word. Besides, I had other reasons to come. One of my college friends, George Bedford, was killed aboard the *Maine*. The least I could do was help to avenge his death, help drive the dagos from Cuba."

Christopher felt a twinge at this second reminder of the *Maine*, but couldn't help curling his lip at Alex's use of the word 'dago.' What does Little Brother think of Theresa? he wondered, or of Fidel and Judith?

Though Alex felt Christopher's distance and his own defensiveness, he rushed blindly forward. "I also joined up because I hated my job at the War Department, and the war looked like it would be exciting, give me a chance to make something of myself."

"Jesus Christ, Alex. Pa's bullshit really did get to you." Christopher immediately regretted these words. He was the one who had abandoned Alex, not the other way around. He was the one who had left the village for the university and the university for Cuba. He was the one who had turned to wave one more time at the small boy crying in the middle of the dirt road. And he was also at least partially responsible for Alex's decision. He softened his tone.

"I'm sorry, Alex. Goddamnit, I am truly glad to see you." He reached out and tousled Alex's hair as he had so often when they were children.

Alex relaxed at the embrace and clapped his brother's shoulders. Then he shared his sense of what had happened in the last few months. As the brothers moved slowly into an easier conversation, they began to talk more like brothers. Theresa motioned Fidel, Judith and the others to follow her to another circle. Michael went along, and neither of the brothers made a move to stop them.

"Chris, you're right—at least about my romantic views. He thought of those distant days three months earlier when he had ridden out into the charged atmosphere of Washington and Santa Fe as a starry-eyed knight errant. "I joined the army with—and because of—a lot of dreams about, you know, glory, cavalry charges, all that kind of stuff."

Christopher smiled. " I can still see you standing behind the counter in that run-down country store, the old man repeating the same half dozen tales a hundred different ways, and you standing there, bug-eyed. He got to you all right. Are you getting your ration of glory?"

"And then some!" Alex said, as his mind raced over the myriad events of the last two months. "I've about decided that the glory is bunk, but I'm doing a good job. I'm a good soldier, a good officer. I'm gaining respect for what I do. For what I do, not for who I know."

Christopher noticed signs of maturity he hadn't expected. "Doing a good job is important. I figured out a long time ago, way back at Georgia Tech, that the fellow who puts out just a little extra effort is the fellow who's going to succeed—at just about anything: his studies, running a sugar plantation, leading men. Or...." His face clouded over a moment. "Or being a lover, or a husband and father."

The brothers were silent, and Alex registered the incredible degree to which his brother had aged during the three years since their last visit. He noticed the veined, parchment skin and the slightly yellowish nails. Christopher's eyes had become much more recessed and his hair had turned white at the temples. It was Christopher's skin that most bothered Alex, however. In addition to the yellowish cast beneath the tan, it was stretched taut over the bones, sharpening his high cheekbones.

"Have you been ill, Chris?"

"Yes, though better lately. I guess I've been too busy to get completely well." Christopher ran his fingers over his face and inspected his hands. "I don't look so great?"

"I've seen better looking cadavers."

"I've had three serious bouts with malaria this past year, plus a few not so serious ones. Had a little one a couple of days ago. Mostly, though, it's the food—or the lack of it. Being a Rough Rider may be one big adventure," he winked, "but being a revolutionary has its drawbacks."

Alex nodded, pleased to discover that his brother had not entirely lost his sense of humor. He saw Chris lift his head, his eyes warming, as Theresa approached,.

"We would like that you and your friend eat with us," Theresa said.

"I'm sorry, Miss Theresa," Alex said. "We have to get back to our regiment. We didn't really have permission to come here in the first place."

Theresa looked confused, so Christopher translated. She spoke to him rapidly in Spanish, and Christopher said: "She's disappointed. Some of the men killed a wild pig this morning, and it's been cooking all day."

"Tell her I'm sorry, Chris, but we must leave or there will be trouble for us. Come to Las Guasimas this evening. I could get a bottle and..."

"That is not possible!" Christopher's face turned to a bitter mask. "This is not the time to talk about it, but you Americans and we Cubans are very uneasy allies."

Alex felt the warmth between them evaporate. "What is this 'you Yankees' nonsense? You're as American as I am."

"No, Alex. I was never an 'American.' What I remember of Georgia is the Old Confederacy, a little of the War and, mostly Reconstruction. I guess that's the one thing I inherited from Pa—an inability to become a Yankee after the occupation ended in '76."

Alex was appalled. "You mean you really consider yourself to be Cuban?"

Christopher saw Michael, Judith and Fidel drifting back their way and rose to his feet. "You still have a lot to learn, Little Brother." His voice was low but intense. "About America, and about Cuba. We've fought ourselves almost to oblivion..."

"That's why we're here, Chris," Alex replied coldly.

"No, you're here because Spain blew up the *Maine*, and because your newspapers and your Colonel Roosevelt and his friends goaded McKinley into war, and because your Senate wants to annex us."

"Nobody's going to annex Cuba, Christopher," Alex insisted, but his voice faltered and he glanced toward Michael. Just the day before they had discussed the latest rumor: Roosevelt had convinced the President that an army of occupation would be absolutely essential. "I'm sure we'll be leaving as soon as we win the war, certainly no longer than a month...or two."

"I'll believe that when you all return to Tampa," Christopher said. He took a deep breath, and proceeded more calmly. "I don't mean you, Alex. I want you to remain here with Theresa and me. There's room for you."

"Chris, I can't stay here. You may be right about Cuba—even right about America, but I couldn't possibly stay." He turned to Michael. "And right now we've got to get back to our regiment. But please come to our camp tonight. After tomorrow's battle I'm not sure where I'll be—or what's going to happen. I need to talk to you again. I want to hear about Theresa and about your plans after the war." He was thinking: One of us, or both, could be dead within twenty-four hours.

But Christopher was adamant. "No, I will not come to your camp. "Everything, EVERYTHING we see and hear and feel since your arrival tells us that you—or at least your army—holds us in contempt. To you we are an ill-led rabble of diseased, starving and illiterate dogs."

"That's not fair, Chris."

"Fuck fair! It's the truth. And you're right—we are poor, diseased, starving and illiterate. But we have a right to our freedom, and we have a right to govern ourselves."

Despite the guilt he was feeling, which sprang from his sense that Christopher was essentially right, Alex shook his head. "No, that's not fair."

Christopher turned to Michael, who had swung up onto his mule. "Am I exaggerating, Corporal?" he asked in Spanish. "Am I being unfair to you *Yanquis*?"

"No," Michael replied, also in Spanish. "You are not being unfair. What you say is the truth. But do not judge your brother too harshly. He has had to learn a lot very quickly. Already he knows more about himself—and about the attitudes you condemn—than he thinks he knows. He is a good man, Colonel."

Alex fumed, grossly insulted that they would talk—about him—in Spanish. By the time he embraced Christopher and mounted his mule, he could barely choke back his anger. "If you won't come to our camp, send word after the battle, so I'll know where to find you." He tried to smile, but ended up glowering down at his brother.

"Very well." Christopher reached up, patted the mule and said, " I want you to stay in Cuba." Seeing the tears of confusion in Alex's eyes, he turned to Michael, offered his hand and said, this time in English, "I look forward to seeing you again also, Michael Archuletta. And I will remember what you have said."

Christopher watched the two Rough Riders disappear into the jungle from which they had emerged. After staring for a few minutes at the almost solid wall of green he walked back to the fire.

* * * * *

An hour and a half later, just as they rode into the camp at Las Guasimas, Alex turned to Michael. "Well, what were you talking about? What did you tell him?"

Michael reined in his mule and looked Alex in the eye. "I told him that he was right in his assessment of American opinion, that we are contemptuous of the Cubans." Alex turned red with anger. More so because he sensed that Michael was right. And he knew that his own opinions didn't differ all that much from those of the American Army. Though Alex sensed the truth, he was not prepared to deal with it. Cursing Michael, he rode off to report to Wood and Roosevelt.

"Lieutenant Jackson!"

At the sound of his name, Alex turned and waved at Freddy and David Vandervoort, who were walking his way. What the hell's wrong now?

"Alex, you'd better get your butt over to HQ immediately. Wood and Roosevelt are really miffed." David grabbed Alex by the arm and headed him in the direction of the distillery.

"Now wait just one minute, Goddamnit! I haven't even unsaddled my mule!"

"I'll take care of your mule, Alex. Get your butt in there. Right now."

"Okay, I'll go peacefully, so let go." My God! but it's been a day. He realized how tired he was, and shivered at the memory of Shorty's bloodless, mutilated body. "What kind of animal could have done such a thing?" he asked, drawing bewildered glances from Freddy and David.

"What?" Freddy asked, trying to hurry Alex along.

"Nothing. I was just wondering what kind of deranged animal would have murdered Shorty like that. These *guerilleros* must be absolute beasts."

"You know, Alex, it may not have been *guerilleros*," David said. "It may not even have been a Cuban." He and Freddy stopped just outside the headquarters building.

"What do you mean?"

"Look," David replied. "You'd better get in there and find out what the colonels want. We'll talk to you about this other thing when you come out. If you do."

Alex caught his two friends exchanging winks. "What the hell are you talking about?" Alex felt too tired to play games. "What makes you think it may not have been a Cuban?"

"Well, Alex, after we l-l-left this morning, an infantryman found a b-blood-soaked lariat in the jungle less than t-twenty yards from where we found Shorty's b-body."

"The lariat belongs to a Rough Rider," David finished. "We're the only troops that carry them."

"Have you reported this to Wood or Roosevelt?"

"No. They know all about Shorty, but they're passing it off as an act of war."

"All right, David. I want you and Freddy to conduct an inspection of all the troops who were down at the beach with us. Check their equipment. Find out if any of them is missing a lariat. Check to see if any of them has blood stained clothing—other than from their own wounds. Also…" He thought for a moment and then shook his head as if denying a persistent but absurd idea. "Go find Michael. Have him help." Without waiting for a response, he turned toward regimental headquarters.

"Jackson! Where the bloody blazes have you been?" Roosevelt glowered at him.

"Well, I…."

"Stow it, Lieutenant," Wood commanded, in his quieter and far more even voice. "We'll be with you in a few minutes. Please stand where you are."

The two colonels, who were alone in the room, ignored Alex and resumed an intense conversation. Left to his own devices, Alex looked around for a chair, saw none close at hand, and realized that they meant for him to remain standing.

He turned his attention back to Shorty. Something about the incident was very wrong, out of place. Why would any Cuban, even if he were a part of the fanatically loyalist *guerilleros*, why would such a political person take the time to knock out an American private, tie him to a tree, then perform such bestialities upon his body? It was too elaborate, too time consuming, too cold.

During his days in Santa Fe and San Antonio, Alex had heard stories about such incidents, stories told by cowboys and usually involving Apaches. Maybe an Indian could do such a thing. But a white man?

Something in the conversation between the colonels snagged his attention. Wood was talking. "If the Regular Army has its way, Generals Brooks and Shafter and the rest will tie everything up. They've made a mess of this campaign, and they'll make a mess of Cuba. They don't know how to govern."

"Well, I'm not staying, Leonard. If the next few weeks turn out like I think they will, I'm going to follow through with Hearst's suggestion and run for Governor of New York."

"I'm not suggesting you stay. I'm suggesting that our army lacks the intelligence and skill to run Cuba." Wood leaned across the table and shook his finger in front of Roosevelt's face. "Look, Theodore, we've been pushing this war for the better part of two years. We've been in on it from the beginning. We've worked with friendly senators, with the Cuban Junta, with McKinley, with the press. And after all that? This army is in almost as much of a mess as Cuba. We can't…"

"All right, Leonard. What do you suggest?"

Colonel Wood sat very erect in his chair, looked at Roosevelt and said, slowly and without even a trace of humor: "I suggest that I become Governor General of Cuba."

Roosevelt slammed his fist down on the table. "Why you bloody, cheeky rascal! And people accuse me of raw ambition?" He drummed his fingers on the table for a moment and broke into a radiant smile. "You do have gall, Leonard. I'll give you that." He began pacing the room. "First, we'd have to make you a general. Second, we'd have to play the army's game, for at least awhile. But third…third, it would give us much tighter control, and a much better chance of cleaning up this cesspool of an island."

"My point, precisely, Theodore. If we get to keep Cuba, which those damned western sugar beet growers are fighting in the Senate to prevent, we'll be able to annex something that isn't an absolute disgrace to the rest of the country."

"And if we don't get to keep Cuba?" Roosevelt prodded.

"Then we'll have done everything humanly possible to make Cuba capable of standing on her own two feet. We'll have improved the health problems, built schools and railroads, encouraged the economy, taught these primitives how to govern themselves, and made the place safe for American investments.

"It's a challenge, Theodore, one helluva challenge. But you know my record, and you know I'm up to it."

Roosevelt nodded. "And we'll make an ally. Don't forget that point. Cuba has been a problem—and a temptation—ever since Jefferson's time. If he'd had his way, Cuba would have been part of the states for damn near a century. Whatever we do here, we have to do it in a way that will guarantee a friendly government."

"The best guarantee of that happening is to create a government of occupation that believes in justice, education and health. The Cubans will have to admire our approach to government. It would be illogical for them not to."

"I hope you're correct in that assumption, Leonard. But you know, the Latins and Negroes are less than famous for their powers of logical analysis."

Alex could hardly believe what he was hearing. Not only were they acting as though they had the power to decide the fate of Cuba; they were actually planning to circumvent their superiors in the General Staff and the War Department.

Despite what he had heard from Christopher, and despite his own weak denials, he could not help but respect the enormous gall of his two leaders. They were right, of course, at least in part. The Army was a mess. Had not their own brigade, particularly the Rough Riders, already displayed more aggressive courage and military skill than the rest of the Army combined?

Roosevelt bent over and clapped Wood on the shoulder. "When

we're done here, Leonard, when we've won this paltry excuse for a war, we'll talk to Hanna and McKinley. I think you're right. I think this is the way to go. Now, let's get back to the business at hand."

Turning abruptly from Wood, he called, "Jackson!" and waited for Alex to approach the table.

"Sir?"

"We've been told that you're late because you went to visit a Cuban camp, and that your brother is a colonel in the Cuban Army. That correct?"

"Yes, sir. He's lived in Cuba since the eighties, as a sugar planter, and he's been in the revolution almost since the beginning."

"Hardly the beginning, Lieutenant," Wood corrected sourly.

"Yes, sir."

"Why didn't he pull out when the current war began?"

Alex was almost embarrassed to answer. "He considers himself to be a Cuban, not an American, sir"

"That's outrageous!" Roosevelt exploded.

Alex tried to explain. "Well, he was married to a Cuban."

"He married a dago?" Roosevelt shook his head in amused disbelief. Alex started to explain that she was part Creole and part African but decided that such information wouldn't help. Instead, he nodded and said, "His wife and three children died in one of Butcher Wyler's concentration camps."

"I'm sorry to hear that, Alex. Had we intervened when this latest war started, we could have saved tens of thousands of lives—Spanish and Cuban." Roosevelt shook his head.

"Lieutenant Jackson." Roosevelt rose again to his feet, suddenly all smiles. "Colonel Wood and I have talked to several people about you. We're quite pleased with your performance—as Assistant Supply Officer and as a leader of men during the battle for Las Guasimas. Leonard?"

"We're promoting you to Captain, as of evening formation. And we're giving you permanent command of "L" Troop."

"Sir, I don't know what to…"

"There's nothing you have to say, Captain, except 'Yes, sir'."

Roosevelt stepped forward. "You've proven that you are a good soldier—as any man from Harvard should be. Right, Leonard?" Wood nodded.

"Thank you, sir." Alex drew himself up to his full height, his hunger, pain, and weariness forgotten. All the dreams of his youth, of the months in Washington, Santa Fe, San Antonio and Tampa detonated inside him. It was the proudest moment of his life. But he had one question for his superiors. "What about my job with Lieutenant Nelson?"

"Nelson has come a long way, Captain", Wood answered. "Thanks to your efforts. We're relieving you of your chores in Supply as of right now."

"But we do have one additional chore for you, Alex, a pleasant one." Roosevelt motioned him to a chair. When the three were seated, Roosevelt leaned over and continued. "We have other promotions to make in "L" Troop. And we want your advice."

Alex came down slightly from his cloud. "Advice about what, sir?"

"One promotion to Sergeant and one to Lieutenant. Who do you recommend?"

Alex wanted to mention David Vandervoort, but shook his head. Whatever else he was, David was not a leader. "For sergeant, sir? Corporal Walker. I have found him to be both responsible and responsive. And for Lieutenant? Michael Archuletta. He's a quiet man of great strength. Self-educated, but probably as well-read as many of our college graduates. Moreover, he's the best soldier I've ever seen. He'd make a splendid officer."

Wood and Roosevelt looked at each other. Each man raised his eyebrows, as if to say: Maybe we've made a mistake. Roosevelt spoke first. "Alex, we can't promote Archuletta."

"Sir?" Alex looked from Wood to Roosevelt and back, genuinely confused. Both men were frowning sternly.

" Archuletta is a good soldier," Roosevelt said. "No question. Several people, including Vandervoort, by the way, have commented on his abilities. However..." Roosevelt cleared his throat. "We're not promoting a Mexican to officer status. It just isn't done."

Alex gritted his teeth. "Archuletta is half-Mexican, sir, but he's also half-Irish."

"You think being Irish is a recommendation?" Wood lifted his eyebrows surprised that a man who had spent four years in Boston could be so naive.

"The man's a damned good soldier, Colonel."

"No need to swear." Roosevelt put his arm around Alex. "Look at it this way. The Anglo-Saxon peoples are better at governing, better at leading men, better organizers. I agree with you about Archuletta; he's an excellent soldier and an intelligent man. But promoting him to Lieutenant would be a disservice to the men under him, who would resent the promotion; and to Archuletta himself, who would come to resent his inability to fit in socially with his new peers. It's not his fault, Alex, and it's not yours. The man comes from the wrong background. Period."

"He has proven abilities, sir. Besides, Captain Luna is pure Spanish."

"Max Luna came to the regiment as an officer. He also comes from one of the oldest families in New Mexico. He has both the breeding and the education. He's a gentleman." Roosevelt dropped his arm from Alex's shoulder. "Corporal Archuletta is a half-breed sheepherder. He's a good soldier, and we'll promote him to Sergeant, right, Leonard?"

Wood nodded. "That's the best we can do, Alex. The man should feel privileged to be a sergeant. Most white soldiers are still privates."

"Alex, old friend." Roosevelt puffed out his chest and glared. "Don't respond. Don't say another word about Archuletta. That's a direct order."

Alex snapped to attention, tightened his lips and stared at the floor.

"Vandervoort will be lieutenant," Wood concluded, "he's got the right back..." Roosevelt made a sharp movement of command and silenced him, then planted his feet in his boxer's stance and shook his finger in Alex's face. "You listened to our discussion earlier, didn't you?"

"I did, sir."

"And you know we're going to have to stay in Cuba, at least for awhile, don't you? And that we're going to have to teach this island of ragamuffins how to govern themselves. Am I right?"

Alex nodded, picturing his brother's gaunt face.

"Have you ever stopped to wonder why? Have you ever asked yourself why the British and the Germans are able to expand their colonies so quickly? Or why those colonies—and their peoples—are so well-governed?"

"Yes, sir," Alex said weakly. Many of his professors at Harvard were unabashed Anglophiles; many others had been trained in the new German tradition of professional and scholarly rigor. But somehow, in ways that he couldn't understand, much less explain, Alex sensed that some vital ingredient was missing in their world views. He believed in the abstract principle; it was the specific applications that pained him. "I understand the theory," he conceded.

"The theory?" Roosevelt shook his head in exaggerated sadness. "The history of The White Man's Burden is a bit more than an academic theory. Its validity has been demonstrated in every one of the major events of this long century."

Alex knew he couldn't argue with Roosevelt. He wasn't sure what posture he would take, even if he could. He knew that Michael was a better soldier than either David or himself.

Roosevelt looked intently at Alex for another moment and then stepped back, not quite satisfied with his new captain's attitude, but willing to drop the harangue, since he'd been able to get in the last word. Wood stepped forward, aware that Roosevelt had once again relegated him to second in command. "Have you eaten, Alex? No? Well, you'd better grab a bite. It may be several days before we get another hot meal."

* * * *

"Christopher? Can we talk for a few minutes?"

He looked to his left and saw Judith standing at the edge of the small clearing, her hands hanging at her sides. He nodded and beckoned her to come over to the rock where he was sitting. "How did you know where to find me?"

"That's easy," she smiled, amused by the question. "You always do the same thing when you want to be alone. You wander off, find a clearing, sit on a rock and stare out over the treetops. Everybody knows that."

"I'm that predictable?"

Judith nodded, sat down next to him and watched the clouds scud over the tops of the *Sierra Maestra*. It had been a good day. There had been no battles. The American supplies of food had increased morale. It had rained only a little. But tomorrow they would again be fighting the Spaniards. And after that? "What will happen to us?" she asked.

"You sound just like Theresa. How am I to know what will happen?" He shrugged. "Some of us will die; others will live. Has that not always been so?"

"That is not what I mean, Christopher."

He shrugged again. "What will be will be. We will follow our orders, which will come from the American generals. We will win this battle and then sit back and wait to see what the Americans want us to do next."

"Why are you talking like this, Christopher? Almost like we've already lost the war?"

He stood up. "I'm 'talking like this' because this is how I feel. I was sixteen years old when the Grand Army of the Potomac, the Yankee army of occupation, pulled out of Georgia. They stayed eleven years after the end of 'The War of the Rebellion,' as they call it. The South was a defeated and occupied country; the occupiers held our culture, our institutions and our people in contempt."

"I'm sorry, Christopher, but that doesn't relate to..."

"Oh, yes, it does! How many times in the last few days have we experienced first hand the American attitude toward Cubans? How many stories have we heard? When they look at us, they don't see worn out, hungry patriots who have sacrificed everything—including their families—for a cause in which they believe. You know what they see? Filthy beggars. They see poor whites and nigger beggars. They see a people more wretched—more inferior—than anything they have ever seen before, except perhaps the American Indian, whose poverty, customs and dark skins they also despise."

"But Christopher. Their ability to help us has nothing to do with how they may feel about us. What do we care how they feel? When the war is over and they are gone...?"

"I don't quite believe they will leave, Judith."

"But just yesterday you were telling us..."

"I know," he nodded. "I know. But I don't think they'll ever leave us alone. Not ever. Not really." He sat back down and stared over the trees listlessly.

"I think maybe you're a cynic," she accused, but immediately regretted her words. This was the man who had, in a very real sense, saved her life, and who had given that life a new purpose. Who was she to judge him? She got up to leave. "I'm sorry, Colonel Jackson. I forget myself."

"No, no. Sit down, Judith." He tried to shake off the mood that had descended upon him two days earlier, which even Alex's visit had increased rather than diminished. "You didn't come out here to ask about tomorrow's battle, did you?"

She sat again beside him. "We all wonder what will happen, but I came for a more…personal reason."

He touched her hand. "Is it about Fidel?"

"Yes," she whispered. "About Fidel and me." She looked up. "So you have known?"

He flashed a broad grin, which made him look younger and less care-worn than he had in months. "Will neither you nor Theresa ever give me credit for seeing anything?"

"It is good to see you smile, Christopher. Maybe we all need to smile more. Sometimes I think…" She stopped for a moment, felt the tears come to her eyes and turned the subject back to Fidel. "What's wrong with him, Christopher? When I try to talk to him about our lives, about what we will do after the war, he pulls away from me, into himself. Lately, the last few days, he has not come out very often. His distance terrifies me."

"It is very simple, Judith. You do not want to live with him in the jungle, with seven children and a dozen pigs."

"But we don't have to do that. I still have money cached at Joseph's shop. We could…"

"Fidel doesn't want to be a Havana shopkeeper," Christopher interrupted with brutal frankness. "Fidel, too, is worried about what will happen to the two of you after the war," he added more gently. "That's why he doesn't want to talk about it."

"I don't understand. In my family we talked about everything, particularly those things that worried us."

"The two of you come from very different lives. You were able to easily talk about what you feel. Fidel must bury what he feels, or at least what worries him. The more you talk about it, the more he'll draw away."

"But I must talk about it," she said, a slight edge of hysteria creeping into her voice.

"Yes, I know."

* * * * *

"I'm not going back. There's nothing left for me in New Mexico," Michael said. Alex was puzzled more by the tone of absolute finality than by the words themselves. "What do you mean? That's where your life is. You have to go back, don't you?"

"Are you planning to go back and pick up your old job as a procurement clerk at the War Department?"

"No, but..."

"The sheep will be cared for, just as they are being cared for now. There is no one waiting for me in the plateau country, no one to miss me."

"Just because your wife died doesn't mean . . ."

"My wife didn't just die, Alex. She was murdered—as you know."

After a short, stunned silence, Freddy asked, "D-d-did you f-find out who did it?" He had been half drowsing, content to lie on his side, eyes closed, and listen to the slow, silence punctuated conversation of his friends. Like Alex, however, he'd been wondering about both Shorty's murder and Michael's reaction. When Michael didn't answer, Freddy repeated his question: "D-did you find out who...?"

"I heard you, Freddy. Yes, I did." He paused. "I found out who murdered Sky Woman." His intensity sent chills down Freddy's spine and caused David to lift his eyes from his book and stare at Alex, with whom he shared a simultaneous knowledge.

Alex wanted to ask, 'Did Shorty kill your wife?' but he already knew the answer. The coincidences of the relationship between Shorty, Michael and himself flooded through his memory. How many times had Michael asked a question or altered a decision when Shorty was involved? The evening in San Antonio flashed before him. Michael had shown no interest in going to town—until he discovered that Shorty was going. Later that same evening, Michael had pumped Shorty for information about the latter's ride through the plateau country of northern New Mexico. Michael had played Shorty like a weak fish on a taut line. It was Michael who had brought Shorty along on the supply detail just three days before, even though the man was known to be one of the worst soldiers in the regiment. Alex wanted to ask about Shorty and Sky Woman, but he asked instead, "What will you do?"

"Stay in Cuba," Michael said, without inflection, as if he had made the decision a long time ago.

"You c-can't do that."

"Yes I can, Freddy." After a moment he added, "I look more like a Cuban than an American. I speak Spanish as well as I speak English. I have a good mind. I can work hard. Maybe I can contribute something to this new country that is about to come into existence. Also, I think that Cuba will allow me to contribute."

As he listened, Alex thought about Michael's promotion to sergeant, and why Wood and Roosevelt refused to promote him to lieutenant. He also realized that he, David and Freddy had all withdrawn slightly from the New Mexican. He raised himself up on his elbow, looked at Michael and said: "I hope you are right." He thought of Christopher, who seemed to share with Michael an underlying strength and hardness. He loved Christopher more than anyone in the world, Charlotte included, and he felt closer to Michael than he had to anyone he had met. Both men were separated from him by the sharp bitterness of personal loss, losses so great that it had convoluted their souls. "Find Christopher," he said quietly to his friend.

* * * * *

Christopher leaned over and shook Theresa. She, too, had been unable to sleep, and opened her eyes instantly. "Are you worried about tomorrow, Theresa?" he asked.

"Yes, but that's not what's kept me awake." She stroked his arm.

Desire for her churned in his stomach. All night he had been succumbing slowly to the sharp hunger. Even during his conversation with Judith, Theresa had been at the back of his mind. He knew he loved her, just as he knew that she loved him. What Consuelo had said so long ago was true; Theresa had always loved him. Even so, he knew that she would never come to him as long as she suspected, even vaguely, that she was a surrogate Consuelo. He couldn't blame her for that. But he knew, as she must surely come to know, that he loved her, Theresa, for herself.

A warmth ran from his toes to his neck and back down to his loins as she ran the tips of her fingers along his arm. "What has kept you from sleeping?" he asked.

"I have decided that you love me," she whispered, without a sign of egoism. "We will be very happy together." The moon slid out from behind the clouds. She was smiling at him, confident both of what she was saying and of his reaction.

In that moment, he felt like a small boy who has been shown something he couldn't figure out for himself. He realized that he felt young, alive, strangely vulnerable. He bent to kiss her and thought. When was the last time I felt like this?

"Wait," she whispered. "Not here." Before he could find the words to protest, she rose from her hammock, took him by the hand, and led him toward his private clearing. When they arrived at his flat rock, she undressed him and pushed him gently down onto his back. As he watched her remove her own clothes, he smiled ruefully: Is this one of the advantages of loving a woman who's been a prostitute? He felt awkward, embarrassed equally by the nakedness of his gaunt body and his throbbing erection, which he covered with his hand. Even before she had finished removing her worn clothing, he felt his senses and mind flowing together in ways he thought he had forgotten.

In the darkness he took in the soft glow of her emerging nakedness, the sharp scolding of a nearby parrot and the distant crack of a sniper's bullet. He knew that neither their love nor their lovemaking could make the war recede for more than a few short moments, but he didn't care.

She came to his open arms, and the world did recede. He knew he would not be able to hold himself back for long; excitement vibrated through every cell of his being. He also realized that it didn't matter. If they survived they would have years to make love slowly, wrapped in a series of nights that would succeed each other with the regularity and rhythm of the seasons. He sensed that she understood his urgency. It seemed to him, for a fraction of a moment, that they were miles apart, connected only by their throbbing loins. He was, for a brief moment, once again with Consuelo in the cane field, but when he opened his eyes and saw Theresa, he pulled her closer, rolled onto his side and held her body along the length of his.

His release came as an explosion, an end to all the guilt and despair he had known since the death of his family. The transition to peace was almost instantaneous. The mindless desire that had consumed him sub sided to a long series, of fading waves, and he experienced a nirvana of oneness he had forgotten was possible.

"I do love you, Theresa."

She was too content to speak.

Chapter Thirty-Six

BALLOON MAY FLOAT OVER SANTIAGO

* * * * *

Washington, June 30.—The reports from Santiago as to reconnoitering parties and efforts of our officers to take observations of the city leads to the belief that the War Department will allow General Shafter to utilize a big balloon as a means of surveying Santiago and all the surrounding country.

* * * * *

THE CUBAN SOLDIER

As the battle progresses the stock of the Cubans is rising steadily. The attitude of the American soldier at first was patronizing—it being inevitable that the Anglo-Saxon should feel superior to all other created things. Now he has discovered from observation that the Cuban is brave, that he understands how to fight the shifty Spaniards, and is death to the Dons. William Randolph Hearst, Editorial: *The New York Journal*, July 2.

Santiago de Cuba

Shortly after noon, General Vara del Ray strode out of Eastern Area Headquarters in Santiago, mounted his horse and, his small staff in tow, headed for San Juan, the City of Saint John the Apostle. General del Ray's job was to defend San Juan and El Caney. He knew that the job was impossible, just as he knew that Spain's position was impossible. Of the thirty thousand Spanish regulars garrisoned in Santiago de Cuba, fewer than six thousand manned the trenches and blockhouses that separated San Juan and El Caney from the invading army. Most of the Spanish army had locked itself up in Santiago; other than the hapless del Ray, the Spanish generals had no interest in sacrificing themselves to save the suburbs.

The Cuban blockade of the three main arteries leading to the city and the naval blockade had done their intended job: more than a month had passed since the last supplies of food, medicine, ammunition or reinforcements had entered Santiago. Several hundred civilians had already died; almost a third of the Spanish Army was hospitalized from diseases related to malnutrition compounded by yellow fever and malaria. The generals knew they were defeated. For almost four centuries Spain had ruled two thirds of the hemisphere. But in less than eight decades, Martin, Bolivar, Juarez, Marti, Gomez, Garcia—thousands of generals and millions of peasant soldiers—had wrested an empire from an enfeebled Spain. Now there was nothing. Nothing. General del Ray exhaled such a long, deep breath that Alonzo de Montoya, his *aide de camp*, voiced his concern.

"It is nothing, *amigo*." The general smiled at his unintentional pun, and decided to share his doubts and fears with his aide. Like himself, Alonzo came from a family that had been sending officers and bureaucrats to the New World for three hundred years. The general laughed, "Once Spain was everything. And now she is nothing."

"Sir?"

"Is that not true, Alonzo?"

"No, sir." Alonzo shook his head. He had been in Cuba less than six months and was homesick for the cafes and music halls of Madrid. To him, Spain was still very strong, very beautiful, exceedingly proud. As was he. "There will always be Spain, General."

"Yes," the general nodded sadly. "There will always be Spain. The heart beats feebly, the cataract-infested eyes still see, even though the arms and legs have fallen away.

"What is left, my son? Dewey has destroyed our Pacific fleet. The Atlantic fleet is locked up in Santiago Harbor. We are about to lose Wake Island, Guam, the Philippines. We've already lost Mexico, and all of Central and South America. We are about to lose Cuba and Puerto Rico."

"No, General." The younger man tightened his lips. "Cuba will always be part of Spain. We have almost 300,000 troops here. We have maybe 100,000 irregular *guerrilleros*. We will win!"

"Alonzo, you are losing control of reality," the general reproved. "You are certainly losing your senses. We have more than thirty thousand troops right here in Santiago, but only a fifth of them are assigned to the defense. Yahhh!" He shrugged his shoulders. "We shall see what we shall see." Del Ray looked around the Santiago Plain and breathed deeply. "At least, it's not raining."

Four miles ahead, the terraced City of San Juan clung to its precarious hold on the steep western slope of San Juan Ridge. As he rode towards the small city and his headquarters, General del Ray's heart became heavier. He knew what would happen within, at most, a very few days. Among other things, he knew he would not survive the battle; of that he could be sure. He had seen, what had the English historian Gibbon called it? The decline and fall? Yes, he had lived long enough to see the decline of a once great empire. He hated being present at the fall.

But first he must see to his family. At least, they would be with him in San Juan when the end came. Better for them there than in Santiago, with its epidemics and its filth. Perhaps they should have stayed in Spain.

But no. He shook his head. The del Rays have always brought their families along. Without our families we are nothing. "Without her colonies, Spain is nothing," he said, drawing another concerned look from Alonzo. What is there left to preserve? Except our pride and our honor? Our honor our honor our honor our honor.

* * * *

Brigadier General Leonard Wood and full Colonel Theodore Roosevelt glowered down at the marching blue coats. From their perch on a small hill overlooking the route of the march, they could view both their own impatiently waiting troopers and elements of General Lawton's infantry division trudging north along a one-time trail now collapsed into a ten yard quagmire of mud and mule shit. Roosevelt looked to his rear, where the cavalry division was sitting in regimental rank, waiting for their turn at the trail.

"Leonard, this is the worst bloody mess I've seen since we left Tampa."

Wood laughed. "Theodore, you said the same thing about the train ride from San Antonio, and about the camp at Tampa, and about the landing at Daiqueri. Right?"

"You bully well better believe it. Of course! Leonard. This dingbat Regular Army isn't worth the powder it'd take to blow it back to Washington. Old Fat Shafter and his geriatric crew are turning a simple little war with a bunch of sick dagos into a Saragossa sea of incompetence."

"Now calm down, Theodore. We'll get there." Wood was in an excellent mood. As far as this brand spanking new brigadier general was concerned, everything was going fine, just fine. Less than three months earlier he'd been a captain in the Surgeon's Corps. As of this morning, he was a general commanding a full brigade of cavalry. Dismounted cavalry, perhaps, but still cavalry. General Leonard Wood turned his mount from the trail overlook, drew himself up a little more erect on his horse and surveyed his command.

It was already mid-afternoon. Since General Lawton's Infantry division had been given first priority to the quagmire, the cavalry was having a long, unwanted day of rest. Quite a sight, Wood observed, as he surveyed the almost two thousand blue coats, the seven hundred Rough Riders, the black faces and the white faces, all backdropped by deep green jungle, the black mountains and perfect sky. Most of the brigade seemed relaxed, stretched out in the grass and perfectly content to watch the sweating, wool-clad infantrymen struggle by. But General Wood knew that their time would come, and that they would have to march all evening to be in position for the early morning attack on the distant ridge. Wood turned his horse and rode back to where Roosevelt was still glowering at the infantry.

"We're never going to get there," he fumed. "Most of the correspondents have abandoned us for Lawton's command. Leonard, we're going to get lost in the shuffle."

"No, we're not. Nothing can possibly happen today. The attack has been postponed; even the Navy has given up."

"I thought this was going to be such a splendid little war," Roosevelt complained, ignoring Wood's remark. "If Joe Wheeler were here, he'd get us up to the front post haste."

"If Wheeler were here, Theodore, neither of us would have been promoted. You wouldn't have command of the Rough Riders, and I wouldn't be a general."

"That's what I'm talking about," Roosevelt interrupted, changing the subject.

They stood quietly for the next few moments and watched part of a battalion of Cuban infantry file by, a hundred or so soldiers of mixed sex and race, led by a tall scarecrow.

"That's who we're fighting for? Those niggers look sicker than dagos. Bloody beggars. At least the dagos are white." Roosevelt shook his head, unconvinced that the Cubans were really their allies.

Leonard Wood did not respond, though he frowned in contempt at the Cubans. Teddy, he thought, you know as well as I do that we're not here for them; we're not fighting for that rabble. We're here for us. And we're going to make something out of this war. Yes, we are! Wood sat quietly astride his horse and continued to scrutinize the units marching by: regiment after regiment of American infantry, interspersed with mixed units of Cubans. Though a few of the Americans were singing, most of them and all of the Cubans sloshed through the ankle-deep muck in silence.

Below them came a commotion on the trail.

"Wait your turn, goddamnit," a soldier shouted.

"Watch your mouth, soldier!" an officer on horse-back shouted. "Make Way! I'm carrying orders." When the rider spotted the two cavalry officers on the hill, he jerked his horse from the muck and cantered toward them.

Captain Phillips, General Shafter's aide de camp, pulled his frothing horse to a halt and saluted. "General Wood. You're next, sir."

"Thank you, young man," Wood replied. "We are ready. Has General Shafter come ashore yet?"

"No, sir. Not yet." Phillips gritted his teeth, saluted again and rode on. Every colonel and general he had encountered since the landing was asking the same questions: 'Has General Shafter come ashore yet? Will the General be in personal command during the assault? When will Shafter arrive at the front?' It was becoming a litany, and he hated it. What could he do? A mere captain? He shared the unvoiced contempt of the field commanders for General Forrest Shafter. He despised the man's undisciplined corpulence, his mindless caution, and his unwillingness to command from the front. Phillips would have paid a year's salary to trade his over-extended errand boy role for command of an infantry company or, better yet, a troop of Teddy Roosevelt's cowboys.

* * * * *

Alex hated marching. He hated the hot, humid sun and hated the sucking muck they were wading through. They had been on the road now for almost five hours, and only the river crossings were pleasant. When they had crossed the first of the three rivers that separated them from their objective, he had been tempted to follow the example of many of his enlisted men, who handed their rifles to their buddies and fell, face forward, into the cool stream. At the second crossing, Bill Pike had been particularly playful. Pike had crashed onto the surface of the shallow river, hit a rock, and come up spitting teeth. When those around him broke into horse laughter, he started to swing his fists, thought better of it, and fell onto his back. For the next minute or so, he snorted like a bull and spat mouthfuls of bloody brown water into the air. "Look at me," he roared. "I'm a sperm whale. Get it! Haw, haw. Get it?"

Shortly after crossing the second river, Alex asked, "What time is it?"

David pulled out his engraved pocket watch. "6:10"

"We should be stopping soon. That's the San Juan River below us, and that's the ridge up to our right, maybe two-three miles beyond the river. San Juan City is on the other side of that ridge line."

David stared at the ridge thinking, so that's where it's all going to happen? He didn't want to kill anyone. Thus far, at least as far as he knew, he hadn't. At Las Guasimas he had just moved ahead with the others, occasionally firing his rifle in the general direction of the Spaniards. Here he was, through no fault of his own, a second lieutenant in charge of two platoons of novice infantrymen trained to fight from horses. A lieutenant! An officer, whose job it was to lead troops into battle. How did it happen? What did I do wrong? Why didn't they make Michael the officer? He's a hard man, a killer.

But he's a dago, he'd heard Roosevelt say. "You think they'll follow him into battle?"

David shook his head. You think they'll follow me into battle? he had wanted to scream. Harvard, Hahvud, how hard. Graduate from Harvard and be a leader. Graduate and be a man, a 'manly' man, Roosevelt would have said. A man of men, a glass of gin. A man of men and glory win . Gory glory, sin win. Christ! He hadn't even played football at Harvard, or baseball, or anything else except an occasional game of chess. He'd studied, day-dreamed, scuffled through the autumn leaves that cluttered the Yard, and sat for hours smoking his pipe along the Charles river. He'd never been a leader of anyone, had never been popular, had never been noticed. He was the very rich, very pleasant and very quiet Jew who bothered nobody. Yet, here he was in Cuba. Because of an impulse, because his participation seemed to be something that might, finally, gain him an iota of respect from his father. Dumb, dumb, dumb. A gun is fun if the war is won, but war is dumb, son. And you are dumb, dumb as your puns. And why am I an officer? he wondered. Because of Ha-vud. Hav-ud. Ha-mud. Mud. Glug, glug. The mud, the mud, the fuckin' Cuban mud. I went to Ha-vud. Roosevelt went to Ha-vud. Wood went to Ha-vud. Alex went to Ha-vud. They're officers. Sine quo non: Me, too.

PART III: A PYRRHIC VICTORY

* * * * *

It was almost dark by the time the Rough Riders made camp on the top of El Poso, a small plateau that over-looked the San Juan River, and almost midnight by the time Alex got his men fed and bedded down, attended a long staff meeting, held a staff meeting of his own and finally stretched out, bone weary, on his blanket roll. Despite his weariness, sleep escaped him. What am I going to do after the war? he wondered. Although he had long ago decided that he would never return to the War Department, he had given little thought to what he would do. Marry Charlotte? Probably. But then what? And why? Why? Why?

Ever since hearing his father's first war story, Alex had dreamed of glory. He knew better now, or at least he thought he did. If glory existed in war, it was only after the fact. Glory was the coloring, the patina, created by time, distance and tall tales. It was a quality best understood and most frequently praised by those whose first hand acquaintance with its terror was minimal, or who had grown old basking in self-congratulatory memories. It was a tale told by an old man, full of dreams and hot wind, signifying bullshit. Alex thought of the Spanish officer he had shot point blank. He may have killed other men; he knew he had killed that one. What had that young Spaniard done to deserve death? And what was glorious about it? He thought of the vultures and land crabs picking at the eyes of the dead and badly wounded. What songs of glory would the parents and friends of those men sing? And what enduring tears would salt the rooms where they once laughed?

Alex tried to move his restless mind to a rosier subject. What would he do after the war if he lived? Go to work for Roosevelt? Stay in Cuba with the occupying army? Perhaps he could go to work for Wood. No! Without ever having discussed the possibility with Christopher, Alex knew that were he to work for an American civil administration in Cuba, he and Christopher would be estranged forever. Stay in Cuba and work with Christopher? Perhaps. But would Charlotte leave the excitement of the capital to live in the Cuban back country? Could he become Cuban? Give up his American citizenship? No.

He was an American. He sensed that the country was just coming into its own, just beginning to gain real stature in the world community. It was a heady period, and he would enjoy it—however ambivalent he might feel about the country's long-term role in Cuba. Christopher was different.

Alex realized that the four years he had spent at Harvard and the years he had spent in Washington had changed him. He sensed the dynamism of his era. The frontier had finally closed. Railroads, factories, huge cattle ranches, mushrooming towns, swarms of immigrants, and more, all contributed to the energy that was America. Henry Adams was right, as was David's hero, Walt Whitman. And he was a part of it. Whatever its faults, he was wedded to America's destiny.

When Alex finally drifted off to sleep, it was almost two. On the battleships and cruisers out in the bay, senior officers were already rising to ready themselves for the long bombardment that would start just before dawn. On both sides of the line, Spanish, American and Cuban troops slept, walked guard, or talked in quiet voices. Everyone knew the battle would be long and hard; many sensed that it would be climactic.

* * * * *

"What does your father say?"

Colonel Carlos Garcia looked at Christopher and shrugged. "What else, my friend? We do what Shafter orders. Such is life." The young colonel turned away from Christopher and the other battalion commanders.

One more moment, Christopher thought. One more moment and I will lose control.

"Hey, Carlos, old companion. Surely, you are joking." Xavier Hernandez was an old man, a veteran of the Ten Years War and a former gunrunner. He had known Carlos since the young man's birth. The colonel failed to keep the patronizing tone from his voice: "Surely, your father realizes what will happen if we follow such a plan."

Carlos whirled back, his face livid. "You think my father wants to do this thing? You think my father has turned stupid? Or soft-headed? Eh? You think maybe he doesn't care for our lives? Or even for the lives of those wool-clad *Yanquis*? Eh?"

"I am sorry, my son, but I..."

"I am not your son, Xavier, even if you have known me forever." Carlos took a deep breath, let it out and continued. "Please, my friends.

One moment." He pushed both hands out in front of him with short, rapid strokes, as if trying to calm expectant children. "I argued with my father about this plan of General Shafter's, just as my father argued with General Shafter. Certainly it is insane. What do you expect?"

Christopher and several others of the unit commanders nodded, impressed. They had never heard Carlos argue with his father, Calixto Garcia, the commanding general of the Eastern Army. They had never even heard of such a thing. And the general had argued with the fat American general? Perhaps there was truly no choice.

"I must get back to my father's headquarters," Carlos said. "I have been honored to serve with you, my friends." He embraced each of the thirteen unit commanders. "These words and embraces are from my father as well as myself. I hope to see all of you again." And he was gone, riding south and west, toward the harbor and the boat that would return him to the headquarters of the Commander of the East.

"Yes, my son," Xavier muttered long after Carlos had passed around the nearest hill. "We all hope to see you again—if any of us live."

The meeting broke up without another word. Each of the colonels knew what he must do, and each knew what he must tell his troops: They would participate with the blue coats in a frontal assault on El Caney. Beginning at the trough of the valley, at the San Juan River, they would cross more than a mile of open country, climb the exposed faces of the ridges, and engage the Spanish fortified trenches. The plan was madness.

* * * * *

The ride back to camp took two hours.

"How did it go?" Fidel asked, rising from the fire to extend a gourd of beans to his colonel.

Christopher looked around, pleased to see his friends, but unsettled by their expectant faces; they would not like his news. Pointedly and without prelude, he sketched out the rough plan. "Tomorrow we will cross the San Juan River with the *Yanqui* infantry. Our battalions will be attached to General Lawton. The reinforced infantry division is going to charge straight up the ridges and capture El Caney. From there we will be able to capture San Juan."

"Ai yi yee!" Fidel moaned, shaking his head. "That will be very hard."

"The charge up El Caney is supposed to be a feint, but it will prob-ably end up being real."

"Why, Christopher? If they give us another day or two, we can take the entire army around the ridge and join the blockade of Santiago. There is no need to capture San Juan City. It is not important."

"We have our orders. I am very sorry."

"But we will lose too many men. So will the *Yanquis*."

"Yes." Christopher wolfed down the last mouthful of beans and walked over to the fire for more.

Fidel followed him, hunkering down by the fire to continue the conversation. "And the women?"

"We will take no women with us, Fidelito. Not this time. We will need their abilities after the battle. We will lose many men, as you suggest."

"What about Theresa?"

"No women. And none of the younger boys. The boys can bring up supplies. All the women can help with the many wounded."

"Yes, that is true." Fidel nodded, satisfied that Judith would not be endangered, and pleased that he would get to fight in what looked to be the major battle of the entire war. As Fidel looked up from the fire, however, his eyes changed expression, became unsettled, even as they revealed his love.

Judith and Theresa had moved up to the fire and heard the last exchange between their men. Theresa stared at Christopher for a moment, furious to hear that she had been relegated to non-combatant. Her face paled behind her swarthy complexion and, without speaking a word, she turned and stalked from the fire. After a short silence, Judith spoke. "So, all of a sudden Theresa and the other women warriors are not good enough for the main battle?"

"It will be a bloody day. Their numbers will not be needed." Christopher tried to stare Judith down, but found he couldn't. "Judith, I'll be damned if I'll sacrifice any more than I have to. It's an insane plan, not of our making."

"But you are willing to commit the lives of our men? It is a bad plan, but you are fighting. Is that not so? But you will not allow Theresa to fight."

"I'm not allowing any of the women to fight, Judith. They will be more useful tending the wounded, and there will be many, many wounded."

"Judith! Be quiet!" Fidel commanded in his most patriarchal tone. "This is our colonel, our commander."

"Ah, so suddenly we weaker vessels are not good fighters," she replied, ignoring Fidel. "Are you afraid your *Yanqui* friends will laugh at you for using women?"

"Judith!" Fidel hissed .

"I don't have any *Yanqui* friends," Christopher exclaimed. Then, more softly, "Except my brother, and he's not a *Yanqui*."

Seeing that their colonel had made up his mind, and that the decision had been unusually difficult, Judith changed her strategy. "So, what's wrong with the *Yanquis*? They have all the ships and all the supplies. Can they not help us with our wounded?"

"I don't think they will be able to help themselves, Judith." He shook his head, envisioning the total disaster that would fall upon the Americans. "They are not ready for this fight. And they will not be ready for its consequences."

"But they are rich, Christopher."

"True enough. But their medical supplies are still aboard their ships. I don't think even their own field commanders know this."

"Then how do you know?" Fidel interrupted.

"General Garcia heard Admiral Sampson and General Shafter talking about the problem. But..." Christopher turned back to Judith. "That's not the worst. The field hospital they have set up on the beach has only three surgeons and is almost twenty kilometers from El Caney."

Judith shook her head. "Many, many men will die before they ever get there."

"Many men," Christopher agreed. He looked to the far side of the clearing where Theresa sat with her back against a palm tree. Her chin rested on her crossed arms. She was glaring at him. "Theresa!" he cried, sounding more like an irate sergeant than a lover. She returned still sulking to the campfire, and he gave his orders, crisply, without the slightest invitation to criticize or second-guess.

"Fidel, you will stay with me until the attack starts. I will give you and the other commanders more specific orders tomorrow, or, rather, later this morning. Judith you will set up your hospital right here. This place is relatively secure from the *guerilleros*, and it is close to the main supply trail. When—and if—medicine starts to arrive, we will be able to get a share. In the meantime, we will care for our own, and our own only. Understood?"

Judith nodded. "I will begin right now, Colonel." She imitated the crisp *Yanqui* salute and turned to put her nurses to work. "Come along, Fidelito. Tomorrow you can be a hero, but tonight you must help me." Without waiting for a reply, she turned and walked towards the tent she used for her hospital headquarters.

Fidel looked toward Christopher, who nodded his approval, and the big man followed Judith, feeling an anger he could not have explained. Ever since the night they had made love on the far side of the harbor, it was as though she had him on a long rope. He was totally controlled by the beautiful woman the *mambises* called the Jewish Angel. What would life be like if he allowed her to lead him into a shop in Havana—or anywhere else?

As he traipsed after her, Fidel thought again of his father's story. Suddenly Federico's inert body rose before him. He shook his head hard. No, Father! I don't want to think of you now. Nor of you, Oinja. Nor of you, Mister Death.

Theresa and Christopher sat alone around the fire for a long time before Christopher finally cleared his throat and broke the uncomfortable silence that hung between them like a shroud. "I am sorry, my little dove."

"We have not been apart for more than a few hours for a long time, Christopher, not since we left Havana." Reproach and anger hardened in her stomach. "Why are you doing this to me?"

"I have already said far more than I intended, Theresa. Please! You must stop arguing with me!"

Just as she was about to retort, Christopher placed his long hand over her mouth. "Listen to me now, Theresa! I am too tired to argue. So listen!" He felt her relax slightly and removed his hand, brushing its back gently across her lips and cheek. "We will need carts to carry our wounded back from the battlefield. This morning, early, take several teams of horses, and borrow at least four carts from the peasant clearings. If you find anyone there—and you probably won't—tell them, as usual, *Para Cuba Libre*. Take the other women soldiers and some of the boys. Do not surrender the carts to the *Yanquis*. They will discover very soon that their few ambulances are insufficient for twenty-five thousand men."

Without looking up at him, Theresa nodded and muttered, "Yes, Colonel, I understand."

Christopher stood and stared down at the curly head of black hair. He started to say something romantic, but shut his mouth and instead touched the top of her head with his fingertips. So much fire and so much pride, he thought. But we shall see, my dove. Maybe we will be given many years to understand each other.

Chapter Thirty-Seven

FIERCE BATTLE ALL DAY BY LAND AND SEA
Whole American Line Advanced Against the Spanish Works

* * * *

BEGAN ATTACK AT THE NORTHEAST OF THE CITY—
MORRO FORTS AT ENTRANCE TO BAY A MASS OF RUINS
Boys of the Seventy-First of New York Have Heavy Losses

* * * *

GEN. SHAFTER SENDS MEAGRE DISPATCHES—
REPORTS OF HEAVY LOSSES

Playa del Este, July 1—The fight has begun. The expected battle has opened. Santiago is being assailed by land and sea.

At seven o'clock this morning General Lawton's advance opened the firing, and pushed forward by successive rushes to capture the fortified positions of vantage about Caney.

The Spaniards replied vigorously, and soon the wounded began coming in on stretchers.

The men from the front told of how the Cubans were aiding Lawton's men and bearing the brunt of the fighting. *The New York Journal,* July 2.

El Caney

Almost 12,000 of Calixto Garcia's troops, divided into three divisions, stood across the roads from Holquin, Manzanillo and Guantanamo. Santiago de Cuba was totally surrounded, cut off both from the sea and from the other major cities of the East. On two of the three highways the Cubans were totally successful. They turned back the Spanish at great cost to themselves, but at even greater cost to the Spanish. Only on the Guantanamo highway did the Spanish column succeed in breaking through to Santiago, but not until July 5, and even then only after losing fifteen hundred of its four thousand troops.

To the south, early on the morning of July 1, a combined force of Cuban and American soldiers initiated a frontal attack on the ridges that overlooked the Santiago plain. Everyone in the city knew that if the ridges fell, Santiago and all of eastern Cuba would fall. Yet the Spanish Captain-General did nothing.

When General del Ray had come to him the day before, the Captain-General had refused to reinforce the five thousand-man garrison on the ridges. Instead, he had satisfied his dwindling interest in the outcome of the battle by commanding del Ray: "Hold the ridge at all costs. Hold to the last man." The Captain-General had little doubt but that del Ray would follow his orders. After all, the old whitebeard was a chevalier from an earlier period. He was a proud vestige of a generation who believed in honor above all else, an expendable anachronism who had lived through decades of Spain's long decline.

This morning the Captain-General grimaced as he descended the stairs of the palace. Heliograph signals flashed from the distant ridge; the attack had begun. He looked toward the ridge for a long time, then crossed himself and hurried down the steps to his morning meal. I hope your sense of honor will pull you through, del Ray, because I can't, he thought. I wish I could help, but the Cuban divisions straddling the main roads can attack Santiago at any moment.

The Captain-General knew that the five thousand regulars defending the ridges could not put up much of a battle. Even the hardened and far more desperate *guerilleros* would not be able to hold out for long. Yes, even the *guerilleros*, fanatically loyal as they were, knew that the end was near. Unlike the commanding general, however, the *guerilleros* had not yet given up; they were not resigned to losing. If the Spanish lost, they could surrender and return to Spain. If the *guerilleros* lost, however, they would lose everything. There was nowhere for them to go.

* * * * *

As he walked back and forth in front of the main blockhouse at El Caney, General del Ray ran the fingers of his left hand continuously through his beard. Though his headquarters remained in the city of San Juan, he had ridden the quarter of a mile up-slope to encourage his troops. Del Ray looked through his field glasses. The Americans and Cubans had barely started moving, though it was almost 8:00 o'clock. Their advance elements would descend to the ford across the rain-swollen San Juan River in fifteen, maybe twenty minutes.

Del Ray turned to his aide. "Remember, Alonzo. The order is to hold our fire until the advance units reach the ford. From that moment on, we will continue to fire, as selectively as possible, until we are all dead."

"Yes, General. But as soon as we commence firing, their artillery will begin firing. Shall we?"

"No, my son. It will do no good to fire at their artillery—until later. When their cannons are mixed with their troops—then you can fire at them. We have three advantages. Let us be sure to use them well."

"I see but two advantages, sir. The steepness and openness of the terrain they will have to cross."

"Yes. But it is already a very hot July day and they are wearing wool. More important, both their rifles and their artillery use black powder. Every puff of smoke will provide a clear target."

At that moment the American artillery commenced firing. A 75 Howitzer shell landed within fifty yards and the two officers sauntered toward cover, each aware of the example they were setting for their terrified soldiers. "General," the colonel said as soon as they were in the block-house, "artillery shells seem to be landing over to the far left."

Del Ray walked to one of the apertures, lifted his glasses and looked out to the southeast toward the far line of blockhouses the Americans would come to call San Juan Hill. "So," he said after a moment. "They are attacking all along the line. They are very brave, and very crazy. Why. in the name of the Virgin, do they not concentrate their assault on one place and send the rest of the army around the ridge? Strange. It would save them many lives."

"Maybe they are not well led, General."

"Hummph, perhaps not. The American generals probably think they know better than Calixto Garcia." Del Ray looked again through the aperture at San Juan Hill, then walked to the southeast portal and looked down ridge at the assault force, which crawled in a miles-long column to the river. "Tell me, Colonel. Do you think Calixto Garcia would have ordered a frontal assault on this ridge line unless there was no other way?"

"Garcia? Never! He values his men too highly to throw them away in heroic gestures."

"The Americans seem to have men to spare. Though their leadership may be poor..."

"But they will still win, won't they, General?" Del Ray didn't answer, and his aide continued to himself: So! It is we who are throwing away our men in heroic gestures.

The American bombardment proved to be weak and ineffective. Of the five hundred rounds fired, most fell short of the ridge or passed harmlessly over, though a few fell in San Juan City and killed several dozen civilians. Only one of the trenches sustained a direct hit, killing three soldiers and wounding seven others. The bombardment was over almost before it had begun.

"The Americans may be a little short of artillery ammunition," the general said, again looking at the river. "Very well, Colonel. The forward elements are into the river. Have the *guerilleros* down slope start. We will wait for more effective range."

The colonel nodded at a signalman, who immediately climbed onto the roof of the blockhouse and flashed orders up and down the lines of connecting ridges. From the ridge itself nothing happened. But the hundreds of *guerilleros* concealed in the down-slope jungle opened fire with devastating results. Within the first few minutes, they managed to kill or wound scores of Americans and Cubans.

General del Ray replaced his glasses and prepared to return to San Juan City. He was satisfied. It would be many long and expensive hours before the invaders would be able to mount an attack on the ridges themselves.

* * * * *

"Goddamnit, Alex! Keep your troop together," Roosevelt yelled, anxious to bully, cajole and otherwise inspire "L" Troop, the leading contingent of Rough Riders. Satisfied that his troop was as together as it could be, Alex ignored him.

The regiment moved but slowly down the crowded trail that fell toward the river. Although the Rough Riders were supposed to stay with the rest of the brigade, already the huge, uncoordinated mass of regiments was blending together. Alex recognized units on his left from the Tenth and Sixth Cavalry, which should still be to the rear. He saw companies of infantry, which should have been far to the front, and a large band of Cubans that should have been at least a mile to the rear. Whatever was happening to the other regiments, however, Alex was satisfied that, thanks to Roosevelt, the Rough Riders were still intact. The man was inexhaustible: He ran his horse, Little Texas, from troop to troop, berating, encouraging, but always leading. This was his chance. The regiment was his. Roosevelt would inspire the troops, himself included, to do their very best.

Suddenly the jungle exploded on the far side of the river. Though he could see only occasional puffs of grey smoke—fired from the old .45 caliber Springfields favored by the *guerilleros*—Alex knew that Spanish rounds by the hundreds were pouring into the ford. Blue-clad bodies floated lazily downstream, many of them accompanied by eddies of pink water.

The units closest to the ford ground to a halt, mesmerized by the slaughter. But the regiments to the rear continued to press forward, anxious to see what was taking place. They pushed the forward units, like an army of reluctant lemmings, toward the river.

Just as the Rough Riders descended to the crossing and prepared to join the blue-coats floundering across the bullet-infested stream, Roosevelt rode again to the front of the formation. "Alex!" he boomed. "Pass the word. Try not to enter that bloody cauldron until the unit in front of us is at least half way across. Then move as fast as possible."

"Yes, sir."

Roosevelt started to ride on, but reined up short, turned back, and added, in flat, even tones: "No one is to fall out of formation! Like at Las Guasimas, the wounded will have to fend for themselves."

"Yes, sir," Alex mumbled, turning from Roosevelt to face Sergeant Archuletta, who had raised his eyebrows and spat. "You heard him," Alex said.

"I heard him."

As they moved down the last hundred yards to the bloody ford, both men thought of the battle at Las Guasimas, and of the wounded who had been left in the jungle to bleed to death, and of the incredible horror they must have experienced, surrounded by no one but the screaming jungle birds, vultures and land crabs. "God, I hope I die instantly," Michael said.

"Yeh, me too. I have always had nightmares about drowning in muddy water."

And then they were into it. They stood on the bank of the river for what seemed like hours and waited for the last of the Ninth Regiment to reach the middle of the ford. Two of the Negro soldiers fell into the river and floated, head to toe, down stream. Alex could not take his eyes off the two bodies. It was as if they were connected by the symbiotic thread of their simultaneous deaths. The two bodies spun with the current, two figures poised to begin a water ballet that would never happen.

"All right! Alex. Get your men across in double time." Roosevelt's voice seemed to boom at them from a great distance. Alex looked to his left. The Colonel sat erect in his saddle, less than twenty yards away. Alex stared into the water at the pock marks that punctured the surface like slanting hail and thought, The man's a fool.

"At the double, for-ward!" he screamed and, without looking to his rear, ran down into the river. At first it was easy. He picked up his feet, pumped his knees, and moved rapidly through the shallows. But then his foot slipped on a mossy rock and he was under the water. He felt arms pulling him back to his feet, and realized that he had lost the rifle which, as an officer, he should not have been carrying in the first place. He jerked his .44 from its holster and stared ahead.

"Move it, Goddamnit!" The words from somewhere to his rear stabbed through him. He tried to run, but found that he could not. The water deepened, first to his waist and then almost to his chest. He was disoriented. For a moment he wasn't sure what he was doing. Several of his troopers had moved out in front of him and were struggling frantically to move through the bullet-torn water. He tried to move faster, but someone was pushing him aside.

"Goddamnit, Cap'n. If you cain't move any faster, let ol' Bill Pike set the pace." That was the voice that had cursed him when he came up out of the water. Alex turned to his right, prepared to reprimand the huge bear, but Pike was in front of him now, laughing at everyone around him, obviously enjoying the danger.

"Sorry, Cap'n," Pike grinned. "Jes couldn't resist a little needle." He turned away, pulling his large body through the river.

They were more than half way across now, and Alex had no idea how many men he had lost. He had given the command to move forward, which was all he could do until they finished the crossing. He concentrated on plowing through the river.

Pike held his rifle above his head with both hands and pumped his arms and shoulders back and forth, using his upper body for leverage. Suddenly he stopped moving and looked up at the sky. "Well I'll be a goddamned hog-humper," he said. Alex looked up. A huge signal balloon carrying two men in a basket drifted towards them, evidently planning to land right in the middle of the trail on the far side of the river.

"Get moving!" Roosevelt yelled from the rear. "Move it! Move it!"

Alex snapped to his senses and pushed for the far bank. "Let's get with it!" he yelled, suddenly, awesomely, aware that the reconnaissance balloon spelled death. Every Spanish rifle within range would be firing at it. If the balloon blocked the trail and brought the crossing to a halt, no one near it would have a chance.

Pike was pushing forward again, still the leader, but frightened for the first time since landing in Cuba. He pumped his shoulders and knees, fighting to get ashore ahead of the balloon. Alex fought to keep up, as did Michael, who was to his left. The rest of the troop was strung out behind, with David bringing up the rear cajoling the stragglers to hurry.

Suddenly Big Bill Pike flopped over backwards in the water. Alex and Michael moved up, grabbed him by the upper arms and dragged him the last twenty yards to shore. A mauser bullet had sliced across the top of his head; his face was already covered with blood.

"Is he dead?" Alex asked, as they placed their burden next to the trail.

"I don't think so," Michael answered, puffing. "But he will be."

"What the fuck you talkin' about, Mex?" Pike looked up, glowering through a mask of blood. "You dumb-ass sheep fucker. They ain't a bullet made that can do me in."

"Bill, we're going to have to leave you here, I..." Alex looked frantically around. Most of "L" Troop had streamed ashore and was moving up the trail and away from the balloon as rapidly as possible. "We've got to go."

"Shhee-it, Cap'n, ya all go on ahead. I'll catch up with ya in no time." Pike was already pulling his field bandage from his tunic and getting ready to wrap his head. "Ya know I gotta hard head."

Alex nodded as he recalled Shorty's story about Pike and the feisty Durango whore. "Come on!" he said to Michael. A few minutes later they caught up with their troop, which had hunkered down in a relatively sheltered depression in the trail. Roosevelt was riding back down the line at a fast trot. "Stay put until we get the rest of the regiment across. Pass the word."

As they scurried up the trail to the head of the troop, Alex and Michael concentrated on keeping their heads down, trying, at the same time, to count their men. When they arrived at the head of the column, they flopped down in the wet grass and tried to catch their breath. "How...many?" Alex gasped.

"One hundred fourteen."

"I got a hundred twelve." He was silent for a moment. "Send for David. Then count off." Almost five minutes passed before David reached the front of the column. "What's the count? Who's missing?" Alex asked, his mind still full of the two Negro soldiers he had watched float serenely down the river.

"A hundred twelve," David puffed.

"Who's missing besides Pike?"

David looked up and grinned. "Pike's not missing. He caught up with us, bloody head, loud mouth and all." David shook his head in disbelief. "That man is something else."

"David, who is missing?"

"Aubrey, Beecham, Kleets. They never made it across the river."

" Shit," Alex muttered, picturing the river clogging with dead and wounded mules and men, and with the living troops still fighting to reach the other side.

Michael stared beyond the river, where the balloon was still trying to land in the trail. Fortunately, for the foot soldiers every time it came close, the light breeze swept it away.

"Here comes Teddy," Michael said, "Jesus, how does he do it? This must be at least the third time he's galloped along the line."

"Move on out!" Roosevelt yelled. "We're all across. Move out before that bloody balloon lands."

Alex jumped to his feet but then stopped, frozen. Everyone around him, Roosevelt included, turned their eyes in the direction he was staring. The balloon had come down hard in the middle of the trail, separating half a troop of Rough Riders from the rest of the regiment and blocking the exodus of the 22nd Infantry from the river.

"My God!" Roosevelt cried, as the Spanish fire increased its intensity, focusing on the balloon. "Let's go," he added, soto voice. The men began to move, their eyes still glued to the crossing, where the blue coated men of the 22nd were toppling by the score.

"Move it!" Alex yelled, and the long column started forward, four abreast.

They moved quickly through the next half-mile of open country, hindered only by occasional snipers. But as they caught up with the Ninth Cavalry, which was being held up by an infantry regiment from New York, Alex heard a scream less than thirty feet to his rear.

"Surgeon!" someone called. Since their path forward was blocked, everyone in the regiment fell flat on their faces in the jungle grasses at the side of the trail, and Alex hurried back to see what had happened. Private Les Baldwin, a short Arizonan, was lying on his back, kicking. His face had already turned dead white. Four of his companions were bent over him, unbuttoning his tunic. One of them looked up at Alex, tears in his eyes: "Gut shot, sir. I don't know. I just don't know."

One of the men pulled the tunic and undershirt aside, exposing a slightly bleeding hole about the size of a dime. "Damn. sir. Ain't that some hole?" the man asked, looking to Alex for confirmation. Alex nodded but thought, yes, but it's not that big. It's the shock that'll get him. He was more worried about the sweating, frozen face of the private than he was about the hole itself. At Las Guasimas, more men had died from shock than from loss of blood.

"What's going on, Alex?" He turned to face Captain Rob Church, the regimental surgeon, who moved quickly to Baldwin's side.

"Looks like a .45 slug, Rob," Alex answered, moving slightly to his left so he could see what the surgeon was doing. Church probed a little, lifted Baldwin's eyelids and said, "Something's wrong. Shock shouldn't be setting in this hard, at least not this fast," and rolled Baldwin gently over on his side. Alex gasped. The hole in the man's back was larger than a fist. Without saying a word, the surgeon allowed him to fall easily back. Baldwin looked up at him, but said nothing. Church shook his head and said, "I'm sorry, soldier," and crawled back to his post at the rear of the column. Baldwin started whispering, and Alex leaned down to listen to the words, which squeaked out between mixed bubbles of air and blood. "Tell Cap'n Robb...ain't his...fault." Alex nodded, removed the man's neckerchief and started to wipe away the cold sweat popping from Baldwin's forehead

"Forget it, Captain."

Alex looked over at Michael's hard, set face, then back down at Baldwin's eyes, from which the light had disappeared. He stood up, decided to take the dead man's rifle, and bent over just in time to take a bullet across the top of his left hand. He jerked to the right just as two more bullets, fired in rapid succession, slammed into Baldwin's corpse. "Goddamn snipers!" he yelled.

Michael was immediately at his side and helped to bandage his lightly creased hand. Alex stared glumly at the bandages. Two wounds already, he mused. What price glory. He then looked out in the general direction of the sniper fire. "There!" he shouted. A green-shirted *guerillero* had tied himself into the branches of a large tree some eighty yards away. Michael nodded and squeezed off three shots before another soldier spotted the well-camouflaged guerilla and also started firing.

* * * *

Juan Medina had climbed up the thick trunk of the tree less than an hour before. He and his two older brothers had spent the early morning hours around his mother's table, eating, filling their ammunition pouches and trying to ignore the old woman's sobs. They had embraced each other one final time, picked up their old .45 Springfields and left the house. None of the three expected to return from the jungle.

Each time Juan fired a round at the advancing *Yanquis*, he crossed himself and said, "One more for you, my father, and one more for Spain." The first time he saw one of his bullets hit an enemy, he sat quietly in his cramped perch for almost five minutes, awed by what his old rifle had accomplished. Though he was almost sixteen years old, this was his first mission with the *guerilleros*. His father had always forbade him to participate. But now that his father had died of the wounds he had received at Las Guasimas, no one had been able to hold him back. His brothers had been fighting the ex-slaves and other human garbage that called itself the Cuban Army of Liberation for almost three years. Now that it was probably too late, he had his chance. He meant to die with honor.

Juan plucked one of his few remaining rounds from the white chamois pouch tied around his waist. He inserted the cartridge carefully, as his brother had instructed. "When you are a sniper," Pablo had said, "every shot must count; every shot must do maximum damage. That is why we file the noses of the bullets." Juan had never seen the effects of an expanding slug, but he had obediently spent the preceding evening filing off the tips of his eighty cartridges.

Now he sat in the camouflage of his tree and watched the enemy scum move east along the river. He knew he would be killed, just as he knew that his cause was just: For God, for the Queen, for the Virgin Mary—and for his martyred father, with whom he would be reunited in Purgatory. Had not Father Salazar said so the preceding evening? He had come to bless the boys and to administer the final rites. He had placed a small particle of ash on each of their heads and then kissed them. "Your stay in Purgatory will be brief," he had said. Juan had wanted to cry. Instead, he had crossed himself, whispered a "Hail Mary" with Father Salazar, and returned to the kitchen table, where the freshly consecrated bullets waited to be filed.

Juan snapped from his reverie. The lead columns of enemy lice had started to slow down and crowd together along the narrow trail. Most of the soldiers were in blue uniforms, but directly across from him, less than a hundred meters distant, several hundred tan-coated men had come to an abrupt halt. He sighted along the heavy barrel of the Springfield, moved it slightly, drew in a deep breath, released half of it, and squeezed the trigger—just as Pablo had told him. He did not move a muscle until his target sprang sideways across the trail and collapsed on his back.

Before he took another shot, Juan counted slowly to two hundred. Pablo had told him: "If you count to two hundred, the smoke from your barrel will have blown away. If you do not, the smoke from your second round will mix with that of your first. Take time between shots." Ninety-eight, ninety-nine, two hundred. Many of his compatriots were now shooting at the men in the tan shirts. This time, just as he squeezed the trigger, his target moved. As he watched the man roll into the grass and spring quickly back to his knees, Juan realized he had only hit the man in the arm or hand.

Suddenly, Juan felt very cold. One of the soldiers was pointing directly at him, and then the tan soldiers were firing at him. Frantic, Juan tried to move his body around behind the trunk, but he was too high, and his feet were tied to the small platform he had constructed. He started to scream: "I do not want to die. I am sorry, my father, but I do not want to die!" At the same time, oblivious to Pablo's instructions, he fired as rapidly as he could load the old single-shot Springfield.

He felt an explosion in his knee and looked down. A bullet had smashed through his kneecap. He stared at the shredded, green cotton trousers, and at the splinters of bone and flesh. He noticed that the blood glinted in the sun. A large fly landed on the blood and he watched the fly circle around the edge of the destroyed knee. Just as the first real wave of pain seared through his shocked mind, a second bullet ripped into his right thigh, and he dropped his rifle. He started screaming again. When the third and fourth bullets hit him almost simultaneously, one in the groin and one in the stomach, he had already forgotten where he was, or why. Even his screams seemed to merge with the sounds and colors of the surrounding jungle. There was something he had to do, but what was it? What was more important than the pain?

All the shades of green turned to reds and yellows and purples. He could feel the sun, but it was very cold. The reds were warm, but they hurt his eyes. His pain was purple, and it ebbed and flowed as it built, like the seventh wave. He tried to open his eyes. The jungle was beneath him, spinning, just as in the dreams he used to have as a small boy. A part of his mind whispered that he had fallen from the tree and was hanging by his heels. That's why. What had he forgotten? What was it he was supposed to do? Father? Purgatory. Father Salazar Father church Holy Father Salazar Father forgive. Yes. Yes! Hail Mary. "Hail Mary full of Grace..."

* * * *

Fidel was furious. The Cubans had never been infantry. And other than short sieges of towns or blockhouses, they had never mounted infantry charges on fortified positions. Because they had always been burdened by insufficient ammunition and arms, they had always preferred surprise and hit and run tactics.

But what were they doing now? What were they doing this day? Fidel looked around at his fellow Cubans. He wanted, simultaneously, to cry and to kill. He looked at the men of his company and at the men of the rest of Christopher's battalion. Battalion? Fewer than two hundred men still on their feet—all ragged, all half-starved, far too undernourished to participate in a cross-country infantry attack on a mountain fortress in the middle of an incredibly hot July day. Already three of his men had fallen aside, stricken by the heat. No one complained—except the officers, like Fidel and Christopher, who knew that the march and long, uphill assault would kill almost as many men as Spanish bullets, and who knew, furthermore, that the whole strategy of the attack was absurd.

The *Yanquis* were having an even harder time of it; he could see that. Their wool uniforms turned them into walking steam baths that metamorphosed to crumbling coffins. But at least they had eaten recently. The *mambises* were without strength, certainly without reserves.

Those who endured did so more from sheer will than from physical strength: They sensed that they were participating in the major battle of the war, just as they sensed that the war, finally, was almost at an end, and that *Cuba Libre!* was finally within grasp. *Cuba Libre!* beckoned them on. *Cuba Libre!* and the deep, bitter sense that there was nowhere else to go—except into a crumpled heap at the side of the trail.

Like the *Yanqui* field grade officers, Christopher rode up and down the column, quietly encouraging his men. On Christopher's next pass along the line, Fidel held up his hand, grabbed Christopher's reins and pulled him off the trail into the jungle. "I do not think our people can go much further."

"I know." Christopher looked down from his horse at his friend, a man who had fought with him in so many battles.

How many has your company lost?"

"Twenty-three."

"How many from the heat and how many from wounds?"

"I don't know how many from what. Some from the heat. And some from three years of poor food, and three weeks of almost no food, and one week of *Yanqui* beans, and three years of old wounds that never heal properly, and too many deaths."

"Yes." Christopher said. "Yes."

He looked back at the trail. He did not want Fidel to see the tears in his eyes. "The *Yanqui* general will want to stop and regroup before the attack. We will have a few minutes to rest. In the meantime, I will try to beg some biscuits from his supply officer." Except for the food provided by Alex almost a week before, he and his officers had been forced to crawl from one American supply officer to another—begging for this, begging for that. Always begging. He hated it, hated himself for doing it, and hated the Americans for forcing him to do it. Each week, each hour, his heart seemed to constrict more and more. For the entire week he had done little else. Slowly, he moved to the rear of the column, where Major Bates, General Lawton's supply officer, shepherded his horde of supply mules. After all that he had done, and all that had been done to him, what was a little begging? His men needed food and the Americans had it. To beg was a required thing, despite the stupidity of his pride. "It's just that I would rather steal it," he muttered, as he rode up to the lead wagon of the supply train.

Chapter Thirty-Eight

SPAIN ADMITS DEFEAT AT CANEY
Five Battalions Under General Vara del Rey Have Been Beaten
The New York Journal, July 3.

* * * *

JOURNAL'S EDITOR DESCRIBES THE CAPTURE
OF EL CANEY
James Creelman, Journal Correspondent, Wounded in
Front Rank of Desperate Charge

* * * *

HEROIC ADVANCE OF INFANTRY UNDER FIRE

With the Army in front of Santiago, July 1—Through glasses our infantry could be seen advancing toward the heights of El Caney. As the cannon at our side would bang and the shell would swish through the air, we would watch its explosion then turn our attention to the little black specks of infantry dodging in and out between the groups of trees. The Spaniards fired in volleys whenever our men came in sight in the open spaces.

Many times we heard their volley fire and saw numbers of our brave fellows pitch forward and lie still on the turf while the others hurried on to the next protecting clump of bushes. William Randolph Hearst, *The New York Journal*, July 4.

El Caney

"They have certainly chosen a hot day, eh, General?" Colonel Alonzo de Montoya looked at General del Ray, who nodded absently. It hadn't rained in two days, and even the men sitting in the trenches, firing passively at the long lines of ants at the bottom of the ridge, were sweating streams. "But I think maybe it will rain later this afternoon, eh?" The colonel pointed at the clouds that squatted along the peaks of the *Sierra Maestra*.

General del Ray lifted his eyebrows slightly and stared through the colonel as if the latter were crazy. "I don't think it makes much difference, my son." He looked through his field glasses at the *Yanquis* and *insurrectos*, who were forming skirmish lines at the bottom of the ridge. "We will all be dead before nightfall. What is the difference if it rains or not?" Then, noticing the confusion and hurt that flitted across the Colonel's face, del Ray relented a bit. "Still, a shower would be nice, wouldn't it? It would make the slope more treacherous for our enemies, and it would help to refresh our troops. Perhaps we should pray for the rain to come."

The colonel glanced away and looked back again, unable to determine whether or not the general was mocking him. "How long before they reach us, sir?"

"Two, perhaps three hours. Perhaps we should form a pool and take bets on the exact time. It might prove to be a diversion and lift the morale of our men."

De Montoya was convinced that the general was losing his mind. The old man was impossibly tranquil, as if he had no worries, or even responsibilities. The colonel saluted, muttered something about "the troops" and departed as quickly as possible.

General del Ray barely noticed the younger man's departure; he was lost in thought. Yes, in some ways it would be good to die. There was little else to live for. He had served his country well for more than half a century; had outlived all of his brothers and both of his sons; had been married for forty years to a soft-spoken though fanatically religious woman who had given him four children. He had written one book on the Cuban soil and another on the African slaves of Oriente Province; and had loved a long series of mistresses. It had been a good life. He thought for a moment of his wife and two unmarried daughters, who were lodged in the rented house in San Juan City, less than half a mile away. I should worry about them, I suppose. But they will be taken care of. They will return to Spain and enter the convent on the hill above Toledo. They will be very pious and very content, and they will pray for my soul, which will do it no harm.

The General pulled out his watch and saw that it was almost 2:00. He picked up his field glasses and climbed the three steps that led from the blockhouse to the connecting trench. The blockhouse had been very quiet. No, not quiet. What was it? Lost in his reveries as he had been, the noise of the rifles and artillery had seemed distant, somehow irrelevant.

As he stepped into the open, however, the battle exploded upon him and his mind leaped back to his duties. He strode through the trenches, giving an order here, a word of commendation there, nods and smiles to everyone. When he reached the western-most trench, he looked down at Santiago Bay, where Cervera's fleet was huddled up against the northern shore. He swept his glasses out to sea, where the American fleet was basking confidently in the sun. When Cervera's fleet is destroyed, he thought, it will be all over for Spain. The Pacific fleet burned at Manila Bay, now the Atlantic fleet is bottled up at Santiago. Two fleets, three hundred thousand soldiers, one empire.

What will happen to the other great empires? he wondered. The German, the Russian, the Austro-Hungarian, the British? How far into the next century will their glory burn? Another decade? Two or three? And what will replace the old empires? The New World? Perhaps. The United Sates? Del Ray chortled. "Perhaps, just perhaps." What would my great-grandfather say? When he was Governor of Florida, Spain owned four fifths of the continent. "Ah well," he shrugged. "Perhaps the Americans will rule their empire with more wisdom than we ruled ours."

When he returned to the blockhouse, a different colonel was waiting with a map. "Ah, General. There you are, sir. I have just finished my intelligence report."

"Oh?" del Ray enquired disinterestedly. "Has your intelligence improved?"

"As we suspected, there are three American divisions. Facing us here at El Caney is an infantry division of about seven thousand men, commanded by a General Lawton. He is reinforced by about twenty-five hundred rebels commanded by Colonel Carlos Garcia."

"Calixto's son?"

"Yes, sir. Our information is that the Cubans are weak and ill-fed. Evidently they are not highly regarded by the *Yanquis.*"

"If that is so, the Americans are making a mistake."

"Yes, sir," the colonel agreed sourly.

"So, my son. We have a reinforced division of Americans and Cubans directly below us. That leaves two divisions for the rest of the ridge line."

"Yes, sir. There is an infantry division under General Kent and a cavalry division—without horses—under General Wheeler. But General Wheeler is sick and General Sumner is in charge. They are headed for San Juan Ridge."

"Hmmnn, a cavalry division without mounts. Are there Cubans with them?"

The colonel nodded. "Another two thousand or so. I don't think we need to worry about the cavalry division, though. Three of its regiments are either Negros or volunteers. We'll turn them back easily enough."

You fool, he wanted to say. Who do you think we've been fighting all these years? Two thirds of the Cuban army is at least part Negro. It's all volunteer.

* * * * *

Nothing can be worse than this, Alex thought. Like most of the men around him he hungered for action, for the release that the attack would bring. Action, movement, a chance to do something. He thought of Roosevelt's toast aboard the *Yucatan:* "May the war last until each officer is dead, wounded or promoted." His father would have loved those words. Now Alex realized he was ahead of the game—twice wounded and twice promoted. He wasn't looking for glory anymore, but still hungered for action, because action meant movement; it meant doing something, anything beyond lying in the dirt and waiting to be shot. Twice was enough for that aspect of glory.

It was time to check his troops. Roosevelt had also said: "Set a manly example. Always set an example. Stand straight up. Inspire bravery." Alex half stood, but when a fusillade of bullets hit the trail just ahead of him and he was forced to run at a crouch, he moved rapidly down the line, checking his troopers, consoling them, reassuring them that, surely, they would move out at any moment.

When he got to the tail of the prostrate column, he found David reading *Leaves of Grass*. "David! What in the hell are you doing?"

Vandervoort looked up, amazed that his friend would ask such an absurd question. "What else is there to do? It keeps my mind off the snipers."

"Look, I'm sure we're going to move out at any second. There's quite a bit of movement going on in the Ninth Regiment and...Here comes Teddy. Put that book away."

"God, I wish we were back in our rooms at Harvard. A little conversation, a bit of sherry, a good book..."

Alex, left him in his reverie. He ran, still in a crouch, up the line to meet Roosevelt who, oblivious to the Spanish fire, was riding down the line on Little Texas. Damned fool! Alex thought. You're going to get yourself killed.

"Bucky's dead," Roosevelt announced. His tone was uncharacteristically confused.

"Sir?"

"Bucky O'Neill is dead, shot while walking the line, smoking a cigarette and inspiring his men. One of his men said, 'Captain, you'd best get down. One of them mauser bullets is going to get you.' Bucky said, 'Friend, there's not a Spanish bullet made that's got my name on it.' Two minutes later a bullet hit him square in the mouth. Jackson, I can't believe it."

I can, Alex thought. He knew that like himself, the former sheriff of Prescott, Arizona had joined up for glory. Alex shivered and looked around. Everyone else in the immediate vicinity was flat on his stomach.

But here he was, a mindless idiot, standing straight up and talking to an even bigger idiot, who was seated on a skittish horse.

"All right! There's the flare from General Wood. Let's GO!" Roosevelt shook off his confusion and regained focus. "Pass the word. No one falls out of formation. If a man falls from a bullet or the heat, that's it. We'll get help back to him later." He charged up and down the skirmish lines, repeating his message. The "crowded hour" of Roosevelt's opportunity had arrived.

"Move out!" Alex yelled, waving his arm in the direction of San Juan Ridge. He started to walk backwards up the hill, yelling to David Vandervoort on his right. "Keep the men spread out. Don't bunch up!" When he was satisfied that his men were in proper intervals, he turned back around, pulled out his pistol, and concentrated on the still distant ridge. The rush of adrenalin was intoxicating, euphoric. He looked to the right and left, conscious that thousands of men were moving up-slope in similar formations, all feeling the same surge of energy after the forced inactivity, all determined to make it to the top of the ridge, still more than a mile away.

The six regiments of the cavalry division moved quickly across the open grasslands, into a thin band of jungle that skirted the main ridge, out into a second clearing, then back into a second and thicker band of jungle. David Vandervoort was excited. He, too, was caught up in the exhilaration of the assault. He was acutely aware that he was participating in something of major importance, a movement of men and ideas that would, in some powerful if still indefinable way, change the history of his country. Images from *Vanity Fair* and *War and Peace* flowed through his mind. He knew that his was a little war, fought on a much smaller scale than the battles of Napoleon. Yet...still. He felt supercharged, more energetic than at any prior moment in his life. "If only it weren't so damned hot," he said to the private several yards to his right. Then they were in the jungle again, trying to slide between trees and cut through the heavy underbrush. "So damned hot, so hot damned, damned so hot," he repeated, poking at the vines with his rifle barrel.

Suddenly, he noticed an odd green shape in a palm tree that stood forty yards ahead of him. "Someone's in that tree!" he screamed. He raised his rifle to his shoulder. But instantly something went wrong. He was sitting on the ground, holding his stomach. The private on his left emptied his rifle at the sniper and bent over David. "Goddamn, Lieutenant! he cried. "Goddamn!" full of fear and pity and knowledge. "They gut shot-cha." The private stood up prepared to move on. "I'll be back with help after the battle. Okay, Lieutenant?"

David watched him go. He was close enough to the edge of the jungle to watch the advance, and saw the same private fall on his face less than twenty yards into the clearing. David watched for a long time, but the private didn't move. Then he couldn't see soldiers any more. He looked down at his stomach, watching as the blood seeped from around the edges of the Whitman he had placed inside his tunic. Sensing that he was about to pass out, David scooted over to a royal palm, put his head and back against the trunk and rested.

* * * * *

More than an hour had passed since they'd started up the hill with the *Yanqui* infantry, and still they were at least two hundred yards from the summit and El Caney. At least now they were close enough not to have to worry about the Spanish artillery, which thundered from the heights just above them; their targets were down-slope, a hell through which Christopher's troops had already come. The racket was awful, like an erratic but unending line of roaring freight cars.

Christopher raised his head just enough to spit out the mouthful of dirt he had eaten. He looked to his right, straight into Fidel's sweating, grime-streaked face. Fidel's eyes were huge with fear and fatigue. "Where did you come from?" Christopher asked. Fidel just looked at him and shook his head. 'Why aren't you with your unit?" he yelled, trying to force his voice above the guttural racket of the artillery.

"I'm deaf," Fidel said. "Can't hear a thing."

"Get back to the rear!" Christopher yelled. He turned on his side and gestured violently down the hill.

"Can't hear you, Colonel. Sorry," Fidel answered in a conversational tone that Christopher had no trouble hearing. Fidel's eyes were flat, almost dead. "I'm not going back."

"What do you mean, not going back?"

Fidel pointed to his ears. "I don't want to be a shopkeeper in Havana."

"Fidel! You don't have to be…"

"Shut up!" Fidel yelled. "I can't hear you. Understand? I can't HEAR you." He turned his back and stared at the obstacle that was holding up the advance on El Caney. The Spanish had rolled circular barbed wire, concertina they called it, across the semi-protected gullies. Seven bodies, Yankee and *mambi*, were draped across its steel thorns. Fidel looked at the wire for a long time, then stood up and sprinted back down the steep hill. Each giant step carried him at least fifteen feet.

"Fidelito!" Christopher screamed at his friend's retreating back. He turned to the front. Both his men and General Lawton's were pinned down by the firestorm that poured from the Spanish trenches. The only way up was through the relatively wide but shallow gullies. Even if they succeeded in cutting the barbed wire, no more than fifteen or twenty men at a time would be able to pour through the opening. How many of those would make it to the top? He thought of ordering another of his men to go after the barbed wire, but, NO! No, Goddamnit! He'd lost three men already on that man-eating wire, and he wasn't about to lose another one. The Yankees had ordered this absurd frontal attack. There had been other ways, other alternatives. The frontal attack was stupid, unnecessary, criminal. Very brave, yes. Very heroic. But very stupid. Nothing but bored officers playing at war, playing with lives, he thought. Playing with our lives.

Two more American soldiers ran up to the wire with dynamite; both were shot before they even touched the wire. When one of their charges exploded, three of the bodies draped over the concertina ripped free. The coiled wire rose in a cloud of rock and grass, and settled gently to earth in almost exactly the same position.

Christopher rested his head on his arm and tried to think. He realized he was crying. He tried to stop the tears; he knew he must do something to protect his men. But there was nothing to do—except hug the earth and pray, or curse. There was nothing anyone could do, except leap to one's feet out of futile desperation and charge the concertina. He was tempted, as the others had been tempted. At least, then, the noise would cease. It would be quiet. He could rest, forever and ever and ever. Maybe that was why he was crying. He was the colonel, yet there was nothing to do. He knew that he wouldn't charge the concertina, and he knew he wouldn't allow any of his men to.

Someone was shaking his shoulder. He stared with a strange sensation of déjà vu, into Fidel's sweat-streaked, almost totally exhausted face. Fidel's breathing was deep, ragged, erratic. He had run all the way back up the hill and was on the verge of collapse, but he was smiling. He held a large wire cutter close to Christopher's face.

"Snip. Snip. Snip," Fidel said. He bent over, kissed his friend on the lips, and was gone before Christopher could grasp what was happening.

" No-o-o-o! Ramon! Stop him!" he screamed at the lieutenant on his right flank. But his voice was drowned out by the cacophony of the artillery and the volleys of small arms fire. Ramon's face was buried between his arms; the young officer didn't even see Fidel flash by.

"Oinja protect me! Mother protect me. Federico protect me. Papi protect me. The saints protect me." Fidel chanted over and over as he zig-zagged the thirty meters to the wire. When he reached it, he stood up straight, raised his left arm in an obscene gesture directed at the Spaniards, and began to cut. He cut through four strands before the first bullet hit him. He braced his feet, shrugged his shoulders as if to shake off a fly, and continued to cut.

"Cover him!" a yankee officer yelled, and the soldiers intensified their fire, a few rising to one knee in order to fire with greater effect.

Fidel did not know that anyone was trying to help him; he had blocked out the world. Since his ears no longer worked, part of the world had already died. He no longer saw Christopher, or Judith, or his two dead brothers, or Federico or Oinja. He was conscious neither of his pain nor of the smells of battle, though he was vaguely aware of the sweat and tears running into his eyes and his open, rasping mouth. He wasn't even aware that he was still chanting. "Oinja protect me..." rose from some deep and forgotten source over which he had no control. The world had died, just as he would die. Only the concertina was alive, but it would die too.

A second bullet hit him, and a third. Still he cut. Snip. One last strand. Snip. He dropped the tin snips, grabbed the wire, yelled *Viva Cuba Libre!* and sprinted across the gully, folding the wire back upon itself. Then he was stumbling. He crashed onto his shoulder, turned an awkward somersault and came to rest in a heap against a rock. He was dead before he stopped moving, but three more bullets slammed into him. Each of the bullets lifted him slightly, as if to rearrange a little more gracefully the contorted bundle of flesh and rags.

* * * *

Then they were through the wire. The advance units of Cubans and Americans, their adrenalin recharged by the Cuban's insanely heroic effort, crashed through the open gully and charged the summit.

Even before the leading edge of the advance had covered the first half of the steep slope, a few Spanish defenders abandoned their trenches. Many of them had watched, mesmerized, as the Negro cut through the wire. Their officers had told them that the barrier would hold. By the time the huge Cuban crashed down the slope to come to rest against a rock, even the youngest of the defenders knew that the battle was over. More of the enemy would die; more of the defenders would die, but the battle was decided.

A little more than half an hour later, Christopher led the advance contingent of Cubans into El Caney. Though many of the Spaniards had fled, many others had fought from hut to hut and trench to trench, giving ground only when killed or seriously wounded.

* * * *

"There!" he yelled, and pointed his pistol at a three man machine gun crew. He fired once and hit the gunner in the shoulder. "Ramon!" Lieutenant Ramon and four other Cubans fired several rounds each at the gun crew, which became quiet. Two of the Cubans turned the gun around and fired into the trenches, from which most of the defenders had already fled.

Ramon and two others followed Christopher into the main blockhouse and discovered a Spanish colonel standing over the bodies of four-young privates. The colonel lifted his pistol and pulled the trigger, but it was empty. He seemed to be in shock; his face was completely devoid of expression. He pointed the pistol at Christopher and continued to pull the trigger, slowly and very methodically.

"What happened here?" Christopher asked.

"They wanted to run away, to abandon the Queen," the colonel answered dully, without interest.

"Shoot him," Christopher ordered. He walked back out of the blockhouse just as General Lawton, commander of the infantry division, rode to the top of the crest.

"Who was that brave nigger?" Lawton asked, wiping his brow with an already filthy red handkerchief. Before Christopher could answer, Ramon's pistol reverberated through the concrete blockhouse. "What's that?" Lawton cried.

"An execution, General,"

"Let me see." Lawton dismounted and nearly collided with Lieutenant Ramon, who was backing out of the blockhouse. Without exchanging a word, the general brushed by the surprised lieutenant and charged into the room where the five dead men sprawled across one corner of the floor. He came immediately back out and announced. "I want an explanation, Colonel."

Christopher forced himself to remain calm. "We caught the Spanish colonel in the act of executing four of his boy soldiers who, he claimed, were trying to desert. So we shot him." Christopher looked Lawton in the eye, saluted, and turned away. The general couldn't believe what he was hearing. " You mean you executed an officer without a hearing?" he cried. "Without a court martial?

Just...?" Lawton snapped his fingers.

"We caught him in the act, General. He admitted that he had shot the boys—without a hearing. There was nothing else to be done." The men glared at each other for a moment, then Christopher added, "This is Cuba, General, and I am a colonel in the Cuban Army. This is our way."

"And how about that big nigger that cut the wire? Who was responsible for ordering that act of incredible bravery?"

Controlling his revulsion, Christopher spoke coldly. "The 'nigger' acted on his own. Perhaps he just got tired—tired of the war, tired of watching his brothers die, tired of lying helplessly on the slope with his face in the mud. Perhaps he lacked faith in the future, General. His name was Captain Fidel Federico." He saluted again and turned back to his troops, who had formed new skirmish lines on the far side of the hill and were firing at targets down-slope towards San Juan City.

PART III: A PYRRHIC VICTORY

On either side of the Cubans, American soldiers were taking up similar positions. The wool-clad troops moved slowly along the ridge, rounding up prisoners, engaging in occasional fire-fights, and trying to patch up the many wounded. Within less than an hour from the time Fidel stood up to cut the wire, El Caney was secure. The Cubans and Americans were in command of the eastern heights overlooking San Juan City. In the distance, now naked to the American artillery, lay Santiago de Cuba, the capital of the East.

* * * * *

General del Ray paced restlessly back and forth on the front porch of his rented house in San Juan. His family huddled inside and watched him through the grillwork. They were afraid of what he would do. Every few minutes his wife or one of his two daughters yelled out the open window: "Father! Come inside. You'll get shot out there."

Del Ray didn't respond. Spanish deserters were streaming down from El Caney, racing desperately to outrun the enemy bullets. After glowering at the desperate men who ran and limped by, del Ray stopped pacing, glanced at the three bleary-eyed women whose faces filled the window, and ran into the street. "Wait! Soldiers!" he shouted. "It must not end this way." He stretched out his arms as if to bar the runaway soldiers. "Stop! Spain must not die this way."

"Out of the way, old man!" screamed a burly sergeant.

"Stop! We must . . ." The sergeant knocked the general over and kept on running. The general rose slowly back to his knees. His forehead was already beginning to swell and his nose was bleeding. But he felt nothing. He stared at the fleeing troops and absently fingered his flowing white beard. Then he remembered where he was, and rose again to his feet. "Stop! Wait . . ." He was no sooner up than he was back down, this time with an enemy bullet through both his long legs. This time he felt the pain. Despite his decades of Spanish pride, distilled through long generations of family service to the Crown, despite all the self-discipline, he could not help himself. He sat where he had fallen and moaned with the pain. Then he began to howl with humiliation and disgust. The last vestiges of pride flowed down his sunken cheeks and wove between the long white years of his beard. Fifty years of service to the kings and queens of Spain, all crystallized in this moment of disgrace.

His troops continued to flow past, the last stragglers mad with fear. Few even glanced at the old man; none made a move to help him. He was just another dying soldier cluttering the steep, narrow street.

After what seemed to be a long time, Angelica, his youngest daughter, dashed from the house and tried to pull the general back towards the porch. The old man, though thin, was very tall; Angelica was tiny. She was moving him, she knew, but too slowly. "Mother of God!" she wheezed. "Please help me." The old man was unconscious. "Mother of God, please!" A young soldier hobbled toward them using his rifle as a crutch. "Please? My father?"

The boy looked first at her and then at the old general. A lady, he thought. His mind raced across a disconnected series of visions: the fine ladies who sometimes sent gowns and mantillas for his mother to mend, and who talked to her as though she were shit; the recruiting squad that had dragged him and his older brother from the marketplace; his brother lying dead in the block-house at the top of the hill.

He realized that this pale, soft-faced young woman was this general's daughter. Tears of rage welled up in his dirt-lined eyes. He leaned more heavily on his Mauser, smashed the woman in the face as hard as he could, and spat on her. Then, in one sharp, unpremeditated move that would continue to surprise him years after his return to Spain, he stood on one leg, swung the Mauser around, and shot the general in the head. Without looking again at the blood and spittle-covered face of the young woman, he replaced the butt of the Mauser under his arm and hobbled down the street.

Chapter Thirty-Nine

BLOOD — BOUGHT VICTORY IN FIRST DAY'S FIGHT
Heroic Charge up San Juan Hill

* * * *

With the American Army before Santiago, July 1—It takes but a few words to tell this, but the fighting was long drawn out. The Spaniards realized the strategic importance of San Juan Hill, as it commands much of the second line of defense and the city itself. So they had concentrated 4,000 troops there, and some artillery.

Their smokeless powder made it somewhat difficult to locate and get the range of the guns, and at times when it seemed that their fire had been silenced, they would open up again.

When in the heat of the afternoon, the order was given for a charge, the men responded with a great cheer. *The New York Journal*, July 3.

San Juan Ridge

How many hours had they been fighting? It seemed like days since he had gulped down his morning hard tack and coffee. No, not days. Weeks. One more rush, Alex thought. One more charge. Twenty more minutes?

"Cap'n?"

What was that sound? His name? The sound seemed to call to him from a great distance.

"Cap'n Alex!" The voice was insistent. He lifted his face from the slope and looked to his right. Bill Pike had crashed down next to him, his usually genial face covered with caked blood and sharp concern.

"Bill? What's wrong?"

"Cap'n. It's them long-tom, horse-cock smokin' artillery dudes again."

"Where?" Disregarding the steady fire pouring from the Spanish trenches on Kettle Hill, Alex leaped to his feet and followed Bill to the right of the skirmish line. But they arrived too late. Even as they ran up to confront the officer in charge, the battery fired its first rounds. The deep roar of the guns was followed immediately by huge clouds of grey smoke that drifted slowly across the lines of prostrate cavalrymen. Even before he and Bill stopped running, Alex yelled at the artillery lieutenant: "Get those god-damn guns out of here, right god-damn now!" The artillery officer stared at the wild-eyed captain and the huge, bloody-headed private, both of whom were waving pistols in his face. The lieutenant could think of nothing to say. "You want to get us all killed, Lieutenant?" Alex yelled.

As if on cue, the first Spanish shells landed thirty yards in front of the guns, almost in the middle of a line of Negro cavalrymen. A severed black arm and hand wrapped in flames landed at the lieutenant's feet.

Alex grabbed the lieutenant and stuck his pistol in the frightened man's mute face. "I wouldn't want to hurt a fellow officer, Lieutenant."

"I would," Pike stared at the officer through the blood that had started, once more, to flow from the deep groove across the top of his head. "You get them horse cocks outa here, little boy, or I'm gonna..." A second barrage from the Spanish artillery exploded in the palm trees less than forty yards to their rear. Though each of the trio wanted to hit the earth, each was conscious of his part in the melodrama, and conscious of the eyes of the artillerymen, who understood profoundly that the Spanish had their range. "I'm gonna blow your fuckin' haid off," Pike managed to conclude. For some reason the concussion of the artillery rounds was causing his head to bleed more profusely. For the first time since getting shot more than half a day earlier, he was feeling the pain. His head was, quite literally, splitting. The pain fed his rage, and his face devolved into a maniacal twist.

"We'll leave," the lieutenant yelled, at least as afraid of the men in front of him as he was of the next Spanish barrage which, he knew, would be on target. "Fall back!" he yelled at his antsy artillerymen, who had already brought in their aiming stakes.

* * * * *

"Let's go, Bill," Alex said, over-awed by their success. Within seconds of their hasty departure, four Spanish rounds landed almost in the middle of the battery, killing two men and destroying one of the guns. By the time the next barrage came, the survivors had moved out.

"We can't stay here. It's suicide!" Michael yelled at Alex. Michael and two privates were checking the wounded

Alex was exhausted, depleted, confused. He looked at Michael, who was waiting for orders, and at Bill Pike, who had collapsed and was cradling his bleeding head in his hands. I've got to do something, Alex thought. I wish Roosevelt would get back. What can I do? Another barrage of shells landed in the lines. Why can't I think? he asked himself through the noise. What can I do?

Suddenly, Bill Pike stopped rocking back and forth. He fell over on his side and became still. Alex bent over, saw that he was dead and, a fog lifted from his mind. He turned to Michael and yelled, "Charge!"

Michael great stared at him. Only Roosevelt or Brady could order a charge. Brady was at the far end of the formation, and Roosevelt had yet to return from his conference with General Wood.

"Charge!, Goddamnit!" Alex screamed. "You wanted something to happen, well—something's happening. Get up!" Alex got to his feet and ran down the line, kicking his prostrate troopers. "Up and at 'em, boys! Let's GO! Get up and fight, or stay here and die." As if to emphasize the unpleasant alternative, another incoming Spanish barrage exploded, this one over their heads. Shrapnel sliced through the air like hundreds of metal scythes.

The men were up and running. Someone to the right blew on a bugle. A second troop rose to its feet and followed the men of "L" Troop. Released from the frustration of their hopelessly exposed positions on the flank of Kettle Hill, the charging soldiers began to shout their battle cry, "Remember the *Maine*!" Troop after troop of Rough Riders rose and started for the top of the hill.

The release of adrenalin triggered a chain reaction. Troops of the First and Ninth Cavalry stood up and joined the assault. Then the men of the Second Brigade—the men of the Third, Sixth and Tenth Regiments—were on their feet and following. Off to their left the First Infantry and the 22nd Massachusetts began to move erratically up the hill. One thousand men, then two thousand, then five. Within minutes the entire western segment of the front was moving toward the connected ridges known as Kettle and San Juan Hills. Each man ran alone, five, ten, sometimes fifteen yards. Then he would drop to one knee, fire, rise to his feet and be off again.

The Spanish line was a magnet that pulled the Americans forward. But if at all able, even the wounded continued their upward push. When a man dropped from the line, he was left to fend for himself.

Though the Spanish artillery fire was heavy, it was becoming less effective; the spotters could not drop their range fast enough to keep up with the charging Americans. And the men were spread out now, five to ten yards apart, running in loosely connected waves of skirmish lines, impervious to what was going on around them.

Then Roosevelt joined them, still astride Little Texas. He too caught the frenzy, totally unaware that he hadn't personally delivered the order to charge. Displaying the kind of mindless heroics that made his men love him and even his most cynical officers emulate him, he rode back and forth along the lines of his regiment—pushing, extolling, encouraging, flashing his well-shined machete in the late afternoon sun. "On, men! On! On! On! On for the *Maine*! On for the flag! On for Old Glory!"

Up, always up. Men dropped by the dozens. Like irregular clumps of blue and tan wild flowers, the heat-stricken, the dead, and the seriously wounded dotted the open green slope. Then the lines divided: the infantry and the Second Brigade headed left, directly for San Juan Hill.

"To the right!" Roosevelt yelled. The word passed rapidly from man to man, and the First Brigade, under the command of the former Assistant Secretary of the Navy, melded slowly to the right and up to the summit of Kettle Hill. Less than two hundred yards now to the squat buildings on the summit, then less than a hundred.

The artillery finally stopped; the Americans were too close for it to be effective. There was less noise now, at least less of the heavy noise that rattled brains. The dominant sound now was rifle fire, the crack, crack of Spanish mausers counter-pointed by the slightly deeper reports of the American springfields and Krag-Jorgensons.

But then a new noise rose up from the ground—a deep, rhythmic rasp. Slowly, yet insistently, it drowned out the other noises of the battlefield. Alex tried to ignore it. He continued to yell at his men, who were also yelling—at each other, at the Spanish, into the air. Everyone was yelling, and everyone was gasping. The super-charged, adrenalin-inspired troops were totally exhausted, but did not yet know it. Nervous energy moved them on up the hill—past the barbed wire, beyond the deepening field of wounded and dead, past the first Spanish troops, beyond endurance, beyond duty, beyond. Always up and beyond.

As they pushed across the second barbed wire harrier, Alex stopped again to reload. His fingers shook. He was panting. Deep, ragged gasps tore from his lungs and exploded through his chapped, open mouth. That was the noise, he realized. That was the new sound sweeping across the advancing line—the thunderous denouncement of over-charged hearts and undernourished lungs. That was the new and terrifying roar that rose to replace the now absent roar of the artillery. A chorus of labored breathing. Ignore it! Alex told himself, as he started across the final clearing. Ignore it! Ignore it!

Then they were there. The mixed regiments of blacks, whites, regulars and Rough Riders poured across trench after trench, shooting and hacking the defenders. Within fifteen minutes it was over; they had captured Kettle Hill. The Spaniards disappeared—dead or seriously wounded, deserters, or, in a few cases, prisoners. Except for the tortured breathing of the victors and the screams of the wounded, the hill quieted. One after another, the men threw themselves down on the ground and tried to catch up with their hearts. A few fell to their hands and knees, some to pray thanks and some to vomit repeatedly before passing out from heat and exhaustion.

"Check your men!" Roosevelt yelled at his officers. Somehow, miraculously, he was still astride his horse, though both horse and rider had been slightly wounded and Little Texas was dripping lather.

What keeps that man alive? Alex wondered, as he turned to reorder his scattered troops. "Sergeant Archuletta!" he cried.

Michael was leaning against a wall. Never, ever, had he exerted himself to such a degree. They had run almost three hundred yards up hill, through the humid yet blistering heat of a tropical July. Despite his fatigue, however, once he understood what Alex required of him, Michael unglued himself from the wall and helped to account for the men of "L" Troop, a job that proved to be almost impossible. The Rough Riders and the other two regiments of the brigade had so thoroughly intermixed during the mad charge that little could be done. Somehow, unaccountably, they had even picked up more than sixty infantrymen, who should have been several hundred yards to the left at San Juan Hill. It would take a week for word to pass through the invading army that almost three thousand Americans and Cubans had died on that sweltering first of July.

"Well?" Alex asked, returning from his own attempt to separate his troops from the melee. "Did you have any better luck than I did?"

"No, sir," Michael answered. "I can't account for twelve of our men." He paused briefly. "I can't even find David."

"I haven't seen him since we left the road. How long has that been? It seems like years."

"About three hours, Captain."

"Surely he..."

"We've got to send men back anyway. We've got folks strung all the way back to the road. No, all the way back to the river. If we don't find them by nightfall..."

" I know," Alex agreed quietly. "But you heard Roosevelt's orders. No one is to leave the front lines—unless they're wounded."

"You're wounded. You can go."

"No, I can't, Michael. Half the regimental officers are dead or seriously wounded. As long as I can stand, I've got to stay."

"Then I'll go. I'll find him." Before Michael could finish his sentence, the battle across the ridge at San Juan Hill moved into the same fiendish crescendo that had just subsided at Kettle Hill. "And here comes Teddy," he added quietly, realizing that he would not have his chance to find David.

Roosevelt rode at a slow walk, his slightly wounded hand resting conspicuously on the saddle horn. "All right, boys. Let's show a little manly support for the Second Brigade." He was surrounded by a dozen war correspondents, who seemed to have sprung from the earth like Caedman's dragon seed. Wearing long dusters and semi-military tunics, they followed the general like a train of expectant retainers. Roosevelt basked in the glow. He knew, even then, that the charge up Kettle Hill was the finest moment of his career, probably the single most exhilarating moment of what he hoped would be a long life. General Wood was still in the rear, and General Wheeler was still ill. HE was in charge. HE had been in the army for less than ninety days and HE was in charge of the brigade. HE was in command on Kettle Hill. The whole world was watching. What couldn't HE do?

As his men lifted themselves from the ground, Roosevelt turned to the correspondents and explained his plan. "We'll provide enfilading fire for the Second Brigade and the infantry. Hopefully, we'll be in position for another charge. Then? On to Santiago. Do you fellows want to stick around for the action? This one you can see from right here; it should be as good as a show at the Apollo."

Frederick Remington looked up from his sketch pad and grinned. "You bet, Colonel. You bet your bottom drawers we do." Most of the rest of the correspondents nodded. As usual, Roosevelt's enthusiasm proved to be contagious. They fantasized about everything a journalist dreams about, everything from six inch headlines to best-selling, eye-witness accounts of Teddy's Terrors and their heroism.

"Good!" Roosevelt nodded. "America will be proud of your contributions as, I hope, she will be proud of ours."

The men of the First Brigade ran, limped and crawled to the far side of Kettle Hill, threw themselves on the ground, and provided covering fire for the Second Brigade and the mixed infantry of Cubans and Americans. The allies were still more than two hundred yards from the crest of San Juan Hill.

"Aim for their heads," Roosevelt yelled, as he paraded back and forth on Little Texas and pointed at the tiny Spanish heads in the distant trenches.

The correspondents were impressed. Though most of them lay flat on the ground, a few knelt on one knee in what they deemed to be appropriately dashing military poses. Quentin Beard, a cadaverous giant from the Boston Globe, dropped his field-glasses and looked up at Roosevelt. "My God! Colonel. They're all so young!"

"That's right, Quentin. Spain's hard pressed. As you can see, however, those manly little fellows can put up one helluva battle."

* * * * *

David could feel the blisters on his face, which had swollen and cracked. His hat had fallen off and rolled away, and he'd finished the last of his water hours ago. Though he knew that many of the soldiers lying dead on the slope had died without consuming their water, there was nothing he could do to get at it. Even if he had the strength to crawl the twenty or thirty yards to the closest body, he wouldn't be able to fight off the two vultures perched upon the dead man's chest and legs. He didn't even have the strength to lean over and retrieve his hat, which had rolled to a stop less than two feet from his right hand.

I wish I'd been shot in the shade, he thought. He tried to move his fingers, but nothing happened. "Damn," he whispered. Ever since propping himself up against the palm tree, he had tried to keep his knees pressed against his stomach and against Whitman's *Leaves of Grass*, his built-in compress, but his knees had long since ceased to press against his stomach, and the bullet-ruptured book of poems no longer staunched the slow seepage of blood from his stomach. I should have brought *War and Peace* today, he thought, and tried to smile at the absurdity of his situation. He sensed that he would die before anyone could return for him.

My sight's going," he mumbled, slightly surprised by the calmness of his voice. "I'm going. Going going gone, said the auctioneer. Going going…" He could hear the parrots screeching in the trees, the distant sounds of battle, which seemed to be getting more intense, more insistent. He heard the whirr-rr-rr of heavy wings and managed to make out through the mist of his fogged-over eyes the red and black shape of the vulture that had landed a few feet away. "Shit!" He dropped his head onto his chest. What would Father do about this? he thought. I wonder what he's going to say when he finds out? I have been such a disappointment.

* * * *

Alex stalked back and forth along the line of prostrate troopers, every one of whom was firing at the trenches protecting the blockhouse on San Juan Hill, almost three hundred yards away. The men fired slowly, carefully, aiming for the round heads that bobbed up and down along the distant trenches. Alex walked stiffly because he was afraid. Even though Roosevelt had abandoned his horse, he was still striding boisterously back and forth, like an indefatigable Simon Legree. As usual, he seemed totally unconcerned for the Spanish bullets. Though not quite as enthusiastically, his officers emulated his example. Even as Alex walked along the line of "L" Troop, however, he tried to shrink inside himself. Being a hero was all right—to a degree—but it had its limitations: Most of the dead littering the slopes of the ridge had died before they could even realize, much less appreciate, their new status. As was most often the case, all died before their grateful and exhilarated countrymen could bestow upon them the rewards of heroism.

"My God! They got Jones." Alex stopped his frenetic pacing and watched four men carry Lieutenant Roger Jones, former captain of the Yale Crew, back over the ridge. Like Alex, the lieutenant had been setting an example for his men.

"Captain! You'd best keep moving!" Michael yelled from off to his right.

Alex nodded in assent and continued his pacing. But before he had taken another step, a Mauser bullet slammed into his chest.

* * * * *

"Alex!"

Voices came at him as from a great distance. They were talking about him. His vision had blurred for some reason, but he could still make them out. There were four of them, and they were bending over him. "Is he dead?"

"I don't think so, Sergeant. Look at his eyes." Someone held a finger in front of Alex's nose. The finger moved back and forth, Alex's eyes followed it.

"Dillon. You still got that compress?"

"Yeh, Sarge. Ah sure do."

"Good." Everything was quiet for a moment. Then: "Lift him up. That's good. Pull up his tunic."

"Ya think that'll hold, Sarge?"

"I don't know. I don't think he'll bleed to death, unless it's internally. But the shock? Dillon, get back to that ranch building on the other side of the hill. Get one of those Spanish blankets." No one said anything for a moment. Then there were other voices, a new voice. It sounded like maybe it was Roosevelt's, but he couldn't tell, and he couldn't see.

"It's your troop, Sergeant. Show me what you can do."

"Yes, sir." Michael saluted and turned back to his remaining men. But I'll be damned if I'm going to strut back and forth like one of those idiotic bantam roosters, he thought.

"Look! They're standing up," Dillon yelled. The Spaniards were standing up in their trenches and firing down the ridge at the advancing Americans and Cubans from the Second Brigade. Somebody to Michael's right yelled. Michael turned to see Roosevelt and half a dozen troopers climb a fence and start across the field in the direction of the San Juan blockhouse. What he's up to, Michael wondered?

Within minutes Roosevelt was running back toward his own lines and waving his hands. The men who had accompanied him remained where they were, an extremely vulnerable group of soldiers who pressed themselves into the ground and fired at the Spanish blockhouse and trenches. "Let's go, Goddamnit. We're attacking!" Furious that no one had followed him, Roosevelt ran up and down the lines, screaming, "Attack, Goddamnit! Attack!"

At first no one could understand what he wanted. Attack what? The Second Brigade and the infantry were almost to the top of San Juan Ridge; they would overrun the blockhouse long before the Rough Riders could possibly arrive.

We'll be a lot more effective right where we are, Michael thought. Here we can continue to supply covering fire. However, Roosevelt had made up his mind: He was not about to let the advance regiment of the Second Brigade, the Negro troopers of the Tenth Cavalry, deprive him of one more chance for glory. Buglers blew Charge, and Roosevelt again began his dash for San Juan Hill, this time followed by the First Brigade and his enthusiastic corps of correspondents.

"All right, men," Archuletta commanded. "Off your asses and on your feet. We're moving out." "L" Troop joined the other troops of Rough Riders, and the long skirmish lines moved forward, first at a fast walk and then at a trot. A number of the Spanish redirected their rifle and machine gun fire, and men started falling into the tall grass.

"Run! Damnit!" Roosevelt stopped briefly, turned to the troops following him, and pumped his arms repeatedly. "Run! Those coons are going to beat us." He turned back to the blockhouse, where the advanced soldiers of the Tenth Cavalry had already reached the outer trenches. By the time the exhausted Rough Riders arrived, the battle was almost won. They poured through the trenches, shot a few cringing defenders, captured eleven prisoners, and liberated a few supplies. But the Tenth Colored Cavalry had already completed the heavy work. The worst was over before the Rough Riders arrived.

* * * * *

The Cubans and Americans had now won the entire chain of hills and connecting ridges that stretched from San Juan Hill in the southwest to El Caney in the northeast. Nothing of consequence stood between the invasion force and Santiago de Cuba.

Michael sat down on the edge of a trench and stared at the bodies crumpled at the bottom of the long slit in the earth. There were other bodies scattered along the trench, most killed by head wounds. Once again Michael marveled at the almost uniform youth of the Spanish soldiers, and then thought of the Rough Riders, who varied in age from sixteen to forty-seven, and of the Cuban soldiers, whose aged varied even more, and whose ranks included many women.

And one of those women is Judith, he remembered, wondering if she had survived the battle. He shook his head. I'm sorry, Sky Woman. He tried to picture his dead wife's face, but couldn't. A profound sadness welled up from the pit of his psyche.

"Sergeant?"

He pulled his eyes from the face of the dead Spanish youth and turned to face Private Henry.

"Doc Church's gettin' ready ta ship the cap'n. You said ya wanted ta know."

"Thanks, Henry." Michael climbed from the trench and stretched his legs. "I'll be right over."

"Where do you think you're going, Archuletta?"

He was already thirty yards from the trench and headed back to Kettle Hill when Roosevelt's voice stopped him. "You are in command of this troop, Sergeant. Where might you think you're going?" Roosevelt stood with his legs apart and his hands on his hips. "It wasn't my idea to make you a sergeant; it was Captain Jackson's. I don't think men of your race should be given serious responsibility. However, you are a sergeant, and you are in charge of "L" Troop—at least until I can transfer another officer. So where were you going?"

Michael hid his fury. "To see the Captain, sir. Dr. Church is getting ready to evacuate him back to the beach."

"Your job is here, Archuletta!" Roosevelt turned on his heel and walked away, followed by a brace of smirking correspondents.

* * * *

Alex opened his eyes. Someone was beating him with rocks. Everything was red. No. There was tan to the left. What was it? His sleeve? Then... What? His head rested on his left arm and he was staring at a pool of blood. The pain was incessant, jolting. He tried to turn his head, and saw a booted foot connected to a tan leg. With every jolt the boot rose up and dropped on his ribs, on his original wound. "Stop!" he tried to yell. Then again, louder: "Stop it!"

"Hey, Corp. They's someone yellin' back there."

"Yeh? Stop the cart and we'll check 'er out." The corporal and driver dismounted from their seat at the front of the springless, large-wheeled ox-cart cart and walked back to the rear, where their cargo of seven severely wounded soldiers lay jumbled in a knot of limbs and blood. "Who said something back here?"

"Me," Alex rasped. "The boot. Please!"

The corporal saw the problem, grunted and climbed into the cart. "Sorry, Captain. It's the ruts. We're going as slow and careful as we can...Dixon! Get your lazy ass up here and help me. The lieutenant's dead. This foot won't be botherin' you any more, Captain. Poor sod."

"Who is it?" Alex wheezed.

"Lieutenant Jones, sir." Jones? Alex flashed back to the night of the poker game in San Antonio. Though Jones had gone to Yale rather than Harvard, Alex knew that he was more than rich and athletic. He had been a brilliant student and, at the same time, an irrepressible snob—sarcastic, petty, condescending, and very witty. So Jones had died as he had lived: making Alex uncomfortable.

"Goddamnit, Dixon. Don't step on that man. He's hurt bad enough as it is."

"Sorry, Corp. It's the weight. Can't seem ta get a fuckin' grip."

Alex lifted his head slightly and watched Jones's boots disappear over the rear of the cart. He noticed that the Yale man's right sole was worn through.

"All right. Let's try this thing one more time." The corporal and his helper were back in the cart. "Maybe with one less we can keep these poor sods from gettin' all tangled up."

"Ah sure hopes so, Corp. That there's the second one we lost, an' we ain't but halfway ta the beach."

"Yeh. Well." The corporal shrugged. "This ride may kill 'em all, boy, but gettin' down to that field hospital's their only chance, so we gotta try."

Half way! Alex thought. Only half way. Maybe that's what the voices had been getting at earlier. He had been sleeping under the warm blanket, but had awakened shivering, even though he knew the late afternoon sun was very hot. There were voices again, and they seemed to be talking about him. "Put him in the wagon, one of the voices had said. "It'll kill him," someone else had said. "Put him in, soldier," the first voice had ordered. It was the surgeon, Rob Church. "I can't help him here."

So that's what they were talking about. Well, I'm going to make it.

The cart jerked forward and continued its slow, jolting trip to the beach. Alex tried to tell from his bandage how badly his chest wound was bleeding. It was sticky, yet Michael must have gotten it tight. If only the pain would go away. Just a little. Some of the other wounded were groaning. He wanted to join in but knew that the drivers were doing the best they could. But why shouldn't I? I don't have to set any more examples. Not now. No more fucking heroics.

Alex let out one long groan, then settled into unconscious, rolling moans in rhythm with each jolt of the springless cart. To the officers, he thought. To the fucking officers.

Chapter Forty

GERMANY FEARS WE WILL BECOME A MILITARY POWER

* * * *

Berlin, July 3—The National Zeitung asserts that the war waged by the United States against Spain is not for humanity and justice, but is based on mercenary motives. It believes that...it will be difficult for the Americans to return to their condition of peace so characteristic of the Republic. Nor will Cuba prove a sufficient indemnity for the great loss of life and property.

The need of a great standing army and a well-equipped modern navy, which has been demonstrated in this war, will make the military element play a leading role in the Republic, as in ancient Rome and the Republics of Cromwell and France. *The New York Journal*, July 4.

South of El Caney

As the Cubans stumbled into their clearing, the women and boys poured from their makeshift *bohios* to help with the wounded. Theresa joined Christopher. "It went well?"

"The battle is over," Christopher said. "Perhaps the war."

"But we lost many men. I count thirty-seven missing. All dead?"

"No." He dropped to the ground, where he remained for the next hour. "The *Yanquis* took six or seven of our wounded to the beach for major surgery. The rest? I think, are dead." He exhaled deeply, suddenly more tired than he could remember ever having been.

"Where is Fidelito?"

"Dead."

"Have you told…?"

"No. There will be a time to tell Judith. She'll be busy for at least several hours."

Theresa was silent. She'd made no move to touch Christopher, but now she reached out and rubbed the back of her hand along his cheek. "I grieve for the dead."

Christopher nodded. Though he heard Theresa's words, his attention stayed with the moans of the wounded, and on the women already keening the loss of sons and husbands. Although he could not speak, Christopher extended his arm and pulled Theresa close. For a long time they held each other and listened to the moans and occasional screams that poured from the tiny hospital. When he finally felt that he was in control of his emotions, he said, "When Judith is finished here, I will send her to Siboney to bring back our wounded."

"No, Christopher. You can't! When Judith finishes she will collapse. When she hears about Fidel…"

"By now she probably knows. Certainly she has been talking to the wounded. Certainly someone has told her."

"You should be the one, Christopher. That is your job."

He nodded, acknowledging the truth of Theresa's words. "We must keep Judith busy, Teresa. When she finishes here we will send her to *Siboney*. She should arrive about dawn. She will work until she drops."

"And that is supposed to help her?"

"Yes! And I will talk with her before she leaves. Now, let me rest." He lay down on his side, cradled his head on his crooked arm and shut his eyes.

Theresa reached out to caress his head, and gazed at his long, parchment face and the streaks of grey that threaded through his brown hair. You have grown old so quickly, she thought. Not even forty, yet so old. When this war is over, my aging love, when this war is over I will make you young again. When he began to snore softly, she rose and walked to the hospital to speak with Judith. At least I can help him with this, she thought.

* * * * *

Shortly after 2100 hours, Roosevelt relieved Michael of his temporary command. Not until long after midnight, however, was the New Mexican able to sneak away from San Juan Hill. He spent the intervening hours explaining the troop to the new lieutenant, a twenty-two year old graduate of Princeton. For the final hour of his sojourn with the First United States Volunteer Cavalry, he packed his few necessities, pretended to fall asleep, then crept from camp in a heavy rain that would last well into the next morning.

His progress was slow. Even though it had been raining for only two hours when Michael approached the San Juan River, the steady downpour had already turned the heavily used trail into a quagmire. Despite the blackness of the night, however, he had no trouble following the trail: Long lines of men, carts and mules streamed back and forth between the beach and the front. Hundreds of wounded were still making their slow way down to the sea, many by themselves, some leaning on the arms of friends, some being carried on litters. Without exception, however, the wounded tried to avoid the high-wheeled, springless carts that carried the terminal and near terminal cases. The word was out: "If you ain't dead when they throw you on one of those rumbling monstrosities, you'll be dead before they throw you off." Each time one of the carts squeaked by, Michael thought of Alex and hoped that he was still alive, that he had survived both the cart ride and the surgery.

Though he had not actually made the conscious decision to leave until that moment when Roosevelt had stopped him from returning to Kettle Hill, Michael knew that, in fact, he had made the decision the moment he had begun to stalk Shorty through the jungle. Unlike the overwhelming majority of men in the regiment, he had never been stirred by patriotism, idealism or war fever. His motives, from the beginning, had been dark. He had been driven to seek out and destroy the man who had killed his wife. His only other interest was in the welfare of his two friends, Alex and David, at least one of whom was probably dead. He would like to see Freddy Nelson if possible, but if he didn't, no matter. Freddy would survive.

Only recently had Michael's motives become more complex. Other than a flock of sheep he had long forgotten and a circular pile of ashes that had already blown away in the desert winds but which would always haunt him, Michael had left nothing behind in New Mexico. He would make his way in Cuba, with the Cuban people, perhaps with? No! He shook his head. Impossible. Still, he couldn't help thinking of her. Judith's face and tall form rose up before him. She seemed almost to shimmer in the rain that continued to fall straight down from the night sky. He shook his head again, aware of the impossibility of his fantasy. That he might have some difficulty being accepted by or proving useful to the Cubans did not worry him. He knew his worth—as a soldier, as a sheepherder, and as a man. And he had met Christopher. He would get along.

When Michael finally arrived at the beach, well before dawn, he had to fight his way through a jumble of carts, soldiers and supplies. If anything, the beach area at Siboney was even more congested and confused than it had been a week earlier. "Where's the hospital?" he asked the first medic he met. The man just stared blankly back, shrugged his shoulders and moved on. Michael had to ask three more times before he finally got directions.

"'Bout a half mile up the beach, west," a lieutenant finally told him.

"But that ain't no hospital, Sergeant. That's a charnel house. They ain't savin' anybody at that sausage factory." Michael saluted, turned, and walked rapidly up the beach. Though he was tempted to pass Freddy's tent by and head straight for the hospital and Alex, he surrendered to a rare impulse and entered. Freddy was alone, seated behind his desk, his head buried in his crossed arms. He didn't bother to look up.

"Freddy?" Michael walked rapidly toward the desk just as Freddy lifted his tear-streaked face to stare uncomprehendingly at the intruder. "It's me, damnit! Archuletta."

"M-m-michael?" Suddenly Freddy was alert, present, almost excited. "Thank G-God! I thought all my friends were d-dead." The tears continued to well in his soft brown eyes.

"Stop blubbering. What's wrong?"

"D-david and Alex. They're g-gone. Our friends are gone."

Michael felt the bottom drop from his stomach. He had been fairly sure that David was dead. But Alex? He shook his head hard. "No!"

"Yes. Alex is d-d-dead, Michael."

"No!" Michael repeated, as if his denial could change reality. "Are you sure?"

Freddy nodded, still blubbering. "At l-least about David. They b-b-brought his body in earlier this evening. I s-saw him. Those awful v-v-vultures had . . ."

"What about Alex?" Michael almost screamed.

"He was still alive wh-wh-when I saw him a few m-minutes ago. They were g-getting ready to operate, b-b-but they said it was hopeless."

"Come on! Let's get over there."

Freddy shook his head. "It won't m-make any difference. When they finish operating, they just p-put the men out in the rain. N-naked, on the ground. They'll all d-d-die."

"I don't believe that. Come on!" Michael turned and bolted out into the rain, which was falling harder than ever. Freddy hesitated a moment, then, more from loneliness than hope, grabbed his slicker and ran after his last friend.

They stood outside the small, tented field hospital where three surgeons and a dozen orderly-medics had already performed more than a hundred and fifty operations in fifteen non-stop hours. None of the surgeons had slept; all three were well past the point of even minimal efficiency. They were short of everything—from blood, to cat gut, to morphine. They even lacked ice. Enough supplies for all their needs rested uselessly in the hold of some unknown transport, the result of the mass chaos at Tampa. Not until almost a week after the last battle would major contingents of medical supplies be landed ashore.

The large, open tent was a production line. The soldiers awaiting their turn on the operating tables huddled or sprawled in the mud, totally unprotected from the rain. When a patient's turn came, he was stripped naked by the orderlies, placed on a litter and carried to the operating table. If the patient died on the operating table—and many did—he was carried out behind the tent and laid in a growing row of corpses whose pale, bluish flesh glowed softly in the wet, moonless night. If the patient survived surgery, he was carried out the front of the tent and, still naked, placed as gently as possible on the sponge-soaked ground. If he was lucky, his waiting friends placed him on a litter, covered him with a slicker, and hauled him off to a dry spot for inexpert but loving care. Though almost all the Cuban wounded were so fortunate, most of the Americans were not: Many would still be lying in the mud at noon when the rain finally stopped. All through the night and early morning, tired orderlies made regular rounds to comfort the conscious and keep the land crabs. Otherwise, there was nothing they could do—no shelter, no morphine, nothing.

"M-m-michael. Here he is."

Michael had been pacing slowly along the lines of post-operative wounded, but had not seen Alex. When Freddy's voice brought him back, he had just decided to go around to the rear of the tent to start checking the corpses. But Freddy's voice had come from the other side of the tent, where the wounded still waited their turn on the operating tables. Michael sloshed around the side of the tent to discover Freddy bent over a filthy, shivering, blood-and-rain soaked Alex.

Freddy looked up. "We've g-got to get him in there."

"How many ahead of him?"

"Too many. F-fourteen or fifteen."

While they were trying to decide what to do, the two orderlies assigned to that side of the tent left to chase land crabs away from the dead. Michael looked quickly around. "Quick! Grab his feet."

"But we c-c-can't do that," Freddy protested. "It wouldn't be f-fair."

"Do you want him to die?" Without waiting for a reply, Michael lifted Alex as gently as possible. Freddy, looking frantically from right to left, grabbed his unconscious friend's ankles and helped Michael move him to the front of the line. They had barely stood up when two orderlies emerged from the tent.

"This man your friend?" the first orderly asked as he gazed vacantly down at Alex. Michael nodded. "Say your prayers, buddy. We're losing about one fer three and going down."

The two men stripped Alex, placed him on a litter and carried him into the tent.

"How long?" Michael called.

The first orderly turned his head. "If he lives 'til they're done? Half hour. Maybe twenty minutes." The two friends sloshed back down the beach through the shallow puddles and steadily falling rain.

* * * * *

Like the American surgeons, Judith had had virtually no sleep for more than a day. With little equipment, no medical education other than what she had learned in the field, and virtually no painkillers, she had been operating on her brothers for what seemed like weeks. Long before she had finished, she was almost overwhelmed by her frustration, horror and sense of personal loss. Each of her patients became Fidelito; when one of them died, Fidelito died.

As soon as Judith had finished operating on the last of the wounded, she stumbled through the rain to her small *bohio* and collapsed in her hammock, ready, finally, to surrender to her private grief. Almost immediately, however, she sensed a new presence and looked up to see Christopher standing, lantern in hand, at her side.

"I am sorry," he said, his rough voice cutting through the silence.

"Please. Go away. Leave me alone." She felt the tears and hysteria waiting to engulf her. "Christopher. Please!"

"I'm sorry, Judith. I'm sorry about Fidel. I'm sorry about the medicine we don't have. I'm sorry about the dead and dying."

"Please! Go away." Her voice was little more than a moan.

"I am also sorry that…you cannot rest, my friend. Not now. Not yet."

Tears exploded from her eyes, and deep sobs tore from her body to join the distant chorus still rising from the scores of women who had lost husbands and sons.

He took her in his arms and allowed her to cry. He held her firmly but gently, trying to will his remaining strength into this woman who, like so many others, had already seen and lost too much.

After several minutes, she pulled herself away, drained of tears but not grief. "What do you want from me?" she asked.

Christopher took a deep breath. During the long moments he had been holding her, he had questioned both his motivation and his judgment. He knew he could find other people to go after the wounded. "You must go to the beach and bring back our wounded. If you don't, those of our brothers who survive surgery will die of exposure."

"I can't do it. I just—don't—have—the—strength. Can't Juanita go?"

Christopher thought of Juanita, the young girl who had lost her foot at the Bay of Baynes. She was learning fast, but not that fast. And he needed to keep Judith busy. "No, I'm sorry, Judith, but many of those men will be near death. You're the closest thing we have to a physician."

She stood up, wiping her eyes with the back of her hand. "I am ready," she said.

* * * *

"Excuse me, Miss. I don't think you remember me, Michael Archuletta?" He faltered. Though she was looking straight at him, her eyes were empty, as if she were blind. She gave no sign of recognition, and made no move to interrupt or greet him. "I'm a friend of Alex Jackson's. Christopher's brother?"

"Michael! They're b-b-bringing him out. L-let's get him to my t-tent." Without waiting for a reply, Freddy dashed through the rain puddles to the rows of post-operative cases. The two orderlies set their litter down, eased Alex to the mushy ground and, without a backward glance, returned to the hospital tent. Freddy tore off his slicker, covered

Alex's still naked body and turned back to Michael, who was still staring into Judith's drained, impassive face. "M-michael. Come ON!"

Michael ignored him. He was as transfixed by Judith's stare. "My friend is talking about Christopher Jackson's brother. Unless he gets good care, he will die."

Judith strode to Alex's side. Without so much as glancing at Freddy, she bent over, stripped away the slicker and stared at the naked soldier. A fine line of blood still seeped from the fresh incision that ran jaggedly across his chest.

"Wh-what is she doing?" Freddy screeched, both angered and embarrassed that the ragged woman was staring at his friend's body

Michael walked to her side and continued his efforts to reach her. "Alex will die without proper care, and he won't get that here. He is Christopher's brother, and . . ."

"I know perfectly well who he is, Michael Archuletta, just as I know who you are. I am not without memory." Her eyes shifted from Michael to Alex and back. "We will take him along, and we will try to see that he lives."

"I will help to carry the litter. He is my friend, my brother."

"Very well," Judith replied in disinterested tones. She started to turn away, but turned back, held for a moment by Michael's intensely green eyes. "Christopher's brother is lucky to have such a friend."

He nodded, forced his eyes to hold hers for another moment, then turned away to bid farewell to Freddy.

"B-but you c-c-can't do that," Freddy stammered as soon as he understood what Michael was up to. "You'll be d-deserting."

"That's right, Freddy. I'm deserting. Everyone will think I'm dead in the jungle. If they ever figure out that I just...left, they'll chalk it up to my 'spic' sense of irresponsibility. As far as Alex is concerned, I'll get word to you—and to the regiment.

"B-but what about you? You'll..."

"I'm staying here, Freddy. For good. If you want to visit, come to Christopher's camp. Otherwise, my friend." Michael shook Freddy's limp hand and nodded at the Cuban soldier standing at the head of Alex's litter. The two men lifted their burden, joined the ragged line of Cuban litter bearers and disappeared into the jungle.

Freddy stood weeping in the dawn rain. He could no more staunch his tears than he could make his feet leave the spot where he stood rooted in the mud.

He felt a hand on his shoulder and turned. "Your strong friend is also a good man. I am sure you will see him—and Alexander—again."

"You s-sp-speak English?" Freddy asked.

"And other languages," Judith answered, amused in spite of herself. Though she had not responded to Michael's inquisitively assertive gaze, she found it easy to be tender with this lonely, aging waif who also seemed to need care. "You had better get in out of the rain before you catch the fever. Your friends will be fine. Alexander is very lucky to have Michael to care for him."

"Yes, I know," Freddy said, adding without even a trace of a stammer: "Michael Archuletta is the strongest man I have ever known. I think he will fall in love with you." He wiped the tears from his face and walked back toward his tent. She watched him disappear into the steady drizzle, and turned back to her desperate patients.

Chapter Forty-One

OUR HEAVY HANDICAP AT SANTIAGO

* * * *

The careful student of two days of battles about Santiago...cannot fail to be convinced that the heavy loss of life on the American side, and the partial check our army suffered, were due most to the Spanish use of smokeless powder and our lack of the necessary equipment of modern war. In the hot skirmishes in the woods our soldiers were utterly unable to tell whence came the bullets that cut them down. Every shot from an American rifle betrayed the position of the shooter.

That our troops should be so sorely handicapped would be incredible if it were not notorious. We the progressive nation, we the inventive, rich and up-to-date people, go into battle with decrepit, antiquated, moribund Spain and find ourselves the laggards—they have the modern tools of war, we the obsolete ones. William Randolph Hearst, *Editorial: The New York Journal*, July 4.

* * * *

VICTORY, BUT AT THE PRICE OF SUFFERING
Road from Siboney to the Front is Full of Wounded Men,
in Wagons and on Foot
The New York Journal, July 5.

South of El Caney

"How is he this morning?"

"Much better, Michael." Judith glanced up from her work. "He has been sleeping better since we got the morphine, and I think the sulfa is fighting any infections."

Michael nodded, rinsed a cloth in a calabash of cool water and bathed Alex's face and upper body. "Did he have bad dreams again last night?"

"They're deliriums, Michael, not dreams."

He grinned. "Delirium is too big a word for an uneducated sheepherder like me."

Judith smiled. "Here, help me with the dressing." For the next half hour he helped Judith tend the dozen men still in hospital two weeks after the last battle. Almost from the first day, they had worked well together, efficiently, each strengthened by the other's presence. Though Michael had allowed himself to fall in love with Judith, he had also tried to conceal his feelings. Thanks to Theresa, he knew that Judith grieved for a man with whom she could never have been happy, and that she had felt guilty for knowing that, even before Fidel's death. Rather than courting her, Michael teased her, helped her with the wounded, listened to her and, when she showed curiosity, talked of his life in New Mexico. They had become friends. As he had done his entire life, even in exacting vengeance, he waited.

During his two weeks in the Cuban camp Michael had also gotten to know Christopher. The two men had taken an instant liking to each other, partly because of their common love for Alex, partly because of the strengths each discerned in the other, but mostly, because each had found a man to whom he could open his soul.

Within a very few days Judith realized that she was relying increasingly on Michael's judgment, steadiness and attentiveness. Had she possessed the time and inclination to think about either her situation or the subtly evolving relationship, she might have been bothered by Michael's apparent selflessness. But she had neither the time nor the inclination. Michael offered assistance and she accepted.

When they finished changing dressings and washing the convalescents, they wandered over to the campfire where Theresa and two other women were stirring gruel and boiling coffee. Like their shared chores, their shared breakfasts had already become a pattern. As soon as she rose from her hammock, Judith headed for the hospital, relieved Juanita and the other orderly, and began her rounds. Fifteen or twenty minutes later Michael would arrive. Without asking what should be done, he bathed the patients, changed dressings, and fed those who were conscious and hungry. Then, their morning chores completed, they would move together to the campfire for a short morning break.

"Good morning Theresa, Augustina, Maria," Judith smiled as she and Michael approached the fire. "It is a beautiful day for the surrender, no?"

"A beautiful morning," Theresa agreed. She stirred the huge pot of coffee with unusual relish. After all these years, she thought. Finally, it is over.

Michael nodded to the women and sat down on a rock, somewhat apart, satisfied to watch their animated faces. He liked Theresa very much and sensed that she would make Christopher a strong and courageous companion.

It was a beautiful morning. Like huge, amorphous ghosts that retreated slowly before the intense tropical sun, tendrils of mist played through the trees and camp. The mists swallowed sound. Despite the presence of more than a hundred men and women in the camp, the clearing was quiet. Even the harsh caws of parrots and the morning songs of hundreds of jungle birds seemed muted, restrained.

"Wonderful day!" Michael turned in the direction of Christopher's voice and stood up, somewhat surprised by the man's appearance. Christopher had changed his ragged ducks and cotton shirt for the worn but clean khaki uniform of a Cuban colonel. In answer to Michael's unspoken question, Christopher explained his uniform. "It has always been easier for those of us who have uniforms to save them for important occasions. Otherwise, they would not have lasted. Like many of us," he added, then shook his head, determined that this day would be one of celebration

"Sergeant Archuletta, would you like to attend the surrender?"

"Certainly. I would be honored."

"I am entitled to an aide. My old aide, my friend, is dead. So, Michael Archuletta, my new friend, as of this moment you are a lieutenant in the Cuban Army of Liberation and my *aide de camp*. You will find a uniform tunic in my *bohio*. Theresa washed and patched it last night."

Michael turned to Theresa, "Thank you, pretty lady."

Theresa blushed. "Thank you, Lieutenant Archuletta. We have lost many of our friends. It gives us joy to make a new one."

"Get dressed, Lieutenant. We will meet General Garcia in less than two hours." The war was over. They had won. Spain was surrendering in eastern Cuba. The drums, the jungle telegraph, rumored that *La Habana* would soon follow.

Ten minutes later Christopher and half a dozen officers rode off at a canter. Though uncomfortable in the uniform of a Cuban officer, Michael was delighted to go along. With the war over and the Americans gone, he would be able to start his new life.

* * * * *

"Judith! Come quick." Juanita's voice carried across the clearing. "It is the *Yanqui*." Theresa at her side, Judith ran to the hospital. "He is lost in his dreams again and he has a fever."

Judith hurried to Alex's side, re-rinsed the cotton rag and bathed his head.

"Is there any medicine?" Theresa asked.

"None that will help with the infection, except for sulpha. But he is over the worst. He will live."

"I thought we were going to lose him last week when he came down with the fever. It is hard on the *Yanquis*, maybe harder than the war."

Alex, confused and frightened, was returning to consciousness. He called for Judith.

She ran the cool palm of her hand across his face. "Alex?" she whispered. "You are getting well, and you are with Christopher.

Your brother and Michael Archuletta are both here." Her English sounded strange to her, rusty and ungainly. It sounded even stranger to Theresa, who understood the language well but could speak it only with a strong accent.

Alex looked up at Judith who continued to whisper his name and bathe his burning forehead.

It seemed like years since he had heard her voice. No, that wasn't possible because he wasn't little any more and she was dead. Yet, he could hear her voice, so he must still be little. She was bending over him and light surrounded her head and she was beautiful. She had always been beautiful. Even when she had died of bitterness and exhaustion, with wrinkles as deep as furrows, even then she had been beautiful. But she wasn't dead, was she? She couldn't be, because she was bending over him and calling his name.

He tried to reach up to touch her cheek, but his arm wouldn't move. Strange, he thought. He knew that if he could raise his arm she would kiss his little fist, just as she had when he was small. But no. That couldn't be. He wasn't little any more. And she wasn't really there, hovering like an angel over his crib. How could she be? But she was, because she kept calling his name in that voice he remembered so well. He felt her cool palm on his forehead and shivered with delight. But it wasn't his mother. She had been dead for years. Perhaps he was dreaming. Yes, that was it.

"Alex, you are safe now." It was Charlotte. He had snuck into her room at the Tampa Bay Hotel. They were lying on top of the sweat-drenched sheets, surrounded by mosquito netting. "You are safe now, Alex," she said. Her face hovered over him and he whispered, "Charlotte, I love you." But it didn't really look like her face. Then there were two faces. That's strange. "You are safe now, Alex, safe with Christopher and Michael." How could that be? Neither one knew Michael, and Charlotte had never met Christopher. How could they say that unless they were in Cuba? No, he was the one who was in Cuba, with Michael. And Christopher was in Cuba. They had seen each other. But Charlotte wasn't in Cuba, and neither was Mother. Mother was dead. Even Father was dead. He was in Cuba now. Someone had died in Cuba. Yes. Bill Pike died, and Shorty. No, Michael killed Shorty. Is Michael dead? Bucky O'Neill is dead. Is David dead? Maybe everyone is dead. Am I dead? Something else died. The stories? Yes, that was it. Father was dead and his stories were dead. All the heroes were dead. No! That's not true. General Wheeler is a hero, and he's alive. But where was he today? At the battle for San Juan Ridge? General Wood was in charge, and he's a hero, but he wasn't there either. Roosevelt was there, and he's a hero. Maybe he knows my father. No, Father's dead.

"Alex, wake up," the voice whispered. It was a soothing voice, but his mother didn't have an accent, and neither did Charlotte. *"Uno momento, mi amiga."* The women were speaking Spanish. Strange. Not his mother and not Charlotte. He remembered now. He was in Cuba and he'd been wounded. His chest. Michael had put a blanket over him. He remembered the agonizing journey. He remembered the rain. It had rained on him, for days and weeks washing away his blood and his life. He was naked. There had been voices and movement and pain. Then it had become very still, and the rain had stopped, and he was no longer wet and cold.

"Alex! Wake up! You need to eat."

He was in Cuba, he was sick, and these haloed heads were caring for him. They spoke quietly in Spanish, which he didn't understand.

"I think his fever has broken," Judith said, wringing water from the rag she had been using to bathe his head.

"Then he will get the chills, no?" Theresa asked.

Judith nodded. "Then we will cover him."

"Did I ever tell you about the time at Federico's? Christopher had the chills and Oinja insisted that I take off my clothes and get into bed with him. Fidelito's mother said..." She stopped babbling, mortified. I'm sorry, Judith. I keep forgetting. I didn't mean to remind you..."

"It is all right, my sister. I have no wish to banish Fidelito from my memory. And I remember his father, the funny, skinny little man the Spanish soldier killed." The two women remained quiet for a moment as they recalled Federico's death and Judith's attack on the other Spanish soldier.

"You were about to say?" Judith asked finally.

"It was nothing," Theresa answered, saddened by the memories washing over her.

"Please, Theresa, go on. I need these memories right now."

"When Christopher was down with the fever at Federico's cabin, he got the chills, bad, and Oinja insisted that I take off my clothes and..."

"And did you?"

"Yes. I had loved him for such a long time, and..."

"Did you enjoy it?" Judith was grinning.

"At first, yes, very much. But then, he kept saying my sister's, kept repeating Consuelo's name and, at the same time, trying to love me like I was her. I had...forgotten that part."

"You're Judith," Alex cried out, "the woman on the beach!"

Both women jumped, startled. Alex spoke in a faint but rational voice. "And you are Christopher's..." he hesitated.

"I am Chreestopher's lover and friend," Teresa said. "And thees ees Judith, your nurse. She and Michael save your life."

* * * * *

"My God, Christopher. There must be several thousand men gathered on that plain."

"Not all men, Michael. As you have already seen."

Christopher's party had ridden over the ridge at El Caney, down through the narrow streets of San Juan City and onto the Santiago Plain. The huge formation of Cubans was drawn up less than a mile from the entrance to Santiago de Cuba, excited, after so many years in the wilderness, to be entering the Capitol of the East.

"If all these soldiers are here, why didn't you bring your troops?"

"They need the rest," Christopher answered. "And I didn't have enough horses for them to come so far."

"But these troops?" He fanned his arm across the increasingly crowded plain.

"You *Yanquis* didn't know how much help we were giving, did you? Most of these men are from the three divisions that blocked the main roads to the city. They kept Spanish reinforcements from pouring in and made it possible for you to win your battles easily."

"Easily? Many, many Americans and Cubans died that day. It may have been quick, Christopher, but it was not easy."

"Hmmmph! You should read the American newspapers. Perhaps I can borrow a copy or two from General Garcia. According to them,

July first was a glorious romp—won by Roosevelt and your Rough Riders almost single-handedly."

Michael laughed. "I didn't know we were that good. What did the papers say about the other Americans? And about the Cubans?"

"Oh, the American infantry is mentioned favorably, especially General Lawton's division at El Caney. But there is no mention of the Negro troopers who actually captured San Juan Hill. And as far as the Cubans are concerned, our help was mentioned, only as an afterthought."

"You seem awfully calm about it all. Aren't you angry?"

"Angry? No. Nor does it surprise me, Michael. The Yankee press has wrung its hands over our starving children and trumpeted an occasional Cuban hero. But not lately. At least since the sinking of the *Maine*, your press has been much more concerned with Yankee vengeance than with the plight of *Cuba Libre*."

"Perhaps you should not have invited America into the war."

Christopher started to speak but clenched his jaw and shook his head. For the next ten minutes they trotted silently down to the rich grass of the Santiago Plain. Christopher's mind flashed back to the *Maine* and to the faces of George Bedford and Ephraim Pratt. Just as they had almost reached the outer edges of the assembled revolutionaries, however, Christopher reined up severely, turned to Michael and said: "I have often thought as much. But what is done is done. And cannot be undone. "Besides," he added, extending his arm and sweeping it from left to write, as if to embrace the entire formation of jubilant *mambises*, "We have won our revolution. Nothing else matters. As of today we are free. "*Viva Cuba Libre!*"

As he followed Christopher into the milling ranks of excited Cuban officers, Michael thought, what a weird assembly. Some of the lieutenants were teenagers and not a few were women. Many of the majors and colonels were in their sixties; others were would-be students. Many wore bandages and some seemed barely able to sit on a horse. But all were excited. Cuba was free. Cuba was theirs.

"Where's General Garcia?" Christopher asked a broad-shouldered mulatto colonel who looked to be about five foot tall.

"Ah! Christopher. How goes it? The general and his son Carlos, they have gone to the city to see the fat general, to find out when we will be able to enter Santiago and accept the surrender of the *pendejos.*"

"Hey, Arturo!" another officer yelled. "Here they come!" The general and his son were galloping toward the formation, whipping their horses with a frenzy that struck many of the officers as uncharacteristic. As word passed back through the ranks that the general was returning, the entire army began, raggedly at first and then with great, united fervor, to chant, "*Viva Cuba Libre! Viva Cuba Libre! Viva Cuba Libre!*" Almost as if on cue, the officer corps rode out at a gallop to escort the man who had led the Eastern Army for so long and so well.

When the two parties met, the officers swarmed around the old general and his son. Carlos was angry. The general looked ill. Only gradually did the mob of cheering officers sense that something was wrong. Slowly at first, then with a rush of understanding, the officers fell silent and gathered around their leader.

"My friends and companions," Calixto Garcia began. "We have won the war. But I am afraid we have lost the revolution. Our *Yanqui* friends have betrayed us."

The general stopped for a moment and stared balefully around the tightly packed, silent group. In the background, the ten thousand man assembly of *mambises* still chanted jubilantly. *Viva Cuba Libre! Viva Cuba Libre!*

"Except for myself and my staff, General Shafter has refused us permission to enter the city." The general's voice became quieter but bitterly sarcastic. "He is afraid, he says, that we will avenge our losses on the helpless Spaniards."

"General Garcia?" Major Allen, an English planter from Del Rio, yelled from the rear of the circle. "If we are forbidden entrance, to whom will the city surrender?"

"To the *Yanqui* generals," Garcia hissed.

"And whose flag will fly over Santiago de Cuba, the Pearl of the East?"

"The flag of the United States of America."

"Never!" The English major yelled. "Never, NEVER!" the assembled officers chorused.

General Garcia nodded to his son, who raised his hands to demand silence. When the angry shouts had subsided to a low rumble, the general continued. "General Shafter has also made it clear that all of the municipal and regional officials appointed by Spain shall retain their positions. The leeches that have sucked Cuba dry will remain in office."

"Machete! " someone yelled. But before the ground swell of anger and frustration could take hold, General Garcia raised his hands and the rising growl again subsided.

"No, my companions. We will not fight the *Yanquis.* We will allow them to occupy Cuba. We will cooperate with them so that their stay may be brief."

"How brief, General?" Christopher yelled.

Garcia turned towards him, stared hard into the gaunt Georgian's eyes, and asked: "How long did the Union army occupy the old Confederacy?"

"Eleven bleak years," Christopher answered as he flashed momentarily on the arrogant Yankee officers and carpetbaggers who had infested Georgia during his youth.

Garcia nodded and continued. "I do not think they shall be here so long. We were their allies, not their enemies. But whether they remain for one year or ten, we will cooperate. We have no choice. It is our only chance for ultimate and complete independence."

The general exhaled a long breath, as if to denote the completion of a much-dreaded task. But with no warning whatsoever, his face turned red. He raised his voice and spat: "We will cooperate, my companions. But make no mistake. We will hate the *Yanquis* forever. FOREVER!"

"Forever!" The officers hissed and mumbled and roared. A captain who had come to Cuba as a Spanish Dominican pronounced a deep basso "Amen!" as if it were a curse.

Michael glanced around the now silent, downcast fighters. Since he was, at the moment, a man without a country, he observed as an outsider. He wanted to understand what was happening with these men and women who had fought so long and sacrificed so much. He thought briefly of the last night in Tampa, when the Rough Riders discovered that they would go to Cuba without half their brothers and without their mounts. But he realized immediately that what he was witnessing on the Santiago plain was far more profound, a disappointment that would alter the Cuban character.

The clouds sweeping down from the *Sierra Maestra* seemed to be bringing more than their daily promise of rain. As they spread rapidly across the plain, the clouds pushed before them an invisible blanket of depression that settled rapidly over the disillusioned officer corps. Though none of the officers had bothered to send a message to the thousands of enlisted men gathered behind them, the *mambises* sensed the disaster. Their chanting had died. Though they waited in ignorance, they now waited in fear of an invisible axe.

General Garcia had pulled apart to consult with his generals and brigadiers. As the conference started to break up, Colonel Carlos Garcia trotted away from his father's side and back to the apprehensive officers. "Colonel Jackson!" he yelled. Christopher nodded and waited. "My father refuses to attend the surrender. None of the other generals are willing to attend either. You and I are ordered to stand in. We will represent him. We must enter the city immediately. Get your staff. Now!"

Christopher was more angered than flattered to be selected. "Why us? For that matter, why anyone? Must we witness our own shame?"

"Get your staff, Colonel!" Carlos ordered. "The ceremony starts in half an hour."

* * * * *

The small Cuban contingent remained mounted and at attention during the entire ceremony. Since they had refused to stand with their *Yanqui* allies, they stood at the foot of the plaza, opposite the steps of the Presidio, upon which stood swarms of Spanish civil servants. The Spanish generals and their huge staffs occupied the west side of the plaza and faced the Americans, who had drawn themselves up on the east side.

Other than the American victors, only the civil servants seemed pleased to be in attendance. They had discovered that they had not lost their sinecures; they had merely traded masters. They would be able to rule and rob as usual. When citizens made complaints and the *Yanquis* came to them for an explanation, they would smile ingratiatingly, rub their hands together, and promise to get to the heart of the abuse.

Among the assembled American officers, the cavalry division had preempted the most conspicuous position. And among the cavalry regiments, the khaki-clad officers of the Rough Riders stood apart from their blue-coated peers.

From his position in the second rank of Cuban witnesses, Michael felt secure, partly because of his position and partly because of his two week old beard. Though he sat his horse at attention, he allowed his eyes to move constantly. He paid particular attention to Theodore Roosevelt.

Michael shook his head as he watched Roosevelt strut back and forth on Little Texas. Virtually the entire American press corps, some ninety strong, led by William Randolph Hearst, had managed to secure seats just to the right of where Roosevelt was trying not very hard to control his spirited mount.

Though he would never forget Roosevelt's slurs at San Juan Hill, and though he despised much that the man stood for, his contempt was mixed with grudging respect and amusement. The man was foolhardy but brave. He was arrogant, something of a bully, and a strutting, pigeon-chested, comic opera hero. He had certainly proven to be a decisive and effective leader who radiated authority and competence.

Christopher's reaction to the ceremony was less detached. As he listened to the speeches and music, and watched the Spanish flag change places with the American, he tasted the bitter gall of defeat. He was ashamed of the tears that sprang to his eyes, but made no move to wipe them away. Had he been willing to move his head even slightly, he would have seen tears cutting furrows through the dust-covered cheeks of Colonel Carlos Garcia. Like Garcia and the rest of the Cuban officers, however, Christopher remained stiffly at attention astride his mount, and endured the ceremony that marked the end of *Viva Cuba Libre!*

As far as Christopher was concerned, the speeches were insulting to Cubans in general and the Cuban Army of Liberation in particular. In a long, bombastic speech, the defeated Spanish general spoke of the bravery and gallantry of the American soldiers, the honor and judgment of the American generals, and the basic fairness and decency of the terms of surrender.

Honor? Decency and fairness and judgment? Christopher wanted to shout his protest, to object to the 'I do's' being exchanged by the noble adversaries. Captain-General Primo, the Spanish commander of the Eastern Army, made no mention of Cuba, no mention of the remnants of empire that Spain was finally losing, no mention of the fact that America had bullied Spain into the war and destroyed both her Atlantic and Pacific fleets. All was forgiven. The two countries were noble adversaries, two macro-knights who had met, clashed and embraced on the field of honor. God, the ultimate judge, had decided in favor of the heroic and decent Americans. Praise be to God!

General Shafter lacked General Primo's elegance. The obese American was sweating rivers during the hour-long ceremony. Nor was he as eloquent as the Spaniard, though he demonstrated copious amounts of pious good will for his vanquished brother-in-arms. He, too, spoke of bravery, of heroic deeds, of the honor, courage and nobility that make warfare both the ultimate test and consummate profession of great men. Like his recent enemy, he made no mention of the Cuban people, the Cuban cause America had, presumably, entered the war to support, or the Cuban army whose multitudinous sacrifices had made the American romp possible.

Rather, Shafter rambled on about the superior attainments of European civilization and the superior moral rectitude of its citizens. America had decided to retain Spain's civil administrators on the job because America knew that only they possessed the education, intelligence and probity to run the country. Such men were the cream of Spanish civilization. They had already spent much of their lives serving the ignorant and unfortunate natives of the province; he was sure they would be of great service in helping America to shoulder its share of the White Man's Burden.

When the handshakes and the surrender of swords came to an end, the *Alcade*, the fat mayor of Santiago, waddled down the steps in a striped cutaway, smiled ingratiatingly at General Shafter, and handed him the key to the city. Shafter smiled back and returned the key. "You have served Spain well," he said. "I am sure you will serve the United States of America equally well."

Then it was over. The two bands played each other's national anthems, the generals embraced, and the participants prepared to return to their assigned quarters. The Spanish soldiers, without their arms but with their pride assuaged, returned to their barracks to await shipment to Spain. The Spanish civil servants, careers and possibilities for graft intact, went back to their offices. The Americans, wallowing in a sea of self-confidence and benevolence, made their way to the heights overlooking the Santiago plain and the beaches stretching east from the harbor entrance.

The small Cuban contingent was the first to depart. Without a sound or a gesture, the representatives of the Cuban Army of Liberation rode stiffly from the plaza. As they passed the halyard where the Stars and Stripes flew above the plaza, the city, and the Plain of Santiago, Christopher wondered when, if ever, the flag of a free Cuba would fly in its place. When the low, black clouds opened, first as a drizzle, then as a torrential downpour, none of the Cubans bothered to stop to don their slickers. For years they had been riding, sleeping and fighting in the rain. Somehow the deluge seemed fitting.

Chapter Forty-Two

CUBANS ANGRY OVER THEIR EXCLUSION FROM SANTIAGO
Refuse to Hold Any Communication with Our Troops
GARCIA OPENLY RESENTS SHAFTER'S ACT
The New York Journal, July 20.

* * * * *

WHAT THE WAR HAS DONE FOR US
Freedom Extended

First, of course, we have the prime object of the war—the rescue of the Cubans from a savage, murderous tyranny that was rapidly exterminating their race. That is being splendidly accomplished, and with it are coming other achievements of the same kind. We have added two hundred thousand square miles of the earth's surface—an area as great as that of France—to the domain of civilization and humanity. William Randolph Hearst, Editorial: *The New York Journal,* July 21.

* * * * *

CUBAN PETITION TO MCKINLEY
Residents of Santiago Beg that Spanish Rule
in the City May Be Ended
THEY ASK THAT THEIR ARMY MAY ENTER
AND THEIR FLAG FLOAT BESIDE OURS
The New York Journal, July 25.

South of El Caney

Within hours after the surrender, the Cuban officer corps divided into three camps: a small group who swore to make life miserable for the occupying *Yanquis* and their Spanish civil servants; another small group who understood the need to cooperate fully with the occupying forces; and the largest group, for whom the latest news was the final straw. It was this group which first opted for home, family and private concerns, and among whom Christopher found himself to be an outspoken member. As a Southerner raised during the eleven years of Reconstruction, he could not visualize himself cooperating with an American occupation. Nor was he sufficiently naive to believe that a poorly supplied and increasingly divided army could drive the Americans from the island.

Almost overnight the decades long coalition of foreign and creole planters, students, merchants, ex-slaves and *camposinos* disintegrated. The war was over. *Viva Cuba Libre!* was lost. And that, bitter stone that it would become, was that. By the next morning more than a quarter of the army had left for whatever might be left of their homes. The camaraderie of common destiny that had melded them together dissipated like late morning mists evaporating in sub-tropical sun.

For what would be the last time, Christopher led his small band of officers down the winding trail that fell from the heights of San Juan Ridge. Tomorrow he would break camp and leave for his long abandoned and thrice-burned sugar fields in Matanzas Province. He would take Theresa, Judith and any of his soldiers wanting to go along. And he would take Alex. As he thought of his brother ,his spirits lightened. After all these years of being apart, they were now together, and would stay together. Christopher glanced at the New Mexican who rode silently at his side. They are so different, Alex and this man, he thought.

As the small group of demoralized officers pulled up before the rain-swollen San Juan River, Christopher turned to Michael. "You say you want to stay in Cuba. Does that mean you never want to return to New Mexico?"

Michael rested his folded hands on the pommel of his saddle and stared across the swiftly running river. "Never!"

"What will you do in Cuba? To live?"

Michael shrugged. "What I must." For the past two weeks he had been asking himself the same question. "Perhaps I will raise sheep. It is something I know, and I have several hundred dollars in a bank in New Mexico, enough to get started."

"Sheep will not do well here; it is too hot and wet."

"Perhaps goats then. Who knows? Goats would do well here. I can sell the milk and the meat. I can tan and sell the hides. I can make cheese." He turned his head and looked Christopher in the eye. "I will live."

Though Christopher was dubious, he kept his mouth shut and spurred his mount into the river. Half an hour later, the group topped a small rise and Christopher called a halt to rest the horses. The men dismounted and broke into small groups to hide from the downpour.

Once Christopher and Michael had found partial shelter under the thick vines, Christopher asked: "You seem interested in Judith. Are you?"

"It's that obvious?"

Despite his own fears for the future, Christopher could not help but smile. This was the first time he had seen Archuletta even slightly disconcerted. So, he thought, that is the way the wind blows. "Theresa claims that I am too often unaware of what's going on around me. She says that I'm too remote, pre-occupied."

Michael said nothing.

"The point is," Christopher continued, "if your interest in Judith is apparent to an insensitive clod like me, Judith must be aware of your feelings. Theresa certainly is."

Michael shook his head. "I didn't realize...I...She hasn't given me any signs that she knows. To even talk like this is not good."

"And she won't, at least not until you say something. And you are right, Michael Archuletta. You must keep patient for many months.

Even then, Theresa says the first sign must come from Judith."

"I would like to talk to you sometime about Fidel. He was your good friend?"

Christopher nodded. "But they would not have been happy together; they were too different. Fidel knew that. So did Judith, I think. Still, they loved each other."

"I am a patient man, Colonel Jackson."

"So I gather." Christopher said, getting back to his feet.

The two men remounted and waited for the others to do the same. "By the way," Christopher asked, "who is Charlotte?"

"The woman Alex loves. In Virginia. She is very rich, and they are engaged."

Christopher chuckled. "You know, I'd always figured that Alex would find a rich wife. I hoped that between us, we'd build one helluva successful sugar plantation. How do you think his Charlotte will like living on a hacienda?"

"I've never met her." He stopped to think. "Have you talked to Alex about staying in Cuba?"

"He's been incoherent for most of the past two weeks," Christopher reminded him. He looked around and saw that his officers were mounted and waiting to go.

For the next hour neither man spoke. Michael had found Christopher's comment about Judith encouraging, though a little unsettling. He had thought that there was more of the Navajo in him, especially after the years with Sky Woman. Yet Christopher, and Theresa evidently, could read him like a book. At the same time, Christopher seemed to approve of his interest in Judith. If he is pleased by the idea, and if Theresa is pleased, then, maybe, things will work between us. Michael smiled to himself, a smile of anticipation and hope.

Though Christopher, too, was thinking about the future, his thoughts were even more unsettled. He remembered the busy and fulfilling years he had spent with Consuelo and their three daughters, and realized for the first time how much he had aged since their deaths a half year earlier. I must start again, he told himself. Theresa will be good for me. And I can be good for her. Courage! he thought. Courage and strength. "Strength! Courage! " he muttered.

Michael overheard and nodded approvingly. "Amen!" he said.

Christopher's mind turned to a fresh concern: Other than the few thousand dollars sitting in a Charleston bank, he lacked capital; he was almost broke. Yet, he had promised to help Judith and his soldiers and seemed about to make the same offer to this quiet sheepherder.

Judith! He recalled something she told him on the day he'd met her. It was in Joseph's shop, that horrible afternoon in February. "This is for the revolution," she'd said, handing him a roll of bills. And when he had enquired further, she confided, " I have more, Mr. Jackson. My stepfather did not spend his money."

My stepfather? Christopher thought of the scrawny, old watchmaker whose hands shook so badly. He must have endured great pain in El Morro, yet he had died without revealing what he knew about *Cuba Libre!* And he died for nothing, Christopher decided bitterly. My family are all dead. Hundreds of thousands are dead. For nothing. *Por Nada!*

He broke into a canter, pulling ahead of Michael. Nothing, nothing, nothing. Consuelo, the girls, Fidel, Federico, those young sailors, the watchmaker...all for nothing.

He thought again of Joseph Rabinsky. Judith had loved her stepfather; they had been very close. His shop was so poor, so squalid. How could the old man have saved so much money? How much? If she would buy part of the land Theresa and Consuelo inherited, there would be money to rebuild. And if she had a strong man, a partner, she could do it—and so could we. If, if, if.

He pulled his horse up short, and glanced back at Michael. For the first time since the so-called surrender ceremony, he felt a glimmer of hope. "It pleases me that my brother found such a strong man for a friend," he called to Michael through the rain. "Cuba has a great need for strong men."

Michael pulled up alongside so close that their horses touched, "Come with us to Matanzas," Christopher said. " All of us—Theresa, Alex, me, and Judith, of course—we will have great use for a man with your strength and patience. We have much to do, much good work." Before Michael could open his mouth to assent, decline or even ask for an explanation, Christopher added: "I do not think you will be sorry."

PART III: A PYRRHIC VICTORY

* * * *

The two women sat on a fallen palm tree, some twenty paces from the hut that housed Alex and the other convalescents. Though they knew that the break in the downpour would not last long, it was still a break. They sipped on their cups of herbal tea and, like so many *mambises*, discussed the future. The drums had already told them that the surrender had not gone well, and that the *Yanquis* had betrayed them. The specifics would have to wait until Christopher's return. Though struggling with uncertainty and dread, they spoke of the future, which was unfolding.

"What do you think he's going to do?" Judith asked.

" Michael?"

"No, I...I..." Judith stammered, bothered by Theresa's response. "I meant Alex, Teresa." Fidel's smiling face floated across her vision, blinding her momentarily.

"I have no idea what he'll do," Theresa replied. "He says he's going back to the states to this Charlotte woman.

"What will you and Christopher do? Will you really return to the sugar?"

" Sugar is all Christopher knows, which is much, much more than I know. Whatever we do, we will do it together." Theresa smiled, confident that she now possessed the strength, courage, and will to move their lives forward.

"And you will be happy, Theresa, won't you?"

Theresa took Judith's hand. "Do not doubt that for one minute. And how about you, my dearest friend? How about you?" Theresa's years as a prostitute had aged her in ways that didn't show in the hundreds of silver threads that peppered her curly black hair. Though she had witnessed much, she had witnessed—and experienced—it over a period of years. Judith, on the other hand, had descended unexpectedly into five months of intense horror. "What will you do now, Judith?" she pressed, squeezing her friend's hand.

Judith's eyes filled with tears. She could only shake her head. From the day of her stepfather's death, she had sensed that this moment would come. Only in the last few days, however, had she understood the degree to which the war had provided her with a refuge from the abyss, the nothingness of her life without her family. For almost five months she had devoted herself to tending those whose pain seemed greater than her own. In doing so she had managed to drown out the faces of her mother, brother and stepfather. But Fidel's death had brought everything back into terrible focus. She had surrendered her heart to him, and he, too, had been killed.

"I don't know what to do. But for a time at least, I will go with you and Christopher."

Theresa continued pressing Judith's hand. "Yes, dear friend, that is best. Now, before we get sad again, let's visit your patients. I would like to talk more with Christopher's brother."

Judith stopped just short of the hospital. "What do you think of this quiet soldier, Theresa?"

"Alex?" Theresa replied, concealing a smile. She knew full well to whom Judith was referring.

Judith, afraid that her patients would overhear, whispered, "No, Michael Archuletta." Then, seeing the gleam of amusement in Theresa's eyes, she added, "As you well know."

"Strength, Judith. He is very strong. Very solid." She stepped inside the hospital and waited for her friend, who was lost in thought again. "Judith?"

Judith followed, still whispering, "What struck me most was his tenderness. I see that. But my first impression was of another quality. Other than those green eyes, which look so directly at you."

"At you," Theresa corrected.

Judith ignored the comment. "Other than his eyes, what struck me most was his tenderness. It is a tenderness coupled with strength." She thought again of Fidel and of her passion for him, a physical passion she would not have believed possible, even after she realized they could never be happy together.

They approached Alex, who was sitting up, resting his weight on one arm, moving his very curious eyes back and forth between the two women.

But before anyone spoke, a distant voice cut through the clearing. "They are back!" The single cry became a chorus. "They are back!" Within seconds almost all the occupants of the camp, including the walking wounded, were on their feet and moving in the direction of the distant voice. "They are back! They are back!"

"Pass the word," Christopher cried as he cantered into the clearing. "We will break camp and leave this place, first thing tomorrow morning. This war is over. We are going home!"

The grizzled survivors of three years of intense suffering and deprivation ran toward him with desperate questions. "What homes?" "How?" "Go where?" "Do what?" "With what?"

Some, who had listened carefully to the drums, shed tears; others, sensing only that the killing and dying had ended, cheered wildly. But most, aware that they would now have to pursue the frayed threads of ruined lives, lapsed into shocked revery. For three years all had been defined by the next battle, and the next meal. War was their universe. The past and its inhabitants had been blown away on the battlefields or starved to death in the *reconcentrados*.

"Colonel!" someone yelled. "What happened at Santiago? What are the drums saying?"

Christopher's face darkened. "I will speak to the battalion in ten minutes."

Ignoring the puzzled, questioning faces, he strode to his hut and collapsed on his hammock. Battalion, hell, he thought. He closed his eyes, but still saw the emaciated faces of the *mambises* who had followed him for so long and at such great cost, only to win so little. He knew what he would say, but he hated to have to say it. He could only amplify what they already knew. The drums, as usual, had been correct. He would fill in the details of the American decision to occupy Cuba. He would tell them of the disgraceful way the obese American general had treated their beloved Calixto Garcia. He would thank them for their loyalty to him and to *Viva Cuba Libre!* He would embrace and kiss each one of his wretched soldiers, offer them work in his cane fields, and send them off to build new lives.

Rather than attending Christopher's assembly, Michael spent the time with Alex, who was finally strong enough to carry on a sustained conversation. Ten minutes after Michael entered the small shack, Alex knew everything Theresa and Judith had been unable to tell him: what had happened at San Juan Hill; how he had gotten to the beach, and from there to the Cuban camp; what had happened to the Rough Riders; and what Michael was planning to do, had, in fact, already done.

"Michael, they'll shoot you if they ever find you."

Archuletta grinned, as if Alex's obligatory warning were nothing more than a symbolic gesture. " I know."

It wasn't just his friend's decision that shocked Alex; he was as shocked by the man's appearance. It was as if the new beard and Cuban officer's tunic underscored Michael's desertion.

To Alex the very concept of desertion was unthinkable. He knew that the Army was less than perfect, just as he and Michael were less than perfect, just as America, the land of their birth, was less than perfect. But America was young, vigorous, powerful, the wave of the future, the hope of the world. One just did not throw away one's responsibilities to, or citizenship in, such a country. Christopher had done it, yes. But that was different; his brother was an unreconstructed Confederate.

Such were the forces battling in his heart and head. But Alex was not just—or even primarily—a jingoistic chauvinist riding this next wave of American expansion. He would miss the quiet, intense sheepherder whom he credited with saving his life. But, he had seen how the Army treated non-whites. Archuletta would never be allowed to fit into the world that Alex still yearned for—the world of position, influence, and financial security. Though he did not want to admit it, he knew that he and Michael had little in common—other than the war.

The two friends remained quiet for a long time. In the background they could hear Christopher's address to his troops and the cries of emotion that punctuated the final gathering of *mambises*. For the first time in months the two men felt a tension between them.

Finally Michael spoke. "You understand what the drums said?"

Alex nodded. "According to Theresa, we did not allow the Cubans to enter Santiago. That seems sensible, doesn't it? A victorious Cuban army would have been hard to control. There could have been a lot of violence." Alex paused for a second and, sensing that Michael was about to disagree, changed the subject.

"I don't understand about the drums. Judith says that most of the Negroes in eastern Cuba, including many of the soldiers, practice a form of voodoo, and that these people can communicate just about anything to any point on the island, in no time at all."

"That's true. But you must understand, Alex, that the Americans kept the Cubans out of Santiago because of contempt. America is convinced that the Cubans, at least for now, are incapable of governing Cuba. Cuba will remain a dependent country."

"For how long?" Alex asked, troubled more by his friend's tone than by the news itself.

"Indefinitely. Your brother is bitter."

Alex could think of nothing to say. Michael rose to his feet to leave, and bumped into Judith, who was on her way in. But Alex had found his voice. "Wait, Michael, you have been a good friend. I owe you my life. Everything. Thank you!" He made no attempt to hide his tears.

"We shall see each other again—my friend." Michael said. As he left the hospital, he met Judith's eyes. Her return gaze was direct and curious.

Christopher came into the shack behind Judith. He had been waiting for the exchange between Alex and Michael to end. Though he had not heard every word, he could tell from the tone, and the long silences, that something important was being said. "How are you doing little brother?" he asked, as he sat beside Alex's hammock. Alex was wiping tears from his eyes.

"Better than it may look, I guess. I think something just ended between me and Michael."

"You had an argument?"

Alex shook his head. "Not an argument. But part of me—and I guess it's an important part—just can't understand what he's doing."

"You mean staying on in Cuba?"

"Yes, Chris. That's part of it. Part, but not all."

"Alex, surely you know that I want you to stay here too."

"I'm an American. I can't do that, Chris."

"We are brothers. What is more important than that?. We need to be together. We haven't spent any time together...for years. The war's over. I have time to spend with you. You're all that's left of my family, Alex. We can build our lives here."

Alex again felt pulled in two directions. "One of the main reasons I joined the Army was to get to see you, to be with you. I've been dreaming about us getting together, fantasizing about it, for months."

"Then stay!" Christopher pleaded He was surprised how much

he wanted this. For years he had gotten along with only an occasional thought about his little brother, an occasional worry about how he was doing in school or at Harvard, an occasional dream about their childhood. It was as though he had found something he hadn't realized how much he had missed. "Stay, little brother. There's a future here for you."

Keeping his eyes locked with Christopher's, Alex shook his head. "No, Chris. I'm sorry, but I'm in love with a beautiful woman. We're engaged to be married. My future is with her—in Washington."

Now Christopher's voice was cold. "We're breaking camp early tomorrow morning. We're leaving for Matanzas."

Alex sat up, felt the blood rush to his head, and lay back down. "Why so soon?"

"Now that the war is over, I want to put it behind me. I want to forget the cost, and the fucking waste."

Alex paused before he spoke again. "Chris, I'm sorry about the surrender ceremony. Michael told me. But it might be the best way to—"

Christopher interrupted, "What would you have thought if you'd been with George Washington at Yorktown? What would you have thought if the French, who came into the war at the last moment, refused to let Washington accept the surrender of Cornwallis?"

"Chris, this isn't the same!"

"But it is. After years of fighting for independence, the Americans are prevented by their new ally from accepting the surrender of the British, and, what's more, they learn that the French are going to occupy the country—because the colonists are too illiterate and unsophisticated to run it themselves. Which, by the way, was likely the case—at least as seen through the eyes of the French. How would you have felt about that, Alex?"

When Alex didn't answer, Christopher added, "You'd be bitter as hell, wouldn't you? And it wouldn't do much to improve your basic suspicions of the French and their motives, would it?"

After two intense conversations in a row Alex was becoming exhausted. "I see your point. But, Chris, you're an American. Certainly you can't…"

"I've lived here most of my adult life, Alex. My family was born here and is buried here. I have known most of my happiness here, most of my happiness and most of my sorrow. I am no longer an American."

"Then I'm sorry," Alex mumbled. His eyelids were heavy and he could feel the sweat popping from his brow. "Maybe we're wrong to stay here, but we won't be here forever."

Christopher shrugged. "We shall see. He glanced around the darkening hut; nodding at the other wounded, who were intrigued by an intense conversation they couldn't understand. After a moment, he plucked a rag from the calabash of luke-warm water. "Here, let me rinse off your face. Alex, we're leaving tomorrow. I'll have four of my men carry you back to your unit." His tone had softened. "Anyway, you don't have to make up your mind now. Or even this evening. We'll have dinner this evening around our last campfire as a unit, enjoy each other's company. When we part tomorrow morning, we'll leave the question open. I just want you to know that you're always welcome in my homeland. Always. Even if only for a visit." He rose to his feet.

Alex rose back up on one elbow, "Perhaps Charlotte and I will come to Cuba on our honeymoon," he offered lamely.

Christopher rolled an eyebrow. "What if she doesn't want to come to Cuba on her honeymoon?"

Alex thought for a moment, then said with a sharp decisiveness that amused them both, "Oh, she'll come!" Then Christopher was gone.

* * * * *

In the morning as the clearing emptied, the jungle sounds gradually asserted themselves. For the first time since his arrival, Alex saw and heard and smelled the richness of Cuba. Still, as much as he loved Christopher, Alex could not imagine wanting to live here. Nor could he even begin to comprehend how anyone could possibly distrust America's motives. Some day the Cubans will learn to appreciate us he thought. Some day our countries will become good neighbors, friends.

"*Señor? Andule, no?*"

Alex looked at the four men standing to his left, suddenly aware of their impatience to begin the eight mile trek to the beach. "*Si, andule, amigos.*" He nodded at the *mambises*, who picked up the litter, and moved with a quiet, purposeful rhythm toward the jungle and the distant beach.

Epilogue

Fred Anderson (b. 1870, d. 1934) stayed in the army and eventually rose to the rank of major. During World War I he served with the Rainbow Division in France, where he suffered a severe case of shell shock. He spent his final fifteen years in a veterans' hospital in St. Louis.

Michael Archuletta (b. 1868, k. 1938) returned to Matanzas Province with Christopher, Theresa and Judith. He and Judith married in 1899 and developed a successful sugar plantation. They had one daughter, Rachael, who was born in 1902. In 1938 Michael participated in one of the abortive rebellions against the dictatorship of General Fulgencio Batista. He was captured, taken to La Punta Fortress in Havana and executed.

Charlotte Boggs (b. 1880, d. 1963) married Alex in November, 1898, the day after Theodore Roosevelt was elected Governor of New York. She and Alex lived in Albany for a year, then accompanied Roosevelt to Washington when he became Vice-President for McKinley's second term. She survived Alex by thirteen years and died in front of her television, where she was watching John F. Kennedy' funeral.

Alexander Dumas Jackson (b. 1873, d. 1950) served Roosevelt in both Albany and Washington. After the defeat of the Bull Moose party, Alex and Charlotte spent three months in Cuba. Upon their return to the states Alex studied law and eventually established a practice in Washington. He joined the staff of Franklin D. Roosevelt in 1933, became an Assistant Secretary of War in 1942, and retired from public life in 1947. In 1950 he was struck and killed by an automobile while crossing Constitution Avenue.

Christopher Jackson (b. 1859, d. 1919) married Theresa, rebuilt his sugar plantation, and became an influential planters in Matanzas Province. Because of the long-term effects of his battles with malaria, he was too weak to travel during the last three years of his life. He died in the influenza pandemic in 1919.

Amos Jordan (b. 1837, d. 1910) retired from the Consular Corps in 1898 and returned to New England. He wrote a biting commentary on American expansion, *The Fateful Decision* and lectured at Dartmouth College. He died in his study while working on a new book denouncing America's 1909 intervention in Cuba.

Judith Sandoval (b. 1873, d. 1954). After Michael's execution in 1938, Judith moved to New York to be near her daughter. When Rachael and her second husband migrated to Israel in 1953, Judith followed. At eighty-one years of age, she died on her lounge chair, gazing out over the Great Sea.

Theresa Valdez (b. 1873, d. 1919). Like Christopher, Theresa died in the influenza pandemic of 1918–19. Of their two children, the oldest, Alexander, was executed at La Punta Fortress with Michael Archuletta. The second died in childhood. Her grandson, Christopher Vero, studied Political Science with Fidel Castro at Columbia University, and was an early leader in the revolution that began in the *Sierra Maestra* and quickly spread across Cuba from east to west, as had the revolution of Jose Marti, Antonio Maceo and Maximo Gomez seventy years before. After the revolution, Christopher Vero taught law at the University of Havana. Disillusioned with Castroism, he served a five year prison sentence and migrated to Canada.

Cuba Libre! did not survive the American decision to occupy Cuba. When the first occupation ended in 1903, General Leonard Wood had done a superb job of building roads and railroads, establishing hospitals and schools and, perhaps most significant, virtually eliminating Yellow Fever. Unfortunately, neither Wood, his assistants, the Platt Amendment, nor the U.S. Congress had done anything to prepare Cubans for self-rule.

Because of the Platt amendment, which gave The United States ultimate control over Cuban foreign policy and, to a large degree, even domestic politics, America re-occupied Cuba in 1909, this time invited by Dr. Tomas Estrada Palma, the retiring president. When America left in 1911, she left behind a long series of dictators, each of which she fully controlled. The revolutions of Batista in the thirties and Castro in the fifties used *Cuba Libre!* as a battle cry. By the thirties, however, that's about all it was—a symbol almost empty of content, though still capable of stirring myths and dreams.

ABOUT THE AUTHOR

In *Kyoto Journal*, speaking of Bird's previous book,
Folding Paper Cranes, an Atomic Memoir, Mike Dillon says,
"This is writing for mortal stakes. And this is history made
personal, where it belongs—set against the devil's logic of war."
With his revisionist novel, *The Scorned Ally*,
Bird returns to his theme of desperate men and women
searching for hope in the ravages of war.

Leonard Bird is a retired English professor
who spent thirty-four years corrupting young minds.
Bird and his wife, the painter Jane Leonard, divide their
time between Grand Haven, Michigan, Durango, Colorado
and San Miguel de Allende, Mexico.

www.ingramcontent.com/pod-product-compliance
Lightning Source LLC
Chambersburg PA
CBHW030425030726
47493CB00022BA/1